CW00848076

The White Blazer

by

P B Alastor

Published by New Generation Publishing in 2020

First Edition

ISBN

Paperback	978-1-80031-838-0
Hardback	978-1-80031-837-3
Ebook	978-1-80031-836-6

www.newgeneration-publishing.com

 New Generation Publishing

CHAPTER ONE

CALIFORNIA DREAMING

It was one of those hot and blue-skied mid-May days, back in the year 2003 AD. The type of spring day that gives us all a great lift and anticipation, for the perfect summer, that's inevitably coming. The mercury was boiling. It shot up the temperature gauge, to just over thirty-one, and as people toiled and stressed in their offices and warehouses, like they do, a self-made man by the name of Charles Edward Barber, was having fun, the son of a gun. He was driving his immaculate 2002 AD white XKR Jag, top open, down a long stretch of road with green each side. It was so hot, his tires were melting into the road, and more grip, meant more speed, baby. Chazzy Barber was on cruise control, completely at one with himself and in love with life. In truth, he was besotted by it, and he felt just like his personalized number plates, 'King Chaz1', firmly seated on his throne. He could have been in California itself, for that's what it felt like to Chaz, not crappy old Tennin, as he lived out his dream of life upon the material plane, pushing that accelerator down hard, as king of the highway, readily chewing on his gum while giving an adoring badass stroke of his Hollywoodian goatee.

There's nothing better than working for yourself, and driving an open top new Jag on a hot spring day when the sap's rising. Chaz was forty-seven, a bit overweight with something of a protruding stomach, with a bronze sheen on his skin, derived from sessions of drugs and sunbeds, and he had been a class one forklift truck driver back in the day. But that was long before he really found himself, and Chaz got a real kick out of doing what he did these days. Ducking and diving, wheeling and dealing in the best traditions, not doing what the system wants its citizens to do, as good upright, stiff-backed citizens. That was the craic! You see Chaz was one of those intrepid folks among us, striking out into the shady areas, where deeper desires and reality lurk and meet. He was at the coalface to coin a phrase, mining the gold and gaining those deeper alchemical insights into the human condition to boot. Chaz knew things, and he always did like a snort of coke from a rolled-up note, and back about a dozen years previously he had more or less drifted seamlessly into dealing. And once he was in it, well Charles Edward Barber, was never one for half measures. It's all or nothing. Do half measures and you'll be turning out coppers and dog ends from your charity shop pockets, so he gave his soul to it you might say. Now the world is full of money, and if you put that much of yourself into life, you invariably get it out. Chaz had enough to swell Swiss bank accounts with a gold ingot or ten with a few little red rubies and sparklers in some clean white envelopes, the Barber Crown Jewels you might say, and all well-hidden.

In 2003 AD, when the buzzword was 'networking', Chaz already had the deep contacts, and now that he was much street wizened, and middling of years, he had a confidence bordering on brash arrogance. It truly was *his* time and now he was achieving everything he ever dreamed, and all made possible by dealing the best 'pub to club, pop and rockstar' dust in the county, possibly the country. Everyone who snorted coke in the Tennin Gap area wanted a bit of Chaz's dust and if they were already snorting it, they wanted more, loads of it. Chaz reckoned that every Tennin bank note in circulation had traces of the firm's cocaine, deep within its grain. Tennin was like a drugs monopoly board with Chazzy Barber as its head gamer and banker. How bad's that, eh? And that was the great thing with Alfredo, Chaz's wholesale dealer. He supplied nothing but the best quality Peruvian cocaine and at reasonable rates to mark up nicely, 'sorted!', as Chaz would say. And it was a given in Tennin, that coke was of the highest quality, and all because of Chaz. If punks bashed it up, they wouldn't sell it to the discerning punters. Every Herbert and Sherbet in Tennin Gap were on it, plus all the respectable hosting their dinner parties, and a goodly number of local dignitaries, who find the time, and have the inclination to take a powder.

Now Chaz's stock had risen profusely since the wharf had been transformed into block after block, after block of new commuting penthouses. The whole bloody lot of them must have been on Chaz's powder, and they couldn't believe how Peruvian pure it was, and what could ever go wrong? Chaz Barber was the type and caliber of person who gave thought to all the angles. He was bomb proof, immaculate and cut just perfect. His old school buddy Alan, who had his own building business employing a dozen or so, and for whom Chaz had done some work previously, also loved a serious bit of coke. For eight years now, Chaz was down on his books as a builder. Heck was he. But the agreement had allowed Chaz to get the mortgage on his house down at Cavell, and for Chaz's side of the bargain, he would supply Alan with a rather generous stash of 'Percy'. Clever little arrangement, with the money going through the books into Chaz's bank account, that was then given back to Alan at a later date in cash. Alan didn't mind, for his wife had a more serious and greedy habit than he had. Chaz tried to be discreet with his dealing, but he loved being brash just a little bit more, and he felt untouchable, and as he always joked, the Tennin Gap police force weren't the brightest, 'The dumb bastards!' Certainly not as bright as Chaz and that golden orb up in the sky today, that made everything sparkle on this very first day of summer, in May.

Now there is always a 'Zeitgeist of the times', and there are always people pioneering that spirit, out there beyond the watchtowers. Chaz reckoned he had gone out from the citadel and found his way to the Temple's treasure troves, deep within the darkest forests of being. That was how deep Charles Edward Barber was prepared to mine, and so quite naturally, Chaz fancied himself as a bit of a visionary, one of those unique people who can see all the trends as they manifest, who can decipher what it all means, and where it was all leading us to. In the New Age money is power, and early in the new millennium, Chaz had risen to the very top. He was admiring his six thousand-pound Rolex watch, whose face caught the midday sunlight, and in that 2003 AD moment, Chaz Barber fully realized that the internet was the game changer. He saw the opportunity and the window was open, so Chaz flew right through the pillars to the new Temple. Everything there, would be hard-core porn, tons of it! He could see that all too clearly and Chazzy Barber was in the business of capitalization, transforming insights into hard-nosed wedge.

But it went further than that with Chaz. Further than a mountain of money. He had the eye of the visionary. The turn of the millennium was heralding great changes, people wanted more, and a whole lot more. They wanted to push all the boundaries, smash them all down, so they could be new people and experience the great ecstasy and joy of sex. Why be hung up and suffer from all that repression? Chaz had read his Freud. He knew how much sex was in people, repressed kinky sacks of it, and where there is a demand for something, the entrepreneurs among us, have to coax and flog it out if need be! Well that's where Chaz's business instincts kicked in. People are sex-mad, all game for it, and Chaz knew how to plug into the circuitry and convert that bacchanal into money. Unconscious desire? Chaz knew all about that, the Capitalist systems built on it. It's all about selling us the dream of getting it on like a sex god, or sex goddess. He would chuckle away to himself as he drove, after all that coal mining, you gain access to the treasure trove. So Chaz Barber knew things all right, and he could see that everybody tries so desperately hard to check themselves, so that they can get to work on time, so they can pay the mortgage, so they don't have to deal with being out on the raft alone steering their own fate towards the new world, but really, they're all mad to get down on it, zonked and drugged out of their miserable square lives, hoping they might gain the knowledge on a wing and a prayer. But Chaz knew things; he had that illumination, and was venerating at the very font. You have to be an explorer and be out there and kinky. It was all up for grabs while you were snorting cocaine and getting down on hard-core, and that golden stud through Chaz's tongue was purely there for oral sex purposes. All the local escort girls pertaining to Chaz's unique tastes had been fully explored with it, fully. Therefore, and without doubt, the working-class enlightened guru, Chaz Barber had arrived, and with that high sun, the light gleamed off the shiny gloss of the Jag and Chaz's accompanying gold. There were his rings, gold sovereigns and his bracelets, all eighteen and twenty-four carats and 'class'.

He gave another quick split-second glance at the six grand Rolex, to keep track of the itinerary in his mind. The last was pure admiration and he hunched his shoulders up and pushed his thick neck out, rather pleased with himself. And despite the copious amounts of drugs he enjoyed, Chaz loved to arrange his day, via a strict timetabling. It gave him that sense of control and order that his liberated lifestyle required.

It had a perfect balance, but today, he was up there with golden eagles. He already had three lines sitting around in the back garden, and he was on top of the highest mountain driving his beautiful white chariot with eyes a bolting. He was impregnable. Chaz Barber, superman, was out on the Atlantic in a superb craft and no ice berg was going to ruin Chazzy Barber's firmly riveted Titanic. He felt like a great king or emperor presiding over his continent as he sang along to the Mama and Papa's. That track was one of his personal anthems and he chortled as he gave his now illegal Dixie horns an airing, passing the son of an old mate in a small opened back truck carrying a number of scrapped fridges. It was the young traveler Paddy Keen who lived on the council, ex-council estate at Tennin Gap, and who was known to purchase a goodly bit of cocaine from the 'Scamp', one of Chaz's big customer franchises within the local traveler community. Chaz poked out his gold studded tongue and Paddy laughed and responded with his hooter.

'Get on it, Paddy!' Chaz shouted, getting a thumbs up from Paddy, who was at that moment thinking about having a line later in the day. It's great when you're living the dream, Chaz thought. You can't fucking beat it. Life is perfect.

And did Chaz look cool. It wasn't just the gold. Chaz had invested his very identity in his clobber. He felt 'pure class' so he had to dress to the party every day, unless he was carping, but that brought in yet another class of apparel! Armani shirts? Chaz must have had twenty-five in his wardrobe, so every day saw a clean, or new one up on the Chaz, with a neat color coordinated tie. Chaz had a selection of over forty and when worn, each would carry the obligatory gold signature pin, that had a skewed symmetry with his gold eyebrow ring, with those skulls set in black diamonds. A cool number that cost him upwards of two G, 'class'.

Chaz confidently changed gear and accelerated, as he loved this stretch of road, and he loved the feel of his feet housed in his trademark alligator shoes. No socks today as feet have to breathe in the heat. Chaz had sixteen pairs, the cheapest fifteen hundred, and today he went for the six grand beggars, his very best Nero Blues, shined up so much that his feet sparkled alligator. Chaz always sported alligator and as a prolific hunting man, those shoes confirmed Chazzy Barber as the king at the very apex of the food chain. His entire body swilled with testosterone. He smiled as the sun glinted off the glass of the Jag and for Chaz everything was dream-like vibes, with his body and sex housed in the most expensive tight-fitting Gucci jeans. Each and every one of us has the chance to choose their own particular pathway in life, and Chaz was a firm, nah staunch believer, in the dictum that once you've chosen it, you've gotta give it your all and flipping well live it.

The all or nothing Chaz gave another quick glance of further admiration of the Blue Nero's, as they really were his finest alligators, and he chuckled to himself regarding his philosophical musings. The only thing life owed to a hot-blooded male like Chazzy Barber, was a bit of pussy or shall we say a harem ton of it, and Chaz liked his shaven, out of preference. His tip for the pilgrims was to always turn the page optimistically, as there's women to shag, gear to snort and money to make on the next one. 'Whoop-hay!', and if you ever get bored, down or depressed about it all, or the missis is an old nag, time to get carping! Chaz's deep self was 'Born to Carp' but in this material world we all have to accept that we are 'Forced to Work'. Chaz worked hard, knocking out his coke and selling and making porn one way or the other, while also having a finger or two in the pie of the carp bait world. He could also be an extremely astute gambler known to go in big when he thought the result was 'nailed on'. No snake oil from anywhere was going to put Chazzy Barber down, on his now rather ample backside.

Chaz did the double overtake up the hill, and got an irascible honk from another road user coming in the opposite direction, and 'so fucking what mate, I'm king of the road,' Chaz thought. The white flash and driving like this in the Jag were all part of the identity that was capped off with the infamous white blazer, Chaz's trademark. Chaz had five white blazers all costing well over the two G and when he was clad in the white blazer he was simply illuminated.

Everything seemed so clean and perfect, as if Chaz had recovered innocence in his wizened experience, and it gave him that measure of panache and profound insight, that he needed to keep ahead of all competitors, and the Tennin 'pig'. Everybody remembered Chaz, when they saw him or met him, and that's how he liked things to be. 'That guy with the white blazer' they would say, and it always led to increased custom, and women were constantly head turning when Chazzy Barber strutted around town, and many more were giving him head. Chaz could tell some risqué stories about slutty women. Feminism or no bloody feminism.

Chaz had the grosgrain collars of his white blazer just slightly turned up and that suited his skewed sophisticated character, and to really put on a show he would regularly have his marginally receding hair bleached to the blazer, 'class'. The smile on his face got bigger as he mused of the likelihood of 'That guy with the white blazer and blue shoes' as being the most commonly heard phrase in the Tennin Gap area. Celebrity, everyone was gagging for it in 2003 AD, and some like Chaz are naturals, have it in spades.

However, everything seemed incongruous to the Californian dream bubble, as Chaz pulled into a working-class estate. He headed to a block of sixties flats, that looked as good as they ever could look, with the clean sunlight, putting the glare on paint peeling, dirty exteriors. He pulled the Jag up in the parking area and took hold of an expensive leather briefcase that was resting on the passenger seat. He put up the roof and locked up with a touch of the keys, and this new man of the millennium sauntered towards the back of the flats, full of white blazered gusto with his rolling of the shoulders rhythmical gait and the sunlight catching those impeccably polished Blue Nero's. Charles Edward Barber was his own superman, true-self honed and fully embodied, chewing that gum.

He approached a first floor flat at the end of the block, that had a gate barring entrance with a sign on it 'Beware of the Bear'. He chuckled, and as Chaz had arranged a time with the gentleman in question, he opened the gate without trepidation and rang the bell. It took up a harsh call to attention and the immediate response was the sound of a big dog barking behind a closed door. Chaz waited for a moment and he could hear a door being opened and a great hound scampering and sliding through the hallway. Within moments the dog was front paws up, barking and pawing away furiously at the potential intruder, trying to get at Chaz through the letter box expecting the postman. The owner, a balding middle-aged man, was violently coughing and apparently battling with the great hound.

'Get down, Zep! Get down, ya bugger!'

The door was slowly opened and the Baskerville brute was desperate to get at Chaz from around the other side of the punter. Chaz instinctively held up his briefcase for safety against the gnashing teeth, like a priest holding up a crucifix to keep the demons at bay.

'Get thee away, Satan! Fuck me mate watch the growler will ya!'

The punter was deeply apologetic and he ordered the hound to settle as he gripped his collar and yanked him backwards.

'Down, Zep! Bad boy!'

Chaz always preferred to turn adversity into something a little witty, his habitual response to life's occurrences and meanderings.

'Well I hope badass don't put his lead into me, mate!' Chaz laughed heartily to his joke and Chazzy Barber did like his own joking turn of mind.

'Sorry about that, mate. Adult Leisure?' the punter asked, and Chaz duly confirmed, that indeed was the wank-fest brand. The dog was hauled into the kitchen and the door was fastened and almost immediately the dog took up a barking harmony with a pneumatic drill that had started up at a road works close by. Chaz was then led into the boudoir that was cram packed full of computers, old and new, big bulbous-backed things. They were stacked high on the dining table and completely covered the floor space.

'My, you've got a lot of computers! Ya in the business?'

The man replied that he was a computer engineer and living in computer shack was all part of the territory. Chaz couldn't resist a joke.

'Come over to mine, it's the same. I'm engineering frigging porn everywhere!' Chaz was off chortling away and the repair man put his card over calling his quite reasonable rates.

'I'll bell ya when I'm in a fix,' Chaz replied, as he shuffled on the settee, opening his briefcase on the small coffee table, finding room amidst the computers. 'But let's get on the frigging porn eh?'

Chaz had some good contacts on the porn scene and all of his DVDs were official and presented nicely in their colorful porny packaging. Chaz bought them in enormous job lots that were housed in boxed cratefuls in the sun bed and gym room, back at the new dream house. All were wrapped in polythene and the briefcase was full of them, with some opened too, that Chaz would use for advertising purposes. Chaz was a great salesman and he always purchased fifty or so of the same titles so that he could fast forward all of his wares and could therefore speak out of a personal testimony, regarding the merits and particular flavorings of each DVD. Being in the game for some time now, he knew that the key was to cater for every conceivable kink and taste. The punter turned one over that looked particularly hard core.

'The BBC are going up where the sun don't shine on that one!' was Chaz's knowledgeable and forthright comment.

The approach seemed to work as the punter took it and this porn cash stream, he had others, was a useful arm to Chaz's business interests. He made a flat five hundred a week on average from this one branch and it was like an insurance policy, just in case the major arm was abruptly cut off with a sword. The punter chose the three, gave Chaz the cash and within a few moments the flash of white blazer was gone.

Out the front in the Jag, Chaz quickly had the roof back off and he put up an eye-catching wheel spin pull away to impress the bystanders, a couple of lads who were swooning at the Jag and a bored one parent mother with her toddler, who was displaying rather a lot of cleavage for a mere trip to the Co-op. Chaz turned heads wherever he went. Some people have got it, and all the rest of us mere mortals haven't, and a man in a Harrods two and a half G white blazer, wearing Blue Nero alligator shoes, while dripping eighteen carat gold has it! It's as simple as that.

As soon as he pulled away, Chaz toked on a joint, that was waiting for him in the ashtray. Drug driving a problem? It never affected Chaz's. But one mission accomplished, it was now a slightly bigger one, up on an estate the other side of town. A trip to Jay and Dai's, a drug dealing duo who operated the Temple Hive estate patch, and who worked the infamous drugs pick up point in the car park by the big DIY store, amongst other outlets. Chaz cut up an elderly woman on a roundabout, by speeding across her while she was slowly crawling around. She bibbed furiously and gestured, and Chaz responded with a quick blast of the Dixie. He couldn't resist.

'Can't wait all day until you've got ya fingers up it, luv! Have a Dixie!'

Within a couple of minutes Chaz was arriving at another block of flats by a modern church community center. Chaz pulled up nearby and raised his hand, as a young guy was looking out of a ground floor flat window, eager to spot him, as Chaz was the man! Dai was a young white youth of twenty-one who was unemployed and lived alone in a nearby block. He had drifted into drug dealing after having struggled with a drug habit. The habit prevented him from holding any job down so why not deal? His mother didn't care that much, as she was too concerned with getting the next bottle of gin or vodka, and his father, well Dai didn't really have one there. He was absent without leave as it were, an approach that was gaining popularity around these blocks. But Dai didn't care; he had enough money to private rent now, and things had never been so much fun and the money that ensured it all continued, was signaled the moment he saw Chaz Barber and the white chariot every week.

'Whoop-hay! Summer's day! The White Blazerman is here, Jay!'

Jay was of mixed race and he too was blighted by the absent father syndrome, although he did still see him on rare occasion. His mother had remarried once in the meantime and then had divorced again and had another partner, and Jay had never got on with either of the guys. The newer partner just couldn't come to terms with Jay's life choices. But this life style that he and Dai enjoyed, was paying the money, 'sorted'.

'Ace one, bruver!' Jay was also on an up as Chaz was indeed the man who made dreams come true. Wherever he got the gear, it was from a secretive but impeccable source, and Jay and Dai had customers everywhere. The pair would drop gear off in the Toyota Spyder that Jay owned, a large part that would be traded on weekday evenings outside that DIY superstore in Tennin's town center. Tennin was known for blinding, blazing coke, but it generally came up on the street, a rather short gram's worth. But people have to make a cut somewhere.

The door was opened to Chaz. He entered with something of a histrionic flourish that was of his want, making incredible gestures like an Italian opera singer with fingers to the lips with a great outward kiss, that said in drug parlance, how incredible the prospective cache of coke was. It was always good, but each batch got just a micro smidgen better, according to Chaz and his marketing strategies. They appreciated Chaz's theatricality. He was a character, and there's too few of those these days. He breezed into the front room, that just had a tatty settee in there, carpet and large screen TV and a dining table with a few chairs around it, where the coke was weighed, bagged or snorted. On this occasion there was a soft porn glamour mag opened out on a center fold, referring to a young woman with whoppingly big tits, captioned 'Magdalena the Shaven Sex Fairy'. Chaz was full of his wares.

'Get on it! Bang on it! Fucking awesome bit of dust, me Herberts! Awesome! I had three lines before I came out and I'm up there like a fucking golden eagle circling around watching all the panto horses, ha ha, and I'm honed and ready to get down that wharf on the muff.' Chaz poked his studded tongue out in a libidinous theatrical flourish.

'Nice one, Chazzy boy, but I thought ya didn't like hairy cunt,' Jay replied, while he was finishing counting out the money. Chaz opened up the briefcase and took the cocaine from its sleeve and put it on the table and explained.

'Just a figure of speech Jay, but Chazzy, like anybody, has his preferences. You'll find a generous supply of grams over the eight there, Jay. Chaz's summer love they call it! Get on it! Get on that sherbet me Herberts!'

'Thanking you oh wondrous blazer king! Many blessings! All there, mate!' and Jay handed over a wad of notes. Chaz thanked him and put the money in the same sleeve he drew the coke from. He could trust Jay so there was never any need for counting. Jay and Dai were immediately up for a line each and Jay took some coke from the bag on a razor blade and was laying two out. He laid the lines neatly next to the center fold, gesturing to the model who was stretched out erotically on a chaise longue in a fairy grotto.

'Like your Natasha's center spread, Chaz. What's all this Magdalena business?' Dai observed and asked.

'Haven't I been telling ya. She's a talented girl Nat. Spreading her wings as they say, Dai,'

Chaz replied without the slightest hint of embarrassment. He had always taught Natasha to enjoy and celebrate her body and if she could make hard cash out of it too, well bring it on! 'That was my idea, the

Magdalena sex fairy thing, Dai. In her game you've gotta pull on everything repressed and tease it all out!'

'Fucking bit of all right!' Dai was gesticulating wanking but knowing these guys well, Chaz played along with all of this good banter.

'Now well out of your crude pond life league, Dai, well out of it!'

They all laughed as Dai snorted a line looking at the naked shot. Apparently, the shoot was done a few months previously, and had been regurgitated in another edition from a few different angles. Chaz explained that the exciting center fold shot was indeed the one that he had commissioned into a large oil painting that was to be found in the Barber's front room at the new abode, above the Great Waldorf settee to be precise. It was vivid proof that Chaz and the Barber's celebrated sex and nudity. How can you be ashamed of the human body and Natasha had the assets, good looking with those big tits that were part natural and part insertions. Those insertions were put in purely for career and financial considerations and Chaz praised Natasha for seeing and seizing the cash nexus. Big boobs are big assets in the New Age.

You don't need to know the theory of relativity to make big money in the 'Now' according to Chaz's philosophies. Just sex, dirty and explicit with three big X's and more and more of it and drugs to smash any repression, preventing you getting home to the bejeweled treasure, equals dosh. These magazine shots titillated, to get people to where they wanted to be, a stoking up that unconscious desire and getting on it. Then it was snorting the lines and opening the doors of perception to that sack of kinky sex. Natasha had appeared in loads of glam mags and was a mega star of the publication *Big Jugs*. For a while she honored in hard-core pornography, and she still flirted, with some big projects in the pipe, although now, she was concentrating her energies in doing just a little shooting like these tasteful pics, allied to a regular two grand a night escort job, catering to the sophisticated tastes of rich Arab and Russian tycoons in London. All very well when you're doing your degree and you want a nice large cash flow to enjoy a particular money rich life style, that as a 'Barber', she was now accustomed to.

Chaz had supported her like a father should, every inch of the way, that she forged with those big cups. Linda, Chaz's long-suffering wife, didn't really approve, but Chaz was an extremely powerful character, and for Chaz none of it seemed an issue. In Chaz's wise opinion, we all have to prostitute ourselves to something or other out there, and it all becomes a matter of how much money we make, while we're doing it. The New Age was all about being open with sex and making money out of it, and if that's what the open led to, 'sorted!' 'What's wrong with glamour and porn?' was what Chaz would always say. Women have got sex, stacks of it, and it seems to go so seamlessly well with money, and it was all the same to Chaz. If people wanted gay porn or whatever else porn, as long as it wasn't fucked up paedo porn, Chaz would buy it wholesale and flog it. He was a New Age businessman, for Christ's sake! Every kink is laden with paves of gold. Chaz had that vision. He knew things and had that deep insight into unconscious desire. It's nothing but sex, sex and more sex.

'Those who are all up in arms complaining about it are sitting around wanking all day over it! The fucking hypocrites!' was a typical riposte that Chaz used on many occasions, even with his mother, who liked to think herself a staunch Catholic. Chaz and Natasha had led Mrs. Barber to believe that Nat did lingerie modeling. However, Mrs. Barber had remembered seeing Natasha's breasts getting that much bigger and she had spoken about a 'shoot' at a country mansion, and something about it all rang a bell of porn in Mrs. Barber. You could say that Mrs. Barber suspected, and she had always been against porn, ever since she had come across those disgusting magazines and videos that Chaz used to have hidden away in his wardrobe in his early twenties.

Chaz left the young dealers, but he would return to this patch again next week with a similar cache, regular as clockwork, with a double whammy likely to be in the offing on the forthcoming bank holiday at the end of the month. He gave a deep breath before pulling away and the next stop was another big cocaine drop to the Waterside crew down at the Wharf. It was an eight ounce down there too and it was all destined to be distributed around the dozen blocks of penthouse flats down that way and any discreet middle-class users in the local Tennin Gap and beyond areas. The operations, which were led by Angusia and Connor her bloke, were discreet as they were 'very' middle class and were meticulous, but ruthless in their dealings with their squad of enforcers. Chaz would regularly return for a second drop of a week, if the demand was great. All sorts of dignitaries and local pillars were on their books, and Chaz was obviously privy to all of their names although he was sworn to confidentiality, unless there were profound issues with authorities of course. Chaz was clever. He liked having some loaded shotguns hidden up his sleeve, metaphorically speaking. It made sense, 'sorted!', and it made Chaz smile too, as he knew that the first woman to head Tennin Council, the forty-six-year-old Sally Brockett, who his wife Linda knew back in the day, regularly had half ounce delivered discreetly via Angusia. Charles would tap his pudgy nose with his index finger. He knew things.

Chaz checked his e mails while he was pulled up in a garage and he had eight new subscriptions on the site worth a score a time, and there had been fifteen kilos of boilies ordered too. Chaz was working with a long-term carp nut friend and business associate called Miko. They were building themselves a viable commercial carp bait that they were hoping to manufacture and distribute more widely. Linda was always urging Chaz to go legit with a carp and angling shop with Miko, to get themselves away from the shadowy drugs landscape. But Chaz always prevaricated, as he loved the anti-establishment and rebel nature of being a drugs dealer. He loved the feeling that he was the dispenser of ecstasy and 'right out of it' vibes! Chaz was like a self-appointed, king of seventh heaven rhapsodies, and heck was the money good. Every Thursday, Friday and Saturday he would knock it out like this, and it'll be six or seven grand profit a week, 'class' and as Chaz reasoned with so much money hidden up in those Swiss bank accounts, if he went down for five, out in two and a half. He would still be quid's in when he came out. Then he could go legitimate. All possible eventualities, had been thought through, so he strode around like an untouchable king.

Chaz was now ordering a big kilo a week from Alfredo and sometimes he went back for a nigh double whammy. Just 'Percy' my Lord for myself and four and twenty drug bird friends, including the ground breaking leader of the council! And just of late the big selling had seen him all right, as he was spending vast quantities on the renovation of the new dream house, a project that was still ongoing.

Chaz purchased one of this three or four carp mags while paying for the petrol, and he was surprised to notice that Joey Olwyn was mentioned on the front page. Joey was a well-known carp fanatic of the Tennin gap area who was one of those lucky lottery winning millionaires. Apparently, he had purchased a lake fairly local, and had spent big money stocking the water and putting in a lodge to cater for the expected 'master carpers'. Chaz took a cursory interested look and put the mag back on the passenger seat. He would have a good read in the evening back home with a few joints and lines of coke, 'snorted!'.

Chaz had another five porn drops to go before downing tools and the next drop was a house over by the local heath. This was to a man who could only take a drop after four o'clock when the wife was off to work. But many clients were like that. They weren't as liberated as Chaz and his Mrs. They seemed so afraid to disclose their dirty lusty fantasy lives to each other. Work it all out, for Christ's sake, and for Chaz the client's attitudes were old age style not the New Age of openness and enlightened consciousness. A myriad of thoughts on various subjects, carp, drugs and sex, were flitting in and out of Chaz's mind, as he worked his Jag up to the heath side houses bopping around to the latest 'Make Luv' dance hit. Chaz was all up for that with half a dozen serious lines up the hooter. The guy on the heath side, obviously had money as the house was large and detached in one of the more upmarket areas of Tennin.

However, Chaz's internal dialogue was interrupted by a cyclist on a mountain bike, who was avoiding each of the deep drain covers that ran along the road up to the heath. Chaz was forced to slow to a crawl and 'Fuck!', 2002 AD white Jag convertibles shouldn't be plugged up by long-haired pricks on mountain bikes. Chaz gave him the Dixie air horn, rather than just the hooter, as if to categorically state, 'get out the fucking way!' But the long-haired one still rode the bike in the same way, oblivious as he snaked his way around the drain holes. A furious Chaz just couldn't pass safely and he remained stuck fast behind him. Chaz felt it incumbent to voice his displeasure.

'Get out the fucking way, longhair!'

The young man, a twenty-year-old builder, had been an enthusiastic and exceptional amateur boxer up until eighteen months previously. He had gradually given up after acquiring a weekend cocaine habit, that ironically, was one that snorted Chaz's superior 'pub to club pop and rock star' up his hooter. But it's a small world. The young guy turned his head around and sneered at Chaz as they approached a set of traffic lights and Chaz inevitably rose to the baited hook.

'Here! Hasn't anyone taught long-haired pricks like you how to ride a fucking pushbike straight! You're all over the fucking road, ya long-haired prat!'

Chaz was never one to mince words, and the young man promptly got off his bike, threw it down by the roadside, before surging forward with vicious intent and giving the front wing of Chaz's gleaming Jag an enormous kick with a steel capped boot. Chaz immediately jutted his head from his shoulders, forgot about his age and condition, which wasn't overly fit, and got out of the Jag to confront the young hoodlum.

'Ya little fucker!' Chaz yelled before lunging at him, hurling a swinging, lumpy looking right hand. But the young fellow blocked it with a snap boxing come karate move, and gave Chaz an almighty right-hand back that gave a resounding crack, sending Chaz sprawling across the bonnet of the car like a beached whale. Then the youngster, who was strong due to his now obsession with a steroid-based weight training addiction, grabbed hold of Chaz with an almost apelike strength pulling him off the bonnet with Chaz nigh strangled by his own tie. He then repeatedly thumped Chaz hard in the stomach. Chaz had never been hit like this before and he gasped in excruciating pain. The young man backed off, having fully won the brief entanglement.

'Ya fat wanker!' the young guy disdainfully snapped, before duly picking his bike up and setting off cycling up the road. To rub the indignity in further, he also gave Chaz the sign, while sneering as he peddled away. Chaz, who suffered from various breathing allergies, was gasping for air with great gulps and he could hardly get his words out, speaking to a guy who had seen the violence and had alighted from his car coming to Chaz's aid.

'I'm fine,' Chaz said. 'I gives him the horn as he was all over the fucking road and then he throws a fucking wobbler. Can ya give me your contact details for the claim?' Chaz asked, pointing to the dent in the side wing.

CHAPTER TWO

CHAZ'S PAD

Chaz and Linda had finally arrived where they wanted to be in life, albeit with a few reservations, and had recently purchased that dream house. Linda had fallen in love with the place the moment she looked at it. It was tucked away down a leafy lane all on its own, that was surrounded by hay fields and a great vista of rape that was across from the house in its full sun kissed golden bloom. The territory was stamped and eked out already. Chaz had placed a personalized house plaque, reading 'Chaz's Pad', on the wooden front gate marking its new inhabitants clearly.

However, although Chaz loved the house and saw its vast potential, he was a little unsure. Less than a mile away up the leafy lane was Tennin Gap House, the old Colditz-looking asylum, come psychiatric hospital. The hospital had been set up in Victorian Britain by the County Asylum board and had become a successful trading colony by the early twentieth century. The vast grounds at the back of Chaz's pad beyond the woods, had been extensively farmed back in the day, but now were merely cut for hay. Chaz didn't like the idea of 'nut-jobs', a stone's throw up the road. Who would? That's the kind of thing that preys on your mind in the dark when you get your head down and the owls are hooting away in the eerie stillness of the night. Fears were for good reason too. Everyone in Tennin knew somebody who had worked up there one time or another, so bizarre and scary Tennin Gap House stories, were known by all. No, Chaz didn't like the proximity, and he only agreed to the move because the asylum was to be demolished in the near future. The council had prepared the area for the now obligatory forthcoming residential and business estates.

But there was no denying that the house had a distinct sense of place about it. That appealed to Chaz. There were two large brick pillars to the fore and the brick frontage wall was probably forty years old or so. The house itself was built at the same time as the asylum and it was eventually one of the hospital authorities doctor's residence's, before being purchased privately by the last owners back in the early seventies. There was an old horse chestnut tree within three meters of the entrance that gave a little shelter from the road. The road was a back entrance to the hospital grounds, that rose up a long drag of a predominately beech-tree-lined and canopied hill, with old iron fencing, marking boundaries both sides. In bygone days, it been used to service the now long defunct hospital farm. On those hospital grounds and in the woods directly behind 'Chaz's

Pad' there were more beech and holly trees and this gave the lane its name, Holly Beach.

At the front gate there was an area of moss and gravel that gave enough parking space for three vehicles or so. Chaz was planning to put a concrete base down later in the summer with some lock up gates. The past owners didn't appear to do anything to the house, apart from tend the gardens. He had also put in planning permission, to carve out a back entrance onto the road with a big double garage around the back of the house. These were exciting times for the Barbers.

Directly opposite Chaz's parking entrance was a wonderful antique art deco and Gothic looking street lamp, that went back to the 1920s and was still in working order, although had been given somewhat to oxidation. The house was secluded a touch as adjacent along the lane was dense woodland that led down to a dwelling at the entrance to the main village road. This was occupied by old Dr. Greene who was well past retirement age although he still worked part-time, and his radiographer wife of nigh twenty years younger.

One of the great attractions of the dwelling for Linda was the delightful gardens which gave such a beautifully scented aroma, that nigh enveloped the house. The previous owners had been keen gardeners all their lives and the front garden was a showcase, with hyacinths and tulips flowering during this period in middling May. There were also rosebushes displaying Lovestruck Red and Daddy's Delight white flowers along the boundary fence near the road. Everyone who came into the garden remarked upon the sweet smell, and the path went right up the center of the plot, so you were surrounded by sweetness. The garden was a beauty on the eye and a balm to the soul and Linda was captivated by it. It was like having your own piece of the Garden of Eden, without the snake. Even Chaz thought it nice. He had shown his mother, who was now in a local nursing home, some snaps he had of it, on his new top-of-the-range mobile phone. How she so desperately wanted to see it in the flesh and be with her only child and son.

The front door had a slate canopy overhead, and was painted an emerald green, with an unusual door knocker, shaped as a spitting snake coiling from its handle. Quite a curiosity and always a talking point. Overall, the house was in need of a little refurbishment as there was an old corrugated porch and walkway at the back of the house, that contained an outside toilet with an old cistern and pulling chain, that Chaz was intending to sort out later in the summer. However, Chaz had done plenty during the winter months and early spring, with new double glazing, central heating, a new roof and much more. Herberts and Sherbets were paying for the lot.

The back garden jutted side on to the house with its small strip of lawn and an area with a couple of small flowerbeds that had neatly trimmed verges. Since coming to the house Linda was reborn. She was determined to keep the gardens as they found them. It was her new enthusiasm and passion. Chaz had recently purchased a large shed that was in position at the end of the small lawn on ground that was part of the vegetable allotment. Linda still intended to work what was left. She was excited at the prospect of delivering her own home grown to the table, although Chaz thought the supermarket much more convenient. To the right of the lawn and beyond, directly behind the house, the garden gathered itself into two acres of unkept land, that once upon a time had been a fruit orchard but by now had run wild. But what potential! When Chaz realized that he had an old apple and pear orchard in his back garden he joked to Miko, that big carp, drugs and porn buddy, that he and Linda would soon be cranking up the ole Adam and Eve juices! Whoop-hay!

There was some work he wanted to do out there to clear it up a bit, specifically an ancient black shed he'd earmarked for demolition. It was away from the house in the old orchard and Chaz joked that it must have been an old man-cave but it just looked an eye sore and would have to go. Beyond that, at the end of Chaz and Linda's land, was an old brick wall some seven-foot-high that was crumbling in places, where trees had grown pushing the walls over, and which marked the boundary on to the vast hospital grounds. There was an area of dense woodland directly behind, before the beginning of the great change. A section of the old hospital ground was now being built on with two enormous great warehouse units being pile driven.

Inside the house, the ample front lounge, had now become *the* place where everything went down, and it was akin to the very center of the king's citadel. New carpets had gone right through the house and with business interests blooming like the garden, no expense was spared. They had plumped for a high price purple glitter twist carpet and it gave a nice complimentary aesthetic with Chaz's new Bluebell armchair, that was a deep violet in cotton velvet. Chaz simply loved the sumptuous quality of high-grade velvet and sitting in it with his white blazer on, made him feel like the king of the aesthetes. There was a luxurious white rug overlain the carpet and everything seemed so clean and perfect, exactly how Chaz liked everything to look to his incredibly cultured eye.

The light was clean too, fixed through a centerpiece Italian cut crystal fitting. Chaz loved style. There was a newly acquired and highly sought-after 1960s, Jason and Michaela Thabane coffee table, that Chaz had purchased from a recent trip to an antiques dealer in London. He went up there with Linda and was after something that would be 'class' in the new front room. But a working table not a mere decoration. He had chosen the

Thabane because of the fantastic engraving on its glass top, depicting the creation of man himself. It cast the nude Adam with outstretched arms, trying to touch hands with God who was himself wrapped in a cloak. It brought something of a gravitas to Chaz's front room and gravitas doesn't come cheap. It cost Chaz nigh seven big ones and was all paid for from the tumultuous demand for 'pub to club rock and popstar' over the Xmas holidays and New Year celebrations. God only knows how much coke was snorted.

The table had now become the chief area for Chaz's cocaine preparation, and of course the Barber's personal joint rolling and drug dalliances. There were also a number of carp magazines on the table as Chaz would always have one on. Reading them was one of Chaz's greatest joys.

Linda, and other guests who might appear, would enjoy the luxury of the grand Waldorf sofa that stretched along the internal wall and which was also a new purchase. All in all, this was that very moment in Chaz's life that he had finally arrived at where he'd always wanted to be, absolutely loaded, so that he could surround his world with art and beauty. The commissioned oil painting of Natasha, that was taken from that classy shot lain on the chaise lounge in *Big Jugs*, was hung above the settee. For Chaz it confirmed, at the center of the citadel, that the Barbers were liberated and cutting edge in the new sexual millennium. The artist who painted it was Royal Academy trained and incidentally Chaz meticulously collected pristine copies of all the magazines that Natasha had appeared in, as she was well in demand, and there had been so many. Chaz swore that when his Nat had become *the* media star of her generation, and Chaz had a master plan, these magazines would be worth the mint. But at present she had her head down studying hard for that media degree. Chaz's wise advice to her was to believe, that glamourous oak trees came from such fantastically sexy and well-proportioned acorns! Those enhanced boobs were great money spinners in the New Age and as they say, she never looked back as they jutted out far and wide these days and Natasha had a razor-sharp brain to boot.

The wall on the right, near where Chaz's velvet chair was positioned, was dominated by two enormous aquarium fish tanks. Chaz was a deep and committed student of the carp species and this gave him a window of opportunity to acquire a nigh third eye vision into carp behavioral instincts. The tanks were three-foot-deep and nearly eight foot in length and both held two of the almost divinely elevated species. They were all three or four pounds in weight with two mirrors in the tank next to the king's velvet chair. Chaz called the biggest 'Hermann the Hoover' as he always seemed to hoover up the red and blue boiled baits that Chaz offered. The smaller mirror was called 'The Beak', as he had a beak of a mouth. In the second tank that led along the wall towards the large screen TV, there was a leather carp and a common. Chaz had called the leather the aptly named 'Alligator Shoe' resonating with those shoes that Chaz simply loved. Who but Chaz wore real alligator around Tennin? The final carp was a female that Chaz named 'Holly Beach' in honor of the dream house although Chaz thought he might rename her 'Wreaker', as she seemed to have a penchant for wrecking all the plants in the tank. Chaz had replaced them three times! Some women are rather recalcitrant, he joked.

Linda didn't really like the carp dominating her front room, but as with most things, Chaz's force of character meant that he always got his way. That tended to be the nature of the relationship because Chaz had *character,* and you can't hold that back. But having had carp in her front room for some time now, they had smaller tanks in their last semi-detached on Tennin's ex-council Cavell estate, Linda had become accustomed to them, and even she found them a calming influence. Chaz would feed them every day with his self-styled carp baits and whatever they ate was recorded meticulously in Chaz's special research books. Trends and patterns would be observed and analyzed, and all the work was aimed towards developing a commercial bait that would be famous among fellow carp enthusiasts. Chaz would sit mesmerized, invariably listening to Bob Marley, satisfying his soul smoking joint after joint, intuiting all kinds of crazy insights about carp feeding habits, that might give him that necessary edge out on the waters and help refine that bait. There was nothing 'smoke dopey' about Chaz. He aspired to climb higher and higher within the carp fraternity and was after a big breakthrough with his tutti-frutti round teaser balls. It would eventually come. The carp would go mad for the little beggars. Then the penny would drop and the carpers would naturally buy them by the sack full and Chaz would be the most famous carp angler in the country. Not bad eh? Chazzy Barber, the veritable king of carp.

In between the tanks was a limestone fireplace that Chaz and Linda had left in, as it was antique and in great condition and it fitted in perfectly with the décor of the room. On the mantel and above were a number of prime iconic relationship and framed family photographs, like we all tend to have. There was the obligatory marriage snap with a youthful looking and thinner twenty-five-year-old Chaz and an attractive young-looking Linda, displaying the freshness, happiness and promise of romantic love. Next to that was another, taken a year or so ago in Ibiza, with Chaz now middle-aged and overweight, but looking as happy as punch, drinking wine from a great ladle. Linda was looking on smiling, at least three stone heavier than the wedding shot. There were others of Natasha, their only child, as a baby and young girl, involved in dancing competitions and even one that was a still from that naked spread in *Big Jugs*. Chaz was proud that there was simply no shame regarding sex in the citadel. We've got to embrace the human body and make hard cash from its primal urges. It's a New Age, for Christ's sake!

But pride of place, at the very center of the mantel, was a neat, inspired piece of wall art, as Chaz had called it. He had recently purchased an old cow's skull with horns at a local antiques auction that was offered up by one Rose Gagnon, who incidentally was born Rose Ashcroft. This had been placed centrally above the fireplace between two diagonally slanting nineteenth century Enfield Martini Henry MK II's, both de-activated of course. These objects were flanked by numerous photographs of Chaz on haunches cradling captured carp, with the one above the cow's head being the most prized. Chaz had always wanted to shine out from the crowd and whenever he carped, he wore his now locally famous, great white shark hunter's hat to do just that. Chaz thought it gave out all the right signals and associations, and Chaz would say, when deliberating regarding the very essence of man, that in the last instance 'we are hunters', rather than being mere fisherman. However, there hadn't been any notable additions to these trophy snaps for some considerable time, and this was beginning to gnaw at Chaz's ego. This failure seemed to be chipping away relentlessly at his hard-won carp king identity. Chaz was a dedicated hunter and it was unfair that he hadn't been rewarded for his gargantuan and boundless efforts the past few seasons.

As well as the fishing photos, there were a number of hunting pics too. One of Chaz holding up a couple of big hares that was taken on a hunting holiday in America during the early nineties, and another with Chaz posing next to a hatch-back vehicle, crammed full of dead geese. Hunting was Chaz's style. He was king hunter.

There were also framed photos of Chaz and his mum that were taken back in Chaz's teens at the family home, a house that Chaz's mum had taken on after the divorce, back in the late seventies. Chaz's dad had gone off with a young female office worker at the cement factory. His mum had the house, while his father had the cash, and there was a goodly bit of that at the time, as the Barbers were originally known for their small chain of sweet shops and newsagents. Chaz's dad had sold those off, when the opportunity came at the cement factory. A Mason friend had worked him in as a head of department. He went on to purchase his own house and when he died, he was smoking and drinking heavily. Chaz's third share of the will put him onto the housing property ladder without too much effort and the house at Cavell was paid off as his mother downsized to help him out too. Chaz had always kept a close relationship to his father, rather than taking sides, but his mother didn't know that he had kept seeing him as regularly as he had. Previously Chaz had never got into a position to buy due to his gambling and drugs habits getting in the way. But now nothing got in his way. He was too astute and he valued the money he earned, and there was always 'Percy' around. How bad's that, eh?

On the far wall to the side of the widescreen, was a large painting of that most prized of the framed carp photographs, again a commissioned work by the same RA local artist that painted Natasha. This was a Barber household famous moment, when Chaz caught his biggest ever British caught carp, a nigh forty-pound specimen from the local 'Ressie' venue, and which was still the record carp for that water. It was likely to stay that way for some considerable time too, as Chaz's 'Humpy Back' as they called him, died a couple of years ago. But that image was iconic. It was *the* proudest moment of Chaz's life and there were sure to be more. He was determined to bag that first fifty! Absolutely determined, and nothing would stop him. Nothing!

Everything internal had been repainted by one of Alan's trusted employees and on the smooth, now lavender gloss lacquer wall by the great settee, was an antique nineteenth century gilt oval mirror. This was purchased many years ago by Chaz and had a fascinating genealogy, originally being owned by a self-styled late Victorian mystic, although that fact was lost on Chaz. But Chaz called it 'The Magic Mirror' as it had become *the* mirror that Chaz used to get into the mind-set of the white blazer, a truly sublime and consciousness changing moment. You're either in the zone or out of it and for Chaz the white blazers were the key to unlock everything. Those white blazers, with their exaggerated peak lapels, had opened the doors to Chaz's true potential. They were that special to Charles Edward Barber.

In the back-reception room, the entrance being from the small hallway by the spiral staircase, there was an expensive sunbed, purchased by Linda when they moved in. It was a top-of-the-range upgrade, and it meant that Chaz was always sporting an around the calendar bronzed Hollywood look. There were those many boxes of Chaz's porn DVDs stacked therein and a small space for Chaz's fitness training. Chaz never touched the exercise bike there, that Linda used sometimes, but he worked darn hard and regular with his many sets of biceps, that kept his enormous tree trunk arms up to strength. Basically, biceps and sunbed with a large joint to unwind, while watching a porn or the carp, was how Chaz liked to 'do' his fitness. To each his own isn't it?

What was noticeable in the front room, was an incongruously placed crucifix at the center of things high above the cow's skull, that seemed a little out of keeping with the Chaz Barber lifestyle. But remember, Chaz was from that staunch Catholic background on his mother's side, and he had always lived in a house with a crucifix up on the wall. It just seemed needed, and it was there to turn to, for that spiritual succor we all need, when things get a little hairy in life, as they invariably do sometimes.

Now Chaz didn't see himself as an old-fashioned man in relation to the new millennium's sexual politics. He wasn't like his stuck in the mud father's generation, who thought that women should be in the kitchen. But it just suited he and Linda's relationship that Linda bossed the kitchen, period. It was her natural domain as it were, where she wanted to be, and to keep her comfortable they had a new dream fit as part of the refurbishment. Linda was on a high and she stepped up to the plate and Chaz did occasionally wash up, usually after the Sunday roast. Domestic chores were shared in this house.

Upstairs held two large bedrooms, and a smaller one and a washroom that had a shower, bath and toilet. All had been given the full makeover treatment. The second of the large bedrooms had a lock, on a spanking new Gothic looking dungeon of a door, and a brand-new crystal door knob. This was the new purple BDSM room, the Dark Room, as it was called. Chaz had left no stone unturned here, and it was fully equipped to 2003 AD cutting edge standards, for shooting kinky liberated films for easy internet consumption. Chaz was on the Zeitgeist of the times and this material was showcased on Chaz's subscription only website. It was the New Age, and according to Chaz, every sex psychologist worth their salt were exhorting all, to experiment and liberate themselves and why not make a bundle out of it too? The filming equipment and all the gadgetry had cost Chaz shedloads and he would get one of his contacts in the porn world to professionally edit the footage. Chaz had pushed out a couple of dozen kilos and more in the autumn and winter months so there was stacks of money to pay for everything. This was more than normal but it had gone out like wildfire due to all of the new inhabitants in Tennin in those wharf penthouses. Many had a habit and Chaz kept fully up with demand so more gold ingots were in the offing. Linda didn't like the continually increased dealing, although this winter had been all about dream house upgrades, and they had to pay for them somehow. But everything was part of the master plan of Chaz's. His dream being that at the opportune time, Chaz would cut ties and go completely legitimate with that carp tackle shop and then just buy 'Percy'. Brave new worlds truly beckoned.

But although they had moved to the new dream house, by 2003 AD, the marriage was under strain as Linda was addicted to valium as well as using coke on a daily basis for self-medication. Linda was more than aware, that the addiction she now had, bound herself to Chaz's lifestyle in the drugs world. Linda was beginning to feel trapped and just didn't know how to speak out or up for herself. She felt encircled, engulfed, but Chaz was a powerful character. She looked at herself negatively in her dressing table mirror as Chaz sat downstairs in the king's chair. She was forty-four now, a bit overweight and caught between looking old and tired and yet retaining something of her youthfulness. But when she faced herself like this, she would invariably end up wanting out of the pain with another line of cocaine. And sometimes she was given to the thought that Chaz had laid the trap. This was the backdrop to the incredible events that took place in Holly Beach Lane, Tennin, early in the new millennium.

The Jag was ensconced in its normal position outside the front gate by the horse chestnut. Chaz had arrived home, and told Linda all the story of what had occurred with the road rage and the fight. Linda took the scuffed up white blazer upstairs and put it away in a wardrobe that held the four others, although they were wrapped in polythene having come back from the cleaners. Chaz was still firmly in position in the kingly seat, next to the carp tanks. He would be nigh immoveable this evening and the Armani and tie were off and Chaz had replaced them with a self-styled carp T-shirt, black with a big red carp on, emblazoned with that caption defining Chaz's very soul, 'Born to Carp, Forced to Work'. He also sported a pair of carp couture shorts that carried the same logo and which displayed his thick but short legs and massive bronzed thighs. For Chaz controlling the everyday aesthetics of our lives makes us feel that much better. Things like that act to validate our inner deepest being. Bring it on!

Linda came down and applied yet another poultice to Chaz's eye and she fussed over him as he winced and grimaced. She also noticed that the Blue Nero's were scuffed. She looked at them knowing full well how much those Nero's had cost and they were Chaz's Sunday best. Chaz was a perfectionist. A badly scuffed shoe inevitably meant a spanking new pair would be in the pipeline and they cost six big ones.

'I think you should go to the casualty, Chaz, just to check.'

Chaz wasn't overly impressed with that idea.

'Huh! And after I've checked in, I'll go off carp fishing because I'll be up there all bloody night waiting, Linda. I'll dare say I'll live, and if it's that bad, I'll sort it out on the morrow. And besides, I got Gray here for two soon and we can't let Gray down on his two!' Chaz looked at the Nero's yet again, sneered and picked the scuffed shoe up and expressed his displeasure and realism.

'Look at it! It'll stick out like a fucking sore thumb. Oh, they'll be all right when I'm running about knocking it out with the Herberts but they're fucking ruined for Royal Ascot, fucking ruined.'

Chaz tossed the shoe aside. Linda was about to say, she told him he should've saved them for Ascot, but she kept quiet, to ensure she wouldn't inflame proceedings.

As Chaz pondered darkly on his Sunday best Blue Nero's, an Audi arrived outside the front and parked up by the horse chestnut, next to Chaz's white Jag and the four-wheel drive Jeep. This was the aforementioned Gray, who alighted from the car in a combat jacket, a man of slim build with a beard, of similar age to Chaz. He immediately noticed the dent on the front wing.   He investigated and looked it over closely.

'Phew! Phew! Chazzy boy, what's all this, mate!'

Gray walked up the garden path smelling the flowers that he had been told about. It indeed looked and smelt like paradise and he thought, with certain reservations, Chaz had indeed bagged himself that much sought-after dream house. Chaz was watching Hermann from the eye that hadn't closed up when Gray tapped on the window.

'Speak of the fellow damned! Here's me Gray!'

Linda was in the kitchen, so Chaz tried to stand up, but he had a muscular spasm in his abdomen as he did so, and he abruptly gave up and called for Linda. Before she arrived at the door, Gray had taken to giving the spitting snake door knocker a bang, thwack, thwack! He just couldn't resist it, and as he waited, he took a further deep breath of the sweet garden aroma. Linda answered the door and quickly explained that Chaz had a row with a cyclist. Gray was looking at the door knocker and Linda looked at it too.

'Snakes are spitting up here, eh!' Gray then turned a little to the garden and took in yet another deep lungful. 'Such a sweet, sweet smell in the air though, Linda,' he added.

Linda explained that all the hyacinths and tulips had really come out. Gray hadn't been up to the new house as Chaz had always dropped the gear into him, but on this occasion, Gray had decided to pick it up, and kill two with one stone as they say. He could see this dream house as it was taking shape, and crucially, get a glimpse of those new carp tanks and carp that Chaz had been raving about. As soon as Gray was inside, he took off his shoes on account of the newly carpeted floor.

'I wouldn't want to put the blackie on your new carpet, Linda.'

Linda thanked him for the consideration. Once inside the front lounge, Gray looked to and fro, assessing the state of things in relation to Chaz's right eye, and then he plonked himself down sitting on a red pouffe up against the Thabane.

'Love the coffee table, Chazzy boy.'

Chaz puffed himself up for the exposition, chewing away as he did so, feeling that profound sense of having fully arrived.

'Cost seven, Gray. Jason, Michaela Thabane, much sought after. See that engraving on it, Gray. The original man reaching out to God! Class, eh?' Chaz expounded.

Gray and Chaz liked to banter. They had known each other since secondary school and after showing his appreciation of the Thabane, Gray turned attentively to the blackened eye.

'Couldn't ya handle him, Chaz?' Gray joked. Chaz guffawed back at him.

'Well I'll concede he was one of those handy youngsters, Gray. He chucked a few at me, winded me as well.'

'Winded!' exclaimed Linda. She then began to explain to Gray that earlier Chaz doubled over on account of his stomach pain. But as she so often would say, nobody could tell Chaz Barber anything, not a thing. Gray made a joke about the blackie not fitting aesthetically with the white blazer. The joke evolved.

'Chuck an eye patch on Chaz and sit at the bar with ya best mate "One Eye"!'

Chaz laughed the suggestion off with an indignant 'Fuck off! I wouldn't sit anywhere with that fucking creep!'

'One Eye' was a fellow fanatic carper who was always trying to outdo Chaz in terms of local carp exploits. He lost an eye in a scaffolding accident in his early twenties and would always wear an eye patch, and the mere mention of his name irked Chaz. Over the last few years many of Chaz's old carp photos had been taken down from the board at the local carp supermarket. There was only the one remaining, the shot of the record 'Ressie' carp, but 'One Eye' had half a dozen with bigger carp than Chaz's, and they were on the wall, surrounding Chaz and taunting him. All were caught from a renowned difficult water that Chaz had always resisted fishing, for time consumption reasons, but which 'One Eye' had seemingly found the magic key and unlocked. It was too hard for Chaz and Chaz had indeed lost the one-upmanship stakes as he hadn't caught a big carp for well over two years, with 2002 AD being his worst season ever. The fact was, Chaz's self-appointed entitlement as king carper of Tennin, was more than slipping, it had already slipped. But Chaz took to bolstering his fragile ego, telling Gray about what had occurred.

'Did I cop him a right hand! I've been telling Linda. It was a fucking peach, mate! He walked right on it!' In fact, Chaz's right hand had come up with a swelling after he caught it when thrown onto the bonnet, so the story seemed credible. Chaz was animated and flushed as he continued the narrative. 'Once he took that fucking number, he backed off cursing and the like and we settled for an honorable draw you might say, Gray. If he had carried on, I'd have fucking murdered him, fucking murdered him!'

Gray went along with it, although he knew full well that sometimes, when it suited him well, Chaz could be very economical with the truth. Chaz explained why events had turned as they did.

'No stamina, these young guns. Shot his load! A case of all that weight training paying off when the chips are down, Gray!'

Once Chaz got into these flights of fancy, his imaginings would virtually become the truth, although sometimes people knew otherwise. Gray accepted the account, but warned Chaz of getting involved with these frisky youngsters as they were likely to pull a blade on you.

'That's what I've been saying to him, Gray,' Linda certainly agreed. But Gray had come to pick up his weekly couple, and he duly put a little pile of notes on the coffee table right in that hand of God, before finally lighting the joint he had been assiduously rolling. Chaz had a small trinket box which he kept a stash of ounces in, down to the side of the chair that he revealed like a magician. It was antique silver with a St. George and the dragon insignia and much loved. Chaz had adopted the St. George myth as his very own and he thought it having a grand significance in the scheme of things. He reinforced his belief system by having an expensive, St. George tussling that old dragon, tattoo on his left calf that was inked by the leading tattooist Joss Van Daniken, who incidentally originally hailed from the same traveler park as Scamp. It was Chaz who recommended he changed his name and it had seemed to do the trick. Everything was branding in the New Age and now Joss had a big studio up town and Chaz had visited him the previous winter. But that tattoo was a very big symbolic and philosophic statement for Chaz, as he would say, that to make the most of our lives, we all have to slay our dragons. Chaz had slayed his, donkey years back when he discovered that he could be another kind of Chaz Barber, the dealer, the dispenser, the one with the gateway keys to higher planes and the seventh heaven and out of your head vibes. Chaz 2003 AD stylee saw himself as the purveyor of those new worlds. He was Chazzy Barber the drugs guru!

'Let's open the box ta get at the magic hooter powder! There's the filthy one and the dirty two ya pirate!' Chaz was always a little dramatic, but the deal was the essential moment of Gray's week and he liked to show his appreciation.

'Love it, Chaz!'

Chaz was a realist, in the sense he knew the drugs world was a day to day, week to week thing. The trick was to make that week to week thing into something more permanent, by being clever. That's why Chaz liked to keep his own customer base down to a select minimum few, who took large amounts, relatively speaking. Let the others knock it out in the little bits was Chaz's way. Gray wasn't greedy and he covered himself with similar tactics a goodly number of rungs down the chain. He would supply a guy named Chopper and the markup was enough to keep Gray with a top up wage and have a little 'Percy' for himself and it meant he wasn't too heavily involved, with Chopper taking nigh all of the risk. Chaz was more than happy to help an old buddy out. He didn't make anything much on the deal but he liked to share that hard cash making love as he had known Gray since they began 'rubbing the One Eyed snake'.

'Yeah, ya got a nice little number going down there with that Chopper guy, Gray. Make hay and barn it while the sun shines and all that mate as ya never know what road ya might go down next in this here game.'

Gray agreed that he saw everything in terms of a week to week thing, and that everything comes to an end, eventually. Chaz and Gray were middle-aged and they thought like that now, but Chaz was living the head trip and his work had built the castle on the ground. This citadel in Holly Beach Lane, firmly built on metamorphic rock.

'How's ya baits?' Gray thought he would shift the conversation onto something that would fire Chaz up.

'Fucking pucker, mate! Like an eighteen-year-old's arsehole waiting to be shagged. And me Hermann is addicted to the blues as much as I am. Watch this, Gray.' Chaz raised himself with great difficulty, wincing with pain, but he was determined to feed the carp. Linda was concerned as he had already vomited up blood in his phlegm.

'I'll live, Linda. God never factored in rest days for the wicked, ya know,' Chaz exclaimed, responding to her fears.

Chaz chortled as the red strawberry boiled baits went down in the tank. They came to rest directly in front of an ornament there, a red telephone box with an octopus poking and wriggling free from it. Hermann came from behind the ancient stone Medusa head that he was hiding behind, and within a few moments the Hoover was on them with his vacuum sucker.

'Get on that sherbet me Herbert! Bang on it!' Chaz winced and laughed and Hermann muscled in on the teaser balls, before Chaz gave his overall assessment regarding the evolution of the wicked prospective commercial bait. Chaz spoke as if he was letting Gray into some exclusive esoteric masonic sect, with Chaz and Miko the grand masters. It was all in whispers and hushed confidential tones, although building inexorably to a grand crescendo.

'I think me and the ole Miko have finally cracked it, Gray. Really do.' Chaz lifted his shoulders in a glorious sense of personal triumph, before surging on. 'Special Assassin Triple X base with a high alcohol E9 additive and no less than *seven* secretive ingredients and attraction enhancers.'

Chaz puffed himself up, self-satisfied in the sheer audacity of what they had pulled off, before revealing all.

'And all boiled up in hemp flavored water with fully active ingredients. Get on it, Gray! Bang on it!'

'Sounds like the carp will get hecking well pissed and stoned on it, Chaz!' Gray replied. How Chaz laughed and Gray agreed with him that Miko had been proved right all along, the carp liked alcohol and dope as much as they did.

Now with the conversation firmly upon carp matters, Chaz was off. Carp fishing was his passion and total obsession, and Gray was a perfect foil, as he used to carp religiously, although he hadn't been for some seven years now. Chaz took a long toke on the joint before waxing lyrical over the big new cooker and big new urns. The scope of this new dream house was incredible.

'Linda's knocking out twenty-five kilos a day, Gray. We sold fifteen on the internet yesterday.' Chaz knew full well that he was quicker than many of his generation to fully recognize the potential and power of the internet going forward. Chaz could see it all clearly, he had that vision, and he elaborated.

'Everything is gonna be internet, mate! It's the Zeitgeist, Gray.' How Chaz liked using that term as he believed with intensity, that he knew that spirit of the times swirling around some place, defining the hip new 'now', and Chaz reckoned smugly that it was plonked down fully embodied in that sumptuous velvet chair. Chaz saw himself as being part of that new Zeitgeist class, the visionaries. He continued with more intensity, as if his every word was impelling the powers of the universe to do his bidding.

'This will be the precursor to a shop and internet business, mate. Mark my words, Gray. Mark my words. And, I'm reinforcing the idea with daily creative visualizations. It's a New Age, Gray! A New Age! And the drugs can open us to a new mind!' Chaz effused.

'And he'll stink the place out,' Linda remarked. Gray replied he could smell them. Chaz then explained that soon all boiling activities would take place down in the new shed, and the front room would smell as sweet as his breath.

'So, it's another big, big summer campaign I gather, Chaz?'

Now that conversation had turned sharply onto carp fishing, Linda thought it wise to extract herself and make a coffee, as once they really got going with carp talk that would be it for an hour at least.

'Massive assault! Fucking massive!' Chaz replied, stating his big intentions.

Linda was out in the kitchen as Chaz talked passionately about possible purchases for the forthcoming season. He had been thinking about revamping his equipment, to bring him back that all important edge. He had to re-bolster his status as a carp somebody with hard cash buying power. He elaborated his cast of mind, trying to sound incisively decisive. You could bear the failure, if it came, better then.

'Probably take the plunge and go for the dragon slayers, mate. You've got to slay the dragons a la St. George in this ere life of ours, Gray, my old son'

The aforementioned dragon slayers were at this precise moment *the* most expensive carp rod on the market, and Chaz thought it about time he had them, although he didn't really need them. The rods he had were expensive too and were hardly worn, but he made excuses to Gray that they were 'short on feel' at extreme distance. Expert carpers are like that, and Gray replied that he knew full well what Chaz was getting at, so it had to be the slayers.

'Road tested as the number one rod on the planet, mate! Like a fucking golden cock!'

How Chaz laughed at his joke but there it was, Chaz just had to have those famed dragon slayers. He also had important other things on his mind too, as lately Chaz had seen the light and had certain realizations. It was a New Age, for Christ's sake. He raised his shoulders a bit more and puffed his big thick neck forward like a male predatorial animal, testosterone overladen, readying for battle.

'And there's a few other bits and pieces I wanna buy, Gray. Revamp!' Now a great deal of Chaz's ego was bound up with all this carp fishing, and with the cocaine safely in his pocket, one could say that Gray was pandering.

'Anything to get that edge, Chaz. It's essential.'

This rather hit the switch as far as Chaz was concerned, and there was such a surfeit of adrenaline swishing through his body, that he was beginning to forget the pain of that eye and abdomen.

'You've hit it on the clit, mate! Right on the cunt button! And there's only so many big carp to go around, mate, only so many, especially the type me and Miko are after. The fucking battleships!'

Linda brought the coffees in as Chaz was using that graphic sexual language, something that always embarrassed Linda, but she would never say anything, although Gray knew how uncomfortable she was with it. Gray remarked that Linda was looking very well and Linda explained this was due to her new-found happiness working in the garden, planting and pruning. It certainly wasn't the enjoyment she gleaned from being a boilie making machine! Gray agreed, that he too just loved that garden.

'Yeah I love the sweet smell out there. Bit like the sweet breath of the White Blazerman, eh? And how's the blazer? Two grand ruined?'

Chaz brushed that one aside. Yes, there were a few scuff marks on it but it wouldn't be too bad after a clean. Gray suggested that Chaz save that one for the rainy days. He then began to peruse the carp tanks more closely.

'And luv the new tanks and the new carp Chaz and that new chair to watch um in, eh? In fact, I luv the new house, mate.'

'Well I had to have a new king's chair to watch me beauties, didn't I, Gray? Best chair I've ever sat in. Sumptuous, is the best way to describe it Gray and the house is *'The Dream'*. Yes, your ole mate Chazzy boy is sure living the dream these days, stoned out me fucking bonce watching me pet carp.' They both laughed.

Things were working out nicely now, although he still had that issue with the asylum in the back of his mind. That very reason why Chaz had resisted the idea of the move. It wasn't the house. The house was fantastic. It was just the position of it and after the laughter, Chaz became more reflective.

'But I've reservations about that old psychiatric hospital up there, mate,' Chaz confided. Gray made a joke out of the issue.

'What afraid they're gonna put ya in the nutty-farm Chaz, eh Linda?' But for Chaz the issue was far from being a joke.

'Nah, I don't like the idea of 'nut-jobs' getting it me back garden, ya know what I mean, Gray.'

Gray knew precisely what he meant, and he wouldn't have fancied being that close to the asylum. It would have spooked him. It was notorious.

CHAPTER THREE

THE SPORTSMAN, THE DRAGON SLAYERS AND THE WISE OLD MAN

The perfect late spring weather continued into the following day, and before Chaz was out on the road, he had an important mixing session in the new shed to negotiate. The shed was a whopper and Chaz had equipped it with some sparkling stainless-steel work surfaces for his bait mixing. He had a smaller one at Cavell, but this one, three times the size, was like heaven in a shed to Chaz. He had a bait mix going on in a big rubber horse feed bucket, kneading away with marigold gloves on, to avoid any hint of human taint. He was inspired and with a few pain killers, the stomach was manageable. He stopped for a moment, before releasing a measured amount of blue dye into the mix. Then he returned to his kneading, working up a mantra, as if to put a spell into the mélange that would give it some kind of magical entrancing power over monster carp.

'Chaz's divine blues, divine blues. You're gonna bring Chazzy boy a big Hermann the Hoov, Hermann the Hoov!' Chaz then picked up a pipette of some kind of deadly enhancer or other and released it into the mix, as if administering a divine sacrament. Specimen hunting wasn't a hobby for Chaz, it was a religion, and only master carpers and males at the top of the hunting chain could be in that exclusive sect.

Linda was engrossed in what she was doing too. She was busily pruning the New Dawn and Strawberry Hill climbing roses which were aligned on cross lattice trellises, that marked the border of the garden to the ancient orchard. She was completely at one with her new hobby and it was so quiet apart from the incessant pile driving taking place over the back on the ex-hospital ground, and the cawing of crows. She was thinking ahead too as she pruned. She intended to sow some Brussels before it was too late, and there was the cauliflower and broccoli to do too. She also wanted to put root veg in with some beetroot, as the soil would be nice and warm with the weather. It was busy gardening day as there was that front garden to keep on point too. As Linda happily worked away, Chaz had just about finished his mixing. It was now time for the vitally important next stage in his procedure. He whispered to himself.

'Bring on the golden eggs, Chazzy boy, bring on the egg,' before calling to Linda with his customary intent. 'Linda! Linda! Bring on those eggs will ya! I need the egg!'

Linda sighed deeply, as there was that usual ordering tone in Chaz's voice. Why did he have to talk like that? Linda heeded the call though, immediately putting down the secateurs and heading for the porch door, as some doves cooed on the back roof, and two butterflies flitted about the back garden around the flowerbeds, on their mating dance. Nature was in Chaz's back yard in its full spring abundance.

While Linda was away collecting the eggs, Chaz had begun mixing yet another big bowlful. This time he was kneading into a red mixture before he stopped and took up yet another syringe and drew liquid from a special bottle marked 'Triple X Assassin'. He checked the liquid's level in the syringe with as much detail as weighing up the cocaine. But this was serious, serious all passion carp business.

Linda knew that Chaz would moan about the eggs. They were all they had in the convenience store and were the smallest and battery farmed, exactly the type that Chaz avoided like the plague. It could only ever be organic farm shop number ones for the 'Passion Reds' and the 'Exotic Blues'. She picked them up out of the big fridge wondering why on earth she had bought them. But maybe Chaz would let it go this once she thought. She appeared back out in the garden with the three trays of eggs, that she placed on the work surface by Chaz. Then she disappeared back outside and picked up her secateurs, praying that Chaz wouldn't notice or might let it go, but knowing full well that Chaz noticed everything, and would never let anything go. Chaz was fiddling around with one of his reels but when he turned, he was disgusted with what befell him. He fumed.

'For fuck's sake, Linda! You've bought me fucking tiddlers! Poxy fucking tiddlers!' he barked. He pulled the box about with utter contempt, 'And, they're out of fucking date! Or nearly! Linda! Linda!'

Linda sheepishly came to the shed, in disbelief as to why she had bought them in the first place. How stupid, but she was having trouble getting her head round anything these days, as she felt so stressed up. She thought it might be early signs of the menopause. But she hoped that a sincerely expressed apology might suffice on this occasion.

'I'm sorry Chaz, but can't you use them this time?'

This made Chaz angrier. It illustrated the very intransigent nature of Linda, as he must have told her a thousand times that when he mixed bait, there had to be complete consistency. Had she ever listened, and more to the point did she ever listen? Chaz was enraged.

'How many more fucking times! This is "Big Fish Assassin Mix!". Eggs on the blink with fuck all yoke and white. It's no fucking good, Linda! No fucking good! Consistency, consistency, always consistency! It's the first principle when you're developing a top-class pro fucking bait! How many more times have I got to fucking well tell ya! You'll have to take them back! You'll have to!'

Linda was motionless for a moment, berating herself for not having gone the extra few miles to the farm shop. Chaz continued his tirade.

'You'll have to! I've knocked up the base with the oil additives. I need the egg! Ya can't be sloppy with "Big Fish Assassin". No fucking way! You should know that by now, Linda. You should know that!'

Linda put down her secateurs in resignation with a deep sigh that didn't impress Chaz one bit.

'And there's no need for all that puffin and fucking huffing!' Chaz pointed at her to accentuate his feelings. 'It was your mistake. You know I need number ones! It's gotta be fresh farm shop number ones for the Assassin mix! It's always organic number ones for the "Big Fish Assassin". Always!'

Linda gave way and now it was a mission to get 'proper' eggs as Chaz called them. She left the house and traveled the five miles to the farm shop at top speed. She knew that Chaz would be mad if she took too long, as the base mix would begin to harden before the egg went in. He would be moaning for a couple of days at least if that happened. But she couldn't understand why she hadn't gone down there in the first place. But there was just too much on her mind.

Before the half hour was up, Linda was driving back up Holly Beach Lane passing the road sign that incidentally read 'Holy' as there was a space in between the 'l' and 'y', as the last 'l' was missing. She had the three boxes of large organic number ones on the passenger seat. Chaz only went organic when he was thinking carp, as carp fishing was all about excessive attention to detail. You have to work darn hard for your fish and as Chaz knew by watching them in the front room, carp are very fastidious creatures.

If Linda had taken another thirty minutes, Chaz would have got a real strop on and thrown the lot away. But luckily Linda made it in time and when she handed them over in the shed, all was well and truly good and 'proper' in Chaz's mixing domain.

'That's me little beauties. Cheers, Linda luv. Even the Hoover would spit um out if I knock um up with stale egg.'

Linda couldn't help but point out, that whatever they were, the supermarket eggs weren't stale.

'They weren't far off it, girl!' Chaz reiterated, thrusting that neck from his shoulders a couple of times.

But with the all-important egg, Chaz was off again in his personal paradise of carp bait preparation.

'So, let's get it wet! Let's get the fanny wet!'

Linda was still in the shed watching Chaz rather dramatically throw the eggs, egg shells and all, into the mix as if anticipating a shocked reaction.

The approach succeeded as Chaz had never done that before while mixing his baits.

'What on earth are you doing?' Linda asked. Chaz was animated. He felt like a pioneer heading out into the unknown, searching for, and discovering new knowledges, that would be held dear for generations to come. Chaz Barber and 'The Crunch Factor'.

'It's egg shells in from now on, Linda. We call it crunch factor. It's something unique that me and Miko have been developing. Carp like crunching with their back teeth, Linda. They find it comforting.' Chaz reached for an appropriate metaphor. 'Ha, ha, like you women and your chocolate, ha ha, and if ya lay a carpet out of um ya gonna get big pit carp crunching and a scrunching.'

Chaz continued, as if delivering some kind of sermon of carp, and Linda listened attentively screwing her nose up as if trying to find the correct erudition.

'Well, other big carp hear the crunch, and scrunching waves ripple out through the water and before ya know it there's tons of carp joining the great crunch and scrunch. So, it's egg shells in this year. It must be egg shells in for crunch factor, Linda!'

Linda thought about crunching away on egg shells and she was far from enamored.

'Well I wouldn't want to crunch on egg shells!' she said, scrunching her face up in disgust. Chaz nodded his head in disbelief. Sometimes.

'Well you're not a big pit flipping carp are ya, Linda!' They both laughed, and then Chaz couldn't but reveal the deeper revelations and secret knowledge. A moment of great significance. 'As I said to Miko. I was smoking a joint and watching Hermann in the tank when the revelation came to me. Like a flash!'

When revealing such important things like this to Linda, Chaz expected and demanded complete and utter attention. Linda looked gripped, hanging over his every word, reading the script, like she was supposed to.

'Soft baits are like substitutes for natural baits. So, we've got to develop a bait that acts like a freshwater muscle or snail. Pure genius eh? Sort of crunchy and scrunchy on the outside and soft on the ins.'

Ideas flowed through Linda's mind as she picked up the train of thought, and she wanted to show how keenly involved in this new revelation she was.

'What, like a French truffle?' she suggested. Chaz sighed deeply.

'Fucking French truffle! No! Not like a French fucking truffle! Like a flipping freshwater muscle! God, you're hard work sometimes, Linda.'

Linda was determined her French truffle suggestion should be seen by Chaz on its merits, and as far as she was concerned, she had witnessed carp being caught on virtually anything. So why not a French truffle and why not a spirited defense of the French truffle? Sometimes she got fed up with Chaz making her feel so stupid.

'Well French truffles are hard and scrunchy on the outside and soft and chocolaty on the inside. Try one. You might actually catch a carp, Chaz!'

Chaz's blood boiled. He didn't have to be reminded of his darn failure and he had to nip such recalcitrance and stupidity in the bud. Linda was the kind of woman who needed good sound advice on anything carp, and anything life in fact.

'Linda, this bait is a complete, nutritious and balanced carp formula. Not a bloody woman's comfort food!'

The previous week Chaz had sat down in front of the carp tanks and scrunched his way through a box of truffles, so Linda couldn't let that one rest.

'Well you scrunched away all my truffles last week getting all comfortable,' she replied. Chaz looked at her considering the context last week.

'That was different, I had a bloody hard day with the Herberts!'

Within a short while, the boilie making process was in full swing, and Chaz was firing off lines of beautiful thin blue sausages with a bait gun. These were then given to Linda who promptly and efficiently rolled them in a boilie tray, creating perfectly rounded divine blues. These then went into another tray all ready for the boil. It was a well-rehearsed ritual and Linda played her part to the full. After the divine blues it was onto the strawberry passion reds and Chaz's mind was given to the aesthetics of shining steel and bright blue and red boilies lain out on the surfaces. Within no time they were there. Twenty-five more kilos ready for the boil!

After all that frenetic work activity, Chaz thought he would get a little time out reading his newspapers and carp magazines. With the summer like warmth and sunshine, he decided to position himself on the small bit of lawn in front of the shed on a carp bed chair. He put it up, but prior to relaxing, it had to be a Chaz Barber fitness work out. This would involve repeated sets of bicep curls and shoulder presses with his dumbbells, undertaken while he was firmly seated in the chair. Chaz was exceptionally disciplined and each exertion would be technically perfect with ramrod straight back with expert breathing. On this occasion his deep inhalations on his efforts, seemed to be rhythmically syncopating with the incessant pile driving that was going on in the ex-hospital farm grounds. After a triumphant last set, he took a long deep breath of satisfaction, and relaxed back into the chair. He picked up a can of lager, cracked it open, had a sip, took hold of a carefully rolled up joint, before reflecting upon this delicious and paradisiacal moment.

'This is the life, Linda! More like California than crappy ol Tennin.'

Linda was blissfully happy working away, and she was just beyond the cross-lattice fencing scratching around with a garden fork, thinking about swedes and turnips and French runner beans. Chaz put on his expensive reading glasses in a studious manner, as if he were to embark on a rigorous course of highly intellectual study. He then took hold of a paper that he would buy as regular as clockwork, *The Sportsman. The Daily Sportsman* was a sex-oriented fantasy paper and it always added humor to Chaz's daily grind. He perused the front-page leader that referred to a woman who had sex with two baboons and an orangutan. This was the kind of exclusive that Chaz loved. He began laughing loudly as he read.

'Fuck's sake! Old trollop here Linda, had a session with two baboons and an orangutan. And I thought *we* were perverted!' He laughed and laughed at his joke, although Linda merely half smiled, as she worked the fork over the earth. Chaz felt impelled to elaborate on the details.

'Says she got bored with the football team that used to bang her. What a slapper! She says she's in love with sex. Well ain't we all, luv! Ain't we all! But ya don't have to let it make a monkey out of ya!'

Chaz laughed even louder at his jokes as the pile drivers still banged away, but Linda didn't laugh. She begrudgingly smiled. Then as Chaz turned another page the quietude descended for a few fleeting moments. The trees at the back of the house beyond the new shed softened the noise of the constant traffic going up the hill, and all you could really hear was the odd car going up the lane at the front, or that incessant pile driver. But it was still a great deal more peaceful than their last home on the ex-council estate at Cavell.

'Wouldn't it be peaceful here Chaz without all that pile driving?'

Chaz was deep into an article about two young women from Longwilly in the West Country, who liked to have as many big cocks as possible down their throats. It was a *Sportsman* exclusive entitled 'Throat fucking and the villages of Olde England' and it was proof to Chaz, that the implications of the New Age were being felt everywhere.

'You're clutching at rainbows! When they've finished, there'll be a great industrial estate at the back of us and before you know it that by-pass will have gone through too! But at least that old asylum won't be there then and thank fuck for that!'

That asylum disquieted Chaz. He had built up something of an irrational fear of the place, but Linda looked at it more pragmatically.

'The asylum never brought noise and air pollution, Chaz,' Linda replied, but that wasn't the point. This new place was nice but it was that asylum.

'You know how I feel, Linda. I've heard too many stories about the fucktards up there. We could do with a twenty-foot barbed wire fence around us, fucking nutty muppets!'

'That would look lovely, wouldn't it! Like a bloody concentration camp!' Linda replied.

It was getting towards one o'clock now which meant it was time for lunch at the Barber household, if Chaz was still hanging around. Linda had meant to purchase an uncut loaf from Moffetts, the local village bakers, when she was out getting the organic eggs. But it just slipped out of her mind. She was just too strung out after arguing with Chaz about those supermarket eggs. But it meant that all they had was her seeded whole-meal. Chaz abhorred seeded whole meal but Linda was hoping that she could somehow persuade him to begin a healthy food eating regime, starting from today, right here, right now. She was forever pointing out to Chaz that whole meal was excellent roughage and fabulously healthy. She'd have to give it a stab, so the boat with the whole meal flag went out. She sounded tentative, although was trying to be decisive.

'I thought it would be nice if we had a whole meal loaf for lunch, Chaz,' she offered with a hopeful smile.

Chaz couldn't believe what he was hearing. How he hated that whole meal bread, especially that type with the seeds that Linda was always stuffing down her chops. She was obsessed with the bloody stuff. He folded up *The Sportsman* in disgust, and rather dramatically threw it down hard on the grass by the chair. He was incensed, maddened that this subject had come up yet again, after he thought that everything had been clarified about whole meal poxy bread.

'Fucking hell, Linda! How many more fucking times have I got to tell ya? I don't like fucking whole meal bread! I know *you* don't like Moffetts uncut white but others find it agreeable and it's called freedom of choice, Linda. I ain't eating fucking whole meal! No way, woman! Those fucking horrible seeds set me asthma off. You know that!'

Linda tried to persist with the idea saying that she only thought it would be better for Chaz's health, that's all. But Chaz would have none of it.

'Well ya thought wrong Linda, didn't ya? And I'm just about sick ta the teeth of hearing all this crap about health foods,' Chaz elaborated with his usual witty flourish.

'Fucking health freaks! They'd have ya on three sticks of celery a day and a fucking iceberg lettuce and ya'd probably be nigh hallucinating with hunger driving up the fucking road. And after ya fucking crashed the car against a lamppost they'd say cod and double chips with a pot of salt are ten times better for ya. I've had uncut door-stopper white since I came off the high chair and I haven't internally combusted as yet, Linda!'

Chaz laughed even louder and in celebration of his wit, he took a great lug from the joint and began coughing and spluttering, before he gave his summation on the issue, freedom of choice being the general premise.

'You're fully entitled to have your own choice, Linda, fashionable whole meal, that will help you crap it out, so artistically, while I'll take mine please, Linda, good ol door-stopping constipation white, thank you very much.'

Linda was boxed into the hangdog corner and she finally revealed the truth.

'We haven't got any, Chaz. I thought I had one in the freezer but I haven't.'

Chaz dug his feet into the lawn, his big legs topping up on the bronze in the high sun. There was only one kind of bread he was going to have and it had to be Moffetts white! Chaz was back with his ordering tone.

'Well go and get some from Moffetts then because I ain't tackling your fucking whole meal. No way! I don't eat the shite. You know that! You've always known it! Always, Linda!'

Linda didn't say a word. She just moved off the premises. She should have remembered and gone to Moffetts in the first darn place. She pulled out of the space in front of the gate a little quickly as her frustration began to bite.

Chaz settled down after Linda had gone. He thought he would take a look at this month's *Master Carper*, one of those Carp monthlies that Chaz so eagerly supported. He turned the cover and gasped at the editorial comment with its header, 'Women catch um on chocolate!'. It referred to a fifty pound plus UK carp that was caught on a chocolate truffle by a woman, Mary Shagnall, who was described as a 'specimen hunter'. Chaz turned the pages and took a glance and then sneered at the exclusive photos that appeared there on page four. The woman, who was forty-nine and came from Grimsby, said she was always dieting and then eating boxes of chocolate truffles, so she thought why not give them a go on the lake. She apparently caught five monsters, four over forty pounds and the biggie up to fifty-three, which was the most impressive haul of big carp anywhere in the country thus far in the 2003 AD season. Chaz got away from that stupid article as quickly as possible. But five big UK carp. Chaz would have given his right arm for a haul like that and his left! She was down on her haunches with the five laid out one behind the other looking like she could have hooked out a whole bloody lake full. Chaz tried desperately to get the image out of his mind. Mary Shagnall from fucking Grimsby! But it must have been a one-off fluke. Like a hundred to one shot winning the Derby. The carp angling fraternity wanted hard scientific male thinking and data with regard the efficacy or otherwise of carp baits. Not bloody women masquerading as men because they didn't have penises, doing as they pleased with packs of chocolate. Women could do football if they wanted to, not that Chaz would ever watch a load of dykes kicking a football about, but never, ever specimen hunting! Men are the hunters and women are the vegetable gatherers with their cooking pots. It was a universal truth and Linda was a living proof of it with her fussing over the vegetable plots and her obsession with that new kitchen.

Chaz stopped for a moment as it seemed that love was in the air and he watched two more white cabbage butterflies as they whirred and danced their way through the garden on their courtship rituals. But then he inevitably broke off his meditation, as he turned the carp mag onto a double page exclusive of the new millennium's must have carp tech gadget, the bait boat with underwater video camera. Now up to this point in time Chaz had hated anything to do with 'plastic' as he called them bait boats. But with such a torrid 2002 AD season behind him, he would undoubtedly be open to persuasion from the right voices, and the winter's drug dealings had left him awash with cash. Despite all the money spent on the house, there was still some forty or fifty grand upstairs, tucked up with the guns in the cabinet.

Chaz could virtually hear the author's voice as he read, and it sounded utterly convincing when you're on a long-term blank. Chaz Barber could not tolerate firing blanks. It was just unacceptable to the great king carp of Tennin Gap.

'Now we all know what some carp folk like me and you might say about bait boats. How they're not *real* fishing. But believe you me, if you can afford one, you'll find the bait boat can be the difference between miserable blanks and big carp-ridden days. Hi-tech precision is the way in the new millennium and bait dropping could triple your big fish take for the season if you take the great leap of faith.'

Chaz read on and this guy Malcolm Peakes, a big name in the carp angling fraternity, had apparently conducted a scientific experiment where he fished with the bait boat and then fished without one. Over the course of six months his results were over two hundred per cent better with the hi-tech gadget. Chaz took a deep lug of his joint. He was just blown away. That two hundred sent him into deep reflection. Why hadn't he converted years ago? It would have been that 'One Eye' who would have been struggling to stay on the supermarket's board, not Chaz. Yes, he was beginning to think a bit different now. He had to be willing to change his mind-set, and why shouldn't better chances of catching carp, accrue to people who had the most money? Money makes the world go around. Tough luck if you didn't have any. It showed you weren't trying hard enough or were a loser, no-hoper dosser. Success with money equates with success in all areas of life. Chaz had earnt the right to capitalize, and yes, maybe this was a period when *all* carpers had to go hi-tech. You can never go back to those fabled 'Good old days' when all you needed were maggots, bread flakes and a flipping split cane rod like he started with on the dykes down Fishgate. You have to move with the times, like Chaz was doing with his internet porn sites.

He continued to be won over by the weight of argument, and was likely to try anything now, beyond reason, to bag more specimen carp. But Chaz felt that now hurting need to re-establish himself as Tennin's number one specimen carp hunting king. They used to call him 'Chaz the Great' down at the 'Ressie'. He kept thinking of that photo up there in the carp supermarket surrounded by bloody 'One Eye' cradling big mother fucker carp. Heaven's forbid, it would be the Mary Shagnall's pushing him off the board next.

As he read, something opened up in his mind. Grand new vistas were caught in the moment like a revelation flash. It was one of those moments of true and pure revelation and Chaz knew the significance. He had to take action now! He had been reading in *The Orb on Sunday* the previous week, that in America there was a new groundswell of activism on behalf of 'gender-benders'. God forbid it would be one of those crazies pushing him off the board next with a huge carp. He had to get a fifty to ensure he stayed at the center. He had too! He read on, transfixed, while also thinking about that forty grand sitting up there in the gun cabinet. Chaz's sap was rising and it did so with a wad in his back pocket.

'And yes, we can all spot carp with the naked eye cruising on the surface but imagine a third eye that sees everything as it really is? Gear up with the video camera that hooks nicely into your cozy bivvy to get your nose into what is really going on down there in the depths. All the expert, fifty big fish a year carpers are already using them! It's the New Age so get a bait boat!'

After reading that, Chaz's head was spinning. A third eye! He jutted his big neck from his shoulders and in that bright light of the early afternoon, he felt as if he had a clear power of vision and insight. How he dreamed of being one of those 'top dogs' as Chaz called them, with their fifty big carp a season. He could see it now. Big photo montage board in the kitchen, full of those fifty carp, with a caption 2003 AD underneath it. Chaz chuckled to himself, the AD reference would give the capture the required gravitas. Yes, with this new-fangled boat he could send the thing out into the lake and it would be like a reconnaissance frigate, discovering where those darn carp were hiding. What a tool! The mother fuckers couldn't escape Chaz's teaser balls then.

Chaz turned the page onto a very auspiciously placed advert, that referred to a micro Panther bait boat deal, that included an echo sounder and video camera, and all for fifteen hundred pounds, reduced temporarily from two G. Chaz was in complete meditation as the doves cooed on the roof and that pile driver kept on cracking down. The advert had been placed by the carp superstore only a mile up the road. The forty grand was beginning to burn an almighty hole in his pocket and his internal carp king voice was on overdrive.

'The third eye will give you that edge, Chaz. You'll have the eye of God and that bait boat will be the difference, between miserable blanks, and fucking heck, you know what a bastard they are Chaz, and big carp ridden soaked days, and all the fifty twenties a season boys are using them Chaz. Big carp soaked days, big.'

Everything was heading just one way, when Chaz's work mobile rang, with its ring tone of the old sixties hit 'She's Not There'. When work came in, Chaz immediately stood to erect attention and became the animated businessman. The Chaz Barber philosophy with business, was that you have to lock yourself in, focus; mean, keen focus! He began stalking around the garden with his mobile all a readied. It was a porn punter on the end of the line, and whenever Chaz talked porn business, the sex power button switched itself on. How he loved the sheer sexual thrill of being involved in the porn industry, gaining that deep insight and experience of all that kinky sex. It gave him that awareness of what women really wanted and that article in *The Sportsman* duly confirmed what Chaz knew all along. It's a New Age and it all hangs out behind closed doors, and be mindful, on look out, for the women who are up for it, gagging for it. Keep clear of the prudes and bigots and man hating feminists. Use your intuition and then it can't go wrong.

'Adult Leisure. Yes mate, six films for forty. Er, whatever floats ya boat, mate. Swedish, German, lesbian and gay gangbang, watersports. Whatever ya like, mate. Yeah, no problem. Where are ya? Hulda Street, Elphame Valley. Yeah, no problem.'

Chaz was organized. This was how he kept his business up and running to perfection like a well-oiled machine. The drop was marked in the itinerary for the day, and while he was jotting in the entry, a female postal worker was walking up the garden path with a small parcel. She too made a deep inhalation of the aromatic scents. She reached the door, frowned at the hissing snake door knocker, before ringing the bell. Chaz spotted her from the garden as the front door approach was in view.

'Hullo there,' he said.

'Parcel for you, Mr. Barber,' she replied.

Chaz was quick to get up to her as he was waiting on a number of personalized printed T-shirts that he had ordered. They were designer shirts that used the famous iconic image of Chaz with the 'Ressie' carp, and another that used that similarly famous iconic image of Natasha. The monster carp snap was emblazoned on two and underneath was the phrase 'King Carp'. The Nastasha T-shirt had 'Porn it!', Chaz's call to the New Age, splashed across it, with the letters covering the image, to bring it this side of acceptable around Tennin.

Chaz admired them and within a few moments he had changed T-shirts and had the pink 'King Carp' on, which would be ideal for that trip to the carp supermarket. Now Chaz had read his Jung as well as his Freud, and he knew that this New millennium was all about men doing their feminine and Chaz reckoned his choice of pink reflected that. It would certainly turn heads just like the 'Porn it!' would. He had certain plans for that one forming in his mind, it would certainly get them talking down in the village. He could assault their narrow-mindedness. Chaz went inside and upstairs, to get a wad of nice clean twenties and fifties from the cabinet, visualizing himself sauntering around in that 'Porn It' top, with all the women giving him the eye. Why not be a fashion leader, Chaz thought as he zipped up his jeans.

After the post office van went down the lane towards the doctor's house, an adder wriggled from the verge and moved in the opposite direction towards Chaz's. The sweltering heat had got the many snakes of the area moving, and this one spiraled a little way, and then stopped, and looked up towards the house, as if on some kind of fixated snake crazy spiraling mission.

Well Chaz was on his mission too. He felt fired up with his new T-shirt on and he toked on a joint as he pulled the chariot away from the parking space by the horse chestnut. Chaz loved the way that the pink T-shirt complimented the perfect white of the Jag. Chaz loved colors and relationships and he would work them to get those heads turning. He was like an artist and he loved the way his tight-fitting Gucci's, pulled at the Barber crown jewels.

Chaz fiddled with the rear view, with his head full of that bait boat and other purchasing ideas. Chaz just had to go hi-tech and Chaz Barber was never one for half measures. He felt up to his moniker, 'Chaz the Great', as he smiled and chewed his way down sun dappled Holly Beach Lane. Why not make the complete leap, he thought, and finally get those three dragon slayers that he had been threatening to buy for ages now? Chaz clicked the CD player and 'Black Magic Woman' from Santana came over his system. It felt right and he sped down the lane, running right over the snake that was slithering up the narrow road. Chaz was on all cylinders turning those heads in that open topped car, with that guitar ringing out. What a blade.

Before hitting the carp supermarket, Chaz took a short trip to the village convenience store, as he wanted the paper to check the runners at York. One of his long-range ante-post Derby punts was running. He also wanted some fags as he had forgot to pick them up from the garden, he was so fired up about the intended purchases. But that was because Chaz simply loved buying carp gear, it was almost as exciting as catching them, or having an hour or two with the escort girls. He could get those to do *anything,* just bung them another half a dozen fifty's, 'sorted!'.

He pulled up into the car parking area, left the joint in the ashtray, and alighted with sheer dramatic energy and with no apparent pain from his abdomen whatsoever. Adrenaline was the drug when things big carp were up and about, and who else pulled up outside Tennin convenience stores in 70K wagons? Chaz chuckled, possibly Natasha Barber might.

There was an old boy about eighty or so with a retriever dog on a lead that was pissing up the railings. The old boy recognized Chaz for being the man who had moved in up Holly Beach Lane, and he was determined to tell Chaz some home truths about the area. Why not, he had the local knowledge and a story to tell.

Chaz breezed out of the shop, giving a glance to the headlines on the front page of *The Orb*, an exclusive on there, that Chaz sighed deeply over. Two hundred killed by mental patients since care in the community introduced next to the 'Greeta is a Man Eater', scoop. He would read up both, especially that Greeta Zadinksy piece, the fifty-two-year-old erotic literary sensation was revealing her quite prodigious sexual appetites, which even raised Chaz's eyebrows. The old boy smiled at him.

'All right, mate?' Chaz acknowledged.

The old boy had his moment now, to open up, and he did so in a gruff gravelly voice treating his information, as if he too was divulging something top secret.

'Have you just moved in up the Holly Beach Lane?' he asked. This made Chaz loiter for a second.

'Yeah, I have, mate. Bought it four months ago,' Chaz replied, thinking for a moment how much work they had already done on the renovation and transformation. The old fellow got straight to the point, as he had that tale to tell, and he couldn't wait to speak it like some old ancient mariner.

'Seen any snakes?' he asked. Chaz looked at him wondering what on earth he was talking about.

'What do you mean, mate?' he asked, and the old boy seized the opportunity.

'It's a snake pit up there and they come out of hibernation this time of year when the heat gets through.' Chaz called his bluff giving his reply an incredulous and hugely mocking tone.

'Yeah, you do say?'

The old boy had tons more stuff to tell to build up the narrative.

'I used to do the boiler maintenance up at the old asylum, back in the day. On a day like this, me and Bert used to watch um sunbathing up on Chalk Hill. We counted a hundred and one, one dinner hour, snakes everywhere. It was that summer of seventy-six, the really hot one. All vipers they were!'

Chaz had heard all these old man tales many a time. These kinds of stories gave them validity, as if they had experienced things that today could never be experienced. He took to being a little flippant with his reply.

'All getting the bronzy on, eh? Nah, no snakes up there now, mate. Just flowers and field mice. The snakes must have migrated on a chartered boat to Africa or something. Sees ya later.'

Chaz made for his car and the reply had maddened the old fellow, who was gesticulating at Chaz with his stick, still adamant that he was right and Chaz was wrong.

'They're still up there and they'll be out. Mark my words! There're loads of snakes up on Holly Beach Hill. Loads!'

Chaz opened the door of the Jag and he couldn't resist one last broadside to such claptrap.

'Yeah, I'll watch out for um with their little peaked caps on, mate,' Chaz said jokingly, but full of derision at the old timer's stories.

Chaz wheel-spun away from the park up, smiling to the strains of 'The Walker Brothers', hell bent on getting to that carp superstore. How Chaz loved the sixties music. He found it came up fresh every time, and when he played it in the Jag everything seemed eternally optimistic and downright sexy, as all that free love swirled around in the air waves. Have some of that, Chaz thought. Chaz's glass was always more than half full of that bullish bonhomie and it was overflowing as he drove his car up to that carp superstore, four grand readied in the skyrocket. The sun was shining for evermore as Chaz momentarily moved his expensive dark glasses with a flicked tic of the fingers, and that high sun shone down and the Jag sparkled like yet another jewel of his crown. His world was perfect. In Chaz's humble opinion, you've got to remain the eternal optimist in this here life. The glass has to be kept brimming. People expect great things and yet they hold up a glass with the bottom falling apart, the dossers. Kevin, the assistant manager of the superstore, noticed Chaz's flash Jag pull into the car park.

'Here he is, the self-appointed carp king!' he said a little ironically to the shop manager by the till.

'He was due one,' the manager Graham replied, knowing full well that this was the time of year when carpers like Chaz, were polishing and rattling their sabers, gearing up for the new season ahead. Chaz entered the shop with a noticeably erect preen about him. As far as Chaz was concerned, he was a somebody in this carp world. He was the gun-slinging carp specimen hunter of Tennin and the most famous of all its carp anglers. Or at least this is what the Chaz had convinced himself he was. He gave a quick glance at the board where the 'Ressie' record snap with Chaz cradling that great monster still held sway, although seemingly besieged by that 'One Eye'.

In fact, the management spoke about the snap as it had been there many years. But they decided they would keep it up indefinitely in some capacity, as Chaz was a habitual customer year upon year. Even though many bigger carp were being caught in local lakes, it still looked big, so why antagonize such a good customer who was bound to be making many more big purchases at the shop? It just made good business and customer liaison sense, and furthermore, they prayed that Chaz would add to his big fish haul. It would ensure he kept on the cutting-edge side of things and that meant diving into the wallet frequently, and he had a big one.

Chaz gave an eye towards Kevin as he entered, and then he sped to the 'master carpers' section, and stood spellbound in front of the top rods, specifically the all-conquering dragon slayers. Four hundred pounds each and pitched as the ultimate in twenty-first century rod technology. Kevin was busily replenishing stock from a trolley and he came behind Chaz.

'You'd be Saint Charles with those beauties, Chazzy,' he japed.

Chaz slowly turned his head from his meditation, stroking and cupping that beard, relishing every moment. Four grand of wedge in the skyrocket and most of it in those clean Bank of England fifties, that he had tucked away in so many escort girl's knickers in his time. How Chaz loved shopping, knowing that he had the sheer power to purchase anything he wanted, anything. Every kinky desire you ever conceived of; all could be satiated. All just like magic! These kinds of things had propelled Chaz to the top of Tennin Gap's tree. But Chaz knew the *real* worth of money and he was prepared to graft it out for every penny that came his way, every penny. If you work that hard to get it, it's yours to spend as you see fit. It's freedom of choice.

'Yeah, they're nice, Kevvy boy. Real nice.'

''Bout the best money can buy, Chaz. The new record went on a dragon slayer,' Kevvy pointed out, hoping that Chaz might dig into his pocket for some big purchases.

You bet that Chaz knew the record went on a dragon slayer, and Chaz was thinking that it was high time that he went dragon slaying. Kevin stood to earn a bonus so he was hoping.

'Yeah, I know, Kevvy, I've heard they're some kinda rod.' Chaz stroked the beard again and Kevin emphasized that they were tops, but to ensure that things weren't all about sales and carp gear pitching, he asked how things were.

'Anyhow, how's tricks, Chaz?'

Chaz gathered himself and opened up, fully aware of who was milling around the store, as Chaz felt his status as a carp master on these premises.

'Agh, the new house. Fantastic, Kevvy boy! And just a little bit closer to my favorite supermarket, I might add!'

Chaz stalled for a moment, stroked the beard thoughtfully this time before continuing, because that darn asylum hovered around his world like that. It seemed to threaten, ominously.

'But a bit too close to those fucking whacky shackers though, mate.'

Chaz couldn't help but air his underlying grievance, but it wasn't long before Chaz could be seen gathering himself ready to make moves. He hunched his shoulders up and preened his neck, looking around the shop, in this re-establishing himself among the elite moment. There were a number of young carpers milling around fairly close by at the mid-price range rods, who had all seen Chaz on the board with that unforgettable shark hunter's hat on. They knew he had that Jag and that must have been fifty grands' worth of car plus the rest, and he was that guy who wore the white blazer and those blue shoes. The flash bastard. They even knew that Jay and Dai scored off him. It had got around, although Jay and Dai tried to keep it quiet. But the goateed Chaz had been seen going into their flat, and it was two plus two equals Chaz was their big dealer dude four.

'Will ya give me ten per cent, Kevvy?'

The big purchases were getting closer, in what was a well-rehearsed routine. Haggling over discounts like this, made Chaz feel embodied in the moment, right here, right now, emboldened by his undoubted purchasing power.

'You always get the five, Chaz. It depends on what you're buying,' was Kevin's worn response.

Chaz hunched his shoulders a little more, knowing that the two young carpers, who had scored Chaz's gear off Jay in the car park last night, were watching him. He cupped that goatee, knowing he was on the stage.

'I was gonna take three dragon slayers, Kevvy, and one of these Panther bait boat packages as advertised in the *Master Carper*, with all the third eye camera gubbins like.'

With that kind of buying there was never going to be a problem with the ten.

'Gladly do ya the ten, Chaz,' Kevin replied.

Within a few minutes all the aforementioned products were on the counter by the till with a whole lot of carp accessories including line, hooks, rigs, bait indicators, carp mats and even a new king-sized landing net and a whole lot more.

'You're hitting the plastic, mate?' Kevin suggested, while ringing up what would be a substantial bill.

'Cash, mate. Pay in cash this time.' Chaz pushed his neck forward, as was his mannerism, like a great turtle pushing its head and neck from its shell. He felt impelled to say something philosophically important and definitive about the overall scene at that time, as Chaz saw himself as one of its leading lights.

'It's the time of the year, Kevvy boy. Besides I wanna go hi-tech. Certain realizations I've had, mate. It's the New Age now, Kevvy, and a New Age for carping. And we've gotta move with the times. All of us. Even the 'master carpers', Kevvy.'

The shop liked the carp brigade to think like this, and it was the way that carping had gone. If you didn't keep up, you just wouldn't be in the mags holding these magnificent fish. Big monster carp cost a lot of time and effort, and some considerable financial outlay. You had to have wedge in your back pocket to catch carp now.

'Yeah, we've all gotta go with the flow otherwise there won't be any carp left for little ol' me and youse, Chaz,' Kev stated, and it all seemed so obvious, now that Chaz had made that leap of faith.

'You're right on the cunt button, mate! Right on the fucking clit!

Chaz always brought his humor back to the downright sexual, because that's where all humor goes in the last instance, according to Chaz. Kevin announced the damage, but Chaz had four big ones in his pocket so he knew it was all covered.

'That will be the kingly sum of three thousand, four hundred and forty-eight quid, Chaz. Ten per cent and we'll call it three four five, plus a very "special" discount for being a very "special" customer, will take ya down to a rounded three big ones as you like to call um, Chaz.'

'Cheers, Kevvy boy!'

Chaz felt carp king vindicated. He dispensed the wedge as if it were no more than chicken feed and nigh all in those immaculate, perfect fifties. One of the young carpers saw how much money Chaz took from his pocket, and he nudged the other into looking too. What a dude!

CHAPTER FOUR

SNAKES IN THE GARDEN

Before ten minutes had passed, Chaz was standing by the carp chair in the back-garden, sipping at a can, quivering one of those dragon slayer beauties, testing its 'feel'. Chaz hunched his shoulders up and smiled to himself. That action was sublime. The bait boat was already out of its boxed packaging, and was by the carp bed-chair, full of reds and blues, destined to be its payload this summer season. After having felt that acute sense of the tip of his new alchemical rod, he broke the rod down and reverentially laid it on the grass beside him. And to think he had three of these beauties. He wondered why on earth he hadn't purchased them before. But then he thought about how much cash he had poured into this dream house. There was lots to pay for, but so what, he thought. He reckoned that with a good bank holiday weekend, he could still purchase those gold ingots, he so desperately wanted to send to the Swiss bank account. Chaz was on the mission, he just had to get up to the twenty, so there was tangible golden evidence that he had finally arrived in the complete and utter big time. Twenty gold ingots, eh? Gold stock Chazzy Barber, 'class', and stuff that down ya pants! And then shove it down the escort girls' throats! Chaz chuckled.

Chaz sat back down on the carp chair, and proceeded to lay a large and quite generous line of coke on the back of the carp magazine. He snorted with an enormous inhalation, and on exhalation he looked the most contented man on the planet. All he needed now was a monster carp and that obligatory trophy snap. He jutted that neck and felt confirmed as badass.

With the sun so bright, Linda reached for the sunglasses. These were very expensive carp specs that Chaz had bought for her birthday. It meant that both Chaz and Linda looked at the world together through carp vision and good marriages are like that, with two people looking at life in the same way, with so much in common. Could any other woman knock boilies out like Linda?

Linda pulled into the opening at the bottom of the lane and that doctor's wife, Catherine, was about to get in her car with her skimpy tennis dress on. Linda had spoken to her once or twice, and they had gone down there, and said hullo to the neighbors, on the afternoon of the house warming party. She also knew she was a chief radiographer at the Tennin General Hospital, the other side of town. But Linda thought she looked a bit of a tart. Her husband must have been some twenty or so years older than her, so it was obvious to Linda what she was all about with that tennis dress up her arse. They smiled politely at each other like 'polite' neighbors do.

By her side on the passenger seat was the bag of shopping, including the essential Moffetts uncut white, that Chaz had virtually been reared on since a young boy. There was also a local newspaper on top of the bag, with a leader that had interested Linda enough to purchase it. 'Big Cats seen on the Triune Way'.   Now the Triune Way was a newish stretch of road that ran along to the River Tunnel approach and which joined up to the road that snaked up Death Hill. Apparently big black cats had been seen down there, and it had become one of those local urban myths that evolve sometimes, akin to UFOs. Unbeknown to Linda, she ran right over the dead and squashed snake as she drove up the Holly Beach Lane. Rubbing it in, you might say.

Linda smelt the flowers again as she walked up the garden path, and she thought they had been truly blessed finding and buying this dream house. They had been so fortunate. It had dropped in their laps. She had said to Chaz, it was like the house had found them, not the other way around! She smiled as she felt vindicated. It was Linda who saw the house advertised in a local estate agent next to her hairdressers. And for Linda the house had something special about it, something unique, that made you feel as if you were far away from the mad frenetic modern world, and only a few miles from Tennin town center. She smiled contentedly and thought she might put last night's chicken leftovers in the sandwiches. Chaz would love that.

Chaz was seated on the carp chair with a beaming smile, as she came up the end of the pathway, and was about to turn the key in the lock.

'Do you want a coffee, Chaz?' Linda asked, knowing that beaming smile well. It was one of those Chazzy Barber 'the world is perfect by me' smiles, that Chaz sometimes had. She immediately knew it had been top-of-the-range carp gear day.

'Love one, Linda.' The big wide grin just got bigger and bigger as Chaz stroked that goatee.

Linda looked at the spitting snake knocker and by now she had come to like it in an odd kind of way. At least it was unique. Apparently, the last owner, who had finally passed away the previous summer, had been a writer of rather arcane books, and his wife had been a supporting actress in many horror films going back in the day, although she had died a number of years ago of cancer. Linda had researched them a bit on the internet and she discovered that the pair of them were deeply involved with their own secret society that brought with it considerable controversy back in the free love 1960s. It was all rather intriguing and Chaz began to take an interest when he discovered these past owners had been sex addicts. He said they hadn't left behind any valuable paintings or whatnot in the attic that they could take to an antiques roadshow though. But he was fascinated and he thought there was something unfathomable, but unbelievably sexy, about the house. His intuition had picked it up and he remembered reading about the couple going back.

While Linda was in the kitchen waiting for the coffee percolating, she read the 'Big Cats' story. There had been a number of reported sightings over the past few weeks, black panthers, and there were speculations as to where they had come from. The favorite theory being, was that an infamous local rock star, who was known to have kept exotic animals, including some of the rarest exotic snakes, might have let a few into the wild, before he died of an overdose, nearly a decade previously. He had owned a massive estate seven miles from Tennin that had once belonged to a liberal prime minister in the early twentieth century, and he was famed for his lurid orgiastic satanic themed parties, that were well chronicled in *The Orb* for many a year. It was known that the previous owner of the dream house had been an associate who influenced Bryan Jonsen, the aforementioned hell raiser, with his esoteric ideas and who regularly attended these rites with his actress wife. Although that itself had become something of a local Tennin myth. Chaz and Linda had spoken about it all and Chaz thought that he could *feel* the sex that was hanging in the air around the house. It was almost palpable Chaz had said, and he thought that augured well for film making. But that local paper just simply loved finding a new angle to bring Bryan Jonsen's infamy back to newsprint, as it always sold a few. Linda quickly logged on with the laptop to do some more research on the couple who had lived at the dream house. Apparently, Diana Desade, as she was known in the horror movies, had also been in porn films earlier in her career, and she was in fact of Russian descent with her real name being Nina Kulagarte and descended to no other than Rasputin, the Russian mystic, she claimed, although it was disputed and probably a lie. Chaz would soon be taking more interest when he knew that. Arthur Ashcroft, her husband, had been primarily known for writing a book on the mystical nature of sexuality, and forming and heading, his esoteric spiritual group, the 'Illuminati Orgia'. Chaz would certainly like all of those associations Linda thought, and all of a sudden, the house and the gardens became that much sexier. Linda began to wonder what had gone on in the house! She frowned, as a few months ago, the painters had shown Chaz and her some odd markings that were on the walls underneath the paint stripped in the bedroom that was now the Dark Room. They passed it off as some artistic daubings of the previous owners, who were obviously creative people. Chaz had joked they probably had satanic orgies in there, and Linda was wondering if that wasn't far from the truth.

Linda found it all exciting but just a little disturbing as well. She had read about how these Satanists sacrifice animals and even babies in *The Orb*, and who knows what went on in the house? It made Linda think deeply for a few moments. She then shut down the laptop and returned to the article in the paper, before pouring Chaz's coffee into his special personalized king carp mug, that carried the image of Chaz and his famous 'Ressie' monster, slapped across his haunches. Chaz just loved to reinforce his sense of success in life. He liked to celebrate the real achievements, and that big carp was one record that was standing the test of time. What a fish!

Chaz was still reading the instructions about setting up the third eye location camera, when Linda came out with the coffee. Linda had decided not to say anything about the research she had just done. It was best left to rest she thought. It might play on her mind and disturb her. But it excited her, it was all so taboo and sexy.

'What do you want in your door-stopper sandwiches, Chaz?' she said jokingly.

Chaz was still on a high with the exhilaration of those new purchases. He was never happier than when spending big wedge on carp gear. Being a carper, set him apart from other people and especially so, being the innovator. Who else would have thought of a bait that acted like a freshwater muscle? He was a leader, and where he and Miko led, others were bound to follow in the end.

'I'll take chicken and pickle and a slap and a tickle please, Linda.' Chaz lewdly poked his gold studded tongue out, looking as explicit and lecherous as he possibly could. But Linda knew darn well he had new fishing gear with that smile on his face. He cupped and stroked his beard.

'That face is telling me you've bought some fishing gear.'

The boy's sized grin just got bigger and bigger. That dishing out the readies had given him a right old buzz and the word *Carp* was like a magical wishing mantra.

'A man has to buy a few new toys from time to time, Linda,' he reflected.

Linda came across to him and Chaz had some explaining to do. Now over the past five years or so, after the introduction of bait boats, Chaz had spoken on many occasions about his displeasure with them. In fact, his hatred, for ruining the great sport of carp fishing, and this was well known and documented by Linda. But that was then. This was right here now.

'I got one of those bait dropper efforts.'

Linda's first response was from the kind of position that Chaz had taught her to think from.

'I thought you said you wanted to throw a brick through one of those?'

Chaz had a few things to get off his chest. The past year had been such a hard time. He put so much work into his carp fishing and last season was strewn with blank session after blank session. He couldn't take blanks anymore and they had been the push that forced him to this realization about carp hi-tech.

'Well I've had some very important realizations lately, Linda. Very important.'

Chaz expected, and Linda showed, a complete attention. He elaborated. 'Look, if I don't go all hi-tech in the new millennium, like all the other "top-dog" carpers, there's not gonna be any carp left for the Chazzy! Nuffin'! It's hard to swallow I know, but it's as simple as that. It's a New Age, and we've got to embrace it Linda, every one of us!'

Chaz then turned his attention to the bait boat that was bursting with the blue and red baits. It was becoming something of a quite startling conversion.

'It's fantastic, unbelievable, Linda! I can precision drop the divine blues and me fruity strawberry assassins anywhere on the lake. Ground bait and hook offerings and the fucking things only got a third eye camera! Third eye camera! What a location tool! The carp can't get a fucking way from ya!'

Linda assessed what Chaz had said to her and she thought it all a bit creepy.

'Isn't that cheating?'

Chaz hadn't thought about it like that, so he had to approach the issue another way.

'Look Linda, carp fishing is all about the "edge". And that's the way it's all gone! And look at me! You still have to put a ton of work in to get a big carp! It's hardly cheating!' Linda certainly knew how much time and effort, and money, the carp fishing took up.

'Oh, I know, Chaz,' she replied, before asking him that essential question that any wife would have asked. 'How much?'

Chaz would always go low on the actual cost, as carp fishing equipment could run away with the Barber's bank account funds, or should we say here 'The Stash'.

'Bargain! With the new rods Linda, well under the two!'

Linda knew by now, that when Chaz said well under the two, he was likely to have spent nigh three.

'Oh Chaz! We could have gone on holiday for that!'

Chaz had to assert his authority. He was the one who did all the big money earning in this household. It was the life style that Chaz had built.

'Look Linda, you've got your bloody solariums that cost the mint and I've got me carp gadgets. What's the difference?'

The new sunbed in the back room cost upwards of ten grand, good enough for a salon and Chaz had lain out prone on it the last six weeks. But it was Linda's request to have one.

'You use that sunbed more than me, Chaz!' she replied, speaking the truth of the matter.

Chaz's blood pressure began to rise sharply, and there was a slightly harsher, more aggressive tone in his voice. What Linda knew as that 'putting her in her place' tone.

'I only use it because it's fucking there! I wouldn't have bought it, would I! It was *you* who bought it Linda, and it's *you* who's just had a dream fucking kitchen fitted. So, could you go and use it please and make Chazzy boy some sarnie! I'm starving!'

Within a few moments Linda was in the kitchen, but before she set about making the king's sandwiches, she rushed upstairs and surreptitiously took a container from deep inside a drawer of clothing. There was a glass of water on her dresser and she took a handful of pills, threw them down her throat and gulped the water.

'Fuck you, ya bastard!' she said to herself. Sometimes Chaz could be a sexist dinosaur. He was old-fashioned in many ways, but that was Chaz and there wasn't any changing Chaz. He was his own man.

Back in the kitchen it appeared that Linda was rather enjoying cutting the door-stopper slices with a long sharp knife. There was a sense of menace and revenge in her actions. There is always a snapping point, and women stabbed their husbands for far less and many times at that. It's all a matter of the relationship's dynamics, and at times Linda felt as if she was caught down a deep pit, full of venomous evil snakes and she only seemed to come out of it snorting coke, before she slid back down into it. But the gardening had become her ladder out and hope. It was all snakes and ladders now.

Within a short while the sandwiches were being enjoyed by Chaz as he lounged on his chair, while Linda had temporarily climbed that ladder, and was bent over investigating vegetable shoots, by an opening in the cross-lattice supports. She had her back towards Chaz and was bent over with a pair of very tight-arsed leggings on. Chaz spotted his chance, picked up the butt end of one of his dragon slayers, stealthily crept over, and crudely poked it underneath Linda's crutch, working it back and forth.

'Like me new rod? The orgasm dragon!' Chaz joked.

'I'm trying to do the gardening, Chaz,' Linda protested.

Chaz walked back to his chair in paroxysm. He sat down and duly fitted the rod back together, admiring his new acquisition, still smirking and laughing out loud. He began quivering the rod again, testing its top end 'feel' as if he had alchemical gold in his hands.

'You loved it, Linda! Getting a butt end poke! Frill of ya day so far!'

Chaz was flying high on that rod tip, it was sublime, otherworldly even, and Chaz was on cloud nine with a sense of reasserted power that spending wads had brought him. He vowed there and then, that whatever was the ultimate best in carp gear, he would purchase it, year upon year and without fail, whether he needed it or not. It was about time the carp king had the very finest on the market. Those Hardings he had were nice but they felt heavy and crap compared to these dandies.

'What an action! Like a golden fucking cock!' was Chaz's colorful way of describing these fantastic slayers. Chaz was veritably purring with them. 'Best rod on the market! It's undisputed, Linda, and every carp expert worth his salt would verify the claim. Yeah, I'm with the 'top-dogs' now Linda!' Chaz was feeling better every moment. The summer of 2003 AD would be dripping big fat monster carp!

'You've got to have the best haven't you, Chaz?' Linda said, just stating the fact without a hint of underlying criticism.

'Fucking right on! Cos as I'm always saying Linda, the best gives you the performance and that's what we're getting from some of those newfangled gadgets we got up there in the Dark Room. Performance!' Linda didn't say anything, but Chaz felt he would follow up his sense of superiority, with another joke or two.

'Expensive, yes granted. But that cock a doodle do machine up there hits the fucking button every time. Ha, ha, as you clearly know by now, Linda!'

Linda tried to hold her anger in, concentrating on her gardening, and incredibly it worked. She remained silent, nigh oblivious, as Chaz returned to his sandwiches, and gave a quick glance at the Rolex thinking about the itinerary. He was so busy he hardly had time to eat, but he was going to enjoy his chicken and pickle. He was famished.

Within a few moments, the back garden had returned to the sound of tweeting birds and pile drivers and the scratching of the fork and the barely audible scrunching of sarnie.

Chaz was thinking deeply as he ate, his mind racing away with thoughts on the future phases of the house and gardens transformation. He had it all worked out.

'I'm thinking bout that extension, Linda. Once we get planning permission that fucking geriatric walkway's a gonna. I reckon on spending eighty or ninety more, and we'll be well over the eight hundred big ones here, well over. Class!'

Linda had now begun watering some seedlings as it seemed that this hot spell was going to continue for nigh two weeks by all accounts.

'Yes, you've been saying, Chaz.'

Chaz took an enormous bite from his chicken sandwich and spoke with a bit still in his mouth.

'And I reckon it's about time Chazzy had his big fucking eagles. Don't you, Linda? Them brick pillars are big enough to take um.'

Linda paused, this was serious, as she just didn't want those silly eagles out there. They were for mansions and country estates. She felt impelled to put up resistance.

'I don't know if I want eagles, Chaz?' she said, rather quietly, although it was clear she didn't want them. But if Chaz wanted eagles it would have to be eagles.

'We've gotta have eagles. Eagles are class! Even "One Eye" has got eagles and his pillars are way smaller than mine.' It was an argument that was irrefutable according to Chaz's logic.

'But I don't know if the house is that sort of house, Chaz. It's, it's more intimate. It's not an eagles' type of house.'

Linda put forward her argument but Chaz wasn't in the mood for debate or compromise. He had spoken about eagles for years and years and they were virtually coming up Holly Beach Lane getting ready to land.

'I'm having eagles. I've always wanted eagles and the house is plenty big enough for big fucking eagles.'

Chaz had spoken, and there was more to his renovation plans. He had been doing some serious forward thinking on those chicken wings.

'I was also thinking of some Greek statues out here around a big tiered pond. You know the kinda thing. A pen for Hermann the Hoover bag you might say and a few big koi to keep him company, class.' Everything had been firmly fixed in his mind's eye. But Linda had to protest. That would be the end of this gardening with a great pool dominating the back with daft Venus statues.

'Oh Chaz, I like the garden as it is. Can't we just build on its natural strengths? That would be more natural. More ecological. The carp can go in the lake like the other lot. They'd like that, Chaz. They really would!'

Chaz had a whole host of strategies to combat this kind of insurgency.

'Ecological! They'd probably die in the "Ressie" choking on local fucking bac-fucking-teria! And don't be so bloody negative and old fogey, Linda. The glass is always half bloody empty with you. Greek culture! Just think of it, Linda. It'll stamp a bit of class on the place. And you want class, don't cha?'

Although Chaz wouldn't have noticed, deep in that old apple and pear orchard, something dark was stirring, even though today everything seemed so bright and crystal clear with the high sun. There was something covered up in that old black shed, an antique that Ashcroft purchased at great expense and had been the focal point of Ashcroft's and Desades's strange rituals going back and it was emitting strange mysterious power.

Chaz immediately got on the blower to Alan, and for Linda, annoyingly arranged for those flying eagles to land the following week. Chaz would measure up the piers, look on the internet for what he wanted, and Alan would send somebody over, 'sorted'. Chaz had always wanted eagles. Linda bit her tongue; she disliked the continual confrontations and she returned to her gardening. Chaz cracked another beer to celebrate the coming of the eagles, fully aware that Linda heard every word of the call. He preened and pushed his head out in his authority, stroked the goatee a few times and then duly returned to the carp mag. Big fucker eagles he had always wanted and big fucker eagles it would be.

Chaz's attention was now turned to that article, Kevvy spoke to him about at the carp superstore. That one about Joey Olwyn's new lake project. After the big lottery win – he shared eleven million with a couple of workmates – he had gone to ground, and subsequently, purchased the obligatory house and gave money to his immediate family. The normal things. Then Joey wondered about what he might do for the rest of his life. It was a no-brainer. He was a carp fanatic, so everything became tunneled carp vision. He bought a deep local chalk pit lake, spent a few hundred grand on imported European carp, and had put in a nice fishing lodge with a café and toilet block, with showers and apparently beer on the house out of the fridge. Good cooked breakfast, no problem. Joey had owned a local worker's café and had been cooking for the past thirty years. He sold up and put the money into the new project. Joey was single now and he was determined to live the rest of his life dedicated to carp fishing. Chaz was looking at a photo of Joey who was early sixties, short and plump, with big ole grey sideburns down a rotund and oval face, holding up the biggest of the stock fish which he had named 'The Pregnant Virgin', a big forty-three-pound carp with a fat belly. Chaz extended his neck as the adrenaline kicked in big.

'Won't be a fucking virgin once me and Miko get hold of her!' Chaz blurted out.

Linda turned sharply from her gardening, dismayed at such a crude comment. Chaz explained.

'No need to foam at the mouth, Linda. This virgin is a forty-three-pound mirror carp, the Pole Star, ya might say. That our local lottery winner, and fellow carp fanatic Joey Olwyn has put in a lake he has just bought with his spare cash. Three hundred carp and some big cats to mop the nuisance fish up.'

The mention of big cats connected to what Linda had been reading in the local paper a while earlier, and there was that serendipity moment. Big cats connecting up to big cats.

'I've just been reading about big black cats down the Triune Way, Chaz!'

Chaz sighed ever so deeply.

'Catfish cats! Not bloody great pussy cats, Linda! Anyhow that fucking cat was probably a stray fucking dog. That's the sensationalist crap that sells that local! Be green haired nutty muppets being carted off by spacemen next. All down on the Triune!'

Chaz had a good laugh at his joke, while that something that was stirring down in the old orchard began to stir just that little bit more. A snake appeared from a hole in the lower part of that old black shed, deep down in the fruit garden. It slithered through the grass, seemingly on some kind of mission or other, and beware of snakes in the grass for they bring the assassin's creed. Or so it's been said.

Chaz was on the mobile to Miko. He had to tell him all about the new rods and this exciting new lake of Olwyn's, who had certainly kept that one quiet. Chaz hadn't got wind of it prior to the magazine, and he had spoken to Joey late last summer at the superstore. But what an opportunity. Chaz envisaged a grand summer campaign at the lake after that fucking virgin, and he was in raptures to Miko about the dragon slayers.

'And the action on them, Miko! I've been showing Linda. Out of this world! Orgasmic! Linda luvs um!' Miko thought that rather an odd comment, but Chaz laughed at his joke as the snake continued its slithering way. It stopped and looked menacingly towards Chaz, sitting there on his throne.

'He's spent three hundred big ones on it mate, with the largest resident, "The Pregnant Virgin", going in at forty-three. Have to make a fucking whore out of her, eh? Eight hundred a year he wants making it exclusive for the top boys. Sounds like us, eh? How about joining up today and hitting it big time this year, Miko? Game?'

Miko had already glanced at the article while he was in the newsagents, and the mag was sitting in front of him on his coffee table at home waiting to be read. But he was well up for it. He also remarked upon how the house was going?

'Brilliant, Miko! Everything's cock up here mate. Linda gets woken up by one every day, ha ha, from that fucking doctor's house. There's an atmosphere up here Miko. Must be all those orgies, that dirty fucker Ashcroft used to have in the house. It used to be all "Free Love" up here, mate! Linda's been researching him and his porny Mrs. on the internet. Nah, joking aside, it's fucking great up here mate, with a few reservations, you know what I mean, Miko.'

While Chaz laughed along to his jokes, that adder was secretly spiraling through the grass in front of the new shed, undetected by both Chaz and the preoccupied Linda. It came to a halt as Chaz's laughter blended with the incessant crack of the pile driver.

Meanwhile, up on the estate, no further than a mile from Chaz, two odd-looking young men had arrived at an old red telephone box. Dan, the bespectacled smaller one of the two, who had a strong largactil-looking shuffle type thing about his movement, had a mobile in his hand, but no credit as usual. The other guy, TV Sam, was his general moniker, although it was TV for short, was rather geekier and stand out odd, with his hoodie jacket, his long green hair and a cap with Dragon Star emblazoned on it in gold. Green hair? TV insisted it would become the norm in twenty years' time when Dragon Star went bongo. TV had informed all the members and prospective members of the asylum's clientele, that eventually everyone would be with the dragon. He had seen it in a vision on shrooms with Keefy. He saw himself kind of rising up in the air and looking down upon all the people, and they were all waiving Dragon Star flags and banners, and then he went higher and higher and there was nothing to behold, but masses of people, the whole of the world's population even, all fans and that of the new cult. Far out, man! TV had never forgotten it.

Incidentally, TV got his moniker because of his avowed transvestite tendencies, and on this occasion, he was wearing his trademark long skirt, bright blue nail varnish and girly bracelets. He was also sporting his new, and for TV, haute couture footwear. What he called 'Jesus's sandals' that he had purchased at a local boot-fair at Death Hill, on the infamously dangerous spiraling rise after the last roundabout on the Triune Way. TV's feet were outsized too, a whoppingly colossal size fourteen and a big fourteen at that!

TV was good looking, or at least women thought so at a glance, and Dan had often said to him that he looked like a rock star, and when he was with Freeda it was a rock star couple. Their relationship was special to Dragon Star as through it, they expressed and embodied, Dragon Star's commitment to love, and cosmic shagging. TV obviously played up to the rock star accolade, as he was the main man these days, but he was gawky and his movements were erratic, sometimes slow and rather too measured, sometimes slow and decidedly unmeasured, but at other times he could move as swift and as agile as a supremely athletic cat. Fundamentally TV was just a one-off oddster and also the undisputed leader of the new Dragon Star children cult.

He parked the big boombox, that he purchased cheap from a charity shop, outside the telephone box. He loaded it with Energy Max Plus, big batteries from the pound shop that lasted about an hour before the monkey on the handle stopped turning. It was 2003 AD and TV was still big on Eminem and he had 'Lose Yourself' playing relentlessly. It was a track that chimed perfectly with the way that he was feeling about life these days.

TV held up an eighteen-carat gold wedding ring, that he had purchased in the town with the birthday money sent to him by his mum and uncle John. It was given to them as trustees from an aunt, and it was a miracle that any money at all found its way to TV. Aunt Joan had told them it was a gift to Samuel so he could buy nice new clothes but they siphoned much of it off for their whisky and drugs. Auntie Joan had looked after TV when he was younger and TV missed her greatly. She had been a mother to him and was now in a residential home with dementia but he still wrote to her regular, saying how thankful he was for everything.

'I can't wait to give it to her, Dan!' TV enthused, with a smile evoking sheer love and feeling.

'She'll love it, TV.'

TV placed the wedding ring carefully back in its little box thinking of his aunt, before slipping it back into the hoodie pocket. His eyes were gleaming as he opened the door of the phone box. There was business to get on with.

'Yeah, won't be a second, Dan.' The idea was for TV, the cult's main man, to take the helm, while Dan looked over his shoulder from a slightly opened door.

TV gathered a section of the local newspaper from his pocket. It was an advert for porn films that Chaz always had in the free press. Over the years it had brought him thousands of pounds worth of work, and it was still making him money. It was that wing of Chaz's business that paid for the food shop and takeaways, although Chaz was realizing that soon his DVDs would be defunct. But that was why he had those subscription websites up and running. Chaz was on the ball, moving with the times. Making money from the old ways and setting himself up to capitalize on the new. And new or old, it would still be going up the hooter. People still need to smash their brains out now and then, despite technological progress. He had read an article recently which said that drug use in the UK in AD 2002 had fallen dramatically from the levels during the birth and early years of Rave culture. Fuck, you wouldn't have noticed that in Tennin. 'Up your hooter! Get on ya scooter!'

'Ya getting some really good blue films, TV?' Dan asked, as he opened the door slightly and lent over TV's shoulder, that he just about reached. This indeed was what TV was going to do with the last of the money, a very generous two hundred. His mother and her sidekick had already had three, and TV knew something would have gone on like that. He wouldn't have entrusted a penny with her, but God bless Auntie Joan. He would love to see her before her departure, but there was no chance of that, however much he wanted.

'Reckon so, Dan,' TV replied, looking at the advert, and then getting a number of fifties ready for the slot. He didn't have much else left now, readies were in the 'special' place, waiting to pounce on the blue films.

Dan loved the excitement that was building up now around these porn films. They would have to be very careful if they played them in the TV room, but TV thought of everything, and he had bought a miniature DVD player that gave them other options.

'I'll watch um and have a wank,' Dan said. TV smirked geekily and added to the folly.

'Yeah, have a party, Dan. Pull it about a bit!'

They both laughed and Dan thought it hilarious. It was what he was seeing in his mind. He visualized getting caught wanking by that battle-axe Nurse Garotte.

'I might get caught wanking by that fatso Gestapo, TV!'

They laughed again, as the Gestapo reference was a running joke between them regarding the way that Doctors Lock and Bolt and Nurse Lavender Garotte run the joint, with 'Locko' being 'The Fuhrer'.

By now the pound shop batteries were moving towards meltdown and Eminem's voice was going all slow, like Lee Marvin's back in long lost days. They were long before TV's and Dan's time, but they heard the track at the hospital on somebody's CD player.

'The Slim Shady's batteries are conking, TV!' Dan exclaimed.

'Sounds like that wandering star bloke, Dan,' TV replied, and they both laughed again. But by now TV was bang on the mission to phone 'Adult Leisure' as it was called, and get those blue films sorted out. 'Don't matter Dan, I gotta ring the porn film, dude.'

Dan thought that in the New Age, TV couldn't be sure of that. That it was definitely a dude.

'Might be a woman doing it all, TV,' Dan replied, and TV accepted it could be, but he played along for a laugh.

'Nah, I know it's a dude, Dan. The alien intelligences are sending me messages!'

They both laughed, and they always had good fun like this.

Back in the garden, Chaz was still speaking to Miko on the mobile, but as soon as he finished the call and put the phone down, 'She's Not There' was off again. Chaz was quickly on it.

'Adult Leisure and other services. What can I do for ya?'

For a few seconds there was nothing and Chaz was staring dumbfounded at the phone.

'Major Tommy, can you hear me?' Chaz asked into the abyss of silence, which was then broken up by laughter that Chaz could hear in the background.

Back at the telephone box, Dan was being a bit of a nuisance. TV had confirmed to him that it was a dude and Dan was so eager to listen in he poked his head across, getting in TV's way.

'Mind, Dan, mind!' TV said, then he turned his attention back on the porn film man, but Chaz had already stopped the call.

Back in the garden the 'She's Not There' ring tone fired off again.

'What's this cunt playing at?' snapped an angry Chaz, as he noticed that the call was coming from the same source. This time TV went for the jugular.

'Do you do blue films?' he asked. Eureka, the Major was actually there! It was probably one of those timid punters, who had trouble facing their sexual urges head on. The Mrs. was probably out of the way upstairs now, or something similar, and the coast was all clear for transgressive porn. Chaz dealt with loads of them.

'I most certainly do, sir! All categories, six for forty! Whatever takes your fancy.'

There was yet another long silence, and plenty of time for Chaz to hear the pile drivers thwacking and the birds tweeting. Chaz sighed and swore before talking back at the mobile.

'Are you still there, mate?'

Chaz had to wait before the enigmatic voice replied again.

'Yeah, I think so.'

The nature of the reply rather humored Chaz, 'I think so', and the guy had said it in that deadpan tone.

'Ha ha, bit of a joker, eh. Give me your address mate, and we can arrange a time for me to do a drop.'

TV Sam turned sharply, and his right shoulder whacked into Dan's head, and Dan cried out in pain. TV was most apologetic.

'Oh, sorry Dan! Er, he wants an address. What shall I say?'

Dan moved from side to side, rubbing his head and screwing his face up. TV had put him on the spot. He even took his glasses off as he was sweating so much. They needed cleaning with a hanky. It all took time, but TV patiently awaited the answer from the oracle, because he was blank. He lived at the asylum and he knew he couldn't mention that. Back in the garden, Chaz was aghast. Who the fuck did he have here?

'I've got a right basket here, Linda!'

Chaz then took the initiative. It was quite normal men prevaricating like this, as they don't want you to drop the porn off while the Mrs. was about. Some women didn't like to think their men found films more exciting than actual sex with them. It was a modern marriage dilemma Chaz had recognized, although it didn't affect the more liberated, like Chaz and Linda.

'It's no problem, mate. If it's not suitable for dropping at your address, we can meet some place quiet like. It needn't be a long transaction.'

The times that Chaz had reeled off that little ruse. TV Sam needed the answer urgently.

'What shall I say, Dan?' he pleaded. Dan put his glasses back on, and shuffled from side to side seemingly about to give TV the answer.

'I dunno, TV. I can't fink.'

Dan didn't like being put under pressure and TV was concerned that his demands had stressed him out.

'Don't stress out about it, Dan. Don't, mate!' TV had the receiver to his ear, and Chaz asked him if he was still there? Chaz was nearly at the end of his patience and was about to hang up.

'Yeah, I was thinking hard,' TV explained. Chaz couldn't believe what he was hearing.

'Well don't think any harder mate, cos I'll still be here looking up at the stars!'

Anything to do with looking up at the stars hit a chord with TV Sam. Stargazing was a big thing with that New Age group he headed and he collected UFO magazines, subscribing to two mags, a UK one and an American one. The self-appointed but obvious, 'no-brainer' choice, as head of the group after Keefy, had to keep abreast of all new UFO developments and movements. It was essential, so naturally TV was excited to hear that this porn seller dude, was into stargazing and alien interventions and all that. He turned to Dan excited.

'He does stargazing, like us, "Dragon Star" Dan!'

This could mean a valuable new connection in the field, and who knows this porn dude might know some brilliant UFO hot spots. Once Dan heard this, stargazing ideas just popped into his head, right out the blue.

'Does he? You can meet him at the flying saucer lamppost, TV!' Dan exclaimed, with an enlightened enthusiasm, and why not, this guy was bound to know it.

'Good finking, Dan!' and TV switched back to the receiver with renewed clarity and energy. 'Do ya know the flying saucer lamppost?' TV asked, fully expecting the porn dude to know it, as TV had written a substantial blog on it. It was on the internet for anybody to read, right across the globe. TV anticipated a billion hits or more, although only six people had read it so far and Dan was one of those. Chaz was perplexed. What the fuck was this guy talking about?

'Nah mate, I don't know that one,' he replied somewhat impassively. Eureka! TV Sam was now clearer about where he might meet the porn dude, the idea just popped out of nowhere into his head. He replied with much more purpose.

'What about the roundabout on the Triune Way, the one with the Salome tulips?' TV knew all his flowers. Chaz had some idea of what he meant, and he thought he could work on this one.

'What? You mean the big one?' Chaz suggested, quite intelligently he thought. TV put him straight, as he knew those tulips and those roundabouts like the back of his hand. Hot spots down there.

'Nah, the big one, is the one with the Red Riding Hoods! It's the next one, the smaller one, with the Salomes.'

Chaz thought that they were getting there at last.

'What the last one before ya start rising up Death Hill where they have the boot-fairs?' The dude had mentioned the boot-fair, so he was spot on TV thought.

'Yeah, spose it is the last one before ya start going up Death Hill finking about it,' TV thoughtfully replied. Back in the garden it was sheer relief for Chaz. He had finally got there. Some people were such fucking hard work.

'Sorted Johnny, no problem. You're only down the road' Chaz made a quick summons of the itinerary diary.

'Got a fucking joker or what on the line here, Linda,' Chaz said, before returning back to the mobile. 'Half nine any good your end?' Chaz asked hopefully. TV was rather perplexed. He looked at Dan with an odd look. He was put out. Johnny? TV was Sam. He wasn't a Johnny! He was TV!

'My name isn't Johnny, Mr. Blue film man. It's TV! It's always been TV!' Chaz was humored and exasperated at the same time.

'TC, eh sorry, mate. Mine has always been Chaz if I remember. I repeat it for the last and final time. Is half-nine any good ta ya?' This was the joker's very last chance. But TV Sam was always decisive when it really mattered and the chips were down. That was why he was leading a New Age cult.

'Yeah! That would work out spot on! Half nine at the last roundabout with the Salome tulips.' Dan was agitated and he fiddled about with his spectacles in a way that confirmed his worry.

'We'll be absconding, TV!'

Dan didn't like the idea of doing that and having Locko on his case. She knew he was scared of Nurse Garotte and she might put her down on Dan's open ward, on overtime, to especially unnerve him. If you crossed Locko you would have that Nurse Lavender on your case. Dan had projected all kinds of things on Nurse Garotte and she frequently turned up in his dreams, or should we say nightmares, as the wicked witch. She terrified him. But TV had been working everything out. He knew they would be absconding, but there was something called the Trust budget. Dan didn't think about such things but TV did. They couldn't do just as they pleased with patients. That wouldn't be cost-effective on the budget.

'The Fuhrer won't section us for it though, Dan. Too much of this!' TV rubbed his fingers together to indicate money, and Dan understood. TV carried on to explain what would happen and Dan knew that with most things, TV was always right. He further elaborated.

'They just won't let us out for a week and we'll have a chance to watch the porn on that DVD player and wank.' Yes, TV had it all worked out. They headed off laughing, with the porn pick up all in the bag.

Dan loved being with TV, things were exciting with him around. There was never a dull day. Dan attempted suicide a number of times, but that was before he met TV. Since then, some four years ago now, he just enjoyed the 'craic', as TV called it. But it was more than that. TV made Dan feel that he was worth something. He felt a somebody when he was with TV.

Back in the garden Chaz was musing to Linda about this very curious punter.

'Half past nine by the third roundabout with the Salome tulips!' he chuckled, 'but the top cats forty quid is as good as the next fucker's, when you've a mortgage to pay, Linda. Put that poxy fork down for five minutes and come over here and sit on the Chazzy's lap.' Linda smiled and came over. Chaz joked, as was his usual want. 'Might get a rise on me dragon slayer!'

Linda sat on Chaz's lap and they began to horse play and Chaz was petting and necking. Linda liked the attention, but Chaz had plans forming.

'Here, I was thinking about a session with "My Little Princess" tonight. You know girl, the usual kinda thing, with a few twists and hard spices that I picked up on a DIY American.'

Chaz and Linda had been married for twenty-two years now and Chaz rarely wanted 'normal' sexual relations. Everything was bound up with his projects and had an ultimate cash angle somewhere at the end. He laughed lewdly as if to eschew any requirements to go into more detail. The dynamic prevailing, was that Linda would do as she was told up there. It was her turn to be fully submissive. Linda seemed a touch ambivalent as she felt pressurized by Chaz to perform these odd kinky scenarios. But Chaz would always work her round. He had tactics, and they usually paid off and Linda had something of an elephantine, greedy drug habit these days.

'Be a devil, Linda. It's all about the holistic integration of your dark sexy side. It's all in that book. You've read it with your own eyes and it's the truth of the New Age, Linda. You know that.'

The book that Chaz referred to, was one that suited Chaz's purposes well, entitled, *Sexual Practices for a New Age*. It was from a Californian writer, who was previously involved with a 1960s Satanic sex magic cult. The writer had forged close links with none other than Arthur Ashcroft, the previous owner of 'Chaz's Pad' and they had met on many occasions back in the seventies. If Chaz had read the book more closely, he would have realized it. But the book was like the Gospel to Chaz, exhorting all to let it hang right out and become more 'holistic' human beings. He picked it up in a second hand book shop down at Fishgate back in his late teens, and it was one of those books that he had always kept and was fascinated by. The drugs helped with the role playing according to the author, and Chaz believed the book validated his sex and drugs philosophies. He had read it loads of times.

'You can stoke up! There's plenty of Charley Farley in the trinket box, Linda.'

There was always plenty of that and the coke meant that Chaz could get her to do anything. He knew how to work Linda around in such matters, now that she had that greedy habit. Blimey, she couldn't get enough up her hooter. She was like an animal for it and worse than he was.

'I might think about it,' Linda concluded. She was never a willing partner here, but she was an addict, although she tried to convince herself she wasn't. Linda extracted herself from Chazzy's lap, and returned to her gardening. She was so happy, that now she had such beautiful gardens and a plot of land to work. She was sure she could persuade Chaz not to have that pool in the garden. The battle of the eagles had been lost, but maybe she could win the next. She could barter participation in the Dark Room activities to prevent Chaz from going through with the idea, and it might be sufficient to prevent him from putting those daft eagles out the front too. You never know. Those tacky, aspirational eagles would annoy her every time she walked out of the house, if they were perched up on her pillars. This house was intimate, it wasn't like that. She frowned and thought deeply for a few moments, and pledged to herself that she would confront Chaz, before Dark Room activities. She wouldn't play, unless the pool idea was abandoned *and* the flying eagles. The ploy had worked in the past.

Once Linda had returned to her seedlings, Chaz returned to the carp magazine. He turned the page and was met with an article regarding a new top-of-the-range rod that had just been marketed by a Japanese company. Chaz scowled as he read looking towards his dismantled pride and joy, the dragon slayer, by his side. He could hear the author of the piece in his mind and he had a harsh grating voice and how it annoyed him.

'This rod is fantastically versatile and has a truly sublime action and feel. We have tested the rod extensively over the past three months and all of the Dream Team rate the Osaki Cobra MKI as marginally superior to the famed 2.12 dragon slayer. Yes folks, in the unanimous opinion of the Dream Team, it's as good as that! Move over, dragon slayer, you're the number two now!' Linda turned as Chaz grunted.

'Fuck it!'

Linda wondered what he was annoyed about, and within a few moments Chaz was seriously thinking about upgrading the upgrade. He could bung Graham a drink or something, to sort it out and get the slayers changed. It looked like it was Osaki Cobra's from now on. The future was enlightened snake! But in this hi-tech age you've just got to keep up.

TV Sam and Dan were busily walking back to the wards. TV carried the boombox on his shoulder, having replaced the batteries, and was listening to a Dragon Star adopted anthem, 'We are all made of Stars', yet was still bounding away, leaving Dan gasping behind. It was because TV was tall and had long legs, and he was as fast a walker as you could ever meet. Dan was trying his best to keep up but it was affecting his breathing badly, and he was sweating profusely in the heat. He needed to stop and have a swig of that Energy Brew that TV had in his other hand.

'Slow up, TV! You're going too fast for me asthma.'

TV didn't mean to race away and put Dan under pressure, but he was thinking deeply. About the one true love of his life. Dan stopped and had to take his glasses off, as they were clouding over with sweat again. He much preferred winter. He rubbed them with his handkerchief.

'Can I have some Brew, TV?' he gasped.

TV gave Dan the drink and Dan held the three liter bottle up with two hands swigging as he was thirsty and dehydrated. He found the sheer size of the container difficult to handle, but TV always went for it, a case of sheer economy. They could afford a three liter bottle a day and this was so important. The Brew was *the* Dragon Star children's drink of choice, and there had to be a ready supply. As TV always said, it gave them the added energy to achieve great things, to push onward, and forward, with the Dragon Star cult and message, and it was the cheapest energy drink on the market too! But TV wasn't thinking about energy drink.

'I'm sorry I was walking fast, Dan. But I fink when I walk fast and I was finking, Dan.'

Dan knew what he was thinking about. He spoke in between his swigs and he was short of breath.

'What bout Freeda?' he said, knowing full well that he was right. It was hard for TV. Things were coming to a head. He knew that the asylum authorities wanted them kept apart at all costs. They might be too much trouble, in more ways than one, if they were together. But they weren't the ones who were being estranged from their soul mate.

'Yeah, been finking, Dan, I'll be lucky if I ever see her again. Let alone talk to her and be with her.' TV felt so depressed about the thought.

'Ya might see her through the window again, TV,' Dan said, trying to put an enthusiastic brave face on the situation, before he swigged again struggling with the enormous bottle of Brew.

Freeda had waved at him only yesterday from the lock up unit when he was smoking by the old beech tree. The nurses had seen him and he was expecting he and Dan to be banned from smoking there any time soon, because no doubt Freeda played up when she saw TV out there. He knew how the regime and Locko's mind worked. Fat old Gestapo-axe would complain to 'The Fuhrer' that Freeda had been 'difficult' because of TV, and then Dr. Lock would call TV in and enforce the ban. Then she would have a security guard out there all day for a few days before budget constraints kicked in and then TV and Dan would be back smoking at the tree.

'I fucking hate this world, Dan. There's always evil snakes getting ready to bite ya.'

'Don't say that, TV!'

'But see her through the windows if I'm lucky. I love her! And there's next week's meeting with Locko. I bet it's about being transferred somewhere hundreds of miles away. I bet it is, Dan. So that me and Freeda ain't any more trouble.' TV gathered himself to declare his intent and he was clearly wrought with emotion.

'I've been thinking, Dan. It's down to the wire. It's all or nothing. I've got a window,' he smirked before continuing. 'And I've gotta smash it, Dan. Smash it in.'

Dan could read into this, enough to know it would be something precarious, in view of the regime and the Gestapo.

'Mind you don't get cut by the glass, TV,' Dan replied, showing concern, but his worry was only further deepened.

'Couldn't give a shit if it cuts me fucking hand off, Dan. I just wanna be with her.'

Dan liked to crack jokes when they were bantering as TV seemed to enjoy his company and when they laughed together it made Dan feel that he was important to somebody. Who else could he crack jokes with like he could with TV? But he just couldn't think of one, but TV knew that he had tried hard too. But Dan wanted to support him.

'They say we can do anything when we set our minds to it, TV. We can make our own world!' Dan tried so desperately to be positive, but TV had come to that brick wall in his mind and in that moment, he had decided there was only one way to deal with it.

'Gonna go for it, Dan. If I chicken it, I'm lost and I might never ever see her again. And it's fucking torturing me not being with her. Torturing me. Like having evil snakes in me brain and the fuckers keep wriggling, keep fucking wriggling!'

TV looked tortured too, and he needed to have a good smoke or two or three. Dan was aware of how much all this was haunting and hurting him.

'I'll pray for ya, TV. Shall we have a smoke at the tree?'

Dan knew he would agree, as TV looked like he could do with a drag or two and they might see Freeda again, and that would change his mood.

'What smoke-the-three like Keefy used ta?'

Now Keefy was a legend among the present clients of the asylum. He had been renowned for wearing a white blazer, nigh identical to that which Chaz wore. An incredible coincidence. Oddly, Keefy, like Chaz, always thought it gave him the edge and a certain confidence, and it was fact that Keefy, knew things that others didn't, like Chaz again, and he was a great friend of TV's, and Dan's. TV had known Keefy from the very first day he came into the asylum seven years ago. They just clicked with each other straight away and Keefy would have been thirty-two now. But he had left a legacy. He was famous in the asylum, for among other things, for his advocacy of a bizarre method of getting a calm on. He reckoned that nicotine, if smoked sensibly, could get you nice and calm, and his thing was to overload and smoke three at a time when you were feeling really agitated. All across the asylum, the nurses were always trying to stop clients from smoking the three, like Keefy used to do. It was akin to an institutionalized act of rebellion done in hiding, yet infrequently, due to the paucity of the fag supply. But there was a will to do it, and when somebody could afford the twenty, it would inevitably take place. Yes, Keefy was a legend and this notoriety hadn't gone away. It was all that Dragon Star stuff that he and TV had initiated. It took hold, and was still influential and that hadn't gone unnoticed by the asylum authorities. Dr. Lock had spoken to an expert on New Age cults and the Trust had decided that Dragon Star business had to be nipped in the bud, before it took greater hold and who knows where cults could go. Dr. Lock had never forgotten that seminar she gave on Charles Manson when training. There were disturbing similarities emerging here, so Dr. Lock had introduced a blanket ban on anything Dragon Star or Keefy. Clients were not to mention Keefy anymore. Dr. Lock had told them all, they needed to let go of him, so Keefy could finally come to rest, because he had been away for ages, and in the interests of everybody's health they should stop smoking the three. It hadn't convinced anybody. Keefy would never go away.

The Trust had stated that Keefy had been transferred to a better hospital, that was more suited to him, and that he had gone away for a long, long time. But TV knew the truth because Keefy's stepbrother had written to him, asking why he wasn't at the funeral. It was a cover up job. Keefy was creating too much trouble. They moved him, he kicked up even more, and they chemically coshed him until he hung himself. But his legend was still strong among the clientele. Dr. Lock was in fact preparing to inform the clients that Keefy had peacefully passed away in his sleep, to clear up the matter once and for all. But she was prevaricating, just in case there was an incendiary response, and psychologists had warned that Keefy could be resurrected, metaphorically speaking, across the asylum. But whatever she chose to do, Keefy's legend was still strong among the clientele, as it was Keefy who had mentored TV, and now TV was an even bigger legend.

Dan liked to smoke-the-three in honor of Keefy, like TV, but the problem with smoking the three was that you would soon get through your packet of ten, and they were so pricey these days. He took the packet from his pocket as TV had spent all his money on the wedding ring for Freeda, and he needed money for that porn.

'Nah, we've only got two left, TV.' They were not destined to get that calm on like Keefy used to do.

There may have been snakes wriggling away in TV's head, but back in Chaz's garden, one slithered its way across the lawn, until it was behind Chaz's carp chair. Chaz heard something that took him from his meditation with the carp magazine and he looked around spontaneously, not really thinking why he had done so. But the quivering, fanged adder was directly beneath Chaz's chair. The snake was a honing in, on Chaz's big juicy tattooed calf muscle. The snake was going for St. George! Linda came out of the old porch threshold, struggling with a couple of packets of seeds in her hand and the fork and spade in the other. She spotted the snake about to strike at Chaz's leg, and she screamed and shouted.

'A snake's underneath ya, Chaz!'

Chaz stood up in a terrified flash and he couldn't believe his eyes. The horrible beggar was hissing and spitting at him. He instinctively grabbed hold of the garden fork from Linda, and spiked the snake right through its body. The snake wrapped itself in agony around the prongs and then wriggled itself free.

'Ugh!' Chaz was noticeably squeamish, but then he grabbed the spade from Linda.

'You'll get it, ya evil fucker!' and with one well executed chop, the snake's head was detached from its body. Clean off with the head, guillotined. Yet both parts, body and head were still alive for a few moments, and the head went straight after Chaz as if on some Satanic retribution mission of pure evil, trying to bite Chaz's bronzed thigh.

'Ya fucker! Ya evil fucker! Ugh! It's fucking head's still alive, Linda. Ugh!'

Chaz managed to flip the monster of a head up the garden towards the shed, until it eventually becalmed and stilled. But Chaz was unnerved and he gingerly picked it up on the spade half expecting the thing to jump straight at his throat. He put the decapitated parts on a compost heap at the bottom of the garden that Linda had been adding to. Chaz was busily reflecting on what had occurred. He was shocked.

'Fucking thing must have come into the garden from that old orchard,' he concluded, and now the apple and pear begun to have an altogether, more menacing atmosphere and wild nature about it.

'Well at least it didn't get ya, Chaz,' said a somewhat bemused and equally terrified Linda. Chaz couldn't get over something he saw in that head though. It was the bloody thing's eyes staring him down. How on earth could it keep coming after him? It was like that Rasputin! Evil! Pure evil bastard!'

Even though such disturbing events had occurred, the world around Holly Beach Lane still continued as if nothing had happened. The pile drivers kept on thwacking and the crows and birds were kraaing and tweeting and a cooing up in the eaves and even the white butterflies were still whirring and dancing through occasionally. But all things pointed towards a tectonic plate of snake having shifted. The wise old man had spoken but Chazzy Barber hadn't listened.

CHAPTER FIVE

TERROR, SUBLIME, CHILLING, TERROR

TV and Dan were up under the smoking tree out on the grounds sharing their final cigarettes, hoping to remain unseen by the nursing staff. They were walking the tightrope as TV tried desperately to get a glimpse of Freeda in the secure unit, across from the cricket pitch. He had to show himself to be seen, and he prayed that it was Freeda who might have spotted him. But his mood was morose and dark; hard reality was biting.

'The one thing you can be sure about life, Dan, is that ya never get what ya fucking want. Never!'

He wanted to kick the beech tree as hard as he could in frustration but those 'Jesus's sandals' as he called them, didn't really give him an option, so he dragged furiously until the cigarette was like a red-hot poker. The more he dragged the more intolerable the moment felt. When feeling like this, he would invariably nick sedatives from the drugs trolley or request a slightly heavier zombie chill.

There was a mass of starlings high above the woods, and they were moving this way and that like they do in a crazy kaleidoscopic manner, although something was amiss in nature's pattern, as they were doing this in mid-May. TV looked up and Dan didn't say anything. It was the best approach Dan thought. TV looked desolate and his mouth took up a disgruntled sneer.

'They look like the great evil snake I got wriggling around in me fucking head!'

The observation disquieted Dan. It was the sheer intensity of TV. When he said these things, an abyss seemed to envelope all, his darkness was that pervasive, and the whole world would reinforce TV's depression. He would get worse, so Dan was worried. He had been there in the Tennin stacker car park, when TV jumped off the third floor because of Freeda. Dan thought he was dead or at least a cripple or something, but TV had fortunately landed on the canvas roof of an articulated lorry. He had got away with a few bruises, but TV was in a similarly black mood that day. When TV was in high spirits, he would laugh that moment off with Dan. It was an apocryphal tale at the asylum, and TV always swore that his dramatic leap was calculated. But Dan knew the TV in the moment before he leapt that day. It was the same abyss settling now and it was palpable. Dan was worried about the future too.

'This 'break out' with Freeda. I'm worried sick for ya both, TV,' he said, and Dan couldn't have meant it more sincerely. He had difficulty

71

holding back the emotion; the tears were welling and TV knew he was upset. In Dan's estimation TV could nigh walk on water, he could do anything, but if the full force of Locko's regime came down, even TV would sink in the end. It would be as inevitable as that HMS Titanic going down, after it hit the berg.

TV knew what the inference was. That the Gestapo would win in the end, but TV's love with Freeda was special, eternal, stronger than the fucking Gestapo. He had to be with her. Freeda was his soul mate. They were made for each other and TV liked the way that Freeda loved him back. It made TV realize that he made a difference to how somebody felt. Freeda looked so happy when she was with him. His very presence took her pain away and being in the same boat in this world as Freeda, gave him a sense that he could make a difference by loving somebody. That had never happened before for TV. But it wouldn't have mattered to Dr. Lock.

But TV also knew that Dan really relied on him to get through up here, and things would be tough for Dan if TV weren't around. By TV's reckoning, Dan wasn't going to win either way, with that inevitable impending transfer to the other end of the country looming. He dragged on the fag again and was pondering darkly, projecting himself into a future where he would no doubt bunk the far away hospital, somehow get back here, and effect the same 'break out' plan that had been forming in his mind. For TV, choice was no choice. No, it wasn't looking good for Dan.

'Whatever happens Dan, you and Keefy are my best friends ever. Best ever, mate!'

Those words really made Dan happy, as he knew that TV and Keefy were inseparable back in the day. But here was TV saying that he valued Dan just as much. It made Dan feel that he really was a somebody. Best mate of TV's and TV was a legend, so Dan had kudos as the right-hand man. But it was more than that. Dan felt that TV really meant it, and nobody had valued Dan's company as much as TV had. He genuinely enjoyed his life when he was with TV and he even thanked and blessed God.

TV knew that Dan was vulnerable and needed reassurance but he found Dan great company. Dan was one of the most important and valued members of the Dragon Star children. They had gone through so much and had even spotted a UFO together down at the flying saucer lamppost. That's how close they were. To be honest, Dan wasn't too sure what he saw, as it was a bit dark down there that night, but he agreed he saw something up there somewhere. But TV needed Dan equally as much to get through asylum life as Dan was a super listener to TV's deepest thoughts and feelings.

'You're a great fella, Dan. I couldn't get by up here without ya.'

They put an arm over each other's shoulder as great friend to great friend, with TV more than a foot taller. Dan couldn't help referring to what TV had said before on one occasion, that when you're in here, you appreciate friendship that much more. He had never forgotten it, because it was true, you were sort of in it together. Dan loved going down into Tennin with TV. It would never be the same without him. They would always get loads of nasty comments down the town but the young of the town were wary of TV. He looked so unpredictable and there had been some rather violent episodes in his back life and they gave him an edge that people would pick up on. The one time a local had really pushed it beyond the verbal comments, he pushed an ice-cream in TV's face, TV responded with a looping great windmill of a punch that knocked him clean over. He got back up, lunged at TV and he took another one and stayed down longer. His mate pulled a blade and TV, who wore a steel-toe capped shoe back then, precisely for protection, did a long-legged kick and smashed it out of his hand in the split of a second. Dan had seen it all happen, and these two locals were supposed to be *the* young Tennin toughies of the moment. The tale had made TV a hero at the asylum and had fully cemented his legendary status. TV, the head of 'The Star' done what he liked, dressed how he liked and if you didn't like it, he would stand up for himself and knock you clean out with one punch. That's what the legend's narrative had been speaking for some time now, and it had acted back on TV so that he would confidently stride out into the town, knowing that if anyone pushed ice-cream in his face again, he would 'windmill' um. But Dan was deeply worried. The world he knew and loved was in danger.

'When ya gonna do it, TV?' he asked.

TV had been doing some serious thinking while he was walking, and he was working everything out in his mind and, unbeknown to Dan, had begun his detailed plans. Sometimes the head of Dragon Star had to be secretive like that, but before he revealed the burgeoning plan, TV took his Dragon Star cap off. He would never go on the wards with it on, as anything Dragon Star was banned. He parted his long fringe to make way for the revelation.

'Next week, before that meeting with "The Fuhrer". Now ya know "Drill-head" has been doing vocational catering,'

Dan knew, as Drill-head had told him, that he had went into the lock up unit and was giving out coffees and biscuits to Freeda. TV continued.

'I gave him a note. Told Freeda to read it and tear it up into a hundred little pieces so that the Gestapo don't get wind of it.'

Dan laughed, but he was so concerned and still didn't know what TV was going to do as TV was keeping it all under the Dragon Star cap, although it was in his pocket hidden away now. TV went all quiet and was thinking some more, and the abyss got deeper. Dan spotted a security guard coming out of the main block.

'They're here, TV.'

They pissed off quick.

Drill-head was busily taking the afternoon tea trolley towards the lock up unit. His real name was Lorenzo Drill and he had got the moniker, after an altercation with nurses and then the security a number of years ago. Lorenzo was caught smoking dope and then he refused to give it up after the staff demanded he did so. He head-butted two security guards who then with another, goaded by Nurse Garotte, tried to manhandle him and search him. Another caught a head-butt so all three tasted the Lorenzo Drill specialty and Keefy, who came to the scene on hearing the commotion, saw Lorenzo butt the three. It was all over quick, but Keefy said to everybody that Lorenzo had drilled them with his head. Thereafter, he was called 'Drill-head', although inevitably Dr. Lock banned the moniker's use, on the grounds that the associations were inhibiting Lorenzo's life chances. But everyone called him Drill-head, and Drill when in the vicinity of the regime's cohorts, who were trained to suggest they all address him by his proper name, Lorenzo. They never did, and eventually the compromise was accepted.

Drill-head smiled to the security and scratched his prematurely balding head and pulled the tea trolley towards the lock up unit with his great big goalkeeper hands. It was all a rattling calling out its imminent arrival. Drill had got on the new vocational catering scheme as he liked moving around the hospital, rather than being tied down to a small area or his room, and he enjoyed seeing people and doing something for his friends. Dr. Lock and Dr. Bolt were pleased too, as he was carrying out his duties efficiently and courteously, and at least it kept him away from being involved with TV. TV with Lorenzo Drill meant bigger trouble. He moved the trolley into the lounge area where the music was coming from.

The estranged lover Freeda was lain on the settee in the lounge, as was her usual afternoon want. She had a minder behind, closely watching her every move as Freeda was considered a danger at all times. She was thirty-one now, of medium build, although she had been a skinny waif in her early twenties and she had long straight black hair. She had a thing about rolling up the ends and chewing and the habit had been discussed by Dr. Lock and Dr. Bolt many a time. Initially they tried weening her off the hair and onto chewing spearmint gum but it hadn't worked. Now she chewed hair and gum at the same time, having a go with the hair for a while before turning to the gum. The chewing had become so habitual, that she didn't know she was doing it, but she demanded spearmint everyday now as well as her hair. Freeda had to have it otherwise she would 'kick off'. Of course, Dr. Lock and Dr. Bolt had discussed Freeda's incessant, obsessive behavioral traits with the psychologist, but it was decided that they would let her chew. The psychologist warned that the energy, if blocked through censure, would probably manifest in more difficult ways. Better the she-devil you knew already, was Dr. Lock's final decision on the matter, so they let her chew to her heart's content. Nurse Garotte was relieved.

Freeda was quirky-looking with a large Roman nose and piercing eyes that were constantly dilated on the medication. Menace pervaded from her and it habitually filled that lounge. It was the maelstrom of emotions mixed with her hi-energy, all swirling around a central core of resentment and hurt. At twenty foot that menace was palpable, disturbing any kind of equilibrium that people in her presence might have. But she had a deeply troubled background, that had greatly affected her emotional and intellectual development. Her incarceration over the years had magnified the effect with heaps of medication, peppered with constant violent clashes. She was willful and the 'notorious' one, in fact the most so in the asylum. She was trouble, big psychotic trouble as despite everything, there was still a fire underneath it all, that existed to state, in an incontrovertible way, that Freeda was here OK. Everything in Freeda, all of her energy, physical and psychic, wanted that which she couldn't have, her soulmate TV Sam.

On this occasion she was deep in obsessed meditation over her new sandals, a birthday present from TV the previous week. Dr. Lock had considered confiscating them, because of the implications, at a meeting that had finalized plans for TV to be transferred to a 'more suitable' unit three hundred miles away. But Dr. Lock had wisely decided not to confront Freeda over the darn things as she was bound to 'kick-off' as the staff called it. The psychologist suggested it was possible that she might get caught in an obsessed kick-off mode. It was a no-brainer. Locko took the virago they knew with the sandals. The sandals in question were the very same 'Jesus's Sandals' that TV wore, although a size or two smaller, a size six to be precise, and of course the shoes cemented their relation. They were the Dragon Star children and they wore 'Jesus's Sandals' and Dan, Drill and Cheryl were going to get some next Sunday, and Arizona and the new Nigerian recruit Abi. TV thought it wonderful that Dragon Star was now crossing continents. The Dragon, as TV had said, was fully inclusive. On numerous occasions he had taunted Dr. Lock that even she would eventually turn Dragon, Nurse Garotte too.

'We don't discriminate, Locko!' he had told her prior to the banning of all things Dragon. 'Mark my words! You'll all be dragons! Wearing our caps! Fucking all of ya!' he had said to them, which further cemented the TV legendary status. Who else spoke like that to Locko?

Freeda was mesmerized by the sandals, although she would look quickly this way and that scowling full of her nervous energy, before returning her gaze to her clad feet. She turned to the minder for some confirmation.

'Do ya like Freeda's new sandals? They're Jesus's!'

He nodded his agreement before Freeda took one of the sandals off and began looking over it more closely. After a perusal and loving smile, she quickly slipped it back on, before raising herself in a jolt, grabbing a magazine from the coffee table, that had a glamourous show biz wedding on the front cover. She smiled enthusiastically and turned the pages to the glossy shots of the bride and groom, before giving one of her perpetual fixated glances out towards the grounds. The minder's eyes followed hers as any sightings of TV out there, had to be reported to Dr. Lock on the mobile. Freeda sat down with the mag and dreamed.

She liked sitting in the lounge. It got her out of the bedroom, and there was that chance of seeing TV out on the grounds around that smoking tree. However, the wheels had been set into motion. Freeda noticed the security guard out there in front of the tree. She turned her lip up and scowled at the minder. Dr. Lock was determined to prevent TV from ever being in sight of that lounge window again until she met those budgetary constraints. But the ongoing dilemma had finally been solved. TV would be sent to Cumbria in a couple of weeks. It would be up to Dr. Bolt to keep Freeda peaceful, with his new medications and syrups during the problematic period. Nurse Lavender Garotte, who would be in the trenches for the regime, battling it out with a maddened, bereft Freeda, was fearing the forthcoming months. It was thought that with increased syrup dosages from Dr. Bolt, eventually Freeda's negative energy would wane, but there might be a few black eyes and worse and most of it coming Lavender's way.

Now when Freeda was young she was very close to her mother. Her mother was an avid music fan and the music Freeda had heard when she was young had stayed with her. But Freeda forgot it all when her mind was confused with all the drugs and emotional disturbances, and it was an Irish nurse Kleeunah, who had helped her remember with some clever prompting. Kleeunah then purchased a dozen or so CDs which were prized possessions that were kept in an old red *Sesame Street* forty-five case, Kleeunah's old one, that Freeda was deeply attached to now. It was clear Freeda was helped by listening to the music, and so Dr. Lock allowed her to listen every day in the lounge, although they knew that everything she played, was in homage to her great love TV. But all in all, the music didn't cause too much trouble. Take the devil you know was always the general policy with all things Freeda.

Another of the clients came in and looked towards Freeda lain on the settee. The minder suggested that she sit up and allow Tyrone to sit down. Tyrone was the only one of her fellow clients that Freeda didn't get along with. He was of mixed race and he was always complaining that Freeda dominated the lounge too much. It was true she did, but his complaints were to no avail.

'Freeda, I think Tyrone would like to sit down, could you move up and sit proper,' the minder said politely, although Freeda merely sneered. She hated Tyrone. He had tried to have her music afternoons stopped after complaining about his headaches. Tyrone didn't push it though and he just sat in an armchair opposite. He was always wary of Freeda as she had viciously attacked him going back. It was at breakfast one morning. They got into a dispute over reading a magazine and Freeda smashed a cereal bowl over his head. He had tried to fight back but Freeda had scared him, threatening to rip his head off before grabbing him by the neck and half strangling him. Freeda goaded the minder triumphantly.

'See! Tyrone don't wanna sit down!'

Tyrone sighed. The minder would write about Freeda's bullying of Tyrone in the daily report. But it was only usual business.

When Drill-head finally arrived, Etta James's 'At Last', one of Freeda's all-time favorites, was playing. It spoke of everything that Freeda longed for. Her Holy Grail was merely to be with TV. When she was with him it was all different.

'Listening to the old ones again, Freeda?' Drill-head said. He said that nigh every day he came through.

'Yeah, Freeda likes the old ones, Drill,' she replied, as she lay lounged out on the settee, enjoying her supremacy over Tyrone, with the minder behind. By now Tyrone had gone off in a huff with his fag packet displayed prominently in his hand, hoping that Freeda might ask for one so that he could flatly refuse and get his own back in some small way. He moaned every day that it wasn't fair how Freeda dominated the lounge.

Freeda was eager for her coffee. She would always have the strongest of coffees from the trolley with her digestive biscuits. Freeda liked her routines. If she had a strong coffee and a handful of digestives at half past one, that was the time, she had to have them. She was liable to do that kicking off that the staff feared, if the routine buckled, so Dr. Lock and Dr. Bolt made sure that Freeda's accustomed regimens were punctual and Drill-head had been specifically ordered to get into that unit on time, at lunch and late afternoons. Anything for the quieter life, although Freeda was never easy, and she clashed interminably with Nurse Lavender.

'Wan it strong again, Freeda?' Drill-head asked, knowing full well, that Freeda always took a strong one. She jumped up with enthusiasm as he poured the coffee, belying her previously lain out apathetic air, and was right into Drill's space.

'Freeda will have her strong coffee, Drill! Freeda will have her strong coffee, please, Drill!'

Oddly, Freeda would invariably refer to herself in the third person like this. Most people thought it odd and Dr. Lock had tried to stop her years ago, but Freeda would have none of it.

'Freeda's gonna talk just how Freeda wants, ta!' was the way Freeda had responded to that particular directive from 'The Fuhrer'.

But something deep within Freeda knew, she had to refer to herself like this, otherwise Freeda might just forget who she was. Exactly why Dr. Lock was trying to end the habit. It was thought she would be less recalcitrant, and might even be peaceful. But Freeda was excessively willful and she wasn't going to take notice of that 'Fuhrer fingy'.

Freeda then noticed that Drill-head was slyly implying that he had something to deliver her, and he popped a note into her hand and winked, all unbeknown to the nurse minder, who had become distracted speaking to another patient who entered. Freeda's eyes were glinting and she had a joyous look on her face once the note was in her hand. She quickly put it in the pocket of her faded, grungy jeans before taking her coffee and biscuits. She knew it was from TV, so she was thrilled.

TV and Dan couldn't get back to the tree because of the security guard, so they fell back to another smoking spot around the back of a ward that was used by the maintenance staff. Dan thought they had just one fag left, but TV had a surprise.

'I didn't think ya had any, TV?' Dan remarked, as TV dramatically revealed a pack of ten from his special Gothic pouch, that he wore underneath his skirt on a belt.

'I bought some from the kiosk when ya went to the toilet, Dan, case we had an emergency.' They both laughed and TV gave Dan a fag, and they both lit up with TV taking an enormous drag that Dan could never have matched due to his lesser lung capacity. But he tried his darn best to. TV exhaled furiously, still greatly troubled.

'I think about her all the time, Dan, I love her so much,' he confessed; a confession that Dan had heard many a time, but he knew how much TV loved her, and how it was reciprocated by Freeda. Dan thought it all tragically sad, he hated speaking about it, but TV's frame of mind forced him to. It was awful. Going back, TV had been placed in that lock up unit for disappearing for two nights and that was when he met Freeda. It was a mutual love at first sight kind of thing, and thereafter the couple brought 'sexual activity problems', as Dr. Lock had called them. For a while they were contained, so they were together some time, before TV was brought back to a more open ward. TV had been madly in love with her since, and the estrangement had made his loss more acute and Freeda felt the same. Dr. Lock gave TV special dispensations and freedoms, to get TV to forget about Freeda. But Freeda was his soulmate.

'I know how much ya love her, TV. And how it's hard for ya both.'

It pained Dan to even speak about it, but TV couldn't hold his emotions back any longer and he broke down in tears, and Dan tried his best to comfort him. TV liked Dan because Dan allowed him to show his true feelings and he always said some nice things.

'You were meant for each other, TV. You're special soulmates, you and Freeda.'

TV agreed with him, but there were still things that worried Dan as he knew that TV would keep his word and make some kind of 'break out' attempt. All the pressure seemed to be coming to a head.

'But how ya gonna break into the lock up though, TV? Locko won't let ya near it,' he said quite realistically. TV had recovered his calm. It was now time to invoke the destiny. He smiled, as if he had everything under control, and that whatever he planned would come to pass.

'I'll do me wires and borrow a few things from the gardener's shed. Tools and that and then I'll go for the dramatic! Like they do in the films, Dan! And I'll shoot up the fucking Gestapo!' TV role-played making merry hell with an automatic and Dan found it funny, but it all sounded unrealistic to Dan, yet TV was animated, obsessed with what he was calling his mission. He had to believe, so he came on with the usual TV Sam bravado, the type of thing that had made him a legend.

'Nothing can stop the leader of Dragon Star, Dan! It's our time! Here! Right Now! It's a New Age, Dan! It's all Dragon Stars!'

TV was super confident and he was desperately trying to build it up, by being more confident. He wouldn't contemplate failure. His mission would be a success, inevitable as the sun rising.

Dan laughed along with TV at the audacity of the plan, although Dan just couldn't work out how he could do it. He was anxious. Yes, TV was a massive legend, but Dan knew that not even TV could beat that system and 'The Fuhrer'.

Chaz was trying to prepare himself as per normal for work after the debacle with the snake. He had placed a cache of DVDs in the briefcase and was tooling up dress wise for the day ahead. He buttoned up the Armani, and began adjusting matching tie in the oval mirror, building up to that sacred moment when he would slip into full character. The world is like a stage and we are all players, was a much-quoted Shakespearean aphorism of Chaz's, and once that blazer was on, Chaz became the bigger than life Chazzy Barber that everybody knew. The dude of Tennin! The one with the Italian cut white blazers and all the gold! The special one in that spanking, shining white chariot of a Jag.

The magical talisman was lain over the Waldorf on a coat hanger with its polythene covering, having freshly returned from the cleaners on the weekend. How Chaz loved a pristine blazer. Meanwhile, Linda was loading a full load of washing into the machine, that was directly outside the back door in the porch way. The back door was open and Chaz stopped for a moment, after he had tucked his shirt in and was straightening his tie. He stroked the goatee.

'That fucking old boy was right,' he mused, raising his voice so that Linda could hear. Linda was just coming through the threshold of the kitchen.

'What do you mean, Chaz?' she asked curiously. Chaz opened up about the old boy's warnings.

'He used to work up at the asylum on the boilers. Reckons him and his mate used to see hundreds of the bastards sunbathing on the chalk, up the hill there. Reckons they're still about, been disturbed. I thought it was one of those old man's tales, ya fucking hear, Linda? '

Linda winced at the idea.

'Well pray we don't get hundreds of um here, Chaz! God forbid they'll give me nightmares.'

Chaz put up his usual bravado. A hundred and one snakes could easily be blasted to kingdom come by Chaz Barber.

'Be a fucking war against the snake if we do, Linda! I'll fucking machine gun the bastards!'

Chaz reflected for a moment, and thought about that old orchard, the obvious source of the intruder. It had rather a foreboding atmosphere now, wild and dangerous.

'I'm not happy with that old orchard. They might be out there, beginning to move, like the old bastard said!'

It was a horrible thought. Evil bastard snakes wriggling everywhere.

'Oh, don't say that, Chaz. I won't be able to go out into the garden without thinking about that head, ugh!'

Linda moved back out to the kitchen again to clean the surfaces, although she just wanted to get away from that talk about snakes. But that snake out the back yard had lodged itself into her imagination. She would have bad dreams; she was sure of it. It would act as a trigger and it would play on her mind, and a hundred! It was the stuff of nightmares. Snakes everywhere! Crawling all over the garden, through the drain pipes and into the house and up the walls. They might even get in the front lounge penetrating the very center of the citadel. 'Ugh!' It was a hideous thought.

With Linda back in the kitchen, Chaz was back concentrating getting into character again for the day's work, putting all that snake business out of his mind. He slipped on the alligators, going for the Blue Nero's with the scuff mark, that he tried desperately to polish out, but had largely failed. But they were more than good enough for crappy old Tennin. It was a no socks day again too. Chaz had decided, that from now, to late October, he would let his feet breathe in alligator and if they began to pong, he would give them a spray. With the shoes back on, he was immediately feeling like the king of the jungle. It was time to stalk down the white blazer.

It was odd this stalking ritual. Chaz really did enter another dimension with the blazer. For Chaz they were like garments invested with spiritual power. Now the robe of Jesus might be an analogy that was pushing it, but something like that. He picked it up off the back of the Waldorf and divested it of its polythene outer shell, handling it with reverence, feeling its sacred ritualistic power. He slipped it on and adjusted himself in the mirror, turning up the collar a little, like he always did, giving him that smart two and a half G rebel look. Linda was still cleaning away in the kitchen. Once that white blazer was on, Chaz was flush with energy. Chaz entered the zone! The place!

'You know I felt bloody knackered in that garden but as soon as the blazer's on. I'm in! I feel clean, perfect, Linda.'

Chaz chuckled to himself, seemingly pleased, as he smiled and flashed his teeth, with the gold cap figuring prominently. Chaz then took up a spray, that he always kept on the table near the front window. He sprayed his mouth before speaking to himself as he peered into the oval mirror. All as per normal and as the work ritual required.

'Coo! Sweet breath and by the end of June you'll be slapping that pregnant virgin forty-three right across your knee, Chazzy Barber, ha, ha, ha, while the bumble bees hum about Linda's big ol bum.'

He chuckled to himself before taking up one of his ultra-expensive Harrods aftershaves that set him apart. The women of Tennin would smell him coming and he'd leave that trace behind to tell them all he'd been. How about that for a craic, eh? Chaz congratulated himself as he liberally applied his Maison St Francis Rouge with its jasmine and wood musk hues. The Tennin women loved them, and there was always the odd one who would look at him smile and politely ask 'What's that aftershave you're wearing? It's really nice?'

'Ha, ha, you're getting a bit of a carp poet in your middling years, Chazzy boy. Ya handsome brute!' Linda came in, and Chaz continued with his sexually framed banter. 'Must be something to do with that masked golden shower exchange of ours, Linda, that has netted us well over the six grand with the kinky fuckers!'

He made an effort to ground the comment in the new reality of this Brave New Age.

'We're all kinky fuckers now, Linda! All the fucking lot of us!'

Linda was silent, then she spoke about her friend June to change the subject. She had begun a new job as a cleaning supervisor, at you guessed it, the asylum.

'I must phone June to see how she's getting on with her new job up the hospital, Chaz.'

Any mention of that place seemed to unnerve Chaz. It was like a phantom, but the place did have a history in Chaz's mindscape. Chaz had never forgot going to a Christmas fair there once, with his mum and dad when he was a young boy. It was dark and lit up with Christmas lights when he left the main administrative building, and it looked like something out of a horror movie. It was like Dracula's castle, or the Bates' house at the Motel and was actually used as an external visual in a British horror film. Thereafter the place always had a hold on Chaz, registering in his young imagination like a haunted house on top of the hill.

'I'll be glad when that nutty-farm is proper dead and fucking buried. But there's no rest for the wicked bastards among us, Linda!' Chaz picked up his briefcase readying himself for the departure. 'Make sure ya feed Hermann and the gang, and do your duties on the box ticking!'

This was a request that was delivered like an order. Those carp simply had to be fed at their allotted times. That was the regime and was all part of the great carp research and study. It had to be detailed, without ever missing a beat and bait. Linda sighed as everything was carp, carp and more bloody carp. It seemed that carp were more important than her these days in the Chazzy Barber world schema of things.

'All right, Chaz, all right!'

Chaz didn't like that tone. Merely feeding the carp was being made into some kind of terrible ordeal to bear.

'Well don't make it sound as if it's so much fucking trouble Linda. You're plopping little round balls in a tank of water, watching, and ticking fucking paper! Anyone would think I had ya stripped to the waist pushing a coal cart all night fucking long! Oh yeah and don't forget to mail out those boilie orders. And try and knock out twenty-five kilo!'

Linda didn't have to go to work. Chaz's business was a job in itself, but at least this bait stuff was legitimate. It was a hope for a better life, even if it meant carp, carp and more darn carp.

'Yeah, no problem, Chaz. Anything else?'

Chaz couldn't think of anything.

'Nah, that's the essential "to do" list, Linda. Be about ten o'clock, the last drop that "Top Cat" twat on the Triune Way.'

Chaz had a ton of work on, with visits and drop offs to make. He gave Linda a quick kiss then made for the back door. He wanted to get that back door wedged up, so that stuffy porch way could get an airing. Outside in the back garden there was a stray black Tom that was a hospital scraps cat, nestled in the long grasses of the old orchard, out of view behind those stinging nettles that lay back behind the far line post, down by the compost heap. Normally he didn't come that far from base as it were, but the warm weather had set him off on his travels. Chaz came out of the porch breezing along, and the door was left open. As soon as Chaz sauntered his way around the side of the house towards the front garden path, the cat saw its chance and made for the door opening. He was in. It was a whole new world for the black Tom as he laid out luxuriously upon the porch carpet near the door, catching the sun's rays and warmth.

Freeda was now firmly ensconced in her private room listening to the '2 Become 1' Spice Girls track on a small CD player with her back towards the door. This was intentional as a minder could be watching her through a peephole. Freeda was busily tearing the note from TV into tiny pieces as TV cleverly instructed. She smiled dreamily, and then as she tore some more, her visage changed to malevolent and moody. While Freeda was shredding, Nurse Lavender Garotte was preparing a small beaker of liquid medication for Freeda, from the drugs trolley. Dr. Bolt had devised a nice daily mixture that had a strawberry taste, or at least, when you first put it in your mouth it tasted like that. It was Freeda's favorite medicine, as she loved anything that was strawberry, even though she didn't like the bitter kick-back taste that it left in her mouth. But then she would have some of her spearmint to counteract it. Nurse Lavender measured the dosage out, sneering as she detested Freeda. She was forty now, heavily built and overweight with great tree trunk arms and flabby, but strong biceps. She was a manly woman with more than a hint of a moustache and her physicality was useful in both areas of her dual life. In her other one, away from the pressure cooker of psychiatric units, she would let her hair down as a baddie in modern women's wrestling, and she had appeared on the undercard of some big wrestling bills. All this energy expenditure made Nurse Garotte into a voluminous eater. Some would go as far to say she stuffed herself, but Lavender liked her food, it was her comfort, and she liked having that extra poundage around too. Having such great bulk is more than useful, when its lock ups and wrestling aprons, so Lavender eschewed all dietary regimes.

Now the advent of the new millennium had allowed people of alternative and diverse sexuality a new freedom of expression and Lavender felt a part of this new world order. When not on duty, she would wear her favored pro-lesbian badge, a rainbow background with Lavender written on it in black. It was subtle and showed her solidarity with the lesbian sisterhood. Back in her twenties, she would frequent all of London's hang outs for risqué meet ups, but now having entered middle age she was settled in a long-term relationship with none other than Dr. Lock, some twenty years and more her senior. The relationship had proved good for her burgeoning wrestling career too, as Dr. Lock was her agent and manager. Their dream was that Lavender would break soon in the USA with her wrestling moniker 'Spiked Lavender'. Things were progressing nicely as wherever she went, she was booed and verbally abused, which was all part of Dr. Lock's master plan on the 'all publicity is good publicity' model. If they got that contract breakthrough, they would both end their stressful careers at Tennin Trust. But in the real world of the here and now in that asylum, the physical power of Nurse Garotte was essential. In the cauldron that was the lock up unit, she was chief nurse in residence in terms of effectively dealing with the problem of the recalcitrant and difficult Freeda Huskit. Nurse Garotte arrived at Freeda's door and knocked, her nostrils inflamed as she readied for the battle. They shared a mutual and intense hatred.

'Miss Huskit! It's time for your medication! Miss Huskit! Miss Huskit!'

There was a rather distinct negative ordering tone in Nurse Lavender's voice and she would never wait until Freeda opened the door, she would just use her master key and open it. She had warned Freeda that she was imminent, and that was sufficient. She would always warn her though. She had done this without fail after catching Freeda masturbating herself on one occasion. The sight of that made Nurse Lavender feel sick and utterly disgusted. She opened the door and she could see that Freeda was visibly trying to hide the bin under the bed, in what looked like a suspicious manner.

'What are you hiding, you little vixen!' Nurse Garotte shouted.

'Nuffin'! It's nuffin', Garotte, nuffin'!' Freeda snapped back aggressively, as was her usual manner. Nurse Garotte shoved the small beaker in front of Freeda, who was seated on her bed readying for more aggression.

'Swallow! And call me by my proper name, please, Nurse Garotte, not 'Garotte', young woman!'

As Freeda took the beaker and put it to her mouth, Nurse Garotte investigated the hidden bin. Freeda launched herself to prevent Nurse Garotte from getting to it. Lavender could see that she had been tearing something up.

'What have you been tearing up! What was it! What was it, Freeda?' she demanded. Lavender's blood pressure was going through the roof, as Freeda screwed her face up and looked daggers back at Garotte, absolutely determined to be a monster. She would never give an inch to the rotten jailor Lavender Garotte.

'Nuffin'! Nuffin'! And Freeda can tear bits of paper up. Can't she! It's a free country, ain't it? Gestapo! Gestapo!'

Freeda had picked up the term from TV. She had forgotten what it actually meant, but when she used it Lavender turned into a raging bull virtually snorting, and Freeda felt as if she was on top, so she would keep using it.

'Don't you call me that name!' Nurse Garotte angrily shouted.

Freeda sneered back at her and held her ground.

'You don't call Freeda names then! Don't call Freeda names!'

Freeda snapped that right back in Nurse Garotte's face and now the argument and battle of wills had begun, there would be no stopping. Nurse Garotte felt impelled to assert her authority.

'I'll jolly well call you what I like, young lady! And I know what that note was! It was from TV! Wasn't it? Delivered by that Lorenzo Drill on the tea trolley!'

Nurse Garotte had that uncanny knack of knowing everything, but it didn't stop Freeda from snapping back at her.

'You know nuffin'! Nuffin'! Go stuff yourself, ya great pig!'

Freeda had learnt that one from TV too. She would push her nose up and off she would go mimicking a pig as best she could. 'Oink! Oink! Oink!' she went, and Freeda reveled. Things could get very personal in the battle and how Nurse Garotte hated that TV. It was TV who had put all these disturbing ideas into Freeda's mind.

'Don't you call me that! You! You!'

Freeda defiantly continued oinking. She loved the power she felt, having that nasty Garotte on the run. Nurse Garotte slapped her around the face as she felt so humiliated and insulted. Freeda increased her scowl and promptly slapped her back. Despite all of Nurse Garotte's wrestling power, it could be more than matched by Freeda's demonic psychotic powers, that she would summons in the heat of battle. This was why the Trust staff used all those subtle tactics to keep her sweet. In this kind of mood, it would take six to pin her down, before Dr. Bolt could get a shot into her. But Nurse Garotte needed help.

'Dr. Bolt! Dr. Bolt! She's kicking off, Dr. Bolt!'

Dr. Bolt was under the more senior Dr. Lock, but he was a right-hand man and the main injection administrator across the asylum. He was suited to the position as he simply loved giving all the clients a helping hand. After all the torrid commotion it was his potions and elixirs that made all the difference, and brought the deviants to their rest. One might call him the Zombie chiller-outer. He had a neatly trimmed beard, and was given to the theory that psychiatric clients have diseases of the brain cells and his injections were like the army divisions fighting and battling those terribly unwanted cells. Oftentimes, he wished he was a doctor back in the good old days, when there wasn't so much meddling in medical affairs by these blasted rights groups, as he would have loved to have been involved with those pioneers who advocated shock treatment. For Dr. Bolt new ways of doing things could derive from a good old-fashioned shock, he thought that it was akin to taking a cold shower after a night on the tiles. It could wake people up and get them out of this most unproductive, sitting around smoking all day mode. Get them shocked and then they might get productive, making tea cozies and sausage dog door stoppers, that incidentally, put some much-needed extra finance into the asylum's coffers. But although Dr. Bolt, bemoaned the cessation of the old ways, he had been incredibly lucky as he had purchased an old electro-convulsive unit at an antiques auction a few years previously and he would spend hours fiddling around with its knobs, while his wife was out fiddling around with a young guy in his twenties who she had met at the body sculpting gymnasium. His wife Stephanie would come home coked and sexed up out of her nut, ironically on Chazzy's popstar cocaine, as Chaz had a four ounce a week drop off, down at 'Charlies', where the manager was in it up to his neck. It's a small world around Tennin. But Dr. Bolt wouldn't have noticed anything untoward, he was always too absorbed in his convulsive unit. He found it most relaxing and therapeutic and 450 volts with their teeth clenched down hard, had always been the best way to deal with the most recalcitrant clients.

When Dr. Bolt heard Nurse Garotte's call, he was looking disturbingly manic, injecting a client in another room, who was being held down by two nurses. He finished and stood up erect looking joyous, anticipating more sport. The most injections he had administered in a day was twenty-three. He had done seven already today and the liquids were all different colors. He simply loved to get through the spectrum of colors a day, he would effuse to his wife Stephanie how he found his job so aesthetically pleasing. He jokingly called himself 'The Rainbow Man', that very morning, before she went off down to 'Charlies' for another strenuous work out.

In a few moments there were two nurses and two security guards, all holding Freeda down while Dr. Bolt plunged in the needle looking ecstatic. It was sublimation and supplication all through the point of a needle. Lavender had a wrestling hold on, and the three others secured her although Freeda had given one of the nurses a black eye in the scuffle, and she had caught Nurse Garotte on the bridge of her nose with a flailing fist. But eventually the four had her secured for the administration, while Lavender's nose throbbed. Lavender kept that grappling hold on and explained.

'It was something from TV, I know it was, Dr. Bolt! A message. I bet these trouble makers are up to something!'

Freeda was still aggressive and she desperately wanted to get that Garotte. How she hated that big fat nurse.

'You know nuffin'! Nuffin'! Oink! Oink! Oink!' Freeda shouted back.

By this time Freeda's voice had really got into Nurse Garotte's mind. She would have disturbing nightmares about Freeda, and on her last really important wrestling bout she had been knocked out cold. All because she was thinking and fretting about Freeda. She hadn't slept a wink tossing and turning. That's how Freeda Huskit could get under a person's skin, and now her nose was throbbing and she knew it was badly damaged too. It would put her wrestling itinerary in jeopardy. This Freeda bloody Huskit could cost her thousands in lost purses. Nurse Garotte almost unconsciously raised her hand as the needle was released by Dr. Bolt. She would smash her nose in revenge. How dare the vixen trash her nose!

'Please, Nurse!' Dr. Bolt intervened, as there were security guards from a private company present. In normal circumstances, he would have let Lavender have a swipe back, and the report would say that Freeda smashed her nose on the bedside table in the struggle. Who would believe Freeda Huskit? The posse of guards left the room as it was a double whammy massive booster and then Dr. Bolt put another double whammy in for luck. He was worried that he might have overdone it in his zeal, but within a few minutes, Freeda was lain out completely zonked and away with the medication zombie fairy's, looking as sweet as a baby. A shot of the Dr. Bolt's would always work the oracle. He took her pulse and opened her eyelids wide, while Nurse Lavender swore and held her battered and twisted conk.

'She'll be fine after twelve hours sleep, Nurse Garotte. She'll wake up like a little baby.'

'Like a little monster! I think she's broken my fucking nose!'

'Please, Nurse, could you temper that language. We are Trust professionals!'

Upon saying that Dr. Bolt looked at Nurse Garotte's nose and it looked like a horrible break.

'My word, Nurse. It's really twisted!'

Nurse Garotte bit her lip, she could have sworn and sworn, but the mystery of the shredded paper, remained a mystery.

Of course, Dr. Lock who shared Lavender's more intimate moments and spaces, heard everything. Lavender had her nose reset and bandaged up immediately, and suitable financial compensation would be forthcoming, and it was decided that a close watch would be made over that Lorenzo Drill and his tea and coffee vocational. Indeed, something was going on, as Drill had been seen flashing about a pack of twenty, and Lorenzo Drill *never* had cigarettes. Dr. Lock thought hard about all the issues, and in the past, she had considerable problems with that Lorenzo Drill. She didn't want them revisited. He had broken many a nose with those devastating head-butts. No, Dr. Lock didn't want a return of that flying Drill-head and Lorenzo's behavior had been positively serene of late, as he rattled his tea trolleys around the wings. Therefore, by the Fuhrer's decree, no direct action would be taken, but all staff, contracted and agency, had to read the Lorenzo Drill tea making memo. It was high alert until further notice. Locko wanted hawk eyes on that Drill-head!

June had been working at the hospital for a couple of weeks now and she was full of it as it was the site of such juicy gossip. It was a perk of the job if you were a gossip like June. She was of similar age to Linda, a little more overweight with black hair that she was always having styled. One might say June was a lifelong slave to the glamour thing and she took it into middle age with a vengeance. You could talk to June all morning about dermal lip fillers, botox, anti-aging creams and practically anything else that might hold up the slings and arrows of the aging process, while she would chain smoke her way through a dozen fags and four coffees, before hitting the mop bucket with a fresh bottle of mountain spring water by her side. She had raked up some eighteen grand of credit card debts and all of it dedicated to the pursuit of eternal beauty. Ray, her husband, knew she had a debt, but he thought it to be about three grand, and he just couldn't understand where all the money was going. He thought she might be a secret gambler.

Going back some, June had been a very attractive young woman, when she could snugly fit in those size eights a few decades ago, but she was still smoking forty a day and it was beginning to take its toll. Her teeth needed treatment now, so the debts were continually increasing but she felt temporarily better on account of the forty hours up at the asylum. She vowed that she would tackle her debts. She was having a coffee with a colleague when Linda rang.

'You're joking! Its head detached still trying to bite him! Oh my God! He's no snake charmer is he, Linda?

June was aghast and Linda simply loved retelling the incident, although it was so disturbing too. It would become apocryphal beyond your very last breath, juicy for gossiping.

'No, I don't think he is, June! Anyway, how's the job going?'

While Linda was on the mobile, she was keeping a cursory eye on the carp. Hermann was hoovering up the baits with a somewhat voracious abandonment.

'It's going fine, but it opens your eyes up, Linda. And by the way, there's a girl on one of the lock up units I do, that looks just like your Nat, drug addict. It's such a shame, Linda.'

Linda was seated on Chaz's velvet chair now, looking at the painting above the great Waldorf settee, the painted image of Nat naked on that chaise longue from *Big Jugs*. She feared Nat's life could run off the rails but she hadn't expressed her fears to Chaz. She thought she needed a close relationship and she hoped she would eventually see how much that Steve thought of her and Linda was sure he would jump and move out from the site on account of Natasha.

'No, not our Nat, Ju. She's preparing for her second-year exams at Uni, she's doing really well, June.'

June had been reading before she started, that students were raking up enormous debts these days going through university.

'Great to hear. Is she still working? I've been reading about some of the debts they rake up these days, Linda.'

'She's still doing her part-time glamour work and things, Ju. Chaz is awfully proud of her.'

Linda thought for moment about Natasha and her lifestyle. At first, she thought it was purely those soft porn shoots. But then there was the money and things like top-of-the-range designer clothes, expensive furs and rented penthouses, costing thousands. Then there was that film. The one that she found among Chaz's magazines while they were at Cavell, and it was still there under the carp tanks, with Natasha on the front called 'Carla, The Gang Bang Whore'. It was a shock when Linda had seen it. She had been naively unaware up to that point. Things had moved swiftly on from there too. The new sports car with her personalized number plate 'NAT FAB1' seemed to embody the misgivings. Part-time glamour work made it all sound above board, and like harmless money-making fun, although Linda, and June, knew full well that Natasha was now caught up deep in the industry. Linda knew she was a high-class prostitute, although she tried to convince herself she wasn't. Linda was hoping that she would somehow grow out of it and eventually get a proper job. But that didn't look likely. The last time she was down at the house warming party, she was talking to Chaz about running a dating agency and Chaz said he was willing to back it up with hard cash. Linda knew that 'dating agency' was a euphuism for escort agency, and after Uni her daughter would likely be a brothel madame. There was also animated talk about Natasha, staying at the house while they were away in Ibiza in mid-July, and Nat said that it would be an ideal location for some glamour shoots. Linda hoped and prayed that her daughter would find a contentment and happiness in it all. But she doubted it. Linda moved on.

'She seems to have taken to it like a duck to water, June. But she always had the figure,' Linda tried to explain.

'She's got the boobs more like it! Oh, yeah, do you want a ticket for "Talking, Hungry Cnuts!" It's on down at the Orchard Garden.'

Linda wondered what it was all about? Hungry Cnuts! What on earth was that? June said that it was all the rage, and Debs was raving about it. June explained it as much as she could.

'It's like a show based on man's fear of hairy cunts with teeth! Like a castration fear. Debs has been telling me! She called it a testimony to the cunt that bites cocks off! Bizarre, eh?'

They both laughed and June went on to say that Debs, who was now doing an 'Access to University' course at a local college, had called it 'Post Freudian Feminism', whatever that meant.

'It'll be a great laugh and Debs says it makes you think as well!'

Linda was up for it, however bizarre it sounded. She didn't go out very often, and she loved going out with her lifelong friends. Talking over the old times, over half a dozen vodkas was fun, and a night out in itself. She'd definitely go, although Chaz hated her having anything to do with Debs, who was now a convert to radical feminism.

'Yeah I'll come. It doesn't matter what night it is, Ju.'

June was excited and she replied she would get the tickets before she launched into some of that juicy gossip that she'd been hearing over the past week or so, and which was a perk of the job.

'The jobs great but you have to watch your step up here, Linda. There's one woman. "Mad Freeda" they call her. She grabbed hold of a male nurse and pulled him into a domestic cupboard.'

Linda obviously put two and two together.

'What and had her wicked way with him?'

June really savored opening up towards the punch line on this one.

'You can say that again, Linda! She said he was full of worms, so she filled his mouth up with vim to get rid of them. Ha, ha. Made him swallow it as well, Linda. He was in intensive care for a week!'

Linda thought she was joking, but June assured her she wasn't, and there was more.

'And would you believe it Linda, a couple of months ago she dug up some garden worms on vocational gardening, accosted a doctor, held him at knifepoint, and said he had too much vim in him, and filled his mouth up with worms!'

'She made him chew um and swallow um, June.'

June's colleague Gloria elaborated as June was relaying the tale, as this was the juiciest of stories and not to be missed. June was laughing away.

'Still off sick! And doesn't look like he's coming back, June!' Gloria pointed out.

Linda was in disbelief, but it made her feel uncomfortable sitting here in the dream house, only a short trip down Holly Beach Lane, away. June went on. She had loads more to get off her chest. She had done the lock up, covering a couple of days, so she had come across this 'Mad Freeda' in person.

'She's got something about her Linda, pervades evil, and you should hear her laugh. It's kind of disturbing you know what I mean, Linda.'

'Worse than horror films!' Gloria pointed out. 'And nothings make-believe with her, June! She'll fly out of a fucking closet and have a flipping knife at ya throat!'

Things were more serious now, and Linda confided, this kind of thing was why Chaz was wary about buying the house in the first place. Why Chaz was eagerly awaiting the bypass and the final end to the God damned place. Even Linda was beginning to fear them up there now, after hearing these horrible stories. But they would have to ride it out. For a couple of years at least.

'Yeah, I'll tell you more about things when we go to the theatre next week. Tuesday, by the way,' June pointed out. Tuesday would be perfect for Linda as that was the night that Chaz was going to a boxing thing. They could both go out that night. What a great idea, Linda thought.

Once the phone call was out of the way, Linda had to set about boiling all those baits. Chaz said he wanted twenty kilos at least, ten of each. She had to fetch them from the freezer in the shed and haul them up to these new urns, she had in the porch walkway. The urns were put in the porch as Chaz didn't want to put heat into that shed through the winter, although Linda had bought a heater, and was running it in the porch, so she might as well have been down the shed. But with the weather, well and truly changed, she would get Chaz to carry the heavy-duty urns down there. She wouldn't need the heat, and it might get this darn boilie smell away from the house. As she opened the back door, that Tom whipped out the back without her knowing. He had been more than comfortable in his new sleeping place and he intended to return.

Linda had to get that work done. She stood in front of the great urns and scooped out a load of baits with a giant-sized colander. Then she laid them out on giant white towels, all lain in the porch, that were heavily stained from all of the blue and red dye. She put some more in a great urn for boiling and looked at the boilies lain on the towels. Their very presence drove Linda spare, but as yet, she just couldn't be bothered in putting them into buckets and getting them down into that shed, ready for Chaz to bag up. She would have a line of coke instead; she was gagging for one. But there was no escaping that smell. It inundated the house, crept through the gaps between the door and jamb, and when it got like this, Linda would open all the windows and spray the house with air freshener that invariably would set off her asthma. For some odd reason Chaz never had any problem with the smell. He was so obsessed with the darn baits he seemed immune.

Linda had her line, felt a little high, and then returned to her drudgery, pouring out yet another great colander scoop of boilies, all blues this time. Linda could never win when it came to these little round beggars.

'Divine fucking blues!' she snarled, utterly fed up with making these infernal baits. Once she had finally finished, it would be back on the fumigation, before she packaged the orders up. There were ten to go out today, which she would post at the village post office in the convenience store. Chaz had brought these bags up from the shed and they were in a cardboard box on the kitchen table. It was a bind but those ten packs would be bringing in well over a hundred and thirty pounds. Linda could see the rhyme and reason behind it all, and as Chaz was always pointing out, 'quids in' justified all of the hardships.

'Work's always uncomfortable, Linda. That's why it's called work!'

Hadn't Chaz nearly got bitten by that great fucking dog the other day. It was all stuff that equated with 'work hassle,' and he had to find a way to deal with all those Herberts! Now that's flipping hassle! But Linda would sigh her way through all the boiling.

While out on his travels, Chaz had to make a visit to Candy Foxes, a gentlemen's lap dance club in the nearby town Foxdale. He had arranged to meet the proprietor there regarding the possibility of some regular business. The venue had come under intense pressure from local councilors after it was thought that eastern European women were being trafficked into the venue and forced to work as prostitutes and lap dancers. However, things had cooled of late, as certain women's protest groups had been supporting the venue, in terms of sex worker's rights, and this emboldened the owner, an Anglo Italian, Giorgio Fiondre, to undertake new ventures. He was interested in the idea of a greater quality drugs supplier, and it had come to his notice that Tennin's drugs were so much purer than the already cut crap that he was getting. He was thinking of more profits and offering higher quality as an alternative to the normal 'bashed' coke, and the Scamp had put Fiondre onto Chaz. Chaz liked the traveler community being involved with him. Who wants travelers on their case? It made potential competitors think twice and Chaz had fifty grand tucked away, especially for paying them if anything came up. Chaz parked up the Jag, in the club's car park, and walked up the small flight of steps and rang the bell. The venue was originally The Foxdale Cinema, going back, some twenty-five years ago. Chaz had the briefcase in his hand with a stash. He was let in by a female receptionist and dance music was already ringing out, bashing the walls. Three or four pole dancers were practicing their moves on the main floor space, and Chaz liked the eye candy. He had come to the club on occasions, although he had never dealt exclusively with the owners. One of the girls who was cavorting round a pole, long blonde hair, wearing a bikini, guessed that Chaz was the drugs dealer that Giorgio was meeting. She worked for Giorgio's daughter's escort agency, an agency that supplied girls to many of the 'gentlemen's' events, in and around the Tennin area. Chaz gave her the eye as she put on the sexy sass around the pole.

'Like your moves! I'll have to hire a private room one night, and I'll pay for a dance and extras.'

'Anytime, sir, book it at the reception, the name's Brooke.'

Chaz was led into a little basement office, and was met by Giorgio's son and a couple of hefty bruiser types. It was Giorgio's son, Salvio who wanted to go big time into the cocaine dealing, it would be available, high quality, from the venue, for 'special' guests or members, but the majority of it, would be bashed out from Salvio's garage business in Foxdale. It was newly acquired, and had a couple of pumps and was out of the way. Ideal for his purpose. Chaz was polite with some club talk, first.

'How's the business these days?' Chaz had read about the problems around re-issuing a license, but he hadn't kept up with the state of play with the vehement agitation for Candy Foxes by those ardent Tennin 'pro-sex' feminists who had persuaded Sally Brockett that new leader of the council into looking at the issue from other angles.

'Great, Mr. Barber, we're even getting dykes in here, paying exorbitant money for a booth and enjoying our raunchy dance girls. We're embracing diversity big time now, and we've even got a gay porn star night going these days – gets the place packed on a Thursday.'

'I noticed the posters; the pink pound is good as anybody else's.'

'Yes, very lucrative and we have great opportunities here, now the heat is off. We're looking for higher quality recreational drug suppliers Mr. Barber, to meet our client's needs.'

Chaz hunched his shoulders. He was going to be the man here.

'Well look no further! We can supply you with our special brand of Peruvian rocket fuel, pure white powder straight from our jungle lab. Best quality coke in the country and at eminently affordable prices that gives our buyers much freedom to sell and cut as they please.'

Chaz opened up the briefcase, took a small bag of coke from a sleeve and placed it on the table for the three to try and consider. One immediately, took some with a blade and laid it out and snorted. But it was all going one way, Salvio wanted high grade coke. Chaz was the only regular source in these parts.

'Can you supply us with a kilo a week, Mr. Barber?'

Chaz fancied a bit of this.

'As long as the money's here every week, you'll get the kilo, all of the same quality without fail. Our firm is built on partnerships and good family relations and we won't tolerate anything else. We play fair. We expect others to play fair with us.'

There was a handshake and the deal was for the first kilo to be delivered at the arranged price for the weekend. When Chaz left, the girls were still working out to dance music on the poles and Chaz eyed that girl up again, and used the opportunity to slip her a card. This was a card relating to his porn business interests with Miko and Vivienne.

'Ever thought of appearing in films? Take my card and check out our opportunities.'

Brooke was impressed and she gathered herself from the pole and took her own card from a bag and handed it to Chaz as Chaz chewed on his gum.

'Here have one of mine, er.'

'Chaz is the name.'

Chaz walked out to the Jag with a sprightly dash in his step, and Foxdale, with its population of eighty-three thousand was Chaz's. Fuck going legit! And that Candy Foxes club was a great opportunity.

After all the work and the visit down to the village post office, Linda returned and re-opened the porch door to get the smell out. She went inside, and the patient black Tom who had caught a bird and devoured it on the lawn while Linda was gone, slipped back inside, and curled up again in a basket of towels that Linda hadn't moved. Linda had a coffee and then went for another line of coke laid out on that Jason and Michaela Thabane coffee table. Coke seemed to come down from the hand of God, to Linda too. But she was getting herself ready, psychologically, for later in the evening. Chaz wanted to do 'that' filming, so she would need to shave any freshly cultivating pubic hair. Chaz hated female pubic hair. Although many women liked all the shaven thing, to please their man kind of thing, Linda detested it, especially so, because she felt she was pressurized into doing it. She looked embittered, when she was shaving the little pubic hair she did have, up there in the bathroom.

'Daddy's little princess will have to shave to please him!'

The afternoon moved towards the day's dusk and Linda was dressed now in fishnet stockings and a black leather micro skirt and revealing bodice. She was still annoyed with the stench that pervaded the lounge though, so she was spraying more freshener, while she was trying to watch a soap. She glanced towards the two small pots of reds and blues on the floor underneath the tanks.

'Pissing boilies!'

Once Linda stopped spraying, she took hold of the St. George trinket box again, emptying the 'Percy' bag as she ran out another generous looking line on the coffee table. Gravitas seemed to be drug-induced in the Barber household these days. But living with Chaz had gradually made Linda into this coke-sniffing fiend. She couldn't deny that in the moment she thoroughly enjoyed it, although she also looked back towards her youth and early twenties, and was nostalgic about her temperance and innocence. For Linda, experience had stained her, corrupted her even, but she enjoyed the high of the moment, and then later on with the come down, she would be more than ambivalent about it all. She would question herself, moving into darker personal enquiry and then, to release herself from an increasing torment, would be drawn into snorting some more. There was always more around. If it wasn't in the trinket box there would be another stash upstairs in the locked unit amid the guns and money waiting to be poured into the trinket box.

On this occasion she just couldn't get enough. She went upstairs and got another 'Percy' bag for St. George. She felt impelled to get drugged out of her head, so that she could face the ordeal of these kinky films that Chaz was so obsessed with. But as Chaz pointed out many a time, Linda didn't mind spending the cash they raked in. Linda was far from extravagant, yet lately Chaz had noticed that her tastes for everything, furnishings, clothes, beauty products and holidays, had all become rather more up-market, and the cash for all that derived from the activities, drugs or otherwise. But there was a brilliant shine going on in her mind, a few minutes after it went up her hooter and the more it glowed, the easier it was for Linda to deal with that Dark Room upstairs. Linda was beginning to hate it as much as Chaz was enthused and inspired by it. There was everything up there, benches, racks, chairs, and hoods and chains of just about every variety and type. There were all kinds of restraints, clamps and what Chaz had named the 'Cock a doodle doo machine', that was just about the most expensive fucking machine on the market. They had shot a film exclusively around 'The Fucker', which was indeed the title of the film, which had netted them upwards of six grand and rising. Anything that can make a rapid quick fire six big ones, was worth developing, according to the Chaz Barber philosophy. He had also spent thousands on those bloody dolls that no doubt he would soon be introducing into proceedings. Chaz was on his mission to keep pleasing all the subscription audience who were paying twenty a month. Linda dreaded to think what they would all look like if you gathered them in a hall. But she knew that Chaz had been talking to Vivienne, Miko's wife, and soon she would be up there, as Linda knew they were pursuing interests. What next, Linda thought? Natasha up there doing some kind of kinky gangbang shoot? It was very likely. Chaz had 'chaperoned' his daughter, right up to her neck in it. He had also been asking subscription punters for any suggestions through e mail, and as a result Chaz's erotic imagination was always bubbling away, thinking out the possible ingredients for the next kinky film or scenario, that the punters would go nuts over. It was all beginning to move into the next phase and Chaz had 'hopes' for Linda.

Linda went for yet another line to get that golden shine brighter, to find escape from all the concern and troubles. She could sense that Chaz's porn business interests were beginning to meet something of a crossroads and

Linda was bang at the center of it. Clients had suggested films involving members with Chaz and Linda or at least sex orgy type films. Chaz knew that the 'old Linda' had red lines, and he was hoping that gradually Linda would loosen up and go with the flow of the New Age. He encouraged the drug use, as that could help Linda cut loose. She could free herself. She had to go with that flow a bit more, embrace the New Age and its realities. Discover her 'Inner Vivienne' as Chaz called it.

Linda topped up with another small, that turned into a biggish line, to get her that bit higher and brighter, and if not exactly 'up for it,' she could at least 'put up' with it. So, you see, those red lines could be relaxed going forward.

Linda then recalled, that she had one last bucket of boilies waiting in the porch, ready to go down to the shed, for the freezer. As Chaz wasn't back, she would weigh them all up down there, and put them in the requisite bags. She could get back, and maybe have a coffee, a fag and another final line. She needed to be a little higher yet for that filming. She needed to be well out of it, with big black dilated pupils ready for smashing taboo as Chaz would say.

Linda picked up the final bucket, and opened the back door and walked along the old porch. It was a windless, clear and silent night. A quite perfect night for stargazing, if that was your want, and the kind of quiet night where sound carries great distance. The light was fading fast as it was gone nine or so. Linda came from the back door on her way to the shed, and she was half way across the small bit of lawn, when there was a bloodcurdling female scream that came up from the depths of the old orchard, piercing the silence. The hairs stood up on her neck. She stumbled and dropped the bucket and was rooted to the spot in fear. Then the diabolical scream rang out again, engendering terror, rape and murder in her imagination. Linda took flight and rushed back into the house and locked the door. She was breathing heavily and had never been so terrified. She thought there was a murderer out there, because that's what it sounded like, and another reality, dredged up from collective memory, smashed its way through on the horror of that scream. She was reeling in shock.

Meanwhile, Chaz was approaching the end of his work day. After the coke deal was set up, he had a waiting on people afternoon, but then eventually it was porn drops, chilling out and watching the world go by, chewing that gum while eyeing the local talent from his white Jag sanctuary. It was now just about dark and he had one more drop to make, that one on the Triune Way, at the last roundabout with the Salome tulips. Chaz had kept up the joke, referring to it all afternoon long, that he was making a drop next to the Salomes.

'Watch out, it might be a mad woman down there wanting ya head off!' the last punter joked and that had Chaz chuckling. What a craic! He popped into a garage and he was in the forecourt getting some petrol when the 'She's Not There' dial tone went off.

'There's somebody out there, Chaz! There's screaming, a woman screaming out in the orchard! I heard her twice! Put a shiver in me, Chaz. I'm, I'm a nervous wreck!'

Chaz tried to get his head around it all, but the first thing he had to do was to calm her.

'Hold on, calm down, Linda!'

But Linda was just thinking practical in terms of what she heard. It was horrific.

'Something terrible has happened out there. Shall I call the police, Chaz?' she asked, although she didn't want to worsen things by mentioning the past. Chaz told her to wait a second, and he parked up in a parking bay away from the pumps. Chaz had it all figured out.

'Now Linda, get a calm on and listen to me. It's probably the vixens. They can sound like that at times. So whatever ya do, don't call pig! We can't have pig snooping around the premises, can we? It's bound to be vixens, girl. Now look, I'm going up for the last drop of the night. I've had a blinding day, monster breakthrough down at "Candy Foxes", new client, the proprietor, going for the pink and dyke pound. So, let's celebrate! Get yourself into your gear, I'll be hitting the Erectafen in a couple of minutes.'

But Linda wasn't really listening to him. That scream was still reverberating around her mind.

'I'm still worried about the screaming, Chaz. It's terrified me!' But Chaz was still dismissive.

'Look, just put it out of your mind, Linda. It's vixens fighting. You'll be scared of your own bloody shadow next! Have a line of Charley Farley. He'll put it all right. Psyche up for the show Linda. We gotta do that filming tonight. It's essential. I'm just about to hit "The Triune Way". Chaz spun his wheels and off he went, kicking up dust in the white chariot, while Linda sat in the Waldorf surrounded by a feeling of enveloping darkness.

CHAPTER SIX

THE FOX, THE PIG AND THE MAGICIAN

Chaz made his way across town heading towards 'The Triune'. Apart from the Candy Fox deal it had been a long hard drugs day. It was a waiting game day and Chaz was always adamant, 'No money, no drugs!' That was one of Chaz's clear red lines and it had always worked for him. Everyone knew the score and it helped Chaz avoid all the criminal behavior, chasing little punks up for five hundred and whatnot. If anybody gave him problems he merely didn't entertain again, or would make the point that the wider traveler community were his bailiffs. Alfredo sometimes pushed levers when it was appropriate too, but Chaz liked to keep everything sweet and those tactics were only last instance gambits. It hadn't been those today, but it was a long wait on that Waterside Crew money. The Waterside Crew, had now become something different as Angusia had taken over as head of the firm down there. Her bloke Connor, who was middle class and discreet, had apparently, unbeknown to Chaz, let his psychotic streak get the better of him and had been whisked away at Her Majesty's pleasure for five years. A particularly vicious GBH that had left one of his organization looking forward to a life struggling in a wheel chair. There were just too many witnesses for him to scare the witnesses off. Connor finally caught up with somebody who owed a goodly sum, outside a mini-supermarket and he lost control and the number plate was taken and CCTV got him on shot. They had kept it quiet as Angusia found it embarrassing, as Connor had fully lost his marbles, going for the guy with a sword and had nigh chopped the guy's leg off. But the Waterside informed the guy that he'd better keep it shut otherwise their would-be future recriminations. The fellow, a disgruntled ex-runner who hadn't been paid, and then had stolen a lump sum of money from Connor, told the police that it was a dispute over Angusia and after he cooled off, Connor, with a little bit of advice from Angusia, flowed along with the explanation. The runner was just happy to get Connor done for the crime, so it was hoped that it would eventually blow over. Angusia said to him that he would be out in two and a half, but she didn't tell him that she was carrying his baby. She decided on an abortion, and getting him out of the way was convenient. She was surreptitiously seeing Salvio, of Candy Foxes no less, and Connor was a psychotic and jealous guy. The sort of guy who chops legs off with swords. But it made Chaz wary when he got the wind of it. That daft bastard lot the Tennin Pig, might be waiting to sit on them down there. But as Chaz knew, things were always fluid and evolving in the underworld, and if you can't stand the heat, get out of the kitchen. Chaz was philosophical. There's only one rule for no trouble. Pay everybody up. Be straight with the criminal underworld. Who wants to be at home with the missus and then a car load of thugs with baseball bats and shotguns turn up? Chaz was a believer in nuclear deterrents, metaphorically speaking, and that's why he loved that big arrangement he had with the county's travelers. His biggest customer Scamp took anything from a half to a full kilo a week off him, supplying that whole traveler community, who were appreciative as it came at a nice discount price.

In the new circumstances down at the Waterside, Angusia, had taken over proceedings as commander in chief, and Chaz had a whopping eight grand to pick up so he wasn't going anywhere. But the cash eventually came in, and was paid up as Angusia rousted them up on her mobile with much animation and plenty of forthright language. The threat of no drugs, next week, always done the trick. The underworld in this part also knew that Chaz and his firm had won a few turf wars, rather ruthlessly and conclusively in the recent past.

However, it proved to be a longer wait than usual and after an hour or so, Chaz decided he would have an hour recreational at a massage parlor down there at the Waterside. Chaz would often use it, when he had an hour or two to kill waiting around, and sitting in that flat with Angusia had made him horny. She had more than ample tits, housed in a push-up see-through bra, covered by a black negligee top. It was all a tease that Chaz rather enjoyed. Chaz bet she had similarly transparent breathable knickers on underneath those designer grunge jeans. He had three coffees and shared as many joints and for a while before that hard cash came in, Chaz was pondering over whether to suggest 'alternative' methods of payment. The idea only momentarily passed his mind, before all the money came in from four sources that arrived virtually one after the other, like buses. But Chaz was ogling Angusia for nigh two hours, so he felt impelled to go in search of that recreational release.

The massage den was in a little cottage down by the scrap merchants. Chaz hated parking the gleaming Jag up there, as it always seemed to get a thick layer of dirt and dust even after a short stay. But now, there was a pop-up car cleaning joint on the site of an old garage next to a demolished old Waterside pub that, you guessed it, was earmarked for yet another block of flats. After the hour with Chantelle and Zarah, why not live like King Solomon and his harem, if you can afford it, he popped the Jag in front of a horde of car washers. It was an opportunity, post sexual assertion, to feel his new millennial sense of power.

'I want it spotless!' Chaz demanded, and the five men worked like donkeys, knowing full well that Chaz tipped big. Chaz was on a whopping high from the session; he had shared a few liberal lines of cocaine with the girls, and had enjoyed one of his favorite threesome kinks, so why not bung them a fifty? Or blow their brains out with a couple? Chaz felt on cloud nine and seventh heaven after that hour.

As the hordes washed and polished, Chaz ruminated upon the afternoons developments and he returned to that Angusia tease. Knowing her guy was away for some time, Chaz had pushed the boat right out, by slipping her one of those special cards, referring her to that internet site. Chaz didn't care if it wasn't her thing, 'nothing ventured, nothing gained' was Chaz's motto, and any woman who was in it up to her fanny in the drugs underworld, might just be open to other lucrative extracurricular activities. Out went the boat, it might catch a stiff one and sail! Chaz had pitched it all very discreetly and he chuckled to himself thinking about it, wondering as they polished.

'If you're into glamour, or know any young women who are up for that kind of stuff, here's our new cards, Angusia. Might be a good opportunity! We all need insurance policies in this 'ere game.'

At least Chaz had made a stab. They finished the clean, and the Jag gleamed again in the early evening sunshine and Chaz slung them a hundred, before doing his customary slide around pull away, to the adoring, celebratory crowd. Time was moving on, and he still had a number of porn drops to make and then he would hit the blue pill again, as he wanted to try out those kinks and shoot the film in the Dark Room. Was there any finite end to the libido of this king carper? Within a couple of hours, it was that last drop of the long day, and Chaz was making his way down to 'The Triune'.

TV Sam and Dan were down there already and TV was transfixed, gazing up at the light of a lamppost, at the third roundabout by the Salomes. The light emanating from that particular lamppost was of a peculiar quality that attracted Dragon Star. TV was pointing out to Dan that it did things to your mind, opened up an inner vision, so that you could look out there into the galaxy, seeing all kinds of things, incredible things and that. Dan was just relieved that it was a more congenial TV now, not the one enveloped by the dark abyss who jumped off the top of stacker car parks, and TV was enthused as it was a rare, nigh perfect night for stargazing.

'Look, Dan! Look! The serpent constellation! Can ya see it, Dan? Look!'

Dan was following TV's outstretched arm and pointing finger as best he could, but TV was well versed on all things of the night sky. TV had astronomy books and all those mags. He was one of those rare people, who could see all the patterns and clusters. Dan could just see stars, loads of them up there. He tried to spot that serpent, he desperately did.

'Er, er there's too many stars, TV.'

'Yeah, I suppose there is a lot up there getting in the way, Dan.'

They both laughed and Dan felt more comfortable now, just getting TV to laugh was a great improvement on the earlier morose state of mind. But Dan thought he would move things on. TV was always reading about UFOs in those swish subscription magazines he collected, and Dan had seen that one down Holly Beech Lane last winter, or at least he thought he had.

'See any saucers, TV?' Dan asked. Generally, for whatever reason, it was always the winter when they saw more saucers, so for TV and Dragon Star there were seasons. TV was still transfixed by the night sky.

'Nah, bit out of season, Dan, always after Halloween and the first frosts.' TV then sparked up with enthusiasm, pointing up at the sky again as he explained. 'Keefy saw loads down here, Dan. That five in formation who were communicating with him. It was here, Dan! It was right here!'

TV had been giving thought about the meeting with the porn dude. He hadn't told him earlier, that there would be two of them waiting for him.

'I'll tell you what, Dan. Hide behind that bush. He might feel intimidated, if there's two of us. We don't want to leave anything to chance, Dan.'

Dan thought that a good idea so he took up his hiding place behind the bush, although if you looked closely you could see him. But at least he was sort of hidden.

Chaz passed the Triune Way road sign and put his foot down. Bowie's 'Starman' was on the CD and Chaz was singing along loudly, lost in his world of Jag, white blazer, a ton of money earned today, new big drug deals and also that high of the 'rumpy pumpy' with the escorts. Wow, he was high, although a little off-key, but Chaz was hollering it out with all his heart. Chaz had always been a massive fan. That track spoke to him about how young people should be allowed to be. Let them do their thing! Everything free and easy, that was Chaz's philosophy. And Chaz loved driving the Triune. You could cruise it, whizzing around, sliding each of the roundabouts, as if you were on a race track. In the 2002 AD 'King Chaz1' he was like a new kid on the Grand Prix block. He was the very king of the highway and he knew the names of all the tulips! He sped the first one with a beautifully aesthetic screeching slide. He felt like the wolf after little red riding hood. Chaz loved accelerating hard away from the first, and his foot went down on the approach to the second, and there wasn't anything to get in his way. Happy days. In fact, that first roundabout displayed a mixture of 'Mystic Hot pants' and 'Flutes on Fire', a fact that didn't register with Chaz. But Chaz could vouch that Angusia's knockers had caught his flute alight! Whoop-hay!

Back at the lamppost TV was still agog, peering into the night sky, as if he was in another world, another planet somewhere, but he was still eagerly awaiting those porn films.

Chaz didn't slow down at all into that second roundabout. That was the craic of 'The Triune'. Hit that second hard and fast and slide around. What a buzz! Get on ya scooter and snort it up ya hooter! However, on this occasion a large shadowy animal whipped across the road in front of him, making its way to the Red Riding Hood tulips on the island and beyond. Chaz tried to take evasive action. He thought he was going to spin around into the barriers at high speed, yet somehow, he managed to keep control of the vehicle and keep it going forward. It was all hair raising, knife edge stuff! But it shocked him. What the fuck was that! Chaz tried to get a glimpse of it, but whatever it was, it had disappeared and was off into the safety of the woods beyond. But it knocked Chaz off his Grand Prix circuit pitch, and a shell-shocked Chaz, approached the final roundabout, 'The Place' at a greatly reduced speed. Chaz looked for his client as the Bowie track faded out on the CD. It was the final track. Chaz turned left and could see the guy, he presumed it to be this TC, head turned away from the road, looking up at the lamppost that emitted a bright violet light. TV was on it; he was the watcher, out there on the ramparts. Chaz swung the Jag around, and pulled up, looking askance at this TC fellow before him with what looked like a skirt on, and what looked like long green hair and a cap. Chaz lent over, and with a touch of the remote, the window came down.

'TC?' Chaz called expectantly. TV Sam didn't turn or even register Chaz, so Chaz thought he would try another tactic.

'Adult Leisure, mate?'

Surely this was the oracle and it seemed to strike the requisite chord as the self-appointed Dragon Star leader, turned sharply and sparked up enthusiastic.

'Oh, hullo, mister blue film. I was looking up at the Dragon Star's totem! The serpent dragon! Look! Up there! Can't you see it! Look!'

TV was excited as it was an excellent night for stargazing with such a clear sky, a quite glorious window into the heavens. Chaz was trying to weigh things up. Now he had come across a few odd characters in his time. But this guy was another stratosphere.

'Now look, mate, I'm not here for the astronomy lesson!'

By now Chaz was lent over, head by the window and he immediately looked down at TV's out-sized feet.

'Fucking hell! Ya got some kippers there, mate, eh?'

TV looked down at his feet and studied them for a measured moment or two.

'They're me Jesus's sandals. Jesus used to wear them. I got um at the boot fair at Death Hill up there. I got a pair for my fiancée too!'

'What, feet as big as yours?'

Chaz was always good with the one-liners, and TV Sam thought it rather funny. The idea that Freeda had size fourteens! It really caught TV's funny vein.

'Ah nah! She's size six Freeda. Do ya know her?' TV asked.

Chaz replied with a firm negative shake of the head and he grabbed the communication back towards that task in hand. Chaz couldn't be wasting time with this twat. He wanted to get that business transaction done and dusted. There was 'that' filming they had to get on with back in the Dark Room. It was essential.

'Anyway, TC,' Chaz said, but this just sent TV off into yet more hysterical laughter. Fancy calling him TC! TV's laugh echoed into the night as the number of cars passing had reduced to a trickle, and it was silent and still.

'TC! TC! I'm TV! TV Sam!' TV was most amused.

'Well I wasn't that far out, mate, was I?' Chaz suggested.

'Only nineteen letters of the alphabet and that's nineteen long letters!'

TV was still laughing. Fancy somebody calling him that! But the sharpness of TV regarding that response, had caught Chaz off-guard, and it made Chaz realize that this guy was a big off with the faeries, so he just brought it back again to the reason why he was here.

'Anyhow, TV,' Chaz said with emphasis, 'do you want these porn films or not?'

'Yeah course! I was just looking at the aurora. I look for flying saucers from Sirius III too! I'm gonna be collected but it's not the season yet. Did ya know?'

Chaz was aghast. Where the fuck did this guy come from? But he immediately was thinking that fucking asylum.

'Er no, I didn't know in fact. But forget your stargazing for a moment now and I'll show you what I got.'

Chaz had the communication back on home territory. He opened the passenger door and had the case of DVDs on the seat. He switched an interior light on, and TV was astonished. The porn dude had a white blazer on and it was just like Keefy's. It was a big moment because the Dragon Star children's sect was big on serendipity. It showed that deeper forces and energies in the universe are at work behind the scenes. For TV this was one of those sublime moments when you could see that hand, clearly. He was twisting and craning his neck as Chaz opened the case and he felt compelled to comment.

'Cor, I narf like your blazer! It's just like Keefy's!'

'Yeah, I like it myself, now.'

Chaz just wanted to get on with business, but TV Sam had a burning desire to know more about the blazer. It looked virtually identical to Keefy's.

'I bet you've climbed a few ladders to get a white blazer like that!' TV exclaimed. For a few moments TV had forgotten about the films. This was a Keefy white blazer moment. Keefy used to 'glide through the ether' with one of these on!

'I do all right, mate. Now I've got…'

Chaz was determined to just get this darn transaction done and dusted, forty quid and home to the Dark Room activities as the little blue pill was beginning to augment the twitch. That kinky American DIY had inspired him for what he had in mind with Linda later. But TV still focused on that white blazer. He was ultra-curious. TV just had to make further enquires.

'Where did ya get it?' he asked.

Chaz was getting more impatient now, usually he would have loved to have a conversation about the sacred blazer but it had been a long hard day, and he had to wait that two hours hanging around on the cash owed by the Waterside Crew, looking down Angusia's cleavage smoking joint after joint. It takes it out of ya.

'I got it up town,' Chaz replied.

TV swallowed his saliva as he had never been so close to something that he so fervently desired, since Keefy was transferred nigh three years ago. He dreamed of getting a white blazer like Keefy, but he had never seen any in Tennin. This dude meant London and TV never got the chance to get up there. But the head of the Dragon Star New Age sect needed one. It would carry on the great legacy. Surely it was written in the stars that he would have one. He tried to get Keefy's from Keefy's family, but the white blazer went back to earth with him. But if TV could get one, he could marry Freeda in it! It would open up all sorts of new things. Neural star connections and that!

'Do ya think you could get me one! I'll pay ya for it!' TV asked, totally forgetting about porn films, because white blazers were synonymous with the founding of the cult, and TV had that legacy responsibility to think about. TV thought he could write to Aunt Joan and plead with her to lend him some more money to buy one. He would pay it back somehow. Surely it wouldn't be any more than a hundred or so he thought, and Aunt Joan had pots stashed away. Incidentally, TV had always asked Keefy how much his blazer had cost, but Keefy always prevaricated, but TV thought about fifty. But as Dan had kept saying Keefy's family were stinking rich and Keefy didn't like anybody thinking him other than 'street'. Chaz was exasperated.

'Look, mate. I'm here to sell ya porn! I haven't got time to worry about shopping for blazers! Anyhow, they're two and a half grand. Could you afford one?'

TV couldn't believe his ears. Two and a half grand! Fuck! Two and a half grand! How did Keefy get hold of that? But on second thoughts, he knew that Keefy's family had money. Dan had always said that, although they never seemed to want anything to do with him. TV hadn't seen any of them at the asylum, never. Chaz was still desperately trying to get on with it, display his porn wares and his patience was wearing thin. This goon was at the last chance corral.

'No idea, mate, but I've got hot Swedish, American, DIY Irish and German!'

TV Sam took a while to respond. He just expected porn films without having to make difficult decisions.

'Wow! It's like being in a sweet shop!'

The naked and porny shots on the covers were swirling around TV's mind.

'Well come on then!' Chaz urged. TV pulled all sorts of faces, poking his tongue out as he agonized over the decision.

'My grandad fought the Germans. I think I'll have German.'

Chaz fiddled with the DVDs, sorting three German that held a couple of films each. But the request rather humored him.

'Erm, Grandad fought the Germans so it must be German. Can't quite get the drift of the logic behind it all. But German ya want and German it is.'

Chaz put the three DVDs in a plain black plastic bag and offered them to TV.

'Forty knicker, mate.'

TV smirked and then burst in laughter.

'Forty knickers! I'd love to pull forty pairs of knickers down, eh? One after the other, eh.' TV joked and nudged Chaz with an elbow. Chaz was a little humored, but he desperately wanted to get away from this nut-job.

'Yeah, well anyway,' Chaz was waiting for the money now, and TV thought he'd better hunt for it, albeit slowly and rather laboriously. He toyed about with the left-hand pocket of the hoodie, turning it inside out. There were sweet wrappers, fag butts and a few pennies with some biscuit and bread crumbs. He obviously wasn't following his true self. But no notes!

'It's not that one,' TV gingerly offered. Chaz looked at him aghast, and thought he might help things along with a little prompting.

'No, maybe the other, eh?'

Meanwhile, behind the bush, Dan was dying for a slash. He just had to go. He tried desperately to hold out, but he would have peed himself if he hadn't gone, so off he went. Chaz knew there was somebody behind there and was a little wary.

'Who's that slashing behind the bush?' he asked.

It felt to TV that the game was up. This porn dude might think they were laying a trap. TV turned over an excuse in the heat of the moment.

'Er, er that's Dan. He's sorta shy.'

TV gave Chaz an inane-looking smile as he began the next round of extended search, within the adjacent pocket of the hoodie. He turned out a few two pence pieces, a winter mixture sweet that had stuck to the inside of the pocket and two packets of confetti that he had purchased earlier in the town.

'My confetti for the wedding!' TV exclaimed. Chaz swore under his breath, and he was about to drive off, when TV put his hand up his skirt. 'Oh yeah! I forgot! My magic pouch! I got my snake's head in it!'

It all seemed oddly preplanned and intentional, as if TV had created this little drama for his own fun and the very mention of a snake's head, jolted Chaz into that serendipity frame of mind himself. It was just odd that coincidence, after the debacle in the garden. How many days in a life does an evil fucker snakes head try and bite ya? TV pulled the pouch out like a magician, as if playing to his audience, and Chaz looked on in disbelief.

'Da! Da!'

TV had purchased the magic pouch in a mysteries shop a few years ago, when he visited the great shopping center. It was black and had moon and star sequins sewn into it, and although a bit tatty now, it still held magical significance and powers for TV. TV then slowly drew this snakes head from the pouch, bringing the porn dude into the great revelation.

'My snake's head! Aunt Joan gave it to me. She didn't like it, my auntie Joan. She had nightmares about it, trying to bite her in the night and that. It's a keep sake from her mum! It's oldie worldie!'

Chaz was bemused. How uncanny he thought. The container was a curious nineteenth century antique that had a gunmetal outer steel shell and an eighteen-carat inner. Chaz noticed that much, being a great enthusiast, for anything gold. It was indeed shaped like a snake's head with two piercing emerald eyes with a penetrating black pupil and an eighteen-carat gold ring in its mouth. TV slowly opened the snake's head, as if he was about to reveal a bejeweled treasure or something, and there they were, two twenty-pound notes that were rolled up. TV slowly drew the forty from it and handed it over. Chaz was mesmerized and in disbelief. What an odd coincidence, and the fucker must have known where the money was all the time. Chaz looked askance at him, but he let it go, as he was just relieved to get the money. Yet in the next split second of a moment as his fingers were centimeters away from the rolled-up notes, they disappeared before him.

'What the fuck!' Chaz had just about enough of this crank, but TV smiled and pointed to Chaz's ear and would you believe it the notes were rolled up behind it.

'I do magic!' TV declared, as Chaz took the money from his ear, dumbfounded.

But the money was in the bin, 'sorted!' But Chaz was overwhelmed by an uncanny feeling that this geek before him had control of the interaction in some odd, unknown and imperceptible way. For a split-second Chaz thought he was engulfed by something unknown and mysterious. TV took the black bag and was already thinking about an endless supply of hot porny films.

'Will I be able to get some more, Mr. White Blazerman?' he asked.

'Chaz is the name. Just phone, but make sure you're ready for a quick drop next time. Money in your hand, ready, like.' Chaz said that much, but in his mind, he was thinking he would avoid this weirdo at all costs. Things then began to take a more unwanted intrusive tone and TV was smiling, with a goading look on his face, that seemed to imply that Chaz was right. TV had him somewhere that he didn't want to be. TV would have called it 'Dragon Starred'. TV pressed home his advantage.

'You live in that house down Holly Beach Lane. The one with the sweet-smelling hyacinths, don't you?' TV blurted out cockily, as if to uncomfortably penetrate Chaz's world. TV had never seen Chaz, but he remembered Drill-head speaking about a guy who wore a white blazer, and TV thought it very likely this Jag before him, was the one he had seen outside the house down by the flying saucer lamppost. TV was on hunches. He smiled with that superior look on his face when Chaz replied.

'How do you know, mate?'

Chaz wanted to probe some answers out, but you would never get a straight answer out of somebody like TV. TV had watched politicians do that and they did all right.

'I could call down next time! You could show me your garden!'

This prompted Chaz to take on a rather more authoritative and sterner persona.

'Look, mate! I don't deal from home. Just ring right! But how do you know where I live?'

Chaz had to follow that one up. This was getting a little disturbing, but this time TV did give a straight answer but with that leering, and for Chaz darn annoying, smug look on his face.

'I use that street lamp by the conker tree for stargazing. I've seen thirteen flying saucers at that lamppost. And Keefy saw a fleet of seven down there! Fucking fleet of seven! That's the "Dragon Star" record! Your living on a hot spot down the Holly Beach! I blogged it!'

This made Chaz snap. He had to take back control.

'Look, mate! I don't want you and your fucking cronies hanging around my house at fucking night, right!'

TV Sam was a bit bewildered, as he didn't think a little bit of stargazing at the flying saucer lamppost should be any problem.

'Oh, I'm sorry, but I was only looking up at the stars minding my own business, free country ain't it?'

Chaz had had enough. He shut the door and done his usual wheel spin, and off he went. Initially, it was in relief, as he had never felt so uncomfortable in all his life. There was something about the moment that assaulted him. A feeling of being caught up in a dark unknown. Once away from that goon though, it immediately dissipated, and thank fuck. But Chaz was still in disbelief. What an odd day he thought. Those snake heads? Chaz would have to sit by the carp tank with a few stiff joints to try and get his head around that one.

The black panther had swiftly made his way through the woods by the road, and he sat on his haunches near the Salome roundabout watching, as the Jag rose up Death Hill disappearing into the darkness. Chaz was still deep in thought about that darn snake's head TV pulled from under his skirt. He shook his head again as he drove and thought about that other head trying to get him in the back garden. It was just so uncanny.

Once the Jag had gone, TV turned and looked up at the lamplight smiling. That White Blazerman had come into the force field of Dragon Star. He had been penetrated by the sect's mystery, and TV felt triumphant with a bag of porn in his hand. It would fuel the fire for Dragon Star's New Age trope that copulation and shagging are the very tool of enlightenment.

'Dan! Dan! I got um, Dan!' TV exhorted.

Six porn films were something of a coup for Dragon Star, a first. Dan came from the bush.

'He heard ya slashing, Dan!'

Dan said that he couldn't help it, he was just bursting to go. TV held the black bag up joyously, but he still wanted to rave on about that jacket. Fancy a porn dude guy wearing a white blazer? And furthermore, it was identical to Keefy's. TV was animated.

'Did ya see his white blazer! Did you see it, Dan?'

Dan had noticed and he had been thinking about it too.

'Yeah, I did, TV,' Dan replied. TV was full of it. He would have given his right arm and his left and a pile of collectible UFO mags for one of those blazers.

'It was just like Keefy's'! Two and a half grand it cost, Dan! Fuck! How did Keefy get hold of two and a half grand?'

It merely confirmed what Dan knew and thought all the time.

'I told ya, his mum and dad were rich, TV. And don't ya remember Drill-head talking about that guy. He saw him up by that big fishing shop TV,' TV remembered.

'Yeah, but Keefy's parents must have been fucking stinking rich, Dan! But we got um! We got um!'

TV done a few crazy dance shapes in honor of them and then he took Dan to the bush to show what they had bagged. They perused the glossy photos on the cases. Real hard-core porn. Even the cases were pornographic. It was a first for Dragon Star!

'I'll be able to wank my way to the enlightenment!' TV joked, and they both laughed but both knew there would be a price to pay, despite happy days on the wanking. They wouldn't get back to the asylum until eleven o'clock, even half eleven, the speed that Dan walked at. It wouldn't be solitary confinement, but Locko would suspend them from leaving the grounds for some time. TV celebrated with a long draught from the three liter Energy Brew. He handed it over to Dan who struggled with it and TV helped him hold it up as he swigged.

It was dark and the moon was full now, and that squashed snake was glistening as a police car turned into Holly Beach Lane watched by a beady-eyed owl swiveling its head around three-sixty. There were two officers in the car, one male the other female. They drove past the doctor's and radiographer's house with the woman Gabi on the blower to base. She glanced up at the bedroom window as Chris drove and she noticed the full light on, curtains open, and a woman up there in just her bra. But she didn't say anything. It might seem a touch voyeuristic to refer to it, as Chris didn't notice, and they were about to arrive at the abode. Gabi had other things on her plate. She spoke authoritatively as she told base the state of affairs after this 'worrying' call.

'We are just about to investigate the reported "female screaming in distress" in Holly Beach Lane, near the old asylum, over.' The voice on the other end referred to what they all hoped.

'Let's hope it was vixens playing. Over and out.'

There had in fact been two murders up Holly Beach Lane, or at least a manslaughter and a murder. The first, well the more recent, was a patient from the asylum. He was walking down Holly Beach Lane, when he got into a dispute with a couple of youths who were goading and humiliating him. The story was well known in Tennin, and Chaz and Linda knew of it, although they didn't like to talk about it, as they tried to enjoy their dream house. It was all in the past. But one of the youths had kicked the patient on the temple viciously and repeatedly, and he died of a brain hemorrhage. It happened no more than ten yards up the road from Chaz's front gate. Chaz did refer to it six months ago when they first looked at the house, but Linda reasoned that it was a one-off incident and the poor patient from the asylum hadn't caused any trouble. That must have been eight years ago or so now, but for Chaz the fact that the incident had occurred by the gate, and he didn't know exactly how near, was enough to taint the idea that the house was a dream house. It was a dream house with a dark compromising cloud around it.

There was also that which was left unspoken, as they didn't know quite where it happened. Back some nigh thirty years ago there was a horrific rape and murder around the vicinity and nobody had ever been charged with it. Chaz remembered the murder. His mum had spoken a lot about it at the time. All he knew, was it happened a long time ago and it had been somewhere in the hospital grounds. It had been a young female athlete out running through the woods and it occurred just beyond Chaz's boundary wall, at the back of the old orchard some twenty-eight years ago to the very day. The murder was well known by the local constabulary, young and old. It was one of its fabled crimes and Chris was a little perturbed as he obviously knew of the murder. He was also fully aware of the unsavory characters locked up in that old asylum. All in all, it was enough to put you on edge.

'Who knows, Gab. I dread to think what they've got straitjacketed up on the hill.'

They drove up to the house and parked adjacent to the horse chestnut. They both immediately noted the light from that old lamppost. When you were investigating something that had such a dark and macabre edge, such things are noticeable. The lamplight created an uncanny atmosphere around the house.

'Wasn't it around here where that murder was committed back in the seventies?' Gabi asked.

'Yeah, just over the back there,' Chris replied, having heard the tale from a more senior officer. But it all placed the 'female in distress' call in a rather chilling context. What if the original murderer was back here some twenty-eight years later? It wasn't impossible was it? Some kind of macabre, twisted and horrific anniversary.

Linda knew, that when Chaz found out that she had called the police, he would go bonkers. But she was just too scared. Fear made her do it. She needed help. She knew what she had heard. She had locked every single door and was breathing heavily as the scream sent her into panic mode. She could hear it in her imagination and that horrific murder resurfaced and hit her in the face. She kept resisting, saying to herself that it must be the foxes, but then she realized that the scream had penetrated to her inner core. That murder had never been solved and Linda knew it could have been out in her orchard for all she knew, and that scream made you think of murder and that horrific case. Linda was greatly relieved when she saw that police car pull up with the flashing light. She quickly finished divesting herself of the micro skirt and bondage wear, getting herself back into casual jeans and top.

'Oh, thank God!'

Within a few moments, the two police officers were walking the garden path with their torches. The perfume was still lingering, although less intense than in the day.

'What a sweet-smelling garden.'

The male officer noticed it, and did anybody step foot in the garden without mentioning it? It was truly memorable, just like that horrific murder that had taken place just the other side of Chaz's boundary wall, and had in fact spilled into Chaz's orchard via the damaged section.

'Hyacinths, among other things,' Gabi replied. Gabi tended to her own garden, so she knew her flowers. They reached the door and Gabi was about to give that brass snake a rap.

'Watch that snake!' Chris made her jumpy and Gabi jerked away from the snake knocker, and rang the bell instead. But the hissing snake rather interested her.

'Odd isn't it?' she said.

After having arrived and been in the area, Chris had begun remembering more about the murder case. It was like a toxic poison trickling back from the diabolical darkness of the collective mind. It had been known as one of the most disturbing killings ever. It certainly hadn't been put to rest. The worst of it was kept out of the press going back, but details were known and continually passed on by the force members and obviously it didn't help with that Ashcroft and his shenanigans being involved with the site. Gabi noticed that Chris was looking rather strained, when a distraught and stressed-looking Linda opened the door. Her demeanor gave the police the sense that something awful had occurred. She was still breathing heavily and deeply agitated. She looked as if she had been scared witless. But Linda never liked to trouble people, that was her natural character, so she was still trying to put on her typically apologetic air. She didn't want to disturb the universe unduly.

'I'm sorry to bother you, really. But it put a shiver up my spine. It really did. Look at me, I'm shaking! It came from over the back in the orchard! It was probably a fox, but I'm sure it was a woman. I'm sure of it. But it was probably a fox like my husband said.'

Linda's heart was pumping furiously and she was sweating with the tension, allied to all of that coke sniffing. That part of her agitation didn't go unnoticed.

'And is your husband there, Mrs. Barber?' Chris asked.

'Er, no, I phoned him. But I'm probably wasting your time.'

Gabi spoke and tried her best to sound confident, but she too was recalling the urban historical myth of that murder and those satanic orgies and whatnot. It had been dredged up out of her memory too. She would have been about ten at the time. It was a particularly diabolical crime and was still there lurking in the depths of the Tennin mind in some way woven into the macabre Ashcroft myth. Gabi's high vis caught the full moon's light and the full moon backdrop had registered in Gabi too.

'Not at all Mrs. Barber. If it was a fox, it was a fox. But terrible things do happen sometimes. You did the right thing, if you were that convinced.'

Linda insisted that the scream certainly sounded like a woman in grave distress.

'It sounded as if—'

Before Linda had finished, another bloodcurdling scream came up from out in the orchard, an exact replica. By now the weather conditions were changing and the temperature was dropping fast, as the forecast noted, that it would be a peculiarly cold night. There was a mist swirling around the orchard and a mysterious power emanating from that old shed. The two police officers had to hold their nerve, but they too experienced the same fear that Linda had with a shiver up their spines. It certainly sounded like murder.

They went through the procedure, alerting base. Gabi took the radio, and Chris was wondering if this was that killer out there resurfacing from nigh three decades ago. It was the grisly nature of the scream that made you naturally think like that. Chris had watched *Psycho II* with Anthony Perkins a couple of nights previously, and all his perceptions had been funneled down some ugly terror pipe. He stood there wondering how on earth he was going to be courageous enough to go out there searching with a darn bloody truncheon. He wanted an automatic shotgun or something. Darn force should have at least issued them with tasers he thought. To say that he felt vulnerable in the circumstances was a gross understatement. He felt terrified. But he would have to meet it. Gabi's radio was crackling away.

'We have just heard what sounded like a female in distress in Tennin Woods adjacent to Holy Beach Lane.'

Linda couldn't help pointing out that it was Holly not Holy.

'Make that Holly Beach and we're going to investigate over.'

Chris told Linda to lock all doors and windows and stay inside while they investigated. His voice was decisive but full of grave concern. He obviously thought it might be a woman out there. Linda had already locked them all up she was so scared. She closed the door and it was now time for the intrepid police officers to head out into the garden and confront whatever was out there. Gabi admitted her stage fright once Linda had shut the door, and that mist swirling around now was enveloping the house and garden in the sinister. Then the old antique lamppost crackled and its bulb blew as if on cue, and the lane was now returned towards its more natural darkness. The light going made Gabi jumpy as she was so on edge.

'It's just that street light going, Gabi,' Chris said, reassuring her.

'That scream was darn terrifying, Chris.' Gabi had to get if off her chest.

'Yeah, let's pray it was a fox, eh?' he replied.

They both took their truncheons from their belts, wishing they had those automatic shotguns. Both were thinking the same thing, recalling all the past horrific details of the case. That killer, back twenty-eight years, had accosted the woman, strangled her, stripped the dead body naked and repeatedly had sex with it, so the autopsy confirmed. Then the mad crazy lunatic had decapitated the body so that there were limbs scattered and just a torso without head, arms and legs. There was certainly a necrophiliac element and the coroner wasn't sure of the chronology of the terror, but it was a complete mystery as to the culprit. Even back then, there were no leads that led to the asylum's clientele, although the case still had associations with that house on top of the hill. As Gabi and Chris walked down towards the orchard, all of this dark past of Tennin woods had suddenly come back to life and was enveloping the air thick. This dark heart of terror had forced itself through the gossamer veneer of a dream house paradise, and in Gabi's and Chris's terms it wasn't just another night shift. There was now a palpable feeling that 'He' whoever he was, the beast, was out there!

Meanwhile, Linda checked the back door, even though she had already locked it earlier, she was so afraid. She returned to the front room looking even more stressed out and worried. She was smoking furiously, and she was now questioning the purchase of the house too. She had begun to recall that murder more clearly. It had been on the main news and was in the papers. But then she lived a good ten miles from Tennin, near Foxdale, so it hadn't been so sharply perceived and registered. Linda was just enjoying her mid-teens without a care in the world, relatively speaking. It was all first boyfriends and the like and she hadn't met Chaz. Her response back then was horror, but her personal one was, 'I certainly won't be running around dark woods on my own'. Linda looked out towards the gate and horse chestnut. Everything was that much darker without the street light, despite the full moon, and it was getting darker by the moment. She was willing Chaz to finally arrive back home, as it was approaching eleven o'clock. It was a nightmare.

'Come on, Chaz! Hurry up! Come on!'

The two police officers kept close to each other and gingerly crept out into the orchard. They shone their torches in all directions around Chaz's land. Both were quiet, deep in their thoughts and deep in that unsolved murder perspective as the almost penumbra-like mist swirled. Chris had recalled all the details of the case and he knew it happened directly around Chaz's boundary wall. In those woods just over the other side to be precise, although dismembered body parts had been found within the orchard. Chris gulped. That scream seemed to have come from well out there, possibly just beyond the boundary wall. Just where the murder had occurred. Then the date, May the fifteenth, came into his mind. He was sure it was the very day of that murder. Surely not an anniversary repeat killing? But they would have to check that old black shed. Gabi could sense Chris's fear as they approached. Murder hung heavy in the increasingly thicker mist.

'Well it seemed to be coming from about here I reckon,' Gabi said, and it helped to break the silence. Chris was resigned to taking the bull by the horns. They had to check the shed; it looked foreboding and then as if on cue, a large rat ran along the shed's rotten wooden floor and knocked into an old hoe that was resting up against the shed wall. It tottered and came crashing down, knocking flowerpots off the benches there, as it did so. But it sounded as if there was somebody in there. Chris gulped harder again, and his imagination was running wild. He envisaged opening the door and discovering the maniac having sex with a dismembered corpse. He gulped again.

'Let's pray he hasn't come back!'

Chris held his truncheon meanly, but in the back of his mind he would run if he thought the odds were overwhelming. He had two young children and a wife at home to think about. He would grab Gabi and pull her off with him, and call for reinforcements. They were both shaking with fear, when Chris put his hand on the door knob. He turned the handle, but it was locked. They thought about breaking in, but the shed had a large window on the other side that was still fully intact, without any glass broken whatsoever. Chris shone his torch through the window. There was nothing but old gardening equipment, making all kinds of dark shadowy shapes, and something mysterious, with what looked like a sheet over it, that had been left. But no dead bodies visible or Holly Beach Lane maniacs.

'Well no diabolical deeds going on in the old shed, thank God,' Gabi concluded, as an owl hooted from the trees, swiveled its head three hundred and sixty degrees and looked out across Chaz's orchard and house, as if claiming it for the damned. They both sighed deeply in relief, and didn't mention their worst fears.

The two officers continued their search around the orchard but they found nothing, and no more screams went up, like the terrible one they had witnessed. They went right out to the boundary wall, but they found nothing but an eerie atmosphere. They went across the wall, where it had collapsed and were within the very area where that murder had been committed all those years ago. It was all baffling, but what a relief, no murder. After five or ten minutes searching into the woods, they decided to go back to the house, although still on edge, and continually watching their backs. Gabi returned to the radio to break the eerie silence, telling base they had searched the area but had found nothing, but the scream sounded as reported. Walking back Gabi recalled yet more about the murder.

'Mary Fielding was the woman's name,' Gabi said, and Chris had already recalled the name in his mind, but had refrained from speaking too much about it all. The case had its fair share of media attention but then as time went on less so. But that was the tactics of the county superintendent. He appealed locally for help and followed scores of leads and interviewed the Ashcroft's extensively and always believed he would get the beast. But they never had, and the superintendent didn't want to unduly publicize the case further, as it merely highlighted the failings of his police force and caused heightened levels of anxiety. The Ashcroft's didn't want any publicity on this occasion and that was fortunate. The case remained open and the superintendent in question had retired deflated and depressed and he never got over his failure, dying after stroke complications in the mid-1990s. Whenever the case was mentioned it always disturbed the more, as one inevitably, thought the maniac was still out there somewhere, leading some oddly baleful double life. It was hoped that he had passed away or was invalided.

As they were walking back to the house Gabi declared somberly that this was proving to be a startling shift, as they wouldn't have expected dredging all this macabre history up.

'Policing, we must expect the totally unexpected, Gabi,' Chris replied.

Incredibly and uncannily, as they approached the house that lamplight crackled and sparked up again, as if being switched on and off by some unseen hand. Gabi jumped out of her skin and Chris tried to reassure her.

'Must be a loose connection, Gabi.'

'Fucking place is spooky, Chris,' she replied.

'More like haunted by the past, Gabi. I wouldn't live here for love nor money'. Gabi agreed that she much preferred her house on the Cavell estate and now Chris recalled that dodgy Ashcroft had lived here too. The one who practiced all the Satanism. It was believed that one of his lot might have done it.

Linda stubbed out a cigarette then immediately lit up another. She had already taken a couple more tranquilizers to calm her nerves, and now she just wanted to smoke, smoke, smoke. She looked at the carp and they were serene and relaxed as they always were. They certainly brought some kind of Zen calm to the room. Then a loud crash came from the kitchen and a wave of fear enveloped her. There was somebody out there. He must have got in here somehow! She instinctively cowered towards the front window virtually stuck-fast in fear. Then simultaneously the two police officers, who had returned to the front from the road side of the house, crossed in front of the window over the narrow pathway there. If Linda had thought things through rationally, she would have realized that it was the police. But it was all too much for her. She was rooted on the spot in sheer terror. She pleaded for help from her very depths. It was an overload of stress.

'Help me! Help me! Please help me!' she cried.

The two police officers thought the same thing. There was somebody inside, and Chris acted quickly taking the back while Gabi tried to communicate with Linda from the front.

'Mrs. Barber! Mrs. Barber! Are you all right, Mrs. Barber!'

Linda was still immobile in the front room, transfixed in fear and anxiety. She too had remembered more and more details of that murder. The terror of the moment had magnified its significance, but she eventually realized that the voice she heard was the police officer's. She moved towards the front door.

'There's somebody in the kitchen. Somebody in the kitchen!' Linda yelled, the dream house rapidly turning into a haunted horror show. In the commotion, Chris appeared back round the front, and yet again he and Gabi set forth to face, whatever it was they had to face, with truncheons up, terror struck and vulnerable. Into the house they went, anticipating a confrontation with some mad axe or knife wielding maniac, welcoming them to the anniversary celebrations. Linda was more than relieved to see them.

'There's somebody out there!' exclaimed the horror-struck Linda.

The police officers gathered themselves to enter the cave of the great beast, but both looked dumfounded by the array of carp tanks, as they moved towards the kitchen door. Gabi courageously swung it open, taking up the cudgels, stepping across the threshold. Why should she think that women had to fall behind? She could clump somebody with that truncheon if need be and Chris backed her up well. She was met by the black Tom on the sink who meowed. He had crept in on an off-chance Linda gave him and had been snoozing on top of a kitchen chair, snuggled in his tail, out of view. She picked the cat up, relieved that the incident had been so benign, and brought it into the front room.

'Here's the somebody! Is he yours?' Gabi said, as the black cat dug its claws in, generating a spontaneous outburst.

'Fuck! You bastard!' Er, sorry about the language, Mrs. Barber.'

Linda was relieved, but she wondered where on earth the cat had come from, as she had never seen one in the garden and that was fortunate as Chaz hated them. Linda opened up the back and porch doors and shushed the cat out into the night, and came back hoping that Chaz wouldn't have a violent reaction later. Chaz was acutely allergic to them. Cat dander pushed him into a severe asthma that could lead to hospitalization, so Linda had more things to worry about. But she regained a measure of composure after the cat had gone, and the police had confirmed that they had found nothing out there. It must have been a fox. Linda got Gabi a plaster as the cat had cut her hand and the blood was flowing. Gabi was wondering if her last tetanus jab covered her, and she was talking about going up to the general for a jab as the cut was bad.

'Thank you, Mrs. Barber, for the plaster,' she said, as she took another furtive glance at the painting of Natasha. Linda was hoping that she didn't inquire further, as Linda didn't share Chaz's enthusiasm for what Nat was doing. She would lie about it if they mentioned it, but the artist had painted the photo quite superbly.

'I'm sorry. I made a right fool of myself. It was just…'

Gabi pointed out to Linda that she didn't have to keep apologizing. 'Mrs. Barber, we heard the scream too and it certainly sounded like a woman. But there was nothing down there,' Gabi insisted, praying their estimation was correct.

Chris was by now transfixed by the carp tanks as they clearly were such a unique feature in the Barber's front lounge. How many people have four-pound monster carp in their front room? He felt he had to comment merely to get the preoccupations away from the macabre.

'These are rather big fish you keep in your front lounge, Mrs. Barber,' he said. The observation rather worried Linda, as she thought Chaz might have contravened some regulation about keeping fish indoors or something.

'Yes, you could call my husband king fisherman or he certainly aspires to be the king! He keeps them to study the species,' Linda explained, liking the opportunity just to get her mind away from all that screaming. Gabi had a relationship with a carp fisherman going back a few years now, until his obsession drove them apart. She probably would have married him too if he didn't have this carp thing. But she was so glad she hadn't, after discovering she was gay, as she had suspected all along. Things were working out well now as she was lucky, her family were liberally inclined and didn't bat an eyelid and she was more than happy living with her partner, an old school friend. But yes, she knew the carp hunter species.

'Does he wait for three days and nights by deep lakes waiting for big fish to turn up?'

Gabi could have chosen a lot of examples that would have made her relationship to carp fishing far less ingratiating, but she wanted to be polite. It had driven her mad at the time to be more precise. But she was glad it did now, otherwise she would have tied the knot.

'You're not married to one, are you?'

Linda thought she might belong to the club of unfortunates.

'Let's say I knew one once,' Gabi said, sniffing the air, registering that smell or should we say that stink. 'I can smell the baits!' she said. Then there was yet another scream, the first for some time, coming up from the old orchard again. Silence descended for a moment as they took it in, but this time there was a distinctive fox like sound to it. They were all relieved and Chris expressed what they all wanted to so desperately believe.

'Well there's our little mystery solved. It certainly sounded like a woman but it was definitely a fox!' But was it?

When the police officers were walking down the garden path towards the gate, Gabi couldn't help but say something about this unique garden again.

'I can't get over this lovely sweet smell, Mrs. Barber! It must be like paradise living here!'

As soon as she had said it, Gabi would have liked to have taken back the comment, as she wouldn't have lived there for a lottery win, after hearing that ghastly scream, whatever it was, and with that rape and murder history in those dark woods. It had all been resurrected in the very here and now, on the back of that horrendous scream. And those Ashcrofts were dodgy as hell and they must have left a trace or two. Linda smiled, but she found the comment grossly inappropriate in the circumstances. Gabi stayed silent. She didn't want to put her foot in it anymore.

'Yes, the hyacinths are out and the lavender is coming through early,' Linda replied.

Linda was outside the front by the door as they left, praying that Chaz would quickly arrive. It must have been well past eleven by now. Where on earth was he? He was well late and although nothing had come of the scream, Linda didn't want to be in the house alone. That scream had terrified her too much.

Chaz was completely baffled driving back home. The coincidence of that darn snake head trying to bite him and that antique snake's head that the nutty farmer had pulled out from up his skirt, was just too astonishing. He was so deep in thought that he didn't bother to listen to any music. But did it all mean anything? Chaz was generally not one to take any notice of tea leaves, tarot cards or anything hocus bloody pocus. But it happened, and it was peculiarly uncanny, and for Chaz if it happens, it doesn't happen without a reason, and in such circumstances, a good one. He was perplexed, but the conclusion he did come to was that TV was definitely from that blasted asylum, and that all of his fears were beginning to manifest. But his frowns and worries, turned into something different when he pulled into the lane, down by Dr. Greene's house. For Chaz caught a rather revealing glimpse of the radiographer wife, curtains wide open, no bra. She looked down at Chaz in that split second, and she didn't make any effort at all to close the curtain. It seemed to Chaz she was just as much the voyeur as he; titillated at the thought she was being looked at.

'Oh yea, tits out as well! You want it, you dirty whore of a doctor's wife!'

Chaz talked his thoughts out loud but before he knew it, he had arrived in front of the parked-up police car by the horse chestnut. Chaz could see that two officers were exiting the garden. He alighted from his car and confronted them.

'Any problems officers? Mr. Barber, the Chaz of Chaz's Pad.' Chaz gestured to that solid oak house plaque, but it was too dark for the police to have registered it. Gabi started to explain what had taken place to an attentive Chaz.

'Oh, hullo, Mr. Barber. Your wife alerted us to what she believed was a female in distress in the back woods but we think it was the vixens screaming,' she said. Chaz was fuming inside although he kept up a cool and calm exterior.

'Well I couldn't comment, officers, but I am greatly thankful that you came at my wife's request.' Chaz walked up the pathway as the police readied themselves to pull away, and as he was doing so another fox scream came up, from down there in the old orchard. The screech had a tinge of female about it, but it was clearly a fox. Chaz uttered a deep sigh.

'Tut! Can't she use her fucking ears!'

Within a few moments, Chaz was in the front room pacing around angrily. Calling 'pig', it wasn't exactly the wisest thing to do when you're in the Chaz line of business.

'Fucking hell, Linda! What the fuck are ya doing phoning pig! And ya could have at least contacted me! I didn't know what the fuck I was walking into, did I?' Linda felt even more stressed. She knew it wasn't the thing to do, but it was that terror she felt.

'I'm sorry, Chaz. I was going to, but I was just too scared. I was shaking, shaking!' Linda replied, still unnerved. Chaz scoffed at the idea. He had heard the bloody thing with his own ears.

'Scared of foxes? Look, I don't want the pig fucking poking around my business. That's all!'

Linda couldn't have been more apologetic, but she insisted that what she heard was what she heard.

'Chaz, please, I'm sorry. I thought a woman was being murdered out there. I can still hear that scream, it kinda said "help me". It was horrible, Chaz. And there was that murder going back, up here somewhere, wasn't there?'

Linda didn't really want to mention it, but she had no choice. Chaz remembered it well, but had conveniently and tactically forgotten it rather better. That death out the front was bad enough. Chaz insisted that he heard the scream himself, and it was obviously a fox, but Linda was still adamant.

'No, it wasn't like that, this was different, Chaz,' she implored, 'and the police officers heard it, and they were terrified!'

Chaz felt like going on a tirade, regarding this bloody house near the asylum, but he thought he would keep his counsel, and he had enough of this fox screaming business. Nobody was hurt, so why ratchet up the conflict?

'Well, let's not go there any more, Linda! That's enough of the screaming bloody foxes for one night!'

Chaz took the white blazer off with his usual reverence, and hung it on a coat hanger on the back of a chair at the front window's table, reflecting for a moment. He would move the focus from fox screams and the disturbing past towards what had occurred on the Triune Way. There was a story to tell.

'You know that fucking village idiot down there on "The Triune", fell in love with the old Barber trade mark, Linda.'

'What are you talking about, Chaz?'

'T bloody C! Or TV should I correctly say. Weird creep! He's only in a fucking skirt and sandals! Fucking great bed stompers, must have been size fifteen!' Chaz chortled and humored himself. 'TV gunboats! Ha, ha ha!'

Linda thought that it might not have been a skirt.

'The skirt might have been one of those sarongs that Beckham used to wear,' she said. Chaz agreed that it could well have been, but that was about the end of any comparison between this TV guy and Beckham.

'Beckham after a year on acid I reckon! And making a simple transaction, six films over from the Chazzy, so now forty quid, yes forty quid from your end, TV! Jesus Christ, fucking hell, God he was hard work! But I could murder a coffee, Linda!' Chaz was relieved the focus had got away from the fox screaming, and he was thinking whether all the drugs and being around the house for so long on her own might be starting to make Linda paranoid. Linda went into the kitchen and begun preparing a filter coffee from the machine. The door to the lounge was open, so Chaz was continuing the conversation, and he had so much to talk about.

'I thought the Chazzy was in for an overnight stay in a sleeping bag! It took him that long to find his dough. And fuck me, he only pulls out this fucking snake's head!'

Linda was just as dumfounded as Chaz, and both were baffled, but Chaz believed there's no mere coincidences. The universe is inextricably connected. Chaz felt sure it was telling him something, and that something was forming in his head. He went on to describe the 'nut-job' who had bought the films.

'And his mind, it was all over the fucking shop! Stars, sandals, my blazer. Yeah, he took a shine to that. Fucking nightmare! Nutty farmer no doubt, Linda. "Care in the community" they're calling it? More like scare the fucking shit out of the community!'

Linda agreed, yes, they did indeed have them up there, and she was just itching to tell Chaz the stories that June had been telling her. But then things took on a more disturbing tone.

'And he said he knows where we live,' Chaz said with a deliberate emphasis and edge. Linda came to the threshold, greatly concerned.

'What do you mean, Chaz?' she asked, really aware these kinds of things would bring an end to the dream house.

'Apparently, he hangs around outside, spying on us looking for flying saucers! Yes, that's the sorta fucking cranks ya get down ya street when ya live here! Reckon he's seen a fleet of them out there!'

Linda clearly didn't like the sound of all this. The negatives all seemed to be coming home to roost. 'You're joking!'

Chaz said, did he look as if he was fucking joking. Linda knew that serious Chaz look. He was looking more fixated and serious than when knocking up his carp mixes. He told Linda about TV giving that lame excuse that he studied the light from the old lamppost.

'They're watching us, Linda! Weirdo fucking nut-jobs are watching us!' Linda was indeed concerned.

'No!' she said.

'A whopping great yes! He said he looks in the garden and he knows all the names of the flowers. *And*, he's waiting to be "collected", as he called it, by aliens. Let's hope they come down quick, and carry the fucker away! And as far as possible at that, the menacing bastard!'

Linda tried her best to put a brave face on it all.

'Oh, he might be harmless, Chaz,' she suggested hopefully.

'And he might not! If he phones again, I'll say I don't work the area anymore. The cunt might get the message and if we see him snooping around out there. We'll phone pig. Nutty fucking muppets, I told ya we'd be plagued with um up here, didn't I? They're a fucking nightmare!'

Chaz sighed and began rolling a joint, still thinking hard about that coincidence. But Chaz was perplexed, fucking snakes everywhere. Linda was reflecting on what she heard and she was becoming increasingly worried, wondering whether the house did have some kind of dark curse or cloud about it. Everything had become so foreboding. She vowed to herself she would go to the library and research that murder case back in the seventies. She wanted to see if she could find some references to the exact location. But then she stood back objectively, and thought about what she was thinking. It was awful, researching horrific murders that encroached on your property. Linda returned to the front room with the coffees and Chaz handed her the joint, although it was likely to magnify her paranoia. Chaz was up for recounting the next part of the strange night.

'What a fucking weirdo night! And then I hit that second roundabout on "The Triune". You know, the one with the Salome tulips, not the Red Riding Hoods, and a black dog or something runs right out in front of Chazzy, and I nearly lost the fucking Jag!'

Chaz had got his tulips all wrong. The Salomes were on that third, but it was still another of those serendipity moments for Linda, with that big cat thing she'd been reading in the local.

'Um, I told you this afternoon about big black cats, panthers, being seen down there,'

Chaz pontificated like a king from the velvet chair. There was no way it was a panther.

'Black panthers don't exist, Linda. They're a fucking myth.' Chaz knew something about these matters. 'A panther is a term for big pumas and jaguars with a melanistic color variant. And anyway, I reckon it was a stray fucking dog!'

'Well that Bryan Jonsen, the heavy rock singer had tigers and things. Even snakes! They say they got out from his old estate when he was high on drugs, having sex orgies. They mentioned it in the local!'

Now that she had referred to that, she just had to refer to the couple who used to live here in the dream house.

'And that mystic who lived here, he was involved with Jonsen and all the satanic orgies with that horror movie actress wife of his with the big boobs!'

Chaz scoffed at the idea, although he thought the cult writer and that wife of his, must have been 'sexy bastards'.

But bringing the subject onto cats jolted Linda into referring to the cat that had got in. She had decided in her mind not to mention it, as Chaz had that aversion thing about cats, but it just slipped out as a response to Chaz's negativity.

'Well, a cat got in here tonight, Chaz.' She kicked herself for saying it. How daft! Well anyone would think a party of back in the day-old tramps had come through the house, the way that Chaz reacted. He liked cats as long as they were hundreds of yards from him. The reaction and its tone were inevitable.

'Fucking mog in here! You know how allergic I am to fucking cat dander!'

The mere mention that a cat had been in the house was enough to set Chaz off. He quickly went for a hand drawer underneath the carp tank and drew out a Ventolin inhaler and began to administer.

'How did the fucking thing get in here! It's set me off, Linda! Fucking cat, fucking dander!' Chaz was breathing badly and was soon purple-faced and looking deeply upset. Linda tried to explain.

'Oh, I must have left the porch door open at some stage and he got into the kitchen. Oh, I don't know. The woman police officer picked him up out there and it scratched her.'

Chaz couldn't believe what he was hearing. Cats and the fucking 'pig' in his house. He was still busily inhaling, coughing and breathing badly.

'Fucking hell, Linda! You had the pig snooping around in my fucking front room! Tut! And fucking stray cats! Cunt was probably curled up in me fucking chair, the way it's setting me asthma off!'

Linda was adamant that he wasn't and she thought Chaz's reaction was probably psychosomatic but Chaz wouldn't have any of it, and he was sure in his mind she had got the bloody idea off that darn Debs.

'What like the idea of a cat is setting me off! Bullocks! There's cat dander in the house. It'll have to be fumigated! It'll have to. I'll never fucking sleep! Never!' Chaz stopped for a second, had another puff on the inhaler, before continuing his tirade. 'You know how sensitive to cat dander I am, Linda! And the fucking pig! I had a joint here this morning you know. And look!'

Chaz pointed to granules of coke that were on the floor by the hip designer table and upon its surface, making it look as if God himself was hurling down coke to be disseminated among the flock. 'And you had um in the front room! Are you trying to get me out of the way for ten years or something!'

Linda tried desperately hard to explain that it was nothing like that. The police hadn't noticed anything, they were merely there for the screaming, and Linda insisted again that the police thought it was a woman in distress too. Chaz didn't want to get drawn into arguing about that fox screeching and he finally put the inhaler down and turned to the carp tanks, while Linda was sure glad that she hoovered and wiped the table down. The police may have noticed it otherwise.

'Enough!' Chaz was exasperated, and he regathered himself as he settled, peering motionless into the tanks. 'Have they had their full quotas?' he asked, desperate to get their conversation away from all this unsettling stuff.

'Of course! It's all in the little book, Chaz. Oh yes, and I rang June and we've arranged a girls' night out at the Orchard Garden. It's the same night you're going to that boxing match. Next Tuesday.'

Chaz assumed that it was strippers and cocks out and that kind of thing. Linda was wary. She didn't want a Debs argument or conflict to develop. If she had said it was a feminist thing with these odd bites-your-cock-off ideas, there would have been more rowing. He would have jumped on it knowing that it was Debs initiated.

'Oh, I don't know Chaz but she told me about her new job at the hospital.'

Chaz sighed deeply again. He was just fed up with the constant reference to that blasted asylum.

'It's not a hospital, Linda! It's a fucking nut-house,' he snapped. It was coming up again and again and again and totally the reason why Chaz was reluctant to buy the house in the first place. And there was plenty more to add fuel to the asylum flames in the offing.

'She said there's a woman up there who puts vim and worms in doctors' and nurses' mouths, Chaz.'

Chaz couldn't resist this one to crack a joke to. 'Yeah, didn't ya know, Linda, they've always gone together like strawberries and fucking cream.' Chaz humored himself so much he felt compelled to continue on this rich vein. 'Yup, everyone's fucking mad for them, Linda! Get ya punnet of fresh vim and worms and get arf free! Fucking nutty farmers! Talk about all your worst fears becoming a nutty fucking reality. Now I've got nut jobs watching me every move, wanting to put vim and worms, and fuck knows what else down me kisser!'

The excitement and the cat dander atmosphere got Chaz's asthma going again, so he reached again for the inhaler, and began puffing some more, while he was also looking at Linda's apparel.

'Anyhow, where's the black leather and fishnets? Its "Daddy's Little Princess" tonight!'

Even after all the commotion of the night, Chaz still wanted to do 'that' filming.

'Well I couldn't very well open the door to the police like that, could I?'

Chaz had got over the asthmatic problems, and was now fiddling around with the St. George trinket box. He was aware that Linda had supplemented it, so had been right on it, but a good stiff line and he would feel much better. 'Why not?' Chaz quipped as he laid the first line out and snorted. 'It's the New Age in a free and liberated country ain't it! And you might have coaxed them into a bi-curious three up! Ha, ha ha!'

Everything is powdered sex in this world, and Chaz believed that you had to ram it hard down the barrel, and get it firing. That's what liberation's all about. Chaz laid a line out for Linda, a little big one. He had plenty of gun powder and he just had to get Linda flying and riding on it and then she would get in that Dark Room.

'Here, have the line, Linda, and then you can get back into ya gear.'

Chaz took another Erectafen from the white blazer pocket, and made a show of popping it in his mouth, his second one of the evening, as Linda prevaricated.

'I don't really feel like it. I can't get that scream out of my mind.'

Chaz didn't like Linda resisting a pre-planned session. This was a 'work' session as much as sex. He was all stoked up for it. It wasn't fair. She would be off to sleep, but with all this built up expectation, he would be up all night masturbating to porn films. Everything had been pre-planned and Linda knew *exactly* what she had to do. Just act in character, like she normally did, and obey his every command. It wasn't hard, was it? He had to persuade her.

'Oh, come on, Linda! All this fuss over a pack of vixens spatting. I've downed the "Erecta". I'm hot for it! And we've got to do that filming. It's essential, Linda. You know that!'

Linda just didn't feel like any of it. That screaming business had scared her so much, and now all this disturbing stuff about asylum patients watching the house. She didn't feel like anything apart from going to bed and falling asleep.

'I don't feel like going up there and doing that, Chaz.'

'Oh, come on, Linda!' Chaz pleaded. 'Have a line. It'll chill ya and get ya buzzed for a session. It'll be good for ya, girl. It'll get all the stresses and strains out.'

Chaz had all the appropriate arguments, and he would generally win Linda over with the weight of them. He had done considerable cutting-edge research on such things. He knew how to talk Linda around.

'And all the top sex and relationship experts are saying it, Linda, role playing is good for ya. It helps ya to break free of inhibitions. Ya smash um down. It's the liberation of the New Age, Linda. And with a long-term relationship like ours, well you've got to explore and be creative haven't ya? You've got to do that, Linda, to prevent it all going stale. You know that, Linda! You know that! Come over and have a line!'

Linda couldn't resist it. She tried to, but then she thought, what the heck, he's right. All the problems of the day, they would all be forgotten with a few more lines of coke, and she would have energy a plenty, for 'that' filming for a few hours. She knelt at the table over the line and Chaz smiled, pleased with what he was seeing.

'That's it, Linda. Snort it up there! You've got to go with the flow more, Linda. That's what it's all about in the New Age. And in the long run those films will raise our standard of living. We'll get more and more twenty knicker subs. Be paying our mortgage. It could help me go legit Linda, so how bad's that eh, class! We can do Daddy's Little Princess tonight and Mummy's Little Soldier tomorrow'

Linda had now resigned herself to do 'that' filming so she would sniff, sniff and snort again.

'Can I have another line, Chaz? she asked.

'That's the spirit! That's more like my Linda!' Chaz eagerly laid out another line, and Linda was on it, and Chaz's smile just got bigger.

The local artist who had been commissioned to do the painting of Natasha had also done one of Chaz and Linda's wedding photo that hung over the fireplace. This was on the landing wall nearly opposite the Dark Room, and as they passed and loitered and Chaz unlocked, Linda cast an eye to the painting. She was flying high on the coke, but Linda was still left wondering how her marriage had become this. Chaz turned the crystal door knob and Linda entered that world of the Dark Room, where all doubts would be annihilated with yet more coke. They were quick to get on with it, and were soon both in character and the cameras were rolling. Chaz was clad in a doctor's white coat, posing as a kind of doctor of kinky domination. He had engaged a devout kinky audience, so Chaz had to keep on serving it up. On these subscription sites, that Linda didn't take any real interest in, he used these bizarre films, with some of the more left field work of Vivienne and Miko, with a few exclusive films starring Natasha. One could say that it was all part of the masterplan. With Miko and Viv on board Chaz was looking towards building something of a porn empire. This was the dream for the New Age visionary Chaz. They had talked about a sex club, which would be sited in Miko's large bungalow with its secluded swimming pool. They would have themed parties there Friday and Saturday nights. Then when successful, the sex clubs would be a new branding idea. They could move forward converting secluded residences with swimming pools into sex clubs. Then it would undoubtedly be a porn channel on the internet and satellite TV going worldwide, giving live footage from the porn venues. That was the dream, with Natasha, who else, as resident host. Chaz didn't really open up on all this to Linda, and if she didn't go along with it, well people do grow apart sometimes, was Chaz's point of view. But he wasn't rigid about it. Linda would eventually smash those red lines and embrace the brand. She just needed to find her 'Inner Vivienne', like Natasha was doing, and get on up for it.

Originally Linda was negative about all of these activities, but Chaz had gradually persuaded her to shoot exclusively with the kinky masks. They worked with the theme of the films and protected her identity, and now the lady behind the mask was something of a mysterious, but reluctant kinky porn star, and her fans on the site wanted more and that's why Chaz wanted her to 'go with the flow' as any sensible person in the New Age did.

The cameras were soon rolling with Linda naked and tied up with all manner of clamps and things, with Chaz admonishing her in his role as the kinky doctor.

'You love being Daddy's Little Princess, don't you, Priscella!'

'Yes, I'm Daddy's little Princess.' Linda knew how to play these kinds of roles. It was like Linda's honed boilie-making skills. She had done it so many times, that eventually she had become the expert. Chaz held a cane and he demanded that Linda turn around and bend over, readying herself for the severe punishment, and there was more.

'And Daddy is taking his little Princess to his dirty grotto because she's full of filth! Admit it, Princess Priscella! Say it! You're full of dirty whoring filth! And we've got to get your filth out!'

Linda just played along in character as she had always done. For Chaz that was the way that those red lines could be ambushed. He foresaw Linda creating a porn star alter-ego like Vivienne. It would come. He whacked her three times with the cane, demanding the admission.

'Yes Daddy, yes Daddy. I'm full of dirty filth, dirty whoring filth!'

Chaz then took a vacuum pump for the extraction enema. Linda was groaning as if she was constipated.

'Daddy shall have to relieve the blockages, my little Princess!'

Chaz knew that it was all going perfectly. 'Class!' The kinky punters would be satisfied and the master plan, regarding Linda's psychological reticence, was being worked. Chaz was on a mission to smash those red lines. They were loosening and soon the dam would burst and the repressed kinky sacks of sex would burst through. Then she would be up for anything, like she needed to be in this Brave New Age.

A short while later, Chaz lounged on the bed in the master bedroom, while Linda was in the bedroom shower unit. Chaz had already showered and he was in his suave white and gold velvet Harrods dressing gown, and he was lying back on the bed, back resting against the head board, rolling a joint. Linda's naked figure was blurred by the wavy glass. Chaz was ecstatic. He really was on a high when they did these films. It was such a buzz and for Chaz this was the real beginning of the new world, and the series of thirty-minute shorts had netted them a dozen grand on worldwide distribution. The internet was amazing, nothing but opportunity and Chaz was quick to seize it. Making a living out of what you like doing. The dream!

'That was great, Linda. Ya kept to the script and concept, just nice. I'll get that for editing. We'll get loads of hits and new subscriptions! It'll sell like hot cakes with the kinky fuckers. Well done!' Chaz liked to give Linda praise when it was due.

'Yeah sure, Chaz.'

Linda was just pleased it was all over. It made her feel dirty inside. Linda didn't really like this kinky kind of sex, but Chaz was pleased and it helped them pay the mortgage. Linda stayed in the shower much longer than she normally did. She found the heat of the water comforting and soothing, and for some reason she just wanted to keep washing herself clean. Then she could begin again all fresh, with the Dark Room business washed away.

Chaz was on such a high he decided he wouldn't even bother trying to go to sleep. He was inspired. He wanted to get at the film footage, get it up and running downstairs on the DVD, so that he knew what they had for the editing process. Chaz would use a contact in the porn world, the Dutch pornographer Dirk Van Dijk who was a first class professional and reasonably priced, who Vivienne had worked with extensively. Chaz always made jokes about his name.

'We'll have to get it to ole Big Dick Dirk, Linda,' he chortled.

It was all a case of getting Dirk some reasonable footage from a number of different angles and he would do his job. Chaz had a number of viewpoints set up in the Dark Room, and every video they had done looked pro after the process. If it isn't broke don't fix it was Chaz's philosophy, and now, he had a methodology going, to get to the final product, and Chaz found that very satisfying. He was always saying to Linda that people don't appreciate the sheer work that goes into these porn films. Chaz was soon downstairs, rolling up yet another joint as the non-edited footage ran on his lounge TV screen.

'Luv it, hot stuff! Van Big Dick will love it!'

Chaz lit the joint and hauled himself up out of his velvet chair, putting in a few extra treat teaser balls down to Hermann and 'The Beak'. Hermann was on them immediately. A wry smile came over Chaz, and he was really enjoying himself still high from the sex and drugs, and that knowledge he was going to make hard cash out of it all. Nothing ever seemed to go wrong these days on that score. He looked towards that classy erotic painting of Natasha, and thought about what that future might hold for his talented and well-educated daughter. He knew she was going to be big. It might even be reality shows he thought, or even porn reality shows, she had the sass. Hermann bullied to get first shot at the teaser balls. Chaz reflected on Hermann's voracious appetite.

'You, Hermann, are as mad for the divine blues, as me and Linda are for kinky sex!'

Linda was upstairs blow drying her hair looking stressed. She clicked the dryer off and put it down on her dressing table. Then she opened the drawer and took out the dispensing container, popping a few valiums into her hand and swilling them down with water. She had felt agitated all night with that screaming, and now the cocaine had worn off, she felt disgusted with herself too. She would need the downers to go to sleep and that scream wouldn't go away either. It was still ringing around her mind.

Chaz sat back down on his sumptuous chair, and kept an eye on the footage while he booted up his laptop. He was firing on all cylinders, accessing an adult contact site that he had been using lately. There were ongoing problems with Linda but he was sure that she would be talked around eventually. Miko was always swinging with Viv. It was a big part of their sex life. Miko would always tell Chaz what they got up to with couples, singles, even gangs, as Vivienne was sex mad. The saucy stories enlivened nights out fishing, and Chaz would always return horny and up for a session in the Dark Room afterwards. But he never told Linda what the big turn on was. Chaz quickly logged onto the site, and was particularly interested in a young couple who lived less than ten miles away. The girl was bisexual and the couple were no more than Natasha's age and she was shaved, just how Chaz liked them. Chaz could virtually hear the girl in his mind talking, and he was really savoring the naked shot of her as she was doing so.

'We are up for anything and gagging to explore the heavy bondage scene. So, gag us please! But we need a more experienced couple to guide us through the bondage labyrinth.'

Chaz's mind was racing and spinning away. He would continue working on Linda. She always gave way in the end, and he could invite this young couple over and get them up there in the Dark Room. Why not eh? Just what the kinky doctor ordered, Chaz thought. They could do some filming to spice the subscription site up, and give the couple a nice fee. It could be the precursor to a more open and liberated Linda. That site had to keep giving the punters variety and diversity. Everything would be diversity in the New Age, Chaz had the insight to fully recognize that. He foresaw Nat, porn presenter, upholding that diversity flag, doing shoots with the BBC. Now that would be something! Chaz chuckled away at his thoughts.

'I think we'll be able to accommodate you, young Eve!' he mused. 'Class!'

Linda got into bed but then came over all hungry. She had to get up and have something. She entered the lounge in her nightdress and felt disgusted when she saw the big screen.

'Oh, do you have to watch that, Chaz?' she said. It made her feel sick having to witness it. But Chaz was adamant, yes, he had to watch the original footage.

'Look, I've got to know what we've got to submit for editing, Linda. It's essential. For all I know, we might have been out of shot or something. I've got to know these things, Linda.'

Linda sighed and suggested that tonight wasn't the right time. She went into the kitchen and began making herself a quick toasted cheese sandwich.

'Do you want a toasted cheese?' she asked. Chaz was still gloating over the young woman and he thought that Linda would quite fancy a bit of her boyfriend too, once she had been persuaded.

'Yeah great, but hang on in there with the filming, Linda. We'll make big dough on all of this. Believe you me. That's a liberated film. It's out there on the edge, exploratory, creative. It's what the kinky bastards are after, Linda. They don't want it pure straight. Everything's kinked in the New Age. It's gotta be kinky!'

Chaz laughed to himself at his turn of phrase. He thought he might have another T-shirt with that on it and a still from one of his porn films. Really shake um up down the village. If there was anything that Chaz detested, it was that small-mindedness.

Linda brought the toasted cheese sandwiches in and Chaz was still ogling the couple but making sure that Linda noticed it, so that he could get a persuasive point of view across and begin to get Linda thinking right. Linda passed him the sandwich, and glanced on the laptop screen, speculating what Chaz was looking at.

'You're not looking at those contacts again are ya?' Linda said with a rather critical tone.

'Couldn't resist a little peep!' Chaz replied, before opening up further. 'Got a young couple here early twenties, nice, and they're looking for an experienced couple who are into bondage, who could teach them a thing or two. Sounds like us, Linda?'

Chaz knew he had the boat right out there and it might just begin to sail, but Linda resisted, and sat down on the settee with a deep sigh. She just had to stick up for herself.

'Chaz, how many more times have I got to say it. "That" sort of thing isn't for me.'

Chaz had been married to Linda for twenty-two years now, so he knew how to approach the intransigence. He had to be assertive, authoritative, make her realize that she was being irrational, that times had moved on. It always worked.

'Oh, come on, Linda! You've never ever given it a bloody chance. How can you say it's not for me, when you haven't even tried it? Go with the flow more, Linda! I was just saying that an hour ago. Go with the flow. That's what it is these days for the sexy devil's sake!'

Chaz chuckled to his joke, but Linda looked across to the footage on the screen, before bowing her head and reflecting. Her very inner being felt compromised, and she wondered why on earth she had gone along with it as it was. It was from a deep inner disgust that emboldened her to speak up this time.

'Well, I don't know if I like what we get up to as it is, Chaz,' she said. Chaz had heard this response time and again, but he knew Linda better than anyone. Better than she knew herself.

'Tut, Linda. You're always negative to anything different, until you get going. And you were begging for that in there tonight, gagging. Admit your own kinky lust for God's sake, Linda. It's essential you do that in the New Age. Essential! Do ya fancy another line? A big "little" one?'

The whole day had been a testing one and now Linda's glass was overflowing with stress and anxiety. But something in her told her that she had to resist. She couldn't just keep on sniffing coke. It was making her high for a while and then it was the inexorable slippery fall back into the snake pit, and then she would reach for the coke and valium ladder again, to crawl her way out of it. But the pit seemed to be getting deeper and deeper.

'Can't you just give it a rest, Chaz?' she said.

Chaz didn't like this kind of attitude. Those films made them thousands and Linda didn't mind spending the proceeds. She was always spending another five hundred on clothes, at the big swank High Grange shopping center. Chaz had readily noticed that she went there far more often these days, buying more than she used to, and it all had to be paid for.

'Look, Linda! It's up to me how many fucking lines or whatever I do. You don't wanna line, that's fair enough. Decide for yourself, cos I'm not the one snorting it up ya hooter, am I! But I'm fucking having one!'

CHAPTER SEVEN

WATER SNAKES

Within a couple of days both Chaz and Miko had purchased a year's membership of Joey Olwyn's lake, merely from what they saw on the mightily impressive new website. Chaz recalled looking around the lake some ten years back, after hearing through the carp grapevine there were a few thirties in there. A works angling society had put a few fish in, and they had grown to a fair size. But things were much more impressive now. Freshly cut swims up to a professional standard had made the lake rather more appetizing to the expert carper. Joey had spent a good few grand on that via a friend's construction company. But it was those big fish including 'The Pregnant Virgin' and the club's exclusiveness due to price, that convinced both Chaz and Miko that this was the lake for them. They also liked the idea of that fishing lodge where you could grab a toilet, a shower and even a few beverages and a breakfast. A carp enthusiast's home from home.

Once having purchased the membership, Chaz and Miko had decided they would fish it on the Friday night. Therefore, on the Thursday and Friday the Barber household was all geared up around the big carp fishing trip to Olwyn's. The word and the world around Holly Beach Lane was all carp, as Chaz enthused about getting those dragon slayers out. He reckoned he would purchase those Osaki Cobras as the season progressed, and he had made a ton of dough out of the spring bank holiday. Jay and Dai and a few others would have an enormous amount of coke as there was the annual dance event at the Tennin show ground, which attracted upwards of twenty thousand for three nights. Then there was Scamp's customers, bang on it, the Waterside commuters going party crazy, and now those Foxdale gentlemen, gays and dykes, getting down on it bigtime and no doubt that Sally Brockett, the council leader, would be sniffing a few up her hooter. But first things first. This important trip to the revamped Blue Lake was a chance to get the rods out, and make that first vital reconnaissance of the water. He could introduce the lake to the Divine blues, and the Tutti Frutti Strawberry Assassins. That big female carp wouldn't be able to resist Chaz's teaser balls. Then there was that New Age bait boat with its all-seeing eye. It was the age of clear carp vision in the dark unknown depths. These were exciting times indeed for the Barber household, and Chaz had arranged a baiting program via Joey on the blower. The idea was to take a hundredweight of bait down there, and Joey would drop it in designated places, in preparation for a monster weekend session in mid-June. The plan being, Chaz and Miko would catch some big lumps, that would give the lake publicity to get it up and running in the *Carp Master's Monthly*. Truly exciting times!

On the Thursday night, as Chaz smoked his dope and watched the carp in the tanks attack the Divine blues and Strawberry Tutti reds, it was all about joyousness and the expectancy of triumph. By the end of June that 'One Eye' would see just how good a carper Chazzy Barber was. He would have another half a dozen new photos on the board. It would be that 'One Eye' who would be pushed to the periphery in retreat. A change was a coming! Chaz would re-consolidate himself at the center of things, his rightful place. Chaz meditated more deeply on Hermann in the tank and he reckoned that nigh forty at the 'Ressie' had been on the board for far too long. Even Chaz expected it to lose center billing any day soon. Pride and place were naturally given to the here and now. But if Chaz got that pregnant fucker up out of the depths, straddled wide on his knees and cradled in his arms, he would finally have one, over that fucking wanker 'One Eye'. Chaz was in deeply meditative mood. With positive affirmative creative visualizations, all part of the New Age thinking for Chaz, catching that carp would be almost inevitable. He saw himself by the bank side with a crowd of carpers around him astonished by the big fish Chaz was proudly holding. But these were superior 'cutting edge' New Age psychological approaches, that Chaz was using. He would corner that pregnant virgin and nail her.

'I reckon by the end of June I'll have bagged that pregnant fucker, Linda. Joey reckons the way it's getting its head down on the trout pellet it might touch fifty by then.' Linda was reading her obligatory historical romance on the Waldorf chiming along appropriately on cue.

'Now that would be something!' Linda stated, yet privately wondering why men had to pull these poor carp about with hooks in their mouths. It all seemed a bit cruel, and she had remembered that carp that Chaz had caught a few years ago. The one that couldn't be mentioned these days. He had kept it in a closed, zip up, sack overnight to take a photo in the morning and it had pulled out the bank stick. Thirty-seven that one went, Linda knew the weight well, and was caught from that difficult water that 'One Eye' had fished regularly. It would have been proof that Chaz could have easily cracked that lake if it was his want. Chaz was angry that he lost his chance to get that all important photo, especially so when 'One Eye' taunted him saying, 'You've been known to tell a few porky's, Sweeny. I reckon ya want a job as a "spin-doctor".' But Linda hadn't forgotten it as when she asked, 'could the carp get out of the sack?', Chaz had told her 'unlikely'. Linda had thought about that poor thing, sitting in the sack waiting to die, or more likely dying of stress trying to get out. It was one of those tales that had finally put her off carp fishing.

Friday was a similarly hot day and the weather showed no signs of relenting. Chaz was praying that it would extend into the Whitsun break as better weather meant more partying, bigger crowds at the dance festival, more drug usage, and more cash binned. But today wasn't about the white blazer, it was carp. Chaz was clad in matching combat fatigues and jacket for camouflaging purposes. He also sported that inimitable great white shark hunter's hat. The hat had made him famous in the local carp world. Chaz was in the zone and it was a big day, a big monster of a day.

Chaz was arranging carp equipment in the new shed, as if he were going on a nineteenth century expedition up the Congo, and if you have never known, carpers tend to do things big. When *real* carpers go on a fishing expedition, they take enough equipment to fill a small truck. Everything from carp chairs, to bivvies and much more were being packed up into Chaz's goliath of a steel-framed carp barrow, the largest and strongest on the market of course, that stood just outside the new shed. Chaz was meticulous in the way that he packed everything into neat holdalls and it had taken him all morning to get everything ready. It would fill that Jeep and the rack, and the storage trailer he would pull behind it. Chaz was chewing relentlessly on gum. He was in the hunting zone!

Linda was pruning some rose bushes in the front garden and she called down to Chaz if he wanted a drink. While she was making the coffee, she picked up one of Chaz's carp magazines from the front room, because she wanted to see the article about the lake that had stopped the Barber household in its tracks. Chaz had tried to push out the weeks coke deals a day early, with varying degrees of success, so that he could concentrate on this momentous first trip to the water, that was set to be Chaz and Miko's first choice lake of the year. Their aim was to do the summer and autumn 2003 AD down there, until they cracked the code. That 'cracking it' meant getting a photo in that *Carp Master's* magazine with that pregnant virgin slapped across their knee. They had a five-hundred-pound side bet, regarding who would catch that fucker first. They were the hunters, hunting down the virgin.

Linda flipped through the glossy mag, wondering what the fuss was all about having to catch these hapless fish. She turned a page and was drawn to the article about the enormous fifty-pound carp that had been caught on that chocolate truffle by Mary Shagnall, the specimen hunter from Grimsby. She couldn't believe it. It was another serendipity moment. She would have to tell Chaz, and she knew full well that Chaz had never hunted down a carp that big.

Chaz readied himself to push the barrow up the small garden to the pathway that ran around to the front of the house. The barrow was enormous and was packed with so much baggage, that Chaz had difficulty seeing the way ahead. He got it up to the pathway and was beginning to pant a little, as Chaz was sweating up heavily in his fatigues and heavy jacket. Linda had warned that he would be too hot in them, but that wasn't the point. He wasn't swanning around trying to get a sun tan. He was hunting and needed serious camouflaging. Linda was fiddling away pruning, up by the front wall. Chaz brought the barrow past another rosebush that was next to the back-path's entry to the front. It was quite a substantial one and the thorns got caught up in Chaz's big carp chair, that needed much more than the width of the path. Chaz was hot and bothered and he wasn't in any mood to show even a hint of patience. The thorn bush seemed to grab hold of the chair as Chaz pushed on relentlessly and of course the chair was pulled out awkwardly from the steel-framed barrow beast.

'Fucking poxy fucking rosebush!'

Linda had her back to Chaz, and was completely absorbed with her gardening. She turned, and Chaz seemed to think it was an affront that she hadn't rushed over to help him. She merely stood there across the other side of the garden with the clippers in her hands.

'Well ya could help us for fuck's sake, Linda! It's a big day! Me and Miko have paid out eight hundred a head for this!'

Linda scurried over and helped him push the overladen barrow around the awkward jutting rose bush.

'Fucking cut that bush back will ya!' Chaz ordered, and while Linda helped to get the barrow back on track, the story about the chocolate truffle popped into her head.

'Did you see that fifty-pound carp caught on a chocolate truffle, Chaz, by that specimen hunter Mary Shagnall?' Linda enthused. Chaz certainly had noticed it, but he would never have mentioned it, and he was more than peeved that Linda had. And how could a woman be a specimen hunter? Play acting. Women wanting to have penises again. But the bloody carp was bigger than anything Chaz had caught by a whopping ten and more pounds.

'Sheer fluke! Carp mistook it for a freshwater muscle! You just wait, Linda, till they get on the "real" deal. The egg shells in! And from now on it will always be the egg shells in, and you just watch how they crack this lake of Joey Olwyn's! You mark my words, Linda! Mark my words!'

Chaz sounded as authoritative as some grand soothsayer writing for the daily newspaper, but Linda saw it all objectively. Chaz's biggest was only thirty-nine. Mary Shagnall had a fifty-three. And the magazine, an authoritative voice, had called her a specimen hunter.

Linda ran forward to open the front gate, checking it with a house brick. Chaz was thinking ahead, once the carp barrow was out there by the Jeep, he would load the lot on, while Linda could go and pick up the garden barrow, that Chaz had stacked up with bait. The Barber's had to attack this with teamwork. Chaz had arranged that pre-baiting with Joey and he was buzzing. There was no way that egg shells in would fail. No way.

'And there's a small barrow load of bait to come up, Linda, please!'

When you're working flat out towards a goal, you always need to share the workload. That was the Chaz Barber philosophy. Linda got down to the shed and there were big blue bottle flies buzzing around the entrance. Did other wives have to put up with giant flies? Chaz always had king-sized maggots about, and king-sized maggots made up into these darn great buzzers. Linda was just about sick of it all and no doubt he had left maggots in there stinking of curry powder. Fancy putting maggots in curry powder. 'Ugh!' Chaz said to her, that it gave them an extra 'wang a dang', whatever that meant. The times she had watched him gluing them to a bit of cork, making what he called his 'Medusa Wig', as he jokingly called it. It was a special rig he used and it all seemed so cruel and creepy to Linda. Fancy sitting there, gluing maggots to a bit of cork? But Chaz was obsessed with that Medusa. He had that gold Medusa ring on his index finger, all part of that St. George philosophy that Chaz espoused, of needing to chop the head off the dragons in our lives. And for Chaz that Medusa was one helluva dragon, turning men into stone! Chaz would have gladly chopped the head off that bitch! That's why he loved that Medusa's head in the carp tank with Hermann. Dragons have it coming to um and when Chaz was stoned, he had those insights about how men, to a man, had to cut the old dragon's head off, making her more amenable to logic and rationality. That was the deeper meaning of the Medusa. Chaz knew things.

Linda pushed the large gardening barrow that was crammed with ten kilo sacks of blue and red boilies up the lawn. There were so many in there, she had to stop and move them otherwise they would have tumbled off. She eventually made it to the front garden stressed right up, and she could see Chaz busily transferring the mountains of carp gear into the back of the Jeep. He had already strapped a ton to the rack. Linda was so annoyed that Chaz had expected her to push this heavy barrow. Why did he have to pack it up like this? If he wanted it that heavy, he should of darn well pushed it himself she thought. She stopped half way up the path exasperated.

'There's rather a lot of bait here for one-night, Chaz,' she whined. Chaz turned and gave her a brusquely edged run down of the expedition, and hadn't he been telling her all morning! Did she ever listen?

'Look, Linda! Joey's gonna do a three-week pre-bait for our monster session. All right! I've been telling you all fucking morning! Fucking hell! What ya got in ya fucking ears!'

When Chaz prepared for such a big fishing trip, the tension in the air was palpable. He put so much work into it and there was always that ever increasing danger of carding a blank. Chaz didn't like to shout it out on the rooftops, but he hadn't caught a carp the last seven times he'd been out. It wasn't good, in fact it had never been so bad. It had undermined the poise and pose of the great white carp hunter. But he was still positive. As he well knew, that glass has to be over half full, riding to the top. He had those sublime new slayers, the bait boat and this fantastic new lake crammed with beautiful monsters, so Chaz was chewing well and stroking the beard. Joey had confided to Chaz, having known each other going back, that he would love to see Chaz holding a fifty as it would be a big sell in the carp monthlies, and would make Chaz 'the' UK carp fishing celebrity with that hat on. So, Chaz was dreaming, yet he was also fearing, another string of the dreaded blanks. Failure had steadily chipped away his confidence.

Linda thought about that reply about pre-baiting, and as she was far less than a carp expert, she saw things from her own naïve but unique angle.

'Don't you think that's kind of cheating? Getting them addicted to your baits?'

When would she actually listen, Chaz thought? He sighed and yet again he had to point her towards how 'carp experts' worked such things. It was no different than people arguing against hunting, when hunting was used for farm and estate management. Chaz might have been a townie, but he wasn't naïve as the average sort of person like Linda, who thinks that all animals are cuddly, fluffy and sweet and you can have them on your lap watching soap operas of the evening. Try that with a frigging alligator.

'Look, Linda!' Chaz hunched his shoulders up, as he was apt to do, whenever initiating Linda into deeper matters such as these. 'Master carpers like me and Miko are confronting a hyper intelligent prey. It's all about a subtle psychological battle of man against fish. You use human intelligence against what is a lesser species, Linda. Although yes, carp are beautiful, beautiful creatures, but us *real* specimen hunters of the prey, have to gradually change their eating behavior, weening them onto our agendas. It's called cunning, Linda, and the real deal carpers, like me and Miko, are cunning men! Not bloody women!' Chaz did seem very authoritative and intellectual talking about carp, Linda thought.

'What, like controlling them?' she replied. Chaz noted more than a hint of criticism, and he went on the defensive. There was nothing at all sinister in the way he went about hunting down big monster carp.

'Look, it's modern carping, Linda, in its advanced psychological aspects. Why do you think I spend all that money on those carp indoors for! To keep pets! I'm a student of carp, not a fucking Nazi for fuck's sake!'

Within a few minutes the Jeep was fully laden as was the trailer, and Chaz was about to pull out. He gave Linda a kiss leaning out of the window while he was chewing that gum. He was excited as all the doubts were being cast aside. Glass half full! Tonight, it would be full of big carp and Chaz would be hauling them out of the depths with his dragon slayers.

'I'll bell ya about how the bait boat goes, Linda.'

'All right, Chaz,' Linda replied. She was used to having to engage appropriately with Chaz on all things carp. 'Have a good time, Chaz. Hope ya don't blank.'

Chaz sneered a little, because that kind of approach was Linda with her glass half bloody empty all the time. She was programmed to be negative. But Chaz didn't want to keep nagging her.

'Oh, I will and oh yeah, there's plenty of Charley Farley in the hooter box so you haven't got a reason to be getting bored have ya?'

Chaz pulled away, with a jeep ram packed full, and he always loved that moment. Pulling away to go carping. When Chaz was going carping, he forgot everything. All the stress, all the hassle, all the lot of it. It was like a Holy day, and Chaz was off to the carp mass. No more of the Herberts for a day or two. Chaz was completely and utterly subsumed in the world of carp.

Now there wasn't pressure on this trip as such, as it was seen as largely a reconnaissance mission in the context of a season's serious carping. Chaz and Miko had quickly devised it, purely to get an introduction and feel for the water, and get that pre-baiting stash to Joey. All in all, the trip wouldn't be too tough on Linda, as he would be back by midafternoon tomorrow and then he could go 'bang on it' for the rest of the weekend, only venturing out if there was a big deal about.

But today was a quite perfect day for a trip to Olwyn's Lake, with the afternoon May sun, high in the sky and only a few wispy clouds to be seen. The lake with its chalk bottom looked tinged with blue around the shallower margins, before slipping away quickly into depth. Back in the day the lake was a working chalk pit and the diggers had hit underwater streams and the pit had virtually come up twenty-five foot in a night. That was going back some sixty-odd years, but all the plant was left at the bottom of the lake which was now nigh on a hundred-foot-deep at its deepest point. Chaz met Miko in the car park where they were personally met by Joey Olwyn, the guy who made this local carp fantasy a reality. What a visionary, Chaz thought. Chaz and Miko were some of the first members, and so they were treated like royalty by Joey. Joey still had the sideburns and he had put on a little bit more weight since Chaz had seen him last, but his enthusiasm for this new venture was infectious.

'It's great to see ya, Chaz, and you, Mike! I'll show you where the carp run, up along the chalk face! It's rich in aquatic worm and they're bang on them! That's where I'll drop ya ground bait in, Chaz.'

Chaz felt confident. It was a case of when the worm runs short, they'd be on his teaser balls. Joey pointed up towards the chalk face that had a path by it, but was inaccessible for angling purposes. That was the place, and he would bait up a patch some sixty foot in length so the pair of them could get their baits up there, in the pocket, as they say. Chaz and Miko were animated, for this was an exciting new world of local carping. It also looked as if Joey would have to do a bit of walking to get the ground bait in from up there at the other side of the big lake.

'Ah, it'll be no bother, Chaz. Give me a walk every day as I want to get some of the weight off. Me cholesterol level's a bit high.'

Joey took them to a couple of beautifully sculpted swims that could take the pair of them, and could be used to put the bait up along the cliff edge on that carp run. Chaz looked out across the deep lake towards the chalk face high embankment, some hundred and thirty yards or so in front of them. Chaz had his deep sage tactical carping hat on.

'Must be one forty, Miko, we'll need the big pit reels!'

'That won't be any problem with those dragon slayers of yours, Chaz,' Joey said. 'They can whip out a bait any kind of distance.'

Chaz didn't like to refer to the bait boat as he liked Joey to think he was casting out there. But before the serious business got underway, they returned to the carp lodge to have a quick drink and snack, and to offload all the packs of bait for the pre-baiting. Chaz opened a pack of passion reds and one of divine exotic blues, and Joey had a smell and feel of the Assassins. He was mightily impressed and Chaz opened up on the secretive bait.

'Yeah, it's some bait you're going to be putting out there, Joey. Revolutionary, we're selling it on the market mate, acts like a freshwater muscle. We've sold two hundred kilos already. Very special bait, "very",' Chaz said with animated enthusiasm. Joey had heard plenty of this in his time but he was impressed by Chaz's talk, but he thought he would use the moment to get some of his own marketing message across. He asked Chaz and Miko to put the word around that he was putting in a further two hundred all over the twenty by mid-June with a few more thirties.

'Eventually, I want the lake to be the best in the country, Chaz!' It was quite a dream that Joey had.

'Fucking ace, mate!' Chaz gloated on the idea, for the lake was so close and convenient, only about seven miles away. It would make things nice and easy with Linda, suitable for a quick shoot of a weekend kind of thing. It was all inspiring to hear and the fishing lodge was really European with its fabulous facilities. There was even enough room for small social gatherings. It was clear that Joey had left no stone unturned. It was all very exciting, although Miko was realistic about it all. Being realistic was Miko's way of preparing for the worst. With the help of Viv he could get porn films out of the can, but carp out of the depths was a whole lot trickier.

'Some head of carp you'll have down there, Joey. Now all we've got to do is catch the bastards!' That certainly was what all the effort was aimed towards, but Joey had other things on his mind too.

'Here, Chaz, do ya like a jellied eel?' Jellied eel? Chaz loved them. Many of Chaz's family had lived up London and whenever he visited from an early age, and that was regular, he would always, without fail, have jellied eels.

'Luv um, mate! Absolutely luv um! I was brought up on um, Joey!' Chaz explained. Joey sparked up. This was a big day for Joey too. There hadn't been many taking membership as yet and he wanted to get carpers in for the word of mouth to get around, and he reckoned Chaz and Miko might get a few big carp out.

'I'll get ya both some. Call it on the house! And there's tins of beer in the fridge, so have yourself a couple!' This new Blue Lake complex was like a home from home, Chaz thought.

Joey almost forgot to tell Chaz and Miko a possible Achilles heel regarding the carp run.

'Oh yeah, Chaz, I would warn ya that there's an old car down there along that run. Ya can see it from the top there. Looks like an old Jag.'

Joey explained that it had been down there years, dumped when the fence used to be virtually non-existent, landing on a shelf and precariously caught over a virtual precipice.

'I'll fish me bait on the roof of the bastard, Joey,' Chaz joked.

By about half six or so Chaz and Miko were in position. All the talking had been done and Chaz was seated on the carp chair finishing off his jellied eel. He was licking his lips; they were that good.

'Fucking handsome! He sure knows how to jelly a fucking eel, Miko. Best I've tasted for years. But let's get down to the real business mate. I'm gonna fish divine blues on two and the strawberry red Assassins on the other Miko.'

They were trying to make their carp bait development 'scientific' and therefore Miko would have the reds on two rods and the blues on the other. There was always the possibility that these fickle carp creatures might go on certain shades of color. Anything is possible with monster carp. Chaz proceeded to put his bait and lead in the bait boat that was crammed full with divine blues. It was an historic moment. The beginning of the New Age of carping and Chaz was at the controls ready to set that boat off in earnest. They were going to smash it! Miko looked towards the bait boat and was wondering why Chaz had become such an evangelist. Chaz looked at him, full of this new-fangled device.

'I knew we had to go hi-tech Miko. It's gonna triple our big fish take. It's been scientifically proven,' Chaz said. Miko was still far from convinced, although he could recognize that Chaz was well into the thing.

'Aren't ya casting the bait, Chaz? he asked, knowing that until only recently Chaz was angrily against anything to do with 'cheating bastard' gadgets. But generally new converts are the most enthusiastic.

'It's a hundred and forty out there, mate. If we cast, it'll take us ten goes to get that bait perfectly in position. Fucking scare the carp away! Joey said that shelf is only twenty foot wide. If you ain't on the shelf, you ain't on the money, Miko! Simple as that. It's all precision in the New Age, mate. And that pregnant virgin fucker runs along that shelf. Sorted! Get the boat out and make a fucking whore out of her Miko. Make a fucking whore out of her!'

Chaz played with the controls and the bait dropper started buzzing and then took off towards its destination at the foot of the chalk face. Chaz was like a big kid with his new toy.

'There she goes, Miko! Off to the new world!'

Chaz was showing off rather. He dropped the bait and hook presentation exactly where he wanted it, at precisely the point where Joey had dropped so much trout pellet. On the carp run! Chaz reiterated what the New Age was all about.

'Carping is all about the precision now! Hi-tech for those who can afford the edge!'

It wasn't long before Chaz had the bait boat filled up with reds and yet another baited hook offering among the load. But little did Chaz know, there were two youths of about thirteen or so who were lying in wait. They were playing but rather bored in the woods nearby inside the lake's perimeter, and they saw opportunities with that bait boat speeding across towards them. There was a pile of brick rubble that had been illegally dumped in the woods when the fence was down prior to the lake's takeover by Joey. Joey had noticed it, but hadn't as yet got around to clearing it up. There were also parts of the fence down around that area, that Joey was intending to repair later in the summer once he was more established. One of the youths had a flash of inspiration and they both rushed to gather the biggest bits of brick rubble they could find. What sport! All with the added bonus of knowing that the fisherman wouldn't have a chance of doing anything about it. They would be home by the time they got around there. There were full bricks among the rubble and even some real heavy blaze furnace bricks. By the time Chaz sent the bait boat on its fifth and penultimate crossing they were armed, lying in wait and ready to pounce!

'Here she comes again, Aaron. The flagship of the fleet!

'Ambush! Sink the fucker! Sink the fucker!'

Both youths opened up, slinging brick after brick down at the bait boat. Chaz was still busily turning the knobs, but Miko spotted what was occurring.

'Chaz! It looks like somebody's chucking rocks at ya boat!'

That boat cost fifteen hundred and had that third eye camera, so Chaz quickly reacted, shouting across the lake.

'Here! Pack it up will ya! Fucking pack it up!'

The youths were still throwing bricks as Chaz kept hollering and one whacked bang into the craft, not sinking it, but had affected its controls, so now the boat was adrift from its helmsman. Chaz knew something had done for it, as he worked them madly trying to get the boat back, but it wasn't moving.

'Thing is indestructible!' Aaron said after yet another brick went straight into the boat, a direct hit. Luke, his mate, picked hold of a heavy engineering brick. Maybe this was end games?

'Feel that then!' Luke put the heavy brick briefly in Aaron's hand.

'Phew huh! Mean bruver! Bunker buster!'

The youth carefully took aim and hurled the heavy brick with as much might as he could muster. It whacked into the boat with yet another direct hit and this time the boat finally split and began to ship water. Chaz was still frantically shouting at them to pack it up but it was all too late. There was nothing Chaz could do! Aaron called out to Chaz in defiance. What an exciting end to the day.

'Here, mate! Ya battleship's just been sunk by stealth fighters!'

Chaz could see the boat disappearing, seemingly sinking into the depths, although it was merely submerged and its top touching the surface. The two youths decided enough was enough. Whooping and hollering they scarpered off into the woods. Chaz was mad. The very first time he had used the boat and the bastard had been destroyed by louts. Miko was more philosophical. Kids were kids and they do these things. But he didn't want to rub it in.

'Well at least you've got your baits out there, Chaz.'

It was one of those Linda-like quips and Chaz boiled. Ten minutes and he had lost the fucking thing. Fifteen hundred quid sunk.

'The little fucking gits! The shits!' Chaz then had a spark of inspiration. 'Stay here Miko, and look after the fucking rods. I'm going to see Joey!'

Chaz was jutting his head from his shoulders like a cockerel, but Joey was cool and calm because he didn't want any negative stories emanating from the opening of the new complex. He had to make a success out of this project.

'I'll replace it tomorrow, Chazzy, but I would suggest not using the bait boat to that area in the future. With the estate nearby they are a bit of a problem mate. But keep the faith! We're win in the end. I'll get a dog patrol and improve the fencing. Here take another pot of jellied eels and one to take home with ya too, Chaz!'

Chazzy's anger subsided after that. At least the debacle hadn't cost him fifteen hundred quid but it was going to be a costly start for Joey Olwyn, because he didn't want that one in the *Carp Masters* monthly. It would be enough to put a hundred anglers off joining.

'Cheers Joey, but keep um all in the fridge, mate, and I'll have um tomorrow dinner time when we go.'

Chaz had just about enough of jellied eels for one day, but at least it wasn't a wad of dough at the bottom of Blue Lake. With that issue sorted out, Chaz could now settle back into some serious carping. It was soon dark and Chaz and Miko were ensconced in their closely adjacent bivvy camps, close enough for conversing. After an hour or so of darkness and Chaz having rolled and smoked a joint or two, his bait indicator was set off. It flashed red and buzzed loudly, and Chaz was up like a flash! Here comes the 'preggers' virgin and he took up his dragon slayer confidently, fully expecting to feel a great colossal lump of a carp on the other end of his line. No way Chaz was going to go back home after a blank.

'On egg shells in, divine blues, Miko!' Chaz triumphantly exclaimed. Miko moved quick too as he was excited at the prospect of landing a great monster carp pushing forty or something similar.

'Are you in, Chaz! Are you in?' Miko shouted.

It was enthralling, riveting stuff, but Chaz turned his big reel and knew darn well that whatever it was, it certainly wasn't a big battleship of a carp.

'Well it ain't a flipping carp, mate!' Chaz replied with a bitter resignation, and disappointment. Miko was shining a torch out into the water as Chaz was bringing the fish to the surface near the bank. Chaz thought it might be a small bream as Joey had said there were a few in the lake. But Chaz soon realized what he had caught and how he hated them.

'Fucking bootlace eel, the wriggling fucker! You pay eight hundred and fifty for a fucking bootlace, fucking eel!'

How Chaz hated catching anything but beautiful monster carp. He was a carp specimen hunter; he didn't want to catch blasted 'nuisance' fish. They should be removed from the lake and left to chance it gasping on the bank.

'Patience, Chazzy!' Miko advised, as he had seen Chaz perform with the so-called 'nuisance' species many a time. But Chaz never had an iota of it with eels. He hated them with a vengeance and he couldn't abide handling the slithering horrible blighters. Chaz merely swung the bootlace on the grass and proceeded to brutally stamp on its head while ripping the hook from its mouth.

'Well that's one less bastard eel in the lake and fucking good o Miko. Horrible little fuckers!'

Chaz baited up again, and this time had to cast his bait, trying desperately hard to get to where he had placed all those baits earlier, prior to the debacle of the sinking. Chaz whipped the rod above his head and went for the long-range big pit cast. It came down well short, just around the hundred mark and the line peeled off his reel. It must have been a hundred foot deep. The carp would need an oxygen tank to get down there. He swore and began to reel back in, but then realized he was hooked up into something.

'Might be some of that old plant, Chaz,' Miko suggested. Chaz put on a lot of side pressure, trying to free the hook but the line was severed with a ping.

'Fuck it!' Chaz exclaimed, as now he would have to reset again in the dark. It took him some time to, as Chaz fiddled around with a torch huffing and puffing. Miko tried to support him saying he would quickly get the hang of the dragon slayers.

'You'll get the next one out there, Chaz. Those slayers have got a nice whippy action!'

The second went about five yards further but it was still thirty yards short.

'Fuck it!' Chaz angrily snapped. Back came the weight and bait as Chaz swore and cursed more. But at least he wasn't snagged this time suggested Miko. When he took it from the water, he realized there was no bait on the rig. He would have to thread yet another boilie. It was tricky enough the first time, as Chaz and Miko had inadvertently chosen the darkest place on the lake and Chaz was far from adept in full darkness. Up at the 'Ressie' it was nigh artificially lit as there was a great 24/7 warehouse one end of the lake. Chaz re-baited and was determined to get it out there. He felt as if he had got used to the whip of the rod, and the weight flew towards the chalk face. It sounded good for a moment but then the reel malfunctioned and Chaz snagged up in a terror of a bird's nest.

'Fuck it! My fucking reel's snagged!'

'I think there's something wrong with your drum, mate,' Miko suggested. Chaz was forced to get one of his older replacement reels out. It was lucky he had them, but they came with a price in terms of confidence. They had older line on them, line that was somewhat compromised, and Joey had warned about those snags, that old Jag for one. All in all, it didn't bode well. Chaz set up again, determined that adversity wasn't going to defeat the Tennin carp king, while Miko just relaxed and drunk a cup of tea. Chaz announced that he was ready to go with a fully set up rod, rigged and baited up and then Miko spotted something.

'Here Chaz, I think you've missed one of your rings!'

'Bollocks! Fuck it!' Chaz lost his cool and hurled the rod down, disregarding the fact that it had cost so much.

'Mind, Chaz! You'll damage that sensitive tip!'

'Fuck it! I'll fish with two!' Chaz just couldn't be bothered to go through that rigmarole again. It would have to wait until first light. Chaz sat down and done what he would always do, rather than keep up the hissing fit. He took a deep breath in, rolled up a joint and smoked it, before carrying on, trying to chill out and feel relaxed. Low and behold it wasn't long before Chaz had another take on egg shells in.

'Are you in this time, Chazzy? You must be!' Miko was just as enthusiastic as there were a lot of big carp in the lake and big carp have to eat like the rest of us. But as soon as Chaz started to turn the reel in earnest, he knew its truth. It felt the same as the last poxy thing.

'Nope! It's a fucking eel again, the fucking things!'

Within a few moments Chaz was stamping on the eel again to extract his hook.

'Not likely to be joining the Eel Preservation Society any time soon then, Chaz!' Miko joked, although he didn't approve of Chaz's actions. But Chaz was Chaz and he explained the rationale of his seeming vendetta against the species.

'Look, I've got nothing against eels, Miko. I've got nothing against them, as long as they keep away from my fucking carp baits!'

Miko reflected for a moment or two, especially after Chaz had talked about all those pots of jellied eels in Olwyn's big fridge.

'Seems to be a lot of them down there, Chazzy.'

Chaz guffawed as he thought that the understatement of the year. The lake seemed to be wriggling with eels. Miko tried to put a brave face on it all, suggesting that they would have to adopt the carp master's stoical tactics.

'We're just going to have to stick at it, Chaz, to get through um to the carp!'

Chaz rebaited and now effortlessly swung the bait to the required area. Miko tried to keep the positive vibes going.

'Beautiful cast, Chaz. You've got the hang of those slayers now, mate! You really have!'

But soon after, Chaz was into yet another eel and he was beginning to reflect over the night's proceedings as he swung it onto the grass for yet more brutal treatment.

'And no wonder he's got a fridge freezer full up with fucking jellied eels! The lake's wriggling with the horrible little fuckers! They must be swarming around on the bottom! Ugh!'

'Probably on that aquatic worm,' Miko suggested. Miko also tried to get Chaz to see things more philosophically, considering the eel species in the wider scheme of things other than carp fishing. 'But they're amazing creatures, traveling all that way to the Sargasso Sea to spawn, Chaz.' Such talk didn't impress the king carp master.

'Fuck up, Miko! I've got brand new line on that reel and they'll fuck it! Crinkle it up something rotten!'

It wouldn't stop. Chaz caught eel after eel with Miko only having one. By the time the dawn came Chaz was resigned to failure. It was a bitter pill. It would be the eighth blank in a row. He felt soured and moody, and had a snort of coke to enliven him, but despite everything, he now had the three baits out on that carp run. The buzzer went off again. Chaz took up the rod and now Miko didn't say a word, that enthusiasm ended many takes ago. But this was different.

'Fuck me, I'm in!' Chaz exclaimed. Chaz knew it was a big fish. It tore into the depths running towards them and Chaz frantically kept up with the line retrieval. Miko took hold of the landing net. 'About fucking time I got into the big stuff!' Chaz smiled as now he realized this was a serious fish. The sun had risen so a nice photo snap was in the offing.

'This fish is gonna make that One Eye's fucking eyeball pop out!'

But then the carp took up another run, and Chaz had a hunch it could be heading for an underwater snag. He tried to turn it but before he knew it, the monster carp was snagged up inside the submerged old Jag.

'Fucking snagged!' Chaz exclaimed, fearing the worst.

'Might be in that old fucking car, Chaz.'

Chaz just let the line go slack but there was no movement. He then tried to apply a little pressure and the line pinged, shearing on the car's metal.

'You fucking bastard!' Chaz shouted out, his voice piercing the quietude of the early dawn. The carp had taken to egg shells in but Chaz was still on a blank and the fish lost in an old 4.2 liter Jag.

They fished hard till late morning without another take, and then returned crestfallen to the lodge. At least Joey cooked a good breakfast, and while he was doing so, Chaz was moaning to Joey about the number of eels in the lake. Joey was trying to explain.

'Now I know there are a good few eel, Chaz, and that's why I'm trying to catch um in traps and knock um out jellied. I'm attracting them with dried blood Chaz from Ripley's butchers. We'll get the lot out, Chaz. Keep the faith! Do you want a few more punnets! On the house!'

Chaz declined and was altogether rather less enthusiastic for jellied eels than he had been yesterday afternoon. As they were eating their breakfast and thoroughly enjoying it, Chaz was trying to understand the night, and what it was telling these master carpers.

'Eels, eels and more wriggling fucker eels! I think these things are sent to try us master carpers and they've fucked me line, mate, utterly fucked it!' Chaz concluded, while cutting one of Joey's big local butcher's sausages. There was no doubt that Joey looked after you. But Chaz was still exasperated.

'Well you had a bend on your rod Chaz. That augurs well, mate.'

'And lost the fucker, snagged up in a fucking Jag! A fucking old Jag of all things! But I wanna know how I catch fucking eighteen and you only have one! What the fuck!'

Miko thought the phenomenon was akin to lottery lines, and by golly he was glad that they avoided his baits. For Miko it was just one of those random things, that are too inexplicable to explain.

'Unless they picked up on your body scent or something Chaz and went for that!' he joked. Chaz smiled and Miko thought it was something of an achievement that Chaz could take all of this philosophically, as they expended a lot of energy, time and finance with all this carp fishing. Chaz got his head down on it all as he steamed into his rashers of bacon. Joey Olwyn sure knew how to cook a breakfast and with half a rasher in his mouth, Chaz expounded to Miko, how he wasn't going to let this one miserable blank on the water deter him.

'We've got to take everything philosophically, Miko. We're master carpers and it's all about the learning curve. Ya gotta take it all on the nose, in this game, mate!' said the wise sage as he began one of his four crispy fried eggs. He shook some salt and pepper on, before continuing his summation.

'It's like gambling. If ya can't take a losing you shouldn't be in the game. Everything in this here life of ours is a challenge, Miko, and we've got to rise and meet it! And the next time we're down here the pre-baiting will have taken effect, mate!'

'We had a take on egg shells in, Chaz! They work, mate!' Miko accentuated the positive as Chaz began the next crispy fried egg.

Joey heard Chaz saying all this, and he vowed that the bait would be going in relentlessly over the next couple of weeks. The idea being that on the third week Joey would back off, so that the carp would be on the 'egg shells in', blues and reds big time when Chaz and Miko returned. Joey said he would bait up another area to ensure the integrity of the bait boat. But Chaz was devising plans already. No, they would have to fish the carp run, but this time Miko would stand up there while Chaz put the bait boat across. That idea made Chaz excited. It showed initiative and cunning. Nothing was going to stop Chazzy Barber, nothing. Joey went out to toilet as Chaz carried on slicing up the last of the egg, before moving onto a couple of juicy looking tomatoes.

'Fucking almost worth joining to get his fucking breakfast!' Chaz said, before continuing his summation with the carp glass half full coming back to the fore again. At least 'egg shells in' had worked!

147

'Let's look on the positive side, Miko. Come a few months Joey won't be doing "any" pre-bait mate. There will be too many members down here. So, we'll kill it here next time. Fucking murder it! Joey will have rid the lake of these pestering eels and we're load up. Take a shed-full of carp! No problem, Miko!'

There was just no stopping the indomitable Chazzy Barber. He was in it for the long haul as Chaz had that mission to re-establish himself in the wider context. He just had to get one over that fucking 'One Eye'.

'We gotta get a shot of that pregnant fucker! Probably go nigh fifty now, mate, the way Joey has been banging in the high pro trout pellet!'

Talking carp could make up for times like these, when you just couldn't catch them. They blanked, but that take and into the Jag meant they were on the scent!

'He wants a fifty out as quickly as possible for his marketing, Chaz. We've got a window of opportunity!'

Chaz tucked into his fried bread and despite the knocks he was still vowing passionately, that they would indeed murder it in three weeks' time. But Miko had to make a joke about it all, to keep it light.

'You'll eat so many fucking jellied eels you'll spew, Chaz!'

'I've had me fill of fucking jellied eels, mate, I can fucking tell ya!'

Joey appeared again and was doing his best to make it all up to Chaz, and he thought he would give Chaz and Miko a free after's if they fancied it.

'Here Chaz, do ya fancy some rhubarb and custard. Had some lovely long sticks in from the allotment!'

Chaz loved his rhubarb and that Joey Olwyn was a good old stick!

Chaz arrived back at the house mid-afternoon and Linda was working in the front garden again when he pulled up. The day was humid but more overcast than of late, and straight away Linda knew that it hadn't gone as planned. Chaz had that brusque ordering tone about him, if he had caught, he would have been on cloud nine, perfect world.

'Linda! Linda! Come and give us a hand getting this fucking gear out the car will ya!'

Linda thought she would tread carefully as it had obviously been yet another dreaded blank. She put her fork down and came straight out.

'How did it go? I thought you were going to phone about the bait boat?' she asked. It was odd that the take it all philosophically on the nose approach, disappeared when Chaz came back to his castle.

'Fucking hopeless! Ya put all this effort in and what do ya get out of it? Fuck all! Nuffin' but fucking water snakes! Bootlace fucking water snakes!' Linda didn't quite understand the drift and she managed to put her foot right in it, but she was only trying to communicate around her husband's great fishing passion.

'Water snakes? I didn't think he put any of those in there.' Sometimes Linda could be as dumb as a pheasant, Chaz thought.

'Fucking eels, eels, ya stupid fucking bitch!' Linda was always apt to say the wrong thing, and she would generally compound the problem, although very innocently.

'How many did ya catch?' Chaz couldn't believe his ears. Did Linda have any tact at all? Or any intelligence?

'Are you taking the fucking piss! Ya princess piss!' Chaz could get vicious but Linda knew that she had to fight back.

'Oh Chaz. I can see you're just in a bad mood because you've blanked!' At least this time she had got it right, and that seemed to ease the tension. Chaz came on like a whining child.

'That's my eighth fucking blank in a row! It ain't fair. It ain't fucking fair! No fucking justice! And to top it all off some fucking hooligans sunk me fucking boat and then I hooked one and lost it in a fucking Jag! In a fucking Jag!' That first point was the first thing that Linda wanted to address.

'What! I thought Joey Olwyn had security fencing and guard dogs?' Linda was saying all the right things now.

'Well not enough by the looks of it, Linda! And the little shites sunk it with bricks or something!' Chaz had opened the gate and blocked it with a brick as the next hour would be the putting all the gear away hour. Linda was concerned about the incident.

'But what about that boat? That boat had a third eye camera. It cost over a grand!'

Chaz pointed out that Joey had been swell over the boat and was going to buy him another one from the superstore tomorrow, and he even said that he would order it, if they hadn't the exact same model in stock.

'Oh, that's not so bad then, Chaz. But how did they get the chance to sink it?' It was still a hot humid afternoon, and Chaz felt tired and brusque and whatever he did to alleviate the bad feelings, he couldn't escape that fact. He had blanked!

'They were forty or fifty foot up on top of a chalk face and they bombarded it the little bastards! All right, satisfied!' This kind of scenario had occurred so many times before. Linda would always say the wrong thing. She didn't mean it. She tried desperately to say the right thing and be sympathetic.

'They were only being kids, Chaz, and I remember you saying that you'd like to throw a brick through one.'

'Shut the fuck up, Linda!' Chaz said with a vicious tone of finality on the issue.

Linda didn't say much else while she helped Chaz unload all the gear, and she left him to it, festering in the shed, while she got on with making a chicken salad for tea. That evening Chaz hardly said a word as he watched the carp, while smoking joint after joint, after joint. It was one of those days that needed to end, so that you can wake up fresh tomorrow having forgotten about it. But Chaz would give his right arm and his left for a fifty! He looked up at the old photo on top of the cow's head and he could see he was certainly looking a little younger back then. He hadn't had a real big UK carp for six long years! Six bloody years! He smashed his fist on the arm of the velvet chair in anger, and then he smashed it down a second time, as he thought about that lost fish. He deserved success. He put more work in than the 'top boys'. Most of his waking hours were focused on carp, well, apart from drugs and porn and getting the knickers off young escort girls and snappy clothes and football, and gambling on football and wads of money. Perfect beautiful wads of that. But it just wasn't fair. He rolled up yet another joint, and Linda had already gotten the message, and she was thinking about retiring upstairs, to get out of his way.   But before doing so, she tried to accentuate the positive by reminding him that he had nearly caught one.

'Fucking nearly! Yeah, I'll say that to "One Eye" when he asks me if I've caught lately. I fucking nearly caught one "One Eye"!' This made Chaz remember that time he lost five grand on a horse in the Arc that was beaten a whisker on the line. Linda had replied then, that the horse ran well and 'nearly won'. Fucking 'nearly'. Chaz whacked his fist on the velvet chair yet again.

'Fucking nearly ain't good enough! I can't get a photo of "fucking nearly"! And I don't get paid out down the bookies for "fucking nearly"!'

Linda had witnessed such antics many a time, so she extracted herself from the inner sanctum, escaping upstairs for her bedtime reading. Chaz held a strawberry red 'egg shells in', between his fingers, smelling the teaser ball, approving his most wonderful freshwater muscle substitute bait.

'There's nothing wrong with our "egg shells in". They're a top bait, a fucking top bait! They just need establishing!'

Chaz dropped some baits down to the carp and Hermann promptly hoovered them up, attacking them with a relish. But that didn't stop Chaz sitting back in the chair looking completely soured. They had that monster session coming up in less than three weeks' time. He wondered if he could take a three nighter catching nothing but fucking eels. But his fears were allied by that pre-bait. You never know it might all just fall into place.

During the course of the evening, Miko phoned and put a brave face on it. They had to keep the pecker up. They would nail it next time, and although Chaz tried desperately to believe him, he feared that Blue Lake now. It was fast becoming a dark deep moody blanking lake, infested by eels. It unsettled him. Catching all those eels had somehow got into Chaz.

It was as if the carp gods were just taking the piss out of him and losing one in a fucking Jag. A blank without anything was better than that. The very thought of another darn jellied eel made him feel sick. But he cast a thought back to that rhubarb. Joey had said he would push him a few bundles of those 'lovely long sticks' next time he was down. Lovely bit of rhubarb.

CHAPTER EIGHT

THE ORCHARD AND THE PRIZE FIGHT

Linda got a taxi and met June and Debs in the foyer of the Orchard Garden. Debs was finishing her Access to University course at Tennin College and was really up for it, as she was in the process of applying for a full university place on a 'Woman's Studies' course. Debs had a faded denim jacket and matching peeked cap, both absolutely covered with feminist orientated badges, finished off with hipster faded Jeans with sewn on feminist slogans, hitched up with a combat brass bullet military belt. But she still had sparkling stilettoes on, as Debs was short and she liked the height they gave her. But those badges. Over the past six months of her relationship with Karenia she had bought hundreds. As Linda and June knew, if Debs got into something, she never did it in half measures. They certainly raised Linda's eyebrows.

'You look great, Debs,' she said politely, as Debs showed all the badges off. Debs said that they were all about women finding their voice, exactly what 'Talking Hungry Cnut' was all about. Linda looked at a few. There was 'Cunt eats Cock OK', and an in-your-face 'I castrate Dick!', accompanied with another, that was Debs' general outlook these days, 'Patriarchy, fuck off!' Linda asked her where she got all the badges from?

'Just going to feminist events with Karenia,' she replied, and both June and Linda kind of grasped that Karenia was significant these days. 'I was here last night with her. It's about time this sort of thing came to Tennin, Linda. You should see the scene with the hairy cunt costume. There's this big cock that comes on June and the cunt starts speaking and the cock runs away. It's all about the castration complex and men's fear of a cunt that talks!'

Linda was certainly surprised and she could recognize that Debs had changed some. But she had always been extreme. She was always the one of the three who drank the most, drugged it the most and both June and Linda used to speak behind her back going back in their late teens, when Debs must have got through a hundred and more one night stands, and now the extremism was her new sexual politics.

But in fact, there had been something of a local furor over the show, as many Tennin residents had complained of the advertising, with its 'Talking Hungry Cnut' posters emblazoned across Tennin. The manager of the theater had written a piece in the local defending the show on Feminist grounds, but seeing that slogan plastered everywhere across town upset the residents, as they didn't know all the fancy theories involved. But bad publicity is always good publicity, and the place was ram packed for both of its nights, and the manager felt vindicated as the show had gone down brilliantly on the first. There was a mixed-race woman selling 'Hungry Cnut!' badges and the three decided to purchase one, Deb's already had two but she wanted that one with the red slogan on a black background. Debs bought June and Linda both a programme each too, she wanted to share the love. She had one from the previous evening, and had underlined sections of it with luminous highlighter pen. She felt like a studious convert to the cause, an evangelist even. The woman gave the badges to Debs who pinned them on June and Linda's breasts. She then took her cap off and put another into the denim, and as she did so the mixed-race woman championed the badges.

'Wear them with pride! They're for a civilization where all women live in freedom! We wear them till the violence stops! Power to the cnut! Power to the hungry talking cnuts!'

'We'll still be wearing them when we're reincarnated then!' Debs roared, and June and Linda laughed as they would soon be heavily on the double vodkas, although they sensed that Debs was altogether cynical about men these days. The woman kept on selling her programmes and as she did so a number of young girls who were also advocates of Karenia, were waving and acknowledging Debs, who had become something of a local Tennin College feminist icon with her evangelical zeal for feminist badges.

'Power to the cnut! Power to the hungry cnuts!' the programme vendor kept on shouting, and it all seemed very cutting edge for Tennin. Linda was shocked to say the least, but she was also interested in reading the booklet to find out more. The three took residence on a comfy settee around a table and decided they would get as many doubles in as possible, before it all started. Debs, who was also in her mid-forties, was going through a bitter and acrimonious divorce that had been a big part of the reason, why her view of men had soured and had become rather poisonous. After the second double she had plenty to say for herself.

'They use ya like a tea bag, June! Sucking out all your flavor and then shoving ya down there with their dirty fucking pants. Yeah, they'll keep the old bag for their emotional prop and mother substitute, while they galivant around with their young fruity Earl Greys!'

All three laughed as they necked another double vodka back. But even after a half an hour, both June and Linda knew that something was definitely going on with Debs and her lecturer Karenia, as her conversation was peppered with continual references to Karenia this, and Karenia that and Karenia this again. Debs had been advised by Karenia to take some of her old friends along to the quite unmissable cutting-edge feminist event. Linda was finding it all so eye-opening. Debs was full of everything, the

T.R.F.W.L.S, a new group that had been set up by Karenia, that protested and campaigned locally in the county on cultural issues. She was itching to enlighten June and Linda regarding their many activities.

'It's been a very, very difficult period, intellectually speaking, for Karenia and the T.R.F.W.L.S, Linda.'

Linda didn't have a clue what Debs was on about.

'I hope you're not planning terrorist attacks, Debs? What on earth does that stand for?' June asked and Debs laughed. But every interaction for Debs these days was a chance to pass on the love, pass on the consciousness, as it was all about consciousness raising now, in the New Age.

'Oh, Goddess forbid, and notice the noun I've used for the head of spiritual affairs, that old bastard God has been toppled off his perch, June. He was a patriarchal construct, June, and we've got an event at the solstice at Glastonbury, worshipping the sex goddess in a few weeks' time. Here, I'll give you a flyer!'

Debs had a leather spiked backpack that was crammed full of her college work, essays, writing pad, and the like and she pulled out the flyers. Debs smiled and expounded on that abbreviation.

'The event is subsidized by the T.R.F.W.L.S, the Tennin Radical Feminist Women's Liberation society, and you've guessed what we're all about.'

Debs looked at June and Linda smugly, as if giving a chance for the uninitiated to join the clan.

'Women's liberation, Linda! Complete and utter, intellectually, spiritually, economically of course, and it's a completely orgasm chasing, pro-sex movement! And that's where Karenia has changed. We've been campaigning hard, real hard on behalf of "Candy Foxes", the lap dance and erotica club in Foxdale.'

June knew of it and she had read something about the issues in the local paper. Linda knew it too, as Chaz had been there in the past, and he had spoken about some new lucrative 'business' he had with the club owner on the weekend, but Linda didn't want to go there.

'Oh, I know, the lap dancing and gentlemen's club.'

Debs was dismissive of the language that June used.

'Oh, times have changed now, June, it's no longer a 'gentlemen's club', fucking patriarchal sexist repression, that was the old sex order!   The clubs fully inclusive and diverse these days June, after the success of Karenia's campaign. In the New Age, we've got to own our sexuality! It's our bloody right! If we want to grind our crotches in a private booth and give other services for a fee. It's our bloody right, Linda! And if a woman wants to be a slutty, whore of a sex worker, it's her bloody right too! Look at your Natasha, Linda! Karenia loves those magazine shoots she does, and she loves her gang bang films. Karenia would love to get her involved in the group. She really would! It would be good for the T.R.F.W.L.S to have active sex workers among our ranks. Look at that!'

Debs opened her jacket up, and June thought she was going to show them the results of a new enlargement, but it was the new Candy Foxes T-shirt, with a sexy image of a woman in a fox costume.

'Two years ago, Karenia was involved with the feminist fucking prude bitches, older women, fucking SWERFS! We hate them!'

'Smurfs! I thought they were those little blue creatures who live in mushroom thingies, Debs!' June had to make the joke, that only partially went down with Debs, who then looked stern and focused.

'No! Fucking "Sex Worker Exclusionary Radical Feminists!" Fucking prudes for short, fucking prudes, who can't own up to shoving a rabbit vibrator up there and getting off on it! Who wants to be a prude, Linda? We've got to own our sexual desire!'

Debs pointed between her legs before hurtling onwards, telling more of the tale of Candy Foxes.

'So, the T.R.F.W.L.S are totally pro-sex, pro-sex worker, pro-choice! And we engaged in a bitter struggle with the SWERFS, bitter, and they were fucking trying to close "Candy Foxes", but we've won! We've won! We put pressure on the local council, who were trying to close the place down, upholding the rights of sex workers, and we threatened to take them to the European Court of Human Rights! And you know what?'

June and Linda were quiet awaiting the answer from the oracle.

'Karenia was awarded a free entry pass for two, Friday night! For life! For services rendered!'

Debs took a long swig of vodka, with her eyes sparkling.

'It's wonderfully inclusive down at "Candy Foxes". Me and Karenia have two hot girls dance for us, each time we go down there, we get buy one get one free, as a special reward, *and* we have "other" services. We're not prudes! I bet your Chaz would agree with me, Linda! If you're against "Candy Foxes", you're a prude and anti-sex! And who wants to be seen as sexless? And prominent local female doctors and nurses can be seen down there. Doing the same thing that me and Karenia are doing. Standing up for their bloody right to get horny and fucking turned on! They buy one get one free too!'

Debs looked straight into Linda's eyes trying to penetrate deeply, trying to speak to an inner lesbian desire that Linda might have, hoping that Linda might see the light and join the Tennin Feminist radicals with Debs and Karenia.

'It's the New Age, Linda. It's all about pushing the boundaries, finding new ways of relating! New ways of expressing our desire!'

Linda had heard that sort of thing before. Debs soon opened up on the programme, as it operated like a tract for staunch believers.

'Oh, this is great! This is what Karenia's into!' Debs enthused. She continued, animated, with yet more vodka appearing from June. 'Here, listen to this! I'll be able to quote it in my final essay! Early Christians worshipped Sophia as the female Holy Spirit and also believed that Mary Magdelene, the former prostitute, was the wisest, I repeat the wisest June, of Christ's disciples.'

'That's because she must have known them inside out with all the shagging!' June joked, and they all cried with laughter, as more vodka was necked back. But Debs kept on, presenting her information as if it was a revelation of some ancient esoteric teaching, that had been miraculously dug up on this girls' night out in the Orchard Garden.

'And Tantric Buddhism still teaches that Buddhahood, and exalted states of consciousness reside up the cunt! Fancy that eh, spirituality up our cunts!' Debs was inspired, over the last six months she had fully subsumed the consciousness. 'And you know they've gotta control that kind of cunt, Linda, because they're frightened, it might bite their bloody cocks off!'

They all laughed again as another double vodka went back and all had drunk enough to really let go, but not enough to go ruin the night. Debs turned directly to Linda, full of passionate energy, wondering what she thought about it all. Debs felt like a feminist lay preacher, disseminating the new truths to her old friends.

'Yeah, it's interesting, Debs,' Linda replied, and she certainly hadn't seen anything like this before. June took Debs' hat off and posed with it on and Debs put up a quick photo on her top-of-the-range mobile. Debs thought that Linda might be helped by doing the same access course that she'd been on. Share the love, eh? Linda, like Debs, only had a secondary education and Debs could clearly see, it just wasn't good enough in the New Age. There were so many new complex issues to think about in the 'Postmodern, Post Patriarchal Age'. The course she was on had got her over this acrimonious break up too. It had truly enlightened her.

'It's eye-opening going back to college, Linda. You must go! You must! It's all so different now! The world's changing, Linda. Who's the leader of the Tennin Council, its first ever woman and Sally bloody Brockett. We all remember Sally Brockett walking through Tennin with fucking Durex hanging off her jacket with suspenders on. And she used to put it about a bit. Didn't she, June?'

'Well I wouldn't want to bitch about women being slags, Debs. But she was a right ol' one! Right ol' one!'

Debs nodded her head, feeling smug and she had more to say about Sally Brockett.

'And keep it quiet the both of you, won't you. Karenia was seeing her a few years ago. Met her at Uni when Brockett was doing an MA. She's a fucking kinky drugs fiend. You wouldn't dream of what she got up to with Karenia, June. But it's sexual desire, Linda! It's the New Age. We don't wanna be prude bitches like them fucking SWERFS!'

June was chiming in with a few memories of the young punk rocker Sally. Linda knew her well too and had said to Chaz that it was something of an achievement that she educated herself through university, becoming an accountant and then ending up where she had. The first female Conservative head of Tennin Council. Chaz was just happy he had one on her with her penchant for dabbling with Peruvian. But Debs had plenty more to say for herself.

'And I think a bit like Karenia now, Linda. You should hear her lecture. Oh. She's fantastic! Fantastic, Linda. All the truth has been repressed by men and men in power, June. All women's truths. It's been a patriarchy and historically our identities have been crushed by men. Fucking crushed. We're told how to be this, how to be that, how to think this and how to shag like that! Fucking men! They squeeze us out like fucking tea bags! Fucking tea bags!'

Linda didn't really understand all these intellectual concepts but she replied that she certainly understood something about being told!

'Hark at the hairy-lipped feminist!' June added, and they all roared again. Linda noticed too that Debs was a little more intimate with the way she touched, while she was speaking to her. She couldn't help but realize the big change. This new all-faded denim and feminist slogan look hit everybody in the face but that didn't stop Debs displaying her ample cleavage to all and a sundry. Debs was also into 'Free Love' these days, that was what Karenia was into, but only with those who took up the feminist cudgels. Although Karenia, who was also bisexual, thought it acceptable, that on occasions when the sex hormones were truly raging, you could 'use' men for their cocks. That was only fair, she had said to Debs. But do it only occasionally, she had advised, when you fancy a bit. Debs was still full of the booklet. She turned a page and began to read it out loud again, as it was all so relevant to where she was in her life right now.

'And it says here, "as a result, we women are born through the word and voice of man, who will even promise our rebirth into his everlasting life while he also decides, how 'we' as women should experience our bodily rhythms and menstrual cycles". Huh! Sounds suspiciously like fucking cunt-head Rick and thank God, that I can talk of him as an 'X' factor these days, Linda. At least I've got something to thank God for! Another vodka? It'll take a couple more yet to get the bastard out of my mind!'

June and Linda both laughed, but they also knew that Debs was going through the bitterest of divorces. It was spitting fire at each other stuff and one of the main reasons was his treachery, his betrayal. She discovered that he'd been having an affair for eight years with her closest friend and confidante, Lorraine. The whole affair had soured her and made her a little twisted. Debs went to the bar for yet another round of doubles, and June was left with Linda.

'Debs has changed a lot since I saw her last, Ju. I hope she ends up happy,' Linda said, sincerely. June agreed and she thought the changes were mainly due to the course and the divorce.

'But she's bisexual now, she told me in the foyer before you arrived, found that with this Karenia woman. I think she's late twenties.' June enjoyed the gossip. 'She's still full of fun though. Same old Debs really! But you seem a little quiet tonight, Linda? As if you seem worried for some reason.'

June had known Linda since they were at primary school, so she knew her well. They also knew Debs from back in those days, so they could always confide in each other.

'Just relax, Linda,' June reassured, 'the reviews say it's hilarious! And they get the whole audience shouting out "Hairy Cunt OK!" and "Bite that cock off!" Debs has been telling me. It'll be a right laugh! And they do a lot for women who are abused all the world over with the charity, and you can see by Debs, it's deep too!' It certainly was the new world opening for Linda but the problem was Chaz.

'What's the problem, Linda?' June asked sympathetically. There was a short pause, and Linda looked downwards first, as if a revelation was in the offing. As if something excessively personal and difficult was coming. June was certainly expecting it. Then it came out.

'It's this boxing prize fight thing he's gone to. He gambles heavily, and he'll be in a stinker if he loses. He was bad enough on the weekend after he blanked with his carping, June. And we've spent tons of money lately, June, tons!'

June knew about these events. Chaz had lost big on occasion, but had generally won big at them. But June knew that Chaz was unlike her Ray, who merely liked to have his harmless flutter. For Chaz it was all about being a big shot gambler. It gave him the chance to strut around in that white blazer and flash wads of money about.

'Well you'll just have to make it up to him if he loses his gorillas!' June suggested. But Linda wasn't sure about sex with Chaz anymore. When was the last time they just had sex with intimacy? All he wanted to do was these twisted films in that Dark Room that he coerced Linda into. Linda was fed up with it all. It was making her feel sick thinking about it.

'Have I? And it's a monkey by the way. Five hundred pounds!'

'Well the monkey's then, but I thought you had a fulfilled and varied sex life, Linda?'

Linda wondered why June had ever garnered that impression, but June was left with a feeling that Linda's marriage was ailing, rapidly.

'Huh! It would be nice if he was closer, if you know what I mean, June.'

As Linda looked into the last drop of her double vodka, she wondered if she too was going to end up like Debs, with a messy and bitter divorce. She didn't want that, but things were getting strained. She knew it was on the cards. She finished the double, and why not get to the bar and get another one in? She wanted to let go, cut loose tonight!

The night proper hadn't started as yet at Tennin's Orchard Gardens, but it had at the prize fight venue. Chaz liked these unlicensed shows. He liked the buzz and it was all about the betting. Chaz had been to a couple of dozen over the years and he was a well-known regular, striding around in the 'work' gear, enjoying that big money, gambling status, 'buying a pig in a poke'. Chaz liked to play to a certain mythology regarding his status and he would punt on the one boxer, as if he was the real deal discriminatory gambler. Up to this point it had worked well. People spoke about Chaz Barber, that bloke in the white blazer, who was lumping on, as if it all meant something and therefore Chaz played on it all, as it puffed him up into feeling like a big shot.

People were watching and whispering as Chaz strode up towards the bookmaker on the premises, Jimbo, who was well known for attending these prize fight nights and could always be seen at local dog tracks and on the rails at the all-weather racing. There was a full house and a bout was taking place, but Chaz wouldn't take a blind bit of notice of those. He would just get into the bout that he was laying the money down on, the big bout, and then sort the other things out, the other attractions, that would take place at the venue. Jimbo was in his late sixties and had been in the game all his life. He worked with his son who was the clerk.

'Hullo, Jimbo! Will ya lay me a dozen monkeys. Yeah six big uns on Phelps?

Phelps was fighting in the main betting event of the evening. It was Phelps, the cultured boxer with a long reach, the young gun, up against the animal banger, 'The Cannibal', who was in his early fifties, but was known to have one of the hardest punches around. He was also as strong as an ox and nearly made it into the UK strongest man series on television. He lost out by a whisker and spiraled into depression thereafter, as he thought it might raise his profile and catapult him into the big time. But this bout was another great opportunity for 'The Cannibal', with its eight-grand purse for the winner, but only two for the loser. When the bout was made it was an instant sell out, as the young twenty-four-year-old Phelps was thought to be a star in the making. He was debating whether or not to turn pro, but his old man had a profitable garage business and it suited him just boxing as a money-making hobby, because he was expected to sort out the garage grind, now his Dad had been diagnosed with bowel cancer. But at this level, things were markedly in his favor. He was a fitness fanatic so he was always fitter than his opponents. It gave him that confidence, and he had been a more than capable amateur boxer too, even winning ABA junior titles and fighting the Olympic Games champion in the seniors final some six years ago where he was closely outpointed. But Jimbo didn't seem perturbed at all in taking Chaz's big bet. He had Phelps marked up at two to one on but offered Chaz more with 'The Cannibal' at seven to four.

'They reckon "The Cannibal's" up for it so you can have that at four to six, Chaz. It's all yours, Chaz!' Chaz couldn't believe his luck. He asked for another two big uns. Jimbo very nigh bit his hand off taking the money. Chaz reckoned that would be a lovely five grand plus in the bin and for what?

'That's great, Jimbo! You're a great layer! But Phelps will box his head off. No problem. Be like taking candy from a big fat pensioner!' Jimbo's son listed the bet as the last of the eight-grand wad of cash was handed over and counted.

'It's all about opinions and laying the money down, Chaz. He's a sly old fox that Cannibal. He's got that big punch power, Chaz, and he's actually been training hard for this.'

Everyone gave heed to the transaction. Chaz had eight big uns on Phelps. It was around the arena like wildfire! Chaz sauntered back over to the bar area not taking a blind bit of notice of the bout that was bumbling on depressively. It was all about Phelps and 'The Cannibal', and winning five big ones, 'easy money'. Chaz fully expected a ton of money being laid down on Phelps, now the oracle had spoken. It usually went like that. Chaz was soon ensconced at the bar knocking back the whiskey chasers with Miko. He had the Jag outside but he was a responsible driver. He would never drink drive, or shall we say, get well pissed and drive. Chaz could take his drink and he was preening, and boasting to Miko about the bet. Miko was much more reserved with his gambling. He was there for the social thing. But for Chaz it was all about cementing his big shot astute gambler status. He explained the going in big.

'We've had nearly a hundred new takers on the site the last couple of weeks so Phelps has got a pack on monkeys, yeah eight big uns riding on his back at four to six. I thought I'd be lucky to get three's on!' Miko thought the bet rather excessive. He wasn't overly sure about Phelps either. Had he ever taken a massive shot like 'The Cannibal' had? Take one of them and you'll be amongst the stars.

'Well let's pray the night don't make a monkey out of you, Chaz,' Miko replied, knowing full well that it might, although Chaz was completely dismissive.

'Oh, leave it out, Miko! There's no way Phelps can lose to that fat git, no way! He's too fit and fast and can actually box a bit. He could be world top ten licensed and he's a fitness fanatic. Ran that Johnson close as an amateur and he's got a shot at the WBC title! Ya always see him jogging and popping out lefts and rights, through the village. The guy can't stop training! Good professional attitude. That young man is solid and he's got that pop, pop, left jab and long reach. And look at "The Cannibal", the fat fucking bastard. It would take him all day to walk to the fucking convenience store and he would probably buy a six pack and a bottle of vodka when he got down there, the fucking piss-head!'

But Miko knew that 'The Cannibal' had a hell of a punch.

'Cannibal's a banger though Chaz and hands of stone! He's been known to knock opponents out cold. You've seen him do it!'

Chaz had at that, but he was still dismissive. Phelps would jab his head off with that snappy left hand he had, and then line him up for the straight right.

'Fucking older than me! And he trains down the Boar's Head!'

Miko thought that he would take the conversation away from the fight. At the end of the day he couldn't care less who won, although he didn't want to see Chaz lose eight grand.

'Anyhow, where's the golden shower and enema girl tonight then, Chaz?' Chaz got concerned.

'Keep it down Miko! Make sure ya keep all that a little secret between best mates'

Miko apologized, but he said he could rely on him. He had known him for forty years! They went to primary school together.

'She's gone on a girls' night out with June and that fucking monster, Debs.' How Chaz detested Debs. He had seen her in that jacket and hat, the all-faded denim look, and had told Linda. 'She looked like the pearly fucking queen Linda!'

But his hatred of her was something unconscious as much as anything. He could see that she was getting bang into things going to college. She was full of it the last time he saw her about six months back. No, he didn't want her influencing Linda.

'One of these male stripper nights or something. Does her good. Probably all suck cock one after another, and she can go where she wants by me, Miko, as long as I can film it and sell it!'

Chaz said that he was only joking. Linda was a great woman, but he didn't really like her going out with that Debs. June wasn't a problem. It was just that Debs. 'I'm sure she's a lesbian, Miko. Nailed on! And a fucking trouble maker if ever I saw one! Full of daft fucking ideas!'

That afternoon, TV sent another message to Freeda, delivered by the Lorenzo Drill method. After the debacle that followed the first message between Nurse Lavender and Freeda, it had been decided that Lorenzo would still continue his duties, as he swore to Dr. Lock that he didn't take anything in. But minders of Freeda in the lounge had to watch that Drill with beady eyes when he rattled in his tea trolley. Freeda dominated the lounge as usual, playing some of her pop favorites this time. It was the Spice Girls and '2 Become 1' about a dozen times and then she done the same thing with 'Come to my Window' as she sat looking out of the window, thinking and dreaming incessantly of TV.

But when Lorenzo did appear, Freeda was as per normal, listening to the old ones again. This time it was a Rat Pack CD, the type of thing that her mother used to play incessantly back in the day, and was again something that Kleeunah had gradually teased from her. Freeda sat completely fixated with a continuous smile on her face, as she enjoyed the warmth that seemed to come from the voice of Dean Martin. It was something she wanted to cling on to, like a raft when shipwrecked out on the Atlantic. There was too much that was simply awful.

'Hullo Freeda! Feeling all right?' Drill-head said. Lorenzo had taken orders from TV to stick the note underneath the large cup with some blue tack. It was a risky move for Drill, but TV gave him a fiver for it, so he took the chance. Twenty fags were on. The minder was a new agency worker and he didn't notice it, and he didn't notice Drill's subtle wink to Freeda either. As soon as Freeda got the coffee, she realized what it was all about.

'Look TV's by the tree!' she blurted out and the minder's attention was diverted, and Freeda successfully tucked the note in her trouser pocket. The minder and Drill-head looked out, and obviously, Lorenzo knew what Freeda was doing.

'Nah I don't think he is, Freeda. Looks like "Long Neck" and "Sidewinder",' Drill said, referring to the two figures that were out there smoking by the tree.

'That fucking Long Neck cunt! He owes me five fags, Drill! He fucking nicked um off me, the cunt!' Freeda snapped, although she smiled to Lorenzo and it was all lost on the agency minder. He was merely gauging the acceptability or otherwise of Freeda's interactions and he asked Freeda politely not to swear in the lounge. She sneered back at him. 'That fucking Long Neck owes me five fags! Cunt!' It was getting close to that 'one shot' of TV Sam's.

During the evening, TV and Dan took to the table tennis table, as was generally their thing of an evening to keep things active. There were a few other patients sitting around and Dan was hitting the ball and TV was exclaiming 'ping', and then when he hit it, it was 'pong'. It was a generally accepted convention between the two, that the one winning easily would do it to take the piss. On this occasion TV was winning by a clear five points, although they were generally evenly matched as Dan had some surprisingly nifty little skills.

'I've sent another message via the carrier pigeon.'

TV couched the information in a little code, but he was still wary of the minder, so he kept it down. Dan was still playing away and he immediately recognized the need to keep it between the two of them.

'I thought the pigeon said he weren't gonna fly anymore, TV?' Dan said, fully on point with the necessary morse. A point was won by TV and TV came to a halt for a moment with a smirk on his face.

'Even pigeons take flight when ya give um the best feed, Dan!' TV joked, and Dan got the gist of it all. But then TV became more intimate and confidential, as the coast became clear when the auxiliary nurse exited for a quick toilet.

'Been finking, Dan. If there was a God, surely God wouldn't want ta see Freeda so unhappy. After everything she's gone through, surely God would allow her to be blessed for a day, even if God couldn't make the feeling last for long.' It all seemed an odd thing to say Dan thought, but he done his best with the reply.

'God ought to bless her TV. He really should!'

'That's what I fink, Dan, and surely God could work through me if I try stuff!'

Dan thought it all sounded a bit portentous. TV served and served out the mystery for the time being.

'We're going tonight at three twenty-eight!'

Dan looked puzzled. Why on earth that time? Then TV told him about the big electrical storm that was forecast during the night, and on the weather at the end of the news, they said it was coming in between three and four a.m. TV said the time just came into his head! Out the blue. Out of the ether! Things were like that with Dragon Star. They just happened and obviously three twenty-eight was important for some reason. Maybe if he set out at a few minutes later they wouldn't get away.

'Three twenty-eight is fate and destiny, Dan. Three twenty-nine! Who knows? Down the can!' TV Sam gestured with a thumbs down and laughed.

Dan smiled and laughed but he was worried. He didn't think it was possible, and he thought that it meant TV would definitely be transferred. But TV was on his 'one shot' mission head, and was nothing but confident.

'The atmospherics are auspicious ya might say, Dan. Bang! Thunder and sheets of rain. Get up and watch from your window, Dan,' TV suggested cockily. Dan laughed and the game broke down, but it all troubled him. TV was such a great friend and was a legend, but that system with 'The Fuhrer' in place seemed all powerful to Dan. It would get cha in the end. Then the nurse appeared back in the games room.

Back at the Tennin Orchard Garden theatre, all three of the women were seated and looking on with excitement and interest, as a black actress was giving her insightful monologue, in what was an intimate setting. They were quiet now, but initially June remarked that it was like somebody talking to you in your front room. It seemed that intimate and personal. The black American actress was late thirties and came across as totally believable, and her story just grew and built to its epiphanies.

'Now men can't love a cunt unless they love pubic hair. They need to raise an altar to the sexiness, the eroticism of pubic hair. And I don't care if they get loose hairs stuck down their throat. They like getting their dicks stuck down ours, don't they?' The audience howled with laughter and there was that recognition that this show was speaking the unspeakable. She continued. 'No, if they don't like a hairy cunt my intuition tells me it's the castration complex, kicking in. They don't want it bitten off, now that could be metaphorical or actual! And that's the only bit of Freud this girl guide is ever gonna take notice off!' There was another great raucous chorus of laughter. The black actress took a sip of water from a glass on a small table before launching herself into further testimony.

'Anyhow, my first and only husband to date, yes I'm still looking for my King Solomon of a man. You know, one who might take me via this hairy, hungry talkative cunt of mine to the seventh heaven or someplace "other".'

Debs smiled at Linda as if to say, yes, this is what she was bang into now, and Linda was absorbed as she wanted to know where it would all lead. The black actress commanded the space and you could hear a pin drop.

'But that first husband, I'll get back to him, he absolutely hated pubic hair. He said it was unladylike, dirty and smelt in a way that he didn't like. Of course, I had to be ladylike enough not to mention his smelly feet and smelly fucking dick!' The laughter went up again and when it died the actress continued, knowing full well that she had the audience in the palm of her hand.

'So boy, did I go through some vaginal deodorant to try and please him. I used so much; I must have paid for the shareholder's dividend.'

The crowd, who were virtually all women, apart from the odd one or two, were warming to her monologue with much hilarity and the laughter was infectious. Although, there was an awareness of the deeper currents that were being intimated.

'So, he made me shave my vagina or "cunt" should we say, as were talking hairy hungry cunts here tonight!'

Her flourish got another chorus of laughter and the openness just made the crowd wanting to respond and laughter was a means of dealing with it.

'But I hated shaving it. Some women might like that sort of thing, but I hated it. And it was the power thing. And now looking back, knowing my castration Freud, I hate it even more. But I done it back then out of some kind of skewed matrimonial duty or something. And shaving it made me feel, well, like a little girl, maybe not quite a little girl, but "girlish", yes like a little girl!' she added, with the last spoken, as if her husband had turned her back into a little girl. The audience were riveted and full of anticipation, as the actress took another swig of water before continuing.

'So then, I refused to shave it. Flatly, I told him straight. It makes me feel like a little girl, I said. And do you know what he says, kind of ironically, "well that's precisely what I want you to feel like, my darling". But I knew deep down that exactly what he did mean. And something just switched on like a light bulb of new consciousness. I saw it all!'

Linda was utterly absorbed in the testimony, as all the audience were. The way the story was being told, it spoke to everybody about that moment, that very moment, when you realize for the first time, that some person has been controlling you and thereafter the game is up. That's the old world and it's under threat from a new.

'I didn't shave it and unbeknown to me, he began seeing this young hot thing about nineteen who *was* into shaving it. But I still refused to shave my lovely hairy cunt. I was getting a little stubborn by then. And do you know what? Within a couple of weeks, I find myself thinking and talking differently. Up to this point I had been talking like a baby in the bedroom. I didn't realize how childlike I'd become. But now I know different.'

The actress gathered herself for a display of defiance that took the crowd further into paroxysms.

'If only I'd known then what I know now! I'd have taunted him. "Afraid of getting your precious dicky bitten off eh? My big hairy cunt will just suck it in and chew it ta bits. Yes, I got you babe! My cunt's got teeth! I dare ya ta stick it up there! I dare ya!"'

Some of the women were in tears laughing, and June hollered while Debs squeezed Linda's thigh rather intimately, just for a second out of friendship, with a little hope that she might find another Linda, who could join her in her great quest. The black actress returned to her monologue after the laughter quietened.

'His teen queen, well she obviously got the hots for some younger cock elsewhere, and he comes crawling back to me, wanting me to shave again. And that's when I let him get inside my head again. He even talked me around to go to therapy regarding our love life. Shit! I must have been nuts! The therapist, she tells me, I should compromise, marriage is all about the big compromise, so shave it, leave the tiniest little line or something, you know, like they do on some of the more refined porn! And she says, with a great knowing wink between sisters as it were, that sometimes we've all got to box hedge clip wild nature as she called it!'

There was yet another uproar of laughter, before the crowd settled a little and she continued.

'So, he virtually press-gangs me to get his own way and yes, I go back on myself and shave it and get so psychologically fucking screwed up, I even start talking like a child again. And that's when I had yet another epiphany. I saw him as he really, really is, with my little ole third eye camera. And he was so ugly, like a jailer, and I knew just where he wanted me in his great scheme of thing. Behind his bars!'

The audience were transfixed and it was like a moment of revelation for Linda. Put like this she could understand how men could control women through subtle psychological ploys in relationships, and there was that serendipity moment of the third eye camera. It felt so uncanny. The actress carried on towards the inevitable punch line. The grand epiphany, where there would be light in the crown and those snakes would be seeing things.

'You know you have to love hair, to love the cunt and to love us women you have to love us as we are. And we have to find out who we are, find ourselves, not be told by men. And the best men are those who want us to find that space, real space, where we can find that out, because then they might meet "The real woman". The ex-husband, he's three years into a ten year stretch for screwing around with a twelve-year-old. Guess that's what he wanted to do all the time.'

There was a thunderous applause at the end of the monologue. The women were all up out of their seats, including Linda and friends. Debs looked overjoyed. It was like a revelation to behold and Debs pointed out that everything in the production was true, derived from personal testimonies of women to the writer, Shrew Jezeb, a pseudonym for Jennifer Cartwright, who was a Berkeley lecturer and feminist psychoanalyst. It all more than spoke to Linda. It was the timing as it were, in the context of her life, and it blew her away and when they came out of the theatre, she quite enjoyed Debs' surreptitious squeeze of her buttocks as the giggling effusive three headed for 'The Stage', a pub close by.

Back at the prize fighting venue, Chaz was still ensconced at the bar while yet another under card brawl was taking place. Would you believe it he was talking to that young blonde lap dancer/escort girl Brooke? There was always a group of girls who would work these shows. It was the first one that Brooke had done with her escort agency and as soon as she spotted Chaz, she made a beeline. Chaz brought her a drink and was quickly down to business. He fancied a bit of Brooke so why not purchase it, and he was talking about a prospective meeting for one afternoon, next week at her place.

'Well it'll have to be "ins" Brooke and both the numbers with any added extras to my taste for the money I'm paying.'

Brooke, who was showing more than enough of her supplemented cleavage was very accommodating. Her friend had spoken to her about Chaz and his money, and that he attended these boxing events. Brooke had the antennae up for him as soon as she arrived, 'that Chaz guy with the white blazer' and she zeroed in on him. She saw for her own eyes down at Candy Foxes, that this guy had money. That jacket and those shoes and the Rolex watch and all that gold. Everything was confirmed when he bought her a drink and pulled out an enormous bundle of fifties. Phew! That guy had some and Brooke would accommodate anything to get a piece of that action. Chaz had dispensed with that eight-grand, yet still had around four on him after coming out with nigh twelve. He just loved giving off that air that he was one of the super-rich. Did any of Chaz's old mates have nigh nine hundred grand tied up in Swiss bank accounts? Sex and money, sex and money, goes together like the bees and honey, fish and chips and strawberries and cream.

Brooke had been so impressed by Chaz and she was determined to bag him as a regular punter. Once a week or even once a fortnight, and she would bag three or four hundred or so, because didn't he say he liked to relax for a few hours with 'up for it' girls? But Chaz just loved that feel of a wad of fifties in his pocket. If you want a bit of fanny, well the rich can just buy it at whim, thought Chaz. Radical Feminism or no bloody feminism. Money spoke in the Old world and money speaks in the New.

'I like to keep all of my clients very happy so they come back Chaz, and I just love a throat fuck, I love it!' Brooke said, giving Chaz a big come on with her glossy plump red lips. Chaz was impressed. She had a dirty smile and dirty mind, and he slipped her a half a dozen or so fifties and put his hand up the inside of her leg. Chaz was hot and his fingers were probing. The dalliance was then interrupted by Miko, who had returned from the toilets. He had a serious and concerned look on his face.

'Bad news from the bogs, Chaz. I was speaking with 'One Eye'.

Chaz withdrew a little from Brooke, as he knew that 'One Eye' was speaking to Miko, so that what he had on his mind, would be passed onto Chaz. It went like that with 'One Eye'. Brooke took to chewing a cherry on a stick, trying to look as voluptuous as possible. Chaz had arranged his deal with Brooke for the night. One of Chaz's special little 'turn on' deals. But he dealt with this issue first, regarding the detested 'One Eye'.

'What, had that pregnant virgin away from the Blue Lake?

Chaz obviously knew full well that 'One Eye' hadn't forked out the eight hundred and fifty as yet. He kept relentlessly fishing that 'Ressie', because it was cheap on his pocket, the skinflint. But there was a more disturbing, deeper undercurrent moving.

'Nah, Chaz, says he's been laying into 'The Cannibal' big time. Had five grand on him at six to four!'

Chaz gulped and strutted that neck a few times. This was more than significant. Chaz couldn't believe what he was hearing. 'One Eye' was a small gambler.

'"One Eye"'! That prick bets in fivers!'

Jimbo had taken the bet as well, deciding that he would merely try and balance his books. He had won big on every bout up until the last and wanted to get out ahead.

The escort girl was looking on and paying attention wondering what the commotion was all about as she sipped her cocktail. Chaz had paid her off to just hang around all night and allow him to touch her up, finger her a bit and squeeze, whatever and whenever he wanted. Chaz liked that sense of entitlement, so he bought it, hard cash. It was all designed to get Chaz hot for that two or three-hours next Tuesday afternoon at her flat. But Chaz was anticipating a certain release after the Boxing show too.

'Well that's what he laid down. Apparently, Phelps has been smoking skunk weed like a demon after a break up with his girlfriend. I don't know where the rumors came from, but everybody is just piling into "The Cannibal".'

Chaz looked visibly ruffled. This wasn't normal, and so he thought on his feet, and had a way of at least retrieving most of his money.

'Miko! Get down there for me and go three grand "The Cannibal". Get some of that fucking money back!'

By now Brooke didn't really understand what was occurring. She just sipped her cocktail, smiled, and thought she would help by slipping her hand under Chaz's arse, giving his balls and cock a pull. It did help but Miko returned quickly with some bad, bad news.

'Jimbo's not taking him anymore. He's only laying Phelps and he's gone out to three to one. It's a free fall and nobody wants him, Chaz!'

Chaz looked as if Death was stalking him, and to make matters worse that fucking 'One Eye' would have a whopping great win on 'The Cannibal'. But Brooke had made his penis erect and he made sure it would keep it up with a blue one. Chaz and Miko went down towards the ring apron with Brooke in tow. Chaz was nigh on a prayer now.

It was clear from the opening bell that Phelps wasn't on his game. His timing was out, he was huffing and puffing worse than the fifty-one-year-old 'Cannibal', who looked overweight, but he seemed inspired as he sensed that Phelps was 'off'. 'The Cannibal' had some debts to pay a coke dealer, incidentally the Waterside Boys outfit, although he had been clean for the training period, the last two months. But he was going flat out for the win. Eight grand in the bin, three to the Waterside Boys, and on the straight and narrow with all his debts paid off, and three grand left to play with. He was darn ponderous and certainly no technician, but my, he was scoring with some almighty swinger body shots in the first round. There were three noticeable ones, and when they nailed Phelps there were audible gasps from the crowd.

'He's a banger, Chaz!' Miko reiterated, and the writing was on the wall just two minutes into the fight. The escort girl who was right there with them down the front realized that Chaz was going to lose and she also caught the drift that there was a certain depth to his finance, otherwise he wouldn't have cared a shit.

The beating got worse in the second round. Chaz was willing Phelps to get that famed jab going but he was jabbing air most of the time or colliding with the Cannibal's gloves. His head and his body weren't right. 'The Cannibal' oozed confidence and he began just walking Phelps down, virtually teeing him up, and when a bout is like that, well the end is nigh, and 'The Cannibal' always had a concussive punch. Crunching blow after crunching blow rained down. 'One Eye', looking from the other side of the ring, had an enormous grin on his face that was edging towards sheer ecstasy and Chaz noticed it. 'One Eye' had inside information on this one. One of his friends was the father of the girl Phelps was still in mourning for.

Another donkey kick punch caught Phelps chin and then another in his stomach. Phelps had never been knocked down as an amateur in over a hundred fights or in unlicensed shows, and he tried desperately to prevent it, and you sensed watching the slaughter that when he did finally go, he would be comatose. It was like the Titanic. Chaz was incensed. Eight-grand! Eight big ones! He had *never* lost eight-grand at a boxing show. He just had to show that wanker Phelps just how he felt, to get something off his chest. Phelps was a disgrace.

'You wanker, Phelps! You fucking puff head wanker! Losing to a fat fucking grandad! Ya fucking tosser!'

Yet another sidewinder bomb whistled through the air and missed by a mile, but then another came across and landed smack into Phelps jaw and down he went. That was it. They would need smelling salts to get him up. Chaz was giving him the wanker sign as the ref counted him out. He could have counted three hundred, and a lot of people were worried, before he finally came around and got to his feet. The crowd cheered with their prayers answered, Phelps was alive and they hadn't witnessed a nigh manslaughter, but what an awful display. Phelps stunk the place out.

'Should have stayed there, ya fucking wanker!' shouted a disgruntled Chaz. Chaz returned to the bar speechless, and he decided that he would leave immediately. He could gain a little recompense with an aggressive throat fuck over the heath with the escort girl. He had paid her well enough. Of course, Linda didn't know all this business with escort girls went on at these shows. But it was all out of sight and mind. Brooke had gone to the women's toilet and Chaz was having a goodbye to Miko.

'Jilted fucking Phelps! The fucking tosser with his puppy love. He's cost me eight G, Miko! And do ya think I would have put a penny on the bastard, if I'd known he had been puffing skunk like a fucking demon!' Chaz was going purple with rage, because when he got animated like this, his blood pressure would go right through the roof.

'One of those, Chazzy. Take ya frustrations out on the escort girl over the heath, mate.'

Chaz took yet another blue pill out of his white blazer, and kept up a bit of bravado to Miko by taking it with a swig of beer.

'Get on it!' he growled, but it didn't stop him noticing that 'One Eye' with his wide grin, looking like the Cheshire cat, collecting that dough from Jimbo, and being paid out with Chaz's fifties. 'One Eye' obviously knew what had occurred, and he was looking over to Chaz relishing the moment, that 'Sweeny Todd' as he called Chaz, was floundering like a beached walrus or even a Phelps! The indignity of it all, and knowing that 'One Eye' had taken seven and a half grand profit. Chaz had as good as lost his dough to the bastard and it hurt bad. 'One Eye' wasn't a 'proper' gambler. The wanker!

The escort girl came out of the toilets smiling. She had made a good night's money out of Chaz, and she didn't have to do much, and she had snorted his coke all night long. She liked a bit of that. The idea was that Chaz would drop her off, but not before stopping over the heath, and she could give him that head and he could go down on her with a bit of frigging. That was the deal, then all the other things were to be played out with a few visits to her flat over the next couple of weeks. 'Sorted!' Brooke was determined to bag Chaz as a regular, so she was up for the deep throat and Chaz felt the urge to be aggressive. 'Sorted!' again, but Chaz was still eight-grand out of pocket! And man did that hurt!

They had already dropped Debs off, and June and Linda were in the cab approaching Holly Beach Lane. Linda was animated about the show.

'It wasn't what I expected, but I thought it was great, June. I really did. Eye-opening. It made me think I suppose.'

They were both a little drunk still, as they topped up with a few more vodkas in 'The Stage', a pub by the theater. There were a couple of young guys in there, giving the three attention and June loved it, and Linda enjoyed the confirmation that young men still found her sexy. Debs had asked both to accompany her and Karenia, to Glastonbury for the weekend in July, although it was more out of hope than anything. But Linda was interested, it just sounded so different. On the way home, June and Linda were being a bit loud in the cab and it induced raised eyebrows on the Asian driving.

'You'll be able to get home to Chaz and tell him about how ya cunt has started hungry talking! I can't wait to tell Ray about it! And watch it. It might bite your cock off!' They both roared with laughter, but Linda's reply seemed to intimate towards deeper currents in the relationship.

'He wouldn't listen to me, Ju. He likes to tell me.'

Linda was rather stumbling her way up the path, but she had really enjoyed herself. She made herself a cup of coffee, and had the booklet in her hand; as despite the way she was feeling, she was captivated by it. It spoke of different worlds and something within her had been stirred, and she couldn't help but be interested by those ideas of sacred sex that Debs was on about. It seemed better than what she was having with Chaz. That was making her feel dirty, unwholesome. By accident she caught her elbow on Chaz's carp mug that sat by the sink as she read. It fell to the floor and smashed.

'Oh my God, I've broken king carp!' Linda was so pissed she just laughed it all off. 'He'll go mad! The carp king broken!' she exclaimed, but she was so drunk, she didn't seem to care.

Although Chaz could obviously get another, this was the original, that held much symbolic and emotional significance. It was an essential bit of the life story. The very first king carp mug. It was a landmark, and Linda picked up all the broken pieces and swept all the smaller chips into a dust pan. That was the least she could do. She staggered into the lounge, and sat herself down on the velvet chair and promptly spilt her coffee all over it. She swore, and then her focused attention went onto the fish tank with Hermann by the red telephone box. She stood up quickly, made a grab for a boilie container, and plopped half a dozen down to Hermann, who hoovered them up like a glutton with 'The Beak' hot on his tail. Linda turned up her face in disgust.

'Addicted! Making them addicted just like fucking me!'

Linda went over to the Waldorf and plonked herself down. She began flicking through the booklet, stopped on a page and began reading. She was still fascinated by it, and a host of the evening's memorable phrases, were flitting through her mind. She could hear Debs voice that now seemed even louder and even more committed.

'Men are always telling us who we are! That's how they keep their power over us, Linda!' These were ideas that were making Linda think, and they had affected her more coming from Debs, a lifelong friend. Then there was that black actress with the monologue that had seemed to open it all up, and whose voice was still reverberating.

'A King Solomon of a man who might take me, via this hairy cunt of mine to the seventh heaven or someplace "other"!', and Linda thought about the final epiphany that made her wonder if Chaz hadn't dug out that snake pit himself, as a trap.

Chaz had his rather aggressive blow job, he did get some of his frustration out, and then he dropped Brooke off. She had the loot so she didn't mind, and had another snort of coke up on the heath, and Chaz said he would text her around Tuesday dinner time, but would expect to be there for two till four. If he was late, he would pay her another couple of fifties. Chaz was generous like that, and Brooke was thinking that she had to serve it up to him, a true porn star fiesta, so that he might come for an overnight stay at a later date. That would pay her rent for the month or more. And she fancied having more of that coke as a freebie. That guy had a pocketful.

Another scream came up from out there in the old orchard. It sounded something like a female scream, but Linda was relieved, the screech was definitely a fox. But it made Linda jumpy. She got up and made a move over to the velvet chair again, and took hold of the St. George trinket box, that was down there by the side of the arm. For a split second she recalled that simpler Linda of a few decades previously, who would never have sniffed coke like this, like a fiend. She liked a few drinks with the girls, but never drugs. How had she allowed herself to get to this place? She had been so carefree, that was one of the traits that had attracted and hooked Chaz, and she remembered herself as being happy back in those days. But then she thought about the gardens and her new hobby, that made her feel good, even a little joy. Maybe her life wasn't so bad but she had a serious drug habit, and the sheer pangs she had for the drug, that alleviated all her tension, and let her feel nice and high for a fleeting moment, were just too much. Within a couple of seconds, she was snorting up a line from the coffee table, and was exhilarated, although she knew darn well that the feeling wouldn't last long. But as Chaz kept telling her, she had to live for the moment. Then the look on her face seemed to infer all the unbearable psychic torment that was mixed with her ecstasy in that fleeting moment. She looked up at the mantel to the wedding photo, with a despairing look on her face. Her life didn't seem so ruined then. She wasn't caught down this snake pit, playing endless snakes and ladders. She glanced towards that photo of Chaz and his record carp and sneered. He looked like the king of a snake pit.

Chaz might have had his throat fuck and bit of fanny but it could never be enough. He lost eight grand on that wanker Phelps and 'One Eye' had one hell of a monster big up on him. What also made Chaz, the big gambler really mad, was that he wasn't on the moment. It rankled him that he didn't have that information about Phelps. How did that 'One Eye' get it? Five grand down? It was hard enough getting him to part with a fiver for a packet of boilies, let alone lump on a fat bastard like 'The Cannibal'. But the fact was Chaz got it all wrong and 'One Eye' had it all right. Chaz felt as if he was the fool guy who lost all his money on a useless no-hoper pothead. He arrived back at the house fuming. He got out of the Jag and made sure he slammed the door and then the gate. Why not? They were his to slam! Chaz had always been a terrible loser, so Linda was well used to these tantrums.

'That fucking wanker!'

Linda heard the gate go, and she knew by his very footsteps what was coming. He'd lost and probably lost big. Chaz slammed the porch door and then slammed the back. He would have to chase it up on the coke dealing all bank holiday weekend, and that would only make his money up at best. Not a penny profit. Fuck it!

'Chaz! Mind the doors!'

Chaz appeared in an angry, foul mood. How dare she!

'They're mine to fucking slam, Linda!' Within a few moments, Chaz was seated in his velvet chair, smashing the arm furiously with his fist. 'Fuck it! Fuck it! That poxy Phelps cost me eight fucking grand! Fuck it!'

Linda just couldn't understand why he had to bet eight thousand pounds. All she done was three or four lines on the lottery, and that was enough of that. She just couldn't believe it.

'Oh Chaz,' she said, sounding like a nag which made Chaz even angrier.

'And that's enough of that, Linda. Eight fucking grand wasted, on that fucking pothead! I lay the fucking bet and then I find out the dosser's been doing puff big time for the past three weeks, coping with his puppy love breakdown. Wanker! Why didn't he just withdraw, the prat!'

Linda had to speak her mind. Fancy betting like that? She just couldn't understand it.

'Well that's what big gambling's like, Chaz. You can't be guaranteed to win every time!'

Chaz exploded. He hadn't come back to the house to be taught by seminar. He was very aggressive.

'And that's enough of the fucking lecturing as well, Linda. I suppose you're learning all that from fucking Debs!' Chaz had always clashed with her, and all this studying had made it all worse as Chaz knew what she was like, when she got that bee in her bonnet. 'Fucking know-it-all! Anyone would think she's a professor the way she fucking carries on. Be a miracle if she's got a poxy O level! She's probably passed her going-down-on-cunt level though.'

173

Linda was angered at Chaz's vulgarity, and she went for a quick defense of Debs in face of his ridicule.

'Well she's trying and she's doing well, Chaz. She got a top grade in her last essay! And she's full of interesting ideas!'

To be fair Linda had been captivated to hear about how Debs had got back into education and was doing so well. One of the reasons Chaz didn't like her now, was because he thought Linda might get similar ones, virtually catching them off her, like a Debs disease.

'Well you be sure not to bring them fucking home here with ya, Linda. Cos they're not fucking wanted! I suppose you pawed over all those stupid bloody badges she wears. What did they say, "down with cock sucking"!' Linda felt so angry. It had been a great night, and now Chaz was trying his best to ruin it all.

'I can see you're just embittered and sour, Chaz, because you lost that bet! You're such a bad loser! You think it's ordained you're going to win every time!'

This seemed to push Chaz over the top. He couldn't have Linda flatly criticizing him, like that.

'I can see what you're asking for, my little princess!'

Linda knew full well where this was all leading and Chaz got up and stalked her menacingly. He turned her over on all fours over the Waldorf and within a few moments had his trousers down and Linda's skirt up over her head. He then tore off her knickers, and within a few more moments had entered her from behind and was violently thrusting away.

'No, Chaz! Not like this, Chaz!' Linda protested.

'You love it, Linda! I'll shag the guilt out of ya! You love it! Love it!'

As soon as the sexual act began, it was coming to its end. But at least the end gave Linda some time to get away from him. She went upstairs, opened the little drawer, and had a few more pills from the small medical dispenser, and cried herself to sleep under the expensive silk sheets, hating herself for getting some kind of warped thrill out of it all.

After the travails of the evening, Chaz thought he would do some serious coke to end the night on a customary high. He snorted a line and then began rolling a joint, while also putting on the DVD that he had shot with Linda, which was destined for the edit. He chuckled and chortled to himself, smoked the joint, had another line and then masturbated, getting off on the film, the throat fuck in the Jag and the forced sex with Linda. 'Get on it! Bang on it!' He came big and massive, although all his load had gone down the throat of the whore. Eventually Chaz got tired and dragged himself up to bed, but at least all the sex and drug highs had made up for losing eight big ones on that wanker Phelps. The digital clock by the bedside read two fifty-eight, exactly the time when TV Sam began to make his first move.

CHAPTER NINE

COME TO MY WINDOW.

THE GREAT ESCAPE: PART ONE

TV Sam got up and took his chance. He had worked it out perfectly. He was determined to go right out the front door with a click of the control panel. Going back a few months TV had seen a nurse punching in her number and he filched her card from her coat pocket, and the office hadn't even deactivated the lost card, so he had the means. He placed clothes and pillows beneath his blankets, so that it looked as if he was sleeping. The idea was to create a diversion, and no other than Lorenzo Drill was the 'diversion man', but this time he was doing it for TV and Dragon Star, although TV bought him another twenty. Drill passed TV's bedside and TV was behind a curtain and motioned to Drill to go for it. Drill went into the toilet and he immediately knocked over a large bin, making a hell of a din, while feigning a collapse on the floor. Drill was well known for his blackouts, and the two nurses on duty had seen Drill go and they immediately went to his aid. The nurses came past TV's area, and he was gone and out of the unit, while the two nurses were helping up a dazed looking Drill-head. 'Sorted!'

TV was on the 'one shot' and nothing was going to stop him. He took refuge behind a tree and looked around to see if there were any security about. This was a big personal moment, but also a big phase of the Dragon Star, New Age revolution, and he sported a hooded jacket that had never been seen before, that was fitting for the special occasion. On the back was the dragon and star, the cult's motif. TV had spent hours over this jacket, all surreptitiously, in Art classes, when the tutor would habitually disappear for twenty minutes or so to have a fag. He also sported that banned Dragon Star cap that had been hidden away in Drill's wardrobe, the usual place for banned memorabilia. TV felt like the man, the leader, fully in the moment and living his destiny.

He looked upwards and menacing clouds were brewing, and the atmospherics were subtly changing, as they do prior to enormous great electrical storms. TV smiled as everything was propitious for Dragon Star, and then he sped off towards the gardener's shed. It was locked, but TV was a genius at unlocking things. If there was a locked door, TV could open it and find out what was hidden behind it. That was a big thing for TV, opening up the doors. How he quite did it, nobody knew, and any attempts to teach people would fall flat. It was something deeply instinctive, a gift that TV Sam had. A gift at opening doors like no other, to find the demons or the treasures and dragons that lay behind them. He would invariably hold three bits of wire of different widths in his hands and fiddle them up the hole, and before you knew it mechanical locks would click, and the doors would open. TV fingered with this particular lock for about twenty seconds, then it went. He had surveyed it a couple of weeks back when the 'break out' plan began to hatch, and it was earmarked as 'easy peasy'. Once inside he knew exactly what he wanted, as he had been watching the gardener closely for some time. He took up a large electric saw and a big heavy sledge hammer, and his intention and mission was to have that big lounge window out. Now the lock up unit was one that did have ultra-strong windows, but TV hoped he could break on through. His guess, and it was correct, was the Trust had probably put in a compromised slightly cheaper version of ultra-strong windows, to keep costs down, when the unit was built a dozen years back. TV made his way over to the unit with the tools, focused on his mission.

Freeda was in her room in her nightdress, and she squinted her eye at the digital clock that read 3:05. It was time. She got up like lightning. TV would never let her down. She had a malevolent look on her face, and she too was switched right on. She would never be happy until she was out of this prison. She was fed up with that big fat nurse, fed up with her. She picked up her beloved purse from a small bedside table and slipped it in her dressing gown pocket. She couldn't leave that behind. It held all her money, best make-up and cherished personal mementoes. She put her Jesus's sandals on over her unicorn socks, knocked on the door and kept knocking, putting on a voice that expressed extreme discomfort. It was the plan that came through, via the Lorenzo Drill vocational tea method, and she knew it off by heart.

'Freeda's tummy is hurting. Please help Freeda! Freeda's tummy is hurting!'

Freeda kept banging the door, and the agency nurses soon picked it up, and they decided to investigate. They were acutely aware of the problem of Freeda, and approached with extreme vigilance.

It was now moving towards ten past, and Dan had set a bleeping alarm in his private room. He was only half asleep anyway, as he was worrying himself sick about TV. He pulled the curtain slightly, and could see TV making his way towards the lock up unit. He knew that TV would be true to his word. He was like that. Dan waved, although TV was too far away to see him. 'Just one shot, TV!' That's all TV would get.

Meanwhile, back in the lock up unit, Freeda was still feigning her stomach problems.

'Freeda feels terrible, terrible! Freeda needs something for her tummy, some Alka-Seltzer!'

The agency nurse opened the door and led Freeda to the drugs cabinet.

'I'll get you something, Freeda.' Freeda knew that she had to get into that lounge, and get the light on, so TV knew that she was in there, because he would be out there. He was like that, and Freeda believed that he could virtually walk on water. If TV said things were going to happen, they always did. He always said he was psychic and he had said he saw them getting out in a dream, running through the rain, and there was lightning and it lit up their faces, and they became famous on this internet thingy. That was ages ago he said that, and Freeda had never forgotten it.

'Can Freeda sit down in the lounge for a minute? Freeda wants to sit down with her bad tummy, bad tummy.'

One of the nurses finished gathering the pills, while the other led Freeda into the lounge. It all seemed innocuous enough. The light went on, and TV was out there in some bushes close by, readying for the moment. Freeda came to the window, looked out, praying she'd spot him. She smiled as she noticed a movement in the bushes and then saw that peaked Dragon Star cap. The 'break out' was on! Freeda returned to the settee with a smile and looked down at those Jesus's sandals. Everything had begun happening since TV brought them for her at that boot fair, she thought. The second nurse came through with the pills and a glass of water as Freeda would rarely get a pill down without one.

'Here you are, Freeda. These should help you.' Freeda took the pills and drank the water, and was having difficulty swallowing them as she always did. There was a massive rumble of thunder as Freeda finally managed to get the pills down. She thought about what TV had said. That there would be flashes of lightning on their faces as they escaped. It was all about to come true!

'Looks like thunderbolts!' Freeda observed, as she gave the glass back to the nurse.

'Yes, it does, Freeda!'

TV was about to go. He saw himself as a medieval troubadour knight, sporting the Dragon Star insignia, hell bent on freeing his damsel in distress. He put the saw down on grass outside the window, and it was time for the charge of the Dragon Star light brigade, with the great sledge hammer. TV was naturally strong but his inner being was tied up with this one, so he was twice as strong as normal. The great hammer whacked into the glass creating a resounding pile driving thwack that resonated right around the hospital grounds. There was a thunderclap overhead as TV slung the sledgehammer into the window again. The alarm was ringing and Freeda was ecstatic. It really was happening. TV was going to get her out of the prison! The nurses were bewildered but they were thinking they could escort Freeda from the lounge. But TV gave her the order.

'Fucking crazy um, Freeda!'

Freeda got the message, and she summonsed a psychotic power that gave her the strength of three. She grabbed hold of the female nurse and threw her across the lounge into a cabinet, as if she was the world's strongest woman. The male nurse made a spontaneous attempt to apprehend her but Freeda pushed him away with ease and great force and then she went hell bent for a nasty.

'If you touch me, I'll rip ya fucking heads off!'

The male nurse cowered away and the two of them nodded to each other and exited hastily. By now, with some continued relentless pounding, TV had made a hole in the middle of the reinforced glass, and he dropped two large sharp kitchen knives through, as well as the lead of the electric saw. TV had thought of everything.

'Plug me in, Freed!' Freeda quickly took the plug, got it into the socket and took up the knives.

'If anyone comes into the room, scare the fuck out of them. Threaten to cut their fucking throats, Freeda!'

Freeda was sneering and smiling at the same time. She was on it with those two knives in her hands. TV had promised to get her out and now TV was doing just that! She held the two knives just waiting for those security to appear. She would show that bearded one a thing or two now she had knives. But she so wanted to hug her TV, who kept telling her to watch that door.

TV had now taken up the chainsaw, a big powerful, heavy one. He had watched the gardener use it and he quickly got the hang of it cutting the enormous pane of glass. By now a couple of security guards were outside, but TV saw them approach and he turned towards them with the chainsaw. They didn't think he would dare, but TV went for the jugular. This was the 'one shot'. He had plenty of lead and he figured he could reach them. He put the saw on and chased, and they legged it off quick with TV accentuating their fear by shouting out, 'I'm fucking mad! Mad! Chainsaw massacre fucking mad!'

He rushed back to the window and began hitting it with the saw again. By now the thunderclaps were getting closer, and were booming, and lightning flashes eerily lit up the asylum grounds. Freeda had those knives in each hand and was watching the opening, poised to pounce like a mad thing, readied to go into a frenzy on TV's orders.

'I'll soon have ya out, Freed! Just keep watching the door!' TV knew that Freeda was apt to let her mind wander. But she was determined to do this for TV.

Dan was watching and couldn't believe his eyes, and with the commotion, lights were coming on all over the asylum. Other patients were up and looking out too, and many were complaining about that terrible noise. Some realized what was happening, as they could see it was TV.

'He's trying to get Freeda out! TV's smashed the fucking window in!' they were saying in the open wards. Three security guards, the entire strength of the site, and all armed with battens, were being informed by the nurses outside the lock up unit.

'She's in the lounge and she's fucking crazy!' the male nurse exclaimed.

'Is she armed?'

The burly bearded security officer, who had scarpered away from TV, sounded professional and calm. But he preferred dealing with this 'Mad Freeda' once that Dr. Bolt had given her a shot or two, although he had the type of cool head you need in these hairy situations. 'Is she armed?' he repeated, and the female nurse took over.

'No, but she's fucking psychotic!' The bearded security guard visibly gulped. But this was his job and role and he felt the implications of the uniform.

'We should be able to handle her.'

He tried his best to exude confidence but he was terrified. He didn't fancy this one bit. The nurses noticed that the other two didn't evoke a great deal of confidence either. This wasn't somebody like Dan 'kicking off'. This was 'Mad Freeda', who was known to have stabbed a few people in her time. By now TV had nearly cut all the glass out, and Freeda was getting too near the window. How she wanted to hug her beloved.

'TV! TV! I wanna hug you, TV!'

But TV was fixated on the mission at hand. He had just the 'one shot' and he knew there wouldn't be another.

'Keep back, Freeda, and keep watching the door!' The security guards appeared on the threshold of the lounge with the bearded leader to the fore.

'They're here, TV!' TV shut down the saw for a moment and told them straight.

'If you get near her, she cuts ya throats!' Freeda didn't move a muscle, she just stood there firmly fixed, looking as if she was spring loaded, brandishing those knives, waiting to pounce. She was the pure embodiment of the kind of unpredictability that petrifies people. And all in her new Jesus's sandals. She put it straight to them.

'Ya get near me and I'll cut ya fucking cocks off, ya bastards!' The bearded security guard weighed up the situation, and thought on his feet in the moment, showing leadership qualities.

'Back off! We'll wait for the police!' He certainly made it sound decisive. The window was about to drop, and TV took up the sledgehammer again to finally knock it out. The whole lot came crashing down.

'I think I scared um, TV!'

TV realized that he had done it and was ecstatic. The window that stood between Freeda and the outside world had been smashed to smithereens. He gestured for her to get a chair to the opening so that she could climb into his arms, and get beyond the jagged glass left in the frame. TV noticed the digital clock in the lounge and it read 3:28. It was fate.

'Come on, Freeda!' Freeda moved the chair then sped to her Sesame Street record case. That had to go with her wherever she went, but she was overwhelmed.

'My TV's freed Freeda! We're going to get married! My TV's freed Freeda forever and ever!'

TV bundled Freeda out of the window, and she was so intent on minding her prized Sesame Street record case, that she dropped the knives as they sped across the field. It seemed that providence was on their side though, as by now the rains were just about to sheet across the asylum's grounds, and this wasn't just a normal storm. It was one of those storms that people remember all their lives. Freeda threw herself at TV when they reached the tree and she sobbed and hugged him, and then some more. She could have stayed there in his arms forever, but TV had to keep them going. White lightning cracked overhead bringing a sublime, unusual light to the asylum's grounds. They parted from their embrace and pressed on, making for the hospital shop as TV had to get them provisions. By now the rains had arrived and were torrential, akin to a mini monsoon and what great cover.

The torrential rain didn't relent and it worsened as a couple of local Tennin police cars hurtled towards the asylum, in visibility that was abominable. Once TV and Freeda had made it to the canopy walkway and the shop, they took a few more moments to hug and kiss each other again, and TV still had the sledgehammer.

'You came, TV! You always promised!'

Everything in Freeda's baggage of life's experiences, seemed to lighten when she was with TV. It seemed like God was blessing her just being in his presence.

'I love ya, Freeda!' These words made Freeda feel so much better. TV was like her healing balm.

Dan had watched the escape and he could see that TV had got her out, as the rain lashed across the grounds and the thunder cracked. He willed them on and he was in elation for the success of it. TV was a living legend at the asylum.

'Ya done it, TV! Ya done it!'

But then Dan stopped when they were out of eyeshot. He went all silent and pensive, as he wondered what on earth TV would do now? A few months earlier he had watched an old documentary on the Second

World War and the battle with the Japanese and he had been intrigued by the Kamikaze pilots. It seemed that TV was in the cockpit.

TV and Freeda were at the door of the hospital shop and TV had his sledgehammer raised. He could hear the police cars arriving in the car park, so they had to get on with it and get off the grounds quickly. He took a whack at the glass of the door but didn't catch it right as Freeda's close proximity had compromised his swing.

'Get back, Freeda!' he shouted.

Freeda was so excited about getting into that shop. It was like a treasure trove to Freeda, and they could have anything, absolutely anything.

'Let's get fags, TV! Milkybars! And those pancake fingys I like!'

'Tons, Freeda!' TV finished clearing out the glass with an almighty swing and quickly had the door open. There were people looking down the walkway towards them, but nobody ran the gauntlet.

'You could have done "wires" on it, TV!' Freeda said, but there wasn't any time for that. When they got inside, they swiftly filled a couple of black bags with food and drink with Freeda making a bee line for those pancake fingys. TV went about smashing the fag screen lock with his hammer, as they had to get a good supply of 'draw'. The rain was still sheeting down and the lightning cracking, and TV noticed that there were some dandy looking big umbrellas. They would need one of them. Then he quickly took off his jacket, and to Freeda's amazement he had another underneath. He turned around to show it off and it was different to his. On the back was a caricatured image of TV and Freeda, with the Dragon Star two fingers up, an image that was now on every year's newsletter, and was owned by Dan. He unzipped it and quickly got it off smiling.

'I made this special jacket for ya, Freeda. And I got ya a "Dragon Star" cap!'

Freeda remembered the photo, and put her fingers up and was blown away. She put it on over her dressing gown and adjusted the hat with an exalted smile on her face. TV thought of everything and Freeda couldn't believe it. Dr. Lock and the big fat nurse would never let them wear those jackets and caps. For Freeda Dragon Star had won, it had 'done them', like TV said it always would.

'Thanks, TV! I love you, TV!'

They hugged, but TV knew they had to get going, double quick. A couple of the patients saw them moving across the grounds in the sheeting rain with that umbrella up, when yet another white lightning strike lit up the asylum. They watched them enter the distant woods but they all kept their silence. Nobody saw anything, would be the general response as nobody would stitch on TV and Freeda. Tyrone had noticed it and he thought about informing Dr. Lock but Drill-head would warn him off by stroking one of his big fists as soon as he rattled that tea trolley around the lock up. The police were soon checking the smashed-out window in the front lounge and then they were at the shop and were realizing that this 'break out' was going to be a little more complicated than expected. The absconders, one of them the most dangerous patient in the asylum, were out there in the wider community, and they had knives.

TV and Freeda got to the safety of the woods, that ran down the farmland of the hospital towards the back of Chaz's abode. They had the big umbrella up and had found some old milk crates and TV covered them with black plastic bags. It was still bucketing down and the thunder was still cracking, but there was some shelter from the tops of the trees and they had found this cozy little place deep in the thick woodland. The rain that made it through the canopy was bouncing off the umbrella, which was a sturdy one and Freeda was snugged up to TV with a radiant smile on her face, as if in the turbulence of a tragic life, she had found that golden moment of contentment. She only felt like this with TV. He was different. Freeda could never get him out of her mind. He was her complete obsession and now she was here with him and that big fat nurse wasn't around to stop it. It was bliss.

'It's nice here with you, TV. It's cozy.'

'That's because our love makes it cozy, Freeda. And I know what we're gonna do. I've planned something special.'

It all sounded so exciting, but Freeda didn't care for anything apart from this moment. She was with her TV and the rain dripping made it all the more intimate and romantic. They were like two drifters off to meet their new world of love, and as deep as you could be in love, and all the forced separation made this being together more special and poignant.

'I just wanna be with you, TV!' Freeda confided, and how she meant it. TV knew though, that they would have to savor these moments. But it was all worth it. He had to be with her. He had too. They were the Romeo and Juliet of Tennin Asylum.

'We'll always be together, Freeda, always! Let's have some of those pancakes together!'

That's why TV got Freeda out because he wanted to do things with Freeda and sharing those pancakes was like a lovers' Holy communion. It was perfect.

CHAPTER TEN

COCK A DOODLE DOO

The rain had been hurtling down over Chaz's house but he slept through it, and didn't hear a thing. But around five o'clock, it was that early morning cockerel from the doctor's that gave the wake-up call. By now the rain was patchier, but it had been an incredible electrical storm. The thunder claps had awoken Linda and scared her, as they were right above the house, and the rest of her sleep was interrupted due to the frequent blasts of heavy rain. Listening to the rain, she could now recognize the wisdom of Chaz to have a new roof, before they moved in. That Dark Room would have been flooded without it. The leaks were right above. Chaz began to squirm though as the cockerel had its cock a doodle doo moment.

'That fucking cock! I'd like to wring its fucking neck!'

People tend to make these kind of off the cuff remarks, but not really mean them. But with Chaz they always bore an undercurrent of real malice and menace. The fact was, if Chaz had half the chance, he would wring the things neck, or at least pay somebody off to wring it. Linda was half asleep and tired, because of the interruptions with the rain, as Chaz thought about how much he could offer for the death of the cockerel.

'Oh, forget about it, Chaz. Go back to sleep. That storm kept waking me up!'

But Chaz was impatient. He had taken just of late to going to bed with ear plugs in, so that he didn't hear the damned thing. But last night with everything going on he forgot them.

'You know I can't get back to sleep once I've been disturbed, Linda,' he angrily snapped. The cock called out again as if to say to Chaz, that yes, it was time to rise and Chaz threw the towel in.

'Oh, fuck it! I'm getting up. I'll have a tea and then go and get the paper.'

Chaz rather liked getting out so early in the morning once he was up and running. With his lungs full of air, he was busily thinking how he would make up that eight fucking grand he lost. The bank holiday weekend was coming up and Chaz was considering getting it out at 'buy one get half free' or something similar. He had the figure of ten grand profit in his mind. Phew! He would have to knock some out! But he already had that kilo for the Candy Foxes upstairs in the safe, that was six made up straight away, and he could buy a full kilo and even another on Saturday afternoon if they all went bonkers over the festivities. He could inform all buyers that it was just a spring bank holiday offer on behalf of the firm, 'Barber's Drug High's Ltd'. With that dance event on, Jay and Dai would be knocking out half a kilo on their own. Chaz was just about to open his front gate thinking about it all, when a police car came up Holly Beach Lane, driven with plenty of intention. Chaz stood back, and was thankful it didn't stop at 'Chaz's Pad'. The police hadn't noticed him and they hurtled on. Chaz frowned, thinking what it might be? There was only one destination up the lane, and it certainly wasn't paradise. It was the back entry to the asylum's old farm. But that was rather an odd way to approach the asylum Chaz thought. What the fuck was going on up there at half five in the morning? He was whistling 'She's Not There' as he walked down Holly Beach Lane, and he walked straight past that decomposing squashed snake, without even noticing it.

Chaz got down to the bottom of the lane and was met by Mrs. Greene-Burrows, the old doctor's wife. She'd come out from her house just after that police car had whizzed up the lane. She was bare legged and scantily clad for her early morning jog, and on the face of it, a bit too scanty, as there was quite a nip in the air. Chaz enjoyed looking her up and down as he approached, while she was preparing at a lamppost, with calf and leg stretches and the like. Chaz talked to himself as he took in the sight.

'Oh yes, you can be in our films, lady, any night you please!'

Chaz was quick-witted in these kinds of scenarios. He had a gift for that.

'Good morning! And such a nice one to get up with the cock!' He thought he would just be able to get away with that one, a quip that had that crescendo of emphasis. Mrs. Greene-Burrows obviously caught the innuendo.

'Oh hullo, yes, they've said it's going to be a very nice day once it gets going. But a quite shocking storm though.'

That storm was inevitably going to be *the* talking point of the day around the village. But Chaz really enjoyed his cheeky innuendo, and he thought this doctor's wife must have been nigh twenty years younger than the old codger, and he probably couldn't get it up. Chaz arrived at the shop and he didn't generally get down there at this unearthly hour. The papers hadn't turned up as yet, and although one of the staff was in, she was waiting on them before opening. There were already two elderly women tying dogs up to railings, eagerly awaiting those papers. Diehards you might call them, and the storm was on their minds and tongues.

'Oh, my word, didn't it come down, Dor! It woke me about twenty to four, Dor! Shocking! And those lightning flashes. I thought he'd got up and put the light on!'

Doreen had plenty to say for herself as well.

'Yeah, I know, Flo, and you should have seen the water running down our front path. No word of a lie it was looking like a river, Flo, and it's ruined all the gardens, ruined them!'

Flo noticed Chaz and being a regular she gave him the lowdown.

'Papers should be here any minute, luv.'

'Oh cheers,' Chaz said politely, before resting himself up against the railings. It was time for a smoke. He lit up, still thinking about his mission to retrieve the eight-grand. Just before he arrived, he did give thought about a big hefty wager on Juventus in the Champions league final in ninety minutes. But then he had accepted that the best bet was that the 'Herbert's and Sherbets' would be sniffing and snorting about three times as much as usual with the extra day off. As he took another drag and was weighing up how much he would require from Alfredo, yet another police car hurtled past at top speed. Something serious was going on, and Doreen could recognize that.

'That's the umpteenth, Flo!' Flo thought that something had kicked off up at the old asylum. The asylum existed as a specter overhanging and waiting to kick off in these parts. But it was grist for animated gossip.

'There's some nasty bundles up there, Flo. Nasty bundles,' Doreen wisely reflected, knowing full well that Flo would agree with her. Doreen had been head supervisor in the laundry, a good few year ago. Then she had ended up on the switchboard when the laundry went private in the eighties. If you had spoken about Freeda to her, she would have known the case. She knew of her when she first came into the hospital some fifteen years ago now. Flo purred in agreement.

'Ooh, nasty, nasty bundles, Dor.' One of the dogs began to bark incessantly as if saying something about the issue himself, which set the other off.

'Sounds like the local canine population are bloody concerned about it!'

Chaz couldn't resist a little early morning joke, and they all laughed as the paper van pulled up just a little late. Chaz bought his paper and strode jauntily back. He was still whistling away not taking a blind bit of notice of the front page, referring to how ordinary people were wilting under the personal debt burden of AD 2003. He was still whistling 'She's Not There!', thinking that it was such a good choice of ring tone. Within ten minutes he was turning into the lane by the doctor's house and Mrs. Greene-Burrows was arriving back home after her early morning run, as if they were fated to meet again. She was beaming with beads of sweat over her, and sweat in certain places of her leotard. Chaz looked her up and down and liked what he saw. Catherine thought his gaze a little intrusive and rude, although she liked being looked at.

'Hullo, we keep bumping into each other this morning,' she politely said, breaking the ice this time, as she wanted to keep communication open with the couple living just up the lane.

'Well you're certainly looking fit and trim and "up for it". It must be all this early morning jogging up with the "cock a doodle doo!" It's working!'

Mrs. Greene-Burrows smiled, and Chaz reciprocated as he passed. Yes, she was definitely, 'up for it', Chaz thought, and then a few yards later Chaz's mobile went. He took it from his pocket, and realized to his astonishment, that it was no other than bloody 'One Eye'.

'Who the fuck! Fucking "One Eye"!'

'One Eye' was alone in a bivvy on the 'Ressie' lakes complex. He wanted someone to talk to about the big success of the nights fishing. To share the enthusiasm and passion. To share the love. He had gone to the lakes straight after the bout on a complete high, after winning that seven and a half grand on 'The Cannibal'. He had the mobile in his left hand to his ear and in his right, he had all the money, wrapped with a band. He knew the score with Chaz's bet and he wanted to rub it in just a little bit. He had the pretext in his mind too, of asking about Chaz's prospective commercial bait. 'One Eye' had one of those deep gruff voices, and the timbre of his voice grated on Chaz.

'Hullo, Sweeny! It's ole "One Eye". How ya doing?' Chaz never trusted 'One Eye'. Chaz had him down as a complete arsehole and he was likely to be up to something.

'And what the fuck are ya doing belling me at this hour for?' Chaz asked. 'One Eye' simply loved explaining.

'Did ya lump on "The Cannibal"? Every man and his dog did! We all had a right ole touch! Must have been bad for Jimbo but he said he took a lot of big money on Phelps early doors, balanced his books. Anyhows, after that seven and a half grand I won, I went down the "Ressie", that's where I am now, Sweeny.'

'Yeah, and?' Chaz asked.

'I just thought I'd ring to share the sessions high. Carp soul to fellow carp soul and the like Sween. I had two after the storm, one just over thirty and a twenty-seven, and I even had time to lose a big un in the reed beds too!'

Chaz went on the defensive. He knew that just over thirty meant that it was bound to be just under. He didn't like to acknowledge anything with 'One Eye', but he would have given his right arm for two carp on the weekend like that. But Chaz was still king, when it came to the 'Ressie'.

'Yeah, but Attila the mirror and "my" humpy back linear, the really big thirties are all dead now though "One Eye". What was the biggest?' Chaz knew all the really big fish intimately at the "Ressie" venue. "One Eye" said that a bloke next to him thought it was "Orange Percy". Chaz scoffed at that piece of information, as he knew that fish well, and he had caught him way bigger.

'As you know, I've had him four times, lowest thirty-three and the highest thirty-six, his heaviest recorded weight. He must be in his dotage these days at thirty, "One Eye". Must have come in like a big ole dustbin lid.'

'One Eye' claimed that the carp had given him a right old battle royal, but he was lying. The fish had come in overly easily and he thought it was a tench or something. But it weighed twenty-nine pounds ten, and he was claiming just over the thirty, as his scales were sure to be out half a dozen ounces. Chaz was determined to get one up on the creep though.

'Well done, "One Eye", but you want to spend that dough you've won on getting a ticket to the new lakes of Joey Olwyn's, if ya want the big stuff. All the "top-dogs" are down there this year, "One Eye".'

'One Eye' was like the equally powerful opponent and nemesis on the other side of the court in a keenly contested tennis match. Back came the ball as awkward to get to as anybody could make it.

'Yeah, nice talking, Sweeny. I'll bear that in mind, but let's hope you have more twenties this year. What was it, one last year at the start? You must have thought you were in for a good ol season, Sween!'

This was the kind of thing that made Chaz's carping full of tension these days. He had to have some big fish again, to stop people talking like this. It was all chipping away at his ego.

'I had some big stuff in France, "One Eye".'

Chaz did catch a few with Miko on a five-night trip to France the previous early September, but the two biggest fish, a twenty-eight and a larger thirty-one, were photographed on a phone that Chaz had subsequently lost.

'Shame you lost your phone, Sweeny, weren't it?' 'One Eye' replied, with Chaz picking up the negative connotation regarding the story. But 'One Eye' pulled the conversation back to the main reason why he had phoned Sweeny Todd. That new bait of Chaz and Miko's.

'I'll have fifty kilos, Sweeny, if you can show proven results with it and not just getting your pet fish on um in the tanks.'

Chaz swore under his breath, and he finished the call right pissed off. But he had been determined not to stoop down to his level and get caught up in a slandering tit for tat. But 'One Eye' had won by knock out. Those carp might not have been monsters, but at least he caught carp, the species he was angling. Chaz was thoroughly carp fishing depressed.

'Fucking wanker!' Chaz walked on a couple of paces, and this time he came right in front of that decomposing snake. He sighed when he saw it as events were confirming that the old boy's snake story was probably not far off the truth. Bloody place *was* full of snakes. Chaz look thunderstruck for a second too, as he again tried to figure out what all this snake business was telling him. Chaz lived by that Freudian maxim that there are no meaningless coincidences, and then something unusual occurred. Chaz had the uncanny feeling that he was being watched and it made him feel strange and uncomfortable. There was something about the dynamic of the moment. As if he were being enveloped by a dark force. It made the hairs on his neck stand on end, and shadowy dark clouds gathered overhead, further emphasizing the feeling, as he still peered, fixated at that decomposed snake. He then turned his head and looked into the dense thickets and woodland directly before him, which jutted up to his dwelling. He heard twigs cracking, somebody or something was in there. The clouds overhead became even darker, lending a greater menace to the moment and Chaz felt unhinged, as if he was about to be accosted by evil. Then there was a cackling female laugh that sounded like a wicked witch in a Disney film.

'Who's there?' Chaz asked, a reflex action, preventing him from becoming completely immobilized. Why did he agree to come and live in this cursed Holly Beach Lane? It had that history. Chaz felt a tingle of fear and then a shiver up his spine. He immediately felt sweaty and oppressed, and sensed that something terrible was afoot. The laugh came again and this time it was closer and even more malevolent. Chaz moved away quickly, and began jogging for ten or twenty uncomfortable looking yards, just to get clear, and every few yards he was quickly shifting his eyes, looking back over his shoulder. It wasn't so much the laugh, it was the sense of menace that he had felt in the moment, assaulting him, in a subtle, uncanny way, that made him think of that darn snake's head in the garden. Thunder began to roll again as he opened the gate, and briskly walked up the path of his darn bloody dream house.

With Chaz gone back to the house, TV Sam, and Freeda edged from the woods onto the lane as TV just had to show Freeda the infamous flying saucer lamppost. Freeda still had her prize possession Sesame Street record case in her hand while TV had the umbrella and the two black plastic bags of provisions. Freeda was joyous but then her face turned to puzzlement as she spotted the snake carcass lying there.

'Ugh! Look TV! A dead snake!' TV bent over and poked it with the tip of his umbrella.

'I reckon he must have run over it in that Jag, Freeda.' Freeda thought that the White Blazerman might like killing snakes. TV sneered with disgust.

'The old ways people stamp on creation. They kill everything that moves. The evil fuckers! But us Dragon Star don't!'

Freeda had another look of puzzlement on her face.

'But we eat fish, TV!' Freeda knew that when fish were taken out of water, they soon looked distressed and within a few minutes they were dead. That seemed to contradict TV's claim, but TV knew instinctively what she was thinking.

'Yeah, but Jesus was a fisherman, Freeda, and he used to feed all the poor and starving people and we've got his sandals on. It's his brand. Like I was saying, everything's branding these days, Freeda.' Freeda looked down at her sandals and then to her Dragon Star jacket, which was making her feel so trendy.

'And we got his badges, TV!'

Freeda put her fingers to her 'Jesus Loves You but I'm his favorite!' badge, and her 'I love Jesus' badge that she had pinned on the hoodie. Kleeunah had got her those. But she still wasn't too sure about the fish, although she thought TV must be right. TV then ushered Freeda over to the flying saucer lamppost.

'Here it is, Freeda. Ya wanna see the light that comes off it. Its fucking wicked, Freed!'

Freeda looked at it and could see it was olde worldie and she wanted to support her TV.

'It's nice, TV. It's well fucking old un it?'

'It's where Keefy saw a fleet of seven in formation. They came up right over that hill.' TV gestured to the area which was looking ominous with dark clouds brewing up. 'It's a fucking hot spot. I blogged it on the internet. It's bound to have a billion hits or something and tons of people all over the world will come down to see this lamppost one day. They will, Freeda! They will, Freeda!'

Freeda didn't say anything because she didn't believe him.

They loitered in the lane a moment, as the clouds darkened further, and then yet another great clap of thunder resounded, before the rain started coming down again. They could see it sheeting its way over the field of rapeseed.

'It's so dark! It's gonna piss down again, Freeda!' TV observed. But Freeda's face was beaming.

'The sun is shining all over, TV, all over!' Freeda said, with a great warm smile on her face.

'It's because we're together at last!' TV replied. 'There's no dark clouds now,' and they kissed and when they parted, they radiated happiness. It was a poignant moment for TV. Freeda glowed when she smiled like that, and for TV, that smile was like the new world, as it was beyond all the darkness and her painful tragedy.

'You look so pretty when you're happy, Freeda.'

Such words were like a healing balm to Freeda. When TV said those kinds of things it really meant something, and she felt better about everything. TV was so special to her. Nobody had made her feel like that.

With the darkness beginning to envelop, the lamp came on and it seemed to accentuate the specialness of the lover's moment. Freeda looked at it in disbelief. It was a lover's light for Freeda. There was something special about that flying saucer lamppost.

TV put the umbrella up as the rains reached them, and they huddled underneath. By then there was the sound of another car approaching, and this time from the top of Holly Beach Lane. TV looked up the road and could see that it was a police car coming down.

'Here they come, Freeda! Back in the woods!'

Once Chaz got indoors, he didn't have time to worry about a mere cackle of laughter. Out of the immediate moment, out of mind to a greater extent. Chaz gathered a heap of cash from the stash in the locked safe, while Linda was in the shower, and then he went back downstairs and got the laptop up and running as he slurped some filtered coffee. He chuckled to himself when he saw that hairydog@Email.com had received a reply from that young 'up for it' kinky contacts couple. He opened it with attachments added, and was positively drooling over some nude and explicit photographs.

'You, little old shaven whore, you! Come to Chazzy, come to Daddy, you little princess!'

Chaz began writing text, as the e mail said they would be up for a meeting. Chaz was excited as he fancied a bit of Eve.

'Me and my wife are just knocked out by your pics and we're very experienced in bondage and role playing, and we have a superbly fitted room with all of the cutting-edge appliances and a few more! We're looking forward to seeing you soon, and in the meantime, here are a few snaps of the wife and me "getting it on" in the Dark Room. We could accommodate you any weekend!'

But Chaz had other things on his mind too. There was that small matter of making up those eight big ones, and getting ahead as many as he could. He grabbed his mobile, the spring bank holiday was nigh coming up and he had to get an order in. Alfredo was always up with the worms. He was out on his back lawn by the pool meeting the dawning sun with his yoga postures.

'Hullo, Alfredo! Chaz is up with the worms with ya today, mate. I could do with another big one for the bank holiday weekend, mate!'

'Sort it out anytime for ya, Chazzy.'

Chaz was thinking ahead. If he could knock it out quickly on that little offer, he might be up for another big one come Saturday with that dance event in the offing.

'Might be another Saturday morning too, Alf!'

It didn't seem any problem Alfredo's end. His European contact had flown in on the makeshift landing strip up his back garden only last week. The vault had a Euro pallet of coke bricks on it.

With that covered Chaz could rest a little. Eight grand gone with the wind, but with this assault, he was hoping to get it all back with another eight profit and interest by the time that ole rave head dance event was over. It was time for a small line of coke to enliven the day, plug him in, 'Get on it!', and why not a triple X porn movie for accompaniment? Linda came down in casual clothes and entered, while Chaz was bent over snorting. She took a quick glance at the opened laptop that was resting on the arm of the velvet chair. She soon caught the drift.

'What's that you're writing?' she asked, putting Chaz on the spot.

'Look, it's an e mail I'm sending to that young couple, Linda.' Chaz was smiling as he spoke, hoping that Linda might be coming around to the idea. Once she hopped over that fence, she wouldn't be able to get enough of it. But Linda was incensed.

'I said I didn't want to get into that, Chaz!'

Chaz began his normal approach of working on Linda. If you keep at something long enough it generally works, was Chaz's philosophy. Just give it patience. Like the way political parties work their agendas, and they got the result, and up to now, Chaz had always got what he wanted from Linda. This was just a bigger hurdle or wall to get her over. Chaz had to be patient and a little tough, nature never hurries.

'Look! Trust me in this, Linda. They are "up for it" or what! We could cut a deal with this couple on films. We'll all get a sexy kick out of it, and make half a dozen grand or something! Class!'

Linda looked at all the money on the table, a nice wad of fifties and twenties.

'What's all that money for?' she asked.

'Well what do you think it's for? I lost big wedge on that fucking wanker Phelps last night so Chaz's "pop and rock" will be buy one, get a dollop free this bank holiday, Linda. Get on it! Up ya hooter and on your scooter!'

Linda stormed out into the kitchen. She just didn't like Chaz getting deeper and deeper and more dependent on drug dealing. It was getting worse and worse and she feared that the bubble would burst. It had to. When Chaz took the boat out, it had to go further and further and yet more out there. Chaz raised his voice from the lounge. It was only rational. He had to make up for that big loss.

'We've gotta make up the eight grand, Linda! It's essential. You know that!'

Linda continued the conversation from the kitchen.

'If you didn't gamble so big, Chaz, you wouldn't have to make up anything.'

Chaz didn't like any criticism of his gambling habits. The sheer fact that he lived in this house and had renovated it with his money, illustrated that he didn't have a gambling problem.

'Do I have any gambling debts, Linda! No! So just concentrate on the breakfast in your wonderfully new fitted kitchen that cost an arm, a leg, and a testicle, ha ha ha!'

Linda recognized it was true, Chaz didn't have debts, but everything was becoming more cocaine, more, and more, and she would never deal with her habit if there was a sack of it upstairs all the time. She came to the threshold again and reiterated her position, honestly.

'Chaz, I only want to see you doing something legitimate that's all. So this dark cloud overhanging us can lift. So the worry can end.'

Chaz had heard all this before a dozen times, and sometime, someplace in the future, he *would* go legit. Hadn't he promised her? But another, rather more present in the moment part of him, demanded copious amounts of cocaine. He got it cheap this way, and my Christ he liked the dosh, and Linda had a big habit and there was that small matter of Alan and his wife with their cocaine pay-off. Sometimes there is only the devil you know, and for Chaz, lots more of him please. Chaz pursued his usual deflection tactics.

'Yes, yes, me and Miko will sort that one out with a business plan in our own time, Linda.'

Linda walked back into the kitchen as she had heard this so many times before too. She wanted to see something concrete. Chaz continued.

'Things are moving towards that, Linda, trust me!' There was a short pause of silence before Chaz struck up another approach. 'Are ya going to have ya hit, girl? Go for the powder, eh?'

Linda called from the kitchen that she might have it later. Chaz grinned, all smug, and held a rolled up fifty-pound note over yet another line, while he was reading a little piece on a forthcoming runner in the Derby in a few weeks. That one at York was a flop which was five hundred down the drain, but this article referred to Kris Kin, which was going to be ridden by Kieren Fallon. It had won the other week, Chaz watched it himself and he marked it up for big wagers. It was a nice each way price and Chaz decided he would go in big, with a bit of wedge from upstairs. The Derby was another of those betting mediums that Chaz liked to hit big. He would try and get as much money down locally with a number of shops, and again Chaz liked to be the big shot, coming in the bookies once in a blue moon, laying down the real big money. The money that got them all talking in Tennin. He reckoned on a two or three grand each way bet. Chaz chortled to himself as he worked out how much he would pick up and saw himself in his mind's eye, entering the local Tennin bookies picking up that big wedge of money. Kris Kin was the one. He would split the money around half a dozen shops and clear their takings out. Chaz began the snort, thinking about that horse, and this was all a process. Once Chaz got it in his mind that a horse was going to win, that was it. He would invest in the thing every couple of days. But as he was snorting, he could hear another police siren. It was getting louder and louder coming down the main road, down the hill, beyond their boundary fence and the new shed.

'Fuck me! There's a lot of ol pig around this morning, Linda! Wacky-shacker must have gone fucking crazy with an automatic rifle or something!'

Linda had begun preparing the fried sausage and bacon. Chaz had three full fried breakfasts a week. He used to have seven but he had finally given way to the idea that he needed to cut down on the fry ups.

'I reckon you should have phoned the police about that woman's voice you heard Chaz. I bet that's got something to do with it, you know' Chaz had half snorted the line and was about to get down on the other half.

'What and have pig sniffing around while I'm fucking snorting! You must be fucking joking, woman! Whatever it is. Let them fucking sort it out themselves, ha ha ha, ha ha ha. They couldn't sort you out with a bag of fucking cooking apples, ha ha ha, ha ha ha.'

The estate police car pulled into the bottom of Holly Beach Lane, and was advancing on 'Chaz's Pad'. It was driven by PC Amelia Wainhurst, who was altogether prim and proper in her work life, but who pursued additional income in her secret private life as 'Voluptuous Angelica', appearing in the same family of magazines that Natasha had featured in. As she drove up the lane she couldn't resist speaking about the notorious previous residents of Holly Beach Lane.

'This is where that sex cult bloke Arthur Ashcroft lived with that woman who appeared in the horror films. What was her name?'

The PC who was in the adjacent seat was used to Amelia's turn of mind, but he had no inkling of her private secrets, but he did recall the couple as they were a big part of Tennin folklore.

'Diane Desade, she was a porn star before that, Amelia. They were involved with all those crazy goings-on at Jonsen's country estate. The unsolved murder was out the back too, over the other side of the wall, body parts were found on Ashcroft's property.' PC David Bridgewater knew plenty about goings-on up Holly Beach Lane.

The siren was turned off as they passed the doctor's house; they had it on to get past all of the rush hour traffic that was bad around Tennin these days. Within a few seconds afterwards the police car was directly outside the front of the house, and Chaz sat there befuddled for a moment with the rolled up fifty-pound note in his fingers ready to go down on it. It was an odd serendipity.

'Fuck's sake, pig!'

Chaz rushed to put the cocaine away, and with the fear of the possible consequences, smashing down on him, he panicked trying to scoop it up into the bag. It went everywhere. Things were worsened by the sound of a dog barking coming from the vicinity of the estate police car. Then the dog was right at the front gate barking even more loudly. Chaz immediately thought 'Raid!'

'Sniffer! Get that fucking hoover out, Linda! There's fucking coke everywhere!'

Chaz then realized he had to do something about the black-market DVDs surrounding him. He turned off the TV and piled them into the cabinets underneath the carp tanks. The police were at the front gate, then walking up the path, with the dog behind on a lead with PC Bridgewater. They both inevitably took to smelling the flowers.

'Sweet smelling garden,' PC Amelia remarked, while paroxysms of movement were taking place in the house. Chaz told Linda to answer the door and stall them while he whipped upstairs. If he had to, he would flush a bag of coke away down the pan.

'What shall I?' Chaz couldn't believe his ears. Couldn't she take the darn initiative for once!

'Just do it for fuck's sake, Linda!'

The two police officers halted when they reached the front door. PC Bridgewater looked suspiciously at the spitting snake, so he rang the bell instead. Linda done her best to be composed, say the right thing, and not trip over herself. But she feared saying the wrong. She opened the door as Chaz passed her with the coke. Linda tentatively put out feelers.

'Yes, er, hullo.'

PC Amelia Wainhurst opened up and Linda was able to breathe a great sigh of relief, before other fears began manifesting.

'We're deeply sorry for any inconvenience at this early hour but there has been a "break out" at the asylum, and we've got two highly dangerous characters on the loose. We'll need to search the woods at the back of the house, with the dog just in case they're lurking out there. Could we have your permission to search please?'

In between trying to keep the dog unexcited, the male officer gave the additional information, that would no doubt alarm all residents living in close proximity.

'They are thought to be carrying knives,' he said, trying not to create too much unnecessary fear. Linda didn't know what to say next, but she felt duly alarmed. The kind of dreadful things that Chaz was afraid might occur up here, were happening.

'Oh dear, well go ahead and search but what do they look like?' Linda asked. The female continued.

'Er thank you, but good question! And we were just coming to that. But have you heard or seen anything suspicious this morning?' Linda hesitated for a moment and then before she knew it, she was referring to what Chaz had briefly spoken about. That odd sinister laugh.

'Hold on! I'll get my husband. He heard something this morning!'

As soon as she said it, she regretted it. Chaz would go ballistic. Linda entered the front room and closed the lounge door for a second, as the police waited outside. Chaz had a hoover going, and was hoovering everywhere around the velvet chair and coffee table. He stopped for a moment.

'They've come about two escaped residents of the old asylum and they want to have a word with you about what you heard, Chaz.' Chaz sighed. He couldn't believe it. He couldn't have made it up.

'Tut! What are you fucking playing at, woman!'

But within a few moments Chaz was at the front door doing his best. 'Can I be of any assistance, officers?' The female took the reins again and Chaz was sure that he had seen that face before. But he couldn't quite place it.

'We are investigating the whereabouts of two escaped patients from the asylum and your wife said you heard something suspicious this morning.'

Chaz opened up and told them about his return from the convenience store, and the woman cackling in the woods down the lane a hundred yards or so.

'Strange, oddly sinister laugh,' he said. The dog began barking louder and PC Bridgewater pulled the hound back out of the way, and was trying to settle him down up the garden path. But he couldn't stop him barking. Then it hit Chaz, like a thunderbolt. He was sure that female PC had appeared in one of Natasha's magazines, *Voluptuaries*. He would check it out as he had the mag in a couple of great piles underneath the far carp tank.

'Sounds like our woman,' the female officer replied. Linda was listening on, back behind Chaz at the door.

'What do they look like, officer?' Chaz asked, a little more assured, now he knew this wouldn't be turning into anything other than what it appeared to be. PC Amelia Wainhurst opened up again.

'Now, I know it sounds odd, but you've got to realize where they are coming from. But the man was last seen wearing a hooded jacket, baseball cap, skirt and sandals.'

Linda exasperated Chaz again with her blurting. But she was only trying to help.

'That's that bloke you saw, Chaz!'

Chaz was incensed and he prevaricated for a moment, trying to make it all up on the fly as best he could. But it was all pressure, he could have done without.

'Well er, I don't know if it was him, Linda? But yes, I saw someone fitting that description by a lamppost on "The Triune Way". I'm sure he had some kind of skirt on. Ha, ha ha, not many blokes around wearing skirts officer is there? Even in these liberated times.'

Chaz had even remembered the glamour model's pseudonym, 'Voluptuous Angelica', as she had appeared in the same edition as Natasha, right next to her in its running order. She was around thirty he guessed and he couldn't wait to check. Chaz was asked to add a few details, and he said that it was last Tuesday while he was going around the last roundabout, the one with the Salome tulips.

'An avid gardener?' suggested the female constable. Chaz enjoyed just kidding them along.

'Of course! Look around you. And ya couldn't miss him. He was staring up at the lamppost to the left there, yeah, where the Salome tulips are.' Chaz enjoyed getting a little personal amusement from his communications with 'pig' at his doorstep, and he could just see that 'Voluptuous Angelica' in that mag, with her legs wide open in his mind's eye. He was darn sure it was this PC in front of him. But Chaz had that insight. People had these dark secret, 'other' lives in the New Age and it gave Chaz an altogether pansophic smile on his face as he spoke. He had her number.

The female PC, the possible Angelica, gave a description of the other absconder.

'The woman is early thirties, Caucasian, long straight hair, thought to be wearing a violet dressing gown on escape. If you spot either of them, Mr. and Mrs. Barber, alert us immediately and in no circumstances, should they be confronted. They have excessively violent histories, especially the woman.'

PC Bridgewater said they would now search the woods and orchard. The dog was quiet.

'At my pleasure, officers, anything to aid their apprehension.' Chaz couldn't resist having a dig at the female PC as he was certain it was her now. Chaz looked at her with eyebrows raised.

'If you should need me, I'll be indoors researching something in a heap of my leisure magazines.'

PC Bridgewater thought it an odd thing to say, and Amelia just raised her shoulders, as if she hadn't the faintest idea of what he was talking about. But she knew that Chaz had opened her closet door. It was an embarrassing moment for her.

As soon as the door was shut, Chaz was in the front room stalking Linda down, but his anger had been tempered with the idea that this PC might have been in Nat's *Voluptuaries*.

'Why the fuck did you have to say I saw the fucking creep!'

'Oh Chaz,' Linda pleaded for him to let it pass, as she was only trying to help.

'And that's enough of the "oh fucking Chaz's". Before you know it, they'll want a statement and that fucking dog will be sniffing me out! Get that fucking hoover going again, woman!'

Chaz then took to the far carp tank cabinet in which he kept the horde of Nat's magazines. He quickly had the edition in question out, and turned to the pages. It was her all right. Linda shut down the hoover for a second as she wondered why he had rushed to get the magazine.

'There she is! That female PC out there, laid out with her hairy twat all open!'

Chaz quickly turned the page.

'And with her fist half up it! Look!'

Linda tried to believe that it wasn't the policewoman. Surely the Tennin police force wasn't into this kind of thing. But she looked at the photos and it was 'Angelica from Fishgate', and she knew it was the PC.

'Yeah, looks like her.'

'It is her! The dirty whore! But get that hoover going!'

Linda switched on, and got going again, as Chaz began cleaning up around the coffee table. He left the mag on the table, opened on a double page X-rated intimate of Angelica, lain on the floor with her legs overhead. Chaz smiled and yet brooded over things, as he plopped a couple of his teaser balls into the tanks, casting an eye towards the spread of Angelica. The baits were still working, if nothing else, as the carp muscled in. But then his mind turned towards the more disturbing, rather than the erotically enticing.

'I knew that fucking Jesus weirdo was out there. I knew it! He's probably been looking in our garden with a blade in his back pocket or down his knickers, the fucking creep!'

Everything was just getting too much for Linda. All the fears that Chaz had, were manifesting as if ordained from some malevolent force in the universe. It felt like being under siege.

'Oh, don't say that, Chaz, please!' Linda moved out from the coffee table, still glancing back towards the magazine, and the transgressive nature of it all turned her on. Chaz noticed her and couldn't resist a smutty joke.

'What the arm of the law does these days eh Linda?' Chaz said, as he sat back down on the velvet chair going immediately for a line, laid out across the Thabane next to that double page spread, seemingly in defiance of the police, who were poking around out the back. Linda saw what he was doing and turned off the hoover.

'Oh Chaz? Do you have to while the police are here?' she pleaded. But Chaz wanted a line and that was that.

'Look, they won't be coming in here, will they? Unless you invite them in to look at her wonderful, wide-open fanny snaps!' Chaz laughed. 'And I'm dying for another one with all this fucking pressure!'

Then Linda suddenly realized that all she needed to do to get a low-down on everything, was to phone June. She would have all the gossip.

'I'll ring June! She's bound to know all about it! And with a hangover too!'

June was in a block of toilets washing the floor when her mobile rung. She rested her mop up and took the call, enjoying every moment of it.

'Great last night, Linda, eh? And I'm still half pissed! I'm still laughing about it all. But ya phoning about the "break out"? It's bonkers up here! Bonkers, Linda!'

Apparently, the knocked-out window was now some kind of extraordinary shrine to the legendary TV Sam. The Trust had put a plastic cover tarpaulin over it and the site had quickly become a bizarre scene of pilgrimage among the clients. No doubt Dr. Lock would tackle that in due course. But for the time being all the patients were busily talking about the sheer audacity of what TV had done, while they peered at the tarpaulin sheet. Who else but TV Sam could have taken out that window with an electric saw? And did you hear him with that sledgehammer! It all added to the powerful myth and asylum legend of TV Sam. Linda told June that they had the police searching the back garden and orchard for them, and she couldn't resist telling June about the female officer who was a glamour model appearing in the same mag as Nat. What a juicy bit of gossip!

'Oh my God!'

June said that there were tons of police up there at the asylum. It was crawling and June got down to the details.

'TV Sam got "Mad Freeda" out of the lock up unit with a sledgehammer and chainsaw, Linda. He took out a window and Freeda was threatening everybody with knives. And apparently she was originally put in here, when she was sixteen, for chopping her stepfather's penis off with a carving knife. Not so fucking sweet, eh, Linda?'

It was all the fears embodied and worse!

'She's fucking mad, June. Fucking mad!'

'That's why she's locked up in here, Linda! And she's the vim and worms girl! And is she dangerous, you wouldn't believe it, Linda. Gloria says she's always threatening to wake people up with a knife in their head! Charming, eh? And it's not just threats, she's stabbed a few people in her time, Gloria's been saying.' June had all the latest low-downs on the escaping story too, lined up like a deck of aces in a card hand.

'How did they get through security?' Linda asked, and June began playing the aces one by one with great relish.

'Too many agency workers not knowing the run of the place, Linda, and we've heard they all confronted "Mad Freeda", and all, to a man, shat their fucking pants!' As June was talking, Linda was wondering whether she would work up there on the cleaning after all, as they didn't need the money. She didn't want this 'Mad Freeda' being a part of her life. But she had to tell June that Chaz had met up with this TV character the previous week. Even juicier gossip!

'You wouldn't believe it, June. Chaz only sold him some DVDs down on "The Triune Way", the other night.'

Sex and that TV. It didn't surprise June as Gloria had told her that he was massive on masturbation. In fact, Gloria held court for nigh half an hour over two teas before they started, so June had plenty of information up her sleeve and how she reveled in it.

'They do it all the time up here, Linda. All the time. And there's more. Gloria has been telling me loads about them. The TV guy, the one who wears the skirts, he's got this weird psycho thing about televisions. He's notorious for smashing them to bits if he gets half a chance. Kicks them in and throws them out of windows'

Linda was exclaiming 'no' in disbelief, and that was inspiring June ever so much more, as she had plenty more big cannons.

'And the wanking. Gloria said it stopped all of a sudden about four years ago. He said he wanted his cock chopped off, Linda.' Chaz could hear the conversation going on.

'It's gets worse and fucking worse. Nutty fucking farmers!'

June continued with the story, making merry over the case in question, TV's penis.

'Gloria said he kept telling the doctors that he didn't get along with it. He said it poked out too much and that it must have been someone else's, and that he was really a woman with a big dick!'

'Oh my God, June!' By now Linda had got the giggles but there was plenty more.

'He was just about to have the op and then he met "Mad Freeda" and changed his mind. And they say it's a big one, Linda. Bout as big as you'll ever see! So, it must have poked out a bit!'

June howled with laughter and Linda gave it a chorus.

'Gloria has seen him wanking too! She said it spurted out like a hosepipe!' Linda laughed so much that she broke down in tears, remonstrating June to stop.

'Oh, June! You're making me laugh so much!' But then a hard dose of reality descended on Linda as June brought it down heavily.

'Might be funny, Linda. But be warned they're mighty dangerous! And they could turn up anywhere!'

Yes, there was humor, but the overriding feeling, was of a worrying and threatening development. Chaz was in the process of laying out yet another smaller line of coke on a snap of 'Voluptuous Angelica'. He had already decided if the police did have to come in for a statement, he would just leave the magazine there on the coffee table, opened on her shoot. But he was concerned about what he was hearing.

'It's all the fears un it! Tooled up fucking nut jobs snooping around, hiding behind bushes, exposing themselves, watching your every fucking move!'

They represented everything bad for Chaz because they were so unpredictable. It was like clowns. Chaz had never liked clowns. He had seen clowns as a young boy at the circus tent along Green Street Meadows and Chaz found them unsettling then, even disturbing. These nutty Muppets were like that. They didn't play by the rules the rest of us have to play by. He snorted up the line and began to think about Linda's safety.

'Might be best if ya locked all the doors and stayed put today, Linda. When ya knocked out all the boilies, just leave them in the porch.'

Linda was incensed. Why couldn't he just stay at home until these two dangerous types had been caught? But when she did criticize or question Chaz, it always seemed to come out sounding so tame. As if she didn't really bother about it that much. But this time there *was* just a little more intensity in her voice.

'Can't you stay at home for today, Chaz, until they've got them?'

Chaz would have loved to have stayed at home. But sheer necessity made that difficult. Money makes the world go round and he and Linda had spent a good bit the last few months, with the house renovations and improvements, that were still ongoing. Expensive process, and Chaz had lent Natasha that forty grand to go towards her Porsche too. Or should we say had given it to her, as it would never be coming back.

'I've got to earn dough, Linda! That fucking wanker Phelps cost me eight fucking big uns last night! And you know I've gotta go in massive on a bank holiday. Otherwise they'll all go down the road to some other fucking supplier. Then we would be up fucking shit creek, wouldn't we?'

This perspective wasn't altogether true, as Chaz's powder was the A game, so the punters would always come to him. But he was in the process of winning an argument.

The two police officers searched the back and were inevitably drawn to the old black shed. It was an obvious hide out, and as soon as they approached it the dog began pulling hard and barking. It reached the door and got up on its hind legs and was furiously tearing at it with his claws.

'Down, Sparky, down!'

The male PC Bridgewater was pulling at the powerful Alsatian, trying to control him as he had obviously picked up on some kind of scent. 'They might be in there! So, watch it, Amelia!'

The male officer tried the door and then like the two before, they looked through the windows to find not a soul in there. They wondered what the dog had picked up on, as he could only be diverted with a few chocolate sweets that were always used judiciously to get that extra bit of dog control. They walked back towards the house convinced that there wasn't anybody out there. But there was.

After their walkabouts, TV Sam and Freeda had found a little safety behind the crumbling back boundary wall and TV was watching the police through a gap. They had the umbrella up and were seated on those milk crates. Freeda was quiet as she was gorging the last of the sweet pancakes. She had been ravenous, but now the hole was nearly filled, and at least it diverted her from that dog barking. But they were snug in this new sheltered spot and TV was thankful that they didn't have to run away from those police and the Alsatian.

'It's cozy here, TV. It's like a holy-day and we've got thousands of fags and pancakes!' TV was still watching the two police officers and dog move back towards the house, relieved.

'Shush, Freeda! They haven't quite gone yet!' Freeda wasn't taking a blind bit of notice as she was so interested in eating the pancakes, her favorites.

'These pancakes are so nice, TV!' Freeda said, as she finished the last and dropped the plastic wrapping before gathering her thoughts towards smoking fags. TV was still watching the police, but they were about to go out of sight now, as they had returned to the house. The black bag rustled as Freeda went for a packet of twenty.

'I'm gonna smoke loads, TV. Loads!'

TV was still looking at that old shed. Now the police had just checked it. If they could get inside; the police wouldn't check it again, or at least for some time. It might be a safe place for a while, TV thought.

'Quiet, Freeda! I reckon we could get in that shed. We could make it our special hide-out! We'd have tools and that!'

After those knives were mislaid Freeda was determined to get another. She had to have knives now she was free. She could scare people with a knife, and the thought of that big fat nurse and Locko was boiling her blood with anger, because she knew they would be out after her.

'I wanna new knife, TV! I wanna get Lock and Bolt. I wanna get um with a knife, TV! And I wanna stick it in that big fat nurse!'

TV started to get worried when Freeda began getting agitated like this. He knew it was bound to happen, yet he wanted their time together to be special, without all the bad things getting in the way.

'Chill out, Freeda! I'll get ya another knife but why don't you smoke-the-three, like Keefy used to do, to get a calm on? He used to always do that, Freeda.'

Just hearing TV's warm voice calmed Freeda, but there was a clear reason why TV had referred to smoking the three. It sparked a significant memory, when she and TV smoked the three in the smoking area in the lock up unit. She had met TV for the first time the previous day when he was sitting in the lounge on one of the armchairs. He used to go on and on and on about Keefy back then, and Freeda never actually met him, but she saw him frequently out on the grounds with TV in that famed white blazer jacket he used to wear. TV was always going on about Keefy's white blazer, so much so, that it used to annoy her, all that going on about Keefy's white blazer. It was only a bloody jacket. But he used to go on and bloody on.

'Don't ya remember, Freed? When we first smoked the three together? And Keefy was out there at the smoking tree in the white blazer!' TV mentioned this, as he knew how much those moments meant to Freeda. She smiled back at TV warmly and thought, I hope he doesn't go on and on about that white blazer, he's a fucking bore when he does that. But she still had such fond memories.

'Yeah, things were fun when we were together back then. The best ever!'

'And that was the most important moment of my life, Freeda. When I was with you, and you were laughing with me.'

TV meant it as well. Freeda had been the changing point. It truly was love at first sight, and Freeda had been swept off her feet. She had always felt TV's love and that was enough for Freeda. In a perfect world they would have been the perfect couple together. But worlds are never like that, although TV meant it; those moments with Freeda were special to him. He had never enjoyed being in a woman's company so much. They just clicked.

TV helped Freeda get the three between her fingers. He made smoking the three seem so very important.

'Right, Freeda, now make sure ya got all three in there like Keefy used to do and I'll give ya a strike.'

Freeda got the three fags into her mouth ready for the big draw. 'Breathe in really deep, Freeda! Really deep!'

TV struck his lighter and Freeda sucked the air in, as if trying to extract the life from the thin air of the Himalayas. TV guided her through the correct breathing. She held it down for four long seconds and then she made a great, slow exhalation, all following TV's prompting. She closed her eyes as she exhaled, and was party to a sheer blissful experience, that only rarefied Dragon Star children can be party too.

'Have ya got it, Freeda? Have ya got it?'

'Oh, I feel so calm now, TV!' she confessed.

TV was an expert at these things. He knew how to get people on that chilled wavelength as he had inherited the wisdom as leader of the cult.

'That's why Keefy used to do it, Freeda. Get a calm on. That's why, Freeda. And smoking one's no good. It's no good. You've gotta smoke three like Keefy used ta! It's gotta be the three, Freeda!'

Freeda took another enormous toke on the three, and this time she coughed and spluttered, and TV quickly put his hand over her mouth to muffle the noise, and thankfully nobody heard her.

By now the police officers were at the door advising the Barbers to keep in touch with local radio updates regarding the fluid situation.

'We most certainly will, officer! Thanking you for all of your trouble. And I hope they get caught soon, as we're gagging to visit my aunt Angelica down at Fishgate later! I love seeing her. I really do! She's quite a sight! And, we don't want them to be hanging around "Chaz's Pad" in the bushes or something when we return!'

Chaz was coming up on all the coke, and he just couldn't resist that one and he was aware enough to notice that PC Amelia Wainhurst knew darn well what he meant. The implications were lost on PC Bridgewater, although he thought Chaz's comments rather odd, although he didn't mention it. PC Amelia thought Mr. Barber was 'on something'.

'Did you notice his eyes? They were nigh bolting out of his head!' she said as they closed the garden gate. But PC Bridgewater knew that everything was about this 'break out'. Clearing this issue up without anything disturbing occurring, was a top priority for the local force.

'We've got other fish to fry right now, Amelia,' he replied.

Chaz came back into the lounge humored, wondering whether he pushed it a bit too far, but so high on coke that he didn't care a shit. He watched the police car depart, and was relieved. But what a coincidence. He would have to tell Natasha!

'Thank fuck for that! And time to get the skates on, Chazzy boy! It's over to Alfredo's, make a few drops, and I need to pop in ta see Mumsy too! So, I'll have to find time for the florist.'

Linda was reflective for a moment, as she still didn't like the idea of Chaz treating this like a normal day, and so not being at home. These two patients had knives, and you couldn't trust them, could you?'

'Do you have to go, Chaz?' she pleaded, with as much feeling and intensity as she could muster. She thought it might just sway him, but once Chaz was committed to a course of action around making hard cash, he was rarely shifted. That large matter of eight grand lost was gnawing at him. If this 'break out' business ruined the weekend, it would take him nigh two weeks to get back into profit.

'Look, Linda, if I don't go out, it'll be tight for those gold ingots and we want another three by the end of the summer. It's essential, Linda. That's security for our future. And I've got to get Charley to Alan, and none of this here would be possible without Al, would it?'

Linda felt stressed and it wasn't just about the 'break out'. She desperately wanted some kind of life change.

'Everything could be sorted if we had your mum here, Chaz. We could pay the mortgage off tomorrow and we would still have stacks of money left and all the gold.'

Chaz was sick of this kind of talk, as Linda was always bringing it up.

'Now how can we have me mum here? The way you two are and the business! Look, just lock the place up! They'll have those two crackers back up there in no time! The place is crawling with "pig", Linda.'

The rain was intermittent now, and TV thought they should make a move on that old shed and set up camp. He reasoned they had a 'window of opportunity' and he referred to it, but Freeda was eating the last of the Milkybars and wasn't taking any notice. He took down the umbrella and rounded up the bags and noticed that the food stock was low. They had taken too much time getting fags, they still had loads of them. TV then tentatively looked over the wall, saw that it was all clear, motioned to Freeda to be ready, and onwards he went with Freeda close behind.

'Quiet, Freeda, and keep look out!'

Freeda glanced this way and that and thought about stealth and the first thing that came into her mind were cats and the way they creep about when they don't want to be noticed. She would be a cat creeping, and she began mimicking as if she were a two-legged creeping cat with her hands up like paws with fingers wide apart. She had a wide grin on her face as everything was fun with TV.

'What you doing, Freed?'

'Freeda's doing creeping cats, so nobody hears her, TV.'

TV thought it fun too, and it would ensure she thought about the way she was moving, when the search parties were bound to be still after them.

'Yeah! Keep creeping, Freeda!'

They arrived at the old black shed and TV tried the door, then pushed it as hard as he could hoping it might open. But it was still sturdy and would have to be tackled with wires. TV studied the lock for a few seconds, taking out a pair of cheap reading glasses this time, so that he could see the details more clearly. He then delved into an inner compartment of his Dragon Star hoody, and took out some thin ones. But there was something about this shed, TV thought. TV was sensitive to aura and things like that and he was trying to get a hook on it. It was akin to a subtle force field and TV was deep in thought. Freeda had slipped off her hoodie, and was busily admiring her and TV emblazoned on the back in that well-crafted caricature.

'I luv our jackets, TV. Don't we look good doing "Dragon Star"!' she enthused.

'They're ace, Freeda! Give it five years and everyone will be wearing them. Mind the light though!'

TV was now back in the moment and he went to work and such old locks were never a problem. The lock released.

'You've opened the door again, TV! It'll be like our house!'

Freeda was excited and at least it would be a safe place to stay for a while, TV thought. They entered and were met with a musty smell and dusty atmosphere so at least it had withstood the storm. This shed had been there the best part of sixty years, but had been well built and maintained, yet everything had gone rusty, before Ashcroft had it repaired by a friend. Freeda wasn't keen but she was with her TV.

'Thanks, TV, for saving Freeda,' she said with a great smiling face and TV hugged her.

'I did it because I love you, Freeda. I wanna be with you always! It was meant to be like that.'

How Freeda loved hearing those words, but she sniffed the air. What a funny place they had chosen to stay in.

'It smells like, like the earth, TV!'

TV sniffed the air. It was a musty old shed that was full of old gardening equipment and had an old work bench running along the wall, that wasn't damp. TV couldn't quite grasp what he was subtly feeling though.

'I never really thought of it like that, Freeda,' he replied, as he hadn't. Freeda became animated with the gardening equipment as she wanted to be positive. It looked like they were going to have to stay here, so she had to make the best of it, and those nurses were always talking about being positive up at the prison, rather than wanting to kill yourself. They were always saying it.

'And look, TV! We've got this lovely barrow!'

TV Sam tried his hardest to make the most of the hide-out but he could tell it was only a matter of time before Freeda would want more. But he still couldn't put his finger on the inscrutable, odd feeling and atmosphere the place had. But he recalled Keefy speaking to him about Ashcroft, the sixties mystic having lived in the house going back, and that he was into some of the things that the Dragon Star were into. Memories came flooding back. He recalled Keefy having a collector's porn magazine that featured that Ashcroft's wife. Keefy used to wank over her and he used to say that she was into Dragon Star shagging and for a spell he swore by her autobiography. Everything is intimately connected, TV thought.

Freeda put her hand into the bucket of the barrow and it disintegrated. She immediately began to look around for something else to focus her attention on, while TV was still trying to work out what he was feeling. She was with TV, so she wasn't going to think about killing herself. She had to keep up with the positive. That's what those nurses were always saying, even that big fat one that she hated so much, so she desperately wanted to find something that wasn't old and rusty. There was a pair of shears hanging on the wall.

'And we've a lovely pair of big scissors, TV!' Freeda put her hand on the shears and the blades came apart and fell on the floor.

'Mind, Freeda! It looks like everything has gone rusty Freed!'

It was a large shed and there was loads of gardening equipment, some of it covered up with old black sheets. TV's mind was averted to a large pitch fork that was resting up against the corner of the shed. But when investigating TV could see this was different. It was a six-foot trident and was brass so was well preserved. He took it up and gesticulated with it, and was thinking about gladiators.

'Look at this, Freeda. This ain't rusty!'

Freeda looked on curiously.

'That might come in handy someday, TV!' she said, and that was exactly what TV thought. 'You could use it forking people!'

TV hadn't thought about it like that, but it did give him options. It might come in handy in tight situations. TV smirked to himself as whatever he was feeling, being alone with Freeda in this enclosed space was making him feel sexy. He could feel himself getting a hard-on.

'Suppose I could, Freeda.'

Freeda's attention was then drawn to an old mattress, that was lain up along the work bench. It had a bed sheet over it and was in reasonable condition, although had caught the musty virus too. But Freeda was still excited. They had been out of prison all this time and hadn't had a shag yet.

'Look, TV! Freeda's found a shagging bed!' They moved the old mattress onto the part collapsed wooden floor and once it was down it was clear that Freeda had things on her mind. She jumped on it smirking while opening her dressing gown. TV would be up for a bit.

'What about a shag to the "Seventh" with a "fizz banger"?', Freeda said, using some of the cult's secret terminology. 'Fizz bangers' and 'Seventh Heaven' were concepts about sexuality, that the inaugural Dragon Star children had developed over many years. It was TV Sam who was largely responsible, albeit heavily influenced by Keefy, but it was TV who had put in the research work in the field, as they say. A goodly number of times in the toilet blocks with agency workers. But Freeda had picked it all up from her mentor. They both smiled as a shagging session was fast approaching.

'Course we can, Freeda. It's about time we had a good shag.'

That was the approach of Dragon Star, breaking into new territory, and meeting sexuality head on, with a complete honesty about lust and desire. It was all about going beyond it all. 'Seeing the Dragon', TV called it.

'I'm gonna suck ya big, enormous spunk chucka first, TV!'

TV thought that a great idea and these were special moments for the lovers. They hadn't had sex since TV was taken out of the lock up unit after being caught having sex with Freeda. But if human beings can be monogamous, TV and Freeda were the monogamists, albeit with a few reservations, and sex to the Dragon Star children was akin to a sacrament. Although Freeda just loved having a good shag with TV.

'I'm getting it, TV! I'm getting the "Fizzer banger snake"!'

The 'Fizzer banger' snake was an idea that TV and Keefy had developed from reading erudite off the wall books on mysticism. One of them being no other than Ashcroft's tome. Sex could really lead us to the new consciousness was the Dragon Star credo, and according to 'The Star' it was best to do it as much as possible. All need to be at it like enlightenment rabbits, was the new call, and the key tenet of the New Age cult's philosophy. Everyone would feel better if they shagged each other's brains out more, was how TV succinctly put it. There had to be a new brain. A new way of thinking, Dragon Star thinking.

'Keep going, Freeda! Like Keefy used to do fizz bang!' TV was now the thrusting master with his oversized and famous penis, so Freeda was undoubtedly feeling something.

'I'm getting him, TV! Fizzer banger! Fizzer banger!'

When the Dragon Star adherents had sex, they would fully immerse themselves into each other, the two becoming one, as they shagged their way towards a glorious merging climax. For TV and Keefy, decent shagging was the way the human race could liberate itself. We all need to shag our old brains out with the white light from the fizz bang snakes. It seemed all esoteric, but as TV would say, it was all underpinned by a good old shag and was therefore accessible to the masses.

It was a beautiful post-coital bliss that TV and Freeda found themselves in, as the sunlight slanted across their mattress. But moments of intimacy were difficult with Freeda.

'Do you remember your dreams, Freeda?' TV asked, in this lover's after glow. Freeda's dreams were bound into her traumatic background, that these moments with TV had given her respite from. Generally, the past would come through positively, and then it would be subsumed by Freeda's abyss.

'I dream of my mummy, TV, when we used to go strawberry picking when I was little.'

Freeda cherished those memories. Strawberry picking with her mum, personified the warmth that she felt with her mother, and which was sorely lacking with her incarcerated life, apart from her friendship with Kleeunah and the Dragon Star members themselves. But none of that could hold back the trauma.

'And he was doing it then! Barry was doing it to me then, TV!'

Freeda broke down into tears and TV comforted her as best he could. TV just wanted her to go beyond all that bad. He tried his best to love it all better, so she could just live in this precious moment.

'Don't be upset by all the horrible things, Freeda. We're together now, and that's all that matters.'

TV made such a difference. When he spoke such loving words, Freeda did feel better, or at least she did when she was with TV. She smiled, thankful she was with him now, although she was wishing she was in a nice house, and not in an old dank and rusty shed surrounded by gardening equipment.

'Yeah it is, TV. You have that dream with the shooting star don't ya?'

This was a dream that Keefy used to have, and he talked about it a lot with TV and then TV started to have it, and more so, after Keefy had died. They called it the blaze of the Dragon Star!

'Yeah! I shoot through the atmosphere in a blaze of light, Freeda!' TV exclaimed. Freeda had heard TV recounting this dream many a time, even back a few years when they were together in the unit, and she remembered just how it all went.

'Is that when the spacemen are coming to get you, TV?'

The Dragon Star children were well versed on anything UFO or relating to visitations from other planetary systems. Keefy had been taking away by aliens twice back in his teenage years, and he was brought back to earth with the Dragon Star light sparking off in his brain. TV had never been taken away, but he was always studying his UFO magazines, and he insisted to everyone that these aliens from other systems were spiritually superior and they liked human beings shagging best. It would be a new enlightenment as soon as people's brains were fully shagged out. That was what Dragon Star was all about, shagging people's brains out! Keefy had said it was like a whiteout of the brain.

'Yeah and I'm free and in this quiet place. There're flowers and that, and they come and collect me. Dan sees it, Freeda!'

It all seemed so odd to Freeda, but the most important thing was being with TV.

'Hope they collect me too, TV,' she said, just wanting to be with him.

CHAPTER ELEVEN

"TIS A LOVELY CARE HOME, MUM"

Chaz was on it, bang on it. Clad in the customary white blazer and dark glasses, he could be seen sidling out of Alfredo's farm house, some twenty miles outside Tennin, deep in the countryside. Alfredo had a farm hand helping him and the ten acres he had was handy, enough room for that landing strip for small aircraft that were coming in every six months or so. Chaz got into the Jag, and locked up a nice cache of coke in the dash. The deal was a whopping two kilo that cost Chaz forty-five grand, all taken from 'The Stash' up in the gun's cabinet, although he reckoned, he still had thirty or forty up there. He would go in with the freebie deal. By now it was a buy three and get the fourth free idea and would involve a little bit of overtime running around to try and set up the opportunity for another load on Saturday afternoon. Happy days he thought to himself, he just had to hang in there, and then the Phelps debacle would be history.

On the passenger seat next to him was a spread of flowers and a big box of Licorice All Sorts. The sun was sparkling off the Jag, and Chaz was feeling that his world was coming back together again, as if there was a benevolent power in the universe seeing Chaz all right, allied with that big bag of hope of course. He got on the blower to Jay, they were up for a six ounce with a two freebie, and they said they would have another on Sunday morning, 'Sorted!' It would be a big piggy bank raid as Jay called it, to get themselves an even bigger piggy full.

There was the smell of rubber when he pulled away. Last night when he lost that dough, he didn't feel in control, but now fully 'back in', he was cruising again, perfect and sorted proper. Chaz had been at Alfredo's for an hour or so, talking about operations concerning Candy Foxes and the like, while Chaz sorted out a kilo of the coke in ounce bags. Thirty-five of the little beggars and he had a kilo brick for the 'Foxes'. He would have it all out in no time. But first he had family duties to attend to.

'Let's go and get an eyeful of little ole big tits,' he guffawed to himself, as he cruised through the delightful rural lanes, making his way to the motorway. The young woman referred to, was a feisty young secretary called Jessica, who worked at the care home on reception. Chaz couldn't stop thinking about her as he drove over there. She usually offered a quite memorable sight.

Within the next breath, Chaz had the flowers and box of sweets in his hands as he looked downwards at the secretary, seated in front of him. Her legs were crossed as she sat typing stuff out on a keyboard, with a big-backed computer in front of her. Chaz loved confronting her like this with nobody around. He could push it out a bit, and on this occasion, Chaz got a tantalizing glimpse up her knickers as he looked down at her in that tight short skirt. Jessica had her usual tight-fitting, slightly open top on, displaying her heaving assets. She placed the visitor's book on the counter for Chaz to sign. Now Chaz had developed a cheeky bantering style with this particular young woman, and Chaz would always be attuned to the type of woman or girl he could get away with such things with. Chaz was fully aware that some women were offended with all of this feminism about, but others were 'up for it'. They had a sack full of that product called sex, and they also liked to make money, just like Chaz. To each his own, was Chaz's philosophy. But Jessica was certainly in Chaz's books, as an 'up for it' kind of girl.

'A lovely day to look down women's cleavages, but too good for work!'

Jessica didn't mind this kind of sexy talk from Chaz. She was bored in her job; and she just liked some sexy attention from this cheeky man, who obviously had pots of money. Chaz was working on her.

'Yes, it is, but I'm not seeing much of it. Stuck in here.'

Jessica sounded bored, as if she was just dying for some exciting things to happen, to end the predictability of her boring life. She was intending to go to the dance event at the Tennin Show ground, but her line manager had been on at her, regarding some reports that she had got behind on. She would have to work the bank holiday weekend, and have days off in lieu. That was why she was particularly bored and pissed off, as she was looking forward to the dance festival with some friends who were into ecstasy and taking cocaine, incidentally, gathered from Jay and Dai up the alley by the DIY store.

'Well I'm seeing a nice bit,' chuckled Chaz. Yes, Chaz had been thinking about Jessica and he thought it was high time to really push it out on her. Give it a try. Why not? Chaz had her down as that 'easy' sort of girl. 'Have you ever thought of being in films? There's plenty of money to be made if you're young, feisty and "up for it".'

Jessica replied with a 'what do you mean?', but her tone was deeply interested, rather than condemnatory, as if she was almost wishing it was porn. Chaz was discreet. He didn't want to have to go into details here.

'Well, here's my card. Excellent rates of pay, although all contracts are negotiable, and I can reassure you, Jessica, that this is a very confidential family company, very confidential.'

Unbeknown to Linda, Chaz and Miko had been making porn films at a local sex club and at Miko's bungalow with Viv directing. They were searching hard now for a stable star and he thought this Jessica might be a possible. Chaz and Miko were obviously geared up for Natasha to get more and more involved after Uni, but they also needed somebody else. With the right girl, Viv believed she could make use of all her experience and gradually build up a heightened anticipation in the punters. The card that Chaz gave her, was for that burgeoning company, and Jessica was more than interested. She said she would take a look and replied in a way that said to Chaz, if she liked the money, she might well be 'up for it'. Chaz suggested that she would have to be very, very 'out there' and 'open'.

'I can be very out there when it all suits me. I'll have a look.'

The communication was interrupted by a driver from a supermarket chain who had the weekly food order.

'Your mother's in the smoking lounge, Mr. Barber. She seems to be doing a lot of that lately.' Jessica smiled and winked, as she anticipated some impending excitement and action. She would look at this website, as soon as the driver was out of the way.

Chaz knew that all of these little sex connections could lead to the Holy Grail, as Chaz was one of those visionaries, who was getting down on that eternal truth, sex and drugs equals money! Tons of it! Women are the repositories of the former, and if you loosen the hold of the gatekeeper at the watchtower with a few lines, onward you press on, towards the hidden treasures. But Chaz tried to put all this out of his mind, as he walked towards the smoking room, but he was still thinking and purring about that Jessica. He would certainly be there at her casting! Who would have thought it, eh? Crying out for it, but Chaz believed anything was possible after coming across that Tennin porn star PC Angelica. Incidentally, Chaz had already phoned Natasha and spoken about her, and Natasha had surprised him further, by saying that she had also appeared in porn films and had done escort work on an agency Natasha was with.

'She'd do anything, Dad, she even does group gangbangs with rugby teams, I spoke to her about it. She said it paid for the extension on her house.'

Yet Nat was surprised as she didn't know she was in the police force. She had kept that secret. But Chaz was now at the smoking room, for his usual quite trying visit, although still steaming after his interaction with hot Jessica.

Chaz's mother was only seventy-six, but she had been an excessive smoker and drinker all her life, and she was biologically ten years older. She was overweight, diabetic and on this occasion was seated by the window, looking sullen and depressed, smoking cigarette after cigarette. She stubbed one out in a full ashtray, and immediately took another from her packet and lit up again, in between a bout of coughing. Chaz entered breezily, it always started like that.

'Hullo, Mum!' Chaz came across to her with the presents behind his back. She lit up seeing her Chaz, but then she tempered her enthusiasm, because it was nearly two weeks since the last time he was here. But first it was the roses, her favorite flowers. 'Love you, Mum! They're a lovely bunch. They smell really sweet, Mum. Give them a smell, go on!'

Chaz's mum smelt them, but showed little sign of approval if her facial expression was anything to go by.

'I'll get a vase in a minute, Mum. Where do you want them?'

'Well I'm certainly not having them in here! Other people will look at them! They'll go in my room. And where have you been? You haven't been for two weeks on Friday!'

Chaz's mum had been counting the days, and there were always too many in between visits from her little soldier Charlie. He was her only child and son, so he was extra special, her Charles, especially so, considering how much difficulty she had conceiving him.

'Oh Mum, I've been really busy at work. But I'm here now, aren't I?'

Chaz was readying himself now for the usual antics. Chaz's mum was obviously led to believe that Chaz was a builder working for Alan, his friend, just like the taxman, but she didn't really believe him. When did Chaz learn to do building? He always worked in warehouses, on a forklift truck and whatnot. She also thought he seemed to have too much money. He had never complained about being short for ten years or more now. Once upon a time he was always on her ear for money, but now he was always speaking about things that needed plenty of it. But he never asked for a loan, and he had told her many times how much all his clothes had cost him from Harrods. Mrs. Barber put two and two together.

'About time too!'

Chaz tried to divert things directly back on how his mother was feeling. It showed how much he cared.

'Are you feeling all right, Mum?' he asked warmly, but Mrs. Barber's visage looked exasperated and full of anger.

'How do you think I feel cooped up in here all day!' she barked.

In these kinds of exchanges, which were the norm, Chaz would do his best to turn her around a little. To make Mum see the bright side of life, and to get her glass half full and rising, regarding her relatively new life here, at this wonderful care home.

'Don't be so negative, Mum. You've got a lovely home here, and it's been a lovely week. Just like summer! Blue skies, sun shining. Haven't you been sitting in the gardens? Beautifully well-kept, Mum.'

How could anyone be positive about sitting in a wheel chair, having to push yourself about or wait for others to push you around. They were always busy and when they did have a moment nothing good would come.

'I don't like the way that care assistant, the big fat one, pushes my chair. Bloody great lump. Anyone would think she's out for the day at the races! She doesn't push them like you do Charlie, all "nice".'

Well at least the response gave Chaz some room for maneuver.

'You mustn't call people "fat" these days, Mum,' Chaz suggested, as he knew how his mother disregarded pleasantries on occasion. 'It's the new political correctness.'

'Oh. don't be so bloody stupid. She's looks as if she's twenty stone! She's not thin, is she? She's fat and lazy, Charlie!'

'Well I'll tell you what, Mum. We'll get those flowers in a vase, and then your little soldier will get you all "nice" and comfy in the gardens. How about that?'

For some reason Mrs. Barber just didn't feel like moving. That's the way this place made you feel.

'It's too cold for sitting,' she replied. Chaz persisted as there were ways of dealing with that.

'I'll put a blanket over you, Mum, and we can sit by the flower beds!' Which sounded nice to Mrs. Barber, but this entire care home environment was angering her. Why did she have to live here all by herself, when she had a son? And he had an empty bedroom at that new house. Natasha lived away now. Mrs. Barber knew that much.

'Very nice, yes very nice indeed. It'll make me feel as if I'm dying. Sitting there with a blanket over me like a geriatric!'

Chaz remonstrated, saying that she would be comfy out there with her little soldier. But Mrs. Barber just didn't fancy it. She'd rather be here in the smoking room, so she took to using another deflecting tactic that she would always pull when needed. It was all par for the course.

'Have you been to church and confessions in between all that work?' she asked as Mrs. Barber was a staunch Catholic. Chaz would always lie to her. She liked the idea of her good boy Charlie going religiously to church in his Sunday best, so why not spin her along.

'Of course, I have, Mum,' Chaz replied, as if there could be no shadow of doubt about it.

But Mrs. Barber knew there were other things in his life. Things that needed confessing about. She had found those drugs in his pockets when he was living with her and his father all those years ago, and there were all those magazines and new-fangled videos in his wardrobe too. She used to watch them when she was alone in the house. They were disgusting those videos, downright disgusting, and she knew, she had watched them all. They were bad influences, encouraging you to do all kinds of dirty things.

'If you keep going to church, you'll stay on the straight and narrow and keep looking like my smart boy, Charlie.'

Chaz thought he would divert things again. He would start informing Mum about how well Natasha was doing.

'Yes Mum, and Nat is doing really well at Uni. She's just finished her second year. Fancy a Barber donning those academic gowns. Showed we always had the brains, Mum!'

In fact, the Barber family were well known locally on account of their former string of newsagents. It was quite a break from tradition, when Chaz's old man flogged them. He had to have brains to run those thought Chaz, but his mum had a wholly negative view of the old Mr. Barber these days.

'Well it must have come from me because it certainly didn't come from your father,' she growled. Chaz pointed out that Dad had gone on to run an office department, down at the cement works.

'But he could never keep it in his pants, could he! Going off with that little slut of a secretary. She was younger than you, Chaz. Disgusting! *And*, she was having it off with that pub manager at The Boar's Head. Did you know that Charlie, the little slut!' That made Chaz recall that he saw the woman in question around the big supermarket in Tennin a couple of weeks previously. She was still about, and was a couple of years younger than Chaz and she had obviously benefited nicely out of the will. Chaz spoke with her for a few minutes and asked how the daughter was doing, Chaz and Linda went to her wedding a couple of years previously. But Chaz dared not mention her, as that would bring up all the business about the funeral, when his mother was livid seeing her. She was no more than early thirties then, 'with her tits hanging out all over the place'. Chaz would then have to agree how terribly immoral it all was, to keep the relative peace.

'Yes, yes, Mum. It was all so terrible, wasn't it? But long forgotten.'

'Forgotten! Some people have got bloody short memories, Charlie! I remember it, as if it were yesterday! Your father caught venereal diseases off her, you know! His penis had warts all over it. The dirty little slut!'

Things were taking the wrong pathway, as Mrs. Barber spat venom when the subject of the newer, younger 'Mrs. Barber' was brought up. Mrs. Barber detested the idea that much of the money went to her, although she didn't realize just how much went to Chaz. She didn't want to. Dad was married to the young secretary for ten years, with just the one daughter.

'Well let's not talk about Dad's penis, Mum. We've talked about that too much over the years.' Chaz chuckled inside, but he had to divert attention away from all that hot conflict stuff.

'The work's been going well, Mum. We've got a ton on!'

'Is it, son?' Now Mrs. Barber suspected her son was a drugs dealer although she'd like to think he wasn't. She also suspected that all this modelling work that Natasha was doing was probably porn. She remembered her talking about that exclusive shoot in the country mansion. Those porn film locations included country mansions. She knew, she had watched stacks of them and there was that expensive car she had. Where on earth did she get the money at her age? Mrs. Barber wasn't that stupid, and when she had come to visit last time, her tits were hanging out all over the place too. A sure sign. But she didn't like to push things. Chaz went on to explain further. He almost convinced himself that he was doing the work when speaking like this.

'I'm working with Alan down at Fishgate, Mum. Putting in a big extension on a house along the front. We'll be down there a couple of months.'

Fishgate. Mrs. Barber had some wonderful memories of that place. As a young woman she would go there with her girlfriends, and she was courted there long ago by Chaz's father. She met him on the dodgems at Fishgate fair in the summer of forty-seven in fact. Then when Chaz was in his teens, they had the caravan down there, not far from the front. They had so many long weekends at the caravan, and Chaz had gone there year after year.

'We used to have nice weekends down the caravan at Fishgate,' Mrs. Barber said.

The Fishgate caravan had many a fond memory for Chaz too. He lost his virginity at Fishgate shagging that young bird, from none other than the Temple Hive estate. All in the caravan, when his mum and dad were out playing bingo. They loved their bingo and thought that Chaz was in the arcades on the pinball machines. He used to joke to his parents that he wanted to go to the caravan and Arcadia. He picked the term up from watching an arts hour on BBC2. His parents never got the drift, but every time he went down there, he seemed to be shagging, while his parents were playing bingo all night long, and that same girl had initiated Chaz into all sorts of kinky activities. She was a couple of years older than him and Chaz tried it all out with the girl from the Hive. Chaz was underage at the time, but it continued for a couple of summers, until she went off with a guy nearly ten years older than her with his brand-new Ford Capri. All Chaz had was a brand new 50cc moped then, but he had fond, fond memories of Fishgate, sniffing around things.

'Yeah, we had some great times down there, Mum,' Chaz remembered, and it wasn't just the entry into the sexual thing. Chaz genuinely enjoyed being with his mum and dad too. They were happy times before the old man started looking up the young skirt. But when Mrs. Barber was talking with Chaz about the family's historical past, it wouldn't be long before the barbs were going in.

'That was before "that" Linda was around.'

Mrs. Barber had never really got on with Linda but then Mrs. Barber remembered everything. When Chaz was first seeing her, Mrs. Barber's marriage was under strain. She knew that something was going on with her husband and that little slut of a secretary, and in her confusion, she had a short-lived affair with the gatehouse man at the chemical works sports and social club. They had sex on a number of occasions over the heath in his Ford Cortina and that was when she saw 'that' Linda over there with a bloke in a Rover. They had passed them on the way out and he was still sitting up at the wheel and she couldn't see Linda. She knew what she was up to. Luckily Linda didn't see her. But she knew what that was all about, nothing but sex, and it was all behind Chaz's back. That's why people went over there, so Mrs. Barber knew the 'real' Linda and she'd been with Chaz six months at least. Yes, she remembered, but Mrs. Barber tried desperately to forget that period, when that slut of a secretary finally took her Albert away from her, to that love nest flat on the riverside. It was that time that Mrs. Barber had also gone out with that young porter at the hospital too. That good looking one rather flattered Mrs. Barber for a short while, and then there was the ugly one with the bulbous nose, who was renowned for having something else that was even more bulbous. She went up that Heath with him, and the young one many times and there was another one in the car with them too. There were other occasions when there were two car loads of them, but just a dozen times or so, although Mrs. Barber thought Linda might have seen her up there. It was all forgotten now of course, so let skeletons be skeletons away from the living was Mrs. Barber's way of thinking. She was very troubled and disturbed back then and those disgusting films had influenced her. But it all came out in confessions, and she was forgiven by the Holy Church.

'Oh Mum, you speak as if she's some kind of bad influence on me. She's a good woman!'

But Mrs. Barber didn't forget things. She might be in a wheelchair but she remembered everything.

'Well how's this new house then? I haven't seen it,' she added tartly.

'I showed you the photos, Mum. It's our dream house and we've got everything straightened out. I'll have to arrange with the manager to bring you over during the summer for a visit, Mum.'

None of this convinced Mrs. Barber. She was in an old people's home. That's what it was, and people died in old people's homes, and that's all they ever did apart from fiddling with jigsaws. She felt imprisoned here, as if the day of the end was looming.

'You don't want your old mother do ya, Charlie? She's no good to you now she's old.'

'Oh, Mum.'

Chaz always got stressed out coming to the home, as this was all par for the course. Mrs. Barber then tried to come at it from another direction and it was a well-trodden one.

'You know that all the money for this here, will come off the value of the house don't you! Seven hundred a week!'

It wasn't about the money. Chaz had two kilos of dough waiting to be made, locked up in that dash. One down to Candy Foxes, a fabulous new arrangement with more demand in the offing too. He would be raking it in on the weekend. He was philosophical now about Phelps. You win some, you lose some, and you win big when all the punters across Tennin, and way beyond, are gagging to pay forty and more a gram for what you bring to the table. With the freebie he would make nigh six grand on that kilo, and nigh seven on the Candy Foxes, and all out by Saturday morning no doubt, and then back to Alfredo's for another big kilo at least.

'Don't worry about me, Mum. The money's fine. Alan pays me well,' Chaz replied, thinking of the bogus payments into his bank account, and then paying the money back to Alan with a bit of coke thrown in. 'Sorted and the punters snorting again!'

'I do worry, son. And the only way I can see out of this mess, is if the fates tear you apart from Linda.'

Chaz could never figure out why his mum detested Linda so much. It all seemed so irrational to Chaz. In fact, Linda had seen her on the heath with the gatekeeper and a car full of men just as Mrs. Barber had feared. But she had never told Chaz. Linda knew they both held incriminating information about each other, and it appeared they both kept their counsel as a result. But there was an ice age between them.

'Oh Mum, me and Linda have never been happier, and we've been married for twenty-two years now. Can't you bury your hatchets after twenty-two years?'

All Mrs. Barber wanted was a different world. Not this waiting to die, interminable hell of a life, sitting in her wheel chair, smoking and sitting in it some more. Having to put up with that Hilda, and social gatherings, which were like a dementia forum. She would have rather talked to a pet budgie.

'Well I've got to live somewhere decent. Death Row they call these places you know.'

Chaz could only say what anyone would say in his situation, but he said it with as much warmly feeling as he could muster.

'You've just got to make the most of it, Mum.'

But that wasn't what Mrs. Barber wanted to hear. She had spent her whole life running after Chaz, making sure that he had everything he ever wanted. Mum was always there for him. But where was her little Charlie when she wanted somebody looking out for her? With 'that' Linda, and she knew what that 'real' Linda was like, performing sex acts in cars over the heath with strange men.

'What Death Row?'

Chaz tried to think about something positive to say about his mother's time at the care home. Something that might raise her spirits, get his mother's glass half full again.

'You like playing bingo with Hilda, don't ya?'

Mrs. Barber had mentioned it once, that she enjoyed playing bingo with Hilda, but it seemed that she had since done some deeper thinking about the care home's bingo.

'It's silly people's bingo. Three pound the top house. It's not the Link Up, "proper" bingo Charlie. And that Hilda, gets on my nerves, always going on about her Ronald! Her bloody Ronald! He can't think that much of her. He's only been in twice since I've been here! Twice! Her bloody Ronald!'

Chaz would always give his mum the sweets at the end of the visit as the visits generally went this way, moving towards a greater and greater negativity. It was a way to end the visit on a positive note.

'Well look what I've got, my mumsy. Your favorites! Licorice All Sorts!'

Chaz took them from the plastic bag and Mrs. Barber, who loved All Sorts, snatched them without saying a word.

CHAPTER TWELVE

BIG CATS AND PORN STARS

Things were moving quickly back at the citadel that evening. Chaz had already gone upstairs and gathered another stash of cash. After the trip to the care home, it had been eight to Dai and Jay, and a further eight to the Waterside Crew and eight down to Scamp, and the rest of the kilo was to be distributed elsewhere in the morning. Every year the dance festival was on, Jay and Dai would deal from a pub near the festival site, called 'The Fur and Feather'. The manager was young, and for once a year, with his pub packed to the rafters, he turned a blind eye. He and his partner also liked a bit of the white powder, and Dai and Jay kept them well supplied free of charge. They would deal there Friday through to Monday during the dinner time and afternoons, and tons of the festival goers used it for a few drinks and a score before hitting the site. This was the third year of the arrangement, and Chaz gave Dai an extra half ounce for the manager, to keep it sweeter than sweet. Chaz's eyes were sparkling, as Dai thought it likely to be a bigger demand than the last two years put together. Everybody they knew was bang up for it, so Chaz was preparing to purchase two more kilos. Generally, Chaz never bought two at a time, as he didn't like the idea of getting caught with too much at the house. His tactics were supply the demand quickly, to get the majority of each purchase off his hands. The law of averages might go his way on a drug bust then. He could get caught with say twelve ounces, bad, or just before an order, it might be down to half a dozen grams personal, pretty good.

Chaz had counted out his stash and had it on the gravitas coffee table, when a flood of calls came in. Jay and Dai had virtually knocked it all out and the demand was ferocious, even greater than anticipated, and that was before they even got down 'The Feather'. Jay and Dai both had money banked in Swiss accounts and a tidy stash that was kept at Jay's sisters. They had decided to go for a kilo and take it from there.

'Everyone's going to Drum and Bass Friday and they're fucking bonkers for it, mate! It's sold out, Chaz, and we've done the eight. Any chance of a kilo?'

Chaz had never known demand like it. But through Friday to Monday it was going to be a thirty thousand capacity sell out, and nigh all of them would be on pills or cocaine, with Chaz's cocaine being the A1 drug of choice for so many. It would be over to Alfredo's on the morrow for two more kilos. Chaz looked at the flyer for the event and it was obviously bigger than ever before, with some real big dance names on the bill. It was the forecast weather too, end of the week through to next Tuesday, was set for twenty-five degrees, without a hint of rain. After Dai, Chaz had a call from Angusia who would love another eight for six deal, and then another three calls came in from other buyers who wanted to take the eight for six. Chaz was totting it all up and his head was spinning, in a Post Phelps money making wonderland. Within five minutes Chaz had seventy grand all counted out in ten thousand wads on the coffee table. He would put it up in the cabinet when he went to bed, but he liked to visually see the money there in front of him, and he liked the way it looked aesthetically with that glamour magazine with the porn PC holding her boobs up, and that design on the gravitas table. All in eyeshot of those sublime carp tanks. It was the life that Chaz had built as it were, and then it was a quickie on the mobile to Alfredo for *three* big ones on the morrow. Alfredo was up for it. With the three-kilo going out he would have ten nights or so in Spain in his holiday home, for a well-deserved break. But he wouldn't be moving till Tuesday. A hundred thousand punters would be turning up at the festival over the three, and God knows how many would pop into 'The Fur and Feather' for a powder. Chaz just hoped that the Tennin Police would prove to be as dumb as they usually were.

Chaz snorted a line to celebrate, one that he laid out across the front page of that mag, with its shot of PC Amelia holding her boobs up. He smirked to himself as he seemed to be developing a fetish. Phelps was history now though. Linda was upstairs having a bath while all this was going on, and after the line was snorted, Chaz noticed that he had an e mail from Jessica. She said she had seen the site and wanted to give it a go, and would be up for anything as she wanted out of that dead end, boring job. She even referred to a long chat she had on the phone with Vivienne and had arranged a date. Chaz was seventh heaven high, zonked from the coke as he watched those carp, while he began dreaming up different scenarios. New Age Man, New Age woman and kinky sacks of sex. What a time to be living, eh! He took up his mobile and phoned Miko and Viv to get the lowdown. He couldn't believe it. The screen test was to take place at the bungalow, next Thursday. The ideas began to evolve fast. They would shoot, with Viv doing the producing with Miko, and another pro camera guy, with the idea touted they would do an exclusive series, with old big Dick doing the post-production. Vivienne was experienced, and knew what the punters wanted, and so many wanted exclusivity, and she envisaged an initial contract of twelve films that gradually got kinkier and out there as the punters wanted more and more. Viv was also talking about future 'interactive' potential. They could offer 'exclusive', 'once in a lifetime' opportunities to subscribers. Apparently, Jessica had sent revealing photos over to Viv and Miko by e mail, and it was clear that Jessica was like a sex bomb, porn star waiting to explode. The idea of the series had already been pitched to Jessica, and Viv liked her answer. She said that she was up for everything and anything, wanted to get 'fully' out there, because she realized that to make the money, and she wanted to make shedloads, she had to be 'Triple, Triple X, and a kinky bit more'. She even raised Vivienne's eyebrows talking openly about extreme scenarios in a way that was totally shameless. Viv had been turned on, and Viv's sheer enthusiasm surprised and excited Chaz over the phone. She generally was realistic and pragmatic, so everything augured well. It seemed that Jessica was the one!

Chaz looked at those horny shots of the PC and it said it all. Every woman he came across seemed to be gagging for extreme sex and making money out of porn, and they wouldn't need to coax the inner whore out of Jessica. Chaz mused about the possibility of hitting the big time. They just needed to develop a brand and they needed that genuine porn star. Chaz had always remembered what Viv had said around the pool on one occasion, about the type of girl you needed.

'You need a star, a real porn star, Chaz. Mysterious, but totally shameless, totally. Punters have to be goaded to attach their unconscious desires to an object. *Your* porn-star. Do that and you make millions. All you need is the candy!'

They had built up the idea. It was a New Age and a porn star could be bigger than a pop star. And then the porn star could be a pop star if she wanted. It was all there, staring these sex visionaries in the face. But they needed the right girl and Viv was really excited as she was sure it was Jessica. It was intuition she said, and Viv had never spoken to Chaz like that before.

'I'll send over her photos, Chaz. They're a knock out! Don't wank over them too much!'

The way that Vivienne was enthusing, it was inevitable that she would make a guest appearance in some of the films, but that would mean her fan base would buy into Jessica. Yes, it augured well indeed. Chaz chuckled, but he understood it all so clearly. It was a New Age. People wanted it! They wanted to break down all that repression, to find that sex that was really there, those kinky sacks of it, and visionaries like he and Vivienne, armed with a potential star like Jessica, and a host like Natasha, were like the chosen ones. The porn evangelists, and it paid well too!

Chaz looked at the tank and then back at the money and the glamour mag that he turned over until PC Angelica was there on that double spread, legs over her head. With the link to Natasha he could get a line to her. See if she was 'up for it' to get on their team. Thoughts floated through his mind. They could get that porn brand down big and no doubt Jessica would be upstairs doing her turn in the Dark Room and maybe this PC Angelica too! They could make dozens of films, all in the dream house!

Chaz looked at the money and thought that yes, he could go tax man legit with the porn brand, and if they hit the porn right on the sex button, opening up the treasure trove, they could start that sex club and then develop a string of them. All ideas that had been touted out there around Miko and Viv's pool many times. Then he looked at the carp tank again, with a wider smile. He and Miko could also have the big carp supermarket! Why not? Maybe, there was a route out of these big coke deals. Then it would only mean that he needed coke for 'Percy' and friends and enough to fuel the stable of porn stars, so all the taboos and boundaries would be smashed with their big black dilated pupils.

Within five minutes, Chaz was simply drooling over Jessica's pics, with her neat Brazilian waxing. Viv had already suggested a series with the waxing, and a series with darn right hairy. They had to cater for all tastes. But Chaz rather liked the waxed Jessica. He slung her over a quick e mail saying that he was overjoyed about the screen test, and thought her pics were 'sexy bonkers, fantastic'. Welcome to the team, the family, Jessica. He sent the mail, and then rolled up a joint and before he had smoked it all, a reply came back over. It was honest and forthright, and darn right sexy. She said she always thought she might end up doing porn as men had always tripped over their dicks to get at her, and why not get paid big for tripping the pricks up, and anything to get a bit of excitement into her life. She was bored, she said she was up for anything. The kinkier the better. It would be something she could get her teeth and cunt into. Chaz chuckled at such a smutty, horny, care home secretary. But it was just what the kinky porn doctor ordered. She even put across her mobile number. Chaz already had an erection on, and after he closed down the e mail, he sent a quick text over to her, asking her if she liked coke? Within a few moments one came back, saying that she was a weekend fiend. Chaz smirked as it was more than likely that she was sniffing up his Charlie! Chaz sent her one back saying that he would pop over for a quick visit at the care home, and drop her a discreet freebie. His mind spun, he would pop over there on the morrow, he could see his mum for a quick half an hour, mum would like that, and he would drag out a double feature of Vivienne's too, as Viv would be mentoring Jessica from now on. Slip that to her with three or four grams. Sex, drugs and money, they go together like milk and honey, fish and chips and strawberries and cream. Chaz chuckled to himself, what an irony, all in the age of feminism.

All the sex business had turned Chaz right on. Linda was ensconced in the bath so he put up the image of the naked Jessica on the laptop, next to the double pager of the PC and masturbated, shooting his load all over 'Voluptuous Angelica'.

He had a busy day tomorrow now. It would be Alfredo, customer deals, the care home, and obligatory porn drops, but he would chase around making up time. The time being used for either a trip to Brookes, if she could accommodate at short notice, Chaz was sure she would, or even one down to the waterside sex den for an hour, with a couple of girls if she couldn't, 'Sorted!' The New Age, Chaz loved it!

Linda finally appeared after the bath, and she went through to the kitchen to make a coffee, while asking Chaz what all the animated discussion was about. She could see the stack of money but wasn't going to say anything tonight. She was beginning to accept it was inevitable that Chaz was going down on a drug bust. It was just a matter of time the way he was knocking it out. Chaz said that he was just talking to Miko about their carp bait ideas going forward, and some of Viv's business interests. Linda didn't want to pursue that one any further. She just wanted to chill out after her relaxing soak. Chaz turned the volume up on the TV as the main news was moving to the regional, and he also wanted confirmation that the weather was going to be as good as all anticipated, for the bank holiday weekend. It was good, perfect in fact, and he raised his shoulders with a smile on his face. He could still make twenty grand profit on the bank holiday. The only thing that could stop it now was a fucking bust somewhere along the line!

The regional news came after the weather, and first up was the 'break out'. It was given top priority. Within a few moments, photos of both TV Sam and Freeda were up on the screen, and Chaz called in Linda to take a look. She appeared just in time and the images were far from flattering.

'Well I wouldn't want to meet them on a long dark night!' she said.

'Dark night! I've met that TV fucker on a dark night. I wouldn't want to be within a hundred miles of um!'

Chaz and Linda were quiet as they listened to a representative of the Tennin Trust, who was warning the public about the absconders.

'We would like to warn the public that Freeda is particularly dangerous, and if you see either of them, don't hesitate in ringing Tennin Police 297324 or dial 999 if the lines are busy. We wouldn't want to unduly frighten the public, but we reiterate, these two are extremely dangerous. Do not, in any circumstances, confront them.'

Linda was unnerved. To think he had been regularly outside, peering into their garden. He might come back and start peering, or something else she thought. Maybe Chaz was right about, this beautiful, but seemingly damned house in the first place. She too now looked forward to the day that Tennin Asylum was finally demolished. She wouldn't have to worry herself sick about warehouse units and new bypasses.

'I won't sleep properly until they're caught, Chaz!' Chaz turned the TV off, scowling. A great day had finished on a bitter, disturbing note.

'They'll happily slit ya throat as much as look at ya. But no need to be unduly frightened. No need at all! Fucking crazies!'

There was only one way to deal with it all for Chaz, and that was to have another defiant line, and a triple vodka chaser. He laid the line and went for it and then poured what looked like a quadruple, and offered his reflections. The magazine had been put away.

'Oh, don't worry yourself sick, Linda. The place is secure and if they come around here with blades, they'll get it with an automatic fucking shotgun, if they wanna be funny cunts. Come to think of it. I'll need to lock that shed up.'

'Oh my God! Be careful! They could be in there, Chaz! And there's two buckets of boilies to go down.' Chaz thought he wouldn't leave anything to chance. He would go down there with a rifle.

There was a slight mist that late May night, and the old orchard had a mysterious atmosphere about it. The place where odd things occur, and as if on cue, that slick black panther, on his territorial creep abouts, deftly slipped over the boundary wall, and stealthily moved through the old apple and pear orchard, as if he had been summoned by superconscious powers.

Chaz went straight upstairs, while the energy was coursing through his veins. He opened up the large airing cupboard and behind it were the safes which secured his money and guns. He opened one with a code and there was a load of weapons inside, both legal and illegal, with two army style automatic shotguns and a sawn-off repeater. The firm's arsenal. He took up a high-powered .22 rifle that Chaz held on a license, which would suffice in the circumstances. It could bring down bison.

Chaz came out the back, carrying the loaded rifle and the two buckets of boilies. He lifted his shoulders up, acknowledging the nip in the air, as the temperature had dipped appreciably, like it can do in May. He made a few more steps towards the new shed, when that fox screech that sounded like a female in distress, went up again. Chaz was jumpy as fear swept through him. The thing did sound like a woman screaming, and a shiver shot up his spine. He put the buckets down and looked out across the orchard with the gun readied, trying to fathom it out. It was complete silence and pitch dark, and he didn't fancy going out there to investigate. It had to be a fox. It had to be. Yet Chaz was left frowning, as he couldn't get his head around how a fox could scream like that. It was terrible. No wonder Linda was worried, and it was uncanny. When he heard that scream, he began thinking about that unsolved murder. It assaulted him, smashed back into his consciousness, and he knew that it happened over the back of the wall. He recalled reading, from someplace deep in his mind, that Ashcroft and his wife weren't in the house when it occurred. They were partying and hanging out at Bryan Jonsen's estate. It all eerily flooded back on that scream and the old apple and pear orchard was now a touch macabre, in Chaz's estimation, and all accentuated by that vaporous, swirling wispy mist. Then another screech went up and this one was definitely a fox. Chaz was relieved, and he pressed on.

Once Chaz was in the safe domain of the shed, he settled, but he still locked the door. He then began weighing out the boilies, putting them in plain sealer bags, readied for the freezer. The next thing on the bait production agenda, was to get a fully designed packaging, so they could be distributed in the shops, and who knows after that, maybe he and Miko could have a small warehouse production unit, knocking out their teaser balls. Chaz lifted his shoulders in anticipation of great things ahead, and he felt less tense when yet another scream went up. It was definitely vixens, and all thoughts of macabre, horrific murders were temporarily banished from his mind, as he became engrossed in his divine exotic blues and strawberry passion reds, inhaling and thoroughly enjoying, that pungent smell. If you can smell boilies you're in carp mode, and he was darn sure, that he and Miko had finally cracked it with those 'egg shells in', despite the eel fiasco. It would all come good in the end, although these little beggars weren't the 'egg shells in' variety this evening, as Linda had forgotten to crack the eggs into the mix. But he was thinking positive tonight after all the successful coke deals, and he was philosophical. Great things come to those who wait, and he did have a take on 'egg shells in'. The one that got away, snagged up in the old 4.2 liter Jag.

'Phew huh, me beauties! That pregnant virgin forty-three, is gonna be slapped across ya knee, Chazzy boy! Make a whore out of her!'

Back out there in the orchard, the panther was motionless in the undergrowth, lying in wait, watching that new shed. Chaz finished his bait packaging and exited turning the light off, locking up, and while he was walking across the lawn to the porch, another scream went up. It sounded like a woman again. Chaz gulped and was back thinking about that horrific rape and murder over the boundary wall. It was Ashcroft's wife who discovered the mutilated body. He remembered that as well. He had read an obituary about her in the late nineties. Apparently, she had mental health issues after the murder, and was a drug addict, right up to her death, and thereafter Ashcroft had gone downhill, until he went into a home AD 2001. It was their daughter who had put the house up for sale, and she was the main beneficiary of the will, as the son died of a drugs overdose way back in his twenties. Chaz looked out at the eerie orchard again and wondered why the hell he bought the cursed place? Then something moved out there, something shadowy. Chaz quickly held the gun up and surveyed, although he didn't have his night sights on. It was something big. But then it was back to silence. He thought it must be a couple of foxes next to each other. They were like shadowy shapes when they moved in the dark, like ghostly apparitions, and he spotted a few more out there. That screech must have been a vixen. It must have been.

However, that rape and murder was still engulfing his mind, when he locked the porch and kitchen doors. Linda was in the lounge on the velvet chair, transfixed by Hermann posturing around the telephone box ornament with the octopus tentacles. She just couldn't wait to say something to Chaz about that scream, and all she could do in response, was to lay out another line from the St. George stash because she felt so unhinged again.

'Did you hear it! That awful scream, Chaz? That's exactly what I was hearing the other night, exactly!' Chaz admitted it terrified him for a few seconds.

'I told you it sounded like a woman screaming!'

While Chaz was in the kitchen getting a snack, the scream was ringing around his head, as if caught in an echo chamber. He was sighing and frowning and visibly concerned, and once back in the velvet chair, Linda was now on the Grand Waldorf, he began to reflect.

'It was a fox, Linda, but fuck, it gives you the creeps with those nutty farmers prowling about! And that fucking murder! Fucking sent that Desade woman off her rocker. Her last film was in 1976. She never worked again.'

'She sold books, Chaz, I read it on the internet the other day.'

Chaz had conveniently forgotten many of the details. Desade had an autobiography, that sold well in the mid-eighties and then another in the early nineties, that both plied heavily on the mystical sex ideas, and those notorious parties, with Desade exploiting her links with pop and rock stars and other media figures. The second was read by Keefy. It told the 'shocking' absolute truth, and Chaz thought he would order it now. The books with their whiff of orgy sex and the spiritual, had kept the couple afloat financially, right up to Ashcroft's death, but Chaz didn't refer to them again. He deliberately wanted to end the talk of that murder, but he had mentioned that unmentionable, and Linda looked terrified, eyes bloodshot and bolting, as she kept hearing that darn fox in her mind.

'God it sounds terrible, Chaz, I don't think I can live here with it.'

'Bloody thing needs shooting!'

At least that would put an end to it, and as soon as he said it, the idea was developing in Chaz's mind. He had the equipment to hunt it down.

'I could lie in wait for the bastard. Fuck, I've done enough hunting in my time, Linda! We could put food down, and I'll get it with me .22 with me Viper scopes. Bang! No more of that fucking scream! I'm not having that in my back garden. No fucking way! Hunting mission! Begins after the bank holiday weekend has settled. I'll bang the fucker out!'

Linda was fully behind the idea. She didn't want all the foxes shot, but just that one, that sounded like horror.

'Well, just wait until those two asylum patients have been caught,' replied Linda wisely.

Outside in the orchard, the panther stretched and raised itself, and began moving stealthily back towards the boundary wall. TV glimpsed it, as it moved through the mist.

'Freeda! The big black cat that Keefy used to see. Quick, look, Freeda!'

Freeda moved quickly to the window. The panther stopped momentarily and turned its head towards the old shed, looking straight at TV. It then moved at top speed towards the boundary wall with Freeda catching a fleeting glimpse of it, before it lithely scampered over the top. Freeda was incredulous, and TV thought it a sign from the aliens. It was all in the unique planetary alignment that was affecting deep nature. It was in those emerald eyes that had met TV's, and TV knew loads of stuff about big cats. He had mentioned all that to Freeda in the past but she had long forgotten. TV used to 'go on' about things.

'It's been in the papers, Freeda!'

Been in the papers. Freeda giggled.

'What has he been telling people what he eats for breakfast, TV?'

TV laughed, sometimes Freeda was very witty.

'Nah, Freeda! They've been seen down the Triune Way and Keefy saw one! Don't ya remember!' Freeda didn't know much about the big black cats on the Triune but she knew one thing. Where there's black cats there's death and that was a big one.

'Only if they walk across your path, Freeda! We only saw one. We were in here, in our shed, and that.'

No, it wouldn't curse TV and Freeda. But Freeda thought the black cat might have walked across the path of that Blazerman, as she called him.

'Nah, he went down to the shed with them buckets, and he had a gun, Freeda! He's got guns!'

Freeda couldn't be bothered talking about guns.

'Who was that woman screaming?' she asked.

'Dunno, Freed. I think it was a fox, Freeda.'

Freeda was adamant that it was a woman. TV thought about it but didn't say anything and the short silence was broken by the hoot of an owl and the whirring wings of bats. It was a touch scary down in this old orchard hideout, and by now the cold misty air was seeping through its porous walls. It was getting colder and damper by the minute and whatever TV was picking up on earlier he couldn't detect it now. He, like Freeda, just felt cold.

'Why did you bring us here, TV? It's all cold and spooky and I want to turn the light on and have a cup of coffee. And I want my biscuits. Two digestive biscuits. That fat nurse always brings me um. My coffee and my biscuits!'

TV kept quiet as Freeda fumbled in the black bag and opened the final remaining can of coke. She had already drunk five while TV had been drinking his Energy Brew. But Freeda sneered as she didn't really want it. She wanted her coffee and her biscuits. She always had them before she went to bed!

'That's the last coke, Freeda!'

'You've got your Energy Brew!' Freeda snapped back at him.

TV then checked the black bag for food and there was nothing. Freeda had eaten the lot. 'You've eaten all the pancakes, Freed, out of that packet as well. You didn't save me any!'

'I like my sweet pancakes, TV, they're my favorites!'

TV refrained from moaning anymore, and then he looked in the second of the black bags hoping for a better result. All that was left was half a dozen packets of fags and a milk chocolate bar.

'We haven't got any food left, Freeda. We had loads. You've eaten it all!'

'We got a Milkybar', Freeda noticed, and TV now had that one last Milkybar in his hand. 'I like my Milkybars,' she added. TV pleaded that he be spared the last as he was starving. Freeda just gave him a disgruntled look as TV began to take it out of its wrapper. There was tension in the air over that final Milkybar. Freeda had already had three, she ate them when they were chasing off the grounds. But that was yonks ago. He broke the tension by breaking the final bar in two and giving Freeda half. But where on earth would they get food, TV thought? Freeda enjoyed the final segment and then she pitched it.

'I'm getting fed up with living in an old shed, TV.' Freeda just had to say it. It was just too old and rusty and damp and cold. At least the prison unit was warm.

'But you said it would be like our home and that, Freeda.' TV was trying hard to make the best of it, but he knew that Freeda was right.

'But it ain't good enough, TV. It's cold, it's dark, and I can hardly see ya! And it smells and that, and it's rusty!'

TV got his little torch out of his pocket. It was only a key ring type of thing and he began to shine it in the shed.

'Tut! Tut!' Freeda was far from impressed. 'That light's fucking stupid.'

To prove her point about the rustiness too, Freeda picked up an old rusting saw from a bench and began sawing its lower shelf, and the saw completely disintegrated. 'See! It's fucking useless this shed, TV!'

TV tried hard to put a positive flavor on things, and he looked at his pitchfork.

'My pitchfork's, a cracking one, Freeda, look,' he said, hoping that Freeda would settle down, for tonight at least. Freeda glanced towards it and tutted again. She wasn't impressed.

'Ya pitchfork won't keep us warm!'

Freeda's eyes had been opened. She could see there were other possibilities. TV could open doors and that.

'I bet that other shed he's got is good. It's more "proper" and got electrics. We could live there, TV. In that "proper" shed!'

It was a compelling argument, but TV didn't fancy the risks. At least they were together here, in this dank, damp, cold and thoroughly miserable shed. But TV had seen what TV had seen.

'But it's too near the house, Freeda, and he uses it for his guns and buckets and that. This shed's safer.'

The argument was all rational, yet it was never going to convince, and keep Freeda quiet. That new shed was bound to be better and it might even have a heater, she thought. She sounded a little petulant now.

'Well I want a proper shed and then a proper house, TV! Like everybody else has. And I wanna cook you a dinner!'

TV liked her intentions here, but he thought it would be better if he done any cooking.

'Nah, I'll do the cooking, Freeda. It's fashionable that men do the cooking so it's not like the olden day times. And I wanna cook ya fish and chips!'

That made Freeda smile. She loved fish and chips. They were her favorite and TV said he was an expert at fish and chips. He used to make them for his aunt Joan and there was more. Fish and chips were important, symbolically, to Dragon Star, and TV knew that everything was product branding these days.

'Jesus fed everybody with his fresh fish and we've got his sandals on, Freeda! We're supporters of his brand!'

Freeda said that she had forgotten about all that, but it was the cold and damp in this old shed. It was taking its effect.

'It makes ya forget about Jesus and his brands, TV!'

The stress of the shed was making Freeda ponder about the gloomier realities of that asylum, that had been her life for so long, not Jesus and his brands. It didn't look good.

'And I want babies, TV! I want babies but I can't have babies, because of them. Cos of that Lock and fucking Bolt. They dun it to me, TV! I can't have babies because of Lock and fucking Bolt!'

TV was greatly worried. This was just what he had feared. He wanted Freeda to be relaxed and calm, chilled out, so they could enjoy this special time together. There was a stream of moonlight coming in from the window that was casting Freeda slightly in its light, and she seemed to be transforming into a manic state with eyes a bolting. It wasn't looking good and something would have to give. Now TV did carry some pills in the snake's head, that were specifically for chilling out purposes, that he took from the drugs trolley. But he wanted to save those. He didn't want to use them all up. TV tried to make it better by holding her hand but she brushed it aside, in her bad temper.

'I want my knives back! Go and get my knives, TV! I wanna get that fat nurse! Fucking knife her!'

Poor Freeda became so angry that she couldn't get her words out. She shook and shook and then broke down in tears, crying her whole life out. TV simply hugged her. He loved her so much.

'Don't get upset, Freeda. You're with me now. Not that big fat nurse. And I've never ever been so happy. I love you so much, so forget about all those nasty bastards. Just forget about them.'

Freeda loved TV too, but she wasn't used to living in an old shed like this. Crawlies had been getting in her long hair, and she couldn't stop scratching. She picked one out of her hair, and it was a little woodlouse that curled up into a ball in her hands.

'There's too many creepy crawlies in this old shed!'

TV could see what she had in her hand as he shined the small torch on it, and the Dragon Star children didn't countenance cruelty to any creatures, although they were allowed to catch and cook fish, as Jesus had done that back in the olden times, when he fed the multitudes. TV espoused the philosophies.

'Don't hurt the little cheesy bugs, Freeda. We mustn't hurt the little cheesy bugs! The "Dragon Star" like cheesy bugs'

'I like them, TV, but I don't want um crawling all over me! Fucking old shed! It's fucking useless!' she snapped.

TV glanced out of the window and he saw the bedroom light going off. The house was in darkness and at least he could divert Freeda's attention.

'Look, Freeda! The lights have gone off. They've gone to bed, Freed!'

Freeda was interested and she was thinking. If they were asleep, why couldn't they try and get into that 'proper' shed? There was bound to be coffee and digestive biscuits and that down there in the 'proper' shed.

'Are they doing fizz bangs, TV?' Freeda asked inquisitively. Sexual couplings in the Dragon Star tradition, could only be affected by fully paid up cult members. Subscription was ten pounds a year and there were thirteen fully paid up members, four up from last year. Associate members were twelve strong having paid up a fiver, but there was tons of Dragon Star stuff that associates didn't know of. All subscriptions were payable to TV Sam, the cult's treasurer, and naturally all of it ended up being spent on fags and UFO mags.

'He's probably shagging her, Freeda, but they wouldn't be doing the proper, proper fizzer banger like you and me do.'

Freeda smiled, but she wondered what TV thought of his wife. He spoke about her when they first came across the house. He said he had watched her when she was bending over gardening a few weeks previously, and said that he liked her big arse.

'Would you like to tie up and fizzer bang Blazerwoman, TV?'

This kind of thing was all part of the master plan. TV was unequivocal.

'Course, Freed! I'll make her "Dragon Star". Put the snake light into her and make her one of us!' Expansion was the great aim of the cult's leader.

Freeda tried hard to sleep as TV requested but she couldn't. She had found a lesser rusty garden trowel and was relentlessly hammering it into the decrepit wooden floor as she was lain out on the mattress. TV put up with it for a short while until it started to really get on his nerves.

'Freeda! Stop that! You're like a woodpecker!'

But there was no stopping Freeda. It was lots of things preying on her mind disturbing her, making her restless, and giving her this woodpecker digging sort of energy.

'Well I wanna knife, TV! Cos I can't have babies! So, get me a knife and then Freeda won't be a Woody Woodpecker!'

'Calm down Freeda, get a calm on.'

TV tried to use a particularly soothing and tender voice. It might just work and then Freeda might settle down and go to sleep. But she was cold and the talk of a 'calm on' had set Freeda's mind racing. She began rustling around for the fag supply, emptying loads of fags from a twenty and putting four cigarettes in each of her hands between fingers and thumbs. She was determined to go for that 'calm on' like Keefy used to do.

'I'm gonna smoke ten fags at once, TV! Ten!' she announced. She really did want to feel calm and it seemed the only way to do it. Get a calm on like Keefy used to do. She held up both hands with the fags in between her fingers. Two dropped out that she had between her thumbs. But there was no stopping Freeda and her stubbornness. 'Gis a light, TV!' TV couldn't quite grasp the logic, because Keefy never smoked eight, he would have coughed too much. He was a bit asthmatic like Dan. So, he popped the question.

'What do ya wanna smoke as many as that for, Freeda?'

Freeda had been thinking about Keefy and she thought to herself, that she was feeling really bad, so surely smoking more than Keefy would make her feel more calmer and better than Keefy.

'I'm gonna smoke myself all calm like Keefy used to do!' she said, still trying desperately to hold those eight fags in her hands, but constantly dropping those between her thumbs and index fingers. TV remonstrated.

'But Keefy only ever smoked three at once, Freeda. Never all that lot!' TV hoped that his protests would bring her to heel. Nobody could ever smoke eight. Not even Keefy. But Freeda was digging in.

'Well Freeda is gonna smoke more, TV! I can't have babies so I'm gonna smoke loads and loads and get more calm! Even calmer than Keefy used ta!' It all seemed logical to Freeda. More fags, more calm. TV reluctantly gave in and snapped his lighter as the owl hooted again. Freeda was on it. She went around the eight, dragging each one alight. TV reflected as she gripped tighter and squashed the ends. By the time she got around the eight, the first couple would have gone out. How could you smoke eight at once?

'It's not a very good example to children, smoking so many, Freeda, and you're smoking eight, not ten!'

'Well I nearly did it!' Freeda snapped back. But she carried on relentlessly. Nothing was going to stop her. She puffed on four of the fags, inhaling deeply and holding for a second before spluttering, and coughing out the vapor. She was doing it, smoking the eight, and what did TV know, about smoking like Keefy used to do? He wasn't even smoking the three!

Freeda was sitting up, and fags dropped from her hands onto the bottom of her dressing gown, that was still underneath that prized Dragon Star jacket. Fags burnt into her gown. She quickly took to brushing them away with the back of her hands. It all proved what TV had been saying all along.

'I told ya, Freeda. Ya can't do it! Nobody can.' Freeda wouldn't admit defeat though. Hadn't eight worked for a little while? She closed her eyes now, as if she was in an advanced Samadhi state of nirvana. She'd show TV that her eight had worked. She had a calm on, bigger than Keefy's.

'But I feel really, really chilled out, TV. All calm! Like Keefy used ta! But even more than Keefy!'

TV relented as it seemed to have worked and they both laid back on the mattress. At least it was reasonably comfortable. Freeda transferred three fags to her left hand and quickly got them going again but then she picked up the trowel. Surely three with a bit of digging would be better than just three on their own, like Keefy used to. She began digging it in again like a woodpecker.

'Freeda! You're doing that woodpecker fing again and it's getting on my fucking nerves!'

Even true love and soulmate things can get bunged up, if you're stuck in an old damp miserable shed for the night.

'Well I wanna sharp knife! I had two! But I haven't even got one now. What ya gonna do about it, TV? You keep saying ya love me. Well get me my knives back!'

TV tried to think of something quick. He had to settle her down.

'Do you have to have them, Freeda? We're into pitchforks now. That's what "Dragon Star" is dead into these days. They work well, pitchforks. The gladiators used them, Freed!' Freeda sneered back at him.

'Freeda don't wanna be a gladiator. And it's a free country, ain't it? That's what you're always saying! An, I want my knives! And I bet that White Blazerman fingy has got loads of knives in that shed with the electrics. The proper, proper shed!'

TV finally gave in. He would have to investigate that proper shed and get in with his wires. But he took the pitchfork with him. Freeda smiled. That bloody useless pitchfork he's got, she was thinking. But it wasn't rusty. It was one of Ashcroft's.

'Now stay here, Freeda, and look after the old shed. Lock and Bolt might be about with the police!'

Now that TV was going to look at the new 'proper' shed, Freeda would stay put and do X-ray eye look outs and she was so happy. She couldn't wait to get in that new shed.

TV crept out looking to and fro, as they were bound to be searching high and low for them. He moved slowly and carefully through the wispy mist and orchard. He passed the garden compost heap, where the severed snake was still decomposing. He smelt a pong but carried on, as the moon shone on the adder's skin. TV finally got to the shed and rested the trident up against it, while he undertook the business of that lock. He bent over and assessed the thing with his keyring torch. He didn't look too bothered, and within a few seconds he had the wires out, and was fiddling away trying to crack the code to the new world. For a second, he thought he might have to go back to get Freeda, so she could hold the torch over the lock. But TV was a genius at opening things and before another minute was up the lock had sprung. He opened the door and looked around for the light switch and hit it immediately.

'Wow!'

He was met by a spotlessly clean shed with all of its brand-new gardening equipment, its electric mower, rows of tools on clips, and many plastic pots and trays of seedlings. He was astonished, and there was a heater too, so Freeda was right. What more could they want? But TV began sniffing. What a funny smell he thought and it was those darn boilies. Now TV had been fishing a couple of times, but had never come across boilies. He went twice, with Keefy and a couple of nurse minders. That was back a few years, with that enlightened doctor on the open ward. But Keefy used maggots. Maggots that were all different colors, so TV couldn't place this odd smell.

TV came before the large freezer and they needed food desperately. There might be something in there that could thaw. It had the key in it so he opened it up. The boilies that had just gone in, were all up at the top and

233

weren't as yet frozen. He whipped out a couple of bags, one blue, and the other those strawberry reds. He opened the seal and yes, it was these round things that were behind the odd smell and luckily these weren't the infamous 'egg shells in' variety. He picked out an exotic divine blue and smelt it and looked at it curiously. It's a sweet he thought and he popped it in his mouth and started crunching. By the look of TV's facial expression, it tasted good!

'He makes sweets! The Blazerman makes sweets!' He couldn't wait to tell Freeda. He then tore the seal from the reds and in went a red. It was strawberry and fruity and he knew that Freeda would love these ones. She treasured anything strawberry. Strawberries were her favorite but TV liked the blues so he popped a load in his hoodie pocket. He then spotted the luxury carp bed chair that lay underneath the stainless-steel bench. He pulled it out with much enthusiasm and could see there was a sleeping bag with it too. Freeda was right all along. This was the 'proper' shed. 'Cor sizzlers on that!' he thought. But TV stopped in his tracks, and gave the situation some thought. Although it might be all right for tonight, it would be awkward staying here. They used it, this 'proper' shed. He then gave thought to what their next move could be, but he liked those sweets, and he was hungry, so he popped in a few more.

It was scary, this old shed without electrics, and with no TV about, things took on more sinister overtones. That owl was still hooting and where there's quiet and owls its eerie. Freeda had heard them doing that in horror films and it made this old shed all spooky. It was also home for lots of little creatures and a field mouse crept his way around the flowerpots. Freeda turned quickly as she was sure that somebody was there. The full moon was casting shadows through the windows and the old sack over the lawn mower was looking like a shadowy figure in the dark of the shed. There was something else at the back of the shed amongst all the gardening equipment that had a black sheet over it. Freeda pulled the sheet clear and looked at it curiously. It seemed odd to her, but she would tell TV and then Freeda looked out of the window and a swooping bat came through the orchard and seemed to be heading straight at her. Freeda put her hands over her eyes, and as she did so the bat rose up into the air and over the roof. But the fear in Freeda was building up, right here, right now, in this dark, horrible shed. Then Freeda began hearing that voice. When Freeda heard voices, it would always be that big fat nurse's, for she was the bringer of dreadful things in Freeda's world.

'You're going to have a room all by yourself, Freeda. And when you have this lovely, lovely jacket on, you'll feel so much better. Won't that be nice! And you must do as Dr. Bolt says Freeda and it'll only be a little itsy-bitsy pinprick! And we're never going to let you see that TV again! Never! And we're never going to let you see that TV again! Never!'

It always ended in that last reproach, and it always echoed in Freeda's mind as if going through a reverb unit set to Gothic Cathedral. It would become lodged and when you're that terrified there is only one human response. Freeda jumped up, picked up the bag of fags, and fled the old shed in distress. She had to get to TV. TV would make her feel better. He was like a magic wand with his better. When TV put his arms around her, it felt so good, she felt blessed. She had to get back to TV. She rushed out of the old shed and scampered towards the new. She could see that light on, so TV was in there. But when she passed the old compost heap, she halted in her tracks. It was the way that the moon was shining upon the decomposing skin of that snake. It glinted and Freeda was attracted to things like that. She frowned when she saw it. But something clicked and she smiled, picked up the decapitated head and its detached body, and put them in her jacket pocket.

Meanwhile, back in the new proper shed, TV had pulled that carp chair out, and had it in its bed chair position, with its deluxe sleeping bag luxuriously lain on top. This was more like it, TV thought. They could snuggle up in that bag and Freeda would love that. Maybe it was the right thing to do, coming over to this new, riskier shed. They could go back to the old shed for days and come to the new by nights! TV had another blue sweet, he had taken to the divine blues, and his back was turned to the slightly ajar door. Freeda thought she would scare him. She pounced before TV knew what was happening, wrapping the body of the snake around his neck and putting the head in his face with a hiss. TV was startled.

'Ugh! What's that, Freeda!' he asked, brushing some of the loose scales off his hoodie. 'It smells!'

'I found it outside! It's my snake!' Freeda triumphantly declared with a giggle. TV looked over the severed snake, and considered what might have led to such an aberration.

'Ugh! He must have chopped it up, Freeda!'

'It might have bitten him, TV!'

That seemed obvious to Freeda. Why would anyone chop up a snake if it didn't try and bite you?'

'Yeah, it might have done and then he chopped it up with a shovel! But I thought you were on look out with your X-ray eyes?'

'Freeda's scared, TV!'

Getting close up to TV was the only way she could alleviate her unease. They cuddled and Freeda sniffed the air and turned up her nose, but then explained what had occurred.

'There were spooks in that old shed, TV. There was this scary art fingy, a woman with a snake fingy and a bloke with horns. Spookers! And there was all these bat fingy's flying about!'

TV comforted her as Freeda was genuinely scared, and he knew her enough to know what preyed on her mind. He held Freeda affectionately, and now they were free, he wanted them to have so many happy times together. That would be enough. But he was curious as to what she saw out there back at the shed. Art fingy?

Freeda smiled, and felt so much better. TV had waved that wand around her, that magic wand of better. TV's right arm came free and he gathered another blue sweet from his pocket and popped it in his mouth. Freeda screwed up her face in curiosity.

'Where did you get those sweets from?'

TV explained everything, all his discoveries. The White Blazerman was a sweet maker as well as a blue film seller.

'Is he?' Freeda enthused. 'What, like Wonka?' It was the only reference that came to Freeda's mind.

'Yeah! Like Wonka, Freed! He's got buckets and bags full. There are loads in his freezer here. Blue and red ones! I reckon you'll love the reds. They're strawberry flavored, Freeda. That's what this funny smell is. It's his sweets, and this must be his little sweet factory. I reckon he must supply all the sweet shops!'

It all seemed so obvious, with so much evidence in front of your eyes. TV opened the freezer top and Freeda was astounded at all those red and blue sweets. It was true! The White Blazerman was a sweet maker!

'Try some reds, Freeda!' Freeda took the boilies and began eating a couple. She had a beaming smile on her face as she was determined to like them. But then her face turned sullen and morose. TV was worried. 'What's up, Freeda? You're not missing hospital are ya?'

It was the intense strawberry flavor. Freeda loved strawberry things but it always made her remember, and tears came to her eyes. TV took her hand, tenderly.

'I just wish my mummy was alive. It's the strawberry, TV, it makes me remember, when I went strawberry picking with my mummy.'

Freeda grabbed hold of TV tighter, thanking God with all her heart that she was with him here and not with those spooks in that horrible old shed or those doctors and nurses up the prison unit. And that was her only prayer. That God would let her be with TV.

'We'll have to go strawberry picking together!'

That was the kind of thing that Freeda dreamed of doing. It was such a beautiful thought and made Freeda so happy.

'Can we, TV?'

'Of course.' That was the reason he got her out. They would have the chance to do things that the hospital Gestapo would never allow them to do. Freeda's attention inevitably drifted towards the bed chair and so it was time for TV to explain that too. 'And look what I've found! He must go camping, Freeda! Keefy used to go camping. He was camping when he was taken away in that UFO by the aliens!'

Freeda had heard all those stories about Keefy and the aliens many a time. Keefy had named his pop group after it. They performed two songs out at the smoking tree with Cheryl on guitar and Drill-head on snare drum and it was all part of a concept album that they were working on called 'The Dragon Star Micro Chip', referring to the chip that the aliens had put in Keefy's brain.

'That was when Keefy had that chip in his brain, weren't it?'

Freeda remembered, but she was getting very excited by that cozy-looking bed. But the chip had always been confusing for Freeda, she visualized a potato chip in some way caught up in Keefy's brain. She screwed her face up and TV knew what was going through her mind.

'It was only a microscopic thing, Freeda. It wasn't like a proper fish and chips chip. Don't you remember me telling ya?'

Freeda looked at TV with suspicion but she had to try out that bed chair. She jumped onto the bed and laid out in pure luxury, smiling. Things were getting better now they had arrived at this 'proper' shed.

'Cor! Ain't this new "proper" shed nice, TV?'

TV agreed. 'Yeah, we've even got a sleeping bag, Freeda!' He leered at Freeda with sexy intentions. Freeda knew that look and she liked it.

'That's all you think about, TV! Getting ya big, big wangher up!'

TV grinned rather inanely as if to confirm that was exactly what he was thinking about. But Freeda still had other things, as well as that kind of thing, on her mind.

'But I still want my knives back! Or at least one, TV! So, I can scare the fucking Christ out of them! The fucking Christ! And you've got to get me a knife! You gotta!'

The call stirred something in TV, so things were looking dangerous for the Barbers. They needed weapons. They might get a little more freedom with weapons and Freeda was so good at scaring people with knives and Freeda knew where they kept them.

'We gotta break into their kitchen. There be knives in there!'

TV thought about it as Freeda nestled into him and the owl hooted again. It would be exciting entering the house, and they could do it with his wires, and Freeda might settle down once she had a knife. Then they could come back out and have fizz bangers on the luxurious bed, all snuggled up in the sleeping bag. It was the best thing they ever done coming to this 'proper' shed.

TV always acted swiftly once he made that all-important decision, and within moments they were at the back-porch door. It was an old lock and TV had his wires out picking it with Freeda by his side, eager for the moment the next door came open. It took a little more time than usual, and

TV had to change wires, replacing a 'fatty' for a 'thinny', and for a moment it seemed that the earth would move, and TV would fail to open a lock. Freeda took up verbal support, as she was dying to get a knife in her hands. That would give her security against that big fat nurse and the other lot.

'My TV can open any door anywhere, my TV can.'

Freeda had heard that idea of needing to be positive, so much at the unit, and she tried desperately to help TV with it. When TV worked, he would always look rather awkward and cack-handed, and on this occasion, it didn't seem to be going very well. He was poking his tongue out a little further than usual, and it was all very tense, until inevitably, he hit that sweet spot. The lock clicked and the door was open!

'We're in, TV!'

TV began whispering. It had to be just whispers from now on. They were about to enter the very citadel of the White Blazerman.

'Quiet Freeda. We gotta be like field mice!'

Freeda screwed up her face and TV struck his lighter to guide the way. Freeda thought she would play.

'But Freeda doesn't want to be a mouse! Freeda wants to do creepy cats again!'

TV gave the nod to creepy cats and they both began a slow-motion, creepy cats creep along the porchway, with it all becoming something of a game.

'I'm going to creep along, TV, until I find my little crackly biscuits!'

TV smirked, trying hard not to break down in hysterics, and went a few paces, and he noticed what looked like an outside toilet. He was dying for a lash. Freeda looked at him, wondering why he had ground to a halt.

'Shush! I'm gotta go to toilet, Freeda. But shush!'

Everything was being conducted in hush hush tones, and Freeda quickly got the drift of it all, putting her finger to her mouth.

'Shush!' she repeated. TV was doing everything right, but he hadn't factored in his own clumsiness. He tripped over a drainpipe surround that was in the porch and he tumbled against some clutter, and a rake that had been left there. The rake crashed to the ground, in a moment that seemed to last an eternity, as both saw it totter and fall, yet couldn't stop it. They stayed motionless and quiet for a few seconds, listening out for any signs that the inhabitants of the house had awoken. TV entered the toilet and was looking upwards, still listening for any movement, but nothing had stirred. He kept looking up and slashed all over the toilet seat and floor.

'Oh dear!'

'You're narf making a lot of noise, TV,' Freeda whispered, as TV continued slashing. He shook it around and then put it away. Then tried to cover his tracks. He awkwardly wiped the seat with some toilet paper, although the floor was covered with urine. But the toilet idea had been firmly planted in Freeda, so now she was dying to go.

'Freeda wants to go to toilet! Freeda wants to go!'

TV came out from the toilet and as yet, nothing stirred deeper within the citadel. Both Chaz and Linda were fast asleep, oblivious. Freeda went into the toilet and TV whispered to her not to make any noise.

'Shush! And mustn't pull the chain, Freeda! No pulling the chain!'

The old-fashioned out toilet with antique pulling chain was just waiting to be pulled, screaming out for it. But Freeda was adamant that she wouldn't. Freeda would never pull that chain. Never.

'That's it, Freeda. No pulling the chain!' TV whispered.

Freeda couldn't help it. She used to use a chain like this at her grandma's house all those years ago and her mind had registered it, so when she got up from the seat, she promptly pulled it without thinking. TV thought the game was up as the water came crashing from the cistern. The Blazerpeople were bound to have woken up. But Chaz snored on and Linda didn't stir either. TV was astonished. He kept telling her not to pull it. He gave a look upward, holding an ear to register any movement, but incredibly there was nothing. But he just couldn't believe it.

'Ya pulled the chain, Freeda! Ya pulled it!'

Freeda looked both ways, and both ways again and reminded TV of where they were.

'Shush! We gotta be like little field mice's, TV!'

TV gave up, and they both crept that little way further, and arrived at the back door proper. This time there was no stopping the wires. Freeda was looking over TV's shoulder, and after a series of pulled faces with his tongue lolling, TV got it, and the lock went, and they entered the new world of the Blazerpeople's citadel. TV struck the lighter again, and could see where the light switch was. He turned the light on, with a click that reverberated, but still nothing stirred. They were astonished. What a magnificent kitchen. This was all worth the wait for Freeda.

'Oh, it's lovely! We can live here forever!'

It was a nice thought, but TV was more pragmatic. He thought they might just hold out here, for a glorious summer spell. Enough time, to really enjoy the success of the 'one shot'.

'We could have it for a holiday, Freeda!'

It was about time they had a holiday. The asylum patients or 'clients' as they were now being called, never had a holiday. Not even a single day out at Fishgate. 'Nuffin'!', as Freeda would say.

'There's never a day out for the bogey people!' was a TV mantra at the asylum that had gained favor with many, as there was an end to trips after Dr. Lock had become 'The Fuhrer', and had outlawed things like fishing and other excursions. That was all about staff shortages and budgetary constraints. Dr. Lock had decided that there would be no more trips on Health and Safety grounds. Locko had such a passion for Health and Safety. It made it so much safer for the clients if they didn't go on trips. A trip was an uncontrollable circumstance and potentially dangerous environment and Dr. Lock was so concerned for her client's well-being.

'Freeda wants to go on the holy-day, TV! Freeda wants to go on the holy-day to Fishgate!'

Freeda had such fond memories of Fishgate. It existed like a glorious idyll, where everything was blue skies, beach and perfect, and she was with her mum. She went there a number of times without Barry around, so Fishgate memories didn't bring Barry to the fore. She longed to go back there and stay at the same caravan park with TV. That would be a dream come true for her.

'We gotta go! We gotta go to Fishgate! And stay in that caravan!'

'We'll go there, Freeda.' Freeda believed him too. Hadn't he got her out of that prison unit with that sledgehammer and that big chain saw fingy?

TV then looked around for a kettle as he, like Freeda, really fancied a cup of coffee. The caffeine withdrawal symptoms were beginning to kick in, because everybody at the asylum would have at least six cups a day. Locko was feted as a heroine for a month or two when she announced that the Trust would be purchasing massive stocks of instant coffee a few years back. It was the calculated tradeoff for no more trips. The Trust was quid's in, as Dr. Lock put it, and for some time it was heralded, as the beginning of Locko's new regime of freedom. All clients could have as many cups as they wanted, and they all got stuck in, so all were addicts. TV spotted the kettle and next to it was a large jar of expensive instant coffee and a biscuit drum.

'Wan that cup of coffee, Freeda?' TV asked in whispers.

'Freeda wants a cup of coffee. And I want my knives back! You promised me a knife, TV!'

After the demand Freeda started giggling and smirking.

'Shush be quiet Freeda, they'll hear us.'

'I was just thinking 'bout that time Drill-head went for the coffee drinking record and puked up over the big fat nurse! It was so funny, TV! It was when we could have all those coffees!'

TV had to laugh a bit himself, it happened when they were all in the lock up together a couple of years ago. Drill-head had nineteen coffees that day, one after the other but TV knew it would be like walking a tightrope coming into this citadel, and the game would be up if the Blazerpeople heard anything and came down. They would just have to scarper. With the talk about Fishgate, he thought they might be able to head there, heavily disguised in some way or other. But he would think about that later. He picked up the kettle and half-filled it, while being as quiet as he could. The water was off on the boil, and TV naturally thought cutlery would be in the drawers underneath the sink where it usually is. He opened one. It was miscellaneous bits and pieces but no knives. But as soon as he opened up the second, there it was, a great big glistening carving knife. Freeda quickly grabbed it. It was like a great talisman. When it was in her hands, an enormous menacing power flooded her. With a knife like that, Freeda was dangerous and powerful, and she knew it. Those doctors and nurses wouldn't give Freeda one of their forced injections, when she had a knife like this. She'd cut them to pieces, and if they came to try and ruin her holy-day with TV, she would stick it in um! Freeda just loved it. It was the best knife she ever had.

'Cor, narf a long un, TV, ain't it?'

While they waited for the water to come to the boil, TV became curious about the designs on the mugs. He picked up one of Chaz's carp mugs, it was the Blazerman on it, holding up big fishes.

'Look, Freeda! He's got his own mugs with big fishes on! He's holding them. Look!'

Freeda perused the mug and she was her usual incredulous, astonished self, as if she had born witness to some ancient esoteric hieroglyphics.

'Oh yeah!' Freeda thought about the curious mug for a few moments, and came to her own conclusions. 'He must do fish and chips! Freeda likes the fish and chips. Freeda likes the fish without bones and chips, TV!'

TV thought it unlikely, but he kept quiet, and looked through some of the other mugs. There were further curiosities. He perused one that was in celebration of Chaz's hunting exploits. In the image, Chaz was outside a hunting lodge with his shotgun resting by him, as he held up two big geese by the neck. This was utterly reprehensible to Dragon Star and their philosophies of preserving life. It was only fish that could be caught, because Jesus had fed the multitudes with fish served up with whole meal bread.

'And look! He's got his guns and he's holding up big goosey ganders! He must shoot them, Freeda! The "Dragon Star" children like goosey ganders.'

The tirade took immediate effect.

'I'll get him with my new knife, TV! See how he likes it!'

Freeda gripped harder with her face, grotesquely distorting. Things were looking worse than inauspicious for the still, fast asleep Chaz, who was snoring away, oblivious.

'Shush, Freeda! We might wake them up.'

The water boiled, and the kettle clicked and TV poured the water for the instant coffees. He opened the fridge with Freeda looking over his shoulder and took some milk, while surveying what they might take, to tie them over.

'We better not take too much, Freeda. They'll know we've been.'

TV noticed an unopened cheesecake, pushed back into the fridge. He pulled it out. 'We'll have this, Freed, for supper!' Her eyes lit up.

'I love my cheesecake, TV. And it's strawberry!'

Then he opened that biscuit drum, and it was full of no other than digestive biscuits.

'Look! The biscuit fairies didn't forget ya, Freeda.'

Freeda smiled and took her digestives with her mug of coffee. It was all because of leaving that old miserable shed. Things were going better now.

'Freeda knew they'd come!'

Freeda dunked her biscuit and took a sip of coffee, and TV had some of his, but TV was curious. He wanted to look deeper into the citadel. He knew it was dangerous and risky, but the Dragon Star clan were renowned risk takers. Many a time TV and Keefy would escape overnight and smoke joints and take 'shrooms' all night long in the woods, and then come back into the open ward just before day break, sneaking in through an opened window, and nobody even knew they had been out. Nobody. Well, apart from a particular agency nurse who saw them come in but didn't say anything as she used to give TV blow jobs in the women's toilets quite regular, until the Gestapo realized something was going on.

'Let's look in the front room, Freeda! But shush! Do creepy cats!'

TV opened the door, and clicked yet another light switch, and both were astounded by what befell them.

'Wow! Big fishes! The White Blazerman keeps big fishes, Freed!'

Freeda connected up one thing and the other confusingly, and she grabbed the wrong end of the stick as they say. This could be unfortunate for Freeda, because if she wasn't checked, she would run with the wrong end, and off she went to build up a whole new world.

'He grows his own, TV! He's probably got a fish and chip van!'

TV thought it unlikely, but then again, he thought he might have. He was a sweet maker, a porn seller and who knows, he might also sell fish and chips in his vans. Anything's possible these days. But the carp transfixed Freeda. She'd never seen fish indoors in tanks like these before. Usually it was those little guppies and angel fish, like in the prison unit. Not these great big fishes. Freeda was so fascinated, that she had her nose nigh pressed up in front of the glass, peering at one of the carp, who was directly in front of her, opening and shutting its mouth. TV was busily perusing all the photos that were on the mantel, and above it, trying to figure out things about these Blazerpeople, while Freeda was looking at those curious fish.

'Don't they look funny, TV! They look like they're sucking schlongers!'

The idea took hold with Freeda and she couldn't help cackling. Big fishes sucking cocks. It was so funny, and the laugh registered in some subtle way upstairs, in Chaz's slumbering consciousness. For a split second he twitched. Surely, he was going to wake up and hear these intruder's downstairs, but in the next moment, he rolled over and was blowing and snoring the more. TV shushed Freeda again and in the doing so, he was distracted from the photographs and was given to taking a closer look at the ornaments in the far tank that housed Hermann, namely the red telephone box and the Medusa head. Freeda was looking with a screwed-up face at the cow's head with its horns trying to figure it all out as she glanced back at the fish-tanks.

'There was horn fingy's in that shed.'

'It's just a cow's head, Freeda. Some people like looking at that sort of thing.' But TV was more interested in the fish tanks.

'Look! A telephone box with an octopus living in it!'

Now Freeda knew certain things that made other things simply impossible.

'You don't get octopuses in telephone boxes!' But TV was adamant that you did.

'Nah, look, Freeda, you can! Look!'

Freeda got her nose right in front of the tank and was silent for a moment as she surveyed the odd ornament. She was in disbelief.

'Oh yeah!'

And there was much more. Freeda had noticed it and was about to comment herself. But TV knew that the head with the snakes coming out of it was that Greek mythic woman.

'And look! That's the Medusa, Freeda! She turns ya to stone if ya look at her!'

Freeda turned her face up again and sneered at the unusual head. She was looking the darn thing in the face and Freeda hadn't been turned into stone.

'Don't be silly! Freeda's still real!' and she pinched her flesh to prove it. TV tried to make Freeda realize that it was all metaphorical and allegorical, whatever that meant, Freeda thought. TV tried other tactics.

'Nah, Freeda, it's make-believe'

'Well Freeda's ain't gonna play!' Freeda snapped. TV went quiet for a few seconds, and then he turned the conversation to the framed photographs, on and above the mantel. He was looking at the preponderance of fish themed photos.

'Look, Freeda! Anyone would think he's married to a big fish!' Freeda looked at the main photograph of Chaz cradling that big 'Ressie' carp and took in the others too, that celebrated Chaz's carp fishing exploits. She screwed up her face again as she reflected.

'He seems to like fish best! Maybe he feeds loads of people from his fish and chip van.'

TV wasn't sure that the Blazerman did have a fish and chip van, but it seemed feasible, although highly unlikely. He looked at his 'Jesus's sandals', for a glance.

'Jesus used to feed loads of people with his fish, Freeda. He had loads of fresh fish to give away to the poor people, loads!'

Any mention of the Jesus of Nazareth placed emphasis back on the footwear the couple were wearing. Freeda looked down at her sandals. She knew they were important.

'We've got his sandals on haven't we, TV?'

TV re-emphasized that the Dragon Star children had bought extensively into his brand at the Death Hill boot fair. Freeda looked back again at her 'Jesus's sandals', trying to work it all out in her mind.

'Did Jesus have a fish and chip van?' she whispered.

'Nah, Freeda. They hadn't been invented back in Jesus's days. That was the old days, Freed. Jesus had donkeys. He used to ride them all over the place.'

Freeda looked around puzzled, and you could she was wrestling, trying to work out all this oddness about Jesus and all the odd things in the Blazerman's lounge.

'Did he go out selling fish and chips on them, TV?' TV thought it unlikely that Jesus did this on donkeys. But you never know. TV had an open mind about most things in the Dragon Star age.

'Nah, Freed! Jesus and his mates all went round on donkeys.' TV hoped the disclosure would bring a clarity, but Freeda was still looking completely baffled.

'What, eating fish and chips?' TV now realized that this one would go around and around, so he relented.

'Yeah, Freeda, yeah!'

Freeda smirked and then giggled. She desperately tried not to laugh too loud, because of those Blazerpeople fingys upstairs. But she was visualizing Jesus and his followers, all on their donkeys, eating their cod and chips while riding no hands.

'What's up, Freeda?' TV asked, and Freeda smirked again, and giggled a bit more, before coming clean.

'Weren't Jesus a fucking weirdo?' TV looked down at his sandals and thought for a moment.

'Spose he was, Freed.' TV's attention was then drawn back to the big carp trophy pics and Freeda was peering with him. 'I used to go fishing with Keefy. He caught whoppers like these Freeda. And you should have

244

seen um. Keefy said they loved the mud and came out of the deep and when he reeled them in, I thought they were black and then in the sun they were brilliant green with these red magical eyes.'

TV put two red boilies over his eye sockets to illustrate the point and held them there.

'They were like magic, Freeda. Magical whoppers with red eyes!'

Freeda was sure now on a number of things about this Jesus bloke and fish.

'Jesus must have caught them, TV,' she said, there was no doubt at all about that. He had that van in the olden days.

'Oh yea, Freed, Jesus caught everything!' TV replied, and he still had those red balls at his eyes. Freeda thought about what TV had said.

'What even the octopuses in the red telephone boxes?' Freeda thought about it all for a moment, but that octopus was still unfathomable. How could octopuses live in telephone boxes? Sometimes, TV got some daft ideas into his head, although she didn't want to say it. She thought it might upset him, and she didn't want to upset the leader of Dragon Star. He was so into all that stuff.

TV looked at more of those framed photographs. Further over to the left of the mantel were a number of hunting snaps with Chaz clad in his military fatigues, and that great white shark hunter's hat. There was one with Chaz and a string of exotic looking ducks that he had shot. TV frowned at the Enfield's as he perused. There was another with Chaz holding up two long eared hares by their ears, and another with Chaz standing next to a hatchback vehicle, that was full of about eighty dead geese. It looked like the wholesale slaughter of the natural world. Meanwhile, Freeda had plonked herself down in the velvet chair and was looking decidedly pleased with herself and cozy. It fitted her like a glove and she was enjoying herself, smiling, as she chewed on her hair.

'Cor! This furry chair! It's really nice, TV! It's all furry! I wish we had one of these furry chairs up the prison!' Freeda said, as she stroked its arm. 'Freeda likes furry chairs! They're all nice and furry, TV!' Freeda then remembered that she had her love heart sunglasses in her big purse. She had to put them on. She thought she would look good in that hoodie jacket, with sunglasses on, in that furry chair. She couldn't hide her excitement.

'Look, TV! Freeda's sitting in the big furry chair with her sunglasses on, TV! TV! Dun Freeda look good, TV!'

'Ya look fucking ace, Freed! But shush!' TV replied, raising his index finger to his lips, as he was assessing and reflecting, on those murders of goosey ganders and things.

'He must have loads of guns, Freed! Loads. Look! And he shoots little quack-quacks!'

Freeda didn't really want to leave that furry chair, as she had taken out her small make up mirror and was applying her cheap lip gloss. She loved applying lip glosses as it made her feel that she was good at making up, without getting in a mess, but she got up and investigated, still fiddling with her lip glosses with those love heart sunglasses on. She would have to try out her cat eyes too. She screwed her face up in disgust, as she peered at Chaz in the photos. It all seemed so alien to the world of Dragon Star.

'And look, Freeda! He shoots big bunny rabbits and holds um up by their long ears! And look! He shot all those goosey ganders and stuffed them in the boot of his car and took them away. He's evil, Freed! Evil!'

Freeda looked down towards their sandals. They were paid up members of the brand.

'I bet Jesus never shot quack-quacks and goosey ganders! He was always out on his donkeys, eating chips and doing good!' Freeda naturally thought these terrible things had to be avenged. Action had to be taken. The Dragon Star could never contemplate such cruelties. Freeda started doing her creepy cats towards the exit door with the long knife held up.

'What ya doing, Freeda?' TV asked. Freeda's eyes were glinting with menace. She had her knife and it was payback time for that Blazerman.

'Freeda's gonna go tip-toe, tip-toe, up his stairs and creepy cat right to his bed and I'm gonna wake him up with my new knife, wakey-wakey! And I'm gonna stick it right in him!'

TV couldn't think of any reason to prevent Freeda from doing it. The White Blazerman was a murderer of poor little ducks, goosey ganders and big furry rabbits. What goes around comes around, was the first plank of the Dragon Star philosophy. It was all coming around.

'Yeah! Teach him the lesson of the "Dragon Star" children, Freeda! But shush!'

Freeda went into creepy cat mode and quietly turned the handle of the door. It squeaked and she looked at TV, and then they looked towards the ceiling listening for movement, but there was nothing. She pressed on and began to creep up the winding stairs. She was going to pounce on that Blazerman like a big black cat!

TV, still fascinated by the treasure trove of oddity that was the front room, had taken to looking at that painting of Natasha, and he was correlating it with the small photograph that was a shot from the glamour mag. Freeda was nigh up the stairs with her raised knife, when TV whispered up to her.

'Freeda! Come and look at this nudey woman photograph! Quick!'

Anything to do with nudey and sex was worth checking out Freeda thought, and she turned around eager, to see what TV had found. She was about to rush, but TV put his finger to his lips.

'Shush! Creepy cats!'

Freeda crept her way down back in her creeping cat mode.

'I'm gonna search for my crackles again, TV.'

They both smirked and giggled with TV trying to keep the noise down but still nothing stirred.

She came into the lounge, and TV quietly closed the door behind her and then went back to the mantel.

'Come over here and look, Freeda!'

'Let Freeda see, TV! Let Freeda see the nudeys!' Freeda rushed over and by now her mind had been diverted from that retribution mission against Chaz the evil hunter. TV showed her the correlation between the two images, that big painting and the small framed photo. TV had cracked some kind of unknown, nudey cipher enigma.

'Oh yeah.' Freeda was fascinated. She looked at the photo and then she looked over at the painting above the Great Waldorf settee, and she kept glancing between the two, digesting it all, reflecting upon the odd serendipity.

'Did Jesus like nudey women, TV?' she asked. Now TV could remember a priest saying that Jesus wept and he was sure you could find one saying he wanked as well. Freeda thought it so funny. She was giggling and smirking away.

'Did Jesus do the "fizz bangs" like we do, TV?'

TV thought that they must have started somewhere, and time was counted from Jesus so the 'fizz bangs' must have come from him, and then they were passed on by Jesus's followers. Just like they were now doing in Dragon Star. It was all connected, or at least it felt like that, when TV was peering and meditating on the light from the special lampposts. Freeda's attention had whizzed off to the marriage photo, that was center stage, or just off center, from the 'Ressie' record carp pic. She was more interested in the marriage photos than the nudes. That photo had pride and place at the center one time, but Chaz had caught that record carp, and that was an important achievement. But Freeda was fixated with the fresh-looking marriage photo, taken some twenty-two years ago now and a small wedding cake decoration that stood on the mantel.

'Look, TV, they've just got married!'

'Nah, that was ages ago. The Blazerman must be nearly eighty now!'

Freeda was nigh meditating upon that photo. She had always wanted to get married in a dress like that, and she wanted to marry TV and have a wedding cake. TV knew what she was thinking.

'You would look so nice in a wedding dress, Freeda. Ya really would.'

Freeda smiled, and TV cuddled her. He had some ideas in his mind that he had been thinking about prior to the 'break out', and which were the main reason for the escape. He had been keeping that under his Dragon

Star cap. But looking at that photo helped Freeda crystallize her deepest yearnings.

'Freeda wants to get married. I wanna marry you, TV.'

TV was determined to make it happen somehow, determined. That was his only real mission now, to get married to Freeda his soulmate. He didn't quite know how they were going to do it. But he believed it would happen somehow, surely it was fated?

'We'll get married, Freeda. I promise.'

Freeda smiled as TV kept his promises. He promised to get her out of that prison and he had done that, so who was to say they wouldn't marry? And why couldn't Freeda get married to TV? That big fat nurse couldn't be right all the time.   Freeda dreamed of that day and she prayed that God would remember her and TV. They had his son's sandals on, and Freeda had the brands badges all over her new jacket.

'And there's their baby, TV!' Both were now looking at a baby photo of Natasha, and TV agreed that it was sweet. Thinking about babies though, sent Freeda into a more disturbing train of thought. Poor Freeda just couldn't escape from her demons.

'Freeda was going to have a baby. TV's baby, and Lock and Bolt took it away from me. They killed it, TV! They killed our baby, TV!'

TV done his best to embrace her in as much love as he could. That's everything he could give her. 'Leave the past behind, Freeda. I'm with ya now. We're together now.'

TV took up his usual 'enthused' diversion tactics. They generally worked well with Freeda in tight spots.

'Look, Freeda! They're on holiday!' TV gestured towards that photo taken around the pool in Spain a couple of years ago, with Chaz drinking from the ladle of wine. Freeda looked closely at the photo with its sunshine, pool and drinks. Desire was being dangled like a carrot as these things were forbidden to Freeda in her prison like existence.

'Freeda wants to go on the holy-day to Fishgate, TV.'

TV was thinking hard about the next steps and a plan was beginning to hatch in his mind, no doubt due to Dragon Star intuition and inspiration. Things happened like that for TV Sam. Answers would just present themselves, all of a sudden, after he had been struggling over something difficult. Dragon Star light would clear the way.

'We are on a kind of holiday, Freeda. And tomorrow we'll make it a real holy-day!'

Freeda smiled as she felt assured, seeing that glint in TV's eyes. They'd go on the 'holy-day' tomorrow as TV said they would. Hadn't he got her out of that prison with that big saw and hammer?

'Will we, TV?'

'Course, Freed!' TV was emphatic. It would all happen tomorrow, and Freeda believed him. For Freeda, TV was so powerful he was like a magician. He could control reality in some unique unfathomable way. TV had shown her. He could open any door with those wires and he could make you see the 'fizz bang' lights with that big wangher of his. And he would get her down Fishgate. They would sit on the beach there with ice-creams, and the sun would be shining and they would have some pictures taken like that holy-day photo of the Blazerpeople. She saw herself sitting on that beach, exactly where she sat with her mum, cuddled up to TV, having those ice creams with the red juice and nuts on.

Freeda's attention was then drawn to the large wide screen TV that was at the end of the room. TV hated televisions, or at least had a certain love/hate relationship with them. Most people at the asylum knew that there was more hate than love. Dr. Lock had to keep TV far away from all televisions, as he had already smashed nine, kicking them all to bits and throwing a further five out of windows. TV liked televisions for a little while and then he lost his temper with them. He said to Dan that it was the cathode rays. They interfered with the Dragon Star light, making it all muddy and opaque, so inevitably at some stage they would get the boot. It was like a pressure cooker thing, and eventually the lid blew, and TV had to destroy and destroy the cathode rays, before he could release the light again. It was something deeply symbolic and philosophical, that he and Keefy used to always talk about. If you gave the screen a good kicking, you smashed the set. You broke through the screen as it were, to find out what was on the other side. To see what's really there. But he would live with this one, as he couldn't smash it tonight. But it still stood there as a massive threat because it was such a big screen.

'The Blazerpeople have got a big TV, TV!'

'Yeah, fucking cathode rays! Fucking fings.'

But Freeda was intrigued. This was the first all-encompassing screen both of them had ever seen. TV felt like kicking it in the moment he set his eyes on it, but he put it out of his mind, as they had to be quiet. But Dragon Star emanations were telling him to kick it in. But he looked away, and his attention focused on a shot of Linda in a bikini, frolicking around the pool on holiday. He fancied a bit of the Blazerwoman. He had watched her bending over in the garden, and he got that erection looking at her, as he hid behind that big tree. He couldn't help it; he had to pull it about and he shot his load over the tree trunk.

'Did Jesus kick in tellies, TV?' Freeda asked.

'He might have done if tellies had been invented in the olden days. But they weren't invented back then, Freeda!'

TV was grinning and leering at Linda, and although he loved Freeda and was her soulmate, Dragon Star had that mission. They were the sex evangelists. They had a duty to shag people's brains out. He would have to do it.

'I'm gonna pull her knickers down and shag her brains out, right out! Take her to seventh heaven and all that!'

It was all part of the urgency and need to spread the Gospel of the Dragon Star. TV was a carrier and he had to disseminate the light bringing seed. It was all part of his contract with the alien intelligences. He and Keefy had even agreed on a date, AD 2025, when the emanations would be streaming in from the deepest reaches of the universe, enveloping the entire planet. Everything would be Dragon Star then, everything. That esoteric knowledge had been communicated to TV and Keefy, by the Sirius Alien Alliance, when they had that pucker bit of dope in Tennin Park, underneath the willow tree. It was twilight and it was just before they got moved on by the Park Ranger. Like Dan said, Keefy must have always been stinking rich because he had that white blazer costing two grand and he regularly had a score of puff.

'Getting your big whanger up! That's all you think about! Let's go back to the proper shed and do "fizzer bangers"! We gotta do some catching up!'

It seemed an almighty good idea, but TV made sure they quietly replaced the cups and he checked that nothing was out of place first, although a large carving knife was missing. Freeda was impatient as she wanted to get into that sleeping bag on their bed in the new shed, and snuggle up to TV. But TV was determined to lock that back door. They couldn't leave any trace and evidence they had been. Now TV could unlock doors better than the best of them, but if the truth be known he wasn't as effective at locking them. He tinkered with the wires as Freeda became more and more impatient.

'I'm going back to our new shed and have some more of those strawberry sweets! And some cheesecake! Um!'

TV was left tinkering with a selection of 'thinnies' and 'fatties,' while Freeda skipped off lightly, excited by the prospect of curling up in that sleeping bag. He looked anguished as he never practiced closing doors. It was opening that was exciting, finding out what lies behind them, rather than taking time shutting them. In fact, he hadn't shut a door for five years. TV stopped for a moment and turned as Freeda was about to leave the porch.

'I've gotta lock the doors up, Freed, so they don't know we've been!'

Freeda just couldn't see the importance. Why not just get back into that shed, where all the action was?

'You're boring, TV, locking doors when we could be doing "fizz bangers" for the "Dragons".

TV was inevitably drawn away and the back door was left unlocked, although if he were to be honest, he didn't think he would lock it. He was a million miles away from getting that sweet spot. So, it was now on to that old door at the back of the porch. This one would be easy. Within a few seconds it was locked. Freeda was already in the shed and had the light on, and within a few more they were cuddled up in the sleeping bag on a lovely comfortable carp bed, feeling as if they were the happiest couple in the whole wide world. It was quiet and the light was turned off and they were at last, together in a cozy intimacy. It was heaven.

'This has been the best day of my life, Freeda. Ain't it great, just being together! And in a cozy sleeping bag?'

These perfect golden moments were overwhelming for Freeda. She couldn't remember a better feeling ever, but that fact was also troubling her. She began sobbing.

'What's up, Freeda?' TV asked sympathetically.

Freeda hit upon the raw truth.

'I'm sad, TV. Because we won't be together forever. Anything good that happens to Freeda, never lasts. It never does.'

TV was philosophical. They had to make the best of it.

'We're together now, so just be in the moment, right here, Freeda. I love you, Freed, and we'll be together forever and ever, in our love and spirit. We're soulmates!'

Freeda felt blessed. For so long this was all she wanted, merely to be with TV, and here she was snuggled up in a sleeping bag with him. It was perfect.

'Thanks for saving me with that electric saw.'

'I love ya, Freeda! I had to!' TV replied.

CHAPTER THIRTEEN

TRAMPS FOR SUPPER

The cock at the Greene-Burrows gave his customary early morning call and he kept repeating it, but it was sometime before there was the sound of rustling movement to herald Chaz's awakening. When he did stir, he was dismayed as he was readily recalling the bizarre dream he had. He hadn't watched *Snow White* for at least fifteen years, back when Natasha was a kid, but an old woman came to the front door selling toffee apples with a big wort on her nose. Chaz went to the bathroom and was sitting on the pan smirking about it all. He remembered it vividly now. Linda had come into the front room as Chaz was concerned with the carp tanks. He had found Hermann floating dead on the surface and there was that center spread open, of that PC Angelica on the table. Linda glanced at it disapprovingly but then she told him there was an old woman selling apples at the door, and that Hermann had been poisoned and there were rumors that witches were about.

Chaz had gone out there and he immediately thought she was a witch in disguise. He said she was that witch in the Disney films and he told her flatly to piss off, but somehow, she cast a spell over him, and she talked Chaz into buying one of her delicious-looking toffee apples. Chaz then remembered himself sitting in the velvet chair with Linda desperately trying to stop him from taking a bite. But Chaz was impelled to scrunch into it and when he did, Chaz could hear that old witch cackling with laughter. She had left her broomstick resting up against the Jag. She picked it up and away she went up Holly Beach Lane heading to that darn fucking asylum. The next thing Chaz remembered, was being in intensive care with his cock shriveled away. Chaz looked down at his penis as he expelled trying to figure out why he had such a weird dream. His penis was still there though. He scratched his head and pulled some paper off the roll, while smirking at the zany craziness of the mind.

Chaz entered the front room, his ample tummy bulging over his boxer shorts. He intended to get some tea on, and he fancied a joint, but as soon as he entered the lounge, he stopped in his tracks and began to sniff.

'What the fuck's that smell?' He sniffed again, turning his face up, trying to think where it might have come from. But he couldn't pinpoint anything, and he didn't recall any smell in the lounge the previous evening. Then Chaz took a handful of boilies and plopped them down to Hermann who abruptly monopolized them, as he scared the smaller carp away. Hermann was certainly on them, and Chaz chuckled approvingly. Carp would make Chaz's special teaser balls their 'go to' bait.

'Phew, Hermann! Get on it! Get on that egg shell!'

Chaz then sat down on his king's chair and he got another waft of that smell again. He could swear it was in the chair and he turned to his side and sniffed it, shook his head in disbelief, before putting the data of the feed in the little black research book. Chaz then raised his shoulders, as he thought he would have his first small line of the morning, which was always a favorite. It set him up for the day as such, but he could still smell that darn smell. He sniffed the air again as Linda flushed the toilet upstairs, readying herself to come down.

'Fucking smell in here?' Chaz reiterated to himself before shouting up to Linda.

'Linda! What you been doing to this fucking chair?'

Chaz was sure that she had put some kind of cleaning powder or something on it. That was the sort of thing Linda would do, he thought, without even telling you. Linda was gathering some dirty washing to bring down.

'I haven't done anything to your blasted chair, Chaz.'

'Well somebody did. The fucking thing stinks! Cheap perfume fucking stink!' Chaz was still sure she had put something on it, no doubt some kind of new dry shampoo, or something cretinous, he thought. When Linda did finally enter in her dressing gown, the front room was being enveloped by the smell of the Wild Fruits of the Forest air freshener, that Chaz was spraying everywhere. She looked at Chaz askance, as he never sprayed like this first thing in the morning.

'Here, was there a fucking smell down here last night? A musty smell, as if we had tramps for supper.'

Linda was still bleary-eyed but she nodded her head in the negative.

'No. I didn't smell anything, but I can smell that air freshener you're spraying all over the place. Tea or coffee?'

Now Chaz realized that the trend and Zeitgeist in post-millennium culture was against sexism, which Chaz thought despicable, so he would always try and get Linda to make decisions. A decision was an opportunity for Linda to empower herself, he would say. He had read tons about what women really wanted now, and he wasn't one of those men who set out to control their wives, like the old-fashioned generations. Hadn't she been to see those strippers on Tuesday night?

'I'll leave you to make the decision, Linda! Either will go nicely with the morning line. And remember, it's a pig day.'

Chaz was about to snort with his fifty-pound snorting note, but he got up, agitated again.

'Fuck me, I can still smell it. Tramps! Tramps and cheap perfume fucking smell! You haven't been putting a cleaning powder all over it, have ya?'

'No! I haven't, Chaz. How many more times have I got to tell you!'

By now Linda was in the kitchen pouring some oil into the frying pan, getting ready to cook the bacon and tomatoes. The rashers were off hissing, while Chaz was still giving that front room the odd intermittent shot of the wild fruits. Linda sighed as she looked at the dirty footprints that were on the kitchen floor. She knew it had rained last night, and obviously thought Chaz had trampled all over the place after he had put those boilies out. She sighed again, but didn't say anything, and was cleaning the floor with a tea towel that she put down and was whizzing around under her foot.

'Get that pig on, Linda!' Chaz jokingly shouted. How Chaz loved his morning bacon and big fry up breakfasts and even more so, since cutting down to one day on, one day off. But with so much freshener in the air, Linda began coughing. It hadn't occurred to her that the footprint was out-sized. She was too concerned by the all-enveloping smell of the freshener that Chaz couldn't stop spraying.

'Chaz! Can you stop spraying that please! You'll put me on my Ventolin!'

Linda cracked six eggs and had them going in another big frying pan. Chaz loved his eggs and he always had four with a cooked breakfast. Linda switched the radio on, that was tuned to the local Tennin station. National news was about to give way to the local.

'The third series of the controversial *Big Brother* begins tonight in a new house in Elstree. This year's contestants include a shopaholic transgendered nurse, a glamour model and activist for the rights of sex workers, a Nigerian dress maker and a controversial former member of the British National Party. The critics and media are negative, but no doubt you, like the rest of us, are hooked! So, tune in!'

The bacon was hissing and Linda was turning the eggs, while she also had some fried bread on the go with the bacon. Next up was tomatoes in with the egg. How Chaz loved his fry ups.

'*Big Brother's* back tonight, Chaz!'

'We'll have to watch it, girl,' Chaz replied, while he was rolling up a joint. Chaz then recalled that dream. He had to tell Linda. 'Guess what, Linda! I was even dreaming about that mad fucking laugh! Fucking witch in my dreams, selling me a poisoned fucking toffee apple at the door!'

Linda laughed, but she said it was understandable as the 'break out' business was disturbing. She was full of the 'Oh, my God's', when Chaz told her the rest of the dream, with his visit to intensive care with his shriveled penis. When Linda returned to the breakfast, the local news was on, referring to the 'break out' as Tennin Police were using it to put across updates.

'The two Tennin Health Trust clients who absconded under the 1983 Mental Health Act, are still at large in the Tennin Gap area. Tennin radio garnered this response from a spokesperson from Tennin Trust late last night.' Linda came to a halt and listened.

'The 'break out's' on the local news, Chaz!' Chaz couldn't believe that they were still running around.

'Ain't they fucking got um yet?' Linda brought the radio into the front room, as she wanted Chaz to hear. A Tennin Police representative was talking now.

'Please bear in mind there have been no confirmed sightings so they may have taken refuge, possibly in a garage or shed, so people must be vigilant. However, a man in Holly Beach Lane, near to the hospital, did hear a woman laughing in the adjacent woods who may have been one of the absconders.'

'That's you, Chaz!' The news item continued and the alert got more alarming.

'We repeat, they're highly dangerous and are known to be armed with knives. If you see them ring Tennin Police on 297324 or 999, and in no circumstances should they be confronted.'

The weather forecast was nice and everything set fair and warm, but Chaz was unsettled as the news gave way to a show of eighties and up to the present-day pop favorites.

'So, they're definitely tooled up, eh? Fucking charming!'

Chaz lit up his joint, as an early morning toke always gave him a healthy appetite. Within five, that breakfast was on a tray before him and he dogged the joint out, carefully preserving it for later on. Crispy local and organic bacon was one of Chaz's favorite moments of the day. He was now approaching high spirits as he realized that by late afternoon that kilo would be out, and that loss of cash on Phelps would be history. Then he had to get that big one to Jay and Dai early evening, which meant he would be around ten grand in profit. He totted figures up in his accounts book and was well pleased with himself. In fact, he was purring.

'Get on that organic pig! Get on it, Chazzy boy. Luv it, Linda. What a day lined up! Knock the rest of the kilo out and then a big one to the deadly Temple Hive duo.'

He then began looking through an accounts book relating to his little porn business. He had arranged drops at specific times.

'And eight, nine, ten drops of the DVDs. Who said you have to kick a pig skin around to get yourself nigh twenty grand a day! Just give the "pig" the fucking run around, while you're filming people shagging! And the time to go for a powder and have a few! Ha, ha, ha, ha!'

Linda came forth from the kitchen with her own breakfast and sat down on the Great Waldorf. She could see the big wad of money on the coffee table and it was all so worrying. Two years ago, Chaz was saying that once he moved into a bigger house and the mortgage was under control, he would cut himself free of all the dealing. They had the house and the money now.

'You're dealing more than you ever did, Chaz,' Linda said critically. Chaz went on the defensive.

'Fuck me, Linda! How do ya think this place was bought? And all the mod cons with it!'

Linda had said it umpteen times before, but she found herself saying it all over again.

'Well it's time we went legit, Chaz. Why can't you just go in with Mike on that fishing tackle shop? And be done with it! And if you had your mum here, you'd have all the money at hand for it. You wouldn't have to touch one of your blasted gold bricks!'

Chaz felt as if he was back in, post Phelps, with everything coming back to normal. Why couldn't Linda just relax?

'Here we go! How on earth can I have my mother here, eh?' Chaz said, with great annoyance. 'I'm sure she'd like to watch you snorting it up ya hooter, Linda!'

'Oh, I just want a new life, Chaz, a clean start.'

Chaz had more important things to think about. What did he want a new life for? He had to get out there and continue being Chaz Barber, cool dude dealer in the alligator shoes and white blazer, driving that chariot about. He was the man, the main man to his many devotees, when he dealt his ace cocaine, and that sheer money power. It made him phallic hot! All the Brooke's and Jessica's wanted a bit of Chaz.

'Maybe next year,' he said, without any conviction whatsoever.

'But you said that last year when we were at Cavell!' Linda replied. Chaz had a ploy to meet her half way, just to shut her up for the day.

'Look, Linda. This year I go in big, right. Get the shed load of dough and then me and Miko will get a business plan up by the end of the year. How's that? Now let me enjoy me hot breakfast, for Christ's sake.'

Chaz had a good laugh at the innuendo, but he meant what he said, although he might alter it as soon as he got out the front gate. Linda resigned herself to a temporary cessation of the pressure.

'Well make sure you don't gamble the lot away then, Chaz!' Chaz accepted that he got his fingers burnt but he promised to lay off the betting until they went to Royal Ascot, which had become a yearly pilgrimage for the Barbers. Chaz was determined he'd go there and get a big wager on the rails that would be spoken about by the TV pundits. That was the mission, although by now Chaz was well into the bacon, but it didn't stop him thinking ahead as he stabbed his sausage. He fancied a cut of that beef joint they had last night for his sandwiches. It would go down a treat.

'Here, when ya finished, Linda darling, I'll have that beef for me lunch, please.'

Chaz loved having his own sandwiches when the pickings were good and that beef was prime local butcher's and very expensive. Chaz finished his breakfast, and put a porn back on to pass the time of day, prior to getting in full character. Linda was out there in the kitchen perplexed, as she was having trouble finding the sharp knife.

'I can't find the sharp knife, Chaz!' Chaz didn't reply as he had the porn turned up loud. Linda sighed and raised her voice. 'I said, I seem to have lost the long sharp knife, Chaz!'

Chaz was well used to this losing and finding in the next breath. If only she'd look a bit more thoroughly in the first place he thought.

'It's where it normally is, Linda. Look properly please,' Chaz said, with a patronizing tone. Linda checked the drawer again. But there was no sign of that sharp knife.

'It isn't here, Chaz. Come and have a look for yourself if you don't believe me.'

Chaz resigned himself to going out there. He would open the drawer and there it would be, as per normal, staring right at him. He sighed and got up, smiling to himself at a lewd act that a woman was engaging in on the DVD. As soon as he went across the threshold in his bed warmer socks, he slid on the wet slippery floor. He flew into the kitchen sink with a whack, and a couple of plates spun to the floor and smashed.

'Fucking hell, Linda! Why not go the whole hog and put gin traps all over the fucking house! I could have broken me fucking neck!'

Linda remonstrated that she had just mopped the floor because of his dirty footprints all over it. Chaz didn't say anything to that, as he knew he had come in with wet soles the night before, as there was a heavy shower early evening.

'Now I don't really expect a load of yellow caution signs, but fuck me, Linda, there is such a thing as a warning! If you were working up that fucking nut-house and I had whacked me bonce, I could have sued ya and took ya to the fucking cleaners!'

Linda apologized profusely and the sound of the kerfuffle was heard by TV who rustled around in the sleeping bag. He heard Chaz's raised voice and thought it was a violent row. He kissed the sleeping Freeda as sweetly as possible.

'Freeda, Freeda,' he quietly whispered in her ear, 'they're having a row, Freeda!'

It had become standard recognized procedure at the unit, for Nurse Lavender, if she was on the early shift, to bring Sugar Puffs. Dr. Lock and the psychologists knew how much Freeda loved them, and it was thought that if the staff brought them every day, it might ingratiate themselves towards her. Now Freeda did smile when Sugar Puffs came but it was for Sugar Puffs and certainly not Nurse Lavender. But this morning she woke as if in her sweetest dream. Morning had broken like the very first, with that big fat nurse not around. She was just here in this warm cozy sleeping bag with her soulmate TV and it was like the most beautiful dream world, one where you have got everything you ever wanted, apart from one thing, Sugar Puffs.

'Freeda! Freeda! They're having a row, Freeda!'

Freeda wasn't concerned. She only had eyes for TV. She awoke with a smile on her face.

'I'm so happy, I'm with you now, TV!' Freeda simply loved being in this comfy sleeping bag with him. It took all her pain away, just being with TV.

'I'm so happy too, Freeda! But he's throwing plates at her! It woke me up!'

There was only one way of dealing with him for Freeda. She would put him straight.

'I'll get him with my knife, TV, for being nasty to Blazerwoman and for killing all those quack-quacks.'

The Dragon Star judge and jury wouldn't take Chaz's indiscretions lightly. The evidence against him was stacked up like those dead geese in that hatchback.

'And he holds up big rabbits by their earseeze, Freeda!'

Freeda took hold of her knife and Freeda knew this was a good one. She could frighten anybody with a new knife like this.

'I'm gonna cut his ears off, TV, and feed them to the rabbits!'

TV thought about it for a moment looking as if he wasn't quite sure. In his mind's eye, he saw Blazerman with his ears cut off streaming blood, while Freeda walked towards a hutch with the two ears in a feed bowl. Then he remembered one of his friends who kept rabbits when he was a kid. They used to feed them together, a big black one and a big white.

'Nah, Freed. Rabbits don't like ears. They like leaves and carrots and that.'

Freeda wiped the palm of her hand across her face thinking about how she might attack the issue from another angle. She recalled a crow, pulling a dead rabbit about on the road with its beak, while she was on an accompanied walk around the hospital grounds, a few years ago. Crows liked ears.

'I'll feed them to the crows then!' she growled. TV thought about crows.

'Yeah, suppose they would eat them, Freeda.'

Freeda smiled as she loved being vindicated by TV. None of those hospital staff ever said nice things to Freeda. It was only Kleeunah who had ever been nice, and Freeda loved that *Sesame Street* record case that Kleeunah had got her. It made her think about 'Freeda's music', that she played every day at the asylum.

'I fancy listening to my music, TV!' she said, because all the good memories that kept her alive, were all contained in that case.

'Yeah, we'll play it later on.'

After the slipping incident, Chaz returned to the matter at hand, that missing knife. On this occasion he just couldn't find it.

'Nah, it isn't here is it. Use the smaller one, Linda.'

'But where has the knife gone, Chaz? It was here yesterday.' Chaz couldn't be bothered with it just now. He had the day's drops and stops on his mind and he was pondering whether or not he might find time, or make it, to visit that Brooke. It would be a tight one, but the idea was circling his thoughts.

'Look, just get the beef sarny sorted, Linda, will ya? I've got a busy day.' Within a few moments Chaz was back in the velvet chair, smoking a joint, smirking to himself as the porn kept rolling on.

'Women will do anything for money, fucking anything!'

Linda pressed down the foot bin to put some wrapping in, and the bin was overflowing with rubbish. She took out the bag and took the keys to the back door and porch, that were always kept behind the sugar bowl. She put the key in the lock but realized that the door had been left open. Linda was surprised, as Chaz was generally vigilant on matters of security.

'You forgot to lock the back door last night, Chaz,' she said. Chaz would never leave doors open.

'Nah, I bloody made sure I locked it with those nutty farmers prowling about. I locked up together like I always do, Linda.'

Linda sighed to herself, as she knew Chaz was wrong, but she didn't want to push the issue and argue. She exited with the rubbish bag in hand, and she put it down in front of the porch's toilet, as she was dying to go all of a sudden. She opened the ajar door and was met with the pool of urine on the floor.

'I'm fucking sick of your piss, Chaz Barber,' she scowled. She quickly put on some marigold gloves and gave the floor a good mop and the seat a clean. He must have been stoned out of his fucking head last night, she thought. Meanwhile, TV and Freeda were still within the sleeping bag cuddled up to each other, and Freeda wanted that blissful moment to last for eternity.

'I luv our new shed, TV, and I'm going to have my Sugar Puffs!' TV was about to explain that all they had left was the remains of the cheese cake and the Blazerman's sweets when he heard the porch door open.

'Shush Freeda, someone's coming out!' TV released himself from the sleeping bag and quickly got himself to the door. He put his fingers to his lips and with the other hand he gestured to Freeda to stay back. TV was watching through the key hole and he could see Linda at the bins. She had two bags, the rubbish and a recycling bag of cans she took from the porch. TV whispered supplying a running commentary. 'She's putting the rubbish out, Freeda.' TV leered at Linda, as she was bending over, moving some pieces of wood lain against the trolley bin. She was so caught up in her thoughts that she didn't notice that odd trident thing lain up against the shed. Freeda was itching to have a look as TV seemed so animated with it all.

'Can Freeda have a look, TV? Can Freeda have a look?'

'Shush! I'm looking at her bum,' he enthused as Linda rose.

'That's all you ever fink about. Getting ya big wangher up!'

TV was still leering as Linda turned back towards the porch.

'Shush, Freed! I can't wait to tie her up and get her knickers off!' Linda had gone, but that big bum had turned TV on. He drew away from the peephole thinking about her. Freeda smirked and thought she would play him along.

'I bet you don't get her knickers down, TV! I bet you don't! I bet!'

The Dragon Star had a duty to disseminate their influences. It was all part of AD 2025 and all that, and the great long-term takeover of the planet.

'I bet I do, Freeda! And I'll get it up and shag her brains out.'

'I said that's all you think about!'

Freeda giggled and began leering at TV, hoping that soon they would be having sex again on that bed chair. But TV's thoughts were still on Linda. It was essential that Dragon Star spread its cosmic consciousness, its magical light. This was why sex was so important to the new cult and TV reckoned this a great chance to put it out there among the masses.

'I've got to give her the "Dragon Star" seed, Freeda, and I'll get Keefy's magic snake going right up through her, into her cosmic sex head. Get her to seventh heaven!'

Back in the day Keefy was always reading those arcane books of his and talking about them to TV, and that's how these ideas had taken off. Puffing on dope and catching the luminosity of the light, with Keefy always talking about his abduction and the alien consciousness threads that were seeping into his brain from the alien's chip. It duly followed that many of the Dragon Star members bragged about their leader Keefy and his magical microchip transmitter and eventually Dr. Lock had him up for an X-ray at Tennin general. Dr. Lock had liaised with no other than Catherine Greene-Burrows over the X-ray and Catherine laughed when Dr. Lock told her that she wanted visual proof to show her clients that there

260

wasn't an alien microchip in Keefy's brain. It didn't matter. None of the clients believed Dr. Lock and it was generally agreed that the X-ray photos could have been of anybody. It was another big cover up job according to Dragon Star. The 'squares' were trying to hold back the cosmic sex light.

All this talk about sex prompted Freeda to put her hand into TV's pants and she began pulling his now erect penis about, all the time giggling.

'Freeda's gonna pull your big wangher about, TV, and make it go spunk cannon!' TV was alarmed.

'Mind, Freeda! Wanghers are sensitive!'

Chaz was laying out a couple of lines of coke on the coffee table, moving the second one about with a razor blade. As he was doing so, he multi-tasked with the laptop checking his e mails. With the two out, he rolled up his fifty and snorted a line and called out to Linda who was in the porch outside the back door.

'I'm running you a life-line, Linda!'

How Chaz liked to have a joke. It's the only way to get through life. Linda was finishing putting some washing in the machine. She was getting worried about her drug taking these days, but it had become so easy just to have another line. The snake pit was sprinkled with it, so she always went back down for more.

'I'll be in, in a mo. Just putting the washing in, Chaz,' she replied.

Chaz was perusing an e mail attachment from that young couple who were into the S&M and Chaz was blown away by explicit shots of the young Eve, pleasuring herself with sex toys. Linda entered and Chaz was raving about having the couple upstairs in the Dark Room, exactly why they had spent so much money on the facilities up there. To push it all out a bit. To fully embrace that New Age of openness, where all the kinky, dirty sex comes out. Chaz's mind was spinning all kinds of erotic fantasies. They could have some fun and make those kinky films to keep the subscriptions coming in. He had to keep working on Linda. The old Linda had to collapse so the New Age Linda would finally be released, like an exotic, erotic butterfly emerging from its chrysalis.

'You've got to have it!'

It was Chaz's estimation that Linda would gradually come round to it, as she always did. He just had to keep plugging away until she caved in. Then the world would be their porn oyster. 'Bring out the whore in um!' It was Chaz's mantra, guaranteed to make hard cash.

'Up for it or what! They love our website and would love to have a session in the Dark Room. To think of what goes on in suburbia these days? Cor! Have them over for a night, eh, Linda? Or even a dirty weekend. And I bet they'll like some hospitality with our Charley Farley!'

Linda was livid. Why couldn't Chaz respect her boundaries and give it a rest? She just didn't want any of it.

'How many more times, Chaz! I don't want that!' Chaz noticed the more strident tone of Linda's voice. But she would eventually give in to the logic. It was all a matter of time. Linda withdrew to the kitchen to pour herself another tea. She just had about enough of arguing with him. Chaz sighed and raised his voice. He just had to keep at her, as he fancied that young Eve. She could have a few more lines of coke and a few vodkas, so she would let her hair down. It was that upbringing and her mum. Their sex lives would be boring otherwise.

'For fuck's sake, Linda, you're holding your life back. There's nothing to fear but fear itself! Always true! Always!' Nobody could dispute such truths and Linda was lured back to the threshold. But Chaz still met a resistance.

'I know what you mean, Chaz, but this is different.' Linda drew a red line under this one, but it didn't stop Chaz. He always had the rational and enlightened answer, always. He was smack on that Zeitgeist too.

'But you know the score, Linda. Ecstasy and liberation are not for the fainthearted, are they?' You can't stay in a square fucking box. No way! No way!' But Linda dug in. These were red lines.

'Well maybe it's not for me!' Linda stormed out the lounge and rushed upstairs. Chaz continued his train of thought, raising his voice so that Linda could get that undoubted logic.

'You're getting caught up in little ideas again, Linda. Go with the flow more, for Christ's sake! It's a New Age!' Chaz looked up at the crucifix with a smile on his face. Linda went straight to her valium as the tears ran down her cheeks. Chaz looked at the line he had lain for Linda and shouted up the stairs again, a scenario that had happened many times before.

'Linda! Ya line is waiting down here for ya! Linda! It won't be waiting forever.'

There was no response. 'Don't fucking have it then!' he petulantly shouted, before proceeding to snort it himself.

Linda sat in front of the dressing table mirror with her palms on her brow staring into an abyss. It felt like her head was going to explode. Chaz's voice was so insistent and overbearing that she heard it all the time, telling her this, telling her that, telling her how to be Linda. But now she was wondering whether she wanted to be 'that' Linda? Chaz's Linda. But she couldn't bear the thought of being alone, and bitter like Debs. Chaz was still at it.

'Everybody's at it. And you've got to be open to new things if you wanna keep sex exciting after twenty-two years, Linda. You know that! And I know you're intelligent enough to know that!'

But something had changed. It was that show she had seen at the Orchard Garden. It had made her think about things and she recalled the voice of the black actress.

'That's when I had another epiphany, I guess. I saw his shadow and I knew just where he wanted me in his scheme of things.'

Linda felt tortured, riven with conflict, and she so desperately wanted not to give in, and just take more drugs. But she knew she would.

Then the 'She's Not There' ringtone went. It was Miko, and Chaz shut the lounge door so he could speak confidentially. The porn was still running on the screen, a young woman entertaining half a dozen blokes. Chaz turned the volume down. He still had that attachment opened on the laptop with the photo of the young woman. He was giving it the eye as he spoke.

'You've got to have it, Miko! Young couple, early twenties. What more does she want? And I'll tell ya, she's a right little shaven peach! But she won't have it! She won't fucking have it! A New fucking Age and my old woman's living in the fucking old one!'

Miko was sitting in a local transit café having some breakfast. The manager was in fact one of Chaz's customers. He was in his late twenties and had taken over the day to day running of the café from his father, who had a heart attack, and was ailing from blood sugar disorders. Chaz regularly went to the café and dealt an ounce and he had already booked a bigger one for the morrow. Miko was tucking into his full fried breakfast and had a sip of coffee to wash it down while he was listening to Chaz. Miko would always try and get Chaz to see things from a broader perspective, and he and Viv thought Linda didn't speak up enough for herself.

'Maybe that sort of thing just isn't up her street, Chaz. To each his own and that? You've got to respect Linda's choices. My Viv is well, "Viv", Chaz.'

Chaz knew what he meant about Vivienne. She had a big sex drive and was mad for swinging and drug-induced sex. Chaz had always thought her rather more exciting than Linda, and he had always been a tad jealous of him.

'Ain't up her street! Whose leg is she pulling? She's always drooling over porn! She'll come around when this young guy has got his cock up her!'

Miko could register where Chaz was at, and he wanted to divert conversation, as he phoned about some news of Blue Lake.

'Anyway, the ins and outs of your sex life are none of my business, Chaz. But what I phoned about was my little reconnaissance last night on this eel-infested lake of Olwyn's.'

Miko had some troubling news. He had gone down there for a quick scout around, like carpers do, after all that frenzied excitement about Jessica, and found that thirty of the carp had died. Some were even keeling over while he was down there. For Miko it didn't augur well for the season

263

ahead. It looked like it was going to be a washout. Chaz took a more optimistic and philosophical tone. His carp glass still abundantly full.

'Thirty dead out of three hundred. Well that might not be so much of a problem, Miko. Life was always about the survival of the fittest, mate. But are they taking!'

Chaz was eager to know that. He just had to have some new photos of big carp perched on his knee with their mouths open. That's what it's all about.

'Definitely not, Chaz! Not one carp has come out! Just eels and more eels, line caught and trapped. Stock seems to be compromised and the lake's a snake pit! Back down the "Ressie", eh, mate?'

Chaz still tried to put a braver than brave face on it all though. The ten per cent were the usual 'non-adapters', when you moved fish from water to water. These things would sort themselves out eventually. Teething problems, Chaz called them.

'They're fucking sulking in there, Miko. They'll soon be over it. The carp are like Linda. They'll hold back until they're gagging for it, mate, and tens on, they'll gag on it, just like that Jessica be gagging on it around your pool!' Chaz chortled at his crude joke.

Linda was still upstairs sitting in front of the dressing table mirror. She wondered how her life had become this negative moment, poised to take yet more medication of one description or other. She just wanted to be numb, to rid herself of inner conflict. She knew the drugs weren't the answer, but they gave her respite. She wondered if heroin might provide her with a bit more. She had read about how blissful it was, as it rushed away all your pain. She could try it a few times before backing off, when she felt better. But Chaz wouldn't help her out there. Smack was a no-go drug for Chaz. That was for no-hopers, in Chaz's estimation. But then she thought of sniffing up more coke. She hated it, but she loved it a little bit more, and a line was always freely available. However, she gained some breathing space from her conflicts, by getting up and walking to the window, and looking out at her beautiful garden. Working out there was the best thing she'd done for years. It was her hope, and her something to hold on to. Her light shining in this dark moment. She eventually decided to put on a brave face and go back downstairs. She wanted to make a last appeal to Chaz in these more than trying circumstances.

Chaz was still talking to Miko. 'Oh, ye of little faith!' was the general tone of Chaz's position, over this temporary setback. He thought the new residents of the lake would eventually settle down and adapt, and with Joey's ground baiting with the divine blues and passion reds, the lake was there to be smashed. Chaz just had to bag that virgin. It was essential, so Chaz could regain his symbolic crown. Linda entered just as Chaz was finishing the call.

'Have ya sorted that sarny out, Linda, darling? Chazzy boy has gotta fly!'

Linda brought out the sandwiches in a lunchbox, with a big slice of Moffetts carrot cake. TV had luckily missed that, the previous night.

'Thanks, darling.' Chaz gave Linda a peck of a kiss in appreciation. Linda felt hesitant in confronting Chaz, but she just had to.

'Er, I've been thinking, Chaz. I know I've already made your lunch, but could you stay around the house today, or at least until we know they've been caught. I feel uneasy with them on the loose, Chaz. I really do!'

Linda hoped that the appeal would work, but Chaz had made his mind up and had sorted his day out. The eight grand may have been recovered, but Chaz had to make profits on top of that. He had to be on the ball for the big dance weekend. He had to get to Alfredo's. There was simply no way he was going to lose out.

'What have I been talking about all fucking morning! It's the big weekender. That's the way this business is. You've got to supply demand and they're going bonkers for it! There won't be a weekend as big as this, all year. And you can lock the doors, can't ya?'

'What and be a prisoner in my own house!' This was typical Linda. Always the glass half empty unless Chaz filled it up for her.

'Well go out then! Use your initiative for fuck's sake! And if ya don't want to, and there's any problems, just call me, I could get back in five as I'll only be local, once I've seen Alfredo.'

Chaz was so selfish. Couldn't he be with her for just one day?'

Chaz knew exactly what she was thinking but he kept quiet. Linda thought for a few moments about going out. She could go to the High Grange shopping center. But she knew she would only hold out for a couple of hours up there, and then she would return and who knows, they might be lying in wait. She resigned herself to battening down the hatches, as she knew that Chaz wouldn't budge. He was stubborn like that. The silence continued until Chaz took the last toke on his joint, and then stubbed the butt out. It was time to get into character.

'Chazzy boy! You can't be a toking a poking the Mary Jane all day long! You gotta supply the vice dens with your magic hooter powder.'

It was the same old bravado but Chaz couldn't miss out on the Tennin Dance festival.

CHAPTER FOURTEEN

"HAVE YOU GOT SUGAR PUFFS?"

Chaz raised himself with an energy that belied the early morning's performance, as it was time to get in character. He refreshed himself with a lovely hot shower, and after inspecting the goatee, he applied a liberal dash of his favorite eau du cologne, Christian Delphian. Wherever he went today, Chaz would leave behind that whiff and trail of Christian. For the perfume of gravitas, Chaz paid a grand a bottle and no other guy would wear that in the village convenience store, the local bookie or in the Waterside sex den. All part of the trademark of the sweet-smelling guy in the white blazer, and Chaz just loved to smell clean and perfect, St. Francis yesterday and the Christian today. He popped on one of his many pairs of Gucci jeans and a new pair of Harrods finest socks. He didn't really like sporting them when it got too hot, but he also didn't want his feet to sweat into the alligator skin of his expensive shoes. Bit of the catch 22s, you might say, no socks yesterday, but Harrods socks today.

There would then be the important choice of which alligator? Today he would go with the dark blue, because how can a man in a white blazer at the top of the food chain live with the same alligator? Once he had his Harrods socks on, it was shoe shining, because alligator has to sing. Chaz took to the shoes with an expensive shoe shining kit that had come from, you've guessed it Harrods. No other man in Tennin shopped exclusively there. But Chaz was that man apart. He slipped the Nero darks on and went downstairs holding a brand-new Armani shirt that was still in its packaging, and a white blazer, all pristine, in polythene, freshly delivered back from the cleaners down in the village. Chaz laid the blazer over the back of the velvet chair and he felt like a clean superman again. He looked outside. It was going to be another warm sunny day. He shrugged his shoulders and preened his neck a few times. Stroked that Christian sweet beard but frowned. Maybe a fruity colorful dash in the cause of the big weekender, would be more appropriate? Everything was up this time of the year. It's all Maypole and the ancient fertility rites and copious amounts of 'enhancers', he thought, so why not put on a show! He went back upstairs and got one of his favorite shirts, a Gucci silk twill. Last year's model was a little too small, as Chaz had put on a bit of weight, and a month ago he had purchased the next size up. It was ready to go. Linda suggested that he put the other in a charity shop, but Chaz envisaged some old biddy marking it up for four pounds fifty or something fucking stupid, and then some long-haired punk on a mountain bike might be wearing one of Chaz's nine hundred quid a chuck shirts, on a building site. No way. It was going to stay on the hanger until he lost the weight with his new fitness regime. The new one was still in its elaborate box and had a beautiful 2003 AD cutting edge design, a tropical Hawaiian motif with flowers, mountains and even a black leopard and an exotic snake on it, yet more of that requisite 'class' that Chaz was always looking for. He took it downstairs, unwrapped it, took the pins out and slipped it on, and he went for a black silk tie, that set the colors off nicely. Chaz smiled to himself in the mirror, and then called Linda out of the kitchen to give her opinion.

'What do ya reckon, girl?' Chaz asked.

'Looks great, Chaz.'

Chaz was now in the zone, and next up was the ritual white blazer. He hunched his shoulders up and stalked it. He was chewing gum and he could see himself striding around with the heat of the day on him, slipping the blazer off and hooking it over his shoulder, showing off that dazzling twill shirt. Then slipping it back on and straightening up a few times to get the women interested. He had to show that shirt off today, but he had to air the blazer. He took it off the chair and slipped the polythene off, revealing its sacred beauty. On it went, and Chaz Barber was in, replete with white blazer power. As he did so the post arrived and Linda went to the door.

There was one for Chaz.

'Looks like one from Harrods' summer lines, Chaz.'

'Cheers, Linda. I'll have a look in a minute.'

On the front of the catalogue was a middle-aged guy, in a new double-breasted white blazer from Tom Davis, the designer that Chaz advocated. Chaz smiled as he admired himself in the oval mirror. Everywhere he went, every day, he could hear people saying 'there's that bloke, that's him'. Chaz was one of those fortunate in life, who are on a stage every moment of the day. Makes the days more interesting than being stuck in a warehouse for sixty hours a week was Chaz's stage philosophy, and he loved these summer climes, when the ladies were stripping the winter layers off and showing that irresistible female flesh. Chaz put on another splash of the Christian for good measure and another. Women, whatever their age, would take a look and have a sniff. The young girls and the more mature. Women simply couldn't resist his charms. Chaz shuffled around in the blazer and flashed his white teeth and that gold capped one. You're one flash bastard, Chazzy Barber! How Chaz loved looking at himself in mirrors. Wherever he went, he would be looking out to see his reflection in glass.

'Why are you so ridiculously good looking, Chazzy Barber? It's because you've got the white blazer on, my son!' He then raised his voice. 'There's a little big one for ya on the table here, Linda!'

Chaz opened his mouth again and squirted in yet more sweet breath spray. He loved the taste of clean mint in his mouth, and would re-squirt at least ten times a day.

'Gold laden teeth and sweet, sweet breath. How can this superman not earn ten big ones a day! Whoop-hay!'

Chaz plonked himself down immaculate in the king's velvet chair, and took the polythene from the catalogue and had a quick look. He surveyed that double-breasted job, and eye-eye, decided within a moment that he had to have one.

'Lovely double-breasted white blazer here, Linda, come and have a look. Be a knockout for Royal Ascot. What do ya reckon?'

Linda agreed and Chaz was thinking of a day out at Harrods before Ascot.

'You can choose your outfit up there as well, Linda.'

Linda liked the blazer and saw it was pushing three grand, but she enjoyed shopping for herself too.

By now the washing machine had gone on spin dry mode, and was at top speed making a hell of a racket, which was fortunate, as TV was thrusting away having groaning, ecstatic sex with Freeda in the sleeping bag. They were moving through the uncharted spiritual realms of Dragon Star consciousness, deep inside the sect's sexy esoteric mind.

'Keefy's snake light! The fizz bang lights!' TV exclaimed.

'Harder! Fizz bang me harder, TV!'

Freeda seemed to be enjoying it. They were on a headlong rush to that Holy Grail of the Dragon Star, the consciousness of the higher planes and seventh heaven. The Holy Grail was an ecstatic cosmic orgasm that broke the confines and frameworks of all known worlds.

'We're nearly there, Freeda! Seventh heaven! The flash! The paradise gardens! We're nearly in!'

Everything was exalted. And harder and faster Freeda wanted it, so harder and faster it went. There was no holding back, they had to have that Dragon Star, shag your brains out, orgasm!

'Harder, TV! Harder! It feels so nice!'

They finally crossed the threshold, with their souls and spirits entwining in the paradise of Chaz's deluxe carp sleeping bag. But Dragon Star thrusting passion was just too much even for a sturdy top-end bed chair, and it collapsed on the last orgasmic-inducing thrust. But fortunately, the commotion and ecstasies of the shed were met with that washing machine whipping away on the loudest and fastest part of its cycle. Chaz and Linda didn't hear a thing, and when TV and Freeda were lying there in their post-coital bliss, the washing machine was coming to rest. It was a propitious coincidence, but TV was just enjoying the moment with Freeda. It was golden.

'Ain't it nice this new shed we've got, Freeda?'

Freeda loved it here. Their lives were changing now they were in the new 'proper' shed.

'Its lovely, TV, and you narf got nice breath!'

'It's the Blazerman's sweets, Freeda. The flavors and all that,' TV said.

These were intimate moments that felt like a great healing to Freeda. She hadn't thought any bad thoughts at all as yet, in this new, 'proper' shed. It was bliss, a sweet kiss, and a haven where the bad slipped away, and Freeda felt less angry, and the hurt of the past was less with her in the moment. All because she was with TV, her long estranged lover, in this brand new 'proper' shed. Everything seemed perfect for those golden moments but it was inevitable. Vestiges of the old hospital routines and influences would be knocking at Freeda's door, as the new 'proper' shed still had its limitations. Nothing lasts forever, and this perfect alchemy of lovers would soon find its obstacles.

'Freeda wants her coffee, TV,' Freeda said, as her body and mind registered the lack of caffeine. TV was more accepting being without any. He just appreciated being with Freeda.

'We haven't got any, Freeda,' he said, smiling. TV didn't like to confront Freeda with the harsh truths, but that was the way it was. All they had were red and blue sweets, a whole freezer full.

'What about that cheesecake?'

They had stuffed that as soon as they had got back into the shed last night. TV was particularly hungry and he had three quarters of it. Nigh all of it surreptitiously. He just couldn't stop himself.

'No, we had that last night, don't you remember?'

Freeda thought for a moment and all she remembered was having a wee small slice. Where had all the rest of it gone?

'We had loads left, loads!' TV picked up the silver tray that housed the strawberry cheesecake. There was hardly a crumb left.

'Fucking hell, TV! You had nearly all of that! Ya fucking pig!'

All TV could offer was a warm smile. He was bloody starving last night, as Freeda hogged all the food they had taken from the hospital shop. He was ravenous. Freeda was deflated. She also began to realize that her normal routine was out. It was like a walking on quick sand moment. How on earth could she get washed up and everything, when she hadn't had her Sugar Puffs? TV would have to find some. He would have too.

'Freeda wants Sugar Puffs. Freeda always has her Sugar Puffs! Always, TV!'

TV was trying to tread carefully, but he would have to tell her the truth. It was always better if you told the truth. But TV didn't like the idea of stacking up a whole load of negatives, so he tried to sound extra nice, as if none of it really mattered.

'We haven't got any, Freeda.'

Freeda snapped back at him. She loved being with TV. It was a dream come true. But you have to have things, don't you? Freeda let rip.

'Dragon Star ain't got nuffin'! Nuffin', TV! We've, we've...' She tried to desperately clutch the answer out of the ether and it came. 'We've got to lend stuff off the Blazerpeople!'

It was all so obvious to Freeda. She bet they had tons of stuff, sugar puffs and that, in that new kitchen. Tons! It all left TV with some considerable weight on his mind. He knew he had to keep Freeda sweet, otherwise she was unpredictable to say the least. But it was Chaz who was to give TV something of a welcome respite from her demands. He was just about to come out of the front door, in full character, holding the obligatory DVD briefcase, packed with porn, cocaine and seventy G. When the door opened, Chaz was still carrying on a conversation with Linda who was at the door. TV heard something out there, and slipped from the sleeping bag, motioning Freeda to be silent with his index finger at his lips again. Chaz began walking up the garden, still talking to Linda as he was leaving, stopping for a moment, a little way up the path. This was TV's chance.

'Quick, Freeda! He's got the white blazer on! Like Keefy's! But shush!'

'Freeda wants to look at the white blazer! Freeda wants a look, TV!'

TV smiled as the diversion was working, and Freeda rushed over and just managed to catch a glimpse of Chaz as he was nearing the front gate. The back garden sloped so she could only see his upper body, but that was enough.

'Oh yeah!' she said in her inimitable way. TV then mimicked how Keefy used to show off in his white blazer back in the day. He would swagger around the hospital grounds real smooth like, with a similar rhythmical gait as Chaz's. Freeda remembered seeing him out there in it, although it was some time ago now.

'Ya can glide through the ether with a white blazer, Freeda!'

Freeda looked perplexed for a moment, and TV told her about how it was Keefy's joke to show how cool white blazers are. Freeda thought for a moment about that Blazerman, and then she thought of TV. He was always going on about them. This was his chance.

'Cor, you know what, TV? You would look really nice in that white blazer. Why can't we borrow it off him? We could force him to lend it!'

TV thought her suggestion interesting and he gave it much thought. TV was a big advocate and fan of white blazers. It was essential that the head of the cult had one, essential, and it would only be fair if the White Blazerman let him borrow it. And there was no reason why they couldn't borrow it off him for good. He wouldn't object, as it was for Dragon Star, and everyone would be Dragon Star eventually, come AD 2025, so TV was now thinking of ways they might force the Blazerman to agree to it.

'Yeah, spose we could, Freeda!'

Linda was sitting in Chaz's chair, perched over the line of cocaine on the coffee table, which Chaz had positioned as if rising from the hand of God. She looked in conflict over whether or not to inhale, but being a habitual user now, there wasn't any way she wouldn't. She sighed before promptly snorting, while giving a few thoughts to how she would negotiate the coming day. She couldn't garden with the ongoing situation with the absconders. That was far too dangerous, so she decided to make twenty-five kilos of boilies. There were sufficient eggs in the fridge and it would pass the time of day, and she could have another line or two when she got bored. She could make those 'egg shells in', she'd forgot yesterday, and Chaz would be in a good mood when she boasted about it when he came home. She could have a trip to the shed to get the necessary enhancers and ingredients. She would have to be careful though.

Linda pulled the washing from the machine and thought she would put it out before preparing to make those boilies. She reasoned to herself that she would worry all day long, if she just locked herself in and done nothing but think about those asylum patients. It would be line after line then. Linda was thinking these things when she took the washing basket out. She'd be careful to look around, she thought. She opened the porch door with the key and crossed the threshold. It was a fateful step. In that split second, she knew that something was wrong as she spotted that odd three-pronged trident resting up against the shed. TV grabbed her forcibly and quickly had his hand over her mouth, before Linda had time to scream. All she gave was a muffled cry. Freeda, with her Dragon Star cap skewed to the side, was gesticulating menacingly with the knife in one hand and the severed snake, head and all, in the other. Linda feared for her life and Freeda was trying so hard to be scary. She sneered at Linda, gesturing as if she was capable of doing terrible things with that knife.

'We're Dragon Star, right! And if ya scream I'll stick it in ya and saw ya head off, right!' Freeda put it to her with a cackle, as if she was on some wild insane and uncontrollable wavelength. Linda was terrified.

'She will, Blazerwoman!' TV said, with a warning that spoke volumes to Linda. TV relaxed his grip and Linda went into survival mode. She didn't know how she would get out of this, but she would try, and her intuition said to her, don't antagonize them. But she was shaking with fear. This was this 'Mad Freeda', June had been talking about.

'I promise I won't! I promise!'

Now the Dragon Star children had the chance they were looking for. That house was waiting. They had claimed the citadel!

'Let's go inside for some breakfast and that, Freeda.'

Freeda was more to the point. There was only one breakfast on her mind. She gesticulated threateningly with the knife again.

'Have you got Sugar Puffs? Freeda wants to know! Have you got Sugar Puffs!'

Linda wondered if this was some kind of trick, but then something about the sincere look on Freeda's face said otherwise.

'Er, no, but we've got muesli and cornflakes.' Linda tried her best, and this Freeda certainly looked mad, Linda thought.

'Muesli?' Freeda screwed her face up, before repeating her demand. 'Freeda wants Sugar Puffs!'

TV was thinking that yes, he did think of most things, but he had neglected thinking about all these little details, relating to Freeda's wants and whatnot. She was going to be difficult he thought, but Linda saw an opportunity and it might just work.

'I'll run down the shops for you in the car and get some. I'll get you loads of them. I'll only be five minutes!'

'Yeah! Get Freeda her Sugar Puffs, right away!' Freeda shouted, but TV saw it was just a ruse to get them caught. He was determined to achieve his aim, to be free as long as possible, so they could have a once in a lifetime experience. They weren't going to be caught out by an act of stupidity.

'You ain't going nowhere! You're with the Dragon Star now!'

Freeda twisted her cap around, so that the emblem of Dragon Star was emblazoned on the front, confirming her membership of the cult.

'See! We're the Dragon Star children. Didn't ya know? And look, Freeda's on the back of our jackets!' Freeda turned and proudly displayed the image of herself and TV on the jacket and Linda smiled approvingly. 'Everyone's wearing them, ain't they, TV?' TV nodded his head in affirmation.

As they were walking into the porch up to the back-door, TV thinking ahead, thought he'd better head off this demand and ensuing further moan, around the issue of Sugar Puffs. It was bound to resurface.

'Freeda!' TV pitched this with great enthusiasm, trying to get Freeda equally enthusiastic. He knew that Freeda paid more attention to him when he did that.

'I know what, Freeda! You can have cornflakes with heaps of sugar on them. Keefy used to love that! He always had cornflakes with loads of sugar. We could have them together, in memory of Keefy!'

TV was hopeful that the ruse had won her over, as they arrived in the fabulous new kitchen. But Freeda wasn't convinced as yet.

'Freeda has Sugar Puffs! Not cornflakes! Stavros has cornflakes, TV, but Freeda has Sugar Puffs!'

Stavros was a great big six foot six, twenty-two stone hulk of a man-child, who lived in the lock up unit too, and who was renowned for using his fist like a great big hammer. It went down on tables and sometimes on people's heads if Stavros was upset. Dr. Bolt had injected Stavros nearly as much as Freeda. He had hit Freeda once, only once, and Freeda responded by putting a chair over his head while he was eating his tea. He had never given Freeda any problems after that. Dr. Lock saw him as the second most difficult client in the lock up, although he never took his anger out on Nurse Garotte, as it was well known that Stavros rather fancied her.

'But this is for Keefy, Freeda! Think about that! Cornflakes in the name of Keefy, the Dragon Star founder!'

But Freeda still wasn't convinced.

'Freeda has Sugar Puffs, not fucking cornflakes! That big fat nurse gets me Sugar Puffs!' There was no easy change in what had become a daily habit.

'Yeah, but she does that so ya won't kick off, Freeda!'

Linda had already offered the cornflakes to TV and he thanked her, and by now Linda could realize that TV seemed to temper Freeda. Yes, it was Freeda who she feared.

'Did the Blazerman cut the head off Freeda's snake?' Freeda asked. Linda had never heard anybody call Chaz that before, but she knew who she meant.

'Yes, he did,' she replied, a little sheepishly.

'Freeda was right! He kills snakes, TV! And the Dragon Stars like snakes don't we? You've got them in your wardrobe! Ain't ya, TV?'

Snakes were an important talisman for Dragon Star. Keefy used to keep exotic snakes, not common all garden type things, when he was a teenager, and it was TV's dream, that eventually he would have exotic snakes too. But it was true that he had them in his wardrobe, photos of them, all colorful and exotic. Freeda had seen them when TV was in the lock up unit. Dan had snakes in his wardrobe and Cheryl too, but these were symbolic of magical snakes, good snakes, not those evil ones that wriggled around in your brain. TV uncovered his gold snake necklace and showed Linda as if to prove the statement. Within a moment Freeda was proudly showing Linda hers. Every member of the cult wore a serpent necklace, it was obligatory and top secret. Dan had one, Drill-head and Cheryl too, and in fact all full members had a gold necklace, while associates wore a silver version, like Stavros. Going back, Dr. Lock had reservations, but it was thought that it was just a fashion statement kind of thing, and not evidence of being in a disturbing New Age cult. The necklace Freeda was displaying was smuggled in via the Lorenzo Drill method, although that was eons ago when Barney Eastwood was doing the teas. Freeda had worn it every day since for Dragon Star, for TV, but especially for Barney. There was some doubt about the fate of Keefy, yet there was never any regarding poor Barney. He absconded while he was on an accompanied walk on the grounds. He legged it, bunked the trains and nicked a bottle of whiskey from a supermarket. He drunk every last drop and then slung himself into the path of an oncoming train on Camden underground. He had always been remembered among the asylum community as Cheryl wrote a song about it called, 'The Ballad of Barney Eastwood'. It became very popular among the patients who would sing it along with Cheryl and the hook resonated with all the clients. 'Barney only wanted to be himself, with his friends, be himself'. It was like a statement of freedom on behalf of the asylum oppressed, and something of a Dragon Star anthem. Eventually Dr. Lock understood all of its implications and it was banned. Cheryl was ordered never to perform it and if she did Dr. Lock would take her guitar away.

'Barney needs to be put to rest now, Cheryl,' was what Locko had said to her.

With the cornflakes out, TV wasn't going to hang about, he was starving. He covered them with heaps of sugar, but he could smell that bloody snake she had brought in and laid on the breakfast table. Freeda looked at the cornflakes, disgruntled. She picked them up and shook a great bowlful out.

'I wanted Sugar Puffs! Not cornflakes, TV!' Freeda decided she would make one last ditch plea for them. You never know she thought.

'I want my Sugar Puffs! You're always saying you love me, get me my Sugar Puffs then! At least by tomorrow!'

Freeda covered them with a heap of sugar and she was hungry so she reluctantly began eating them. She held the knife in her left hand with it stood up on the table, with the spoon in the other.

In between eating his cornflakes, TV was making the coffee. He was thinking about that decomposing snake. He couldn't have that on his breakfast table.

'Freeda! Take that snake's head off the table! It fucking stinks!'

Freeda knew that kind of thing shouldn't be on tables, and she snatched it up and put it in her hoodie jacket pocket and although she began wolfing down her cornflakes, it wasn't the same as Sugar Puffs. But she kept wolfing them down and she stopped for a moment.

'Sugar Puffs! Freeda has Sugar Puffs! Freeda never has cornflakes! Never!'

TV sat down but he could still smell that darn snake in her pocket. You don't go around with old dead snakes in your pockets.

'Freeda, I think we ought to put the snake and that out the back. Stick it in the porch. It's unhygienic having it in the house!'

Freeda looked at TV curiously and tutted and sighed, and promptly got up still tutting, and put the carcass on the washing machine outside in the porch.

'Fucking hell, TV! You said I could do fings!'

She returned and took hold of the cornflakes packet and bolshily poured out a load more into her cereal bowl. Then she covered them with another great heap of sugar, and TV smiled. He knew she'd like them. TV then began fiddling with a yellow cloth that he had neatly tied up in a deep pocket in his hoody jacket. Freeda looked on curiously shoveling the cornflakes in as TV began to unravel it. TV had worked on this in art classes too, a yellow cloth that had a dragon and star design on it, with Dragon Star emblazoned above it. The art classes had been a window of opportunity with a new tutor, who wasn't versed in the appropriate TV Sam protocol around image making. He opened it out. He had saved it for a special moment like this.

'Look, Freeda! It's our new flag!'

Freeda looked at it excitedly, and by now she had forgotten about the Sugar Puffs as those cornflakes were filling the hole nicely.

'Let's put it up in the garden! We can put it up on the poles!'

TV thought about it, but couldn't resist it, despite everything. He just had to see it flying. It would be confirmation that Dragon Star was kicking off big. Freeda took her last spoonful of cornflakes and delivered the bowl into the sink, and they were off with Freeda clasping the knife in her hand showing it to Linda, making sure she didn't try an escape. They arrived at the line pole and TV threaded the flag through the rope. He had chosen the one down the far end of the garden by that stinging nettle patch, to keep it out of the way a bit, and he was thinking how he might get the flag up there. There was a step ladder in the new shed but it wasn't big enough to get TV up the top of the high pole. Freeda had an idea.

'There's that ladder by the old rusty shed, TV!'

TV got Freeda to guard Blazerwoman, while he went and got the ladder.

After initial vigilance Freeda's mind began to wander. All her attention was on TV bringing that ladder back and Linda had a chance. She could knock that knife out of her hand, or even make a running dash for the front. But Linda thought about it for too long. TV called back as he arrived at the old shed.

'Make sure you watch her, Freeda!' and Freeda fixed the blade back on Linda.

'Fucking watch it, Blazerwoman!'

Before getting the ladder, TV thought he would take a look at the so-called 'spookers' that Freeda had seen in the old shed. Now that Freeda wasn't there to distract him he noticed something unusual in the atmosphere around it. TV was sensitive to auras. He entered the shed and the 'Art Fingy' was only partially covered now, and TV wondered why he hadn't noticed it last night. TV pulled the black sheet off and was astounded. It was a life size cast bronze sculpture, dark and shining. Freeda was right they were like 'spookers', TV thought, and he guessed it must have been something to do with that Ashcroft bloke who used to live there in the olden days. But he had to get that ladder and get that flag up.

TV struggled getting the ladder free from dense brambles, thinking about the odd couple, but eventually it yanked out. He checked its rungs and it didn't look too bad, and he brought it back to the pole and lined it up against it from the grass. He tested it on the bottom rung and was thinking about safety.

'I know what, Freeda, get Blazerwoman to stand on the bottom rung for me, to keep me safe up there.'

'Freeda wants to stand on the bottom rung, TV! To keep ya safe! Freeda wants to!'

'Nah, Freeda, yah gotta keep a check on Blazerwoman with the knife! Let Blazerwoman do it!'

TV started up the ladder, while Linda steadied and Freeda still held the knife pointing towards Linda, who was obeying every order diligently, hoping that something or somebody might end this knife edge ordeal.

'You mind how you go on that ladder, TV! If you fell off you would fall in the stinging nettles.'

TV was slowly ascending, testing each rung as he went, as the crows cawed and the pile drivers pounded. He got up as far as he needed to, put the flag up and stopped it with a couple of line pegs. Once he had sorted it, he would talk about what he'd found in the old shed. But the Dragon Star flag was so important.

'I won't fall off it, Freeda, it's a good strong ladder.'

TV put one foot down in the descent and the rung cracked and TV's weight was all going forward. He tried to hang on to the pole and down he went, into that dense patch of stinging nettles. Freeda smirked and giggled.

'You wanna watch old ladders, TV!'

The stingers broke his fall but his legs were heavily stung because he had that skirt on. But although he was complaining, it was still a momentous moment when that flag went up. For TV it was bigger than the first flag on the moon! The house had changed hands. It was claimed as the Dragon Star citadel, and TV said it was a forerunner of AD 2025, when that flag would reign supreme. Freeda was very proud of TV as she looked up at that flag flying. The wind had got up and you could see TV's artwork clearly. Dragon Star was in the wind!

When they went back inside, it was still breakfast to finish, but TV had all those nettle hairs all over his legs and the rashes were covering them. His concern wasn't 'spookers' now, it was his legs.

'Me legs are flipping stinging all over!'

'Blazerwoman, she must have some stinging nettle cream!'

Linda did have some antihistamine cream upstairs, and the pair followed her up. Linda thought it might ingratiate her to them, so she was eager to help. But when she passed the Dark Room with them to get to the large bathroom, fear flooded through her. The Dark Room was locked up, but it was the fear of what might occur, if they somehow got into it. What all the prompts might set off. Freeda halted up there on the landing in front of the painting of Chaz and Linda's wedding day. She was all quiet and really taken by it.

'Freeda really likes that painting, TV!'

TV looked at it and thought it divine.

'It's beautiful, Freeda, beautiful, it's when Blazerman and Blazerwoman got married Freed.'

Freeda looked at the painting and she thought that TV and Freeda could have one like that, when they got married.

'Wouldn't it be nice if we had a painting done of us like that, TV?' TV held her close.

'I love you, Freeda. But me legs are fucking stinging!'

Linda was grateful that the wedding painting had diverted attention away from the Dark Room, and luckily TV and Freeda, were more concerned about TV's stinging, rash-covered legs. TV literally covered his legs with cream and took the tube downstairs with them, but neither noticed, or paid any attention, to the room with its crystal door knob, and that mock up dungeon type door, painted black, with the sign 'The Dark Room' on it. TV and Freeda had breakfast to finish with their toasties and coffees.

Back in the kitchen, TV was finishing preparing the filter coffee, and he was looking at one of Chaz's personalized mugs, the one with Chaz holding up two long eared hares. Freeda was shaking some more cornflakes into her retrieved bowl with another heap of sugar.

'I thought you didn't like cornflakes, Freeda!'

'I don't!' Freeda was blunt and surly. 'But we ain't got Sugar Puffs, so I got to, TV!' TV was still perusing that hunting mug, and Freeda glanced at it and caught the drift.

'The Blazerman holds up dead bunny rabbits by the earseeze, dun he, TV?'

TV poured the coffees out but didn't use that particular one.

'Yes, he does, Freeda. Big, big bunny rabbits! With big fluffy ears!'

Linda was sitting at the table just smiling, and keeping up the smiling, hoping that the events wouldn't move into some awful dark place. Freeda was still nonchalantly spooning the cornflakes in.

'Us "Dragon Star" don't like people who kill bunny rabbits, do we, TV?' Freeda scowled at Linda as she was the Blazerwoman and she was behind these kinds of atrocities. 'We would give them lettuces and carrots and that, wouldn't we?'

TV looked down towards his sandals and Freeda naturally looked down towards hers. They were in the brand.

'That's right, Freeda! Me and Travis used to feed them with nice juicy carrots. And we've got Jesus's sandals on!' Freeda was pointing down to them and Linda was still smiling, trying to appease her.

The last of the cornflakes were spooned into Freeda's mouth and then she began to squirm in her chair. Now that the cornflakes were over, she began thinking about those big fishes, and that octopus in the telephone box and that big furry chair. She had to have a sit in that again.

'Freeda's gonna sit in the furry chair, with her sun glasses on, and watch the big fishes, TV!' TV tried to keep her in the kitchen while he was finishing off the toast, but Freeda was so eager to see those fish again. They weren't like the guppies and angel fish in the prison fish tank.

'All right, Freeda, you look after Blazerwoman in the front room, while I finish making the coffee and toast!' Freeda was up ready to dash, but any talk of toast meant that Freeda had to have her marmalade with no peel.

'Two toasties with Freeda's special marmalade, TV. With Freeda's special marmalade!'

It was repeated for good measure, but Chaz never had marmalade and Linda had been watching her weight, so she stopped having it ages ago. But there were jams. Chaz was bang into the village shop homemade jams these days.

'There's no marmalade. Er, Chaz has jams. There's blackcurrant and elderflower.'

Freeda screwed her nose up.

'Flowers! Freeda has toasties with her special marmalade. I want some, TV! Get me some! Get me my special marmalade!' There were a few seconds silence, before Freeda scraped her chair and raised herself quickly. 'Freeda's gonna sit in the big furry chair. It's so nice and furry, TV! But I want my special marmalade! I want it!'

'Blazerwoman can sit in there with ya while I finish the toast, Freeda,' TV suggested.

Freeda went into the lounge with Linda in front of her. She waved Linda to sit on the Waldorf, and then plonked herself down in the furry chair. She shuffled around, enjoying its luxurious feel with a great smile on her face, with that knife firmly in her right hand. Then she rested the knife on the arm of the chair, and gathered her cat eye sunglasses from her purse, and put them on. Then it was the Dragon Star cap off and tossed on the table, and she took a hair brush out of the purse and adjusted her hair, before gathering some and chewing.

'Dun Freeda look good with her sunglasses on?' Linda nodded her head. 'TV! TV! Freeda's sitting in the big furry chair with her sunglasses on again, TV! TV! Freeda's in the big furry chair!'

She quickly took a spearmint from her purse, unwrapped it, popped it in her mouth and then she got her lip glosses out and small make-up mirror, and looked at herself, smiling, and began making up, applying her lip gloss as she chewed. After thirty seconds or so, Freeda put the lip gloss away and then turned and focused her attention on the big fishes. She began smirking, leading to a burst of laughter, while she was watching Hermann in the tank. TV was quickly to the threshold.

'What's up, Freed? What ya laughing at?'

'You falling off that ladder. It was so funny! You fell right into those stinging nettles! I knew you were going to fall off it, TV! Freeda knew!' TV pulled up his skirt, revealing his rash-covered bare legs, and pronounced bulge from his pants, that caught a disbelieving Linda's eye. It was true, he must have a whopper, she thought.

'Flipping hell, Freed! My legs are killing me!'

'You shouldn't have been climbing up old ladders, TV. Freeda wouldn't have climbed up it. Everything in that old shed was rusty. I could see you were going to fall off. I knew that rung was a bad one!'

TV was quite peeved.

'You could have told me, Freeda,' he whined.

'Nothing I said would have stopped ya. You wanted to put that dragon flag up!'

TV dropped the issue, and that meant that Freeda did. Then Freeda began moving rhythmically, side to side, with a great smile on her face. How she enjoyed being in that velvet chair.

'But it's good in this big furry chair, TV. It's Freeda's big furry chair!'

'Nah it's not furry, Freed. It's velvet. But watch her and make sure she don't do monkey business on ya, Freeda, trying ta trick you and that!'

Freeda switched her attention back on Linda with the knife threateningly pointed.

'Don't you do monkey's on, Freeda!'

'I promise I won't! I promise!' Linda replied, praying that Freeda wouldn't turn nasty on a whim. TV went back into the kitchen to sort those toasties and jam. He looked at the two jars and thought elderflower might just be a jam too far, so he went with the blackcurrant with a charm offensive, coming to the threshold again. It worked with the cornflakes.

'Freeda! Me and Keefy used to have blackcurrant jam, from the breakfast trolley! The Dragon Star children are really into blackcurrant jams, Freeda! It's really nice, Freed, you've gotta try it, made from real blackcurrants from the bushes!'

Freeda had a sour, non-believing look on her face.

'Flower jams! Freeda ain't fucking eating them, TV. It's a free country ain't it!'

Then Freeda's attention was pulled back on those exciting big fish. She had never seen such big fish indoors in tanks, and that octopus coming out of the telephone box intrigued her. Then there was that head with all the snakes coming out of it. Freeda scowled at that. She rushed over to the second tank near the widescreen. This one had the sunken ornamental Titanic split in two at its bottom and that crocodile's skull. Both were perplexing Freeda. Linda looked at the knife resting there on the table, as Freeda had her nose right into that fish-tank. She was deliberating whether or not to strike out, grab it and take her chance. But she just couldn't do it, something told her, just be calm, smile and pray. Surely something would turn up and end it all. She prayed that Chaz would come home for something or other, sometimes he did. Freeda was still fascinated by those carp though, as she obsessively chewed her hair.

'TV! Come and look at the big fishes! They're sucking wanghers, TV! And there's that crocodile's head!' TV was still adjusting the toaster, trying to get his own toasties just right.

'Yeah, it's a big crocodiles head, Freed, I've seen it, but keep a watch over her, otherwise she'll try and escape!'

Freeda immediately rushed back to the coffee table, snatched up the knife, and turned it on Linda.

'You try and escape, Blazerwoman, and Freeda will do a fucking mad-diddlo on ya! Like this!'

Freeda tore up the arm of Chaz's velvet chair with repeated and disturbing looking thrusts with the knife. Linda looked on terrified.

'I promise I won't! I promise!' Freeda showed her the blade again with a nasty-looking screwed up face of a look.

'You be good then!'

TV took a quick glance through the threshold, and saw what Freeda had done to the armchair.

'Oh, don't knife up the furry chair, Freeda. You'll ruin it for sitting in.'

Freeda lounged back in the chair, although the arm had been torn to bits.

'It's only a little rip, TV!' TV investigated further.

'It's not, Freeda. You've knifed the fuck out of it!' Freeda laid back in apparent luxury, trying to show that the rips were nothing. She snapped back at him.

'It's only a little rip! And Freeda still likes her furry chair!'

TV investigated the torn shredded arm. He didn't really want to make any more comments to worsen the argument, but he had to say something. He had been looking forward to sitting in that chair himself and watching those big fish.

'It's not a little rip, Freeda, you fucking mashed it!'

Freeda snapped back again.

'Freeda still likes it, TV!' She took to caressing the right arm of the chair.

'It's still nice and furry this side!'

'Fucking ain't the other though, Freeda.'

TV gave up on the velvet chair, but he told Freeda to keep watch over Linda. She nodded her head, and TV went back out into the kitchen to finish sorting the toast. Now Freeda was vigilant looking over Linda, who was quiet and subdued, seated on the Waldorf with the false smile on her face, but only for a few seconds. Her attention was inevitably drawn back on those fish-tanks. She'd never seen such big fishes, close up looking at her like that. She peered into the tank transfixed, and without thinking, casually took three or four strawberry passion reds from her pocket. She popped them in her mouth, as if she was eating popcorn at the cinema. Linda was amazed.

'They're Chaz's, boilies!'

Freeda rushed across to the kitchen threshold with the news for TV.

'They're called Chaz's boiled sweets, TV! Chaz's boiled sweets!'

TV was still adjusting the toaster, trying to set it just right. Chaz liked toast lightly done and TV liked his slightly burnt and crispy, and TV wanted it slightly more burnt. He turned towards Freeda giving thought to what he heard, and her face turned from elation to deflation.

'They're not boiled sweets, Freeda. They're too soft to be boiled sweets. Boiled are all hard-winter mixtures and the Foxes. Don't ya remember?' Freeda realized what TV meant and she turned towards Linda on the Waldorf.

'Don't you lie to Freeda! They're too soft to be boiled! If you keep lying, Freeda will put vim in your mouth! Or worms! Won't I, TV? Won't I do it, TV?' TV made himself visible at the threshold.

'That's right. Ya did it to that doctor bloke ya didn't like, didn't ya, Freeda? And there be tons of worms around after all that rain!' Freeda nodded and smiled as she was vindicated.

'See, Blazerwoman! We'll collect um up and that, and stuff um down ya kisser! So fucking shut up will ya!'

Linda gulped, and she didn't put anything past this 'Mad Freeda', and she resolved to be ultra-careful. That knife could be plunged into her any moment. Freeda gradually quieted, as she found her repose in the velvet chair again, and now her attention was divided between long looks at the carp, in between quick checking glances towards Linda, and then an appreciative stroke of the furry chair and then a quick glance to the Natasha nude above the Waldorf. But then she halted and fixed her eyes firmly on Linda. It didn't look good.

'We're born again, me and TV. Did ya know, Blazerwoman?'

Linda just smiled and Freeda sneered as she wanted a reply.

'I said we're born again, Blazerwoman! Did ya know?'

Linda tried her best to negotiate the tricky pitch of the conversation.

'Er no, I didn't, but very nice!' Linda prayed that her answer would placate her. Freeda took up the issue with TV. It was TV who talked about all that stuff. She rushed toward the threshold.

'We're born again! Ain't we, TV? Ain't we born again?'

TV had made four slices of toast but he was still turning the settings of the toaster trying to get his perfect. He turned his head.

'That's right, Freeda. This is our new life now. Dragon Star and that.'

TV said they were born again, so they must have been born again, according to Freeda. Freeda rushed back into the lounge to tell that Blazerwoman a thing or two.

'See! And have you seen TV's tattoo? He's got a big black cat! Come and show Blazerwoman, TV! Come and show her your tattoo cat, TV! TV!'

TV entered enthusiastically. It had cost a lot of money that tattoo, but he had left the toast burning on too high a setting. He came to Linda and turned his leg around, so the panther tattoo on his calf was in eyeshot. He had it done some time ago now, when everybody was talking about panthers being spotted on the moors and it had been big national news. It was a good move as big black cats were popular again, becoming something of a Tennin urban myth now.

'Freeda's gonna have one done. Ain't I, TV? And we saw one in the back garden didn't we! Snooping about! Didn't we see one snooping about, TV?'

'That's right, Freeda. He's out the back. We saw him!'

'See, Blazerwoman!' Then Freeda put the knife back on the coffee table and she started up a stalking and preying game with her hands up as if mimicking paws. It was playful but it unhinged Linda.

'TV's gonna get ya with his panther claws! And his pointed teeth!'

Freeda kept repeating her little mantra while shifting side to side and TV played along.

'Nah, Freed! I've got fangs. Panther fangs, Freed!' TV jutted out his teeth, smiling.

'And you've got sweet breath, TV! Breathe over Blazerwoman with ya sweet breath! Breathe over her!'

TV grinned inanely, and breathed all over Linda, who just smiled, and all she could smell was those darn boilies. They both lolled their tongues out ominously too, TV's all blue and Freeda's all red, as both had kept slipping a few in now and then. But out in the kitchen, smoke streamed out of the toaster, setting the fire alarm off. Linda was relieved there was a diversion.

'The toast! I've burnt the flipping toast, Freeda!' TV rushed into the kitchen with Freeda close behind.

'Freeda wants to see! Freeda wants to see it burning!'

TV quickly pulled the plug on the toaster and opened the back door. He had done it all quickly, and after a few more seconds bleeping, the alarm went quiet. TV was quick to see the danger.

'You need to get back in there, Freeda! Quick! You haven't got your knife!' Freeda rushed back into the front room, but Linda had done nothing. She sat their terrified and motionless. Linda had considered making a dash for the front door, but it all seemed to unpredictable. Linda just didn't want to give this 'Mad Freeda' a pretext. She was just too disturbing, so she just had to sit it out and smile. Her hope was that something or other would turn up soon, with the police searching high and low for them. But she was so angry about Chaz's selfishness. None of this would have happened if Chaz stayed at home. Freeda grabbed the knife and pointed it straight at Linda.

'You watch it, Blazerwoman! You just watch it!'

Freeda's attention momentarily wandered, and she was pulled towards the photos on the mantel. She recalled what TV said last night, about the ones with the fish.

'Is Blazerwoman married to a fish?'

It was an odd question but Linda smiled, closely watching that knife.

'Erm, I suppose you could say that sometimes,' she replied, still beaming.

Meanwhile, in the kitchen, TV had become interested in a pot of runny honey. He scooped a big spoonful out, and popped two of the blue sweets on top of the honey, and gorged it down, pulling an approving facial expression. He had to tell Freeda. She'd love it with those strawberry sweets.

'Freeda! Freeda!' I've found some honey and it dun arf go good with the sweets! I'll—'

Before TV could get his words out Freeda was in the kitchen. She had to try the honey with the Blazerman's sweets, but it all gave Linda yet another chance to make a dash. She deliberated again. She wanted to go, but she feared that Freeda would come dashing through at any moment with that knife. Linda just thought about it too much and the chance was lost again.

'Freeda wants to try the honey, TV! Freeda wants to try!' TV immediately saw more danger. Why couldn't she just sit in that furry chair?

'Get back in your furry chair, Freeda! To guard her, Freed! Get back in your furry chair!'

Freeda rushed back, looking more crazed and more determined to make it up to her TV. Linda was shaking with fear as Freeda came at her with the knife, waving it around malevolently. She pleaded with Freeda not to hurt her, but Freeda had to show she meant it.

'Don't you fucking dare! I'll stab ya! A fucking hundred times! A fucking hundred!'

To Freeda's way of thinking, the more excessive the threats the more TV would be pleased with her. But TV came to the threshold. He thought she was being far too excessive.

'Oh, chill out, Freeda! Not a hundred! That's a bit over the top! Have ya breakfast, Freeda. It's done, ya coffee and that! And we've got that honey!'

Freeda's attention was diverted back to those toasties and coffee.

'Freeda wants her coffee, TV! Freeda wants her coffee and toasties!'

TV entered with all the breakfast on a tray including toasties, jam and the jar of honey. With the honey and sweets idea still firmly in her mind, TV took the dessert spoon and filled it with honey.

'Pop ya red ones on the top, Freeda.'

Within a few moments Freeda had one dessert spoon-full, thought it tasted delicious, and then she had a second. TV was still joking, holding two red boilies at his eyes again, looking at himself in the mirror and then trying to get Freeda's attention.

'Look at my big sweetie eyes, Freeda!'

TV could see that Freeda had so much in her mouth, she couldn't say anything much.

'Ain't they nice, Freeda? Ain't they nice?'

Freeda laid it on thick as she reclined back in the furry chair with her arms laid out. She closed her eyes and held an expression as if she had just tasted nirvana, responding dreamily with an appreciative 'um'. Then after a few more seconds of Dragon Star samadhi, everything in her bodily and mental make-up said, time for a fag. She jumped forward with an abrupt jolt of intent.

'I'm gonna have some fags with my coffee, TV! Freeda always has fags with her coffee!' Linda saw a great opportunity to appease them. Anything to avert a chilling end to her fate.

'There's six hundred in the drawer over there! They're all yours! A present from Chaz and me and you would never hurt people who gave you presents, and loads of fags, Freeda, would you? People who give you presents are friends, aren't they?'

TV was there like a bolt as Dragon Star always needed more fags, due to their relentless chain smoking. He opened the drawer of an antique sideboard that jutted up to the front wall of the building, and true to her word, there were three packets of two hundred, that hadn't been touched.

'Fucking hell! There's loads, Freed! Loads!' The fags were well and truly sorted.

'I'm gonna smoke eight at once like I used to TV!' TV had already passed a packet to Freeda and she was eagerly taking that wrapping off and pulling out loads of fags. She was on it, a mission!

'Nah, Freeda. Eight was too many. You smoked three like Keefy used ta. Don't you remember? It wasn't eight. Eight weren't any good, Freed.' Freeda was screwing her face up as TV spoke. She wanted to smoke eight, but it was true, she did recall smoking three. But she wanted to smoke more. That was in the old days when people used to smoke three.

'Ya smoked three to get that calm on, Freeda. Three. Don't you remember? It weren't eight, Freed.'

TV was beginning to stress Freeda out. She wanted to smoke loads, real loads, and they had more fags than they ever had.

'Keep your flipping hair on, TV!'

TV kept trying to get Freeda to remember. She must do he thought, as it was only the other day. Freeda sighed and finally gave in to end the squabble.

'All right! All right! For fuck's sake! Freeda won't smoke the fucking eight. Fucking hell TV! Ya kisser's going snap, snap, fucking snap!'

The argument broke down into uncontrollable laughter, as Freeda made a snapping gesture with her hand like a bird's beak. Freeda looked joyous as she loved to laugh with TV. He made her feel that her very character was valued.

With Freeda temporarily out of the velvet chair, she was seated on the pouffe, getting those three fags in position, TV took his chance to get into the furry chair himself, because he wanted to watch those carp. Freeda swiftly had the three fags in her right hand between her fingers, TV clicked his lighter, and Freeda took to sucking hard to get the three going. Once they were, she took an enormous toke, held the smoke down for a few seconds and tried desperately to stop herself coughing. She raised herself from the pouffe and sat down next to Linda on the Great Waldorf and she spluttered the smoke out. TV was now lain back in the chair with a rash covered leg hooked round the right arm, with his skirt disheveled and his bulging pants showing. He, like Freeda before him, was now engrossed in those carp. Freeda had now settled into smoking the three, but she wanted more. She wanted TV involved, not this taking no notice of her, while watching those fish.

'Urm, three's really, really nice. You can get a "calmer" on like Keefy used to do! Try three, TV! Try three with Freeda, TV! TV!'

TV sat there mesmerized by those carp, but when Freeda got something in her mind like this, she would never stop, never.

'TV! TV! You gotta try the three with Freeda, TV! Be in Freeda's team, TV! TV!'

Hermann was subtly moving his tail in the tank and TV was bewitched. He began talking, but his focus was on Hermann.

'I'm watching the big fish, Freeda. I will in a minute but I'm watching the big fish!'

With TV preoccupied, the irritated Freeda turned to the Blazerwoman, because everybody had to smoke-the-three with Freeda.

'Have you ever smoke-the-three, eh, Blazerwoman?' Freeda took an enormous inhalation of the three, and exhaled the smoke in volumes. She went for TV again. 'TV! TV! Freeda's smoking the three like you told me to, TV! TV!'

TV had an itch and he scratched his privates, quite spontaneously, without any lewd intention. He was still transfixed by those carp.

'I'm watching the big fishes, Freeda,' he said impatiently now. Freeda sneered a little, and grabbed hold of the fag packet, pulling out a load of cigarettes and she started to put them in Linda's fingers.

'Well, Blazerwoman is gonna smoke-the-three with Freeda, ain't ya, Blazerwoman?'

Linda knew that she just had to play along with all this and not antagonize this 'Mad Freeda'. Linda done her best to be enthusiastic.

'Yes, I am, Freeda.'

Freeda smiled. It was all so much fun, and with the fags in between Linda's fingers, it was time to teach Blazerwoman how to actually smoke-the-three.

'Ya gotta get them in between, like the way Freeda's doing it. That's it. Give Blazerwoman a light, TV! Give her a light so she can smoke-the-three with Freeda! So, she can be in Freeda's team, TV! TV!'

TV was still lost in his meditation on that carp by the red telephone box, and then he looked over to the carp in the far tank with that Titanic at the bottom of the ocean.

'Have ya seen that boat at the bottom of the other tank, Freeda? It's the Titanic at the bottom of the ocean!'

Everything Titanic-related had profound associations for the couple. Freeda and TV used to watch it in the lock up ward on the DVD. They watched it thirty-seven times together and one day that watched it four times, back to back. TV counted them, and they would mimic the I'm flying' scene there in the lock up unit lounge. While this was occurring, Nurse Garotte was vehemently against it. She thought it might presage a major problem if the pair were flying like that in the lounge. Freeda jumped up with the three fags in her hand still. She used to love doing that flying with TV. It was so romantic! They even did it on Valentine's Day! That was before TV kicked the screen in.

'Let's do the flying scene! Like we used ta, TV! Like we used to up the prison!'

'But we haven't got a crate, Freeda,' TV replied. Back in the day, to appease Freeda for a while, before things started occurring that made the liaison between TV and Freeda untenable, the agency nurses brought in a plastic milk crate that Freeda could stand on, when they done the flying scene. Freeda had such fond memories of it, but there was an enormous fight when Nurse Garotte eventually took the crate away and TV kicked the screen in. Nurse Garotte had never forgotten it. She got a fat lip, a black eye, and had a mild bout of concussion, and she didn't even inflict any hurt on Freeda. No, she never forgot it, as she was off work and wrestling for a month or so.

'Look, TV! We can use this fingy here!'

The 'fingy here' was that leather pouffe by the coffee table. It was spongy, but crate-sized, and Freeda clambered on top, while she was still smoking the three with an enormous drag, a hold for three and exhalation. TV got up for this little role play as that period was like an iconic one, when love first blossomed. They had done this, countless times.

'Close your eyes, Freeda, no squinty eyes and stretch your arms out and fink you're on that big ship Freeda, make-believe!' Freeda still held her eyes open, as she was curious about the ornaments in the second of the carp tanks. She screwed up her face.

'How did that crocodile's skull get in there, TV?'

TV looked closely at the skull and began thinking about the shoes that were by the velvet chair. He went across to the chair and picked them up, another pair of Blue Nero's and perused them, trying to get his head around the odd symmetry.

'Dunno, Freeda, but Blazerman goes around in these crocodile skin shoes. Blue ones. Look!'

Freeda was screwing up her face trying to figure everything out. Then TV tossed the shoes to the floor. He wanted to get on with this exciting little role play.

'Stretch your arms out wide, Freeda!'

But Freeda was still perplexed by the crocodile's head and the shoes.

'How does he get the skin off crocodiles?'

'Nah, the poor people in Africa and that, kill them, Freeda. And then he gets them made into shoes and that,' but TV wanted to get on with 'The Flying'. 'But do ya trust me, Freeda? Do ya trust me?'

''Course I do, TV! Course, I trust ya! You got me out of that prison with that big saw. I'm flying TV! I'm flying!'

'Keep your eyes closed, Freeda, and look with your inner eye, your inner eye! Imagine yourself flying to seventh heaven to the Dragon Star! Ta seventh heaven, Freeda!'

Seventh heaven meant only one thing to Freeda.

'Are we gonna have a shag later, TV?'

''Course, Freeda!' The little love play ended with a deep passionate kiss, before Freeda toppled off the pouffe and down went the three fags on the carpet, but TV cushioned the fall. Linda had watched it all sitting on the settee, and by now the three fags in her hand had gone out.

As soon as Freeda got back on the sofa, it was time to relight the cigarettes and get back into smoking the three. She had to get her team up and running again. TV sat back in the velvet chair and was immediately re-mesmerized by those carp. Freeda stopped and looked back over at that far tank. It was the crocodiles head.

'Does the Blazerman keep crocodiles?' TV was now transfixed by the carp.

'Nah, I doubt it, Freeda. They'd chase the postman off!' TV and Freeda burst out laughing, they were having so much fun together, but now it was smoke-the-three time again.

'Gis a light, TV!' Freeda turned towards Linda ushering her towards the lighter. 'Come on, Blazerwoman, get um alight!' TV clicked the lighter a number of times but he wasn't really looking, as he was completely absorbed with Hermann again. Freeda jostled Linda into position to get the fags lit up.

'Light um up Blazerwoman, and then ya got to drag um all at the same time. Hasn't she, TV!'

'Yeah, like Keefy used to do, Freeda.' Freeda got Linda to get the three alight, and exhorted her to inhale them all together, to get that big, big 'calm on'.

'Deep! Really Deep! Look TV! Blazerwoman's smoking the three like Freeda and Keefy do. Look, TV! Breathe in deeper, Blazerwoman, like Freeda does. Look, like, Freeda!'

Freeda dragged on the three and Linda smiled and dragged on the three exactly like she was supposed to. TV was still looking and thinking about those big fishes, while going back to scratching his testicles. Freeda kept on.

'Why can't you smoke-the-three, TV? We can all get a big calm on! TV! TV! Stop looking at the big fishes, TV!'

The growing tension between TV, who wasn't taking much notice, and Freeda, came to an end when TV came to an observation. He was looking intently at Hermann.

'The big fish do look like blowjob fish, Freeda!' Freeda burst out laughing, the connection had been remade.

'I told you, TV! Freeda knew. The Blazerpeople have them with chips!' Linda couldn't help but put Freeda right on that point.

'No, we don't eat them, Freeda. Chaz keeps them like big goldfish. He watches them and feeds them,' Linda explained. Freeda couldn't believe what she was hearing. Goldfish?

'What? You don't eat fish and chips? All the Dragon Star children eat fish and chips! Don't we all eat fish and chips? Dan does and Drillhead and Cheryl, and Keefy used ta like them, didn't he, TV?'

TV confirmed the truth that it was all linked back to Jesus and Galilee.

'Course we do, Freeda. Dragon Star have always eaten them, Freed!' TV was still transfixed by those carp. But he added, 'and Jesus liked his fresh fish Freeda. He always did.'

'See!' Freeda emphatically declared, before she took another great drag on the three. Linda tried to support Freeda as she was beginning to learn something about survival tactics in this odd, terrifying new world.

'Me and Chaz love fish and chips, Freeda. We really do.'

Freeda thought for a moment, and then turned to her Jesus badges again, that she wanted to show off to cement the Dragon Star children's relationship with him.

'Have ya seen Freeda's badges? Look! We got "Team Jesus" badges, ain't we, TV! We do stuff for that Jesus bloke!'

Linda said that they were very nice and Freeda recalled what was said last night about Jesus and fish and chips.

'You've got that fish and chip van, haven't ya?'

Linda was quiet, looking perplexed, as she didn't want to say the wrong thing. Freeda turned towards TV for the confirmation. TV knew that Jesus had one. 'They've got that fish and chip van like Jesus used to have. Haven't they, TV?' TV could now see that Freeda was getting confused. He had to try and un-confuse her, make her understand it all.

'Nah, Freeda, you're getting it all mixed up, Freeda.' Freeda screwed her face up, wondering what TV was coming at her with now. He said that Jesus had a fish and chip van last night.

'Fuck up, TV! Ya fucking said he had one last night!' TV tried to explain.

'Nah, nah, Freeda, fish and chip vans weren't invented when Jesus was about, Freeda. Don't ya remember me telling ya? Jesus had them donkeys. I was telling ya, don't ya remember? Jesus had donkeys back in the olden days. He used to ride into cities on um and that, with his mates, Freeda.'

Freeda looked even more confused, but she thought she had it all figured out now. She turned to Linda, to tell the Blazerwoman how it all used to be back then, back in the olden days.

'Blazerwoman, did ya know that Jesus used to sell fish and chips on his donkeys?' Linda prayed, she played it safe.

'No, I didn't know that, Freeda.'

Freeda couldn't believe it. But then she could, as she knew that the Dragon Star children knew loads of stuff. She smiled as they were privy to the secrets, so she could understand why Blazerwoman knew nothing. But she couldn't believe it a bit more.

'Ya didn't know that Jesus done that? Ya didn't know? TV! TV! She didn't know, that Jesus bloke used to sell his fish and chips on his donkeys, with those disciple fingys. Ya don't know much do ya?'

'No, I don't, Freeda,' Linda cautiously replied. By now Freeda noticed that Linda had stopped smoking the three. There were three fags resting in the ashtray on the side of the Waldorf about to go out. Freeda gave Linda a nudge.

'Come on Blazerwoman! You've gottta smoke-the-three in Freeda's team!'

Linda picked up the three and puffed away again, and TV was still sitting there mesmerized by those carp.

CHAPTER FIFTEEN

THREE DUCKS A FLYING, THREE PIPES A PIPING AND A WIDESCREEN DANGLER TV!

A lock up gate opened and Chaz drove the Jag up the drive and parked outside the large detached bungalow. The area, near Galverstone bike and car racing track, was renowned for being a haunt for shady criminal types. This was Miko's bungalow, the site frequently used for filming porn, and which would be the place for Jessica's screen test. Miko and Viv had a couple of well secluded and covered acres and Viv was hot about directing and starring in the anticipated forthcoming series. Chaz was soon out the back around the pool with a glass of wine and a joint talking porn. There would be the screen test and then the following week, Jessica would do a thirty-minute solo, all geared to stoking up interest in their new would be sensation. Chaz vowed that he wouldn't miss it for anything, and Viv reiterated how Jessica was 'up for it big time'.

'We won't have to make a whore out of Jessica Miko!'

Chaz looked at a prospective running order of films in the series and it was hoped that Chaz himself could do a few impromptu appearances, beginning from four in. That narrative line had Chaz and Vivienne picking up Jessica in a park while she drank a coffee and then taking her to Miko's bungalow where they subjected her to an S&M-type ordeal with a gang of four, well-endowed men, appearing out of nowhere. Jessica agreed to the idea. 'Well it is porn for God's sake,' she said, fully anticipating what she was getting herself into. It made Chaz horny, thinking about it all, and he put across a saucy text to Jessica while they were smoking that joint, telling her that within half an hour he would be dropping off a freebie. Jessica replied quickly while she was administering in the care home, saying that if the money was there, she was up for anything. They had agreed a sizable fee to rope her in and she was hoping to end her job as soon as she had that first payment, although Vivienne convinced her to keep up with the day job. They had to wait and see how the punters and market, took her first film appearance. But they were more than hopeful.

When Chaz got back in the Jag, he couldn't help checking the stash of money, and kilo or so he had in the dash. He had already been to Jay and Dai's and dropped the kilo, the most they had ever had, and he had made another delivery down at the Waterside that ended up big too, another twelve ounces. He has also slipped another eight deal to Scamp and a few others too, including the first delivery to Candy Foxes, and all in all, it meant that Chaz virtually knocked out three kilos in a day, without having to make that many drops. He was nigh eighteen grand up on the day, with everything moving blindingly in the right direction, and it would be to that care home next. But Chaz then looked at the beef sarnie and cake he had, and he couldn't resist a quick park up close by, and he ended up in a small lane in a clearing. He thought he would have five minutes there. That was the beauty about being self-employed Chaz thought, you could have a break, nigh anytime and anywhere, as long as all the punters were happy. While he was tucking into that beef sandwich, Chaz noticed a money spider crawling up the arm of his white blazer. Chaz watched the spider inch his way up his arm, no doubt spinning Chaz even more new clothes and spanking good fortune. It had been unbelievable over the past ten years or so. Nothing except tons of money and it was all from that simple formulae: sex and drugs equals chalupa and filthy lucre. And then give it more sex and drugs and you get more chalupa and a little bit more dirty lucre. It never failed, that's the way human beings are wired. Chaz knew how it all is, like Miko's astute Viv, and hadn't Chaz seen that opportunity, in that Jessica? It's only the visionary who can tease that kind of talent out. They had high hopes she was going to hit it big, because she had that triple X factor about her.

But that money spider set Chaz's mind off on a flashback. To that moment back in time when the light came in, when Chaz began to believe that things could change. That dreams could come true. He had forgotten it, like you do, but that spider had taken him back there. He realized now it was the most important iconic moment of his life. He was working then at a warehouse down by Tennin Creek. Work was a little slack that day, and Chaz was waiting on a couple of trailers to come in, that had been delayed. It was a long wait, as they had been held up due to a road closure, and Chaz dozed off in his jumbo forklift. He woke up suddenly when called by a workmate, and he was in disbelief, as his predominately white sweat shirt under his high-vis, was covered with small money spiders. In the locker room at the end of the shift, his workmate thought it showed that Chaz was destined for better things. Those money spiders were spinning him new clothes, and these clothes he was wearing now, that he dearly loved so much, and the world that Chaz was living in, had been spun out of that moment. Chaz could remember his very words, as they put their work gear in their lockers.

'I fucking hope so, Andy! Cos, I don't wanna be driving a fucking forklift all me life. I can tell ya, mate!'

Chaz started the Jag up and left the engine ticking over for a few moments, before he turned it off and thought again. That really was the moment when it all began to change. Now it was nine hundred quid a chuck shirt's and a grand for the eau du cologne. Not bad eh? Chaz had seen the light and it made him believe there was a different life ahead for him. It didn't have to be overtime, and more overtime, fuck that! Now everything was money, and more money, life was perfect. 'Sorted!' New house, new Jag, even his wardrobe must have been well over a hundred grands worth, as his alligators had cost him fifty. New investments, a carp shop in the offing, good coke, plenty of toke, good marriage and a little bit of behind the scenes rumpy-pumpy too, and ten or so ingots banked with a couple more in the pipeline. How about that? All he wanted now was that pregnant virgin slapped over his knee, and a front page on *The Carpmasters Monthly*, and to be at that casting video, involving big tits Jessica next week. All this and a fine wife too, who could knock out a hundredweight of boilies and do a turn in the Dark Room to boot. 'Sorted!' Had life ever been so good? And Chaz saw the future in terms of sex clubs, sex channels, with Natasha as a broadcasting host, an idea that he had already touted with her. She was 'bang up for it'. Chaz smiled as he had been reading only yesterday in *The Orb*, how dissatisfaction with modern life was increasing. What the fuck? The twats need to snort his grade A white powder up their hooters. Chaz kept smiling and basked in his total freedom, by taking a quick look around him and laying a swift line on a porn mag that was in the side pockets. Another mag featuring that PC Angelica, he had a couple and Chaz had a thing about her now. He laid the coke over a front-page snap with her holding her boobs up, fifty-pound note rolled up, 'Up ya hooter! Snorted!' What a life, and next up was a number of DVD drops. 'Whoop-hay!'

Nothing much had changed back at Holly Beach Lane. Freeda had begun another fresh three and Linda was being instructed to do the same. It was a team effort this smoke-the-three thing, and with the knife in her left hand and the three in the right, Freeda inhaled slowly, real slowly. Then she put the knife down and dug Linda in the ribs with the fingers of her left hand, alerting her to keep watch on how the experts of the three were doing it. When Freeda exhaled she was still basking in a nirvana paradise of the seventh heaven. She went all dreamy and Linda was doing her darn hardest to be dreamy with her. Anything to prevent this moment from turning ugly.

Meanwhile, TV had changed his perspective slightly, and was now looking intently at the wide screen TV. He had never kicked in a whopper like that. He had thought about watching a porn on it, there must be loads of porn in the Blazerman's house, stacks, but now he had other thoughts. TV kicked in tellies. It had become his personal statement and trademark, and much of his notoriety had come about because of smashed, kicked-in screens. It was what TV liked to do, there was something deeply transgressive about it, and TV was always saying that you could never become a full associate member of Dragon Star, if you sat glued to the telly all day long. It was those cathode rays. They controlled your mind, getting you to think how the cathode creators wanted you to think. All square like, in straight lines. You had to bend it like TV and the spiral, and the Dragon Star was the hope, the light, found in studying star configurations and alien intelligences and doing tons and tons of cosmic 'between the worlds' shagging. Bigger meant more cathode ray mind control, and TV kept looking at the dwarfing screen and a violent outburst was visibly welling, all born from the conflicts of the old dispensation butting up against the new Dragon Star shagging enlightenment. He was in the zone and now all he could hear was Freeda annoyingly getting at him in the far distance, but all of his deepest inner being was in a dynamic relation with that wide screen. He smirked, as he saw himself in his mind's eye, flying through the ether, and kicking the fuck out of it. He had read tons about how important creative visualizations are when you want to get stuff done in the New Age.

Freeda was away in another dimension now, even though she was but a few yards from him, still teaching that Blazerwoman how to smoke-the-three, like Keefy used to do. She could see TV was in his television hate trance, but she had to show TV how good her team was at smoking the three. It was essential.

'Look, TV! Look! Ready Blazerwoman! Freeda is your leader. Your smoke-the-three leader. Look, TV! Freeda and Blazerwoman are smoking the three like Keefy used to do! Look, TV!'

TV didn't take a blind bit of notice. He just looked more intently at the widescreen, his toes twitching in his 'Jesus's sandals'. He saw himself doing a Kung Fu kick on that telly with the flat of his sandal, like that footballer did that time to someone in the crowd. Pow! He was bearing down on that moment. But Freeda just wouldn't stop.

'Light up three, TV! Go on, TV! We can be the smoking three team! Smoke three with Freeda like Keefy used to do! Like Freeda and Keefy!'

TV then turned and he had a dark look on his face. He looked manic and Freeda knew he was going to kick it in.

'Give us your knife, Freeda!'

Linda thought the end was nigh. She burst out pleading.

'Please don't hurt me! You'll get into trouble if you hurt me, and you don't want to get into trouble. And we've got money you can have. Loads of money. You'll be able to buy nice things! Loads! Loads of things!'

Freeda screwed her face up, annoyed at this outburst. This was Freeda's smoking the three time that Blazerwoman was interrupting here.

'Shut the fuck up, Blazerwoman, will ya! You're getting on my fucking nerves! We don't want loads of fucking fings! We've got to smoke-the-three ain't we, TV! We're supposed to!'

Freeda took a long drag on the three, looking at TV for approval, before she handed him the knife. He took it and Linda pleaded again. TV pulled a determined and disturbing looking face with the knife firmly in his hand, waiting to strike. He then rose with a speed that belied the way he was lounged out in his dark mood, moved on the screen and repeatedly stabbed it, like a madman.

'Fuck the set! Fuck it! Fuck it up!'

For the coup de grace, TV stepped back a few paces before launching that flying Kung Fu kick, smashing the screen yet further with the flat of his Jesus's sandal. Then he ripped the thing off the wall as if he was a wild animal and gave it another great kick. It was shocking stuff. But this time he caught the front of his toes and he cursed the screen as he hobbled about.

'Fuck it! You bastard! Bastard!'

The set was completely smashed to bits and TV plonked himself back down into the chair, but doubling over because of his toe, grimacing due to the intolerable pain.

'Phuu! Me big fucking toe! It's killing me, Freeda!'

Freeda took a quick blast on the three and offered her opinion.

'You wanna watch yourself, TV, with all this climbing up ladders and kicking in tellies ya doing,' Freeda said, concerned, but then she recalled that moment when TV fell off that ladder into those stinging nettles and she burst out laughing.

'It ain't fucking funny, Freeda! You wouldn't like it if ya fell in a load of stingers and me big toe's flipping killing me!'

Freeda tried to hold her laughter back, but she smirked and burst out again.

'I knew that ladder was no good. I knew it!'

There was then a short silence, as TV looked at the debris and despite that throbbing toe, he was mesmerized by those sandals. Freeda explained the situation to Linda.

'TV doesn't believe in tellies. It's them ray fingy's they do.'

Linda smiled a little, so grateful that the knife wasn't used on her. TV was still perusing those Jesus's sandals and his big toe was going vroom throb and he was bending over rocking in pain.

'I knew they were proper, proper Jesus's sandals Freeda, but me flipping toe's fucking killing me! It's throbbing like fuck!'

Freeda looked down at the identical pair of sandals, albeit size six, on her feet, and immediately it was obvious to her.

'Jesus would have kicked in tellies if they had been invented back in the olden days! Wouldn't he, TV?'

'He would have kicked in thousands, Freeda! All the tellies up the hospital. All the tellies all across Tennin! Jesus would have kicked them all in, Freeda!'

'He'd have to watch his toes!'

Freeda burst into hysterical laughter. How could Jesus kick in so many tellies? Sometimes TV said some daft things. Freeda then turned towards Linda with an adamant 'see!', to validate TV's claims, but that toe was still throbbing.

'Cor, me big toe dun arf hurt, Freeda!'

Freeda looked this way and that, and the idea popped in her head, that TV ought to put his feet in a bowl of water. That's what people usually did when they hurt their feet, and there was a bowl out there in the kitchen.

'Do you want me to get ya a bowl of hot water!'

'Just warm, Freeda,' TV replied. Freeda was up immediately. She wanted to show her love to her soulmate. She turned towards Linda.

'Stay put there, Blazerwoman, smoking the three! Freeda will get the bowl of warm water. Freeda will get it for you, TV. Freeda will get it and make your toes better!'

Freeda rushed out to the kitchen and turned the tap on, and waited till the water was warm. While the water was running Freeda was drawn to investigating the food cupboards and the fridge, to see what food these Blazerpeople had hidden. She found a nice farmhouse cake that was another from the village bakery, they would have that later, but she turned her nose up at that elderflower jam in the cupboard. By the time she returned to the water it was coming through piping hot and certainly not just warm. She picked the bowl up and carried it through to the front room, the water nigh filled to the edge and was steaming.

'They've got a nice big cake out there, TV!'

'Yeah, we'll have it later, but is it just warm, Freeda?' TV asked, although he had the majority of his attention bound up with watching Hermann and the Beak in the fish-tank.

'It's all nice, TV, to make ya feet better!'

Freeda was so happy that she was helping her TV. She put the bowl down, pulled the coffee table out a touch and put that bowl right by his feet. TV plunged his feet in without thinking twice as he was still mesmerized by those carp.

'Agh! Fuck! It's boiling, Freeda!' TV screamed. 'Me fucking feet!' Freeda had to think of something.

'We'll kiss ya feet better, TV! Come on, Blazerwoman, we gotta kiss TV's feet better!'

TV was rubbing his feet as they were scolded.

'Nah, just get some cold water in a jug or something, Freeda, and we'll put it in ta get it just right.' Freeda rushed out and found a jug and this time filled it with cold water. She brought it back in and poured it all in the bowl which overflowed. TV wasn't taking chances and he took his feet out of the way with quick evasive action. Freeda explained.

'It was the Blazerpeople, TV! They tricked Freeda with their boiling hot water!'

After another jug of cold, the temperature of the water became just right, and TV had his feet in, trying to soothe the pain away.

'I reckon Jesus must have put his feet in a bowl of water after all his walking, Freeda.'

Freeda looked at the bowl, and she liked the idea of putting her feet in the water too. It was a big bowl and hers would go in there. Hers were only little small feet, not big kippers like TV's.

'Freeda wants to put her feet in the bowl of water, TV! Freeda wants to soothe her feet like Jesus used ta!'

It was all so much fun. She took her sandals and unicorn socks off and sat on TV's lap, and in went her feet. Both TV's and Freeda's were in the bowl together.

'It's all sort of intimate ain't it, Freeda?' TV suggested. Freeda had a warm smile on her face.

'Who would have thought it? Tootsies together in the bowl and watching the big fishes? And that big fat nurse not about!'

It was certainly food for thought. Freeda took some of the strawberry sweets from her pocket and TV asked for one, so now they were eating those boiled sweets, with their feet intimately touching in the water. They were lovely moments, but once the water had got a bit cold TV had enough, and it was feet out and they got a towel from the washing basket from the porch. Next it was sandals back on and Freeda returned to the Waldorf next to Linda.

'Do ya like our Jesus's sandals?' Linda kept up with her appeasing tactics. It seemed to work.

'Yes, they're very, very nice, Freeda.' There was only one thing to do, thought Freeda.

'TV! We've gotta get Blazerwoman a pair! So, she can be in the Dragon Star Team! We've got to get her some, TV!' TV might of had his feet out of the bowl but that toe was still throbbing. But why not he thought.

'Yeah, I can get her some when the boot fair's on again, Freeda!'

Freeda was looking at Linda, as if to say, you will be in our team soon, but she felt mischievous, thinking about some of the things that TV had said earlier.

'See! You'll be in Freeda's team and guess what?' Freeda started giggling and Linda smiled back at her. 'Guess what?' Freeda nudged Linda in the side, giggling some more. 'TV fancies you! Cos when ya bent over the bins, TV said he wanted to pull your knickers down! Didn't ya, TV! TV! Didn't ya say you wanted to pull her knickers down? You said it, didn't ya?'

TV was a bit petulant with his reply. Freeda didn't have to say that kind of thing. It was embarrassing.

'Well, she's got a nice bum, Freeda, but it doesn't matter, does it? I still love you.'

Linda smiled, praying that this wouldn't go somewhere intolerable, but Freeda would never stop when she got that ball rolling. She nudged Linda a second time.

'And guess what, Blazerwoman. My TV has got the biggest wangher-dangher in the whole wide world! Aint' it true, TV? Ain't it true? Get ya big wangher out and show it her, TV! Dangle it out, TV!'

Luckily for Linda, TV went all shy.

'I don't wanna get it out. I don't wanna, Freeda. I'm watching the big fishes and me toe flipping well hurts. I don't wanna get it out!' But Freeda was on to something that was entertaining her, and she just wouldn't let it drop.

'But Blazerwoman wants to see it. She's dying to see it! She's gotta fing about it! Ta see how big it is, TV.'

Freeda was giggling away, and Linda was just smiling, not knowing what to say. Freeda had plenty more though.

'She wants to suck it, TV! Don't cha?' Freeda said, still sniggering and nudging Linda. 'She wants it stuck in her mouth, so it goes big, big dollop! It's bigger than a horse's! Ain't it, TV? Ain't it massive, TV?'

TV was blushing because Freeda was making him feel so uncomfortable.

'It's not bigger than a horse's, Freeda, it might be the same size, Freeda, but not bigger.'

Freeda burst into hysterical laughter. She was having so much fun, and she kept goading and goading some more. Eventually, TV relented, he quickly pulled his pants half way down, stood up and raised his skirt, giving Freeda and Linda a clear sighting. Freeda kept on laughing, as TV quickly sat down again, pulling his pants up. Then Freeda was at it again.

'Did ya see it, Blazerwoman? Did ya see the big wangly dangler?'

'Yes, I did,' Linda replied, praying that this wasn't going to end up with some kind of bizarre, terrible ordeal at her expense.

But Freeda wanted to keep playing this one out. She was giggling and having fun and TV's big dangler was so funny.

'Get it out again, TV! Show us it again. Get the big wangler out again, TV, cos Blazerwoman's got this fing about it. Go on, TV!'

TV was visibly annoyed with Freeda. It was all so embarrassing.

'Nah, not until it's got the whomper on, Freeda. She's seen it dangling. I'm not gonna get it out again, until it's got the whomper on.'

Freeda then got closer into Linda's personal space, making Linda feel extremely uncomfortable.

'You wanna see it Blazerwoman, when it's got the whomper! It's like a bundle of rhubarb sticks. All long uns, ain't it, TV? Ya pants stick up like a tent, dun they, TV?'

Linda felt more and more uncomfortable as Freeda dug her in the ribs yet again.

'Do ya like ya rhubarb, eh, Blazerwoman? Do ya like your big sticks of rhubarb? Eh?'

Linda smiled. 'Er no, but I'm glad for you, I really am,' and then she pleaded again. 'Please, don't do anything nasty to me! Please!'

'Freeda wouldn't do anything nasty. The Blazerwoman is invited to our wedding. Ain't she, TV? As long as she sucks ya.'

Freeda held the tension for a second. 'Big toe!'

Freeda was in a fit of hysterical laughter. It was all so funny but TV was still concerned by his big toe, in between his continual obsession with Hermann and the Medusa. TV was nigh in a deep meditative trance peering into that fish-tank, although he was still lending an ear.

'Course, she is, Freeda. They're flipping mesmerizing these big fishes. I'm even forgetting me big toe's hurting.'

'Freeda wants a look! Freeda wants to look at the mesmerized fishes!' Freeda rushed across to the tanks and put her nose right up to the glass, while TV was thinking about the idea of the marriage.

'And you'll be getting loads of presents bought for ya at the wedding, like all brides do Freeda. Won't she?' TV said, turning towards Linda for support. Linda saw another opportunity to be ingratiating, and at the same time, she was praying that the police would come or Chaz would come home, anything to bring it all to an end.

'Yes, she will, and Chaz and me will be buying her loads, loads!'

Freeda turned her head and looked at Linda smiling, as she loved that idea of having presents bought for her. The last presents she got was at Christmas, from her friends at the asylum. TV orchestrated that from the open wards, even though Dr. Lock prevented presents coming to Freeda, labeled directly from TV. It had been decided that any renewal of their relationship, or glimmer of hope that it might be renewed, would cause behavioral problems in Freeda. Therefore, it had to be stopped. But Freeda got a secret letter at that time via a bribed agency nurse who was infatuated with TV, that informed her that certain presents were from him. Dr. Lock subsequently discovered from Lavender, that this agency nurse had been alone with TV in one of the toilet facilities and it was decided that the Trust didn't want her services any more.

'Who's Chaz?' Freeda asked. TV informed her that was the Blazerman's real name. TV was still thinking ahead and some ideas were forming.

'And you'll be getting a new dress, Freeda.' TV was sure that Linda would have some smaller clothing, some of her olden day clothing from when she was skinnier. Woman always done that he noticed. They always hoped to get back to the good old skinnier days, when they were size eight or so. She's bound to have some small stuff, he thought. It could give Freeda a chance to dress up, rather than just be in her knickers, hoodie and Dragon cap.

'Will I, TV? Freeda's always wanted a wedding dress, TV!

This moved Freeda's attention away from the carp tanks, to the framed photographs on the mantel, specifically to that wedding snap. She looked at the photo and was enamored. It embodied everything Freeda desired. She wanted to wear a wedding dress, and feel all special and get married, and she wanted to be in a photo like that with TV, more than anything in the world. She got closer up to the photograph and was in deep thought. She was captivated by that white dress, and it made her remember the bridal doll she used to play with when she was at home with her mummy. She found it comforting combing its hair, after Barry had been nasty to her.

'I wanna doll, one that's getting married, so I can comb her hair again. Like I used ta.'

TV intuitively knew what this was all about and he took hold of her hand tenderly. Freeda loved TV's affection and she sat on his lap on the chair hugging and kissing him. With the talk about weddings, and wedding dresses, Linda saw another chance, as upstairs, she still had her wedding dress, that was kept in a large decorative box with her necklace, jewelry and tiara. It might fit Freeda too, as Linda was a few stone lighter back in the day.

'There's loads of nice dresses upstairs for you, Freeda, and there's a beautiful wedding dress. And it's yours, Freeda, as long as you don't hurt me. Please don't hurt me, Freeda, please,' Linda pleaded.

The knife was resting on the coffee table and was out of Freeda's consciousness, as everything was weddings now.

'I wouldn't hurt Blazerwoman? Would I, TV?' The couple were still cuddling up together on the velvet chair with its slashed-up arm.

'Course you wouldn't, Freed. I told ya things would work out, Freeda! Wedding dresses and that! I told ya, didn't I?' TV then looked intently at the ripped arm chair. For a number of seconds, it seemed he was in another world detached. Freeda looked so happy and excited. It was as if all her dreams were coming true, and all because TV had saved her from that prison.

'Have you got any electrical tape, Blazerwoman?'

Linda thought that TV might be thinking about taping her mouth up, and who knows what else, so she played it vague.

'No, I don't think we have,' she replied, but Freeda remembered seeing some when they broke in, when TV was getting her a knife. There was some tape in the drawer next to the cutlery.

'There's some in that drawer, TV!' Linda was relieved, when TV came back and proceeded to repair the velvet chair.

'I just had to repair it. It was getting on my flipping nerves.'

After the arm was repaired Freeda wanted more cuddles in the chair.

'Let's do more cuddling in the chair, TV!' TV put the tape on the coffee table and began cozying up.

'If she does lies to us, TV, we can tape her kisser up with that tape, and do fings to her!' Freeda suggested, and what that might be was something too horrible for Linda to contemplate.

'I would never lie to you, Freeda. I never would.'

Linda prayed but she was incensed with Chaz for being so selfish.

Unusual things were occurring, in another area of Tennin. Chaz parked up the Jag outside a terraced house, and proceeded to get out of the car with his usual measure of panache carrying his briefcase. A couple of girls in their late teens were walking along the path on the other side of the narrow back road. Both the girls were showing off plenty of leg and cleavage in their cropped shorts and skimpy tops. They both looked at Chaz as his whole demeanor attracted like a magnet. He looked so different and obviously wealthy. Chaz could see that they were slyly eyeing him, so he engaged in a little cheeky innuendo banter, as was his usual want.

'Lovely day ta show it all off, eh?' It seemed the right comment, as Chaz certainly cut the dash with that white blazer and twill number up and the new Jag parked. If they had given him half a chance, he would have found a way to pop one of those cards over that he gave Jessica. But they shyly smiled and carried on walking. But they were mighty impressed, and they soon started to look behind themselves, still smiling. They loved the way that Chaz dressed. He looked flash and kooky and they also looked admiringly at his car.

Golden moments like these truly bolstered Chaz's ego. No older than eighteen or so, but they were 'up for it', in Chaz's estimation. A little shy granted, but in truth, they were wanting it big, real big. He noticed number seven, strode confidently to the door, pressed the door bell, while he looked up the road towards the two girls. They were still in view as the road went up on a slight incline and they kept looking round. Chaz smiled and waved and they were both smiling and one waved back. The door opened with Chaz grinning and in good spirits, and before him was an elderly gentleman of about eighty, who had lived at this address for upwards of fifty years, and had spent the last ten alone, after his wife had died. He had an old tweed blazer on and trousers that could have done with an iron, and a neat old-fashioned tie and white shirt that looked a little ochre tinged and thin on the collar. All set off with his best brown brogues.

'Adult Leisure!' Chaz announced. Henry was delighted to see him. This was an exciting day.

'Oh, come on in! Please do! We'll conduct business in the front room,' Henry suggested. Chaz raised his eyebrows at the front room, as on entry it felt akin to going back in time to his childhood, where the front room in some of his aunties two-up two-down terraced houses, were there for show. There was a small dining table by the front window with a table cloth on it and ashtray that hadn't as yet been used. Chaz looked curiously at the ashtray as it was circa sixties, push top spinning away type, that Chaz hadn't seen for donkeys. The bloody place was like a museum, Chaz thought, and he couldn't but notice that old biscuit barrel on a coffee table in front of the fireplace. It must have been forty-odd years old if not a day and the table was also circa sixties that was covered in old photographs of Venice. Henry thought it very cosmopolitan, and it held great sentimental value. Chaz frowned, as he hadn't seen one of those since his early teens. He sat down at the dining table, and Henry pulled the curtains over as he wanted things very discreet. Chaz looked above the old fireplace that had a gas heater in front of it with a companion set. His mum used to swear by them back in the day, even after they went gas. He remembered her defending them against his father on 'ornamental' grounds. Memories came flooding back, as Henry excused himself for a toilet, leaving his pipe and tobacco tin and a curious looking matchbox that was nigh antique. It was a red strike match called 'Brichetas' that Chaz hadn't seen for twenty-five years, but he remembered using them the first time he smoked Park Drive when he was nine. They were the young pyromaniacs match of choice going back, as you could strike them on any surface. Half of Tennin heath went up from a strike from the 'Brichetas'. But how was this old boy still using them? Then Chaz was startled by a bird that came out of its turret door on a large cuckoo clock on the far wall, striking out its three o'clock call. Chaz felt impelled to investigate. The thing was quite a grand affair, with water wheel and even a figure of a beer drinker sitting at a table who smashed his beer down, setting the wheel in motion. After three cuckoos, and a reverberation of springs, the bird disappeared. Chaz smiled. It was riveting stuff. But there was more. The clock then played a little melodic wedding piece and a couple danced about the face. Chaz thought it rather sweet. There was so much here.

Henry returned, breezily and excited, and Chaz couldn't help but remark, upon the three plaster ducks that were on the wall in flying formation, of a design that was mightily popular way back in the fifties and early sixties. Chaz remembered them well; they adorned the wall on the Barber's front lounge in the early sixties, accompanying the early flights of imagination he had back then.

'I haven't seen ducks flying like that for a few year,' Chaz remarked, and Henry said he liked the ducks, and that he liked to keep the front room for best.

'I like to keep things like they used to be. Do you mind if I smoke a pipe?' Henry asked.

'Nah, go ahead, mate, you're in your own castle ain't ya? I couldn't begrudge ya a bit of the ol pipe,' Chaz said.

'Henry's the name.' They shook hands very firmly like gentlemen do.

'Nice to be acquainted, Henry, call me Chaz.'

Henry greeted him, giving Chaz a little firmer gentleman's handshaking. It always helped cement a business arrangement, Henry thought. Then things went quiet for a few moments as Chaz watched Henry slowly opening his tobacco tin, and then even more slowly packing his pipe with tobacco. It was deliberate slow-motion stuff. Chaz looked again at the 'Brichetas' box with its 'Use Matches Sparingly' advice on the packet. He felt obliged to comment.

'That's an old box of matches ya got there, Henry.' Henry looked anxious all of a sudden, as if some greatly held secret had been uncovered, leaving him vulnerable. But Henry rather warmed to this Chaz, so he thought he would open up a little, as he reckoned Chaz to be the black-market type of gentleman. All of a sudden he became enthused, but whispered in hushed tones, very hushed tones.

'I'll tell you a little confidential story, Chaz. A story between fellow gentlemen.'

Henry winked and Chaz nodded, curious as to where the old boy would take him. Henry continued.

'I used to work down at the wharf on the barges back in the good old days, Chaz.'

'Yeah I know the wharf,' Chaz replied as he frequented that area very regularly, and had worked down there in that warehouse back in the day.

'Oh, it's not like it used to be, Chaz. I used to work for Mills & Johnson's. Used to have a dozen barges a day down there. Well me and the wife Elsie.'

Henry motioned to a few photographs of Henry and his wife on the mantel. The obligatory wedding snap, and a few holiday photos that corresponded with the Venice table, with another of the fiftieth anniversary that Chaz acknowledged with sympathy, before Henry continued.

'Well we had the gas put in and it meant we had the coal shed out the back empty. It was a few years after they introduced the smokeless fuel zones. We couldn't afford the smokeless Chaz, so we had to go gas. Now

Fred had a truck then and we had a barge, half full of these "Brichetas" and they weren't properly documented.'

Henry gave a knowing wink and Chaz nodded in the affirmative.

'Sometimes you have to seize that window of opportunity. Keep this between gentlemen, Chaz, between gentlemen.' Chaz was floating along with it all.

'You can rely on me to keep my counsel, Henry.'

Henry looked around as if to make sure that nobody was listening in.

'We saw it as an investment, so we had three thousand boxes.'

'What ya still got um out there, Henry?' said Chaz in an interested disbelief.

'Keep it between gentlemen.' Henry hushed his voice a little more, for the punchline revelation. 'Must have five hundred left. You can have half a dozen boxes, Chaz. The Brichetas are a wonderful match!'

Chaz chuckled away to himself, but he wanted to keep in with this old Henry.

'That's very nice of you, Henry. Very nice.'

'I'll get them for you when I go out the back,' Henry replied, winking his eye.

Chaz was rather enjoying a little bit of people watching time, wondering why on earth would somebody want a coal shed full up with darn boxes of matches? Chaz looked with suspicion when Henry took one of his old red tipped 'Brichetas' from the box. It had a bulbous and irregular head. Henry struck the match on the side of the box and it didn't quite fire. He tried again with a harder strike and its head flew off like a rocket and Chaz had to take evasive action on behalf of the white blazer and nine-hundred-pound twill. Henry's suave demeanor broke down as the head burnt the tablecloth.

'Oh, fucking hell! It's fucking one of them!'

'It's Henry with his box of Exocet missiles! I used to play with "Brichetas" when I was a boy, Henry. Sometimes ya used to get ones with the irregular ends. Like that one!'

Henry was most apologetic. Then he lit another, making sure he did so well away from Chaz and he puckered up on his pipe. This all tickled Chaz and then he dramatically broke the ice, knowing those glossy hard-core covers would make old Henry's knees tremble.

'Right, let's get the adult leisure opened on the table, Henry! Before ya burn your house down!'

Henry rather appreciated the wit, and he was warming to this dapper-looking Chaz, but he was thankful that match end hadn't ruined the Adult Leisure gentleman's blazer. Chaz opened the briefcase, and all the shiny porny packaging stood out amid the rather drab front room. Henry began pumping away on the pipe, much liking what he was seeing.

'They're all pretty darn hot! What's your thing, Henry? The entire dirty canvas of tastes are catered for!'

Henry meticulously put his pipe back down neatly on the tobacco tin and opened up about something, that Sylvester was reinforcing on the phone that very morning. Sylvester was a close friend, who was participating in the 'special' day's remembrance celebrations, who had a somewhat severe disposition, and whom Henry found 'difficult' and stressful. But it was a very confidential disclosure that Henry was making.

'There was something I forgot to tell you, Chaz. You see I'm getting them for a party we've got going. Myself and some very good old friends. We've invited a young woman too and they want exclusively kinky German, exclusively.'

It was a big confession of secret personal information from Henry, but it was nothing to Chaz. He was used to every kink in the book being asked for and a few more. Sexual energy is very diverse, and the Chaz Barber philosophy was any expression of it, is paved with gold and precious jewels.

'Ya can't beat a bit of kinky German to get the ole sex demon going at a dinner party, eh, Henry?' A revelatory spark went off in Henry's mind. What a coincidence, how uncanny?

'That's just what Cyril's always saying, Chaz!' Chaz began looking through the DVDs for German, and incredibly he didn't have any with him. He sighed.

'Would you believe it, Henry. Sod's Law! I've brought just about everything else out, except the bloody German! Hold on, Henry, mate. I might have some in the Jag.'

Chaz went out to check what he had, because he had quite a few in there. He recalled that TV crackpot had some German off him, but he looked up the road hoping to see those two girls hanging around. Now that would be something, but they were nowhere to be seen. Chaz got into the car and searched a cache of films but there wasn't any German.

'Fuck it!'

Chaz was annoyed, but he immediately started thinking the situation through. No-one needed to tell Chaz Barber how business works. Satisfy Henry, and probably the other old dudes would be buying off him too, and then some more old dudes, that they knew. Might be another ten customers, and that could mean another ten subscribers, and that could also mean ten new ones to buy into their new porn star Jessica. Keep him sweet, Chazzy boy. Everything is in the long game. But he thought about those Swedish and American, and a few others he had with him. They were all hard core. He would give them a stab. The door was on the latch and Chaz entered. Henry was still at the table looking over the assorted

DVDs puckering away on his pipe, thoroughly enjoying himself, with his reading glasses magnifying the titillations.

'I'm sorry, Henry. I haven't brought any German out. But I can assure you the Swedish and American films are just as kinky, and I've got some blinding, bloody blinding DIY Irish here! You're fully entitled to have them extensively previewed, to see what floats ya boat, Henry'

Henry lit up his pipe again and puffed and puckered, so that he had the required nicotine shot, before briefing Chaz on the requirements. Chaz had to wait a few long seconds for the reply, that seemed to come within a halo of piped smoke.

'No, it must be German, Chaz. Sylvester was over there serving in the army and he likes the way German women speak and Cyril's the same too. It makes them reminisce about the old German whores they used to know, and the young woman we've got coming to join us, is German, Chaz. It's all part of the remembrance celebrations.'

Henry felt compelled to make the point, as he had promised Sylvester and Cyril that he would get the German. It was all about creating the right atmosphere, according to Sylvester, the perfectionist. Henry's pipe had gone out and he was tapping it and knocking it on the table edge, trying to dislodge some compacted baccy, getting it ready for yet another naked flame. He sprinkled in some fresh, waiting for Chaz's reply. Chaz was now resigned to another approach, more time consuming, but it would have to be adopted. He tried to be as buoyant and positive as possible, as he was thinking ahead towards that goal of more future custom, in the host of pies he had his fingers in. The inconvenience wouldn't be too much of a problem, he could pop the remaining kilo of coke and all that cash in the house. He liked to get it out of the car.

'I'll tell you what, Henry. How about it, if I pop back home to get the German, and I'll be back here in about half an hour? How's that sound?' Henry thought that a grand idea.

'Sylvester and Cyril would be pleased if you did that, Chaz. They really would.'

Chaz left the house and opened the door to his Jag again, humoring and resigning himself to the customers' requirements.

'We must please the Sylvester's and the Cyril's, Chazzy boy!'

Chaz got in the car and sped up the road. Once he got on that main drag, that ran a couple of miles up to the asylum, low and behold, he spots those two young girls loitering around the chippy. Chaz gave them an airing of the Dixie horns, and the two girls immediately knew who it was, and both were smiling as the Jag went up the road.

With all the exciting talk of new dresses, there was only one place Freeda wanted to go now, and that was upstairs and the master bedroom. She and TV walked Linda up the stairs under close scrutiny, but Freeda just let herself go when she saw that bed through the opened door. She hurled the knife down and began to jump about on the big double bed with those silk sheets.

'Ain't it great, TV!' Freeda couldn't believe it. She would be sleeping with TV in a big proper double bed. She had never done that before and it was so 'cushiony'. 'We'll have to stay in bed all day long, shagging, TV!' TV was delighted too. What an opportunity!

'Yeah, we can shag all day and all night, Freed! There's no doctors and nurses to stop us now, Freeda!'

Linda didn't want to say anything, but she hoped and prayed that did have a shag, as they might forget about her for five minutes and she could escape. TV asked Linda to show Freeda the dresses and Linda opened the wardrobe, with her eyes registering the knife on the dressing table. If things turned darker, she would go for it, for Linda had a certain fear about being upstairs with that darn fully equipped, and potentially horrific Dark Room, waiting to be explored next door. It was beginning to prey heavily on her mind. But Linda didn't want to hurt anybody, but she was prepared to defend herself against an evil attack. This 'Mad Freeda' was so unpredictable.

'I've got loads of dresses here, Freeda, and you're welcome to have any of them, as a special present. Any you like!'

This made Freeda feel like a woman again. She took out a couple of dresses and put each to her body, looking at herself in the wardrobe's mirror. She fell instantly in love with an old red garish-looking party dress, that Linda had kept for sentimental reasons. She wore it on the night that Chaz proposed to her at a local Chinese restaurant. He seemed so gallant back them, going down on one knee like he did, asking for her hand, like a knight or medieval troubadour. That was way back then, but now Freeda was full of the dress.

'Oh, look at this one, TV! It's so nice. A real, real party dress!'

Freeda was twisting and turning with it pressed to her body. All the women in the magazines wore party dresses like this one, Freeda thought. 'It can be my dancing dress, TV!'

'Yeah, you'd look a bit of all right in that, Freeda!'

Freeda couldn't wait to put it on and she caressed it, a wonderful new dress. Then she turned towards the dressing table, and opened the top drawer and it was full of make-up. Freeda loved make-up, her make-up was so precious to her, and all in that purse with her money. She had things purchased from the pound shop or the bargain bins, and much was bought her by Kleeunah, although now, she was running short.

'Look at all the make-up, TV! Freeda will have to be made up for her special day! And the Blazerpeople will have to come, won't they, TV? I like Blazerwoman!'

Linda had yet another chance to grab the knife. She wouldn't have rationalized why she did it. It was more a sense of some impending, foreboding event, she was fearing. It seemed to her that it was almost inevitable the Dark Room would have its part to play in the ensuing drama, and Linda just snapped under the intolerable burden of it all. She made a desperate lunge for the knife. Yet as soon as Linda had the knife in her hand TV reacted like lightning, in a way that belied his normal demeanor. But that was the unpredictability of TV. He kicked the knife from Linda's hand with the flat of his Jesus's sandal in a flash, leaving Linda cowering in the corner holding her hurt wrist, thinking her end was nigh.

'I told ya they're Jesus's sandals! They do miracles!' But TV doubled over in pain, as he caught his bad toe. 'Oh fucking hell, me big toe! It's flipping killing me!'

By this time Freeda had gathered her knife and she was exhorting TV to allow Dragon Star to deal with her.

'She tried to trick us, TV! Get up on that bed, Blazerwoman! We're gonna slash you down and you're gonna be "Dragon Starred".' TV agreed, as the new cult had to have its initiates, and why not Blazerwoman? There was a pressing need to "break out" of the asylum to gather new initiates, for that great rush towards AD 2025, the groundhog year.

'Yeah, that's what we'll do, Freeda, mash her brains up and reset um in "Dragon Star". Make her one of us!'

Linda pleaded, as she now feared the worst. She berated herself, it was so stupid, and she even had Freeda pacified through her clothing and make-up. But it was just the fear that something dark and horrible was to befall her, that did it. It was the proximity of that Dark Room, and what could become in the wrong hands, a chamber of horrors.

'Please I'm sorry! I didn't know what I was doing! Please don't hurt me! Please! I beg of you, don't hurt me!' Linda gingerly got onto the bed and cowered, terrified that something diabolical would take place. But with Linda out of the way on the bed, Freeda's attention was immediately back on the dress.

'Freeda is going to put the party dress on, TV! She'll feel good and best in it! And I'm going down to get Blazerwoman's handbag, to borrow it. She said I could, didn't ya, Blazerwoman?'

'Yes, you can have it, Freeda. It's a present for you.'

'Freeda likes handbags!' Freeda had noticed that handbag downstairs, but she became sidetracked by those big fishes in the tanks and her smoking the three team, to get around to acquiring it. But things were different now. She saw herself in her mind's eye in that party dress, and it would go well with that expensive and 'proper' handbag. She could be made up too, and then she would look like the women do in the films and when they go to parties. It was so exciting being out of that hospital prison as she and TV could do things now. She rushed downstairs and picked up the Betty Storm handbag, one that had cost six hundred quid and was a present from Chaz. She rushed into the kitchen and poured all of its contents out on the kitchen table. There were a few things she put back in, a lip gloss and some foundation, but the rest of it went the way of the bin. Freeda then took her own purse from her hoodie and put it in the handbag. It would be safe there, and then she bolted back upstairs as she couldn't wait to get in that dress.

Freeda put the red dress on in the bathroom and soon had the bag slung over her shoulder. She had picked up some of Linda's make-up from the bedroom and put it in her new bag, and she was making a mess, putting on eye shadow and lipstick. Back at the asylum Kleeunah had helped her with her make-up, and when she left, some of the other agency nurses helped her, as Freeda had never really learnt herself. But that pleasure was eventually curtailed by Dr. Lock, as it was thought to be 'destabilizing,' as Freeda always thought she was doing herself up for TV.

'Freeda will look good for TV!'

While Freeda was in the bathroom Linda was guarded by TV, who held the knife but wasn't threatening with it. Linda was still cradling her wrist, while TV opened up a little about Freeda's life.

'When Freeda comes back in, can you say that she looks nice. Some people have a hard life, don't they? And Freeda's like that. For some people that's their life, ain't it? Having a hard time.'

TV looked morose but serious when he was talking, but he was honest and confidential. He knew people had negative views about Freeda, and too many didn't have compassion for her. She was just a 'Mad Freeda'.

'Yes, it is.' Linda tried to show empathy, and what she did show encouraged TV to open up a little more, and a few things just slipped off his tongue.

'She's always crying cos of what Lock and Bolt did to her. And she gets angry and they give her forced injections and put her in a straitjacket. You wouldn't like to be in a straitjacket? Would ya? And they won't allow us to be together. And that's why I got her out. She's calmer with me because I love her. Me and Freeda are soulmates.'

Linda didn't want to get involved, fearing that she would say the wrong thing, so she just took it all in, while nodding her head and acknowledging sympathetically. Freeda rushed from the bathroom in the red dress but she came to an abrupt halt by the Dark Room. It had a small sign on the door, 'Dark Room in use', in bright red that matched the color of Freeda's dress and it caught her eye. The door was black, and Freeda knew it was a dungeon door and she was fascinated by that crystal glass door knob. Freeda had never seen one of those before. She hadn't noticed it when she was rushing to the bathroom with the dress. She turned the door knob excitedly, but it was locked, and Freeda gave a puzzled look. She tore off, back to the master bedroom.

'Look, TV, my new dress!' TV embraced her. The dress was a perfect fit, and TV kissed her and the thick messy lipstick was transferred to TV's lips and cheeks.

'Ya look great, Freeda! Real sexy! Like the women do in the mags.' Linda could see that TV was expecting support.

'Yes, you do, Freeda! You look so wonderful!' Freeda felt special in her new dress. She so much wanted to look like the women did in the magazines.

'I'm so happy, TV, that I've got a new dress. I needed a new dress, didn't I?'

'Yeah, ya did, Freeda, but ya look great!' TV was thinking about the make-up. It was a bit of a mess and maybe Linda could make Freeda up properly. She'd like that, he thought. 'And let Linda put some make-up on ya, Freeda. Linda's brill at lipsticks and eye shadows and that. Ain't ya, Linda? She's like Kleeunah!' TV had gathered the name from one of the birthday cards that were on the sideboard, which read 'Happy birthday Linda, from your loving husband'.

Freeda was happier when Kleeunah was working at the asylum. She had done so much for Freeda and it was all appreciated. Freeda would never forget Kleeunah.

'Kleeunah was Irish and she was a goddess, weren't she, TV? And she brought all my music back!' That was what Kleeunah had told Freeda about the origins of her name and Freeda had never forgotten it. 'And she married Kevin, like in the Irish fairy tales. Didn't she?'

'That's right, Freeda. You remember everything. Sit in the chair by the dressing table and Linda will make you up, like Kleeunah used to do, Freeda!'

Freeda sat in the chair and smiled, as she loved the way that Kleeunah used to make her up. Kleeunah had made Freeda feel special, and Freeda was so excited that she was shifting her head this way and that, telling TV all about it.

'I'm going to be made up like Kleeunah used to do it, TV!' She remembered how Kleeunah used to do it and she had so much fun that time Kleeunah made her up for Halloween.

'Oh yeah, TV! Can Freeda have scary make-up like Kleeunah did for that party! Halloween and that!' TV looked at Linda and Linda nodded her head, as if to say that she could do that. Freeda was still constantly fidgeting.

'Keep your head still, Freeda,' TV asked, and Freeda instantly stopped moving her head and she was completely still, as this was so exciting. Being made up all scary like that party.

'I'll be like a statue, TV! For the scary, scary make-up!'

Chaz was on that mission to get back to the house, grab the German and whizz back to Henry, 'sorted!' He got temporarily blocked in some heavy traffic, and thought he would give Linda a ring and tell her he was popping back. He had a few jokes to tell her about flying ducks and German whores. And that Firestarter turn with the 'Brichetas', tickled Chaz too. He held his mobile to his ear as he was driving, and the ring tone kept ringing. He recorded a message and was expecting one back immediately, but nothing. He was baffled. What the fuck was she doing?

It was a big day for Henry and an even bigger one for Sylvester. He lived the other side of Tennin in what was known as the more 'well-to-do' part of town, and the day gave him a wonderful opportunity. Sylvester was also a new post-millennial bachelor, as his wife Agnes had died five years previously. He stayed in the semi-detached bungalow they had lived in for the past forty odd years, and chances like this came around once in a lifetime. Now Sylvester had, in the past, been renowned for being a bit of a ladies' man, and he had really cranked up the effort for this dinner party at Henry's. Yesterday he had his mustache trimmed at the barber's. He always went for the English style that parted at the philtrum, giving him that debonair, suave look. He had also made a successful liaison with a local escort agency, and had hired a very attractive and buxom young German girl for a 'Porn Star, triple X-rated experience with extras to your choosing', from the great number offered from Mia, an amply built young girl of twenty-four. All to take place in the back room at Henry's 'two-up-two-down'.

Sylvester was something of a local celebrity these days too, as he had been a red beret in the Second World War, and had parachuted down in Arnhem as part of 'Operation Market Garden'. Over the past few years he had got into celebrating anniversaries of the emancipation of Europe, and wherever a commemoration was being held, you were likely to see Sylvester there with his campaign medals and parachute regimental beret. It would have been Normandy for the fifty ninth, but Sylvester's diary had become rather cluttered. But next week he was finally going to have a hip operation on the NHS at Tennin General, and about time too. He didn't want to go into his savings for it, as he had made some big purchases lately, and the greyhounds were getting beaten, so he had to endure the pain. But this week was all about the meet up at Henry's, which he had meticulously prepared for. He had put his pin striped three piece into the cleaners and it was going to be the full Montague Burton for Sylvester. He had a cleanup of the hair down at the barber's too, with a close shave to accommodate his fabulously expensive wig, and his false teeth had been in the ultrasonic orthodontic cleaner overnight, so they were sparkling white. Sylvester swore by orthodontic cleaners. However, like always, when he looked at the mirror with his teeth in, it looked like there was one too many in there. He vowed, like always, to get himself a new set once the greyhounds started winning, but in the moment, he cut his dash with the dentures devil he knew.

Now when it came to putting on that pin-striped suit, it wasn't quite like Chaz with the white blazer, but Sylvester still felt elevated. Pin striped always made him recall his 'demob' suit that he received when he eventually came back to 'civvy street'. Directly after the war Sylvester had been in Western Germany as part of the newly formed NATO alliance activities. Cecil, the other member of the triumvirate, had met Sylvester out there in Germany too, and they had always kept in touch.

With the orthodontic white teeth in early, Sylvester had been veritably whizzing about and most importantly, he had been to the doctors and consulted. He had played the hand of cards that Sylvester had boasted, and would you believe it, everything seemed to be dropping right for them. He had told his doctor that he was enjoying a relationship with a woman of sixty-two who had a very demanding sex drive and he pleaded with the doctor to prescribe him, this new wonder drug Erectafen. Sylvester had no ongoing heart issues and was generally healthy due to his daily walks with his retriever dog and twice weekly golf, although all of this, had ground to a halt due to his hip issues. It was a close call, the doctor didn't want to prescribe, but Sylvester suggested it would be age discrimination if he didn't, and that swayed the doctor's decision. Sylvester put them in the inside pocket of his jacket and he admired his moustache. He wanted to be perfect and neatly turned out for this young German lady. He slipped a packet of Executive Gold cigarettes in the pocket of the jacket. This was designed to impress her, to show her the caliber of gentleman that Sylvester was, but while he was working out his selections, he would have a couple of Navy Cuts. Sylvester had an account with a direct phone line bookmaker, that was very confidential and discreet. It was a service favored by dignitaries, old army colonels, lords and baronesses, and Sylvester loved the kudos it brought him. Today he had gone for a multiple bet comprising of four greyhounds, all trained by trainers he knew personally. When the local dogs at Tennin were on in the afternoon, he would phone around a few of his greyhound trainer friends and get all the insider information. But sometimes dogs slip round bends and get bumped off course which can be vexing when you've a few hundred down. He had trained a few dogs himself going back, but he packed that up seven or eight years ago when he finally realized his mobility problems were severe. He found it difficult getting down to pick up the feed bowls and he just couldn't keep up with paying an assistant. But he would go to the dogs religiously every Saturday night, so he kept his eye in as it were. But once the bets were phoned through, it was all stations towards Henry's and that meant just one thing.

Now apart from racing greyhounds and World War Two anniversary commemorations, Sylvester's other passion was for classic cars. He would go out at least a dozen times through a season as he had a 1967 E-Type 4.2 Coupe, all in old English White, and worth well over the hundred grand, as it had low mileage and had been superbly rebuilt. He just had to take it out but he never really liked leaving it down Henry's road, as there were unemployed youths down there. Yet he desperately wanted to impress this young German whore, make her realize it was the very crème de la crème of gentleman she was 'entertaining'. Now, Sylvester had taken the trouble to really stand out at this party, by purchasing a new pair of leather loafers. They were as expensive as Sylvester could hunt down, and neither Henry or Cecil were as fastidious with their footwear. You can tell a man by the shoes he wears, was Sylvester's credo, and it was sure to impress this young woman. But by necessity Sylvester had gone slip on and now he was just praying his penis would stand up like it used to, with these Erectafen wonder pills.

Sylvester slurped another coffee looking out for the post and he couldn't believe it, the post woman had arrived outside, with a long looking parcel. Sylvester was delighted. He thought it wouldn't arrive on time, due to problems about stock. It was that expensive leather horse hair flogger. He and Cyril had been into that kind of thing with the German whores and they wanted to re-visit one of those evenings they enjoyed, some fifty odd years ago while they were staying in West Berlin. Henry had got a couple of bottles of Smirnoff in and at great expense Sylvester had purchased some cocaine. *You Only Live Twice* was Sylvester's favorite Bond movie, and this was the Second Coming! Sylvester had remarked last year to Cecil that it was something about becoming an octogenarian, 'We've got to squeeze a bit more juice out of it, Cecil!' and they all agreed. Market Garden was hairy, so why not walk the tightrope once more.

As Henry's was only a few miles away, Sylvester thought he would take the E-Type down the M69 for ten miles just to get the engine warmed. Back in the day he had liked all the Jazz but his penchant these days was for MOTR and he traveled towards Fishgate enjoying Perry Como, with his favorite 'It's Impossible' featuring prominently, as he sailed along in the fast lane with the idea, he would do a loop back to Henry's and warm that engine up. He pulled up at a garage to fill up, and was almost jubilant that he managed to get out of the low car without a hint of pain in his hip. Some days were like that, others were terrible. He would dose himself up with so many painkillers that he would fall asleep in the chair while he was watching old war movies and he would wake up startled in the dark, thinking he was back in Arnhem. He was intending to buy some extra strength paracetamol, but his mind was so much on taking an Erectafen, he forgot, and he couldn't be bothered to get out of the vehicle again. But he smiled, looked at himself in the rear mirror and popped another one in, fully expecting to go back in time to that virility of 'the class of forty-nine'. He was on a high with that hip being more considerate this morning.

It was quite a drive up from Fishgate for Cecil, as he wasn't the most mobile of eighty-four-year-olds. He used a buggy and had rails put around the small coastal bungalow he lived in, positioned where the Fishgate sands met the firmer inner terracotta. Cecil had been on his own for some ten years now. He had divorced and his ex-wife lived along the front at Fishgate with a younger lover.

Now Cecil had been on the phone to Sylvester a lot recently and he thought the 'special' meet up was a grand idea. Why not have a few more parties before you finally meet your dotage, and over the past month, by golly, had Cecil put the preparation in. It was fair to say that Cecil's manhood had rather shrunk since its glory days. He had always remembered it, as larger and obviously more erect and stand-uppish. But he had been persuaded by a local friend at the British Legion Club that penis pumps could give you that extra fillip. Well this party was a social event and Cecil didn't like the idea of missing out with this hot young German girl with her 'entertaining', and his penis would be on public display. He had to be prepared, so for the last month it had been nothing but weights, exercises and those pumps and he had been avidly measuring his stretched-out penis. He was sure it had grown by three quarters of an inch and he hoped that these new wonder pills that Sylvester had finally got hold of for the big day would do the rest. He had read in *The Orb* that a man of seventy-five had an erection for twenty-four hours after an Erectafen, and with this woman being with them for six, he agreed with Sylvester's estimate, 'It'll be like having eighty eights' down our pants'. But Cecil was determined to augment that with new fitness levels. He had undertaken a hectic chair yoga exercise campaign and had been walking his Labrador out on the dunes for the past six weeks, wearing those weights on his penis.

It was a hectic time for Cecil, and it was also hectic back at Henry's 'two-up-two down,' as that rotary telephone in the back room, where the majority of the 'entertaining' would take place, just wouldn't stop ringing. Henry had struggled for an hour in the morning getting a double mattress down in that back room, and he covered it with spanking new silk sheets, that cost them hundreds. This was lain there, its edge up against the fire surround. The idea was the German whore could cavort and perform in a number of ways, upon the mattress, among other things. The back room was where Henry lived and he had a telly in there with this swish new DVD player that Henry thought very modern, which had only been purchased recently, in response to this reunion idea that Sylvester and Cecil had cooked up. Sylvester had organized everything with something of a military precision with help from Cecil. Now Sylvester had loads of porn back at his house, but they were all videos. He hadn't bothered to go DVD and Sylvester thought it wise to have a DVD player, as the German whore might think them a bit old fogey if they didn't. It was just a case of waiting on Adult Leisure for the films.

Sylvester turned right by the pub and was approaching the left hand turn down to Henry's house feeling like a tornado with his K Tel CD on now, with 'Telstar' blaring from his speakers. He felt young again and his penis was certainly on the twitch. Sylvester smiled to himself, that 'Telstar', sounded as futuristic today as it did back then, when Sylvester was the logistics man at a warehouse, and he would drive that Austin Frogeye Sprite, and was knocking off that young office worker. How he smiled with nostalgia. He saw her in Sainsbury's last week with her husband, she was mid-sixties now, and he acknowledged her, and Sylvester was thinking, back in the day when that Frogeye was rocking and rolling. He had popped in another Erectafen when he halted at a set of traffic lights out of town and the big dosage was kicking in. One might be good, but surely three would be better! He smiled; it might be up for seventy-two hours! As he was slowing, driving down the hill towards Henry's he passed the same two girls who Chaz had seen, on their way back home. Sylvester's blood was up, and with 'Telstar' on the waves he gave them the eye. Both were looking back at the Old English White E-Type smiling and Sylvester was on cloud nine. Even young girls appreciate a manly man with class and wealth, and that expensive wig was taking at least twenty years off him. That's what Sylvester was thinking, and he couldn't wait to hand the pills around to the boys. Share the love, eh? That Telstar was still orbiting around the earth, so why couldn't Sylvester be orbiting his way around the love hives, and things are best when they are shared Sylvester thought. This German whore was there for that, she was costing them enough.

Sylvester parked the Jag up directly outside Henry's. One hundred and fifty grands worth. No wonder the young girls were turning their heads, Sylvester thought. He had read recently, that in the new millennium, 'old is the new young and eighty is the new sixty-five' and Sylvester had that Jag, the wig and the cultured English mustache, so he could be taken for sixty-two, he reckoned. It was like the good old days were coming back and let the good times roll was Sylvester's motto. He struggled and used a stick to get himself out of that low seat usually, one of the reasons why he didn't use the E-Type very often. But this time, with those young girls just passing, he tried valiantly to get out breezily, without the stick. It was a gross miscalculation and he got a hoot from a passing car as Sylvester only gave a cursory glance before opening the door out onto the roadside.

'Oh, fuck me!'

The girls passed, and they wouldn't have been impressed by the way Sylvester gathered himself from the E-Type. It certainly wasn't 'breezy' and Sylvester got a shooting pain in his left hip, the one to be operated on next week. The spasm was so great, he had to hang on the Jag's door for dear life, dislodging that wig in the process. His body was wrought with pain. It would have to be a thousand mg of paracetamol before they started 'entertaining'. Henry had been looking out for him, and noticed he looked in trouble. When he came out, Sylvester was rested up against the wing of the jag, immobilized, with the wig disheveled and nigh falling off his head.

'Are you all right, Sylvester?' Sylvester took a deep breath and that pain spasmed through his hip again.

'Does it fucking look like it, Henry?' Sylvester would have fallen over, if he wasn't resting up on the Jag. He blew out a deep intake of breath, before having another gulp of air that he hoped would prevent him from passing out. If only he had an oxygen bottle in the boot.

'Shall I call an ambulance, Sylvester?' Henry was very concerned as Sylvester looked rather white and peaky.

'No! No! Just give me a few moments, Henry, and I'll be fine,' Sylvester said, as he tried to straighten out his wig from his reflection in the glass.

'Where's your stick?' asked Henry, as Sylvester had always sworn by that stick to get him out of that, low to the ground, sports car. In fact, last year the E-Type had stayed in the garage most of the summer. But he made the Tennin show ground's Classic show, as his son drove it down for him. But Sylvester was determined. He had to make the effort for this sex party. That Jag was a head-turner and would make this German whore think a bit.

'It's inside,' replied Sylvester, still breathing with deep, deep recovery breaths. 'And there's a holdall on the passenger seat that needs to come out, Henry.'

Henry was excited as it contained those accoutrements that Sylvester was enthusing about. At the same time that he gathered it, a middle-aged woman was pushing a pram by.

'What, did you get that monster Rabbit Vibrator, Sylvester?', Henry asked, with a knowing grin on his face. Sylvester gave him a severe look.

'Be a bit more discreet, Henry!' The middle-aged woman heard and quickly turned away, and Sylvester thought it most embarrassing. With that wig still slightly skewed, once the woman turned the corner, she burst out laughing. But at least Sylvester had stabilized and had recovered his mojo, and now nobody was about, he opened up on other things he had purchased, which were in the black holdall. He had got these from a mail order company, that a fellow mature member of the sports and social club had put Sylvester onto.

'And there's the two-pronged dildo in there, Henry,' Sylvester said quietly. Henry was animated carrying the bag, but he could see that Sylvester was still in pain. He held the stick, but was still resting up against the side of the Jag, taking deep breaths.

'Was it wise to bring out the Jag and put it up this road, Sylvester? It's worth a hundred and forty thousand, you know.'

'You don't need to tell me how much the bloody thing's worth, Henry!'

Sylvester was known to be sharp-tongued at the best of times, but Henry liked to give good advice. That was part of his character. He looked out for people.

'You should have used your bus pass, Sylvester!'

Sylvester looked at him, disgusted. Wasn't it bloody obvious why he had brought it out? It was showing that Sylvester was of a certain level and caliber.

'Shut the fuck up, Henry!' Sylvester snapped, and when Henry was on the sharp end of Sylvester's tongue, he would always watch his step. But he still had things on his mind that he felt impelled to ask about.

'And did ya?' Henry asked, regarding those all-important Erectafen pills. Sylvester, who was now readying himself to go with the stick, turned up his mouth and moustache with a beaming grin, that could only mean one thing to Henry. It was on! Sylvester locked the car and thought he'd better ask Henry about the other pills.

'Have you got any five hundred milligram paracetamol, Henry?'

'I might have, Sylvester,' Henry replied a little vaguely.

'You either have or ya haven't! You're always pussyfooting, Henry. You're like a bloody washer-woman.' Henry, who was a touch more mobile that Sylvester, thought on his feet.

'I'll let you in, Sylvester, and then go around the chemists.'

'Cuckoo! Cuckoo! Cuckoo!'

The cuckoo sprung forth from his turret and called the half hour. The beer drinker raised his glass and knocked it down on the table, setting off the wheel and that melodic ditty. The suitably dressed couple went around and around. Sylvester was captivated, as he had never seen the antique cuckoo ever work. Henry had always threatened to get it repaired. He had been threatening for long as Sylvester could remember, and he had finally taken the plunge into Henry's New Age of the Cuckoo!

'You had your clock repaired then, Henry!' Sylvester remarked, raising himself from the table smoking a Cuban cigar, while Henry was perusing those sex toys. Henry was fascinated by the two-pronged glass dildo that Sylvester purchased as a showcase.

'The rabbit stimulator has got an on/off switch down the bottom, Henry. There's not much doubt how you might use the other.' Henry agreed that it looked self-evident. But Sylvester wanted to know more about that cuckoo clock.

'Quite a song bird, isn't he, Henry?' Sylvester remarked, while perusing the clock which had seemingly come to life. Henry puckered up on the pipe. It had been an excellent new investment.

'I had it fully restored down at Davis's. Done a great job, Sylvester! Great job.'

Sylvester agreed, and thought he would take a vodka. The idea being that if they did decide to drink heavy, they would stay over at Henry's and have a breakfast out. But now that Sylvester had recovered his sang-froid, it was time to get that formal jacket off and roll the sleeves up. He had assumed that Henry had acquired the German films, as that was his part of the preparation, as well as the Smirnoff, although Sylvester had brought a couple of bottles of champagne, that Henry collected from the boot of the car. Sylvester liked to think of himself as the main man of the show as it were. He saw himself as a natural leader, and he was sure that this young German woman would be mightily impressed by him. Sylvester was already considering hiring her personally for the bungalow, if she was up to his taste. Henry tapped his pipe, and readied himself for a light and pucker up. There was this delicate situation to inform Sylvester about, and he knew Sylvester could be difficult, and very belligerent. He struck up another Brichetas and would you believe it, the same thing occurred as earlier, and the head of the match zoomed off, and hit Sylvester's brand-new white shirt.

'Dah! Those fucking stupid matches!' The match head spelt disaster as it made a burn mark on the pure white of Sylvester's shirt. It was ruined as far as Sylvester was concerned. A very expensive Marks and Spencer one too! It was all a case of being properly turned out!

'I'm sorry, Sylvester, that occurred earlier with that Chaz of Adult Leisure,' Henry explained. 'I'll put in a written complaint and put in a claim on your shirt, Sylvester.'

'What with those darn matches from 1969! Don't be so bloody daft, Henry! Stupid fucking things. What sort of person has three thousand boxes of fucking matches in their coal shed? Fucking idiotic!'

Sylvester hated anything like this. He was a perfectionist. How could he greet this young German whore with a brown mark on his pristine white shirt? Henry said he could borrow one of his. Sylvester had reservations, but he thought he would take a look. Sylvester swore under his breath as he sat at the table, exasperated, that he couldn't just whizz up to the shopping center to sort it. But there was no more whizzing about like that, although Henry veritably zoomed upstairs, and was searching through a selection of suitably white shirts, that might go with Sylvester's tie. Henry was on an appeasement mission. He would have liked to have got Sylvester upstairs to take a look himself, but that might prove too dangerous, as the stairs were narrow and steep and Henry couldn't cope with any more of the high drama. Sylvester was stressing. Things couldn't have gone any worse. He knew darn well that white shirts of Henry's wouldn't be perfectly white, and they would have threadbare neck lines. Henry didn't share Sylvester's fastidiousness when it came to shirts. But at least everything was going to plan, so Sylvester thought the issue around on the philosophical side. You've got to expect these kinds of setbacks when you're in 'civvy street'. But he could still afford himself a wry smile, looking at the double pronged glass dildo, by him on the table. At least he knew where that one was going.

Henry brought a couple of shirts down, and Sylvester gave the excuse they weren't his cut. Bloody tatty garbage he wears, Sylvester thought. But he decided there and then, that he wasn't going to put on one of those blasted charity shop woolens, Henry wore, and he couldn't really put the pin striped suit jacket back on. It would be all too stiff and formal when he had to be footloose and fancy free. Like they were in West Berlin.

'Why don't you try and use your tie to hide it up, Sylvester? It's a long one and you could tuck it in your trousers.'

Sylvester considered the idea for a moment and made the effort to stand up. A sharp pain went into that bad hip of his again, and he grabbed hold of the table to take the weight.

'Mind yourself, Sylvester! You shouldn't get up like that,' Henry said, showing concern for Sylvester's welfare. He had been waiting a darn long time for that hip operation, and Henry thought he needed to get up there without any further complications. Sylvester looked in a mirror that Henry had up over the fireplace, and it was obvious that however he wore it, the tie wouldn't cover the burn mark.

'Might be all right if me tie was wider than the length of me cock, Henry!'

Sylvester sat down, deflated and gave it some more thought. He might be a fastidious bastard with the shirts, but possibly this German girl wouldn't notice it if he touched it up with a bit of whitener. 'Have you got any Tippex, Henry?'

Henry duly brought the Tippex and Sylvester touched the burn mark up and Henry agreed that it was effective, which still left Henry needing to tell Sylvester about the hold up with the films. He would have to light that pipe up again. He picked up the box of Britchetas, which was a danger sign to Sylvester, who would be more than bloody angry, if Henry put one on his best pin stripped 'demob-style' suit.

'Here now, Henry!' Sylvester warned, and Henry turned away to shield Sylvester from another errant antique match. Henry struck it and lit the pipe, really puckering up readying to impart the news about the hold up.

'Where's these kinky German films then, Henry? We can have a little peep show at em! Find the best bits!' Henry was still puckering up like a mad thing, and was sheepish with his reply, as he knew full well that Sylvester wouldn't be pleased.

'Well he's been, Sylvester,' Henry replied, prevaricating again, before he turned and struck another Brichetas.

'What do you mean, he's bloody been?' replied a concerned Sylvester. 'Have you got the bloody kinky German, Henry?' Henry turned and puckered a touch, if the truth be known, he was terrified of Sylvester.

'That mark you know; you can't see it, Sylvester.'

Sylvester obviously knew Henry like the back of his hand, and he always stalled like this in his usual pussyfooting style, when the prognosis wasn't good. He would have to persist.

'For the third time! Have you got the kinky bloody German, Henry?' Sylvester demanded, more aggressively.

'As I was trying to tell you, Sylvester. He came, but he didn't have any German and he's gone back home to get some,' Henry pointed out. 'He's a very dependable man, Chaz is his name. We took up a gentlemen's agreement, Sylvester. You mark my words, Sylvester, he'll be back. We took up a gentleman's agreement! Very firm handshake, and I've got that nice new DVD player in the back-room, Sylvester.'

'Not much fucking good if he doesn't come back with the films, is it? The bloody *Sound of Music's* no bloody good!'

Henry tapped his pipe on his tobacco tin, turned away from Sylvester and struck another Brichetas, done his usual puckering up with an enormous inhalation, before he placed his pipe back on the tin. Sylvester was still smoking his Havana with its slobbery wet end.

'Er excuse me, Sylvester. I've got to lay a few hot snakes.'

'Well make sure you wash your arse! You'll be strangling the snake in public later, Henry!'

Henry rose and went out into the kitchen and beyond, where the new toilet and bathroom were. Henry had that fitted some five years back, after he realized his bladder was too weak to be climbing those steep stairs every few hours. While Henry was out there on the toilet, the old rotary telephone in the back room was ringing. Henry was on the dump, so he called out to Sylvester to catch it. The phone was on a little coffee table, next to the tatty lived in armchair, that Henry had out there.

Cecil had driven half the way up from Fishgate, and he had stopped in the motorway services café, but he was no more than twenty minutes' drive away. He was in a quiet area of the restaurant on his up to date mobile phone. Cecil liked to think himself 'up with the times' and he was an advocate of anything and everything 'cutting edge'. One had to embrace change, was Cecil's philosophy.

'How's it all shaping up then, Sylvester? Has he got the German?'

'No, he hasn't, Cecil. But we've got a gentlemen's agreement that he is going to get um with a very firm handshake,' Sylvester explained sarcastically. Cecil was also concerned about the German lady who was attending the party.

'Oh, but is it all OK with the German whore, Sylvester?' Cecil asked, knowing the films were one thing, but everything hinged on Mia arriving.

'Of course it is, Cecil! She will be arriving at six o'clock and will be "entertaining" till twelve.' Cecil then looked around, making sure he wasn't being overheard.

'And did you get that glass dildo with the twisted shafts?'

'Of course I did, Cecil! When I say I'm going to get something it bloody well comes. It's not on gentlemen's agreement license!' Cecil thought he would change the track of the conversation, and refer to Sylvester's togs, as he knew he would have made a titanic effort.

'I suppose you're wearing that new poplin button cuff shirt you were speaking about last week. Must look nice, Sylvester.'

'Of course I am, Cecil!'

Cecil was bemused at the abrasive tone, but he gathered that something had gone on. However, he had to ask Sylvester if he managed to secure the Erectafen, as nothing would stand up without those. Cecil had also read the article on the drug in *The Orb* and this would be an excellent opportunity to test its 'scientific' claims.

'And did you get the special?'

'Now you don't need the assurance of a gentleman's agreement with that either, Cecil. And you know what Cecil, he's finally got that cuckoo clock repaired!' Sylvester said to a shocked Cecil. He had never seen the thing work.

'Has he? He's been threatening to get that done for ten years or more.'

'And the rest! Thirty's more like it!' Sylvester replied. Neither of them had ever seen it work.

When Henry came out from the back, the pair took up their positions, each smoking at the front room table. If felt like one of those long-extended waits for something. Sylvester smoked that cigar right down to the butt and then lit up another. The cuckoo came out from the little door again, springs reverberating, heralding that passing of time, that was weighing heavy, in Henry's front room.

'Cuckoo! Cuckoo! Cuckoo! Cuckoo!'

It was four o'clock now, and they were still waiting and the whole scenario irked Sylvester. This was the time when they should have been out there in the back room, watching those German DVDs and stoking up for the party. The films were essential, and Sylvester wanted them left continually running through the evening, to generate the right atmosphere. Henry didn't like pressurizing Sylvester but he had been known to like a few drugs back in the day, as he had become hooked on combat amphetamines during the Second World War. He didn't like to speak about his experiences back then, as he still had occasional nightmares about it all. He was a rear gunner in a Lancaster Bomber and carried out forty-three missions over Germany. Henry had offered to put some money up for that side of the party, but Sylvester had been adamant that he would pay for it all. Henry puckered up on the pipe, which had gone out again, so he gave it a rat-a-tap-tap on the table edge, packed it with fresh tobacco and struck yet another Britchetas match. He puckered up again, took up a large inhalation, and then came to the point that was on his mind.

'Did you get the cocaine, Sylvester?' he finally asked, knowing full well that Sylvester had been withholding the declaration, because of the lack of the kinky German films.

'Of course I've got it, Henry. When I say I'm going to do something, I actually do it! I don't pussy foot about!' Sylvester gathered the cocaine from the inside pocket of his jacket and dramatically threw it down on the table. There was a gap in between the curtains with the light coming through, and Henry, wanting complete privacy, quickly pulled the curtains firmly shut. Henry was surprised, as he thought that getting a cocaine stash for the night, was all Sylvester bravado. He hadn't been a drugs dabbler in the past and here he was, with a packet of cocaine. Henry looked at it and fiddled around with the packet.

'I thought we'd all celebrate with a line when Cecil makes it, Henry. We can make it a declaration of intent. It's high grade. I had a line before I set out in the coupe.' Henry pawed the bag over, and wondered where Sylvester had got it from. Now Sylvester used a different linguistic sensibility, inappropriate to the age, yet understandable, if one gave Sylvester a little sympathetic consideration. He had used the powers of deduction that some young youths in the 'Bull and Head', were drug dealers. He had spoken to one in the toilets, a 'half-caste chap' as Sylvester called him, who was very discreet and who looked surprised, but had taken Sylvester's request on its merits. The young man had said that they didn't deal directly at the pub and Sylvester was asked to meet up near the local DIY superstore, any time after eight, in a more secluded road near the main car parking area, illustrating that Tennin was a small, small world indeed, and that Jay and Dai had a modicum of decency about them, as Sylvester was obviously more than vulnerable.

'Why don't you give Adult Leisure a ring, Henry? Just to see how he's getting on with those German films?'

Henry took to the phone book and sorted out Chaz's number, phoning him up on the old rotary dialing telephone in the back room.

'It's on answer, Sylvester,' Henry called through.

'Well keep trying, Henry. Things come to those who keep trying!'

Sylvester's patience was wearing thin. He had watched an old adaptation of *Oliver Twist* the previous week, and he still had the film in his mind. It was that waiting around expecting somebody to turn up, who eventually doesn't idea, that was to the fore. Henry came back into the front room, and sat back down and began packing the pipe again.

'No, maybe he'll ring back in a minute, Sylvester? He was a very nice gentleman. I'm sure he will.'

'Well let's hope we're not buggering around waiting for Oliver bloody Twist!

Sylvester was snappy, as he was getting more and more anxious about the evening's proceedings.

'Cuckoo! Cuckoo! Cuckoo!' The bird was off again and Sylvester was sure it was coming out on the quarter.

'No, it's on the half pasts, Sylvester. He wouldn't cuckoo on the quarters. He would wear his springs out.'

Sylvester sneered at the cuckoo clock and sniffed a line of coke up through a fifty-pound note. He brought a bundle of those out to show the German whore he was a gentleman of means, even though the proceedings were taking place in Henry's two-up two-down.

'Give it five minutes, Henry, then give him another ring.'

CHAPTER SIXTEEN

THE DARK ROOM

Back in the bedroom, Linda's mobile went off in the handbag that was slung over Freeda's shoulder.

'Don't touch it! Don't touch it, Freeda!' TV shouted. Freeda quickly jumped up, now with her Halloween make up on. Her lips were black and glossed, and shaped like the Joker's, with black configurations around her eyes that were highlighted with blue and red eye shadow. The beloved sunglasses were put away now and she looked 'well scary' to TV and with her long straight hair and tendency to sneer, Freeda looked like she could frighten anybody. All she needed was that long knife in her hand.

Freeda reacted as if she had a venomous adder, coiled around her arm, and she hurled the bag across the room as the dialing tone 'I Will Survive' was reverberating from the bag. Its message resonated to Linda like a mantra. She was determined to do just that, survive. TV acted in the moment, pulling the phone from the bag, and promptly stamping on it as hard as he could, as Freeda looked on. She reflected, as he kept stamping until the mobile was crushed under foot.

'That's the third miracle you've done with Jesus's sandals, TV,' she said. TV looked down at the smashed remnants for a moment, and his sandals.

'Yeah, spose it is, Freeda!' was TV's deadpan reply.

Chaz needed a miracle. He was totally pissed off, as he was stuck steadfast in a steadily worsening traffic jam, caused by an accident that had gridlocked all the local roads. Tennin was a busy place and intersection, and had the big river tunnels too, and anything like this would create mayhem. He tapped his mobile and looked at it in befuddlement, as he couldn't make out why Linda's phone had gone completely dead on him. He tried again and again, but nothing. He sighed. What the fuck was going on?'

Back in the two-up two-down prospective site of the sex party, the doorbell went. Cecil had finally arrived, and he was still wearing those weights on his penis, as he hoped he would get that little bit more stretch and length, right on the wire. But when he entered, he knew that something wasn't right. It was the atmosphere.

'Cuckoo! Cuckoo! Cuckoo!' The bird came out of its turret and Cecil couldn't believe it.

'So, you had the clock done then, Henry!'

'Fully repaired, Cecil. Two hundred pound at Davis's. He's done a great job!' Henry replied, as he lit up his pipe yet again. There was a line of coke on the table and by it two Erectafen.

'It's all ready for you, Cecil. A nice fat line and a couple of bonk pills,' Sylvester said. Cecil smiled and began to remove his jacket when he noticed that mark on Sylvester's shirt.

'Here, it looks like you've got Tippex on your shirt, Sylvester!'

Sylvester scowled and asked Cecil not to go there, and Cecil, who was always deferential, promptly shut it, as he could tell that something had occurred that had irked Sylvester.

'That's a nice wig you've got there, Sylvester.' Cecil tried to make it up with some positive comments. Sylvester looked daggers at him, as he had clambered into Henry's with the thing lop sided, and those young women had seen him, which had been enormously embarrassing. Cecil thought he would tread carefully indeed, as Henry offered to hang his jacket up.

'Thanks, H, I thought you would have been in that back room watching those German porn films Sylvester.' Sylvester uttered a deep sigh, before opening up.

'As you can see, Cecil, you can rely on good old Sylvester for the cocaine, the prick pills and the German whore, but you can't even rely on Henry for the films! But you can rely on him for a reconditioned fucking cuckoo clock!'

'What's happened? I thought this was our reunion, remembering the time with the German girls?' Cecil was wondering what on earth was going on? Henry had to say something and he was puckering up on the pipe for dear life, to get that all-important nicotine hit, so that he didn't bottle it.

'Er, Chaz from Adult Leisure has been Cecil but he's gone back home to get the German. He should be back any minute. We made a gentleman's agreement Cecil.'

'And he's still isn't fucking here!' stated Sylvester rather brusquely. 'Give Adult Leisure another ring, Henry, for fuck's sake!' Sylvester said, in a rather demonstrative and authoritative tone. Henry promptly put down the pipe on the tobacco tin, and went out into the back room. This time Chaz took the call as he was stuck in that jam.

'Hullo, Chaz, how are you doing with those German films? The boys are here now, relying on you, Chaz.'

Chaz informed him about the jam and assured him that he would be back as soon as humanly possible.

'No problems, Henry. Adult Leisure will have the German to you in no time!'

Henry went back in the front room, and fiddled about with his pipe again, tapping it and packing it.

'Well?' Sylvester asked with a cutting edge.

'Adult Leisure has got stuck in a traffic jam, Sylvester. But he's vowed to honor our gentleman's agreement,' Henry explained, and so they waited.

Back at Holly Beach Lane, TV was looking through Linda's wardrobe. He was deep in thought regarding his bridegroom clothing. He liked his skirt but he didn't really like dresses. He had gone off them after he had decided he wouldn't have it chopped off, because Freeda seemed to enjoy it so much.

'Are you going to have a new wedding dress, TV?'

TV wasn't sure what he was going to wear yet on the wedding day.

'I dunno, Freeda,' he replied. Freeda thought it might be a good idea if TV looked in Blazerman's wardrobe.

'He might have some good stuff, TV!'

Linda saw yet another chance.

'Chaz has got some lovely trousers and jackets and he would love to give them to you as long as you don't hurt me.'

Freeda was in disbelief.

'Are you thicko or something? TV don't wear trousers! It's one of those white blazer fingy's he's after. Ain't it, TV? Ta lend it! Ain't it, TV?'

'Yeah, like Keefy's, Freeda!'

TV was animated anything white blazer and even more so, now that he knew how much that white blazer of Keefy's cost. Two and a half grand!

TV opened Chaz's enormous triple wardrobe, a wardrobe way bigger than Linda's, and with the first door he opened he was met by the jackpot of jackpots. There they were, four white blazers, three in polythene coverings, but all pristine, hanging there ready for wearing. There were also many pairs of trousers, mainly expensive jeans, but also four or five pairs of white trousers too, that gained TV's interest. TV rapidly filed through the blazers first.

'Fuck! One, two, three, four white blazers! All like Keefy's, Freeda! I can lend them all! All of them! And I think I might get back into wearing trousers again. Look! They would go well with the blazer for the wedding and that, Freed!'

Freeda couldn't believe it and she was so happy that TV was happy.

'Oh yeah! I'm so glad for you, TV! I bet Jesus and his donkeys are glad for you too, TV!'

TV was so excited. Everything seemed to be coming together. He thought he would never have a white blazer but now miraculously he had four! He thought it must be some mysterious force from the mystical world and alien intelligence, working in his, and Dragon Star's favor. It was a moment of incredible importance. TV could divest himself of the old world. He wasn't going to be one of the Dragon Star children caught in a hoodie anymore. The cult's leader had to have white blazers like Keefy, that was all about the legacies and that. TV quite liked his arty hoody, but he thought lieutenants could wear Dragon Star hoodies from now on. He thought about it a minute and it hit him like a snake bite. It was all foreseen a number of years ago, when he and Keefy picked magic mushrooms from the cow fields over the other side of the asylum. They dried them out and each had a bundle and they saw seven heavens and seven new earths. Keefy saw four and TV three, and TV swore he saw himself in a white blazer and then there was a woman in white with him too. That was before he met Freeda. He was under a tree and TV was sure it was all a premonition. There was that tree outside and Linda had a wedding dress that Freeda could wear! But those magic mushrooms had allowed the space for new Dragon Star neural connections to emerge. Fuck those old jackets and hoodies, he thought. They were just too common. New neural connections required new white blazers and now TV, the cult's leader, had ten grands worth! TV smiled as he saw himself slinking around, swaying his shoulders to and fro, being a real somebody in a white blazer. He slipped the polythene covering off one of the jackets, and treated it with a similar awe to that of Chaz.

'Put it on, TV! Put it on! You're look good in it, TV!'

TV smiled as if he had just had the cream when he put it on. The TV world had irrevocably changed. Four white blazers and seven heavens, it confirmed that he was the one. Now he did feel reborn!

'I've always wanted one! Always! And now I got four, Freeda! They came along like fucking buses, Freed, glide through the ether with Keefy blazers!' He shuffled around, feeling so good. 'They'll make me own his legacy! Keefy will always be with me now, now I got his blazer on, always!'

Freeda looked on admiringly. The blazer did suit TV, and he had a beaming smile on his face. Freeda put her hand on her hip striking a pose, and turned up her black Halloween joker lips.

'You know what, TV? Ya look a real bit of all right in that blazer. Don't he, Blazerwoman?'

Linda nodded her head in agreement and TV was inspired.

'I fink I will put the trousers on, Freeda. Try um, see if they'll be all right for the wedding and that!' TV took off his skirt and Freeda was looking down at his pants. Freeda began playing around again.

'Get ya wangher dangher out again, TV! Give us a flash!'

'Nah, nah, I'm putting on me white trousers, Freeda!'

TV just had to put those white trousers on, right then and there. But with that skirt off Freeda just wanted some more giggly fun.

'TV! Blazerwoman wants ta suck on ya bundle of rhubarb! She likes her big long sticks!' Freeda smirked and began nudging Linda in the ribs. 'Go on! TV will let ya!' Freeda then remembered what she had found, that funny room with the crystal door knob. 'And I nearly forgot, TV! Guess what! There's another bedroom, TV, and it's locked. It's called the Dark Room! And it's got this funny door knob fingy!'

Linda lost her breath for a second. This had been the fear in the back of her mind all along, and heaven help her if they got in there, she thought. But she knew the lock was solid and they would have to smash the door down to get in there. She prayed they wouldn't do that. But it didn't look good. There was that sledgehammer of Chaz's out in the shed. They might hunt for something they could use and find it.

'There's always fings behind locked doors, Freeda. Always!' This was yet more excitement for Freeda. The Blazerpeople must be hiding things. They had to find out what they were! They had to!

'Let's go and open it then, TV! See what it is they're hiding!'

Linda's heart sunk. Her first thought was that TV managed that escape, cutting that window out, so why couldn't he smash his way into that bedroom somehow. Her mind turned back to that sledgehammer. June had said he used a sledgehammer when he broke into that unit.

They exited the master bedroom and were there before the door. TV read the 'Dark Room in use' sign and thought it rather odd, and that made TV even more curious now, regarding what was behind that locked door, and he was astounded by that door knob.

'Fuck! Crystal glass!' he exclaimed.

'I said it was, TV! Freeda said it was a funny door knob!'

TV turned to Linda for the more pertinent of the issues regarding the door and the secret room.

'Give us the key, Blazerwoman!' TV demanded. Linda tried to sound emphatic, hoping that might persuade them to give up their entry attempt.

'Chaz has got it on his bunch of keys,' she said, with complete assurance. But that wouldn't bother TV. He could open any door whatsoever, anywhere in the universe.

'You keep Blazerwoman covered, Freeda, while I do me wires.'

Freeda began taunting Linda, and Linda had that horribly uncanny feeling that this was going to go somewhere, she desperately didn't want it to go.

'You watch my TV! He can open any door with his wires! We got in here last night with his wires, with his wires! So, he'll get in your secret room with his wires! Ya can't hide fings from me and TV very long!'

Freeda drew the knife menacingly through the air, and now it had been confirmed, how they got in the house last night, and took the knife. Linda was more concerned. If he opened the back door that was locked, why couldn't he open this one?

'And no monkeys! No monkeying!'

Freeda held the knife to Linda, who was swallowing hard trying her best to refrain from that. TV went back to the master bedroom, and gathered his wires that were in the hoodie jacket pocket. He was soon kneeling down tinkering around, poking his wires up into the lock, trying to hit that sweet spot. 'What's behind it, eh? What you Blazerpeople hiding?' Freeda asked. 'What ya got in there?'

With the way that TV was approaching the lock, Linda couldn't see how he would open it. He looked so frigging awkward fiddling about with those wires, yet she was still fearing the worst.

'What you hiding?' Freeda repeated her demand. Linda tried to sound blasé, as if it was nothing out of the ordinary.

'Oh nothing, just a spare bedroom for sleepovers, the usual thing.'

TV's tongue was hanging out, as it always helped him concentrate when doing his wires. He knew he would get it though as it was a basic lock and TV would always unlock those.

'What with a funny door knob fingy! Freeda don't believe ya, Blazerwoman! TV said there's always fings behind locked doors. Didn't ya, TV?'

'Always is, Freeda! That's why they lock um up! They didn't lock their bedroom up and they had all the white blazers and that in their Freeda, so. I got it!'

Linda's knees knocked when she saw that TV had indeed opened, the cutting edge, superbly equipped dungeon of a Dark Room. The surprise! TV and Freeda were astounded by the room replete with its dungeon horse, benches and racks on the wall and all the rest of the paraphernalia, all surrounded by mirrors.

'It's a pervert's dungeon, Freeda! The Blazerpeople are perverts!'

Freeda looked at Linda aghast, screwing her face up, but she was fascinated, and her eyes were drawn to the plethora of masks upon the wall, including doggy masks with zipper mouths and gas mask looking things, as well as simple Venetian masks and blind fold type things. There were racks and clamps and restraints, gags and dildos and all sorts of insertion plugs and even one with a long fox tail and another with a long black cat's tail. TV recognized the filming equipment and everything seemed to click.

'It's where he makes his blue films, Freeda!'

Freeda had become increasingly preoccupied with the doggy masks, thinking them odd and very funny.

'Oh yeah, but look, TV! Look at the doggy masks! The Blazerpeople must put them on and pretend they're doggies!'

'They're perverts, Freeda! Real perverts, and real perverts dress up in rubber suits and wear doggy masks! They're always doing it.'

Freeda picked up the fox-tail plug and showed it to TV.

'And what's this for, TV?' TV looked at it and knew what it was for.

'They stick it up each other's bum-holes and they pretend they're zoo animals and that!' Freeda turned her face up, wondering what on earth these Blazerpeople were about. She was speechless, and she kept taking glances at Linda and then she looked back at the odd butt plug in a complete disbelief.

'Let's have her on the bench, eh, TV?' Freeda suggested.

'Yeah, we could tie her all up with the straps and fings! It'll be fun Freeda! And we could stick the furry tail up her bum-hole!' Freeda laughed hysterically. It sounded all so much fun doing things to the Blazerwoman.

'Sit on the bench, Blazerwoman!' Freeda demanded, as she waved the knife menacingly and drew its blade closer and closer, towards Linda. Linda thought this was really it. She was nearing some kind of macabre and horrific end games, now they were in this horror chamber. But she had to try something, anything. She just had to.

'I wouldn't do anything nasty, Freeda! There'll be people after you. The police and doctors!' Freeda's anger boiled over, and she swished the blade agonizingly close to Linda's throat.

'Shut the fuck up! Shut it, Blazerwoman! Don't you talk to Freeda about Lock and fucking Bolt! And that fucking fat nurse! I'll fucking knife um! Fucking stab um!'

Freeda took her anger out on a small cushioned bench and she tore it to pieces with the knife, stabbing and ripping it repeatedly. Linda broke down in tears under the strain.

'Please! I'm sorry! I won't mention them again! I'm sorry.'

TV was concerned again that Freeda was getting unstable.

'Calm down, Freeda! Why don't you smoke-the-three again, so ya get all calm like Keefy used to do, Freed! Yeah, smoke-the-three, Freed! Give the three a try again!'

TV had already transferred fags into the white blazer that he was proudly wearing, so he quickly had them out and was offering them for Freeda to take. To the relief of Linda, Freeda put down the knife, coming round to the idea, and she took the three fags from the packet.

'Yea, Freeeda will have the three TV and smoke herself calm. Freeda will have the three like Keefy used ta.'

But the high emotion was just too much, Freeda broke down in tears and TV was quick to comfort her, enveloping her in his arms.

'You're with TV, Freeda, and I love you. Don't get upset. We're together now.'

Freeda felt so much better when she was hugged by TV, and she could smoke-the-three and get a calm on like Keefy too. Life was so much better when she was with TV.

'Freeda will have the three, TV!' Freeda fumbled the fags into position. 'Gis a light, TV!' she asked.

'That's it, Freeda! Get the calm on like Keefy.'

TV flicked his lighter and Freeda concentrated hard, getting all three alight and then taking a long slow inhalation. She held it down for a few moments, putting on the best dream-like persona she could muster, before exhaling the smoke slowly with closed eyes. Then she held herself in a complete stillness, as if experiencing some profound nirvana like high, in utter meditative tranquility. She took another long one and done exactly the same thing.

'I feel just so calm, TV!' Freeda said, nodding her head imperceptibly from side to side, with that dreamy smile on her face. But then Freeda's natural energy came crushing through the dam. The calmer Freeda, moved towards the hyper. She took a rapid quick-fire lug on the three and turned her head sharply towards TV, like she normally did, snapping out of the meditative.

'Are you gonna give Blazerwoman loads of loves bites?' TV thought about the question a little, before delivering his answer.

'I might, Freeda, but love bites are for you, Freeda, generally speaking.'

Freeda put her face right into Linda's personal space.

'See! TV's not going to give you love bites Blazerwoman! Love bites are for Freeda! See!' By this time TV was thinking about what they might do for a bit of fun with the equipment.

'Let's strap her down on this exercise horsey fingy, Freeda! We can tie her up with all these cuffs and fings!' Linda couldn't help but make her pleas again.

'Oh, please don't hurt me? You're nice people, and nice people don't hurt people!' she exclaimed. But it fell on deaf ears, as Freeda's patience was wearing thin by Linda's constant outbursts.

'She's getting right on my nerves! Right on my fucking nerves!'

Freeda then got right into Linda's face again. 'Shut the fuck up! And get on that bench for the nudey stuff! Get on it, Blazerwoman!'

Linda laid out on the bench and TV began to investigate the chains and straps, trying to discern what did what and the like. He took some straps over Linda's legs and also pushed her legs wide and began tying them to a metal connection to the horse, especially designed for the purpose.

'I reckon it goes over like that, Freeda, and this like this!' Linda was tightly fastened to the bench, and whatever was going to happen, she had no means of preventing it.

'Tie her up proper, TV! And we can do fings! Do fings to her!' Freeda shouted.

'Please, please don't hurt me! Please!' Linda cried.

In a short time, Linda was chained and restrained, with her legs spread open, as she lay on the horse. TV finished tying the straps and things and Freeda was curious about that filming equipment. TV explained the mystery to her.

'He does blue films as well as sweets, Freeda. The Blazerman must be stinking rich!' It all seemed so obvious to TV.

'And I bet he makes tons out of that fish and chip van! I bet he does! But that Jesus bloke never ever, never ever, had a fish and chip van, did he, TV?'

TV had remembered seeing colorful illustrations of Jesus feeding the multitudes in the leaflets that came through the letterbox when he was living at his auntie Joan's. The painted image flashed through his mind.

'Nah, Freed! He had baskets, Freeda, fish baskets!'

Freeda frowned as that seemed to contradict with what she was led to believe.

'You said he had donkeys!'

TV tried to explain the misunderstandings again.

'Well he did, Freeda. But he carried his fishes in the baskets, on donkeys, and then he gave them to the poor and starving, Freeda. They used to weave loads of baskets back in the olden day times.'

Freeda looking intently at TV, frowning as she tried to contextualize these new additions to the Jesus narrative.

'Cor ya know what. I'm un arf hungry, TV,' Freeda announced rather unexpectantly, now that TV was speaking about hunger and starvation. But TV thought it best that they finished getting the Blazerwoman's clothes off first. Then they could go searching for food. Freeda's thoughts were displaced from food and hunger for a few moments.

'Yeah! Let's take all her clothes off, TV. Get um off and look at her hairy beaver! Let's do it TV! Let's do it like the shoes tell us to!'

Linda pleaded again to leave her alone, but Freeda couldn't understand it. The Blazerpeople had 'nudey' pictures down in the front room, and yet Blazerwoman didn't want to be seen in the 'nudey'.

'Fucking square bush! And her front room is full of nudey pictures, TV! Fucking square busha!

'Let's have her knickers off, Freed! See her beaver diva, hairy beaver!'

Linda had a pair of tight black slacks on and TV released the ankle straps for a moment, so that they could get them off with those knickers. Linda still pleaded with them to leave her alone but TV wanted her strapped up and stripped, so that they could do fings. With her legs unrestrained again TV and Freeda quickly had the slacks off, and then it was time for the knickers.

'Knickers off!'

'Yeah, and see her beaver diva, hairy beaver!'

The knickers came down and TV and Freeda were astonished by Linda's shaven fanny. Freeda burst into hysterical laughter.

'Er, she's like a little girl, TV!' Freeda exclaimed. TV wasn't too keen himself, but he was still leering.

'Spose she is, Freeda! But I like my beavers all hairy, Freeda, like yours!' Freeda thought those truths were like givens.

'TV likes hairy beavers! He don't like your one, Blazerwoman! TV would never poke his wangher-dangher up ya beaver! Never!'

This was incontrovertible according to Freeda. TV hated baldy beavers.

'Nah, Freeda! Nah! I've still got to shag her brains out so she's in with Dragon Star, Freed. We gotta think of the neural connections. Don't you remember?'

TV then had an idea inspired from looking at all the pervert masks. He picked up a doggy style one, and was quiet for a few seconds as he perused. Freeda began giggling as she found those doggy masks so funny.

'Here, Freeda! Let's put one of these pervert masks on the Blazerwoman, and she won't be able to see us!'

It all sounded so much fun to Freeda and she just couldn't stop giggling.

'Don't the perverts mask look funny? It's like a doggy, TV!'

'Well they're for perverts, real perverts, Freeda!' Within a few moments, TV had the mask on Linda, and she was still pleading, her voice reverberating in the mask. Freeda had just about enough of this Blazerwoman. She shouted in her face aggressively.

'Shut the fuck up! Zip ya kisser fucking up!'

TV zipped the mouth up on the mask which made Freeda hysterical again. Everything was so funny. TV then took his pants off and he stood there with his white blazer on, sporting his enormous erect penis. The 'whomper' as he called it, was on!

'It's standing up like a flagpole, TV!' TV looked down.

'Spose it is, Freeda! Keefy used to say that.'

Freeda interrupted his flow as Keefy wasn't like TV.

'But Keefy never ever had a dangler like yours, TV! You told me.'

Freeda was getting mistaken again, TV thought. He tried to explain as best he could.

'Nah, Freeda, nah. I wasn't gonna talk about Keefy's knob, Freed. Nah, Keefy used to say there's a sex snake down in women's bang holes and when ya shagging, ya bringing it all out, Freeda, and fizz banging and all that.'

'Well your dick narf looks big! Poke it up her! Do ya genie on her, TV! Shove it up her! Shove it up her and shag her brains out, TV!'

Within a few moments, TV was having sex with Linda, humping away furiously, clad in the white blazer and Dragon Star cap, with more than enthusiastic encouragement from Freeda.

'Shag her brains out, TV! Shag um out and make her Dragon Star! Get her in our team, TV!'

TV was pounding away finding a pulsating rhythm, and Linda was trying desperately hard to hate every single moment of it. But this impossible situation was making her respond to TV's massive penis, and his now pounding and long deep penetrative thrusts were putting vigorous and erotically arousing friction on her clitoris. She was trying to fight her erotic responses, which was unfortunately making her darn more erotic. What a cock! TV could sense what was happening.

'She's coming up, Freeda! I'm stoking her up! She's loving me cock! Loving it! It feels all different, Freeda. It's this white blazer, it's making me cock all different, like a magic sparkler!'

Chaz had put on his David Bowie Greatest Hits CD, and was engaging in some enthusiastic singing, temporarily forgetting the issue regarding Linda's phone. That would be sorted out once he got home. He slid his wheels a little round a roundabout, while in tandem to the intro of 'The Jean Genie'. It was a particular favorite of Chaz's, that went back to his mid-teens. It was 1972. He recalled the party he and Miko went to, where Miko shagged Viv for the very first time up in Gonzo's parents' bedroom. Miko spilt that bottle of vodka all over the bedroom floor and left a used condom under the pillow. What a craic. Chaz laughed to himself remembering the night. That party of Gonzo's was something else and he paid for it too, being grounded for God knows how long. Chaz and Miko still referred to it occasionally when they wanted a laugh fishing. Chaz was going out with Sharon Darby back then and he shagged her three times after Miko had done Viv. He was just sixteen and after a crowd of them did the vodka, Chaz and Miko finished off downing loads of barley wine. They kept drinking and drinking with both ending up chucking it all back down Gonzo's bog and to think that Miko was still with Viv after thirty-one years had passed, and after her becoming a porn star. He chuckled as a woman motorist gave him a bib for cutting her up with his fast-erratic driving.

'And one up ya back passage, luv!' Chaz shouted, before Chaz got on that long stretch of road, Green Street Meadows, where he loved to put the foot down. He was flying, singing the lyrics, whoop-hay! He would get home, the long-haired greenie. He wouldn't make women's knickers. He could have them off all day long, in the sex dens if he so desired, and then get that kinky German back to Henry and the boys. What a craic! And how Chaz loved the freedom of his life style, ducking and diving, wheeling and dealing with a bit of powder up ya hooter, get on your scooter. All in that New Age when the new woman was 'up for it', and even time for those flying ducks and Henry's fucking cuckoo clock! 'Whoop-hay', for a second time. Chaz had a toke on his joint and was up from that little big line that he snorted from PC Angelica's naked body. He had wanked over her twice already.

Meanwhile, things had developed back in the Dark Room. TV was still humping away on Linda, who was strapped in tight on that bondage horse. And on each thrust, and now they were long and deep, he was trying to disassemble her brain, to make it amenable for the transformation to Dragon Star. The light bringer was humping, and Freeda was giving much rapturous and vehement support.

'Shag her brains out, TV!'

TV was ecstatic. He had never known sex like this. There was something truly cosmic about it. Something of the star children. It was out there, man!

'She's loving it, Freeda! She's loving it! It must be the white blazer. It's giving me cock special powers, frigging special powers, Freeda! It's like a flipping crazy sparkler!'

Freeda was resolute in her rapturous approach.

'Ooh! I wanna bit of it, TV! Freeda wants a bit! But shag her brains out first, TV! Shag um out with ya special cock!'

Chaz approached the turn into Holly Beach Lane firing on all cylinders. He certainly let himself go! He always turned into Holly Beach Lane far too fast, and he would then slow appreciably as he went past Dr. Greene-Burrow's house, hoping to get a sighting of that horny wife of his. Chaz was sure that woman was well 'up for it', and was obviously not getting enough. Catherine was working in the front garden with those extremely tight multi-colored running tights on, and she was bent over with her bum up in the air. Dr. Greene was sitting in the shade, reading some hospital reports and protocol, as he was still on the board. Catherine stood up straight, as she knew the sound of that Jag approaching, and hers and Chaz's eyes met, as Chaz quickly passed. Catherine Greene-Burrows acknowledged Chaz with a courteous smile as Chaz continued in his high spirits.

'Whoop-hay! Bum up to fuck and giving Chazzy boy the eye, eh!'

Chaz was having so much fun, he was nigh back round that party at Gonzo's!

To keep appearances up, Catherine turned to her husband, shaking her head a little, as it was strict etiquette to criticize such a man. But if the truth be known, she was fascinated. He was a touch debonair and had style, and she thought he had a striking élan and gusto. There was a spunk about him that Jeremy certainly didn't have. But she had to keep appearances up.

'Anyone would think he's at Silverstone, Jeremy. He's like a fifty-year-old adolescent.'

Jeremy's attention was turned away from internal hospital business, that was referring to complaints regarding one of the top surgeons at the general hospital.

'I suspect he's a drug dealer, dear.'

Chaz parked the Jag up by the horse chestnut. He would get in there, grab the German, put the coke and money under the tanks, have a quick line and out the door. He might even catch another tantalizing glimpse of that horny doctor's wife, posturing out there in those tights. Pudenda phew! Chaz had been masturbating thinking about her for ages. He reasoned that it was the fact that she was fit, but also from the doctor's class as it were. He had told Miko jokingly while they were fishing, that he wished she'd subscribe to his sites. It was a fun comment, but he also meant it, as Chaz reckoned, she probably surfed the internet for kinky porn to get her fingers and vibrators poking. Chaz thought that anything was possible in the sexually liberated New Age. He would have her tied up to that horse! Horse bag of coke on and snorted! Set the cameras rolling!

Up there in the Dark Room, the cock genie was still humping and building up to that tumultuous moment, and he had somehow managed to magically coax Linda with him. She was in ecstasy, moaning and a groaning, in a wave field of sex and more ecstatic sex. Linda felt as if she was going to explode like a nuclear sex bomb and TV was exhorting her, to join him in the seventh earth and the seventh heaven of the Dragon Star.

'White light, the snake, the fizz bang snake!'

TV was incessant. He felt like a King Solomon with enough sexual power to service a thousand women or more, and every one of them would become Dragon Star. It was the white blazer. It was making his cock fizzle and spark like a god's! But Freeda wasn't present now. She had been drawn back into that big bedroom with all the make-up, and she was applying a few touches of lipstick and eye shadow, to an already dramatic and scary look. Freeda loved looking like this, and she was practising her scary faces in the mirror, and posing with her knife raised like a 'Mad Freeda'. You never know when you need to put the shits up someone, and it was such fun looking like Halloween, and she was still shouting out some vocal support for the self-styled sex guru.

'Give her the spunk hose, TV! You're the one with the white blazers now, TV!'

TV could hear Freeda faintly in the far distance, but he was in another consciousness world of magical sex, and Linda was now moving in perfect harmony with his thrusting, wanting every last bit of orgasmic ecstasy she could garner from that incredible cosmic cock.

'The seventh heaven! We're nearly there! Nearly there!'

Freeda was still staring in the mirror, poking her tongue out that was bright red from all the coloring from the strawberry boilies. She couldn't wait to have a shag with TV again, with these white blazers of his. It was such a good idea to lend them. It seemed to have done something magical to his cock and she could hear Linda's moans and groans getting louder and louder and more intense. She smiled and then heard the front gate go. She was quick to the window, and she caught a glimpse of Chaz in the white blazer sauntering up the garden path. Freeda rushed to the Dark Room to tell TV, and by now Linda had gone beyond just groaning, she was responding with a deep filthy lust. She wanted more and more of that cock! That incredible cock that was beyond belief!

'Yes! Yes! Fuck me harder! Harder! Give me more of that cock!'

Freeda came in and TV told her the state of ecstatic play. He was Dragon Star zonked.

'We're nearly there, Freeda! Nearly there! And she's loving it! She wants more and more cock, Freeda!'

'The Blazerman! He's coming through the gate, TV! He's here, TV!'

TV tried to take it in and come to a path of action, but there was no stopping. He was hurtling towards that infinite cataclysm of pure ecstatic Dragon Star consciousness. He was responding to Linda's calls for deeper and harder, and he felt his whole body and mind were like a white blazer, at one in a cosmic cock hungry cunt.

'I gotta finish the fizz bang! Get the seed up her, Freed! Trip him as he! Oh, the white light, the fizz banger! Oh yes, the Garden!' TV tried to be coherent, tried really hard, but Linda wanted more of that threshing machine cock, loads more, and his cock was feeling so good!

'Fuck me harder! Harder, you bastard! Harder!' she wailed, as proceedings reached an orgasmic fever pitch.

'She's gonna come massive, Freeda! Massive! It's the white blazer. Me cock's got special powers! It's fantastic, like a fucking magic bonk wand!'

Freeda looked bewildered, but then there was a visible sense that she had some kind of inspired idea. She held the knife more tightly, and her eyes were glinting like a Queen of All Hallows' Eve. All ready to confront that Blazerman.

Chaz came through the front gate and he didn't bother to close it properly, as he anticipated coming back out in five. He sauntered round the back, his mind contemplating that doctor's wife. He would definitely walk down that convenience store *very* regularly of an early morn to get to know her a little better. Chaz was so tied up with thinking about that doctor's wife that he forgot to take the coke and money out of the dashboard, but he immediately came to an abrupt halt, when he saw that darn odd Dragon Star flag flying away, in the now stiff breeze that had got up. He also looked bewildered at that trident up against the shed. Who the fuck put that there?

Chaz could hear something or other going on inside. He went through the porch wondering what was going on? TV was trying to keep the noise level down, but Linda was just making too much, and the sound of his thrusting into the sex horse was virtually coming through the ceiling. Chaz came across the snake carcass on the washing machine and looked at it in a total disbelief. Was Linda starting some kind of snake cult?

'What the?'

Within a few moments he was in further disbelief in the front lounge confronted by the smashed screen and a commotion going on upstairs.

'What the fuck, Linda! Linda! What the fuck's going on?'

Chaz strode out the lounge. He whipped upstairs, blood up, to the sound of Linda in the throes of orgasmic ecstasy, and as he was doing so, he had to endure the ignominy of hearing Linda shouting out that lust. It was hard to bear but he had to investigate.

'Give me more of that cock! Give me more of that fucking cock, you bastard!'

The Dark Room's door was ajar and Chaz opened it, and took in the sight of TV in one of Chaz's white blazers with that long green hair and Dragon Star cap, now turned around backwards, shagging Linda who was overflowing in ecstasy. TV turned around and gave Chaz an inane smile.

'Oh, hullo, Blazerman. I was just shagging ya wife's brains out!'

'You green-haired bastard!'

Chaz lunged into the Dark Room, and he hadn't noticed Freeda who was crouched behind the door, holding a bondage stick that she struck across Chaz's pathway, tripping him. Chaz stumbled as Freeda checked that powerful angered forward momentum, and within a moment the 'Mad Freeda' had pounced. Her knees were pinning his shoulders down and Chaz was shocked that she had such an incredible manic strength, that he just couldn't budge. She held the knife to his throat with her eyes bolting with that hideous Gothic make-up. He tried to move her again summonsing all his strength, but he just couldn't, and the more he tried, the greater the force he was met with, and it didn't yield. This 'Mad Freeda' certainly looked like one, but the strength of her seemed unreal. She was like a monster.

'I can hold you down, Blazer-Dicky! One move and your fucking head's off! Head's off!' Freeda couldn't help but notice Chaz's colorful shirt.

'Cor, he narf got a nice shirt on, TV!'

Meanwhile TV was still thrusting deep into Linda, and they were nearly there. It was the fuck of all cosmic fucks. TV was effusive. What a fuck!

'Has he? But I'm gonna spunk her, Freed! And we're gonna come! I'm in! The white blazer! It's spunking!'

Linda was still shouting out her lewd desires, just letting herself go, on this incredible ecstasy ride. She wanted more, more, more! She was howling out for it.

'Yes! Yes! More of that cock! Give it to me, you bastard! Fuck me harder! Harder, you bastard!'

Freeda taunted Chaz menacingly with the blade, exhorting TV to go for that ultimate Dragon Star fuck.

'Shag her brains out, TV! Make her see dragons! The fucking dragons, TV!'

They finally came together in a shuddering climactic Dragon Star orgasm, that smashed all known boundaries, and their ecstatic cries could be heard reverberating through the house, spilling into the air waves of Holly Beach Lane, mingling with the caws of crows.

CHAPTER SEVENTEEN

THE MIRACLE OF JESUS'S SANDALS

Linda was still naked and strapped down with the doggy mask on, and Chaz, if not quite thinking on his feet, was having to think of something quick, while he was being pinned down by this mad lunatic. He just had to try something, and in the last instance everybody is susceptible to the charms and snares of money, when you haven't got any, and Chaz had a veritable wad of notes in the blazer, although most of the cash was in that plastic bag in twenty pound bundles of a thousand. But the Waterside Crew's payment was there in an envelope.

'I've got money! Loads! I've got eight grand in my pocket! It's yours! Just let me get it out!' Chaz exclaimed, holding the faith that money could get him out of this fix. But Freeda wasn't overly impressed.

'We got money! Freeda's got money in her purse, ain't she, TV?'

TV was still lying on top of Linda, with his penis still inside of her, planting the cosmic seed. But he turned his head as the Dragon Star children needed money to cement their legacy, and TV had never seen eight grand in a wad before.

'If you've got eight grand, fucking prove it, Blazerman! Right here! Right fucking now! Fucking prove it!' There was no denying TV's interest, and Freeda took up vociferous support.

'Yeah, fucking prove it! Fucking prove it, Blazerman!'

'It's in my jacket pocket. Let me get up and I will give it to you,' Chaz emphasized, and TV was desirous to investigate such a claim. Eight grand! Eight for the Dragon Star's treasurer!

'Get off him, Freeda, but cover him with your knife. I've got to let me spunk seep into her fanny properly! But no monkey business, Blazerman! No funny stuff!'

Freeda raised herself off Chaz, but held the knife fixed at him, speaking through its menacing power.

'Yeah no monkeys! None of those big fucking monkeys, right!'

Chaz put his arm into his blazer pocket and took out the envelope packed with cash, as Freeda taunted him.

'TV's spunk is all in your Blazerwoman's fanny. TV's dragon spunked her! Ain't ya, TV!'

'That's right, Freed! It's still seeping in!'

Chaz took the money from the envelope and splayed the wad of notes open to impress this mad 'nutty farm' duo. The sight of that *real* money was enough of an incentive for TV to withdraw from Linda. He naturally took the money as head of the new order, and he couldn't believe it, when he had it there in his hands, a great wad and eight fucking grand.

'Fucking hell! Look, Freeda! We've got money! We're fucking loaded! It's me magic cock, Freeda! It's bringing us money, tons of it!'

'Freeda's got money in her purse, TV!' Freeda exclaimed. 'Tons of it,' but TV was saying that this was real big-time money, and it gave TV an enormous wide grin on his face. There were subtle forces behind the scenes, helping them, creating certain auspicious circumstances. Freeda was thinking about money now, the sort of things she knew you could do with it.

'We can go shopping, TV! And go on a cruise! And then come home for a cup of coffee and then go shopping again!'

'And go on another cruise, straight after, Freeda!' TV replied, as he was dead sure they had enough money now. Chaz saw his chance opening up and with these types, who were 'shot through', in Chaz's estimation, anything might work. He done his best to make it sound as if there really, was only one thing for them to do now.

'What are you waiting for then? Get out there and spend it! That's what money's for! You've hit the jackpot! Get out there. Go for it! Show the world you're loaded now!'

Freeda gobbled it up, hook, line and sinker. She would just love to go shopping like all the women do, and buy just anything she ever wanted. TV could do it as well!

'Let's go to that new shopping center, TV! The one Kleeunah used to go to! The big one!'

Chaz thought that this might just work. Just make them feel you're being helpful, was Chaz's modus operandi.

'Go for it! You've got the money now! Be trendsetters! Get up there and flash that cash around, like your millionaires! I'll even drop you up there! How bad's that, eh? It's only famous people, who've got the dough you two have got now!'

Freeda was sucked in, but there was no way that TV wasn't going to see Chaz's chicanery.

'Nah, Freeda, we'll get caught! He's trying to trick us, Freed! But we've got money now! We've got dosh for Dragon Star's legacy!'

Freeda wasn't quite sure what TV was talking about, but she knew it meant they weren't going shopping like the Blazerman said.

'See, Blazerman! We're not gonna go shopping wasting all our money. Right! We're gonna keep our money! We're savers, ain't we, TV? We like hoarding our money!'

TV backed Freeda up, saying that Dragon Star was putting it all away for a rainy day.

'We'll save it, Freeda, for when we go down Fishgate!'

'I wanna go to Fishgate, TV! And sit on the beach with ya and have a big cornet!'

The way that Blazerwoman had responded to TV shagging her in that white blazer hadn't gone unnoticed by Freeda, and she was itching to try it all out.

'TV,' she asked intimately, 'can Freeda have one of them new spunk cannons you got now, TV? Like ya gave the Blazerwoman!' She felt impelled to ask, as TV was going on and on about how that white blazer was making his cock all special. TV looked down at his penis. It was back to a dangler.

'Yeah, course, Freeda. But it'll be a while before I can reload, Freeda! New whompers take time.'

'Then we've got time to have more of his sweets, TV,' Chaz was obviously curious.

'Sweets?' he asked, thinking that Linda might have had some chocolate truffles hidden away somewhere that they found. But he soon began to realize what it was all about.

'You know what Freeda means, Blazerman! The blue ones that TV likes and the strawberry ones that Freeda likes!' Freeda took the last couple of baits out of her pocket, showed them to Chaz with a satisfied smirk on her face and popped them in her mouth.

'Um, these strawberry sweets that the Blazerman makes are so lovely, TV! Um!'

The penny dropped and Chaz was quick to exploit an opening from the boilies.

'I'll make ya buckets of them! Buckets! But we'll need eggs, more eggs, and we'll have to go to the shops to get them, down in the village,' Chaz explained. But none of this tricked TV. He saw two enormous boxes out there in the fridge, there must have been fifty out there.

'We've got eggs! We've got loads out there in the fridge, loads!' TV snapped, and Freeda backed him up wholeheartedly.

'See! We don't need eggs! Me and TV have got loads! Loads of eggs!'

TV had said they had and TV was always right, Freeda thought. Things turned darker again as TV thought they had to put an end to this Blazerman trying to trick them. They needed to scare him a little bit.

'Keep his throat covered, Freed, and slit it if he tries any more of those monkey tricks!' This was accompanied by a vicious sneering throat slitting gesture that Freeda reciprocated. Freeda thought she'd better show this Blazerman Freeda meant business, Freeda's business.

'And if you don't watch it, Blazerman, I'll have ya cocky, right off, chop it off! Clean off!' Freeda broke into disturbing laughter, as she taunted Chaz with that knife. 'And don't think Freeda wouldn't do it!

Because Freeda's chopped them off before. Ain't I, TV? Ain't I chopped cocks off, TV?'

TV baited her, so as to inform the Blazerman of what had occurred to Barry's dick.

'Yeah, tell him about it, Freeda! Tell him!' Freeda was laughing while she recounted the story as it was a personal triumph, ending her long-term abuse by her stepfather. Freeda's real father had died in a motorbike accident, when she was just over a year old, so she never remembered him. But she had always felt there was something missing. But she got back at that Barry in the end, and it was Freeda's fightback.

'I sliced it right off, see! And Barry screamed and when the ambulance came TV, Barry was still screaming! And in between the screams he was fucking whimpering, like a little fucking baby! Cunt! I got him, TV! Fuck to Barry! And fuck to Lock and Bolt and that big fat nurse! Fuck um all, TV! Fuck um all!'

Freeda's anger boiled over, and she dug the knife deep into the seat of a bondage chair in the Dark Room and was tearing and ripping the seat to shreds. Linda, still spread-eagled naked on that horse, was pleading through the doggy mask to TV and Freeda.

'Please don't hurt us! Please!'

Freeda had enough of this Blazerwoman shouting out things. She stopped her ripping with the knife, and addressed her.

'That Blazerwoman fingy!' Freeda went right up to her and shouted right into Linda's doggy masked face. 'Fucking shut it, Blazerwoman! Shut ya fucking kisser up!' Linda went quiet as TV reflected on that Barry story, that Freeda had been recounting. It was like a long delayed reflective reaction.

'I spose he must have been screaming with his cock chopped off, Freeda,' he mused. Freeda burst into more hysterical manic laughter, with a look of sheer triumph and joy on her face. She knew instinctively it was an iconic moment, and if the truth be known, she wouldn't have been alive if she hadn't chopped it off. She would have killed herself.

Meanwhile, TV's attention was turned by some of the odd bondage and kinky sex gadgets, that were in the room. His main interest was that expensive top-of-the-range fucking machine on wheels. Freeda was looking at Chaz lain on the floor, hunched up against the wall. She frowned and she was thinking deeply about him, and then she finally came to her macabre solution. It was back to those ears again.

'I'll tell you what, TV! How bout if I chop his ears off like they do in those gangster films! It would be good, TV! Really good!' Linda couldn't bear what she was hearing. It was horrible. She began protesting again.

'Please no! Be nice! Please!' Linda exclaimed. Freeda was just about sick of this Blazerwoman, she just wouldn't stop shouting out things through her doggy mask.

'She's getting right on my fucking nerves, TV! Right on my fucking nerves!'

Freeda went right up to Linda again and shouted into that funny doggy mask for the umpteenth time.

'Shut ya fucking kisser, Blazerwoman!'

TV didn't really like the idea of chopping Blazerman's ears off. He had some plans lined up, and to put them into action, Blazerman had to have his ears on. He had to.

'Nah, Freeda! He won't be able to hear things, Freeda! I told ya that before and that, Freed,' But TV thought that it would be wise to scare that Blazerman. He might shut it then and keep quiet. Yes, he deserved to be scared.

'But you could do his cock like ya did Barry's, Freeda!' Chaz was terrified and driven to say something in defense of his manhood.

'Please, please. Show some decent humanity! Show us that you're, good decent people! Good decent people. You've got a Jesus badge on there, look! Jesus would want you to be nice!'

Anything like this might work, Chaz thought. There was no real telling with these nutty farmer fuckers. But Freeda scoffed at this kind of pleading from the Blazerman. She and TV had seen what kind of things he was doing. They had seen those photographs on the mantel. Freeda taunted him.

'Oh yeah! You weren't so nice to the goosey ganders and the quack-quacks! Was he, TV? He killed them all! All of them, TV! Didn't he?'

It was all stacking up against Chaz Barber.

'And the big fluffy bunny rabbits, Freeda! He was hanging them up by their ears, their big long ears, Freed! All dead fluffy bunny rabbits!' Freeda pointed the knife down at the cowering Chaz and confronted him.

'See! You're not nice and good! You did that ta big fluffy bunny rabbits! Didn't he, TV?'

TV felt obliged to say something on behalf of the animal friendly philosophies of the new cult.

'The Dragon Star children would never do that, Freeda! Never! The Dragon Star only catch fish like Jesus did, Freeda! They would never kill fluffy bunny rabbits, Freeda. Never, Freeda!'

Within a few moments the duo had taken up the 'They'd never kill fluffy bunny rabbits!' mantra. They kept chanting it and chanting it and the chant got louder and louder and they stamped their feet in unison and rhythm, with hands in the air. Freeda wielded the knife and TV spontaneously picked up a dildo accompanying her and the chanting got quicker and quicker until reaching its inevitable crescendo, with Freeda's anger boiling over. 'They'd never kill fluffy bunny rabbits!' She plunged the knife into that bondage chair, ripping the seat to shreds.

Chaz's life was hanging on a thread that could be broken any moment. He was held over a precipice, balancing on the whims of this 'Mad Freeda' with that knife in her hand, shouting off about fluffy bunny rabbits. Every fear that Chaz had, in coming to this dream house, had become, not only realized, but magnified, ten-fold. He was living his worst nightmare now.

TV was drawn back to his curious engagement with the fucking machine, trying to find its on/off switch, and he wasn't really noticing how Freeda was moving towards a terrible denouement with the Blazerman. TV just wanted to find out how the odd machine worked, but Freeda had the blade directed with a fearful intensity at Chaz, as he cowed in the corner.

'Freeda's gonna chop your head right fucking off! Right fucking off! And put it out to roast on Fishgate pier in one of those heatwave fingys!'

Chaz was thinking about just going for it. It wasn't far off the last rites, and he would have to take his chance. Freeda turned towards TV who wasn't taking a blind bit of notice as he was fiddling around with that fucking machine.

'Wouldn't it look good, TV? TV! Wouldn't it look good?'

Freeda had always remembered Fishgate, although even those nice memories were counterbalanced by the darkness of Barry and his sexual abuse. But she recalled the sunshine and the caravan park they had stayed in a number of times, and by coincidence, on one occasion, positioned right next to where the Barbers had their caravan going back. If Chaz had a vivid enough memory and knew the actual facts, he would have realized he and Linda met Freeda as she played outside her caravan on her much-loved *Sesame Street* pedal car. It can be a small world. Freeda always remembered holding her mummy's hand on the beach, licking ice-cream. That hand was a loving hand, but even though she blocked out Barry at Fishgate, as much as she could, the sheer trauma that was Barry meant she couldn't for long. He was always abusing her. TV was only half listening as he was still perusing that bizarre machine in search of the elusive 'off we go' switch.

'Spose it would, but Fishgate's a long, long way, Freeda.'

Chaz was still hanging over the precipice with these perpetrators of dark torture deliberating on a whimsy. He had to try another ruse, and if he interested them in eight grand, why not go further and offer them more. Chuck um the seventy!

'Please! I'll make you both filthy, stinking rich! I've got seventy grand; you can have it right now!'

But TV sneered back at Chaz, and Freeda followed TV's lead. The Dragon Star weren't materialistic. Money was a means and nothing more was the cult's philosophy. TV spread out the wad of money they already had, as if he had it in his pocket all the time.

'We got loads of money! Look! Tons!' and TV was backed up by Freeda.

'Yeah shut up, Blazer-Dicky! We've got money. Me and TV have always had money and Freeda's got loads more money in her purse, haven't I, TV?'

The two were resisting simply being bought off, and the way forward was clarifying in Freeda's mind's eye. She fired off her intent with loads of enthusiasm.

'I know what we could do! We could put his head on that washing line pole in the garden, so we didn't have to go all the way to Fishgate! What about it, TV? It would go with your flag! Let's do it like those shoes keep telling us to!'

TV was still searching for that elusive switch on the fucking machine, but now his mind was diverted. Freeda had spun that 'head off the Blazerman' idea right out, now it was his turn. TV was enthusiastic, and Chaz was rapidly coming to that moment, where he would have to just take his chance and to hell with the consequences.

'It would be like a totem pole, Freeda! And ya could put his dick on the lawn for the foxes like ya did Barry's. And we'd be famous, Freeda! Fame's massive these days! And "Dragon Star" would be mega, mega famous!'

Chaz was now primed and ready to strike. He reckoned if he could get that knife, he could stab one of them and the other might just break down. It was his only chance.

'What, more than those *Big Brother* blokes, TV?' Freeda replied, knowing full well that the Big Brothers, whoever they were, were famous. Everyone was talking about them in the ward, everyone.

'Loads more, Freeda!'

Freeda couldn't believe it. To think that her and TV could be the most famous people in the whole wide world. TV elaborated.

'Everybody would be talking about us, Freeda! They'd write books about us. And there'd be documentaries on the telly about us. And there'd even be a Hollywood movie about us! There's bound to be!'

Linda just had to have her say again. She was distraught but she had too.

'Please don't do any nasty things to us! Please!'

But Freeda didn't hear her pleas. She laughed hysterically, as she found that doggy mask so funny.

'Don't the Blazerwoman look all funny, all nudey in her doggy mask, TV! Shouting out fings!'

The odd irony was the crazy sex machine became something of a temporary savior. TV was about to answer Freeda, but he finally found that switch, clicked it, and set the machine off, with the ginormous phallic knob thrusting back and forth. It was the fucking machine savior as Freeda's attention was diverted away from the decapitation.

'Look, Freeda! It's a fucking machine! A big wangher dangher fucking machine! He must stick it up Blazerwoman's fanny when he's doing his blue films, Freeda!'

Freeda hadn't seen anything like this before, and she wanted to get close up to it. She was in disbelief.

'Freeda wants to see the big fucking machine! Freeda wants to see it wangher danghering!'

For a second, Chaz thought he might have his chance to get to the door, but it was gone a moment later, as TV held Freeda to her discipline.

'Nah, Freeda, keep him pinned down! It's got wheels, I'll bring it over.'

Freeda was astounded as TV wheeled it across to her and then put the brakes on. But as it was wangher-danghering away, TV became fascinated with admiring himself in the many mirrors of the Dark Room. It was the white blazer. He had never seen himself in a white blazer before, and he had wanted one for donkeys' years. He still didn't have anything on though, apart from that blazer and a T-shirt with Dragon Star emblazoned on it, and those now infamous sandals of Jesus's. But he didn't care because it didn't matter. Everyone had seen his big wangher dangling, so why not let it freely dangle.

'Dun I look good in the white blazer, Freed!' Freeda wanted to support her TV.

'You look like a real White Blazerman, TV. A *real* one, without ya pants on!' Freeda giggled hysterically. 'Not a pretend one, like him!' she added.

Freeda gestured with her knife towards Chaz, as if he was garbage. 'But that fucking machine TV! That wangher-dangher fucking machine! Ain't it funny, TV? Ain't it funny?'

The machine was still wangher-danghering and thrusting away, but TV remained in the rarefied zone and air of the white blazer. It was unreal that now he was actually wearing one like Keefy's and to think how it made his cock feel like a wizard's wand. He wanted to show it off to people. This was the real TV, wearing the white blazer so he had a special "Dragon Star" cock!'

'Wait till Drill-head and Dan see it! All the members and the associates and that Delgardo in Spain and Anton in Brazil, Freeda!' TV enthused, somewhat transfixed by his mirror image. He was already thinking about sending the oversea members of the cult, photos of himself in the white blazer. All of the Dragon Star had to see TV, the cult's head man with a white blazer on, like Keefy's.

'You'll have to put a pair of pants on, TV!'

It was all about origins and the sense of history with Keefy. Continuity and all that. But Freeda was thinking about that machine thrusting back and forth, as TV shuffled around, still admiring himself in the mirrors. This was a suave look. It was all how it was supposed to be, befitting the new leader of the cult. But Freeda was perplexed by that darn machine.

With all the talk about chopping his head off and putting it up on the line-pole in the garden, Chaz just had to make his move. Their concentration had wandered, but Chaz wanted to pre-empt them before it returned. If he could get that knife he would wound one of them, and then release Linda and get out of there. With Freeda's attention on TV wearing that white blazer, Chaz acted swiftly and punched Freeda's wrist as hard as he could. The knife flew from her hand and Chaz quickly retrieved it from the floor, just what he'd hoped. This was end games now. He was going to stab Freeda, he didn't really want to, but it was survival. He just had to do it.

But Chaz hadn't factored in the incredible speed and agility of TV Sam. As soon as Chaz had the knife in his hand, and had it raised in earnest, TV kicked it out, with the flat of his Jesus's sandal, and with the other foot he kicked Chaz as hard as he could in the stomach. The blow was on the already damaged muscles, and Chaz was in so much pain, he now had little chance of making any impact. He groaned and was expecting the worst. But with the deed done, TV was now reiterating how special these Jesus's sandals were. They were like special protectors.

'We could do anything with his sandals on, Freeda! Anything!'

But the kick had been right on that bad toe of his. The one that had taken the strains of the kicked in widescreen.

'Another miracle, Freeda! The fourth! It's proof that Jesus is alive and kicking, Freeda. But keep the knife at his throat!'

TV had a laugh at the joke but he hobbled and grimaced, 'Fuck it! Me big toe flipping hurts again Freeda! It's fucking killing me!'

'That toe of yours been giving ya some trouble lately, ain't it?'

Freeda returned her attention towards their prisoner Chaz. She waved that knife at him but Chaz was disabled somewhat, because as soon as he moved, that stomach gave him pain. Freeda had a good plan to keep this Blazerman quiet.

'Shall I slicey, slicey, from this side to that side! He'd shut the fuck up then!'

TV was reflecting, but brought himself back to dignity by pulling his pants up, while still admiring himself with that white blazer on, in the myriad of mirrors. He had a wide grin on his face and the ecstasy that blazer brought him, filled him up with endorphins, that counteracted the throb of that big toe. That fucking machine was still fucking away relentlessly, and Freeda wanted an answer. She fancied cutting the Blazerman's throat. Her wrist hurt and fancy picking up a knife and threatening them with it?

'Shall I cut his throat, TV?'

'Hold on, Freeda!'

TV brought a temporary demise to the tension with a new diversion. There was a large wardrobe along one of the walls and TV was curious. Anything was possible with these Blazerpeople. He slid the door open that was on runners, and there was yet another treasure trove of the weird and wonderful. Staring at him were two silicon dolls, 2003 AD top-of-the-range. One was a lifelike male with an enormous veined penis. The other was a similarly looking lifelike porn star beauty of a female. There were also a couple of odd torsos on a shelf, a male half body with a large penis and a vagina and anus too. Like a best of all the worlds non-binary gender, multi-tasking doll. Chaz had paid thousands for them. TV was astounded.

'Look, Freeda! They've got sex dolls. I've read about them in the papers! Look! Weirdy sex dolls, Freed!'

Freeda rushed over to the wardrobe and Chaz looked to the door as he toyed with the idea of trying to get there. Chaz moved but flinched in pain, and TV saw him with that intent, so he sneered and gestured, as if to say 'you move and I'll give you another kick'. Freeda screwed her face up, frowning in disbelief at the male silicon, nigh full height doll, that had a sculptured torso, perfectly defined with that big cock, but crucially smaller than TV's. Freeda smirked, then looked dumfounded, thought a bit, then smirked again as the doll had an uncanny resemblance to TV. All it needed was a green wig and a Dragon Star cap and of course the white blazer now.

'It looks like you, TV!'

TV was still admiring himself in those mirrors and he wasn't paying close attention.

'Nah, Freeda, it's a weirdy sex doll, Freeda!'

Freeda kept claiming that it looked like him, and he eventually took another look. He stood in front of it and even TV was puzzled. He could see that uncanny resemblance himself.

'Spose it does a bit, Freed!'

Freeda inevitably became interested with the torso that carried all genitalia.

'Look! This one's had its head chopped off! It's got boobies, a big wangher-dangher and a fanny, TV! Look!' she said, pulling it about exploring its oddity. TV reflected on the weird doll for a few seconds.

'It's got everything, Freeda. They must do kinky films with um!'

TV looked around the room and at Chaz, and ideas came to him. He thought it would be fair if Freeda had a crack of the whip.

'Freeda! I know! Why don't we tie Blazerman up and that, with the cuffs and chains, and then you can have ya sexy-thang with him, Freeda!' The idea seemed to hit the right note.

'Oh yeah, TV! My sexy-thang! I've got to have my sexy-thang with him, TV, haven't I?'

But Freeda kept glancing at that odd sex doll that looked like TV. It was all so odd at the Blazerpeople's house.

Meanwhile, TV was trying to figure out a bondage swing that had a pillow type thing on it. He was thinking about Blazerman and Freeda, and he noticed how Blazerman seemed to be in pain with his stomach. He wanted to show compassion, as that was the philosophy of the burgeoning cult. Their goal was to bring love, peace and unity, all with a cosmic shag, wherever they went. It was the credo of the Dragon.

'We could put him in this swing fing, Freeda. He would be comfortable with his head on the pillow, Freed!'

But Freeda had other fingys on her mind. She wanted to look at those big fishes in the lounge again.

'But Freeda wants her sexy-thang downstairs, TV. I want to see those big fishes sucking scholongers and the octopuses, in that red telephone box fingy!'

'Yeah, why not? If that's the way ya want him, Freeda, why not?'

TV helped Chaz up and Freeda came up with a good idea. She said that Blazerman wasn't the *real* Blazerman anymore and that he should have his blazer taken away, so people wouldn't get confused between TV and the old Blazerman.

'He's got his flashy shirt! He don't need it, TV!'

'Yeah! That's a great idea, Freeda! Take it off, Blazerman!'

Chaz took it off, struggling a little, as he felt a few spasms in his damaged muscles. With the blazer off, they sat Chaz in the bondage chair, yet another of the top of range items that Chaz had purchased which was solid and weighty but ripped to pieces.

'Well strap him in, Freeda, so that he can never, ever get away!'

There was plenty of strapping around for that.

CHAPTER EIGHTEEN

FISH AND CHIPS AND POLITICAL INCORRECTNESS

'Cuckoo! Cuckoo! Cuckoo!'

The bird came out of its turret, announced that it was a quarter past five, and disappeared just as quick. Henry looked up at the clock rather concerned, as the bird shouldn't have come out on the quarter. It was a half past and the hours bird, and it all added to the knife edge tension in the air. It was the intolerable wait for Adult Leisure that was doing it, with the additional problem of Sylvester's text to the young German lady. It was all on yesterday but the text he sent half an hour ago hadn't got a reply. Sylvester rang her but her mobile was on answer, and he left a message. But there was still no reply.

'Can't you stop that pestering cuckoo, Henry. The bloody thing needs shooting!'

The cuckoo, seemingly in defiance of Sylvester, came out for an impromptu off the cuff 'cuckoo' and went back inside his turret. 'Fucking turn it off, Henry!' Sylvester snapped with a touch of genuine Sylvester venom. Cecil could recognize Henry was under pressure as he was terrified of Sylvester in such a foul mood.

'I think you ought to take it back for Davis's to look at again, Henry. It shouldn't be coming out on the quarters and when it feels like it. It would become rather annoying if it did, Henry,' Cecil suggested. Sylvester's patience wasn't wearing thin, there just wasn't any.

'He's gone well past fucking annoying. I'd stick it up out the back and fucking shoot it!'

Sylvester struggled up with his stick and turned the cuckoo off on a switch, although he hadn't done that properly, and it was still set to go off on the half past. Cecil was similarly annoyed about this Adult Leisure hold up, as he had come up with this wonderful re-union idea, and he could appreciate how much of a perfectionist Sylvester was. That was Sylvester's character. Henry sat down again and was now under attack from both sides. Cecil had to have his say.

'It's bloody disgraceful, Henry. Me and Sylvester liberated Europe for the likes of him! Get him on the blower again, Henry!'

Henry got up again and went back out to the rotary telephone, dialed and there was no reply. He waited and waited but there was nothing. What was happening? As he put the phone down another Luftwaffe salvo hit the front room.

'Oh, for fuck's sake!' Sylvester reeled.

'What's up, Sylvester?' asked Cecil, knowing full well something of great significance had come through as a text.

'That fucking German whore has pulled out! The fucking whore! That's what's fucking up!'

Cecil was aghast.

'What? She can't do that! We've already paid her three hundred, Sylvester!'

'Well, she fucking well has. Says one of her kids has gone down with diarrhea and sickness.'

As he spoke, yet another text came in suggesting the meet up should be postponed until next week. Same day, same time, and same place. But it wasn't that easy for Sylvester, as he had to go in hospital Monday next for his long-awaited hip operation. 'Cuckoo!' The bloody thing seemed to come out of its turret specially to rub it in to Sylvester's wounds.

'Poxy fucking bird!'

Sylvester threw his vodka glass across the room at it and caught the decorative edge of the clock. Henry was accepting. He realized how Sylvester was feeling and Cecil put the debacle into its context.

'It's turning out worse than Market Garden, Sylvester.'

'At least we had the bloody chance to shoot at Nazis there Cecil!' When Cecil got like this, he could be very difficult and abusive.

It wasn't much better than Market Garden back in Holly Beach Lane as Chaz was now strapped down hard in the chair.

'Right, Freeda, you get that end and I'll get this, and we'll carry him down.'

Freeda was still fascinated by those doggy masks, and there was another one up on the wall exactly the same as the one on Linda.

'Shall we put a doggy mask on him, TV, so both the Blazerpeople are like doggies?' It was all such good fun. When Freeda reached for the mask, she came across another that was behind it. The same thing but with a black penis as a nose. Within a few moments Chaz was a doggy too, but with a big black cock of a hooter, and he was now readied to be hauled downstairs for a sexy vigil with Freeda in paroxysms.

'TV! The Blazerman's nose. He's got a big black dick, TV! Look, TV!'

They desperately struggled to get Chaz and the chair to the stairs, and saw it was going to be awkward carrying him down, as Chaz was a heavy lump, but TV had an idea.

'I know what! We can slide him down, Freeda!'

Once they got the chair down a little way, they let it go and TV helped it round the bend and then gave it an almighty push and it slid to the bottom like a mat on a helter-skelter. Chaz landed awkwardly, crying out in agony as TV and Freeda hooped and hollered.

'He's on the helter-skelter at Fishgate, Freeda! Whoop-hay!'

Then they hauled the chair and a groaning Chaz into the front lounge and set it up, in front of the coffee table. It took a bit of effort but as soon as the chair was in position, Freeda had plans for that 'sexy-thang'.

Now Dr. Greene-Burrows didn't think it a good idea in the circumstances, but Catherine insisted she go out for a jog. She had missed her habitual run in the morning, after Jeremy had dropped a pint of milk in the kitchen and she cleared all the glass up, but now she was determined to get it in before tea. She intended to run up the lane and take a pathway into the large asylum fields for her usual three miles. That afternoon a pair of half kilo weights, especially for runners, had arrived in the post, and she wanted to try them out. She chose her fireworks blaze leotard as she loved the freedom, leotards gave her running action. It was a recovery run on her schedule today, a training regime all progressing to the Tennin half marathon in July, and she came past 'Chaz's Pad' completely unaware of what was taking place. She glanced at the Jag and thought about Jeremy. He could be so staid and unexciting. She also thought about Chaz's style again. It was certainly unforgettable; with that white blazer and those colorful shirts she had seen him in, and those expensive shoes. He certainly cut a dash, she thought. As Jeremy said the other night in bed, he was likely to be involved in 'marginal activities', but there was still a whiff of excitement around him. She passed, and off she went up Holly Beach Lane, in her brightly colored leotard as Freeda entered the lounge, busying herself with her sexy-thang.

'I'm going to pull his pants down and suck his wangher!'

'Yeah, he's all there for ya, Freeda. Yeah, give it a suck. He probably does it to his sex dolls, the pervert!'

'Yeah, he's a fucking pervert with his weirdy dolls! Fucking pervert hooter! Pervert hooter!' Freeda shouted into Chaz's masked face.

Freeda laughed and went for it, unzipping Chaz's jeans and dragging his trousers and pants down, and further bursting into hysterical laughter, upon seeing the Blazerman's penis. It was so much smaller, tiny, compared to TV's big whopper.

'He's got a little wangher! He's got a little weeny dicky, TV!'

TV was more interested in looking at himself in the oval mirror. He just couldn't get over it. He had a white blazer on, but he glanced over and took a look.

'It's tiny, Freeda! It don't dangle like mine. I can't believe it, Freeda!'

TV was still shuffling in front of the mirror, giving himself differing perspectives. He knew he looked so photogenic in it. But the leader of the Dragon Star children, had to be like that. He had to have shining star quality and stand out beyond the crowd.

'I've got so many white blazers now, Freed! And they make me cock all magical! It's like a fucking bonk wand! I fink I'll shag her brains out again. Me cock's telling me to do it! I've gottta shag her brains right out, Freeda!'

Freeda had moved her 'sexy-thang' on a level or two, and she was giving Chaz some kind of oral sex experience, but his penis just wasn't responding. It just couldn't get hard. TV was still obsessed with that mirror and his blazer, and his magic wand *was* beginning to twitch. It was getting the whomper back on! He had to get it up Linda again.

'His dicky won't get hard, TV!'

But TV's cock was, and it was beginning to burst upright out of his pants.

'He's old and that. They don't go on standing up forever, Freeda! They sorta lie down and forget to get up again!'

'He's fucking clapped out! His knob's fucking useless!' All of a sudden TV fancied more of those sweets, and some honey, and Freeda could have some too.

'I'm gonna get more of those sweets, Freeda, out of the shed. We can have them with that honey, Freed!'

'Yeah, I can have my strawberry ones, TV! I like my strawberry boiled! Um!'

Meanwhile, Linda was still strapped tight onto that bondage horse, there was no way she could escape. She prayed that Chaz was all right, but she feared that something terrible had befallen him. The sexual assault and rape had created an awful ambivalence in Linda too. She resisted that penis. She had to. That TV was raping her – that's what it was, rape – but eventually that cock had carried her away on a tide of erotic ecstasy. She loved it. The more she fought against it, wishing that she wouldn't experience pleasure and intensity, the more she had felt it and thoroughly loved it and furthermore, she was hotly desirous for more! It was as if that TV had carried her over some kind of threshold. But then that rational mind kicked in. She had been tied up and raped. There was nothing consensual in what had taken place. TV had forced it upon her. It was an outrage! But Linda was agonizing as she so desperately wanted TV's cock up her again. She ejaculated merely thinking about it, because the experience had overwhelmed her. She wanted more of that cock! That perfect cock! That TV had a magic wand in his pants. He was a sex god!

TV went back out to the old shed with Freeda in hot pursuit. He reckoned that both the Blazerpeople weren't going anywhere, so it didn't matter. He stood at the porch opening, making sure that nobody was around. But it was all clear and down to the new shed they went for more sweets.

Chaz's legs were strapped to the chair's legs, his arms to its arms and he was even fastened across the chest, until he could only move his head. He turned it to the right to look at the mantel piece. He focused his eyes on Jesus on the cross, that stood high above the cow skull and all the photos, up there on the middle of the breast. It was there precisely for faith purposes when times were bad, and times had never been as bad! He was lucky he hadn't had his head sawn off, yet an hour or so ago, he had been laughing at flying ducks and a cuckoo clock! It made him feel ill, but Chaz still prayed that God would get them out of this ordeal unscathed. But the way that Linda had responded upstairs. No, Chaz didn't like that. What the hell was going on?

Within a few minutes, TV and Freeda had bowls of sweets and honey on the coffee table, and Freeda was on top of Chaz going for the hump with a mouthful of strawberry passions and honey. She was doing her best, humping up and down on Chaz, and red honey saliva was running out of her mouth, dribbling all over him. But TV wasn't taking much notice. He knew that she would never get to seventh heaven with the Blazerman. TV was pinning those delicious blues with a cocktail stick he had found, and was thoroughly enjoying dipping them into the honey, getting that extra flavor, while he was ensconced in that furry chair. Freeda was sneering and becoming quickly disgruntled with Chaz and his penis, and she also fancied sitting in that furry chair again. She wanted one up the prison now. But TV looked comfortable though, with his feet up on the coffee table and he was utterly spellbound by those big fishes. Freeda was still trying but she recognized that it was all futile. She came to an abrupt halt with an admission of failure.

'He's fucking useless, TV! His cock's fucking useless!'

TV was meditating upon the subtle movement of Hermann's gills and fins in the tank, and he was thinking about Jesus's sandals and the way that Jesus fed the multitudes with his fish. But TV smiled, as seventh heaven and new earths, and cosmic shagging weren't for the unenlightened. That was for fully paid up members of Dragon Star and ones who had been receptacles of the seed.

'I told ya, Freeda, his nob's fucking clapped out.'

TV had his attention bang on 'The Beak' when he popped Freeda the question.

'Do ya fancy fish and chips, Freeda?' We've got loads of um here, Freeda! Loads!'

Freeda was still on top of Chaz on the bondage chair ready to give up once and for all, and she really felt hungry. She fancied some fish and chips.

'Freeda wants some fish and chips, TV! Freeda wants the fish and chips!'

TV raised himself in a flash and promptly extracted the flapping Beak out of the tank.

'It'll be fresh, Freeda! Like the fish in Jesus's baskets!'

Freeda had to get off this flaccid Blazerman, but she had eaten so many of the darn strawberry boilies that she heaved and puked the bile all over Chaz. Chaz was afflicted with nausea and he was heaving and puking in his mask. He felt disgusted. But the carp was flapping furiously about in TV's hands and out it went as it continued beating away on the white rug next to Chaz on his bondage chair.

'Er, it's flapping! It's all flapping about, TV! It's all flapping about and that!

TV hastily retrieved the fish from the carpet.

'Spose it is, Freeda!' TV took the waggling fish out into the kitchen, where it managed to get out of his hands again, through its sheer slippery power. By now Freeda had finally given up and decided enough was enough. Sex with the old Blazerman was boring.

'He's useless at sex, TV! Useless!' Freeda protested, as TV looked around for something to deal with this fish that just wouldn't stop flapping.

'I told yah, his knob's clapped out, Freeda!'

TV opened a drawer by the sink and found a rolling pin. He grabbed it and without hesitation, gave the big fish a good whack on the snout and then another one. Both solid blows. The fish gradually but inexorably flapped, then twitched to its rest. It was a nice fresh fish.

'It's stopped flapping about now, Freeda!'

Freeda, now off Blazerman, sped out into the kitchen with all her usual zest and high energy. She wanted to see that big fishy ready for cooking.

'Freeda wants to see! The fish that's stopped flapping, TV! Freeda wants to see it!'

The carp was now lying on the surface by the sink, ready for filleting.

'I'm making fish and chips for ya, Freeda, and it's gonna be nice, cos I wanna show how much I love ya, Freeda! Look, it's all ready and fresh!'

Freeda smiled lovingly and she bent her head over the sink with her nose nearly touching the fish's skin. She then turned sharply, because fish and chips were her favorite meal.

'Freeda wants the fish and chips! But no bones, TV! Freeda don't like bones! They get stuck in my throat! Freeda has her special fish, special fish with no bones!'

TV looked at Freeda a little anxiously, as he was now under pressure to serve up the fish without bones. He wanted to say that the special, was fish that was processed, that was filleted before packaging. But he knew that wouldn't be enough to appease Freeda. He'd just have to give it his best shot. With Chaz and Linda nicely trussed up, Freeda hung around the kitchen to help TV make the fish and chips. TV filleted the fish as best he could, and even knocked up some batter and the fillets were frying in a large pan and Freeda nearly had her nose in it. TV nudged her.

'Mind, Freeda! It'll spit you in the eye, like a big snake!'

TV handed Freeda the steel turner.

'You look after them, Freeda! But turn them over and make sure they don't burn! I fink I'll go and get Blazerwoman.'

'All right, TV!' Freeda said, determined to turn the fish over, so that Jesus's fresh fish didn't burn. TV stopped at the kitchen threshold for a moment. He couldn't resist it.

'I fink I might shag her again before I come down, Freed!'

'All right, TV!' Freeda replied again, while concentrating on cooking the fish. TV moved through the lounge warning Chaz not to try any more tricks.

'And don't you try anything, Blazerman, with ya clapped-out cock! Cos if you do, Freeda will have it off! Clean off! Right!'

Freeda rushed through into the lounge laughing, taunting Chaz who didn't say a word. He thought he just had to sit it out patiently and pray. She turned and rushed back out to the kitchen to get back to her fish and chips. She was determined they wouldn't burn. But then she felt as if she wanted to taunt that Blazerman in his flashy shirt and doggy mask a little bit more. It'd be fun. She rushed to the threshold, reinforcing TV's threats.

'And don't you try and escape from your chair old Blazerman, cos if you do, Freeda will have your little weeny dick off!' Freeda laughed her way back to the fish in the pan. She was so determined not to let that fish burn and she kept telling herself in a mantra to keep the vigilance. 'Freeda mustn't let the fish and chips burn! Freeda mustn't let the fish and chips burny, burny! Freeda wouldn't let the fish burn! Never! Never in a hundred years! She would never mess up the fish and chips! Never!'

TV entered the Dark Room, but before he got down to yet more disseminating business for the legacy, he thought he'd better remind Freeda again about making sure. He went back down the stairs a little and shouted down.

'Make sure ya turn the fish over, Freeda! Will ya!'

But Freeda was being diligent. She was watching that fish cook like a hawk, but she rushed through the lounge to get to the foot of the stairs.

'Ya can count on Freeda, TV. She'd never let the fish and chips burn in a hundred million years!'

Within a few moments Freeda was back in the kitchen turning the chips this way and that, while TV set to the ongoing vigil of shagging Linda's brains out with the white blazer. His cock was ramrod hard and TV could feel its arcane esoteric power, as he plugged it into Linda's sex circuitry. Dragon Star had to shag people to the stars and now TV had the chance with that white blazer on to smash Linda's brains with the cults cosmic orgasmic light. His thrusts were long, hard, powerful and deep, with those mad staccato phrases. Once TV got into rhythmical gear, it sounded like the entire upstairs was shaking and reverberating, in some colossal and magnificent sexual power. Freeda looked to the ceiling from the kitchen, thinking the ceiling was going to collapse, so Freeda knew something very special was happening. TV had always gone on about this kind of stuff. He had warned her, as the leader of the cult, he would initially, have to 'put it about a bit'.

Freeda felt compelled to go back into the lounge and taunt that Blazerman some more, because he didn't have a special cock like TV's. His was like an old clapped-out banger, and he couldn't get it up, but TV's was like a skyrocket, that was a gateway to the galaxies, all down there tucked in his pants, waiting for the rock hard whomper. She went right up to the doggy mask, laughing at the old Blazerman's hooter cock, and she shouted right in that doggy's face.

'TV's shagging Mrs. Blazerwoman's brains out again! Making her one of us! Not one of youse! And there's nuffin' you can do about it is there, big nose! Nuffin'! Not nuffin'! Sitting there with that big cock on your nose! In ya flashy shirt! With ya pants round your ankles!'

Chaz just had to say something back and his response was spontaneous.

'You're evil! Pure evil!' Chaz muffled through the mask.

'Evil! TV's not evil! He's got to put his seeds about for the Dragon Team!'

Linda tried to restrain herself again. She thought about that Zen like detachment that she had read about in the paper a few weeks ago, but it was all useless. There was something about that fantastic golden cock, and as soon as it was up her, it was abandonment. She wanted more and more, and lashings more after that. All resistance was just smashed down each time TV thrust it back and forth like a great threshing machine. Linda was a bacchanal, wanton for the god.

'Fizz bang light! Seventh heaven!' TV exclaimed, moving towards incoherence yet again, as he exalted in the ecstasy.

'Fuck me harder! Fuck me harder you bastard!' was Linda's lewd response, that reverberated and echoed around the house. Freeda heard it all and rushed from the kitchen and sped upstairs. She just had to watch it and give vocal support. She entered that Dark Room exhorting TV to sow that seed for the dragon.

'Spunk her, TV! Shag her brains out and spunk her! Give her the dragon! Give it to her, TV!'

Linda was moaning and groaning in pure exalted ecstasy, as TV led her up into those super orgasmic realms, that were pivotal to the cult's philosophies. He turned his head for a moment towards Freeda, and restrained from his deep thrusts, although Linda was goading him onward, as she just wanted more and more.

'She hecking loves me cock, Freed! She loves it! But you're supposed to be watching the fish and chips, Freeda! They'll get burnt! Get down there and turn the fish over, Freeda! Get the fuck down there!'

TV returned to his deep thrusting and Linda was responding, gripping her sphincter muscles and pushing her sex power to meet that god of a thrusting magical cock. Her desire was nigh manic now. It was building and building. She was lust incarnate. That magical sex organ was blowing her brains out. She could feel it erasing layers and layers of sediment in her brain, it was bringing light to a darkness in her mind. She was seeing things she had never seen before! New worlds!

'Yes! Yes! That cock! Give me more of that fantastic fucking cock!'

Chaz could hear all the ecstatic grunts and exclamations and he grappled with the indignity of it all. He felt disgusted with her. She was acting like a cheap whore.

At that very moment the elderly fellow who had warned Chaz about the snake-infested Holly Beach Lane, was walking his dog past the horse chestnut tree. The dog stopped and had a pee up the tree, on what was one of the old fellows twice weekly long walks up to the back entrance of the asylum, and low and behold, up went that lurid and crazed, lusty ecstasis, of Linda. Being out of the way Chaz hadn't bothered about sound proofing and the top section of the back window behind the plush velvet curtains was opened a tad. Linda's lewd wails pierced the Holly Beach Lane quietude.

'Give me more of that cock! Harder, you bastard! Harder!' The old fellow was astonished.

'Flipping heck, Butch!' he said in jest to his dog, while raising his eyebrows in utter disbelief. Catherine returned down Holly Beach Lane on her run, tiring now, ready to get back indoors for a hot refreshing shower. She passed the back of the house when Linda's hotly desirous cry came up again.

'Fuck me harder, you bastard! I want more of it! Give me that cock, you bastard! That incredible fucking cock!'

She heard it all as she wasn't moving very quickly, and she was shocked. She reached the horse chestnut and the elderly fellow turned to her with an apt one-liner as she passed.

'Looks like some women are getting it these days,' he said, and Catherine smiled. She jogged down the road and had never felt such a turn on in all her life. The sheer ecstasy and lust of Linda had overcome her. That guy must be something else, she thought! She just couldn't believe it! What on earth were they doing! She could tell the woman had some kind of mask on as the voice sounded muffled. It just made it more transgressive and erotic. When she got in, the house was empty as Jeffrey had gone to chess club. She went straight up into the bedroom and masturbated herself, and it became extremely vigorous, fingers and then a shameless abandoned fist, as she fantasied about that man in the white blazer. She kept hearing the woman's voice in her mind and felt ablaze with a hot bacchanalian lust, taking herself to an intense shuddering and throat groaning orgasm. It was all so spontaneous, so shameless, and now that house just a hundred or so yards up the road, embodied something dark and shockingly libidinous. She had never heard such wanton cries of lust. Those orgasmic cries called out an erotic liberation that shocked Catherine to the core. How she wanted to taste and gorge on that ecstasy. That man in the white blazer was now positioned firmly in her imagination, as some kind of white-hot sex god, who had an enormously powerful transformative phallus down his pants. Things could never be the same as Chaz had become the site of her deepest and filthiest projections. She proceeded to fuck herself with Jeremy's drink bottle, she was so horny.

After the temporary end to the Dark Room activities, TV unfastened Linda's spread-eagled legs and arms. He then tied her arms behind her back with some of the Velcro restraints, but he kept the mask on. Now that the head of Dragon Star had sown, he wanted to investigate what Linda had said earlier, about that wedding dress. He thought it was sublime synchronicity working.

'Please don't hurt us, TV! Please!' Linda pleaded as she grappled with her feelings. That orgasmic excitement had undermined her deepest sense of self, it was the sheer intensity of her desire. She had exploded with sex power and even as she spoke, she felt the desire relentlessly building for that cock, that wondrous cock!

'You said you had a wedding dress?' TV asked. Linda jumped on the idea, as this might help bide time, until surely somebody would come to the house and end it all.

'Yes! And a necklace and tiara. They're in a box in my wardrobe. You can have them. A present from me and Chaz.'

It seemed that things were beginning to work out well TV thought. An unseen hand was working overtime in his and Freeda's favor. He was inspired, anything was possible with white blazers and Jesus's sandals.

'It would make Freeda so happy if she got married like normal people do,' TV confided.

'She can have them! I'll show you. But please don't hurt us! Please!' Linda pleaded again, although she was feeling that desire, such hot pulsating desire between her legs. She tried to hold herself back but she had that glass of sex juice, full and overflowing with dark eroticism, her rational intellect was trying hard to deny it, but was being smashed to pieces under the onslaught.

'We won't hurt you. You're one of us now,' TV replied, fully convinced that the Blazerwoman had been dragon shagged. But the transition would take time, and for safety purposes, TV tied Linda's legs together, just in case she tried to get out and alert the police. He then picked the naked Linda up in a traditional fire safety carry, and took her to the master bedroom and plonked her down on the bed. He just had to check out that wedding dress.

'It's all in the black box at the bottom of the wardrobe, TV,' Linda said with a glimpse at TV's manhood tucked away. She had now taken to watching for that moment it might get that hard on. What on earth was going on? Linda was struggling as her entire body and psyche were throbbing with lust for that cock, that fantastic cosmic cock!

TV quickly had that big black box out and opened its lid. There it was. A pristine wedding dress that had been put away twenty-two years ago, yet was still perfect. TV opened up, as he held the wedding dress and began to confide in Linda.

'Wow! Freeda will love this! She deserves a wedding dress Linda! Freeda's had such a terrible life. Barry abused her from six years old, until she cut his dick off. And then her mum killed herself, when she found out what had been happening behind her back. He controlled Freeda, so she couldn't speak for herself, speak out for herself. But love makes it better, don't it, and we love each other.'

Linda looked reflective as TV looked over the wedding jewelry, a tiara, necklace and earrings. TV just couldn't believe the way that Dragon Star was manifesting everything and Freeda would love wearing these.

'Freeda will look like a princess! Like a real bride,' he exclaimed.

'Everything is a gift from me and Chaz but please don't hurt us, TV. Please!' The plea was largely aimed at Freeda, as Linda could recognize that TV could influence her.

Freeda had given up any thought of having that 'sexy-thang' with the Blazerman, but she was still drawn away from the fish and chips cooking. It was those big fishes and tanks in the front room. They were like a magnet. They were so different from the guppies and angel fish at the unit, that she liked to watch in her quieter moments. Freeda was entranced with her face near the glass staring at Hermann, talking to herself.

'Big, big fishes!' and Hermann was seemingly staring back at her. With TV upstairs, Chaz thought that he would try a ruse on her. It might just work. He just had to try something and obviously Freeda was the weak link. If he could just, break that link! He appealed to her with a gentle voice with his deepest feeling.

'Freeda, Freeda my dearest,' he asked.

Freeda turned from the tanks sharply, and looked at the Blazerman with his doggy mask on and that funny cock nose. She smirked, but there was a curious look on her face. Chaz continued with his soft voiced tactics.

'Freeda, if you untie my hands and feet, I'll be able to feed those big fishes with you. They would like that, Freeda, and it would be so much fun.'

Freeda frowned at Chaz but his mode of expression clicked with her. She liked the idea of feeding those fishes. She rushed towards Chaz and began undoing the fastenings without saying a word. She giggled and smirked again at that big penis nose jutting outwards, but she was doing exactly what Chaz wanted. Chaz had already schemed a plan in his mind. She would let him loose, and he would persuade her to get that head in the carp tank. Then he would fight the pain and make that rush, as best he could, to the front door and escape. Within no time the place would be crawling pig, it would be all over.

With Freeda's attention diverted away from the fish and chips cooking, it was inevitable they would burn. Off went the fire alarm, upsetting Chaz's plans. Freeda rushed out into the kitchen but she didn't do the obvious thing and turn the heat off, or take the pans from the heat plates. She was quickly glancing round the kitchen looking for the alarm in the hope she could stop it. Frustratingly, Chaz hadn't been undone enough to break out. He was stuck fast as his legs were free but his hands were not. He crouched up with the bondage chair strapped to his arms and uttered a cry of pain, as the weight of the chair pulled on his stomach muscles. Chaz thought about going for the door, but how on earth could he open it, and that bondage chair was heavy. But he had to try. He could push down on the door handle with that mask. It might work and that black penis hooter, might just get him out of this scrape. He struggled out there bent over, as if he had a two hundredweight sack on his back. Freeda rushed into the front room, and she could see the Blazerman trying to open the front door with that big black cock on his hooter. Chaz was contorted with his body wreaked in pain. He pushed it down and tried desperately to hook open the door. But Freeda got him and dragged him back into the front room.

While all this was going on, TV was on the toilet having a crap. He called out to Freeda and when he did return down the stairs that fire alarm was still bleeping madly, but the bondage chair was back in its allotted place. TV grabbed Linda from the bed and carried her downstairs with a fire service carry, while Freeda had rushed back out into the kitchen trying to do something with that grating high pitched alarm. She was desperate to stop it.

'TV! Come and stop it, TV! TV!'

TV entered with the naked Linda over his shoulder into the smoke filled lounge. He couldn't believe it, but he had no inclination that Chaz had nearly escaped.

'Ya let the fish and chips burn, Freeda!'

Freeda tried to divert the criticism, because she knew she hadn't tended the fish and chips properly. But at least she had got that Blazerman back in the lounge. TV didn't have to know that he nearly tricked her.

'You're like a fireman, TV!'

TV plumped the naked Linda down on the settee, and couldn't help correct Freeda's politically incorrect language.

'You're not supposed to say fireman anymore, Freeda,' TV replied, although not offering any explanation. It sounded suspicious to Freeda, something that Lock or Bolt and the big fat nurse were up to.

'Who says! Who says Freeda can't say things!'

TV tried to explain, saying that's how it is everywhere these days but it was all unconvincing to Freeda, and she had plenty to say about it. She bet it was the prison and those nasty doctors and nurses. Why couldn't TV see it?

'Well if it's the Gestapo saying it, TV, Freeda ain't taking no notice!'

In pure defiance Freeda went right into Chaz's personal space, shouting right into that funny doggy mask. 'Fireman! Fireman! Fireman! See!' She turned triumphant to TV.

'Who's gonna do anything about it, eh, TV? The big fat nurse ain't here!'

TV didn't reply because he didn't want to complicate things, but he did notice that the leg ties on the Blazerman were undone. He began retying them and Freeda naturally tried to explain what had occurred.

'He tricked me! He tricked me with that pervert's mask on, TV! He said he was gonna help me feed the big fishes. But he tricked me with that big blackcock on his nose! That's what he did, TV!' The fire alarm was still bleeping away incessantly as more smoke began to funnel into the front lounge, and Freeda had her hands over her ears, as the alarm in the front room was madly bleeping too. 'Oh, turn that noise off! It's giving Freeda a headache! Turn it off, TV!'

TV rushed into the kitchen and opened the back door and turned that heat off. He quickly whizzed along to the porch door and opened that, so that the smoke could clear. The fish and chips were completely black and charred into charcoal. After a short while the alarms came to a halt but the meal had been lost to the kitchen bin, and TV berated Freeda, but tried not to overdo it and upset her. But he rued leaving Freeda all alone cooking.

'We've still got loads of big fishes left, TV! Look! Loads of fish and chips! Blazerman grows um here!' Freeda explained.

'But I asked ya to watch um and not let um burn, while I was shagging her brains out, Freeda.'

Freeda knew she hadn't been good at cooking, but she just couldn't see why TV was making so much fuss. They had loads of those big fishes.

'Fucking hell! Keep ya hair on, TV!'

Freeda then looked at the naked Blazerwoman in her doggy mask. Above Linda was that naked painting of Natasha. It just all seemed so odd to Freeda. Everything was all nudes in this Blazerpeople's house.

It wasn't long before there were only two carp left in the tanks, one in each, and then on the instructions of Freeda, TV was required to put one from the far tank into the tank next to the furry chair.

'We gotta have the two in this tank! Cos it looks good, TV!'

But this time TV would oversee the cooking from start to finish, until the fish and chips were on the plate. He had firmly retied that Blazerman to the bondage chair, and Blazerwoman was lain on the settee with her ankles bound and her arms tied behind her back. While TV was cooking the fish and chips, Freeda was rushing in and out of the lounge, as she wanted to catch a glimpse of those two-remaining carp from the furry chair. She was still obsessed by them.

'TV! We mustn't have any more of the big fishes for fish and chips! Must we, TV?'

TV was tending to the fish and chips out in the kitchen and he called back to her.

'Nah, we'll have to eat some other stuff. Its good fun watching the big fish, Freeda!'

Within a few more moments, Freeda had returned to the kitchen to work with TV on the meal, and Linda, still lain on the Waldorf, whispered to Chaz asking him the obvious question of what they were going to do?

'Well I can't do a fucking lot while I'm strapped to this fucking chair, Linda, can I?' Chaz replied from behind his doggy mask. 'I knew we should never have come to this fucking damned house! I knew it!' he added scornfully. Chaz refrained from saying anything about what had taken place upstairs, but it was a major reason why Chaz was so churlish. Linda felt ashamed of herself. But she didn't want to mention it. She was tearful and she prayed that somehow, they would get out of it all. Chaz's trousers and pants were still around his ankles, stretched out across his bound legs.

'Well let's pray pig comes back!' Chaz added, as it seemed their only chance.

'They've got to, Chaz. They've got to!' Linda replied, and it was a rational argument. They were likely to return with the Barbers so close to the asylum. Surely, they would search a second time.

As the food neared completion, TV and Freeda brought Chaz and Linda into the kitchen to have a sit-down tea. They carried Chaz on the bondage chair and plonked him down around the table, and TV picked Linda up again and placed her on the chair next to him. It was time for the bizarre tea party.

'Tea's ready!' TV announced, having done a real proper job on the cooking this time. Freeda was so excited. Who would have thought?

'Isn't it nice to have tea like a proper, real family, TV!'

TV said that it was 'real proper, like they do in proper families, at the tea table and all that' but it did seem rather different than the normal family tea, with Freeda holding her long knife firmly clasped in her grip on the table for 'security'.

'Dicky and Blazerwoman have come along, haven't they, TV? And Blazerwoman is all in the nudey with her doggy mask on! And Dicky's got that big black cock on his hooter! And he hasn't got any pants on! Has he, TV?'

TV turned his head away from his food preparation.

'He's got his flashy shirt and tie on though, Freeda.'

'I like his flashy shirt! You know what, you'd narf look nice in one of those shirts, TV.'

TV didn't reply but he had seen another one in that big wardrobe and he began to think about it. It would go nice with his new white blazers.

While TV was making tea, they also searched for real strawberries and despite Linda swearing they didn't have any, TV was forced to make the search. The Blazerpeople hid things and Freeda was sure the Blazerpeople were hiding them somewhere, to try and keep them for themselves. The Blazerpeople were like that.

'They hid that wangher dangher fingy, TV! I bet they hide their strawberries. I bet they do!'

The search was all to no avail so it would have to be Blazerman's boiled sweets and custard for Dessert, but Freeda loved those sweets.

Freeda couldn't stop giggling and smirking as TV placed the four plates of food around the table with the fish and chips and sweetcorn perfectly cooked, as TV had done loads of cooking with his aunt Joan back in his teens. He was looking well pleased with himself.

'I told you I'm good at fish and chips, Freeda!'

Freeda loved her fish. She liked her *special* fish, when the fish didn't have any bones in. Back in the past she had some bad experiences with bones getting stuck down her gullet. She had never forgotten them, never.

'And we've got fresh fish from the front room without any bones, haven't we, TV! There're no bones in it is there, TV? No bones! Freeda don't like bones!'

TV was adamant. All bones had been fully removed and Freeda kept going on about how much she loved her fish. She always had it Fridays up at the prison unit, and then it was kippers on Tuesday mornings. She picked up her fork and was about to start on her dinner with the long knife still in her hand.

'Freeda! Ya don't eat dinner with that kind of knife, Freed!'

Freeda put the knife down with a jolt and picked up her dinner knife. She looked at Chaz and smirked and then at Linda and smirked again. It was those pervert doggy masks they were into wearing, and that one that Blazerman liked with the dick on his nose! It was all so funny.

'Aren't the Blazerpeople funny, TV! Freeda has never, ever had dinner with people with doggy masks on.'

She looked at the fish and it looked nice, but she had her doubts about whether it would be like her *special* fish.

'I'm going to have some of my fish without bones first, my *special* fish, TV,' Freeda declared. 'I love my fish without bones, TV! Um!'

Freeda was sure that TV had got all the bones out, but she was still a little suspicious. TV tried to assuage her fears. He had got a lot of bones out of that fish.

'It's a lovely bit of fish, Freeda. Lovely bit,' he kept reaffirming, 'and there's some fresh orange juice there too!'

'I love my orange juices!' she replied, as Freeda had juice every day at the asylum. That was another of Freeda's 'keep her sweet' treats, and part of Dr. Lock's overall strategy of giving them something of what they want, before resorting to coercion, containment, and darn right muscle if need be, although the asylum had gone futuristic over the past years, with the plethora of Dr. Bolt's *special* syrups available. But Freeda was so hungry. She attacked her fish with such great relish and was thoroughly enjoying it, incessantly telling TV how beautiful the fish was. But then the flow of positive fish and chips energy came to a grinding halt. Distress signals were up. A bone had become lodged in her throat and she began to choke a little, with TV looking decidedly uncomfortable.

'It's a lovely bit of fish, Freeda,' TV repeated, hoping that the bone would dislodge and that would be the end of it. But it didn't, and Freeda began to choke and cough more violently with her face getting redder and redder and she was honked off bad.

'You said there wasn't any bones, TV! And Freeda's gotta fucking-bone stuck!' she replied, distressed and angry.

'I tried to get all the bones out, Freeda. I really did, honest!'

Freeda sneered at TV. She was so annoyed. He knew she only liked her *special* fish. She was scathing.

'You know I don't like bones!' Freeda began yet another bout of deep coughing, that was making her asthmatic too.

'Drink some of your orange juice, Freeda!'

Freeda took hold of the glass but she was barking badly, and TV was looking concerned. He helped Freeda drink some more, and with TV fussing over her, Freeda managed to stabilize. As soon as she did, she quietly pushed the fish to one side of the plate. TV was relieved.

'I think Freeda will go on to her chips now, TV.'

Freeda was hungry and the chips and golden corn didn't cause her any more problems. She was quiet as she ate, but as soon as the last chip and last bit of corn was off her plate, she got something off her mind, that had been troubling her.

'Now we've finished our fish and chips, TV, will we be force-feeding the Blazerpeople?'

'Corse we will, but it's not force-feeding Freeda,' TV explained. Freeda had other ideas on the issue.

'Well they do it at the hospital, TV! That fat nurse does it when people don't eat fings!'

TV knew what Freeda was alluding too. It was that tragic affair of Barney Eastwood. TV took up the narrative, so that Freeda could remember more clearly what had occurred back then.

'But that was Barney Eastwood, when he went on hunger strike Freeda. And then it became a battle of wills, Locko's and that against Barney Eastwood's, Freed.'

Freeda remembered loads of stuff about Barney Eastwood.

'Barney Eastwood's dead now, ain't he, TV? There was that song about him!'

TV smiled, but he didn't want to talk about Barney. That upset him too much, and he gestured to Freeda to take up the force-feeding. Freeda unzipped Chaz's mouth zipper and she laughed again at the big black phallic knob that poked out like a nose. She was excited as this was the chance to have some fun with the mummy's and daddy's games.

'Open your mouth, Dicky, cos Mummy is going to force-feed ya.' Chaz was rather reluctant to do so, as he didn't like the idea of playing along with these mad hatter games. But Freeda was nothing but persistent and she admonished her Dicky.

'Open your mouth wider, Dicky! Otherwise Mummy will get all cross and go mad, mad diddlo with her big long knife!' In her gathering excitement she turned towards TV. This was so much fun. 'We're lucky these doggy masks have got a hole, TV!'

'That's right, Freeda! You can get loads of food through the hole! Loads!'

Freeda couldn't wait to start shoving it in. TV scolded Chaz for not complying to Freeda's demands.

'Open ya kisser, Blazerman! Open it! Open ya fucking kisser!'

'Yeah, open ya fucking kisser!' Freeda shouted, so Chaz opened his mouth and Freeda crammed it with chips, and she just kept shoveling them in, chip upon chip. 'I'm gonna put hundreds in, TV! Hundreds!'

TV was eating his fish but he was noticing that hundreds and hundreds would be far too many. He had to say something. There would be too much mess on the tablecloth.

'I fink you're putting too many chips in his mouth, Freeda,' he said, but Freeda didn't take any notice whatsoever, and she kept cramming in chip upon chip, forcing Chaz to keep his mouth open. Scolding him when need be.

'My Dicky loves his chips!' she replied, thinking that it was all part of the game. 'He loves his chips!' Freeda kept shoveling chips and they were slobbering out of Chaz's mouth.

'I said I think you're putting too many chips in his mouth Freeda!'

TV said it again but this time a little louder. Freeda was enjoying this playing mummies and daddies.

'My Dicky loves his chips! But he's just not chewing them nicely enough TV! He's a bad, bad boy! And Mummy will have to give him, her big long sharp knife, if he doesn't eat all his chips up!' Freeda relented for a moment, as she took up her long knife. 'He's not the White Blazerman anymore, is he, TV? You're the proper, proper Blazerman these days! Ain't ya, TV!'

TV was spoon-feeding Linda with little bits of food that weren't causing the same problems.

'Yeah, that's right, Freeda. I've got it now! And I've got five of them, Freeda! And I'm gonna shag Linda's brains out in all but one of them! I keep getting the whomper!'

Freeda just laughed as it was all so funny and especially the Blazerman with that ridiculous nose of his.

'That's all you think about, TV! Shagging Blazerwoman's brains out with ya big wangly dangler!' Freeda was now ladling heaps of sweet corn into Chaz's already crammed mouth, as if the game had turned into some macabre satirical torture. 'Open wider, Dicky! Otherwise Mummy will smack, smack your big fat botty!' Freeda burst out into yet more hysterical laughter, as Chaz swallowed and choked on chips, and the sweet corn dribbled out of his mouth.

'What's up, Freeda?' TV asked.

'Dicky's big fat botty, TV! He's got such a big fat botty!' Freeda said giggling but TV knew, from watching the morning TV, that bottom smacking was illegal these days. You just couldn't do it anymore.

'You're not supposed to smack botties anymore, Freeda!'

Freeda had heard all this type of thing before and she guessed where it came from all right.

'Who says! Who says, TV?' Freeda demanded, and she wasn't going to take any notice, and she bet it was that big fat nurse because she was always trying to stop Freeda. TV tried his best to explain.

'That's what it is these days, Freeda. No botty smacking. They tell you nearly every day on TV, Freed.'

Freeda hadn't heard anything so absurd. If she wanted to smack Dicky's botty, she was going to smack his big fat botty.

'Well after tea, Freeda's going to get Blazerman out of his chair and she's going to smack, smack his botty, TV. And who's gonna stop Freeda! Eh! Who's gonna stop me! That fat nurse ain't here!'

Chaz spluttered on his food, but he felt it incumbent to try another escape ruse. This Freeda was like a child he thought, so why not speak to her as if she really was his mummy. He had to try something, even if it was all a bit pot luck. Something daft might work.

'After tea, Mummy.'

For a moment Freeda looked at the Blazerman a little distrustfully but then she reasoned that it was all part of the game of mummies and daddies they were playing.

'Yes, little Dicky?' Freeda replied, and Chaz had to try something and he went for it. You never know, it might just work.

'Wouldn't it be good Mummy, if you phoned all your friends at the hospital. I think they must be missing you, Mummy, and they'll want to give you a big, big party.'

Linda had the feeling that something like this was inspired. This kind of thing might just trick them and talk of a party seemed too exciting an opportunity for Freeda to miss. She loved parties.

'A party for me, TV! Freeda wants to go! Freeda wants to go! I can show Cheryl my new dress, TV!'

Chaz may have been able to trick Freeda easily, but he would never trick TV.

'He's trying to trick ya with his baby talk, Freeda! So, we give everything away and get caught! So, you'll be back with the big fat nurse!'

Freeda got up abruptly grabbing her long knife off the table, gesticulating with it as if she was about to hack at Chaz's penis.

'Please, no!' Chaz pleaded. Freeda was just about to go through with it and dismember Chaz's manhood, just like she did Barry's, so TV felt compelled to act. TV didn't want to see either of the Blazerpeople hurt. That kind of thing wasn't why he had done that great escape with the electric saw. It was for love and freedom and something special.

'No! The "Dragon Star" children don't wanna to hurt people, Freeda. I've got something else planned. It's a real big surprise for ya.'

369

Freeda screwed her face up, wondering what TV was arranging for her. Big surprises for Freeda was an idea she liked. She smiled with anticipation. It sounded all so exciting. She put the knife down and returned to the mummy and daddy's games, as the sweet was being served, waiting for that big surprise. With the cutting edge dissipated, TV also played along with the game, that Freeda was enjoying so much.

'Let's feed the children, Freeda. There's one for the Blazerwoman and one for the Blazerman!' TV said, as he plonked the bowls in front of them. 'But we'll have to wait for the custard to cool down a little bit, Freeda,' he added.

Now, the custard was smoking hot, but Freeda, always a little impatient, wanted to press ahead.

'My little Dicky loves his hot custard, TV. He always has seconds! Always! Open your mouth! Wider! Come on little Dicky boy, open it, otherwise Mummy will chop, chop, chop off your willy!'

Chaz reluctantly opened his mouth wider and Freeda rammed the boilies and hot custard in, burning Chaz's mouth. He expelled the custard, choking and splattering with a pained cry.

'Naughty little Dicky! Bad Dicky!' Freeda pushed Chaz forward in the bondage chair and began slapping him hard on the back. 'Bad boy Dicky! Trying to eat that much in one go! Mummy 's angry! Bad boy!' Freeda turned to TV, who was trying to cool the custard down on a spoon with blowing, before he fed Linda. But Freeda wasn't going to bother about that. Her Dicky liked his custard piping hot!

'I love playing mummies and daddies, TV!'

TV thought that it had been good fun too, but now TV was considering other things again.

'After tea, Freeda, I fink I'll go back upstairs and shag Linda again. I've got to finish getting her in Dragon Star.'

Freeda was getting a little bit jealous of all this attention that TV was giving the Blazerwoman.

'Freeda will come and watch ya do ya fizz bangers, TV,' she said, hoping that afterwards it would be all for Freeda.

TV was in the process of thinking everything through. They would have to make sure Blazerman was gagged, otherwise he might shout out stuff while TV was shagging Blazerwoman. TV and Freeda then carried Chaz back into the front room on his chair and when TV temporarily removed the doggy mask the sheer strain on Chaz could be seen. He looked ten years older, sweating, red faced and glass eyed. The ordeal was taking its toll. TV went upstairs and collected a roll of heavy-duty tape from the Dark Room, that was there exactly for his purpose. He came down and began to tape Chaz's mouth up, winding the tape around the back of his head a number of times, and as soon as he began, Freeda wanted to have a go.

'Can Freeda do it, TV? Can Freeda tape his kisser up?'

'Course ya can, Freeda. So, he can't shout out fings to the police and that, Freed.'

Freeda scolded the Blazerman. How dare her little Dicky shout out things that Mummy didn't want him to shout!

'Bad boy Dicky. Mummy will have to smack, smack his big fat botty! See, TV! Freeda can say it! Smack, smack, smack the big fat botties!' She burst into cackling laughter as she went around Chaz's head time and time again with the tape, until the whole reel had been used. Once she had finished the roll, she picked up the doggy mask with its black penis protuberance. She was still smirking and giggling. 'Can Freeda put the doggy mask back on him, TV? Can I, TV?'

'Course, Freeda!' TV replied. 'That's why I got you out, so you could do fings, Freeda.'

Freeda then had a wave of inspiration, it was designed to get TV away from his obsession with the Blazerwoman. The old Blazerman had that big fat botty. Why couldn't TV put his whomper up Blazerman's big fat botty? The old Blazerman could be with Dragon Star too!'

'Here, TV! I got an idea! Why don't ya shove ya dick up his bum! Make him "Dragon Star"! Go on, TV! Shove it up his bum!'

Chaz couldn't say anything clearly but there was some mumbling going on underneath the thick tape and doggy mask. Raped by that creep! But TV was more interested in getting Blazerwoman in the seventh heaven. He was working towards that. He had got her there a little bit, and he needed to get her there a little bit more. He hoisted Linda over his shoulder again. The whomper was on!

'Now you just wait here Dicky and don't go away!' Freeda said, as TV just stood there with the naked Linda over his shoulder.

'He won't go anywhere strapped in that chair, Freeda. He's like all the animals caught in his traps. What goes around comes around, eh, Freed?'

Freeda had heard TV always saying that. It was the Dragon Star way. Freeda followed upstairs just wanting to be around her TV, but she was getting really annoyed with all of this shagging the Blazerwoman.

Linda was carried off back up to the Dark Room and her feelings were ambivalent again. As soon as she entered that darn room, she wanted that cock up her. How she wanted that cock! It was like an insatiable desire. Her mind admonished her for feeling like that. She mustn't be wanting it! She and Chaz were being held hostage and threatened with knives, but something just happened, when she was carried into that Dark Room. It hit her like a thunderbolt and the only thing she wanted, and wanted obsessively, was that fantastic cock! TV's cock opened up a door into some infinite orgasmic ecstasy and Linda just wanted more and more. She was gagging for it, and this time TV tied her into a bondage swing for a bit of variety.

'I'm gonna put her in the shagging swing, Freeda!' TV was quick to get Linda into the seat, spreading her legs. Freeda didn't say a word, she was looking perplexed at that sex doll that looked remarkably like TV.

'It'll be something new and wondrous, Freed. And ya know what! I fink I'll put on a fresh blazer, so me dick's more special. I got loads!'

TV left the Dark Room, with Linda now trussed up in the bondage swing with her legs spread-eagled. Freeda was thinking to herself about that doll and some wild ideas came to her mind. There was an odd green wig among all the accessories. TV had green hair and that wig would look good on that doll. It would make it look even more like TV. She then rushed into the master bedroom, where TV was sorting another white blazer out. By now TV had dispensed with the one that he had used while shagging and cooking, and had taken yet another one out of the wardrobe, entranced by its sacred power. He divested it of polythene and was soon sliding it on, admiring himself in the mirror as he shuffled around preening. How he loved white blazers. He was just like Chaz with them.

'Cor, I feel so clean and perfect, Freeda! I'm gliding through the ether like Keefy! And me cock, look! It's rock hard again, Freeda. It's fucking golden!'

Freeda's hand went down to pull it, as it stood hard and erect, thrusting out of TV's pants. TV assured her, that after this one last, final shagging out of her brains, that would be it. It would only be Freeda after that. The seed would have been disseminated, and TV reckoned that Blazerwoman would shag everybody, and pass it all on. That's how it was going to work and after a good bit of shagging, and then more and more of it, the cosmic light would be shooting up and out in all directions!

Freeda couldn't wait, as she was getting fed up with TV shagging Blazerwoman. He just wouldn't stop. They went back into the Dark Room and TV stood before Linda in the swing and how Linda wanted that cock! That fantastic, phallic wand of a cock! She tried to resist it, but then she just gave in to its power. It touched her thigh and that was it. She wanted it. It was like a god!

'Get it up me! Get that cock up me, you bastard!' Linda shouted and TV duly obliged, and while he began working Linda up, with his long deep thrusts, Freeda took hold of that sex doll and that green wig and exited, with a plan beginning to evolve. She went back into the master bedroom and took hold of that white blazer that TV had left strewn on the bed. She put the blazer on the doll, and then hauled it downstairs, with some mission or other on her mind. A couple of weeks previously, Freeda had seen the telly talking about odd art works and she thought Freeda would do one. Why not? TV had said it tons of times that he got her out of that prison unit, so that she could 'do fings'. Within a couple of minutes, she was outside with the TV doll, and she set it up right in the center of one of those small flower beds. It was as if TV had come up out of the spring flowers, with a big whomper on. It did make Freeda laugh. It was just like that art fingy on the telly. Freeda then rushed back through the house to that Dark Room, as she wanted to support her TV, shagging Blazerwoman's brains out, for the legacy fingy, for the last and final time. She was sure he would finally get them out, and fill her up with dragons. TV's cock was huge!

The old boy had gone up to the top of Holly Beach Lane, and after a few laps of the asylum's football pitch, he had turned, to make his way back. He was now well on his way towards 'Chaz's Pad'. He was talking to his dog, as dog owners tend to do.

'We'll be passing that shagging shop again, in a minute, Butch.'

Meanwhile, Catherine had changed into some casual clothes, and she thought she would take her Bolognese out for a short walk. She generally did this regular, and when she came from the garden, she felt impelled to go back up Holly Beach Lane, past Chaz's house. It was as if something deeply anticipatory, and downright lascivious, was forcing her to go that way. She would only go a little way past, the now fascinating and mysterious house, and then come back down the lane, albeit slowly, loitering a touch. Her Bolognese didn't need much exercise, but what she had heard deeply intrigued her. Whatever that man in the white blazer was, and he was probably involved with drugs, he had something that her loving, but staid, partner Jeremy certainly didn't have. Catherine was enthralled.

CHAPTER NINETEEN

HOP IT!

THE GREAT ESCAPE: PART TWO

With Freeda upstairs giving her vocal support, Chaz had some kind of chance. He had noticed those fastenings around his legs weren't as tight as previously, and this enabled him to get a good grip and firm base. He stood up and tried to see if he could move with the chair strapped to his back. He cursed those darn narrow Gucci jeans that he couldn't get off his feet and which were stretched across his legs with the pants. But he was lucky she hadn't covered his eyes with that tape. Then he heard Freeda coming downstairs, and he moved back a yard and sat firmly down. Chaz watched her go past him with that sex doll with a white blazer on it, and he wondered what on earth she was going to do with it. But she looked pleased with herself when she passed him again, going back upstairs, some five minutes later, and Chaz could see that she'd left the back door open. He wondered if that porch door might be open too? There was a chance, so he had to make his move. He stood up again and began moving with that heavy bondage chair strapped to his back, and, with great effort, he found he could move with small pigeon steps. Then inspiration. He made the leap into the bunny hop and with continuous bunny hops, although strenuous because of the weight of the chair, he managed to get himself to that back door. He could hear Freeda exhorting TV onwards and upwards and Linda was groaning and moaning, carried along on the sex god's relentless waves. But Chaz had his chance. He might just be able to bunny hop and pigeon step his way around the back and through into the front garden. If he made that horse chestnut tree and the road, somebody would see him out there and then surely this ordeal would come to its end? Chaz shuffled and bunny hopped his way to the back door, breathing heavily, through the hot silicone rubber mask. There must be search parties out looking everywhere for these two darn crazies? He just had to take this chance while he had it. He could hear the sex ordeal in full swing now and the pounding and thrusting made that bondage swing creek like an old swing in the park, and there was much vocal support from Freeda.

'Shove it up her, TV! Shag her brains out! Shag um right out!'

TV was shoving it up all right and Linda was responding with that lewd, crude lust again.

'Give me more of that cock! Give it to me! Give it to me, you bastard!'

374

It was a lot to take, the sheer indignity of hearing his wife shout that. Like a cheap whore and for that creep, and nutty farmer. Chaz muffled something or other through the mask again and then found that he had to bunny hop the rather high threshold, between the back door and the porch. You don't normally register such things, but you do when you're strapped in tightly to a bondage chair with a doggy mask on. But he took the leap of faith and bunny hopped, and nearly made it with a flying leap, but unfortunately, the back legs of the chair caught the edge of the step, and Chaz crumpled to the floor in a heap. He uttered a muffled cry of pain, but luckily, he fell wedged up against a washer basket. Those bondage and doggy mask gods were with him! Chaz's breathing had become even heavier with the stress and effort of it all, but he managed to haul himself up, to begin that great escape bunny hop towards the porch door. He could see that it was open. He had to make it, and get out of this Godforsaken house. Three more hops and he would reach it, although he was gulping for oxygen. He couldn't get any through his mouth, and his nose was blocked with his hay fever and cat dander allergies.

Up in the Dark Room, Freeda was still giving her earnest support, but she was thinking about the front bedroom. She liked playing with that make-up, and she was getting bored now, just shouting out things. But she still done it with conviction for the cult.

'Poke it up harder, TV! Make her see the Dragon! And the flying saucers!

TV was humping away furiously and everything seemed to be going wonderfully well.

'I've got her flying on it, Freed! It's me blazers! Me cock's like a god. She can't get enough of it, Freeda!'

About time he used it with Freeda was what Freeda was thinking. She was fed up looking at the Blazerwoman all nudey.

Out in the garden paradise, Chaz was still intent on his mission. He was determined to get to that front gate, whether it was open or not, and there was that chance that it would still be off the latch. Sometimes he would swing it back and it wouldn't shut properly. He prayed that it was ajar. He bunny hopped around the side of the house and he breathed a great sigh of relief when he saw that gate open.

'What the fuck!' Chaz muffled under the mask, when he cast his eye onto the back garden and saw that sex doll with the green wig and white blazer and a darn Dragon Star cap on its head. The bloody thing looked uncannily like TV. What a fucking horror movie!

The old boy who had warned Chaz about the oncoming plague of snakes, had now just about reached Chaz's house. He was whistling away as he loitered around by the flying saucer lamppost, opposite the horse chestnut. But he had to have a quick slash, he was crying out for one, bursting to go. The pile-drivers were still pounding away, and the old boy hadn't heard the landing sound of the metal bondage chair, as Chaz hopped and scraped his way up the front garden path. He was too concerned about being seen having a slash. But he had to go, as he was literally bursting. Just as he started to relieve himself, he could see that woman he spoke to earlier, approaching with a Bolognese dog on a lead. Another filthy lusty wail came from the house, and before he knew it, Catherine was there with her dog. It was like a serendipity all over again, and the old boy hastily put his penis away and zipped his flies up. It didn't look good as Mrs. Greene-Burrow approached as the old boy got his zip stuck. He tried desperately to unzip it but eventually gave up trying, as it began to look as if he was trying to expose himself.

'Give me that big fucking cock, you bastard! Give it to me!' Linda wailed, piercing that quietude with her lust again, exactly when Catherine passed with the Bolognese.

'Sounds like he's got a big one!' the old boy joked, and Catherine frowned and smiled as she passed. She went quickly now, and didn't look behind her, and after a few further steps she heard the woman's wail and frenetic cry again. She stopped by a tree a little further up the road, but in earshot of what was coming from the house. Catherine looked from behind the tree and she knew they were in there, at it, behind that heavily curtained window. She tied the dog up, looked up and down the road and could see the elderly fellow further down, about to go out of sight. She couldn't help herself. It was the transgressional and spontaneous element of it all that Catherine found so exciting, and she could see exactly where it was coming from. With one hand, she pulled her knickers down and spread her legs behind the tree with her back partly to it, and she masturbated, as she continued to listen to Linda's ecstasy, looking up at that open window. She entered a deep erotic intensity, and as if by association and her own sexual lusting, she seemed locked in some vast dark erotic force field that was radiating out from that house, shamelessly through the air waves. It was the way that Linda was ecstatically shouting. She was overflowing with filthy lust, and Catherine was uncannily at one with it, as she masturbated, groaning and moaning, and not caring now, if anyone walked by. She just had to own and become this unbridled lust. That dandy of a man was blessed by a sex god.

The birds were still cawing and squawking, and to Chaz's frustration, when he reached the gate, he could see that the old boy and his dog were down the road, oblivious to him. He mumbled through the tape but just couldn't garner his attention. The old fellow looked this way and that, as if alerted by something out of the ordinary, but then he just carried on down the road towards the doctor's house. Half way down, and out of sight of Chaz, the old boy came across the carcass of that snake that had been there a couple of weeks. It was well decomposed now, but it proved that he was right. Holly Beach Lane was infested and they were out of hibernation. He poked it about with his stick and then looked up the road towards Chaz's house, shaking his head.

By now Chaz had reached the gate. It was ajar and he bravely hopped right at it, and somehow it opened. He breathed as deeply as he could through his nose, although he felt he was going to faint and pass out, so great was his difficulty. He then gathered himself for the final push, to the road itself. If he could get himself there, surely it would be freedom and the end of these tribulations. Surely! But he rested for a few moments to gather himself, before the big bunny hop push!

Freeda had rushed out to the master bedroom while TV and the Blazerwoman were shagging away, to and fro, on that swing. She was getting more and more jealous and a bit more after that, but she knew that it was for the legacy and whatnot, and TV did say it was the last time. But as soon as she was at that dressing table and among all that make-up, she quickly forgot anyway. TV liked the blue sweets, so he was bound to like Freeda having more of that blue eye shadow. But then she heard something. It was an odd scraping sound outside the house, so she got up and went to the front window to investigate. She was shocked to see Blazerman getting through the front gate on his chair.

'Blazer Dicky!' she shouted. She just had to get to that Dark Room to tell TV.

TV and Linda were swinging back and forth on that swing, hurtling towards yet another tumultuous cosmic orgasm.

'Keefy's snake! The snake garden, we're nearly in!' TV exclaimed, as Linda was still shouting out that mantra in homage to that magnificent orgasmic-inducing cock. The cock that broke through all boundaries.

'Oh yes! Yes! Come on! Give me more of that cock! Give me more of that fucking fantastic cock!'

They reached a wondrous Dragon Star orgasmic release as Freeda rushed in. Out in Holly Beach Lane, Catherine heard everything. Every last orgasmic howl and wail of it. She wasn't there yet, but she would be soon, and she kept frigging herself as she leant back on the tree. She wanted her ecstasy to go on and on for an eternity. She just had to have sex with that man. She had to have that cock up her. She came powerfully, with an enormous thrusting feeling. She was overtaken with her lust, ablaze with desire, to be up there with that sex god, with his fantastic cock.

'The Blazerman, TV! He's gone up the garden path! He's up there hopping about on his chair, TV!' Freeda exclaimed. TV was high on sex, and he had difficulty coming back down in the moment. He had taken the Blazerwoman to where the Dragon Star children go. He was zonked, totally zonked and buzzing for sex.

'I got her in the garden, Freeda! I got her in the emanation fields. She was like three new earths!'

TV was still in his post-coital high, but Freeda knew that time was running out. If he got away, hopping about all over the place in that chair, the police and Locko would find him, and no doubt the big fat nurse. Freeda could see it clearly.

'Listen to me, TV! Blazerman is hopping about on his chair in the garden! He's hopping all about!'

Finally, the reality kicked in. You can't live in the ecstasy garden for very long. He withdrew his golden cock, picked up his hat from the floor, that he had lost while frantically shagging, and rushed out with a mission to get that Blazerman back inside, with Freeda in hot pursuit.

While TV had wasted precious seconds loitering in his post-coital ecstatic states of consciousness, Chaz had managed to get to the road. He was pushing and hopping to freedom! He prayed that whoever came, wouldn't be scared off by his mask. But he had made the Great Escape happen. He got himself out into the very middle of the road and plonked himself down. He was exhausted, tears were flowing, but he couldn't go any further. Those stomach muscles were screaming with pain. He prayed that within a few moments 'pig' might come up the lane, and this nightmare would finally be over.

If Catherine had come back round the tree, she would have caught a glimpse of him with that mask and protruding black phallic nose, but she was deeply involved in her delicious orgasmic ecstasy, with her fingers going vigorously in and out.

TV didn't notice that sex doll perched up in the flowerbeds, in the frantic attempt to get out there quick. They rushed up the garden path and they could see Blazerman out there in the middle of the road.

'There he is! Trying to get away, TV!'

Catherine heard voices and they were close. Yet she was impelled to continue. That was part of the excitement. The sheer transgression of masturbating secretly in a public space like this, and risking getting caught and who knows where that might lead. She just had to take it to the very limit and she was nearly there. She would go over the very top and come like the wife of that sex god of a spunky guy.

TV could see the danger now. All it needed was a car coming up Holly Beach Lane or a dog walker and the game was up!

'Quick, Freeda, before the police see him!'

Chaz swore to himself when he saw who it was apprehending him.

'Gotcha, Blazerman!' Freeda growled. TV lent the chair back and Freeda lifted from the front. They carried him behind the horse chestnut tree and it was a timely move, as Catherine glanced around her tree, to check if anyone was close. There was nobody there and she continued. She had to keep going. Her ecstasy knew no bounds. She could sense her orgasm would be more intense and pulsating than the first, and she just longed for that cock, that fantastic cock!

TV and Freeda were just in time with regard the other direction too, as a car turned into the lane down by the doctor's house. It was a late middle-aged local couple who were taking their dog up to the asylum woods and grounds. They had noticed an increased police presence in and around the village, but had no idea what was going on. There were no sightings in Tennin reported and it was thought they had got away from the town in the early hours by car. The police superintendent believed that somebody on the outside had aided them, given them a lift someplace, and this seemed to be part confirmed, with the report of a sighting of the couple, in a Vauxhall Corsa on the road to Fishgate, noon after the break out. Resources of the county constabulary were now more concentrated on Fishgate.

But TV and Freeda only survived by a cat's whisker. They could be seen for a moment or two as that car approached, but they weren't noticed. But the wife, sitting on the passenger's seat, did notice Mrs. Greene-Burrows, and she couldn't believe it. They drove past and she caught a shocking flash of Catherine nigh naked and masturbating. She looked over her shoulder to see more and, in that brief moment, she knew who it was. It was shocking. She had recently been X-rayed by Catherine up at the general hospital.

'Did you see that woman masturbating behind that tree!'

Her husband, a balding recently retired sixty-five-year-old, hadn't seen anything and was in disbelief.

'I know who it was. She gave me that X-ray a couple of weeks ago! Filthy woman!'

TV and Freeda hauled Chaz up the garden path with great effort, but as they turned the corner to get around the back, they got him caught up with the overhanging rose bush. There was another muffled cry as loads of the thorns dug into the bare flesh of the hapless Chaz. Chaz was genuinely fearing for his life, as these two mad loons were sure to enact a terrible revenge. They moved him around the back, and this time TV couldn't help but notice that sex doll, standing up in the flowerbeds. He just couldn't understand why on earth she had put it there.

'What ya put that there for, Freeda?' he asked.

'I thought it would look good, TV. It's like saying TV was here, OK! It's like an art fingy!'

'Nah, we'll have to move it, Freeda. We've already got the flag up! It might give us away!' TV intended to come back outside and get the sex doll, after they had got Blazerman safely in that front lounge. But then he gave the doll a second look, and he thought Freeda was right. 'But it looks

379

great, Freeda! You've got real imagination! You really have. That could win one of those Turner prizes for Art, Freeda. It's like the New Age man, all dragon starred!'

Freeda smiled with the vindication and compliment, and smirked and giggled at the joke, but TV would have to move it, after they got the Blazerman back inside. They had been lucky to evade a sighting with that fiasco out the front. But TV didn't want to say any more about it, as he was planning something special in his mind, and he was sure it would all work out. Circumstances were auspicious. It would have all the blessing of the unseen Dragon Star power, but there would have to be urgency. TV could see that it was only a matter of time. It was now or never!

They rested for a few moments with Chaz on that chair around the side of the house, out of the road's view. It was a quiet moment of reflection, and Freeda was looking at that flag flying on the line pole. She was thinking about what she suggested earlier and what TV had said about fame.

'It must be great being famous and all that, TV,' she said. 'Everyone wants to be famous these days! It's like saying "I was here" and everybody knowing, ain't it?'

'We'll be famous for "Dragon Star" one day, Freed, it's definite. AD 2025 that's the date, when everybody, the whole wide world will be "Dragon Star". It's on me birthday, Freeda.'

Freeda had heard all that before. TV's birthday was July the sixteenth, so naturally Dragon Star day would be July the sixteenth, AD 2025. But she was here now and was looking at that line pole, as the pile-drivers pounded their final rhythm of the day. It was late afternoon and TV looked at Freeda with curiosity.

'What ya looking at the line pole for, Freeda?'

Freeda was thinking about fame now, and she burst out with a torrent of energy.

'Let's put his head up on it! Like we said we were gonna! We'd be famous with all those documentaries. People would never forget us, TV! They'd always be wondering why we dun it! We could get that step ladder out of the proper shed. You won't fall off it like that old ladder!' Freeda smirked as it was so funny when TV fell off that ladder and into the stinging nettles. Chaz could be heard mumbling away through his mask and taped up mouth. He envisaged a horrible, terrible finale and now expected death. He was nigh at those pearly gates. Freeda was still enthusiastic, still on it.

'Let's do it, TV! It would only take five minutes. I can get my knife!'

Chaz prayed, but feared the worst, butchered to death by this 'Mad Freeda'. He kept repeating the Lord's Prayer to himself. It was only the big boy who could help him now. TV reflected for a moment in the peaceful quiet, seemingly having the power over life and death. He was weighing things up; he was thinking ahead about his plans as Freeda desperately tried to sway him.

'Let's cut his head off! Oh, go on, TV! Let's do it! Like those shoes keep telling us! Then we can put it up on the big pole! Freeda can stand on the ladder and keep it safe for ya!'

The crows cawed and that pile driver still pounded relentlessly as TV kept thinking about fame. But he baulked. The decapitating would be rather messy and gory, but yes, they would be famous, that's for sure, and TV was more than aware of how famous 'fame' had become. TV had been telling Freeda just a short while ago. There were a few raspy kraas, and thankfully TV's better instincts held sway. He had other ideas planned. Ideas that had been the inspiration for 'The Great Escape' and it all added up to the longest few moments of Chaz's life, as TV deliberated. He had poor Chaz dangling by his feet, hanging over a pit of deadly venomous snakes, that meant only one thing, certain death. But finally, he made that decision, and gave Chaz a helping hand out of that snake pit.

'Nah, Freed, you're getting it wrong, the shoes tell ya to run faster or get yourself a good job and that. They don't tell ya to chop heads off. And I've got a plan, and it wouldn't work if we chopped his head off. He wouldn't have a head, Freeda.'

Freeda was crestfallen as she liked that idea of being famous. Everyone wanted to be famous.

'But we could be more famous than the Big Brothers! You said it yourself, TV!'

It was true, TV knew they could be.

CHAPTER TWENTY

THE SACRED MARRIAGE

There was a sense of urgency about TV when they re-positioned Chaz back in the center of the citadel strapped on his chair. He undid Chaz's hand fastenings with something in mind. He then began putting Chaz into his hoodie with its TV and Freeda caricature on the back.

'What ya doing, TV?' Freeda asked.

TV had reached that critical moment and he knew the window of opportunity was small. It was now or never.

'We're gonna get married, Freeda, and the old Blazerman is gonna be the priest who does it! So, we can't chop his head off! We can't, Freeda!'

Freeda's eyes bulged and focused in a realization she just couldn't believe. She had fought long and hard with that big fat nurse about marrying TV. The big fat nurse had always said it was impossible. She taunted Freeda that she could never marry TV. But now they were going to prove that horrible nurse was wrong all along. It was the dream come true for Freeda. She lit up.

'Freeda is getting married to TV! You'd better put some trousers on, TV! And we'll have to leave his head on, TV! He's got to have his head on!'

TV said he would wear the white trousers and a new fresh blazer, and there were those flashy shirts up there. He could wear one of those. TV smiled, put a tender arm around Freeda and hugged and snuggled her.

'That's why I got you out, Freeda! So, that we could get married and it's all gonna work out!'

Freeda couldn't believe it, but after a few seconds, she soon began believing, because when TV said things were going to happen, they always did. He always said he would get her out of that prison unit, and he did. TV always said he could open any door. He opened all the Blazerpeople's doors, even finding that wangher dangher fingy. TV did all that, and if TV said they were going to get married, then that was that, they were. TV said things and it all happened. Freeda's world had turned upside down, and all for the better. She was going to wear her wedding dress, and it was all because of TV. And when they were carrying that fat Blazerman down the stairs, TV had said that all the seed sowing with the Blazerwoman had ended. He may have had a relapse but that dissemination business was all over now. Everything was for Freeda, his one true love, from now on. The whomper was all for Freeda, and she was effusive.

'We're getting married at last! We'll have to invite Dicky and Blazerwoman! We'll have to, TV!'

'Yeah, course, Freed! And I've got a nice wedding dress and special things and a wedding ring too!'

Freeda remembered women talking at the bus stop to her mother, all those years ago, saying that things always worked out in the end. For the first time Freeda really knew what they meant.

'Things always work out in the end don't they, TV?'

Freeda was joyfully happy as she never thought that would happen to her. Never worked out, was all that ever happened to Freeda. Or at least, apart from Kleeunah's kindness, nothing did, but TV tried to support her in her newly found optimism. He held her hand softly and squeezed, because TV understood all her hurt.

'Even after all the bad, they work out, Freeda. We've got to believe that! We've got to!'

They naturally found themselves in the furry chair with Freeda lain across TV. They were intimate moments. 'And ever since I was sectioned and I met ya, I've loved ya. You suit me, Freed. And I wanna be with ya for the rest of my life! For the rest of my life, Freeda!'

Tears flowed down Freeda's cheeks and how Freeda wanted to be with TV forever and ever too. He had a gift of just touching Freeda and things were better and Freeda loved cuddling with TV in that furry chair. TV smiled and he knew that this joy in the moment together, here and now, had to be fully appreciated. He tried to get that idea over to Freeda, so she could see how special these moments truly were.

'Keefy used to say we've got to enjoy every minute to its full, Freeda, because the space people are coming to collect us.'

It all seemed so strange and mysterious. Freeda didn't understand it all, but she was just thankful that she was in the furry chair with TV.

'It's all weird, ain't it? Like Jesus and his donkeys,' Freeda reflected. Yes, it was all very weird and wonderful, and TV gave a thought to that Blazerwoman Linda upstairs. He reckoned the Dragon Star was truly inside her now. The snake of illumination, TV called it. Now every time that Linda had sex it would be Dragon Star sex. That's why TV had to disseminate the cult's light and put it about a bit. It was for the legacy and all that. TV was still thinking about the space people.

'I see them coming in my dreams, Freeda!'

'What, loads of donkeys?' Things seemed to be getting even more mysterious for Freeda but TV pointed out that no, it wasn't the donkeys.

'Nah, Freeda! The space people! I'm at the Sea of Galilee where Jesus went fishing. He caught loads of whoppers! Like the ones we cooked, Freeda!'

He was going on about that dream again and for Freeda, it all meant that the Dragon Star children were close, very close to this Jesus bloke. This was just more confirmation of that, and Freeda said they must mean a lot to Jesus, her and TV, because they had his badges and his sandals. Chaz was trying to say something through the tape but it was still too tight for him, but the intent hit some kind of connection with TV.

'I think he's trying to tell us that Jesus would be happy, Freeda, if we didn't hurt anybody and he would be really happy if we were nice.'

'That Jesus was a nice bloke weren't he?' Freeda replied. TV kept on talking about all the links between Dragon Star and the Jesus of Nazareth.

'He was a diamond geezer, Freeda; he fed all the people with those fish!'

Freeda looked down at her sandals and then at TV's, and then she thought about those fish and chips, and shoveling chips into Blazerman's mouth. Then she looked at those carp in the tank. They were indeed close to that Jesus bloke.

'We've got his sandals on, haven't we, TV? And we fed the Blazerpeople with fish and chips! Didn't we?'

For TV there was so much happening, astrologically speaking. That was why he had chosen this week for the break out. The planets and stars were aligned.

'We did, Freeda, and the space people are gonna collect me there at Galilee when I've got flowers in me hair, Freeda!' Freeda had seen documentaries about hippies.

'What, like one of those hippy fingys?'

'Well, Jesus was a hippy, Freeda. Me and Keefy used to read about how he used to do "shrooms" an' all that. Jesus used to trip out fucking bad, Freeda, on "shrooms"! He saw all the revelations tripping. But you're the best fing that ever happened to me, Freeda.'

Freeda smiled dotingly and TV began to sing the marriage song doing a verse of 'Da, da da da, da da da da'. TV knew the first verse off by heart, because of his hope for the escape and wedding, and he added a little flourish to make it personal.

'Here comes the bride, all dressed in white, radiant and lovely she shines in the light! Gently she glides, graceful as a dove, Freeda's with her TV, her eyes full of love!'

TV got up out of the furry chair with Freeda following him and he kept going back around the verse, teaching her the words as he went. Freeda was trying to get the full words off pat but it was happening all too quick, but her face was beaming. They began dancing around in a circle with TV singing and Freeda now beginning to pick up all the words, before they fell into a heap on the Waldorf settee. These were joyous, special moments for the lovers. They were free just to be together, and Freeda was so glad, now that TV had ended all that shagging with Blazerwoman. It was making her feel so jealous. This was her special time with TV, and she was going to get married! Then TV had an idea. He thought he might do something symbolic to mark this place, they had found beyond all the pain of the past. Something that would put an end to all of its negative influences. TV had seen something like this on breakfast TV and they could do their version.

'I know what I'm going to do, Freeda!' he announced. TV began to move towards the kitchen. 'It's to mark the end of the old and the beginning of the new marriage, Freeda.'

Anything to do with their marriage was exciting to Freeda. She took a quick glance at the carp in the first tank. Freeda was still captivated.

'We're going to get married aren't we, TV?' Freeda asked, sounding as if she wanted desperately to have that fact reconfirmed. She had become so used to the big fat nurse taunting her to the contrary.

'It's true, Freeda, it's really true,' TV replied, and Freeda's face beamed the more, as TV returned to the front room with a pair of scissors and a big fruit bowl, that he placed on the coffee table. He began playing around with the scissors. It was a new game, and Freeda just loved playing new games with TV. He began to explain.

'We're gonna snip the past away, Freeda. People always do that, so they can move on from all the bad. They shed it like a snake sheds its skin!'

'What like that snake we found, TV?' Freeda asked. It was a connection.

'Yeah like that snake, Freed. But we're gonna snip the bad all away with the snip, snip, snip the scissors tune, Freeda!'

TV began snipping the scissors all around Chaz and Freeda was having trouble figuring out what TV was doing. But she then realized what good fun 'snipping the scissors' would be. TV took up the rhythmic ditty that would accompany the snipping.

'Snip the scissors, snip, snip snip! Snip, snip, the scissors snip!'

The outlook was altogether foreboding again, as events descended back to square one. Chaz was praying it wouldn't turn into a blood bath. But in this horrible sublime moment as those scissors snipped, Chaz had realizations. Facing death's door, you naturally turn to higher powers, asking for a divine intervention. It was an awe inspiring, redemptive moment for Chaz. Chaz prayed with all his power and love of life. Surely the time wasn't ripe for his death. He had a great wife and daughter, grandchildren to look forward to, hundreds of more kilos to buy, and porn films to make, and he desperately wanted to see Natasha thriving in whatever field of the media she chose. Although he sincerely hoped she would make up into a porn channel host, with a few wisely chosen forays in front of the camera herself, to keep the mystique at fever pitch. But none of that mattered to Freeda. Freeda just wanted to do that snip song. It looked so much fun doing it around the Blazerman, scaring him to death.

'Freeda wants to do snip the scissors! Freeda wants to snip um, TV!' TV wanted to show Freeda something else too, and he took the confetti from the hoodie jacket that was on Chaz.

'Look, Freeda! Look!

'What is it?' Freeda asked, screwing up her face.

'It's wedding confetti! I bought it in the town when I went out with Dan! They always sprinkle confetti at weddings! It gets in the bride's hair and that! It's all bright colors, Freeda!'

Freeda simply loved that idea. Anything to do with her wedding was so exciting.

'Freeda wants the confetti in her hair, TV! Freeda wants it, Freeda wants it in her hair!'

But before the wedding and confetti in her hair, there would be the game that TV was playing.

'First we're gotta do 'snip the past away confetti'. It's a new game Freeda. Everyone's doing it!'

Freeda was a little dumbfounded, as she thought the snipping was all about snipping Blazerman. Having fun with scaring him and that. TV took some porn magazines that were in the cupboards underneath the fish tanks. He just needed something or other to snip up. TV had the magazines out on the coffee table, as he was now sitting in the furry chair with Freeda on the arm, and he noticed that image of God, clasping the outstretched hand of Adam, as previously it was obscured by a newspaper.

'Look, Freeda! It's God and the first man, Freeda! On the coffee table!'

'Oh yeah,' Freeda was in further disbelief, as TV opened up the glamour mag that had Natasha on the front. He immediately recognized the correspondence with that painting on the wall above the big settee, and he wanted to get the center page spread out. This was that big iconic moment of Natasha's burgeoning career. The center page from *Big Jugs*. He opened it out and there it was, Nat on a chaise lounge, naked, exactly as she was painted on the wall.

'Look, Freeda! That's her on the wall there!'

Freeda couldn't believe her eyes. It seemed all so unbelievable, as if she and TV were cracking the arcane code to the secrets of the universe.

'Oh yeah. And she's got that shaven fanny thing again, TV! Like Blazerwoman!'

'That's right, Freeda, and I'm gonna cut up all the nudey women and the big fish men, Freed!'

That would all be part of the rite. Everything would be as confetti when faced with the cult's cosmic light. TV looked up at the mantel piece, stood up and went across to check out the photograph of Chaz and that 'Ressie' carp status symbol, directly above the cow's skull. Then he looked at the painting that hung above the second of the carp tanks, making connections. When he had gathered those porn mags from underneath the tanks, he recalled that he caught a glimpse of something like that. He went back searching underneath, and pulled out the magazine in question, that had the corresponding photograph of Chaz on the front page. It was Chaz's claim to fame, in the carp angler's sense of the term. The article had been part of a piece on big European stock fish, that had been placed in British waters, and Chaz's big carp was one of them.

'Look, Freeda! It's Blazerman with the big fish, Freed!'

Freeda was incredulous yet again. Everything was so surprising and mysterious since they had left that prison. It was obviously all about the Dragon Star light and neural connections and all the nudey stuff.

'Oh yeah! Ain't it big? He must do loads of fish and chips, TV! Loads!'

'Probably does, Freeda!' TV pulled that double page center spread out of the porn mag, and began snipping the naked Natasha up into little pieces. 'As we do the snipping, Freeda, the old world and everything in it falls away. No more Barry, the hospital, Locko or Bolt!

'And that big fat nurse, TV!' Freeda replied, 'we don't want that fat nurse about!' she added. Lavender was well known, nigh notorious, for her gargantuan appetite. She would attempt to diet at times, but she couldn't find one that could accommodate the little pleasures in life that she enjoyed. She always said to Julietta that she never smoked, hardly drunk and that she needed the weight for her wrestling career, in the ring and on the asylum's wards. But it was a good excuse anyhow, and Julietta used to laugh at the joke, but fighting Freeda Huskit's stubborn will wasn't any joke.

'She's always eating those meat pies and doughnuts, TV! She's a pig! A big fat greedy pig!'

TV started grunting like a pig and Freeda burst into laughter as she learnt this off TV and that big fat nurse used to go mad when she done her 'oinking'. Dr. Lock always lectured Freeda why she shouldn't do it, how it upset Nurse Lavender so much, and Freeda smirked as she was thinking how she would always say 'Yes, Dr. Lock, Freeda's sorry, Dr. Lock, Freeda will never do it again, Dr. Lock'. She would refrain from doing it for a month or two, until she started it all up again. Freeda smiled to herself, as it always worked, but now TV was chanting a new mantra as he snipped and it soon had Freeda carried away.

'No more Barry and the big fat nurse, Locko or Bolt!' No more Barry and the big fat nurse, Locko or Bolt!'

It gradually built up momentum and they chanted triumphantly, with their arms extended overhead, like football supporters, who had just won the great big cup! It was no more Barry, the big fat nurse, Dr. Lock, or Dr.

Bolt and Freeda just loved chanting it out. It was like a pure catharsis and what freedom.

'No more Barry and the big fat nurse, Locko or Bolt! No more Barry and the big fat nurse, Locko or Bolt!'

Down at the bottom of Holly Beach Lane the Greene-Burrows were taking in a relaxing evening in the front lounge. Jeremy had plenty of DVDs that were bought for him last Christmas, a Robert de Niro box set among them, that he had never got around to watching, and so after tea he decided to watch one with Catherine, who was at the table with a laptop. Jeremy was reading the back of the DVDs and was looking over one.

'It's about the rise and fall of the Las Vegas mob, dear, not that I like gangster hoodlum films but it seems well acclaimed, Catherine, with good performances.'

'Well go ahead and put it on, Jeremy, you've had that set since Christmas and you haven't watched any.'

Jeremy was in his rocking chair watching the film while Catherine, still turned on by what she had heard, was secretly trawling the net for sex sites. Things can sometimes be fated and she tried a few different extreme S&M websites, before coming across one called 'Secret Pleasures'. This was Viv and Miko's website with stacks of content relating to Vivienne and her interests, but there was also a link to Chaz's website. She clicked the link and was met with the host of the site who was none other than Natasha who was introducing herself. This was a new state-of-the-art and cutting-edge interactive site, using the very latest in Web cam technology, offering subscribers real life content. Natasha had done the recording around Viv's pool and it then flashed to the Dark Room in the house, while giving viewers or potential subscribers insight into the content. Then there was another trailer of this young woman with a group of men, having sex around a white Porsche and then it hit Catherine. She knew this woman. She had seen her that afternoon, Chaz and his wife knocked at the door to meet their new neighbors. They shook hands and exchanged pleasantries, and then when Catherine was walking the dog, this woman got out of that white Porsche in front of the gate. It was her, she was sure, and she found herself completely turned on and intoxicated, and then there were snippets of films involving Chaz and Linda in a mask. She looked at the trailers and knew it was him and his wife. Within a few moments she had her debit card by the laptop paying a subscription. To think all this was going on up the lane in that house. She felt as if she was joining some kind of underground sex cult.

Back in the house, Freeda was even more inspired as TV began to fiddle about with that pervert's mask, as he needed to take it off Chaz for the wedding ceremonies. But all of the talk of doing things symbolic and like play, had given Freeda an idea. She could chop off that big black hooter cock on Blazerman's nose. She smiled to TV mischievously as if to say this was a trick, and TV had an inclination of what she was up to.

'I'm gonna chop off his cock! I'm gonna chop it off, TV!'

'Yeah, chop it off! Right here! Right now, Freeda! Chop it off! It'll be a right ole laugh!'

Chaz mumbled away, trying to protest, and he anticipated a pain so excruciating that it would be like a death. 'Oh, Father which art in heaven!' How Chaz prayed and he reacted by forcing himself against his fastenings like a vain, but inept attempt, at pushing towards freedom. But it was impossible. For Chaz, it was akin to being in a chair, waiting to be tortured by the Nazis, 'forgive us our trespasses', but Freeda had the knife in her hand and she smirked with TV, and put the knife right by that big black penis nose.

'I'm gonna saw it off, TV! I'm gonna saw the cock off his hooter!'

Freeda began sawing through the black cock and Chaz could recognize what she was doing and he continued praying, 'forgive those that trespass against us', that she wouldn't set about his manhood. TV held it as Freeda sawed and hacked her way through. When it came off, she held it up like some odd trophy of her hunting prowess.

'Got it, TV!' And I know what we can do! We can stick it up his big fat botty. Let's do it, TV! Let's stick it up his big fat botty!'

Freeda raised the penis nose above her head in triumph and she just had to celebrate it with that chant. It was 'No more Barry and the big fat nurse! Locko or Bolt!'

She kept repeating it with TV laughing, and she gesticulated with it as if it was a dildo.

'Freeda's gonna give him it! Fuck his bum, TV, with her big black cock!'

How TV laughed but he still had that sense of urgency. It was all good fun but they couldn't get waylaid with sticking dildos up Blazerman's bum. Time was of the essence. He began taking the perverts mask off him. Freeda was a little deflated. But TV had to move things on.

'What ya taking it off for, TV? He looks good in his doggy mask!'

TV had the wedding ceremony on his mind.

'Nah, Freeda. Priests don't wear um when they're marrying people. He'll have to have his mouth free, Freeda!' To divert things away from that dildo business, TV took up the previous mantra that Freeda relished chanting.

'No more Barry and the big fat nurse, Locko or Bolt! No more Barry and the big fat nurse, Locko or Bolt!'

Freeda joined in excitedly and it was hands in the air time again. How she enjoyed shouting that out. It was so much fun being out of prison with TV.

The two carp remaining looked on, no doubt praying that they wouldn't be taken, gasping out of the tanks in the name of feeding the multitudes. Chaz couldn't help but confront TV when his mouth was finally free of that tape and that mask. He was looking watery-eyed and white and aged about twenty years now. That mad duo had made the very hair on his neck stand up in that garden, when they were deliberating around the line pole. It stood even more erect when he thought his penis would be severed off in his own front lounge, his own citadel, by an insane nutty farmer. His castle besieged by the Barbarians!

'You know you won't get away with this, TV! No matter what happens!' TV had gone beyond caring. He had a mission, and a mission only.

'Who cares, Blazerman! Me and Freeda have never got away with anything, have we? So, nothing will change, will it?' Freeda couldn't resist a snap right into Chaz's face.

'Na nuffin'! Nuffin' Blazerman! Nuffin'!

Chaz thought quickly, he had to try something. He was trying to prize a dark rock so that a little chink of light might come forth from the other side. This TV loved the white blazers as much as he did. He could appeal for mercy through the white blazers. It was a case of living by the white blazer and dying by the white blazer.

'Please, TV! Remember, I gave you five white blazers! Five blazers, mate! Would you have been able to get one if it weren't for me and you wouldn't hurt a nice fellow who gave ya five white blazers? You're the main man, the man with the white blazers now! And it was all because of me! All because of me, TV!'

Chaz was laying it on thick and it certainly made TV stop and think for a few moments. It was true what he was saying. He had always wanted a blazer like Keefy's, and it was the old Blazerman who had given it to him. But the marriage was the main priority, and TV pointed out that Blazerman was going to marry them and do it properly. But by now Chaz was going for broke. He had to try anything to get himself out of this hell on earth. He just had to keep trying things. He had a few more ploys up his sleeve and he was thinking ahead too. There was a kilo of coke in the dash out there and a ton of money. Getting them looking out there might lead to them getting caught but that carried a mega risk for Chaz. It had to be the St. George and the Dragon first.

'Do you like a bit of coke?'

'Yeah! Have ya got one of them big bottles!' Freeda asked, as she fancied some coke, in fact she was dying for some. Coca-Cola was another of Freeda's treats in the unit. She always had two cans a day, supplied by Dr. Lock herself. If she misbehaved it would be no cokes.

'Nah, I mean the *real* deal. Cocaine! Get on it! Be like the rock stars and jet-setters. Best gear you could snort in the whole of England!'

'Drugs, he means, Freeda! We can have a drugs party! Where is it, Blazerman?'

The St. George tin was underneath the discarded newspaper by the side of the furry chair. Chaz turned his head and could see the edge of the tin.

'It's in that tin underneath the paper! Get on it! Get it up your hooters!'

TV jumped on it and opened the tin. There was nothing in it but a few grains, evidently Linda, had snorted the lot and hadn't replaced it.

'Ya fucking lying bastard! There's nuffin' here!' TV exclaimed and the angry Freeda set about the old Blazerman whacking Chaz around the head with that big black cock as TV threw the St. George tin to the floor.

'Ya fucking liar! Where's the bottle of coke? Freeda wants her fucking coke!'

Freeda gave Chaz another whack over the head with the big black cock. 'Where's the coke! Where's the bottle of coke! Ya bastard! Freeda wants her coke!'

'We haven't got any bottles of coke!'

'Ya lying bastard! Your tricking Freeda again saying you've got loads of bottles of coke!'

She proceeded to whack Chaz over the head four times with the big black cock, still calling Chaz a lying bastard.

Chaz's head throbbed and he was dazed, but he felt impelled to keep on trying.

'If you let me phone the hospital, the doctors will come down here to help ya!'

Freeda, dispensed with the cock and picked up her knife from the coffee table. She gripped it harder. How she hated those doctors and that fat nurse.

'If Locko comes down here, I'll fucking kill her! And that fucking Bolt bastard. Cunt! And I'll get that big fat nurse! I'll fucking get her, TV! I'll give it to you, Blazerman! I'll give it to you!'

She picked up the black cock again and whacked Chaz another three times before she felt compelled to stab that knife in something. She didn't want to put any more rips into the big furry chair as they were using that to cuddle up on, so she took to the Great Waldorf and gave that half a dozen disturbingly manic thrusts and cuts.

Chaz was thinking in the moment. He had to refine the idea. But he was having trouble as he fought the symptoms of concussion. Chaz was wincing in pain as he spoke and he could feel his head throbbing.

'Well "they" don't have to be invited to the wedding proper. Let me phone, so all your friends can be invited! They would all love to come! Cans of coke, booze! Food! Everything!'

Chaz turned directly to TV trying to appeal to the degree of rationality that he did have, praying that he could finally trick him into making a fatal mistake. Then it would be the end games. Chaz was using all of his ingenuity, fighting his dizziness.

'All real weddings have lots of guests TV. You know that! They always do! And your best mate Keefy can come. You'll be able to show him all your new blazers! All five of them! How about that, eh? And you'll be able to flash all that cash about, like rich and famous people do!'

Freeda was up for it. Coke and cakes for everybody, at her and TV's wedding! And count Freeda in on anything that meant, Dan, Angelo, Clara, Cheryl and Drill-head, and the rest of them were there. She would even invite Stavros if he promised he wouldn't hit anybody over the head with his hammer fist, and they would all love to see Keefy again. They had to go for it!

Chaz thought that he might just be getting somewhere, that breakthrough might be in sight.

'They can all come, TV! Get um down here! Have a great house party for ya wedding reception, mate! Go for it!'

Freeda was all over the idea but it didn't work. TV knew what this was about, and he went close up to Chaz's face, like Freeda had done previously, and told him how it was.

'You're like a big bull in a field, ain't ya? With the shit piling out of ya big fat arse!' Freeda was quick to the wavelength.

'Yeah, Blazerman! Bull shit! Bull shit! Nuffin' but bull shit out ya big fat botty! You said you had big bottles of coke. But you were fucking lying! Bull shit! Bull shit! Out of ya big fat botty!'

They laughed and laughed and inevitably took up another rhythmic chant as they danced around Chaz on the chair.

'Bull shit, bull shit out of ya big fat botty! Bull shit, bull shit, out ya big fat botty!'

TV played along picking up the sawn-off cock nose and took up another chant and Freeda followed in turn.

'Shove it up his arse and get the bull shit out his botty! Shove it up his arse and get the bull shit out his botty!'

They were in hysterics, but TV had no intention of doing it. It was just threatening fun, and besides, TV just had to crack on with the marriage. TV gave some clarification.

'Me and Freeda are gonna get married in real, real secret. And Keefy's dead. So, you don't know fuck all. You're just an old clapped-out, Blazerman!'

Whatever ruse Chaz tried, he just couldn't get one past TV. Freeda backed up her TV by having another shout right in Chaz's face. Chaz fancied spitting in her eye. But he thought he'd better not.

'Keefy's dead right! Fucking bull shit botty! Ya fink you're so fucking good in your flashy shirt. Don't cha? Well TV's getting one. Ain't ya, TV?'

TV acknowledged her, as he would certainly try on that other one he had seen. He then threateningly snipped the scissors a few times and handed them to Freeda. It wasn't looking good, but if she did sever his cock off, Chaz would spit in her face then. Chaz looked across to the far carp tank and the Titanic ornament. He would spit in her eye, a big horrible gobby one. It would be his way of going down like the Titanic. But TV's patience was wearing thin, and there was a nastier edge to his tone now. It was time for more sinister games.

'Here, Freeda! Do the snip, snip, scary, scarum snip to scare the fuck out of him!' Freeda loved a game like this one.

'Freeda wants to do it! The snip, snip scary scarums, TV! Freeda wants to do it!'

Chaz was scared witless as TV mimicked the snip with his fingers, teaching what was expected from Freeda, by snipping all around Chaz's body. It would be Freeda who would wield the real 'scary scarum' scissors. TV took up the abominable chant again.

'Snip, snip, the scissors snip! Snip the scissors, snip, snip, snip!'

Freeda took to the game with abandon, she picked up the scissors and snipped them close to Chaz's flesh, snipping everywhere, a mere centimeter from his body. The depravity of these nut jobs! Poor Chaz envisaged himself being snipped to death with a pair of scissors. He closed his eyes and prayed to God again for deliverance. What had Charles Edward Barber ever done to deserve this? Throat fucking a few escort girls he had given a wad of money too? Trod on a few horrible fucker eels? Shot a few geese and what not, on hunting holidays to help the American economy? Scared an Albanian drugs gang off the Tennin landscape with a couple of automatic guns? Paid off a few local traveler bailiffs to exact a bit of pressure and leverage on non-payers of cash? You've got to pay your dues haven't you, whether you're underworld or on the straight? And Chaz would only enforce like a hoodlum in the *very* last resort. Chaz's drugs were all about giving people a good time. They were only recreational. He was the bringer of ecstasy and the seventh heaven vibe. Everyone needs to get high, now and then. Surely the big boy would countenance that? All work and no play would make Chaz and all the rest of us dullards. But Chaz was living by drugs, sex and money and it would have to be that unholy Trinity to get him out of this darn shite. Surely it would save him, because in the New Age they are the savior, according to Zeitgeist Chaz. He pleaded desperately; they already had a pocketful, but a bucketful is always that much better by most people's evaluation. Surely it was worth another hit.

'I'll give ya more money! I've got loads! Fucking loads! You can have it all! You'll be rich! Stinking rich!'

It was worth a stab. There was nigh seventy in the car with the cocaine and there must have been fifty or sixty upstairs with the guns. He would go with the car first. He had already thought about the cabinet upstairs. But it would be like rolling the dice of life and death. What if they got the guns? But TV couldn't believe it. To think the Dragon Star children could be bribed to do things for money. They had five white blazers now, anything was possible. They were the rightful custodians of the white blazers. And they had money, tons of it! TV sneered at Chaz.

'We got white blazers and we don't need any more money! We're Dragon Star, we've got fucking loads. Look!' TV took the big wad of money from his pouch and spread it across his hands. 'Money? Fucking loads! And we've always had shedloads, ain't we, Freeda?'

Freeda naturally backed him to the hilt.

'We've always had money, see! And Freeda's got more money in her purse. Haven't I, TV?'

TV promptly gave half of the notes to Freeda and they both spread the cash out in their hands. They were in this for things other than just money, as long as the coffers of the treasury were full. Then TV gave a grand theatrical fling of the notes into the air.

'See! We just couldn't give a shit about money! Not even a dog shit turd!'

'We don't give a turd, a turd on a stick about money! See!' Freeda backed him up and she copied him, with another fling of the notes in the air and all over the floor, with many coming to rest upon Chaz and the bondage chair.

There were a few seconds silence as TV and Freeda looked at that money all over the floor. It was a hell of a lot. Freeda finally broke the deadlock.

'Shall I pick it up, TV?' Freeda asked. 'We don't want to lose it.'

TV thought again, yes, it was true, that wad might come in handy.

'Yeah, we might need it come to fink of it, Freeda. But don't you think "Dragon Star" are materialistic, Blazerman! Cos we're not! We're into cosmic shagging, peace and love ins!'

'Yeah, were always shagging! See!' Freeda blurted.

They gathered up the strewn cash and Freeda remarked again on how much money they had. Freeda had never seen so much, and TV had never had this kind of cash. TV put it back in the magic pouch for safe keeping, and with the money sorted, and out of the way, Freeda wanted to get back to that exciting snipping game. But TV had a number of things on his mind now. There was the wedding, but that cocaine was interesting. Fucking drugs party!

'Let's cover his gobber up again, TV! And I'll do the real snip the scissors, snipping! Let's cover up his gobber, TV! Nobody will hear him screaming then!'

Chaz pleaded for mercy again, crying, praying that his distress might make these two freaks, show some humanity. But TV had to change the direction of events. They had to marry nicely. It had to take place in this front room and it could look nice if they got that smashed-up telly and glass out.

'Nah, we can't snip him to death, Freeda. It'll be too messy, blood and that, Freed. It'll be all over your new party dress, and me white blazers! And the wedding dress! And we need him alive to be the priest to marry us, Freeda!'

'Nah we can't ruin my wedding dress, TV!'

Freeda was in disbelief. This was going to be a real wedding.

TV then thought he'd sort out the cocaine.

'You said you had drugs. Cocaine? Have ya got any, Blazerman? We wanna know?'

It was a calculated risk on Chaz's part. If the situation broke up at the wrong time, it could be a long spell at Her Majesty's pleasure. But he gambled.

'Look in the dashboard in the Jag. There's a kilo out there in a bag with a ton of money. The keys are in the pocket of the blazer I took off. Get it and go on the run! Like they would do in the films!'

Linda had been lying there strapped down in the Dark Room unable to move. She heard shouting coming from downstairs, and she just prayed that Chaz was all right. She had thought about shouting for help, but Freeda had already warned her she'd cut her throat if she shouted stuff out. But she was so hot in that mask and really thirsty. She could hear them coming upstairs and going into the master bedroom and while in there, TV realized that the white blazer was on that sex doll in the garden. He would have to go out there to get the keys, but first he wanted to check up on Linda while Freeda sat herself down at the dressing table, engrossed with Linda's make-up. When TV appeared, Linda complained of being thirsty. TV shot downstairs to fetch a bottle of water for her. As TV came past Chaz, he thought he would quickly tape his mouth up again, so that he wouldn't shout out things. He couldn't be trusted and TV decided to search the Jag later. They would have the wedding and reception and then leave the house in the Blazerman's Jag. There was much to do. TV returned to the Dark Room and began undoing Linda's straps and chains, and he also took the mask off, so she could drink. It was a chance for TV to confide with Linda about his feelings and his hopes, that she would help him in his mission.

'I promise we won't hurt you, or your husband. But will ya make-up Freeda for our wedding? Its why I got us out. Cos, I wanted us to get married, even if we never live together. Getting married is a really special thing to me and Freeda. It's our dream, and you could get dressed up smart for the wedding! That would be nice that would.'

Linda gave thought to what he said, and she agreed, as long as TV kept that promise, not to hurt either of them. The more Linda considered the idea, the more she thought it might work, to take the edge off Freeda, to pacify her and keep her on her better behavior. That was Linda's hope, so she agreed.

So now Freeda was going to get married at last to TV. She was sitting at the dressing table so excited, and that big fat nurse was wrong all the time. They had all been proved wrong. She was thinking these things as she was looking into the mirror and she had to wash all that spooky Halloween stuff off. She shouted out to TV.

'TV! I need to get all this black make-up off! I look awful!'

TV came in with Linda and suggested that Freeda had a shower.

'Then Linda will make you up all special for your wedding day, Freeda!'

This was confirmation to Freeda. It was all true. It was going to happen. She kissed Linda in her gratitude and rushed off to the bathroom. There was that shower in the master bedroom, but she was gone, and so Linda had a quick shower herself before she got changed. But freshening up, gave her the sense they would get out of this situation. She felt clean and fresh and more positive and she felt clear in purpose. They just had to play along with this mock wedding thing and she would wink to Chaz downstairs when she got there. Yes, that could be the way they approached it and Chaz would get it immediately. She just hoped something terrible hadn't already befallen him.

After the shower, Linda got herself into a trouser suit that she had worn at Royal Ascot the previous year. She had kept it for another event that might come along, and nothing had, but it had been cleaned, and was sitting there in the wardrobe for an occasion. TV thought it would look just right and there was an elegant straw hat with a ribbon that went with it. It was all perfect and Linda made herself up, while Freeda was in the main bathroom showering, and still singing that wedding song. It had been on her mind, and in the relaxed moment of the shower she remembered all the words, and she could be heard singing as Linda finalized her outfit.

Freeda came back into the bedroom with a towel around her and she confronted the wedding dress that was hung on a coat hanger over the edge of the wardrobe. The dress took Freeda's breath away. It was all true. That wedding dress made it true.

'It's true! Freeda is going to get married to TV!'

'Yeah, we are, Freeda! And Linda's gonna make you all beautiful and special for your wedding.'

'We'll have to tell Dan!' Freeda exclaimed, and TV would love to get Dan involved.

'Yeah, we will, Freeda! He knew that I got you out to get married, Freed! Dan was the only person I told! And we'll have our photographs taken, Freeda!'

Linda nodded her head as TV looked at her. Yes, she could take photographs of the wedding.

'We've got a terrific camera but you mustn't hurt anybody, Freeda, on your wedding day. It's a time of love and celebration, and being nice to people. And not hurting people.'

Linda was praying that this request might do the trick. Freeda took the dress and held it up to her body in the mirror. If she could get that wedding dress on and marry TV, she would never hurt anybody, never.

'Freeda wouldn't hurt anybody on her wedding day,' Freeda replied, as the dress was just so beautiful and it was likely to fit well, as Linda was of similar height and weight, back when she married. That was twenty-two years and forty pounds less ago! But the dress was transporting Freeda away to the place of her dreams. Everything had been special since she was with TV.

TV took yet another pristine white blazer, and this time trousers to match from Chaz's wardrobe. He also went for the older, smaller version of Chaz's twill shirt.

'I've gotta have a flashy shirt, Freeda!'

TV explored the shirt more, pulling it about on its hanger and he could see that it was slightly different, but so appropriate. It had all the colors of the other, but had a dragon on it. Like a Dragon Star psychedelic shirt. It blew TV away.

'It's got a red dragon on it breathing fire, Freeda!

'Dragon Star must have put it there for ya to find, TV,' Freeda said, and TV agreed. But the world is mysterious like that TV thought, and he found a nice matching black satin tie, that complimented the loud, brash, and vibrant colors of the shirt. He considered the trousers, and although they were a little short in the leg, they would be fine with a belt hitching them up from the waist. But he had to have them now, as they would look so aesthetically right with the accompanying blazer. The groom gathered his clothing, he was still in disbelief, a white blazer and a Dragon Star shirt? He collected the necklace and tiara from the bottom of the black box. He would give them to Freeda later, they'd be more special then.

'I'll have a quick shower and then go downstairs and get ready for ya, Freeda.'

TV kissed her and left the bedroom, and Freeda kept holding that wedding dress close. That big fat nurse was wrong. Wrong all the time. That wedding dress was Freeda's heart.

After TV left the bedroom, Linda set about preparing Freeda for her wedding day. Firstly, she blow-dried her hair and then she helped Freeda get in that wedding dress. It was a nigh perfect fit and as Linda zipped up the back, she couldn't help but feel a deep compassion and sympathy for Freeda, who kept relentlessly asking her for confirmation, that she was marrying.

'Freeda is going to get married to TV, isn't she?' Freeda asked a number of times in one way or another, and that vulnerability and doubt, touched Linda. She had never had anything, Linda thought, and she also thought about what TV had said earlier about her stepfather. Linda became determined to make Freeda up as best she could, and surely it was the key to keep her contained. It was all about mere survival.

While he was in the shower, TV thought more about weddings. There were always flowers at weddings and there was a ton out there in the garden. He thought he'd pick some and make some pin on roses. There were loads on those trellises. He could cut them off with the clippers, he saw down that proper shed, and he could roll the stalks up in some silver foil. TV knew that the red rose was a symbol of eternal love, and what would be more appropriate? Their love would last for an eternity, at the very least. They would never be parted. It was written in the stars and they were the Dragon Star children. He was thinking about the cocaine in that dashboard too.

Freeda was speechless. She was standing in front of the full-length mirror in her wedding dress. She was 'special' Freeda now. The dress looked wonderful. It was like a healing balm to her soul and she even had some long sparkling cuff style earrings on, with the phrase 'eternal love' engraved on them. The gem's sparkled and they were reborn again, as was the dress. She looked perfect, smelt perfect and felt even more so. Dreams really come true sometimes.

'Does Freeda look beautiful, Linda?'

'You look wonderful on your wedding day, Freeda, just wonderful,' Linda confirmed, and with the special personal attention given to Freeda by Linda, the Blazerwoman had become Linda. Kleeunah was the last person who had helped Freeda like this. She had won a massive measure of friendship.

'This is the very best day of my life, Linda. I've always wanted to get married to TV! I've always wanted to!'

Freeda looked so happy, still in disbelief that her life could turn out like this. She was looking as good as all those women did in the magazines who get married. Freeda knew she looked beautiful, and she thought of her mother.

'I pray my mummy is looking down on me in my wedding dress.'

'I'm sure she is, Freeda, I'm sure she is,' Linda replied.

The police had followed the lead into Fishgate and had searched the resort as best they could, especially so when they were told by the Trust representative that Fishgate might be where they headed, as Freeda talked frequently about Fishgate in the unit. They had that initial sighting ten miles or so from Tennin and then another, reported on the outskirts of Fishgate. But there were a lot of goths and hip young things down at Fishgate and it had been a case of mistaken identity. But the police still thought that it was likely they were there, but well holed out. It was just a matter of time before something else came through. Back in the local Tennin area, all the immediate vicinity had been searched. It would be a case of keep searching, as they had to be apprehended. Since Chaz though, there hadn't been any leads whatsoever, and if they were there the police thought they must be holed up in a shed or on a farm, or in somebody's house. Both the police and the Trust were fearing the worst and hoping for the very best, and if the truth be known, they fully expected something in between.

TV popped out into the garden in his pants and Dragon Star T-shirt and white blazer, but he intended to get properly dressed when he returned to the front lounge. The first thing he wanted to do was sort those flowers out. He took the roses off the trellis with the snips and handling them made him think. He could make a hand bouquet for Freeda like all the brides have. But he would have to be quick though. Time was of the essence. He picked a selection of flowers from the front of the house, making sure that nobody was around, or walking past to see him. TV knew something about doing bouquets, as his aunt Joan had worked in a florist, and TV helped her regularly. He collected a selection of different shades of yellow spring flowers and a few tulips, and some Calla Lilly, as that front garden had such variety. TV would set them off with some blue larkspur and some clever greenery. Everything went into a bucket. But before he came back in, he just had to check that dashboard, to see if Blazerman was telling the truth. He said there was stacks of money and cocaine in there. He went down into the garden and confronted that sex doll. It was like looking at himself, the likeness was so uncanny. The keys were there in the inside pocket and TV quickly went out to the Jag, shaking his head, still in disbelief. He opened the car's door but he could see a group of people, who were approaching up the lane from that house down the bottom. It looked bad. There were a crowd of a dozen or so and of course TV thought it was a search party. He got into the car and laid low.

It was in fact 'The Tennin Ramblers', and today they had decided to cover the asylum area on a long walk, to try and contribute to the general search. TV's heart was a thumping, but the walkers all rambled past. They hadn't seen him. TV then opened the dash up with a little key that was on the ring and there was a plastic carrier bag that carried the one full kilo and other ounce bags, and stacks of cash.

'Fuck! He was telling the truth!'

TV couldn't believe it. He only ever had cocaine a few times, and that was bought by Keefy, but now he could get smashed, and they could get Dan down for a legend of a wedding party!

As soon as TV got back in the kitchen, it was an enormous line out on the table and snorted through a twenty-pound note. But he couldn't believe how much money they had now. He decided they would have the wedding and then get the fuck out of Tennin. Drive that Jag someplace, as he kind of knew how to drive. He would guess the rest. But with euphoria overcoming him as soon as he snorted, the added energy helped him to get all the preparations done. He felt like superman on a wedding mission. He took to wrapping those roses and creating his hand bouquet, and in between, he began searching the kitchen fridge and all the other cupboards for food. He had seen those bottles in the fridge earlier, but now he was looking with his wedding reception and party eye. Wedding receptions always have stacks of food and drink, and TV's and Freeda's had to be like that. The first thing he came across were the two large bottles of champagne that were sitting there. These were earmarked for a little family get together, around the wedding anniversary, that was a couple of weeks into June. TV couldn't believe his luck. It must have all been written in the stars. Real champagne to toast the wedding, tons of food for the reception, and cocaine to get out your nut. There was even a chocolate cake in the cupboard and chocolate cake was something that Freeda loved. And there was everything in that fridge, absolutely everything, cheeses, salads, and in the freezer box there were pizzas, and now TV had tons of energy. He was coming up big on that coke and he couldn't resist another line. Then he rushed to the threshold and called up to Freeda and Linda to wait upstairs, until he gave the go ahead.

'I'm gonna get it all done special for ya, down here, Freeda!' he shouted up. Freeda didn't mind, as Linda could take more time fussing over her, and it was exciting having to wait. It was like Christmas and TV wouldn't be long as he would work fast.

The more TV looked in the cupboards the more he found. Pickled onions, pickled walnuts, he loved his pickled, and the array of cheeses was mind boggling. They would have a cheeseboard and he would have to get Dan down! He could sneak past the concentration camp guards, TV thought, with a smile on his face. Everything was tons better than he imagined. But he would have to clear out that front lounge, get that smashed widescreen out, and give it a good hoover. He went to Chaz and undid the tape and asked him where the hoover was, and Chaz directed him to the back-reception room opposite the front door. He picked up the hoover and was astounded by that grand solar bed and the stacked-up porn DVDs, like the ones he had bought on the 'Triune Way'. There were thousands of them. But it was other things that interested TV more now. He found some LED lights and bunting flags that Chaz had bought and used for that house warming party in early April. He also found some festive sparkling angels with pipes, with lights inside, the kind of thing you see in pound shops, but these were rather more elaborate and up-market. TV couldn't believe his luck; he even found a small sewing box with pins and safety pins. He was on a mission. He would make that front lounge look something else and do it quick too. He prepared the cheeseboard and cut up a whole meal loaf neatly, and there were biscuits and crackers and all those pickles. He popped the pizza in the oven and then while it was cooking, he began to furnish the front room. He used some garden gloves to get that glass out and he dumped the smashed TV down by the rubbish bins. Then when he went back, he was coiling that bunting and the LEDs all around the light fittings and the fish-tanks. Chaz didn't say a word. Nothing bad was happening and time was passing. The longer it all went on, the greater likelihood they would be discovered, and Chaz was praying hard that 'pig' would come back through that gate again. Where are they, when you really need them?

Then TV began fiddling about with an item in his magic pouch. It was something that he had ordered as a personalized message from that wedding shop in Tennin. It was some bunting that said 'Freeda and TV', with a big love heart in the middle. He had kept it secret and special for Freeda and he taped it onto the wall, and everything, the cow horns, the guns, the carp tanks, the coffee table, and the velvet chair itself, was given an appropriate lift with some tinsel. Finally, he put those angels around the room, on the mantel and on top of the fish-tanks, and the large coffee table. He also took Linda and Chaz's bride and groom wedding cake decoration and put it on that chocolate cake that was ready to go in the kitchen. He finished his bouquets and pin on roses, and stopped for a moment and smiled. All this had worked out better than he had ever dreamed. Fancy Freeda having a proper wedding dress? It all seemed fate and destiny and it was time now for TV to get properly dressed too. What a shirt! TV slipped the Dragon Star twill over his T-shirt and then hitched up the white trousers, before putting on his black satin tie. He would be the hippest bridegroom in town. The pristine wedding blazer was lain over the Waldorf, and this one was all for Freeda. He had officially ceased all white blazer shagging with anybody now apart from Freeda. He took the blazer reverentially from its polythene and slipped it on, admiring and straightening himself out in the mirror, putting a comb through his long green hair. He then pinned that eternal red rose on the lapel and whatever happened, TV believed they would be together for eternity. And looking at himself dressed like this, was a moment of sheer personal triumph. The Dragon Star forces had been released and everything was now perfect for AD 2025, when the world would go all Dragon Star, due to the sheer enlightenment from the emanations. Then everybody would shag like crazy in the name of the avatar of the New Age. It was amazing. It was all kicking off, and kicking butt big and he turned to Chaz with a sneer on his face, but Chaz's eyes were closed. He had never prayed so much, and so fervently. It had to come to an end. Something had to occur that would change the state of play. Chaz prayed for that divine intervention. He would become a born-again Christian, if he got out of this, such was his suffering.

If ever a woman was supposed to be in a wedding dress, as a realization of self, it was Freeda. She was at the top of the stairs, radiating happiness, waiting to come down. She felt perfect and in the personalized moments in the bedroom with Linda attending her, she had transcended all the tragedy of her life and all its pain. She wanted to be here in this moment forever, wearing this beautiful wedding dress that trailed behind her.

'Thank you for helping me on my wedding day, Linda. You were nice to Freeda, really nice, nice to Freeda like Kleeunah used to be.'

Linda breathed a sigh of relief. It seemed this was the way to pacify Freeda, and she felt touched, because it was a heartfelt thank you. Linda had hope now, her hunches were proving correct. Keep her in the wedding zone and then Freeda's better instincts could be appealed to. Those that moved towards union and love, rather than psycho-conflict. Surely Freeda wouldn't do anything terrible in that wedding dress?

TV had finished his preparations. The food and drink were brought into the lounge, and placed on the large coffee table and with the curtains now drawn, the LED lights and bunting, and those angels and the tinsel brought with it a special intimacy.

'Are you ready now, Freeda?' TV shouted up.

Freeda and Linda had been waiting for this moment for the past half hour and more, because a couple of hours had passed. But the waiting had made it all the more exciting.

'We're coming down TV! We're coming down!' Freeda shouted back, her breath taken away by anticipation. 'Can you bring my handbag down for me, Linda, please?' Freeda asked, not wanting to ruin her look, but she had to have her new handbag. TV had brought along a CD that had the bridal song as its first track, an instrumental, and he put it on the player and began to sing the first verse, exhorting Chaz to give him strong support.

'Here comes the bride all dressed in white, radiant and lovely she shines in the light! Sing it, Blazerman! Sing it with me! As if ya really mean it! Sing it, Blazerman!'

Chaz, who had been half-heartedly singing, raised his voice with a little more forced enthusiasm, sitting there in his bondage chair, still strapped in, and looking like some off the wall Dragon Star priest with the hoodie on, caught with his pants down. Freeda came down the stairs and appeared, looking stunning in Linda's wedding dress with her hair done up, with Linda holding the short trail in attendance.

'You look beautiful, Freeda! Like a goddess!' TV gushed, as Freeda came through the threshold into the lounge. Freeda's face lit up. She was astonished by that room. It did look special, everything glowed and Freeda felt blessed. Linda looked composed in her trouser suit and Ascot hat and she gave a quick look to Chaz, that spoke volumes about their need to just flow with these events. Chaz caught the drift. Freeda had a good look at TV and smiled, and thought he looked so smart and loads better in his white blazer and trousers, and that loud shirt. He looked like a rockstar or film star.

'And you look great TV! Like, like...'

Freeda had difficulty in finding the words, yes, he did look like a film star but he was all the New Age and Dragon Star shagging, and that, and then it just popped out.

'Like a messiah!'

TV was more than surprised. The reply was like a rabbit unexpectantly coming out of a hat. But then he looked over himself. He wondered why on earth Freeda had said that?

'Yeah, I never really thought of it like that, Freeda! It must be all the white! But you look so beautiful!' and TV had things to enhance Freeda's radiance. 'Now, close your eyes! Close your eyes, real, real tight, Freeda! No squinty eyes! It's gotta be a surprise!'

Freeda closed her eyes but she was so curious. She couldn't wait to see what TV had for her.

'I would never ever cheat you with squinty eyes, TV! Never ever!' As soon as she said it her left eye was slyly opening.

'Nah, Freed! Ya mustn't look! Keep them shut tight until I say when.'

TV placed the wedding necklace around her neck and fastened it, and then placed the tiara on her head before attaching the red rose.

'What ya doing, TV?' Freeda asked, enjoying every second of the attention.

'Keep your eyes closed, Freeda!' Linda couldn't help but arrange the veil as TV moved Freeda in front of the oval mirror. 'Now you can open them!'

Freeda couldn't believe it, she looked more like a wedding bride than she had upstairs.

'A necklace and a princess's crown!'

TV smiled and held the rose on the white blazer's lapel.

'And look, Freeda, we've got red roses on. They mean we're together in love for eternity. That's what red roses mean!'

Freeda smiled with all her love, and that smile meant everything to TV, it showed it had all been worthwhile. It was like an incredible healing. It meant so much to him and TV had more to give her too.

'Here's your bouquet, Freeda. I made it myself, Freed! All brides have them, Freeda!'

Freeda's heart was in her throat. She had seen brides holding these and when she held it, looking at TV, and that bunting celebrating Freeda and TV's marriage, it reinforced what she remembered from being at the bus-stop with her mum. Dreams could come true and things did work out in the end. Everything seemed to sparkle golden, and TV had loads more for Freeda. 'And I've got this for ya, Freeda!' He held up the ring. 'It's your wedding ring! Dan was with me when I bought it, Freeda.' Freeda raised her hand to take the ring, but TV said he would give it to her during the ceremony. 'That's what happens, Freeda!' He then took another ring from the blazer pocket, the one that Dan brought, so Freeda had a ring to give to TV. 'This is the ring that Dan bought for ya with nearly all his birthday money, Freeda. It's the groom's ring. It's for you to give to me. That's how much Dan thinks of us, Freeda!'

Freeda became so overwhelmed by everything, she began to sob. Seeing that bunting spelling out the marriage and the lights and the cake and food, and seeing TV, looking just like the grooms do when they marry was just all too much. Freeda wanted to be in this moment forever and those little angels were calling out her name.

'Look, Freeda, even the angels are blowing their pipes and singing for us! Everything is in harmony now!'

Freeda was in disbelief. But it was all true!

Chaz had the hood up on his jacket, as TV thought it made him look more like a priest, and he was still trying his darndest to extract himself from the humiliation.

'I've got to have my hands and legs free, TV, to preside over a proper marriage. Priests are never, ever tied up like this in real churches, are they? They're always standing up!'

TV was just about fed up with Chaz trying to trick them and he lost his cool.

'You'll do it tied to the chair, Blazerman! And if you try any more tricks on our wedding day, I'll tell the bride to dig it in your thigh! Get it!' Linda protested. TV had promised. 'Yeah, but no tricks! If there's tricks, he'll get it!'

Within a few minutes, the officiating priest was ready to marry the love-struck couple. Chaz took up the gauntlet. It seemed the right thing to do in the odd circumstances, but he was still tied up and strapped to the bondage chair with his trousers and pants stretched across his ankles.

'We are gathered here today to bear witness to the marriage of TV Sam and Freeda, who have a great and abiding love for each other, and who now wish to be brought together in the sanctity of God's marriage vows. So, if there is anybody out there, who objects to this marriage taking place, raise your voice now, otherwise God's will shall be done!'

There was a complete silence, but for the birds singing and kraaing outside, and Freeda's heart was singing with them. It was real. At last, Freeda was getting married to TV.

'There's nobody, TV!' Freeda exclaimed, so excited that soon she would be married to him.

'That's because our marriage was made in heaven, Freeda! It was God's plan for us!'

Freeda loved TV talking like that. It made it feel that it was all fated, and meant to be. Their destiny.

'It always works out in the end, TV, doesn't it? Always!' Freeda said, and TV agreed.

By now, Chaz had begun to immerse himself into the role of priest, administering for the sacred union of the lovers and it was working. Everything was a matter of stalled time, and in this mood, Freeda wasn't likely to go the 'head on a pole' route.

'The exchange of the rings please and firstly the ring for the bride!'

TV took Freeda's hand and placed the ring on her finger and God had remembered her at last. She was transported to a world of love beyond her wildest dreams.

'I love you so much, Freeda,' and Freeda replied with the same feeling towards her beloved groom. Chaz was asked to continue with a nod from TV.

'And now for the groom's ring,' Chaz exclaimed, further recognizing that this mock wedding ceremony was the key to prevent 'Mad Freeda' from flashing that knife around, threatening to cut his penis off. He gave a smile to Linda, as if to confirm they would keep proceedings at this pitch, if possible. Linda gave Freeda the ring from Dan and she helped her place the ring on TV's finger.

'I'll have to thank Dan TV,' Freeda said, and TV agreed, so they would phone him as soon as the marriage ceremony was over. Chaz carried on with conviction, realizing that this development might just work the oracle.

'With the rings exchanged, I shall continue. Do you, TV Sam, take Freeda Huskit for your lawful wedded wife? In sickness and in health and for better and for poorer?' TV looked deep into Freeda's eyes, and to think that all of this was made possible by that big electric saw.

'I do with all my heart,' TV said lovingly, before Chaz proceeded. 'And do you, Freeda Huskit, take TV Sam, for your lawful wedded husband? In sickness and in health, and for better and for poorer?

'Of course, I do! I love TV! He saved me! And it's God's plan!'

Chaz pronounced them man and wife and the pronouncement couldn't have been more real for TV and Freeda. They were married now, and TV gave Freeda a long kiss, before he turned on the CD player again, onto the second track on the disc. A church organ boomed through the lounge with the wedding march, like a real proper wedding. And as the music rang out, Linda threw confetti over the couple and took photos. It was as if God's very angels were blessing their marriage.

The sun was going downwards, yet still bright and streaming into the front garden, and TV thought it would be wonderful to have more photos, out there with the spring flowers around them.

'We can make sure nobody's around, Freeda!'

TV slipped around the back and there was nobody about. They would have to do it quick. TV knocked on the front door to give the all clear. Freeda came out, gloriously happy and the couple stood together up by the gate. Linda threw the last of the confetti over them, and then she moved backwards, taking loads more snaps. Freeda couldn't contain her joy. To think it had actually happened.

'We're married, TV! That fat nurse was wrong, TV! We did get married!'

TV was so happy. He had done it.

'I said we'd get married, Freeda, didn't I? And you look beautiful! My wife's so beautiful! Doesn't my wife look beautiful, Linda?'

Linda agreed as she kept taking photographs. When they arrived back in the front lounge, TV began pressing the mobile that he had taken from Chaz. They just had to tell Dan, and Freeda was bursting to speak to him. The joy and love had to be shared.

'We've got to tell Dan, TV! We've got to!' Such married bliss.

CHAPTER TWENTY-ONE

TILL DEATH DO US PART

Dan was alone, seated in the television lounge with a cup of coffee. The TV was running but he wasn't taking anything but a cursory notice of it, and he was gloomily depressed. He was missing TV already, as TV helped him get through hospital life. He liked cracking jokes and laughing with him and nobody appreciated Dan like TV. TV made his life fun, and without him it wasn't fun at all. It made him feel that he was in an asylum and everything was dark and oppressive. How he wanted TV back there. It would never be the same without him. He felt empty at breakfast, dinner and all afternoon. It was going to get really hard and nasty he thought, and nasty could get really bad for Dan, as he was a self-harmer in depressed Dan mode. He would sit around bringing up, and then reliving all the bad, just like he was beginning to do now. Then the ringtone of his mobile went, and he perked up immediately, when he heard TV's voice the other end. He couldn't believe it.

'Dan! Me and Freeda have just got married like I said, Dan. And Freeda was so happy ya brought the ring, Dan! Really, really happy!'

Dan looked around concerned as he didn't want anyone to know who he was speaking to, even though there was nobody in the lounge. He spoke with a close watchful eye on the door. He would quickly end the call if need be.

'I'll have to whisper, TV! They're going full on bonkers up here, police and that! People are running around with their head's half off! They questioned me and I told um I know nothing. But where are ya? I'm missing ya, TV!'

Freeda was urging TV to give her the mobile. She just wanted to express her great joy. She had to tell Dan about her wedding and looking beautiful; it was the best day of her life, and she wanted to tell Dan how much she loved TV. But TV kept hold of it, as he tried to explain to Dan where they were, and what was happening. He could do that better.

'You know that house by the flying saucer lamppost? We're in there, Dan. Why don't ya come down? You'll be able to see Freeda in her wedding dress. She looks so pretty, Dan, and we've got bottles of champagne and tons of cocaine. Tons of it! Like the films! And we've got a wedding cake and fucking stacks of money. Fucking stacks! It's all come good, Dan! It's that blue film man's house!'

Dan couldn't believe it. How did TV get in there? But TV was one of those people that make things happen, and does what they say they're going to do, so it didn't surprise him one bit really. Freeda was veritably itching to speak.

'Let Freeda speak to Dan, TV! Let Freeda speak to Dan!'

How Freeda wanted to just share her joy with loved ones. Everything had become so exciting, but TV wanted to say just a few more things first.

'Just a sec, Freed! Come down, Dan, cos Freeda looks so beautiful. And I gotta white blazer on like Keefy's Dan. You wanna see it! I've got loads of them. "Dragon Star" is really beginning to happen, Dan! It's really kicking off! Like I said it would, Dan!' Freeda was still pestering, so eventually TV had to give her the moment. 'Here's Freeda, Dan!' he exclaimed. It was all so exciting.

Nurse Lavender Garotte never usually worked in Dan's more open ward, but she decided to get some overtime in. There was a late shift going and while Dan was speaking, she had come on shift, and had been briefed by the Ward Leader with regards running around the drugs. She had some liquid medication for Dan on the trolley, a new fruity pink syrup from Dr. Bolt.

Dan detested Nurse Garotte too, as all the patients did, and he was just thankful that she was rarely on his ward. Dan was sensitive and that Lavender nurse terrified him. Freeda was effusive.

'We got married, Dan! Freeda got married to TV, at last! The big fat nurse was wrong all the time, Dan! We did get married! Can you hear our wedding music! And we've got bottles of champagne, Dan! And big bottles of coke!' TV made sure the church organ wedding song was on a loop to keep the right atmosphere up.

'And thank Dan for the ring, Freeda,' TV said.

'Yeah, and thank you for buying me that ring, Dan. TV loves it! Thank you, Dan, we love you lots!'

Those words meant so much to Dan. Spending that money he had in his bank account on the ring was more than worth it. Dan explained about the day he and TV bought the wedding rings. It was fantastic. Everything had worked out.

'You deserve good things happening, Freeda, and I was with TV when he bought your wedding ring. It cost him all his money, Freeda, and then I bought that groom's ring for ya to give TV.'

But Freeda was so excited, she just had too much to say.

'I've got a wedding dress, Dan, and I'm like a princess! And there's all confetti over us, like proper weddings and TV has got Keefy's blazer on and a flashy Dragon shirt! Come down, Dan! It's by the flying saucer lamppost!'

Dan was so pleased for her, but then Nurse Garotte was calling for him out in the ward.

'Mr. Clarke! Mr. Clarke, your medication!'

Her voice was enough to visibly unhinge poor Dan.

'The Gestapo's here. I'll try and get down, Freeda.'

Dan had reduced his voice to a whisper but it was too late. Nurse Lavender saw him flustering around trying to get the mobile into his pocket, as she was about to open the door. She put two and two together. Dan had been speaking to TV and Freeda. She could read all the signs.

'Mr. Clarke, here's your medication! And who were you talking to?'

Nurse Garotte had always terrified Dan and she knew it, and she was trying to be as frightening as possible. 'Who were you talking to!' she demanded to know.

'Nobody! Nobody, Nurse!'

Dan put his hand out for the medicine and took it quickly, praying that Nurse Lavender would go away and tend her flowers, or pester Drill-head or something, but she didn't. She persisted, as she knew it had been TV.

'Give me that phone! Give it to me! Otherwise I'll transfer to this ward full-time, Mr. Clarke, and give you hell! You'll be six foot under the mire!' Dan gave up the thing immediately. She really was as scary as the Gestapo. Six foot under the mire, Dan was hardly five and there was no way that Dan could have Nurse Garotte on his case. He would commit suicide if she was after him, day after day. He would hang himself, without a doubt. Nurse Garotte found the previous call and phoned back. Back in the lounge TV naturally thought it was Dan, phoning back to get a confirmation or something.

'It must be Dan, Freeda! It must be Dan! Yeah it is! Hullo, Dan! What's up?' TV said. He gulped when he heard Nurse Garotte on the other end of the line. He couldn't have dreamed up a worse nightmare.

'A ha! Just as I thought! TV! Now you jolly well come back to the hospital immediately. Right this minute!'

'Fuck off, ya fat Nazi monster!'

TV ended the call, but he knew that Nurse Garotte would confiscate Dan's mobile, and then it would be a tracking of the number down to this house. At least TV was aware of the implications. Nurse Lavender was fuming, flames were nigh snorting out of her nostrils. How dare she be spoken to like that! She was in such a rage that she gave the phone back to Dan without thinking, when he reached out for it. She went off in a complete huff and puff and then realized that she should have confiscated the thing. She returned to the lounge, but Dan had scarpered. Nurse Garotte informed the Ward Leader and within a few minutes the security was told to apprehend Dan Clarke immediately. They just had to get that mobile! But Dan was away, and he was cutting across the grass fields as fast as he could, huffing and puffing his way towards the smoking tree with a half empty king size bottle of Brew in his hand.

Back in the lounge, things were tense, but TV had the resolve to just carry on, as if nothing had happened. Everything was a matter of time he thought. They just had to enjoy every moment of this special wedding day.

Freeda was still high about the idea of Dan coming down to join the party. They had two bottles of champagne!

'Dan's coming down to our wedding party, TV!'

But Chaz was still trying to work one on them. He had to try. He saw yet another opening.

'You'll have to go on a honeymoon! Won't they, Linda? Married couples always go off on their honeymoon! You gotta go!'

Talk of the honeymoon set Freeda off. Blazerman was right, all married couples did that, and she and TV had to be the same, so their wedding was all proper.

'Freeda wants to go on the honeymoon! To Fishgate! Let's go to Fishgate, TV!'

Chaz had to keep trying. The ruse might just work, and that would be that, game over.

Why don't you just set off right now! We can get you a taxi to go anywhere, or I can drive ya in me Jag! Go down the south of France! Go for it, like proper married couples do, when they've got stacks of money like you two have. Just do it!'

Freeda was so excited, but France, no, she would be more than happy with Fishgate. She wanted to go to that place on the beach where she sat with her mum. She could be there with TV and Blazerwoman could take loads of photos. And they could stay anywhere, they could go to that caravan park and it was true, Dragon Star had stacks of money these days.

'We've got to go, TV! We can pick up Dan by the flying saucer lamppost!'

But TV knew that this was yet another trick, and TV was more urgent now. He expected Garotte to get that mobile traced. He would have to end all these tricks once and for all. He didn't really want to do it like this, but they had to.

'He's trying to get us caught again, Freeda! Give him a stab in the thigh! Give him a dig so he gets the message!'

Linda tried desperately to stop the drama moving backwards, appealing to TV, regarding his promise. But TV was trying his best to keep things restrained.

'You promised not to hurt us, TV. You promised!' she said.

'But he keeps trying to trick us!' TV replied, with a noticeably rising anger. Freeda fell back into her threatening mode as this old Blazerman was ruining her wedding. She snatched up the knife that TV had placed underneath the coffee table for safe keeping. Chaz began to beg and vowed to himself that was it, he had to ditch such tactics.

'No Please, no! The police will come and get ya!'

But Chaz had to be taught a lesson, to end all this tricking.

'Give him a nick, Freeda! Just a nick so he gets the idea!'

Freeda was quick to it with a sneer. This old Blazerman had to shut his kisser up. She nicked his thigh, while TV covered his mouth to stop any cries of pain. Linda protested as Freeda slipped back into her psychotic. She liked scaring people with knives.

'No! That's enough, Freeda! That's enough! Ya don't wanna get blood on your wedding dress!'

Freeda dropped the knife instantly. TV was right. She looked so beautiful, and if she messed up her wedding dress, everything would be ruined. It was special, she couldn't mess it all up. But TV said, at least the old clapped-out Blazerman knew they meant it now. No-one messes with Dragon Star. Nobody!

'Yeah, we mean it, Blazerman! Nuffin' stops the Dragon Star children! Nuffin'! Not even the big fat nurse! Nuffin'!' Freeda snapped, as TV released his hand from Chaz's mouth. Chaz was grimacing and his thigh was bleeding, and the concerned TV turned to Linda.

'Have you got any bandages?' he said.

'Yes! Yes!' Linda exclaimed, running out to the kitchen with TV close behind her. The commotion over the wound was soon over though, as things quietened, on Linda's realization that the wound was only superficial. It wouldn't be a problem, although the bandage was bloody. Chaz was noticeably flinching when Linda was dressing the wound but the atmosphere was calming and more importantly Freeda, nor TV, had any blood on their wedding day clothes.

It was only a little nick. TV was chilled and Freeda was now returning to that wedding high.

'Fancy me marrying you, TV! Who would have thought it? We proved that big fat nurse wrong. Didn't we, TV?' TV held Freeda closely to him.

'I always knew we would, Freeda! I could see it in the stars! And let's have some champagne and toast our marriage. And then we can have the food and play the music, and have a dance as bride and groom!'

'And Dicky can be the man who does those special speeches, TV.'

TV thought that a great idea.

'Yeah, Freeda! He can be the best man and he'd better do it properly! And Dan can be the real proper one when he gets down. He'll make it. I know Nurse Garotte was on the phone shouting, but I bet he got out when she wasn't looking Freeda! That's the sort of thing that Dan does. He sneaks off! He's good at sneaking off! Nobody notices him!'

TV laughed, emanating warmth, as he had great affection for Dan. Freeda thought that TV deserved two best men, it would be a great idea, and TV just prayed that Dan would make it.

With a couple of bottles of champagne, they could also crack on with a toast, and do it again later when Dan came. TV uncorked the first bottle with a hoop and a holler and poured four glasses on a tray. He released one arm of Chaz's, and then offered the champagne. They were all ready for the special toast.

'Let's toast to the marriage of Freeda and TV, the special, special marriage of Holly Beach Lane!' TV announced with such pride and joy. Freeda joined in too.

'Yeah, drink to me and my husband, TV!'

All four touched their glasses and Chaz and Linda both raised the toast and drank the champagne; however reluctant Chaz was. But as soon as the toast was over, TV fastened up Chaz's arm to the chair, to prevent any more of that funny business. TV wanted to wait for Dan, but he knew he might not make it, so they had to press on. It was time now for the wedding food and Dan could still have some if he came late. TV had cut up a whole meal loaf, and Freeda, still thinking they were playing mummies and daddies, naturally wanted to feed her little Dicky.

'I'm going to let my little Dicky have some whole meal bread, TV! My Dicky loves his whole meal!' Within a few minutes, Freeda had stuffed Chaz's mouth to full capacity, and it looked as if Chaz, had a whole meal bread tennis ball stuck in his mouth, with bits of bread dribbling from it. Freeda was reveling in being mummy again as Chaz expelled the slobber.

'Naughty, naughty little Dicky, spitting your bread out! You've got to eat it all up! Otherwise Dicky won't grow up all big and strong for Mummy.'

Freeda then came on with a rather more aggressive tone. 'Open your kisser, Dicky! Fucking open it!' she shouted. TV frowned as he wanted to divert Freeda away from those games. They still had the best man speeches, and then the wedding cake stuff to get through, and if Dan did make it, they had the booze up and the cocaine. Fuck Locko, they were gonna raise hell! It was going to be champagne and cocaine in the name of Dragon Star's first celebrity wedding!

'Nah, don't play mummies and daddies anymore, Freeda, cos it's time for the special speech from my best man. So, don't fill up his mouth anymore, Freeda! He won't be able to do his speaking and that. So, don't put any more food in there, Freeda!'

But Freeda was still relentlessly shoveling in the whole meal bread. However, she stopped and smiled, and eventually relented, as she looked forward to that speech.

'Oh yea! And he's bound to say nice things! They always do, don't they, TV?'

There was a quiet in the room as Chaz prepared to make the speech with a few coughs and a clearing of his mouth of gooey bread. It was unsightly, like a baby messing with its food on a high chair.

'Isn't he messy with his food, TV?'

Tensions had eased, Freeda had been pacified by this wonderful marriage ceremony, but Chaz was still aware that she was unpredictable. He still had to be careful. Chaz began making a stab at the speech as best he could.

'Let's all raise our glasses to the special marriage that's taken place here today. And all I can say, er, is that this special wedding couldn't happen to a nicer bloke. Now I know I haven't known TV for very long, but I'm sure he'll be a good loving husband to Freeda, and TV and Freeda will make such a perfect couple. How bad's that?'

Freeda was smiling, as Blazerman was saying such nice things, like best men should and there was more.

'And I've noticed that Freeda is turning over a new leaf and she would never, never hurt anybody now she's married to TV. Now she's really, really happy.'

There was a few seconds silence and Chaz hoped that he had pulled it off successfully, and he had, because Freeda was beaming.

'Yeah, that's true, TV! Weren't that nice? I knew Dicky was really nice! Let's have another toast! For our special marriage, TV!'

TV was up for that, and he poured out another glass of champagne and then cracked another bottle so they would continue to have full glasses. Linda played along and toasted, and she thought she would let herself go and drink, as it might ease her fears, although the potentially violent atmosphere had given way to something a little more benign now. TV went over to the music deck and Freeda was effusive. She wanted music from her special *Sesame Street* case.

'We can play that one I bought ya, Freeda, all the old ones!'

'It's Freeda's special music, TV. My special music!'

The CD in question was a compilation of old acts from the fifties and early sixties that Freeda loved. Although there were some 1990s pop acts in the case, most of the music was old, as that's what her mother played when Freeda was young. The very first track was the Etta James track that Freeda played relentlessly in the lock up unit, thinking of TV.

'It's my song, TV! Freeda's song!'

They were up swaying together and Freeda shed tears of joy. Her life had seemingly caught up with her song, and TV was in her arms and was hers at last.

'The skies are blue now, Freeda, and we're in heaven! Whatever happens we'll always be in heaven together, Freeda!'

'At last, TV! At last! We're together now! Aren't we?'

Linda was sat on the Waldorf and despite everything, she couldn't help but be moved, by the couples display of warm affection for each other. It was an odd feeling, being touched, but that was how she felt, and for Freeda this was three minutes of the most perfect healing and redemption.

The song was Freeda's song as it contained all her longing to be with TV. Dr. Lock had torn them apart but now TV was holding her in his arms and they were married. The new life had begun, and Freeda's heart felt healed by the warmth she was feeling.

'We'll be together forever now won't we, TV?'

'Of course, we will, Freeda! We were meant to be together.'

The second track on the CD added to the warm feeling that was being evoked as the afternoon moved into early evening. The track was Dean Martin's 'Volare' and TV knew that Dean Martin was another of Freeda's favorites.

'It's Dean Martin, TV! My mum's favorite!'

The couple just kept on swaying together.

'That's why I chose it! So, that she can be up there looking down on us, Freeda! She'll be so happy you got married at last! Things do work out nice sometimes.'

Freeda nestled her head on TV's shoulder and cried into the white blazer, thinking about her mum. But she felt enveloped by TV's love and all she could feel was love.

'I told ya we would get married, Freeda, and now we're married forever,' TV quietly confided.'

'I knew I would marry you in the end! I knew I would, TV!'

'Do you remember that first time I met ya, Freeda, in the lounge. I fell in love with ya at first sight! And you're so beautiful. Doesn't my wife look beautiful, Linda?'

'Yes, she's very beautiful on her wedding day,' Linda replied, trying to hold back her tears. Freeda reiterated again and again that this was the most special day of her life.

'The best, TV! The best!' she said. This was how a wedding should be.

Things began to lighten even further as they had another glass of champagne and everything sparkled for the newlyweds as Louis Armstrong's trumpet began, and TV swayed with Freeda. They were together as one. Linda was drawn to take some more photographs and the angels were singing with love.

'We're married now aren't we, TV?'

'We're married forever now, Freeda,' was the response that Freeda kept wanting to hear, as everything in her life was generally taken away. She wanted no more than to hang onto these precious moments in that front lounge, that was the warmest place on planet earth. La Vie en Rose! The bliss.

CHAPTER TWENTY-TWO

HERE COMES THE CAVALRY

Far away from the wedding and hostage bubble that was 'Chaz's Pad', Linda's close friend, June, was in the lounge of her house watching TV. The regional news was on and June was dragging on a cigarette reading the paper. The news item was referring to the 'break out' and June immediately put the paper aside and listened with interest. The two absconders were still at large and were highly dangerous.

'Ooh, I must ring Linda to check if they are all right, Ray,' June said. Ray also suggested that she ought to keep on about that part time job. It would do Linda good to just get out of the house a bit more.

'She's sitting around doing too much coke!' Ray said, and June knew that Ray was right. They were worried about her. Linda was in a place where she just needed something else, to get her away from her incessant drug taking. June pressed her mobile; Linda's line was completely dead.

'Um, that's odd, it's dead, Ray.'

Ray suggested they should try the other number, Chaz's dealing hotline. He had it on his phone, so he gave it a ring. He got through, but there was no answer and Ray recorded his message. He waited for a response as he knew that of an evening, Chaz always had this phone with him, whether he was at home, or out on his rounds. But nothing came back and June didn't like it.

'I don't like this, Ray, with these two crazies on the fucking run. And that Mad Freeda sounds like a right old head case. Let's pop over and check, eh.'

Ray agreed that it might be the best thing to do to be sure.

Back in the wedding parlor, the celebrations were at fever pitch. The wedding music was still playing on the CD and now it was the turn of Sammy Davis Junior and 'Mr. Bojangles', another track that Freeda loved, as her mother used to play Rat Pack records all the time. It was Kleeunah who had helped her remember those nice moments of her childhood, by prompting her with different music until Freeda found the treasure trove.

'Oh, I love this one, TV! Do ya dancing, TV!' she exclaimed, and TV danced one of his own interpretations, which he had done way back when he was in the lock up unit with Freeda. Freeda clasped her hands and caressed her wedding ring with the fingers of her right hand. The moments were golden.

'Freeda thanks God for today, TV! For our special wedding, our wonderful wedding.'

'Yeah, we're blessed, Freeda! Look everything's sparkling, it's all around us sparkling.'

'Let's have more champagne, TV!'

TV thought that a great idea and he poured yet another glass of bubbly. Freeda's words touched Linda, who could see these moments were Freeda's redemptive ones.

June and Ray turned into Holly Beach Lane, after having seen a number of police vehicles in the village and vicinity. They passed the doctor's detached, and were soon to arrive at the house as they sped past the Holly Beach Lane road sign. They parked up and were at the gate. June breathed in the late spring garden with its sweet aromas. It really was a special garden, like the Garden of Eden, June thought. It was just so beautiful. However, she gave Ray an odd look when she noticed the curtains drawn, a little early for that. June and Ray both knew instantly that something was up. They walked up the garden path and June spotted the odd sex doll that stood erect in the middle of the flower bed in the back garden. She just pointed at it in disbelief.

'What the fuck is that!' Ray exclaimed, and June gestured to him to keep quiet. They stopped and heard female laughter, an odd cackling laugh and June recognized it immediately. She nodded her head to Ray as if to say, 'That's them in there'. It was a heart-stopping moment. They quietly turned back and were at pains to get out of the garden, without making a noise. June was quickly onto the police with her mobile behind the horse chestnut, and they wouldn't be long in responding, as they were still in the village.

'I work at Tennin Asylum as a cleaning supervisor and I recognize her laugh. You can't mistake it really. They are in there, without a doubt!' June explained. The officer on the line said there would be a response team up there as quickly as possible, but he insisted that in no circumstances, should they get involved.

Meanwhile, in the lounge, Freeda was urging TV to put the CD back to the first track, to 'Freeda's song', and she was badgering him to phone Dan again. She so desperately wanted to show Dan her dress and tiara.

'Phone Dan again, TV! Phone Dan! To see when he's coming, TV! Phone Dan!'

TV felt unsure about phoning him because of Nurse Garotte. She had probably confiscated his mobile. But Freeda kept pestering him so he gave it a ring, hoping for the best, and praying he wasn't met with the Gestapo on the other end of the line. He was so relieved.

'He's on the line, Freeda! Have you left, Dan? Freeda can't wait to see ya. We've got so much to show ya, Dan!'

Dan had just exited from the hospital perimeter and was at another smoking place in the woods that TV and Dan used. He had stopped for a quick fag, and some Brew, to calm his nerves after he had left the grounds. He thought that Nurse Garotte was probably out after him and it made poor Dan all jittery. She might be on that pushbike she used to ride. It was his worst nightmare, like being in a horror movie with the ghouls chasing him. TV thought that Dan sounded scared.

'I'm on my way, TV. I think they're after me! Garotte and that. I'm just having a fag and some Brew down by the old tree stumps. But how did ya get married, TV? How did ya do it?' Dan just couldn't work it out, but then TV seemed to always achieve the impossible. How could anybody, apart from TV Sam, have devised a break out like that and get away with it? Nobody, except TV. 'How?' Dan asked again and TV began to tell him. It was all so clear.

'Ya know that guy with the white blazer, the porn dude? He's a sweet maker and a priest, Dan, and he married us! And his wife's this great photographer and he gave me all his blazers Dan! And he donated a load of money to "Dragon Star", Dan!' That seemed all very handy Dan said, and he asked to speak to Freeda again.

'Freeda! Dan wants to speak to ya!'

Freeda loved hearing those words, and she took the mobile up inspired, still wanting to tell all her friends about the wedding.

'We got married, Dan! Ya gotta get down here! I've got my wedding dress on and you should see me! Everyone's saying how beautiful I look, Dan! And I got a wedding ring from TV! I look so beautiful, Dan! You should see me! And TV's got loads of white blazers and this flashy shirt with "Dragon Star" on it!'

Dan was so happy for Freeda but he was so worried too. But he longed to see her looking like that and being happy. He just had to get there. He would push on once he'd finished his fag.

'I can't wait to see ya looking like that, Freeda. TV is always saying how much he loves ya. He always is, Freeda!' Freeda couldn't help but repeat what she had been saying on the last call.

'And we love you so much, Dan! And we've got food and music, Dan, and loads of champagne, loads. Its where the flying saucers are, Dan! That funny lamppost!'

Dan knew where it was all right, but he reckoned it would take him at least fifteen minutes to get down there, even more. The call ended with Freeda saying again that she couldn't wait to see him. But then Freeda heard footsteps and speaking from outside, and she inquisitively took a peep out of the curtains. She could see police cars out there. At that precise moment the CD jammed at the end of the Sammy Davis track. The music had ended but the show must go on.

'The police are here, TV! The police are here!' TV took up the mobile as he wanted to say goodbye to Dan. There was a poignancy and finality about it.

'See ya, Dan! You're my best friend, Dan. Best friend ever! I loved being with you, Dan. We had some great times. We had the craic!'

When the call ended, Dan was tearful and worried. He could tell that TV was concerned about something happening, it was in his voice, and Dan wanted to get down there as quick as he could, so he could be with them. He yearned to see Freeda in that wedding dress. But how on earth did TV get Freeda a wedding dress? Dan couldn't work it out, but he pressed on, thinking that TV could do virtually anything, even walk on water.

Chaz breathed a sigh of relief, and he looked up towards the crucifix, thanking God. There was a light now at the end of his dark tunnel. He prayed that they would get out of this without 'Mad Freeda' flashing that knife about anymore. TV rushed to the curtain and took a peep outside, and could see a couple of police cars at the gate and in the road. Police were blocking the road off with a number of plastic bollards and tape. The end games were on the player now.

'I bet they got Locko and fucking Bolt with them, Freeda!' TV exclaimed. 'And the big fat nurse!'

The thought that the Gestapo were out there, flipped Freeda out from the wedding sparkle. Even when Freeda had her perfect moment, they came to ruin it. It was always like that. They ruined everything. She grabbed hold of the knife and gesticulated with it, and this time; all her psychotic rage took hold. Nurse Garotte, Bolt and 'The Fuhrer', as TV called her, were like touch papers ignited, and Freeda viciously thrust the knife into the arm of the velvet chair. She slashed it repeatedly, so now both arms had been lacerated.

'I wanna fucking get um! Knife um!' she shouted, in a demented anger, hitting the panic button.

'Freeda! Smoke-the-three like Keefy! Smoke-the-three like Keefy used to do, Freed! We've got tons of fags, get a calm on!' Freeda dropped the knife and broke down in tears and TV comforted her. She had that awful realization that the warmth of this front room, the perfect moment of it all, had ended, like all nice things did for Freeda. TV tried to comfort her as best he could.

'Settle down, Freeda, I love you, Freeda, TV will always love ya. But settle down, Freed.'

'But what we gonna do, TV?'

'I dunno. But I'll think of something,' Freeda bawled into TV's arms and both Chaz and Linda remained silent, but Chaz smiled to Linda. That end was very near now as Freeda found some solace locked in TV's arms.

There were five police officers outside and they were briefed to wait until the Doctors of the asylum were on the scene. Gabi, who had visited the house regarding the screaming foxes, was outside by the horse chestnut. She had been on the blower and was talking to a colleague.

'The doctors should be here any minute and the armed response will take another fifteen or so.' A stage was being set.

Dr. Lock had an angry and stern looking face on, as she drove her Mercedes from the hospital car park, heading towards Holly Beach Lane. Next to her was her right-hand man of the liquid cosh, the inimitable Dr. Bolt, who had trimmed his beard quickly, to appear more professional and had packed up an enormous bag, full of his elixirs and potions. Dr. Bolt was looking even more gaunt than normal, due to his training for the annual Fishgate ultra marathon. He looked a little mad and ecstatic. He was still on a dizzying high as yesterday he had finished another of his epic research papers entitled, 'The Brain Disease Epidemic in the Twenty-First Century', and for Dr. Bolt, Freeda and TV, were particularly diseased specimens. But in the moment, he was determined and steely-eyed, relishing the opportunity to utilize the full arsenal on the maleficent duo. Dr. Bolt saw himself as one of the true outback pioneers, like the first man to explore the Grand Canyon or something. He was sure that generations to come would be indebted to him.

Nurse Lavender Garotte was in the back seat, gorging on a steak and kidney pie. She was about to have her break when the dream team had got the call. Now she didn't mind losing her break for such a good cause, but there was no way she was going to forego her steak and kidney puds. She had warmed them up in the microwave before they set off as she had to be fortified for any pushing, shoving and holding down work, she might have to do. But she was also annoyed at the inconvenience. She and Julietta had planned a night out. They had hired a booth at Candy Foxes which was all part of their 'let the hair down' monthly visits, where they would get pissed on champagne and expensive wine, and have 'fun' with the dancers. It was obviously off now and both were snappy as they had booked tomorrow off to give them a long weekend to recover from the debauchery. Dr. Lock, Julietta, noticed her wolfing down a pie using her fingers. She raised her eyebrows but didn't want to berate her. Minds had to be concentrated on the task in hand, but she also knew that Lavender was disgruntled because of the likely cancellation of the long-awaited night at Candy Foxes.

'You'll have to forget about partying tonight, Lavender. We've got a job to do!'

The Trust Executive had already been on the phone to Dr. Lock regarding his hope that the two miscreants hadn't given anyone cause for litigation. It was early in the new financial year and the budget had already been planned out and it was a tight one. Yes, it was a great worry with Freeda Huskit at large, and especially so, since they had been taking undue risks on security staffing of late to cut costs. However, none of this registered much with Dr. Bolt, who was emboldened and a touch euphoric. A fantastic window of opportunity beckoned.

'If we can get those high levels of largactil and lithium into their blood streams, their psychic aberrations will be substantially mitigated, Dr. Lock.'

'Get them zombie chilled I say,' Nurse Garotte remarked, as she sneered and tore into her steak and kidney, feeling bad-tempered, as she really fancied getting down on it at the new revamped Candy Foxes. She had been on shift two hours longer than normal already too. They were two long hours and she was famished, and she had been looking forward to having that Brooke dancing for them in the booth. She had told Julietta that she would have to eat on the move, and she was determined to get that vixen out of that house in no time, so they could still enjoy their night out. Julietta had already said, that was definitely off, and although she understood that Lavender was hungry, it was the uncouth manner in which Lavender went about it all, that made her angry. But Lavender was bad-tempered. She had been hot for the 'Foxes'.

'That isn't a helpful comment, Lavender dear. Dr. Bolt and I are discussing medical procedures!'

There was a noticeable censorious tone in Dr. Lock's comment, and Nurse Lavender duly shut it, as her big fat biceps bulged out of her short-sleeved tunic, readying for action. Dr. Bolt was even more emboldened, he breathed in deeply, his nostrils inflamed, as this was like a great passion. He loved his work; it was for the community at large. He was the SAS medical commando behind enemy lines, fighting hard against those diseased cells, that were endangering the beautiful world that we all know and love. Someone had to fight those Nazis bastards and Dr. Bolt flew the flag.

'The diseases must be infecting clean cells by now, Dr. Lock! They must have their new syrups! It's imperative!' Dr. Bolt exclaimed, his eyes verily popping out of his head. Nurse Garotte had a mouthful of pie, still gorging away, and Dr. Lock was of the opinion that her colleague Dr. Bolt might be on something, but she held her counsel.

'Huh! She never had a clean cell in the first place! The vixen!' There was pure hatred in Nurse Lavender's voice, born from many a bitter struggle between the two and to think she was ruining a night that had been planned for countless weeks. Dr. Lock could see in the rear mirror that bits of steak and kidney pie were dropping from her fingers and mouth. How disgusting! She couldn't put up with that! The car was a brand new 2003 AD Mercedes, sporting Julietta's empowering new personalized number plate, 'Top Lock'. She only had the car four weeks. They pulled up at traffic lights.

'And please! Can you mind my seating, Lavender dear! It's not much to ask is it?' Dr. Lock said with a severe scolding tone looking at Lavender's swollen conk in the mirror, that was still on recovery. It made her look so ugly, Julietta thought. Nurse Garotte went very quiet but it didn't stop her eating.

A few moments later they turned into Holly Beach Lane and came towards Dr. Greene-Burrow's house. Nurse Garotte knew where the destination dwelling was, as she remembered it from those times, she and Julietta done their fitness cycling up the lane. Dan was out for a walk with TV on one occasion and saw Nurse Garotte riding her bike up Holly Beach. But all the staff knew where old Greene's house was anyway.

'It's just up here, Julietta darling, past old Dr Greene's house.'

'Huh! And no doubt she's sunbathing half naked, trying to attract the rough. The slut!' Dr. Lock declared.

'I reckon every bloke on the staff, even the porters have shagged her, Julietta. It's well known she puts it about!' Nurse Garotte replied in a condemnatory tone. Dr. Bolt was keeping a quiet counsel, and it was an embarrassed one at that, as it was well known, that he had hiked in Appalachia for a period with the radiographer Catherine Greene-Burrows. He had said he was working on some medical textual matters with her at the time.

'I think she suffers from low self-esteem, Lavender dear,' Dr. Lock replied, desperately trying to bring the discourse back to a requisite standard of decency, after having smashed her. Catherine was in fact noted for being highly professional at her job but a 'bit easy' when out of it. They passed Dr. Greene-Burrow's abode and Nurse Garotte opened up yet another steak and kidney, heralded by the rustling of wrapping.

'Oh, for God's sake! Not another one, Lavender?' remarked Dr. Lock with an acerbic and disgusted tone. Nurse Garotte had something of a manual workers hole to fill.

'I missed dinner, Julietta,' Lavender replied, making her predicament known yet again.

'But two pies! Anyone would think you were an hod carrier, Lavender!'

While they politely bitched and argued, Dr. Bolt caught the first glimpse of the house.

'There it is!' and within a few seconds they had arrived. The police officer could see who it was, and he temporarily removed the cone in the road, so they could park up near to the house by the Jag and the old tree. It was rather congested around the house now, with the Jag and the Jeep, plus police vehicles. But there was no more talk of that radiographer slut. They were professionals now in the conflict zone.

'We'll coax them out of their bolt hole in no time!' remarked a quietly confident Dr. Lock. But as soon as she put the handbrake on, Dr. Bolt quietly reiterated the fears.

'I just hope they haven't put the householders through some kind of ugly ordeal, Dr. Lock, as the Trust will be liable, you know.' Dr. Lock was silent but Nurse Lavender had to open up even though she was still eating.

'Huh! When Freeda Huskit is let loose, there is *nothing* but ugly ordeals! That vixen will cost us a stinking fortune!' Dr. Lock lost all patience with her.

'Lavender! Do you have to speak while you're eating those fucking pies! It's such a turn off!'

The principals put on their best air of authority as they stepped from the Merc with Nurse Garotte in close attendance. She was still jiggling around with a pie and Dr. Lock gave her a vicious-looking glance that said 'Put it away, Lavender! You need to be more professional!' Nurse Lavender promptly slid the half-eaten pie in its wrapping, back in her tunic pocket. Meanwhile, Dr. Lock was met by the female police officer, who she found rather appealing. Julietta had a thing about women in uniforms, as Lavender well knew. The policewoman informed Dr. Lock about the state of play and was holding a megaphone in her hand.

'The two absconders are holed up in the house and we suspect they are holding the occupants, the Barbers, hostage, Doctor.' Dr. Lock was always decisive in these kinds of dramatic situations. People look towards those in authority to take the lead like that. It inspires confidence in the foot soldiers. The first maxim for Dr. Lock. She ran to form with her normal air of supreme confidence.

'Thank you for your brief, Officer. Could I borrow?' she said referring to the megaphone. She continued, 'We are sure we can coax these two out with a few carefully chosen psychological ploys Officer. We know them like the back of our hands!' Dr. Lock stated, quite categorically.

'Inside out, Officer!' Dr. Bolt substantiated the claim. The police officer was suitably impressed by Dr. Lock's assured self-confidence. She thought that this Doctor had an *air* about her. Dr. Bolt had the back of the Mercedes open, digging into an enormous bag of his wares and potions. He took a couple of syringes and popped them in his tunic. He was continually backing up Dr. Lock. They were truly a superbly gifted medical team.

'They must have their largactil and lithium. The new fruity ones! We have to combat those diseased brain cells!'

Nurse Garotte couldn't help but be scathing on her assessment.

'Huh! She must only have about three to combat!' As Nurse Garotte spoke, she took a sly gorge of the steak and kidney, hardly appropriate. Dr. Lock could see that the police officer thought such remarks to be less than professional, and she took Lavender aside and spoke to her quietly. This nonsense had to end!

'Please, Lavender dear. We are representing the Trust. Not swigging the beer down at the Ivy Leaf! And for the last time, put that blasted pie away!'

Dr. Lock was getting decidedly angry with Lavender and her darn pie eating. But Lavender knew she'd better come to heel, and quick. It was only a month ago when Julietta made out that new will, making Lavender the chief beneficiary. Everyone thought Dr. Lock was fifty-four or five, yet they doubted the accuracy of that information, but in reality, she was sixty-three, but still with great powers. She held the megaphone up, directed at that front lounge. She projected her voice with all the power of Dr. Lock and it was to be megaphone diplomacy on this occasion. Her voice boomed and echoed in the leafy quietude.

'Freeda! TV! We know you're in there! This is your good friend Dr. Lock and we all hope you're not doing anything nasty to Mr. and Mrs. Barber. The Barbers are nice people but we've all been missing you so greatly on the wards!' Dr. Lock turned to Gabi, the police officer, smiling.

'Logic doesn't compute with these two, Officer.' She then motioned towards Nurse Garotte. 'Get the cigarettes, Lavender!' While Lavender acquired the two packets from the back seat, Dr. Lock took up the megaphone again. 'And we've come down here with four hundred, yes four hundred cigarettes, two hundred for each of you. Nurse Lavender brought them out of her wages as a coming home present. She misses you so much, Freeda!' Nurse Garotte screwed her face up in disbelief, mumbling under her breath.

'Huh! Misses her! And as if I would buy that vixen anything!'

But Nurse Lavender went to the gate and held up the two packets of fags with rather a false smile on her face. By now the megaphone had been given to Dr. Bolt who was itching to contribute.

'And we've got some wonderful, wonderful new medication, TV. It's a new fruit syrup that Dan's been having. He's been saying that it makes you feel as if you're floating on air and he's said he can't wait to take it with you, TV! And you, Freeda! Everyone is saying how good that new fruity one of Dr. Bolt's tastes! What are you waiting for? Come out and taste some!'

Nothing stirred, but then Dr. Lock could see the side of the curtain shifting and what looked like Freeda peeping out.

'There she is, the monster!' Nurse Garotte snapped, as she still paraded those fags as the bargaining chips. Freeda could see Nurse Lavender holding up the packets of fags next to those hated doctors Lock and Bolt.

'It's Lock and fucking Bolt, TV! And the fat nurse has bought us fags!'

TV wasn't so easily taken in. He knew this triumvirate like the back of his hand. They dealt with snake oil, nothing but pure unadulterated snake oil.

'Lying bastards! That battle-axe wouldn't buy you fags, Freeda. They've come to drug us so, we're better, sitting in a chair cabbaged! And they would never let us see each other again, Freeda! Never!'

'But we're married now, TV, and Freeda's got her wedding ring!' How Freeda wanted to stay put in these beautiful golden moments but TV knew the score.

'That won't stop them! Not Lock and Bolt!'

Dr. Lock persisted as she knew that persistence was the key here. She had to keep pushing and pushing, until their wills and resistance broke.

'So, if you come out now, Freeda, you'll be able to chain smoke-the-three, like Keefy used to do! We won't stop you today, Freeda, as we've all been missing you so much! You're such a sparkling person Freeda! Everyone loves you at the hospital. And we all want Freeda back on the wards! We all do!'

Nurse Lavender gave another sarcastic scoff of disbelief, but Dr. Lock continued.

'And Clara and Angelo are always saying how much they miss you. And Lorenzo and Dan have been very, very upset indeed. They've even been crying and you like Lorenzo and Dan don't you, Freeda? And Keith phoned and said he wanted so dearly to come to the homecoming party, we're going to give for Freeda and TV! There will be loads of jellies and ice creams, Freeda! And we've brought in your favorite Neapolitan ice-cream!'

This kind of talk inspired Dr. Bolt to take up the gauntlet. He knew exactly what they needed.

'Remember to mention strawberries, Dr. Lock! She'll come out here like a jumping bean for a bowlful. Then I'll take my chance and get a syringe in!' Dr. Lock thought this a wonderful idea and a certain ploy was set into operation immediately.

'Lavender! Go to the convenience store and get some strawberries and cream. They might come in handy. But I don't want any of that steak and kidney pie muck on my driving seat please!'

Nurse Garotte got straight into the driver's seat and pulled away in the Merc as Dr. Lock continued phase two of the megaphone diplomacy, her voice reverberating as the light started to fade.

'And oh, yes, Freeda. Dr. Bolt's new medicines taste just like strawberries and you love your strawberries don't you, Freeda? And we've even got *real* strawberries and cream out here, freshly picked from the strawberry fields!'

The constant barrage of goodies were winning Freeda over. She bubbled with enthusiasm.

'A party for us, TV! For our wedding! And new medicines and strawberries! We haven't had strawberries for ages, TV! And they've got fags and my Napoleonic ice-cream!' Freeda began to open the window but she was restrained by TV. Chaz looked at Linda and winked and she got his message that they just had to let this ride out and it would soon be all over.

'Nah Freeda! It's Neapolitan, with the chocolate, strawberry and vanilla and that. But it's a trick, Freeda! Keefy's dead and they wouldn't give us four hundred fags. Pouffe! They'd fucking disappear like a conjurer's trick if we went out there. All they'd give us is liquid coshes, Freeda, get us on a poleaxed vibe.' Freeda screwed her face up, but she knew that TV was always right, she couldn't trust them lot. But TV had something cooking.

'But they trick us, so we're gonna fucking trick them, the bastards!'

A plan was hatching. It wasn't a freedom plan, it was more about revenge, and go on another run for a spell plan, because after today and the wedding, they had nothing to go back for and TV knew he would be transferred to somewhere the other end of the country. Freeda supported him. She was married to TV now.

'Yeah, let's trick Lock and Bolt and that big fat nurse, TV! Because she doesn't smell like lavender! She stinks, TV, like a fucking sewer! Holding those fags up smiling! And she wouldn't buy Freeda Napoleon's ice-cream!'

TV broke down in laughter and Freeda joined him and they hugged each other and they kept laughing and hugging and it all calmed TV's nerves a bit. But really, he was worried about how it all might end now, although Freeda was just happy to be with her husband TV. He looked so smart in that white blazer and the flashy Dragon Star shirt.

Chaz couldn't refrain from trying to help things along, to end the stand-off.

'You ought to go out there. A party for ya and they'll let you live together, forever!'

For the first time, and with the tension rising, TV lost his composure.

'Fucking shut it, Blazerman! Show him the knife! Real motherfucking bad! Right on his throat, Freeda!'

Linda sighed, and pleaded for mercy, but why couldn't Chaz just sit still, and let fate take its course? He had to keep interfering, and Freeda, emboldened by TV, stuck the knife right at Chaz's throat. Chaz was gasping as Freeda looked straight into his eyes, putting it to him, full of 'Mad Freeda' now.

'Freeda's got this 'ere knife right. Right here right! So, shut the mother fucker up, Blazerman!'

She drew the knife away a few inches and Chaz nodded, wishing he hadn't said a word, and TV stressed that he was in the last chance saloon. But he had been given plenty of them.

Outside Dr. Lock was still persisting. It was all about more of the same until they cracked, and they surely would. It was just a matter of time. Dr. Lock was a firm believer in that old maxim, 'Bread and Circuses', and in this scenario, that manifested as strawberries and cream and much more within the context of a party. There was a clinical method to Dr. Lock's madness from the megaphone.

'So, come out and smoke-the-three like Keefy used to do, and then have some strawberries and cream, Freeda!   And we've just had a text from Keefy that he's just arrived at Tennin train station! You'll be able to eat that Neapolitan ice-cream later with Keefy!'   Freeda's intensity with that blade lessened on hearing Dr. Lock throwing out the goody bags again

'Smoke-the-three and that Napoleon's ice-cream, TV.'

'The lying bastards!' TV exclaimed, and he pulled the curtains a little and opened the window, movement that gave Dr. Bolt the message that things were opening up nicely.

'Now, we're getting somewhere, Dr. Lock!'   Dr. Lock gave a smile of smug assurance. She wasn't the lynchpin of that hospital without reason and 'The Dream Team' knew these two reprobates inside out, outside in, and had them sussed around the other side too. They watched expectantly for positive developments as TV was at the window.

'Fuck off, Locko! We know you made Keefy kill himself cos of all ya chemical coshes, ya bastards! But his memory lives on in the better people. The decent people of the world! The "Dragon Star" children. And mark my fucking words, Locko, AD 2025 it's payback time!   The dragon's gonna get ya, Locko! It's fucking gonna get ya with its fire!'   Freeda was at the window with vocal back up.

'And the dragon's gonna get the big fat nurse, who Freeda hates! Yeah, stuff ya ice-cream up ya arse, Locko! Stuff that Napoleon! It's all dragons now! Dragons!'

Dr. Lock scoffed when she heard the ridiculous barrage of comments. She had banned all talk of the Dragon Star children, nearly three years ago, as Julietta feared it was the emergence of a warped cult. She wouldn't put anything past that TV. She recognized his power of influence over the other clients.   She had an eye for such things. She had read biographies of Charles Manson and had written a professionally acclaimed dissertation on the character type. She had concluded that TV was similarly dangerous with all of his cult business. It was a clear case of delusions of grandeur, and a thirst for power, all born from TV's own personal short comings. She had spoken to Lavender about him at considerable length, saying that he had similar character defects as Hitler or other dangerous demagogues. They had heard rumors that he and Keefy had started some kind of worldwide organization. It was very disturbing.

Freeda lent around TV and showed herself in her wedding attire. Lock and Bolt were bewildered.

'Yeah, we fucking hate ya, Lock and Bolt! Fucking hate ya! And that big fat nurse! We hate ya! Hate ya!' Freeda really enjoyed shouting that out. Usually, when she did that, a forced injection was the immediate response, although it might take the posse to hold her down before Dr. Bolt plunged the needle in. But she was with TV now and she could do things and get away with it. Then it was the inevitable. Freeda began the 'No more Barry, and the big fat nurse! Locko or Bolt!' chant and TV joined in enthusiastically and they kept chanting it and chanting it and Dr. Lock sighed and tutted to a serious and intent looking Dr. Bolt. But it was the kind of thing you could expect from these two miscreants.

'Was she in a wedding dress?' Dr. Bolt asked as the chanting continued unabated. Dr. Lock merely shook her head not really knowing what Freeda was wearing. After the outburst, and that incessant chant, the police officers were beginning to doubt the approach, but Dr. Lock was at pains to point out certain realities within a 'scientific paradigm', and she purveyed excessive self-confidence. She wouldn't have climbed Everest without it!

'It's all bluster, Officer. The key to the character type is to keep at them, with sacks of goody bags and they're always swayed.'

But the chant went on behind the curtains and could be heard through the slightly ajar window. Dr. Lock looked over Gabi rather intently, knowing that she was impressing this dish of a police officer and Gabi got the subtle message. Dr. Lock continued.

After this fiasco has ended, Officer, it might be wise if the police force liaised with my department, regarding the character type,' Dr. Lock suggested quietly. Gabi got the drift.

'Well I would certainly put myself forward as a candidate for that dialogue, Doctor!'

'Here's my contact card.' Dr. Lock slipped Gabi a card.

'Oh, thank you very much.'

Dr. Lock smiled, she already saw herself behind a locked door in the liaison room at the asylum with this young officer, so she attacked the megaphone again with an uprush of power. The chanting had died as Dr. Lock raised the megaphone and addressed TV. But then TV began shouting from inside the lounge.

'You're murderers! Ya fucking murdered Keefy! Ya Nazi bastards!'

'Now you know that's just not true, TV. Keith has gone away for a very long time, as we want him to get better again. But he's said he's well enough for your homecoming party, TV! So, come on out now and have your strawberries. They've been freshly picked by Lavender! And the best we've ever tasted!'

All the talk of real strawberries was proving irresistible to Freeda. They didn't have any in the fridge in the Blazerpeople's house and she was still certain they were hiding them, but she would love to have a bowl. She really would.

'Let's go out and have the real strawberries, TV!' She turned towards Chaz looking at him with disgust. 'Freeda is fed up with those sweets of his! She's fed up with them! If I eat another one I'll be fucking sick TV!' But TV was adamant that it was all a ruse and a trap. But he had a plan now.

'We're gonna set one up for them, Freeda! We'll trap the fucking Gestapo! Nobody can do "Dragon Star" over! Nobody!'

'Yeah, we'll trap that Lock and Bolt and the big fat nurse! That's what we'll do, TV! See how they like it! Yeah, we'll trap them!'

Freeda looked at TV curiously, as she didn't really know what the hell he was up to. TV Sam did though, and he could be seen at the window again.

'All right, Locko! We'll agree to come out and give ourselves up as long as you bring the strawberries up the path and give them to me at the front door! No funny business! And then when we've eaten our strawberries and cream, we'll come out and go back to the hospital, right! Everything dead and buried!' TV exclaimed. 'Waiting for the resurrection and the dawn of the Dragon!' he added cryptically.

Dr. Lock naturally thought this confirmation, that her ploys were finally breaking them. It always went like this. She explained to Gabi and the police officers.

'He always speaks in wild riddles. But as we've said officers, they're easily swayed as they have limited reasoning faculties.'

It all seemed so easy or at least it would be, once Lavender got back from the convenience store with those darn strawberries and cream. Dr. Lock spoke to Gabi confidentially about those anticipated, future Tennin police force, Tennin Asylum, liaison activities.

'Looking further ahead, Officer, I think those liaisons can be carried forward on an informal, personal level, don't you think?'

Gabi loved the turn on, being cleverly set up for the seduction, by this powerful, sexy domineering woman. Everything seemed all so easy, or at least it would be, once Lavender got back from the convenience store with the strawberries and cream.

CHAPTER TWENTY-THREE

END GAMES

Nurse Lavender was just about to pull away from the convenience store. She had the punnets of strawberries and fresh farm cream in a bag next to her. There were also cream doughnuts and a giant bottle of coke. Lavender always had cream doughnuts and coke after her pies, and feeling famished after a long hard shift, she had to have her doughnuts with a few swigs to wash them down, despite Julietta reprimanding her for eating on duty. She had a space in the car for a tuck up and she looked at the cream and jam and just couldn't stop herself. She fumbled the packets and began wolfing one down as she sped off, the cream oozing out, dropping on the edge of the driver's seat. Lavender was a somewhat messy eater.

'Fuck it!' she shouted, and within a couple of seconds she had taken another ginormous bite and with her concentration on her driving, she couldn't stop cream and jam oozing from the doughnut, falling on the edge of the seat again. She gave Julietta a few thoughts as she gathered another cream doughnut. She had noticed there was a certain tension between them at the moment and Lavender was sure it was because she had been putting on weight. She would go on a diet immediately and she could see that Julietta had eyes for that police officer. She knew when Julietta got the hots and it was of concern as Julietta was so aggressive sexually.

Meanwhile, back at the house, TV was putting a plan into operation. The first thing he needed were those fastenings. He quickly returned to the lounge and although he apologized to Linda for doing so, he couldn't risk her tricking Freeda, and so he had to fasten her wrists and feet.

'Stay on guard, Freeda!' TV's tone of voice implied that it was imperative, as he shut the front window. He then left the lounge, and went upstairs, clear in his own mind on his course of action. TV had returned to that psychological moment when he went for it at the asylum. 'I'm just going upstairs for something, Freeda.'

'All right, TV,' she replied. Once TV had gone, Chaz was at it again, working on Freeda. She had proven to be exceedingly easy to trick with any kind of ruse and he put on his child like voice again, certain that he could talk her around his little finger.

'Mummy! I think you should take your little Dicky and Blazerwoman out to meet the people with their big loudspeakers, Mummy. They'll give you fags and you'll be able to smoke three at once, like Keefy used to do at your big party, Mummy.'

Freeda was confused. She looked at the old Blazerman with a puzzled look. She thought she had finished with all the games like that. Chaz continued, sure he was going to get somewhere this time, although Linda just wanted him to shut up. But Chaz had all the prompts off pat and he couldn't just sit there passive and docile like Linda, that wasn't his character. He had to keep trying, pushing right to the end.

'Just untie me, Mummy, and we can all smoke-the-three like Keefy used to do!'

It worked, because Freeda began to untie Chaz's fastenings. She had enjoyed that Freeda's Team business and this was a chance to get it up and running again. Chaz winked across to Linda as if to say, this is it, we're nearly over the line. He would get her out into the kitchen and then he would belt off and get that door open. Chaz reckoned an armed response team was out the front. They had to be, and if he could get out there, while TV was upstairs, 'pig' could get in the front door and then it would be all over. He could quickly put that cocaine and all the money in a cupboard underneath the carp tanks. But the idea of getting busted with over a kilo of coke was certainly a concern as well as these two nutters, and whatever the ordeal threw at him, he had bruises and a big lump or two on his forehead, at least he was still thinking straight. Freeda untied his legs and was beginning to work on his hand fastenings, when TV could be heard coming down the stairs. He had been doing his wires up in the master bedroom.

Nurse Lavender was enjoying her third cream doughnut. She was waiting at traffic lights and took the moment to have a good scoff, as she listened to her and Julietta's favorite song, 'Come to my Window', although the track had been somewhat sullied since that Huskit had taken it up as some kind of anthem looking out of that unit's window. She would announce to Julietta that she intended to go on a diet, to get back to her old weight, the weight at which she met Julietta. She was sure that the reason their sex life was tailing off right now, was her weight. She was sure of it. Lavender had been Dr. Lock's lover and partner for over seven years now, and they lived in a detached house a dozen miles or so from Tennin. The relationship had been kept 'hush-hush', so the patients didn't know anything. Obviously, it was common knowledge among the regular staff. But such was the power of Dr. Lock, they kept their counsel to the degree that their 'clients', didn't know one way or the other. They just got caught up with rumors. Of course, Freeda had referred to Nurse Garotte with 'inappropriate' comments, as TV suspected she was gay and involved with Dr. Lock, and he would joke that Locko was probably shagging her with a dildo. Freeda had picked the ideas up and used them determinedly against Lavender, another reason why Nurse Garotte detested her, and such things upset Lavender, who was a sensitive woman away from the asylum coalface. Dr. Lock was layered with a much thicker skin. She was like the armadillo, after having put up with the likes of Freeda and dozens of others, who were 'difficult', for the past three decades and more. Dr. Lock had nine lives and nine layers of armadillo.

Nurse Garotte turned into the lane thinking, if only she could get that bigger contract with that new Australian wrestling federation that Julietta was pushing for. Nothing had come as yet from the application to America, but Lavender was hopeful about the Aussie. If they could get a contract, they could both retire, travel and enjoy their lives and not have to put up with darn Freeda Huskit! Oh, the bliss! Live the dream, Lavender! And that was a fantastic new pitch that Julietta had made last night with Lavender's CV over the internet. The idea being that 'Spiked Lavender' could disappear, and then resurface underneath an anonymous diamante mask, pursuing somewhat dubious choke hold and dirty forearm punch tactics, so that she could be *the* big baddie draw of the Aussie circuit. Her new moniker would be 'The Hooded Strangleress', with the hook being, that all other woman wrestlers would attempt to wrench the hood off her head. Pure wrestling show business, and Julietta was certain that a large contract was in the offing, and they were thinking of relocating down under, if it transpired, and behind the scenes down under, the big Aussie money players were drawing up a concrete contract offer. It was just the type of showbiz catch they were looking for. They were on the cusp!

She passed old Dr. Greene's and noticed that radiographer slut was working out in her garden with dumbbells, wearing a leotard. Catherine was curious as to what was going on up the lane. She caught Nurse Garotte's attention, and smiled as they were fellow Trust employees. Lavender met her with a polite smile back and she rather admired her trim, athletic-looking body, and Lavender began thinking about that decrepit Dr. Greene. She could see the attraction of Catherine Greene-Burrows, and Lavender rather liked a mature woman, although the sheer authoritative power of Dr. Lock blew her away. She was Lavender's femme dominatrix and Julietta liked to take control everywhere, and especially the bedroom, or in that quiet room where she would meet Gabi, the police officer. She would have Gabi's knickers off within five minutes and her fist up her and Gabi would be abandoned, hooked by the power of her dominance. That was inevitable as soon as Gabi gave way and allowed Dr. Lock's sexual aggression to ravish her and that was why Lavender didn't like the way that Julietta leered at her.

Before she knew it, Lavender was back in the war zone. She parked up, and gave the strawberries and cream to Dr. Lock and by now Nurse Lavender, had finished four cream doughnuts and unbeknownst to her, she had a large blob of cream around her mouth. Julietta was scathing and she was starting to find Lavender something of a turn off, with all this gargantuan eating.

'I suppose it's a packet of cream doughnuts now is it, Lavender? Yes, it's all around your mouth, dear.'

Dr. Lock gave Nurse Garotte a particularly dirty look and then turned her attention back on the job at hand. Living the dream hadn't as yet landed on the runway, and she was just about sick of Lavender's lack of professionalism, in these more than trying circumstances. If she wasn't sleeping with her and involved intimately, she would have formally disciplined her. She would confront her in the bedroom when they finally did get home. They were shop window of the Trust. Dr. Lock turned towards Dr. Bolt, who was aware of all the shenanigans going on, but who would never say a word. He was very professional at holding his counsel.

'Erm, let's see if these can bring an end to this little drama, Dr. Bolt!'

Dr. Lock took to the megaphone again, flushed by strawberries, confident that the end games were nigh. It was megaphone diplomacy phase two, as Dr. Lock went back into the fray.

'TV! I'll bring the strawberries and cream right up to the door and then after you have finished them, you can both come back to the hospital. How about that? OK?' The letterbox took long-seconds to respond and open with TV speaking through it. Those snakes on the door were still spitting out their furies.

'Bring the strawberries up and give us fifteen minutes to eat um and then we'll come out, Locko!' Dr. Lock breathed a deep sigh of relief as now everything was moving to plan, and she praised Dr. Bolt for coming up with the idea.

'It really was key here, Dr. Bolt, an incredible flight of inspiration!', she remarked in measured tones, that brought a smug, self-satisfied smile from Dr. Bolt. Then Dr. Lock turned to the police officers, including Gabi, and spoke as if she had the situation under a firm, dominating control. It was an expression of Dr. Lock's will. She commanded and others followed, or fell into obedient line. 'As I have said, officers, there are certain psychological ploys that never fail with these character types, and my colleague Dr. Bolt would fully agree with me here, "type" is the operative term.'

The police officers, especially a swooning Gabi, were duly impressed. Everything seemed to be proceeding as planned because these medical professionals knew best how to deal with their client group and Dr. Lock was beginning to think again about that long-awaited party night at the 'Foxes'.

There had been the crackle of police radios and another police officer informed the medical team that the armed response's arrival was imminent.

'You surely don't need armed response teams if you've a fresh cache of strawberries and cream, Officer!' Dr. Lock joked, fully anticipating the forthcoming end to the tense standoff. The officers laughed along like a pack of devotees and the end games were about to come to their tutti-frutti finale. The acting chief officer was tentative, because of the air of undoubted authority, that Dr. Lock evinced. She was a natural born leader, who was rather more experienced at leading, than the young police officer, who in all intents and purposes, wanted to check Dr. Lock's hastiness. Dr. Lock took up the megaphone again.

'TV, I'm coming up the garden path with the strawberries and cream!'

Freeda was so excited that they were bringing those strawberries and cream. They could have them in the front room with the Blazerpeople, and listen to more wedding music.

'Strawberries, TV! They're bringing us strawberries!'

TV was by the door and he was instructing Freeda what to do next. It was all part of the master plan he had hatched. Meanwhile, out the front, Dr. Lock was about to open the gate and walk up the path. The male police officer in charge, implied that he should follow too, but Dr. Lock was adamant that she had everything under control. A too visible police presence might unhinge TV, and anyhow, this was nothing compared to some of the scrapes, she had been in during her career. She was nigh strangled once, going back two decades and had nearly caught up with a vicious machete chop from a patient on another occasion, but had parried the blow with a karate move. A black belt, third dan, was another one of her long lists of accomplishments. That Everest climb was the hardest route and with the national medical federation mountaineering team, and she had done countless Ironman triathlons going back a few years, scooping loads of woman's veteran cups. She was a powerful cat with a few lives left, thank you, and Freeda didn't bother her, like she did Lavender. The Freeda's of this world were just part and parcel of the territory. In metaphorical terms, she was like a T34 tank, cleverly bulldozing its way through any recalcitrance that might occur from her client group.

'No, you stay here, Officer. I can deal with this now we've got the strawberries!' Dr. Lock then went back to addressing TV. 'I'm coming up with the punnets, TV!'

TV was still speaking through the opened letterbox.

'We can't wait for the opportunity, Locko. Bring um up and we'll open up!'

Dr. Lock gave the officer the megaphone, opened the gate and walked a couple of paces up the path. She stopped for a moment or two, breathing in the sweet aroma of those glorious late spring flowers. Spend a little time smelling the flowers, was Dr. Lock's philosophy of life, that's why she frequented that Candy Foxes. That was why she had invited that police officer up to the hospital, why she had slipped her one. But she pressed on. The door opened to her and she was in disbelief when TV and Freeda appeared on the threshold. They looked as if they were a pair of fashionable media personalities 'Just Married!'. She was astonished. TV smiled and put out his left hand awkwardly for the bag, while Freeda backed off into the house, but then TV dramatically pulled his right hand from behind him and he had a sawn-off shotgun.

'Welcome to our shotgun wedding, Locko!'

TV was ruthless. He shot her a number of times at point blank range, the first into her chest and another few when she went down. Infamy and fame were beckoning.

'You got her, TV! You got the Fuhrer fingy!' shouted Freeda excitedly, and then TV quickly closed the door and gave Freeda the bag of strawberries. Outside, Nurse Garotte was screaming and Dr. Bolt was in disbelief.

'He's killed Dr. Lock! He's murdered her! In cold blood! The bastard! In cold blood!' he exclaimed, as Nurse Garotte and Dr. Bolt crouched behind the car. Lavender had a quick snap at another cream doughnut in between, shouting out for her partner and lover.

'Julietta! Julietta!'

The pain was too great, and Lavender rushed into the garden to see if she was still alive. She reached her and quickly checked her pulse with tears streaming from her eyes, and her face turning blood pressure high red with feelings of anger. She wanted revenge, because the unthinkable had happened, Julietta, her lover, her soulmate, was dead. Shot in cold blood by TV Sam and that Freeda 'She-Devil Monster' Huskit.

Dan heard the gunshots. He was now walking down Holly Beach Lane, only a few minutes away from the house and could just about see the back of it. He stopped and looked concerned, as he knew where they had come from. He thought and hoped, it might be a farmer shooting rabbits or something, as they frequently did that around the area. But he sensed it was something more significant and distressing. He took his packet of fags from his pocket, took one and lit it, looking even more worried, dragged at it, had a final swig of Brew, before setting off again.

TV was now upstairs with a much more powerful weapon than the one he used out the front. This was a full military capacity automatic shotgun. Freeda was behind him as TV was about to pull down the sash window.

'Ya got her, TV! Ya got her!' Freeda enthused.

'Yeah, fuck the bitch! She got us enough, Freeda!' But TV had a plan. 'Freeda! Go downstairs and keep watch! If they try and bash the back-door in. Call me!'

'All right, TV,' she replied. 'We can have the strawberries together, TV! We can sit in the furry chair!'

TV hugged and kissed her tenderly, and Freeda smiled, she didn't care what was happening, she only wanted to be with TV. That's all that mattered to Freeda. Once Freeda was out of the room, TV finished pulling the sash down and Nurse Garotte scampered behind the rose bush, which then allowed her to slide down a slight bank into the back garden out of range. She was confronted by that sex doll. She felt she was being taunted by that murdering bastard because that's who the doll was. The shell-shocked Lavender now realized that Julietta had been right all along. This TV Sam was dangerous cult leader material. She went into the woods and returned to the front of the house distraught and full of tears for her lost lover; her life turned upside down. But she was eager for revenge.

The armed response team had arrived and another was on its way. They were being briefed, but as yet were not in position as more sirens could be heard in the distance. TV shouted from the upstairs window.

'The wheels have turned for once, Bolt, ya fucking coshing bastard! Have a fucking syrup! This one's from Keefy!'

The police weren't sure what he had, weapon-wise, but they soon knew. It was definitely a military style automatic shotgun he had up there now. TV shot out a full cartridge, spraying the end of the garden around the vehicles and horse chestnut tree. One of the police officers was hit and then one of the armed response team, as cartridges ripped through the vehicles, including Chaz's Jag. It was a shocking burst of fire and the police were pinned down, terrified. TV continued through four cartridges and he planned to save the other couple for downstairs, as Tennin Trust ambulances were now hurtling towards Holly Beach Lane in force.

Dan stopped again and his hand was shaking, as he puffed hard on his fag. He knew that whatever was happening, with all the shouting going on, it was TV and Freeda. He was fearing the worst as yet another volley of shots rang out. It was pandemonium. He dropped his finished fag and pressed on to the sound of multiple sirens, that were now turning into the bottom of Holly Beach Lane. He had to see TV and Freeda, he had to!

Chaz closed his eyes. The darn bloody incident couldn't have got any worse as those were illegal weapons that TV was using. He thought about that kilo of cocaine that was probably out there in the kitchen. He had to at least get that out of the way and had already began thinking about that gun. He could plead guilty and could say that he got carried away with guns after hunting expeditions in America. Yes, that would be the approach, he could say that he lost himself in American macho gun culture. But now Chaz had two things on his mind. Surviving, and preventing the police from finding the coke and the nigh seventy grand!

For a few moments, there was a temporary silence and the crows could be heard cawing away. Nurse Lavender arrived back outside having gone through those woods adjacent to the small back lawn. She was emotionally distraught and stressed and the only thing she could think of doing was eat. She took up yet another cream doughnut. She had the last few in her tunic. It was her way of handling the stress, and she was sick behind the wheels of the Merc. That was just horrible, looking into her dead lover's eyes, checking a nonexistent pulse, and her tunic covered with Julietta's blood.

'The bastard! He shot Julietta in cold blood! In cold blood, while she was bringing him strawberries, the bastard!' exhorted Nurse Garotte incensed with rage. She would love dearly to get him in one of her chokes. The darn bastard needed a good garroting. The nurse's thirst for revenge was shared by Dr. Bolt. His nostrils were like bellows snorting, hell bent on getting that TV Sam lain prostrate, the police could hold him down while he gave him shot after shot after shot. How dare this hoodlum, shoot dead his much loved and respected colleague. His anger overflowed.

'If the bastard wants a fight, I'll take it to him, Nurse! I'm no Dr. Pisspants! You just wait till I give him a shot of the Dr. Bolts! I'll give him half a dozen coshes, the bastard! Prototype concentrates! I've got a dozen in the bag!' Dr. Bolt wasn't going to hold back, it was the sheer outrage that meant he had rather contravened the Trust's professional code. But he was the second in command, so was now the first, and would be expected to negotiate further with this murderer. This was no time for being a gutless wonder. Nurse Lavender was now in tears, distraught as the tragedy had fully come to roost.

'Dead, poor Julietta, dead!' She wiped her mouth and licked her fingers and thought she might have the last of the cream doughnuts and in such a stressed situation, she like Dr. Bolt, expressed herself in ways, that with more reflection, she would rather have not.

'I'm lucky Julietta made that will. It would have gone to probate without it, Dr. Bolt! And all sorts of rogues would have come out of the woodwork! Like bloody woodworms. Those bitch sisters never accepted her, never! They would have wanted their bloody penny worth though! I can tell you, Dr. Bolt! The nasty bitches!'

After that outburst, Nurse Lavender fancied another cream doughnut as a stress reliever, but she had done the lot. But she, like Dr. Bolt, was thirsting for revenge. She'd get that TV with one of her expert mandible choke holds. Big fat fingers under the tongue, jabbing into the soft tissue down his throat. She'd make him squill like a vixen and then she would nigh wrench his head off with a camel clutch! The bastard!

TV loaded the gun, the penultimate cartridge, and went downstairs. Freeda was out in the kitchen, still singing the bridal song, putting the strawberries into two bowls she had found, with some cream on top. She brought them out into the lounge as TV came in.

'TV! Let's eat the strawberries together in the furry chair!'

They squeezed themselves onto the furry chair and found room to each eat their strawberries.

'It wouldn't have been right if we didn't have any strawberries, TV!'

TV ate some and smiled and then clasped Freeda's hand tenderly. He didn't quite know how they were going to get out of this one. But he felt so happy.

'Whatever happens, Freeda. I've never been so happy as today. Getting married to you, being in the white blazer. All my dreams have come true.'

Freeda naturally thought that being married meant that everything had to work out.

'But we're married now, TV! After our strawberries, can we have some more wedding music on! And another glass of champagne! That's special for our wedding, ain't it, TV?'

'Course we can, Freeda.'

'And, TV! After we've eaten our strawberries shall we put our feet in a bowl of water again! Freeda liked that! It was all nice, Freeda really liked that!' TV thought that a lovely touch.

'Yeah, mind, Freeda, I'll get us a bowl.'

Chaz and Linda remained quiet, not really knowing what to say. They were just praying they could get out of this horrific and unpredictable situation, and Chaz was worried sick about the illegal guns and the rather thorny matter of that cocaine.

Within a few moments, TV and Freeda had their tootsies in the bowl, eating their strawberries, and with it all being quiet, Freeda didn't have a care in the world. She was totally in the moment like TV said. TV picked up the CD control and moved on the music. It was 'That's Amore' and Dean Martin was back, bringing more warmth into the lounge, and now as the light faded, the LED lights and angels looked all the more impressive. It was a romantic three minutes and Freeda and TV were like the eternal lovers, smiling together and swaying in the furry chair.

'Ain't it nice, TV, tootsies in the bowl together, and we'll have to go to a fish and chip shop in Fishgate! We can go there in Blazerman's Jag!'

TV smiled and drew Freeda closer to him.

'Corse we will, Freed. We're married now and all the angels are singing for us.'

And for the duration of the track, Freeda and TV were in a perfect bliss. They beamed happiness. They finished the strawberries and poured another glass and it was intimate feet in the bowl with glasses of champagne, and yet another toast for TV and Freeda's special wedding in Holly Beach Lane. The perfect moment that was glistening bejeweled and golden, lasted for a wee short time more, until it was Sinatra and 'That's Life' and reality bit into TV. He had to get up. It was feet out of the bowl, all strawberries finished and back to the automatic shotgun.

'I gotta keep firing, Freeda!'

'Shoot them all, TV! All of them! Then we'll go down to Fishgate and have some more fish and chips!'

TV pulled the sash window down and began spraying yet another magazine of rounds all over the place. A marksman was hit to the side of the house in the woods as TV took a wide trajectory. Then he turned to the cars parked outside the garden, ripping through the vehicles, nigh shredding Dr. Lock's Mercedes and the horse chestnut. He kept everyone pinned down, clinging onto faith, as the Police sirens were still going off in all directions, responding to TV's armory. But luckily, Dr. Bolt and Nurse Lavender both escaped being hit, but shots missed Lavender by a fraction and she was sure it was fate. She would survive this ordeal; higher providence had a life mission for her, and she had that hunch it was going to be a new life as 'The Hooded Strangleress', down under, with that diamante mask. She could do it in memory of Julietta! TV stopped for a moment. He was inspired, blood up, this automatic shotgun was pure heaven and retribution.

'What goes around comes around. That's life, Dr. Bolt!'

Freeda backed him up.

'Yeah that's life, Bolt, ya bastard! Keep shooting, TV, and they'll go away! Keep shooting!' Freeda backed up her shouting with the chant, 'No more Barry, the big fat nurse, Locko or Bolt! No more Barry, the big fat nurse, Locko or Bolt!'

TV had decided to save the last magazine for an escape plan he had hatched, but with Freeda egging him on, he reloaded and just kept firing and spraying the cartridge everywhere. The last cartridge inevitably ran out. The gun was just a toy now.

'Fuck it! That's the lot, Freeda!'

'What about that small gun you had, TV?'

It was an odd serendipity down at Dr. Greene-Burrow's. Jeremy and Catherine tried to work out what was going on? Jeremy thought it a drug bust as yet another police car past. He spoke as the gangster film was banging away on the DVD.

'Huh, it's like having Al Capone living up the road.'

TV rushed upstairs and found a couple of cartridges for the sawn off, and he had to save those for the Fishgate run attempt. But the reality of the situation was finally dawning on Freeda. That lot outside weren't going away now that TV didn't have the big gun going, but she still had faith in him to get them out somehow. TV could do anything! He got her out of that prison unit and scared everybody away! He would do it again! He could walk on water and it was Fishgate or bust.

'Let's go to the seaside like we said, TV! We can go to Fishgate! That place in my photo! Let's go, TV! Let's go to Fishgate!'

But reality had dawned. TV loaded the sawn down gun, and they sat back down on the furry chair, cuddling. By now it was a quarter to nine and the light was beginning to fade into twilight, but inside that front lounge, the lights and angels sparkled all the more. It made everything more poignant and Freeda just broke down and sobbed.

'I wanna be with you, TV! We're married and we need to be together now, don't we?'

TV comforted her as best he could.

'We'll always be together, Freeda. Always! Now I've got a plan!'

Freeda's hopes were raised as TV was good with his plans. He fiddled with his magic pouch and brought out that snake's head that had startled Chaz. He slowly opened the head.

'Now if anything bad, real bad happens to me, Freed. I get shot or something.'

Freeda wanted to blot this kind of scenario out. She couldn't face that. It would be the end. She would die of a broken heart. She burst into more tears and TV squeezed her trying desperately to comfort her. He had a little bag of pills in his hand and he popped them into Freeda's. 'We'll always be together, Freeda, we'll go to heaven and be there at Fishgate forever! Right there on the beach with your mum.'

As if on cue, Dean Martin's 'Memories' was the next track, and TV said everything in his few words. 'Think about it, Freeda! We've been blessed. Getting married and this house where we cuddled each other on the furry chair, me in my white blazer and you in your wedding dress. We're blessed, Freeda! We're like angels together!'

Freeda beamed. The only thing TV could think of doing was to show that he was happy! Another glass of champagne! He wanted to accentuate all the wonderful things that had taken place. His heart was singing and his smile was warmer and bigger.

'I couldn't care what happens. I'm just happy I married ya. That's why I got you out and it all worked out! Everything did! We caught stars, Freeda! The Dragon Stars!'

Freeda was just so happy hearing TV speaking like that. She would cling onto this moment as the tears flowed down her cheeks.

'It's been the best day of my life, TV! The best of Freeda's life! Can we have "Freeda's song" on again, TV?'

'Course, Freeda! We can do our wedding dance again!'

They both raised themselves from the furry chair for the last time as the intro of the Etta James begun. They swayed and danced together smiling, their eyes melting, and their hearts joining for ever more. Two ambulances had already left and one more arrived with yet another injured marksman being stretchered inside. It was still shocked mayhem out there, and they obviously didn't know how many rounds TV had left. But they were envisaging a long, tense stand-off. Dr. Bolt was considering the situation rationally.

'It's going to be a terrible night for the Trust, Nurse Garotte. Terrible!'

Back in the front lounge, TV and Freeda were swaying with each other and Freeda bawled her life out on TV's shoulder as they swayed. TV tried to just wrap her in a cocoon of love. But everything had been worth it. Everything, and TV was sure that Dragon Star would be famous now! Everything was moving towards AD 2025! It was kicking off!

Meanwhile, the forces of order were getting organized again, and Dr. Bolt took up the cudgels to move things into the final phase of megaphone diplomacy. He had spoken to the acting chief officer. They were concerned about the hostages. They had to get those Barbers out safely if at all possible. There was a censorious parental air about Dr. Bolt's tone as he tried to fill Dr. Lock's shoes, but he was more comfortable standing behind her.

'TV! Your aunt Joan wants to know if Charlie and Linda are all right? She hopes you haven't hurt them, TV! She wants you to be nice to them, TV!' It was a clever ploy from Dr. Bolt.

'The murderers! Murderers!' Lavender snapped. 'How dare they!' and by now Freeda was at the window, determined to have a say, after she heard that Bolt shouting his mouth off out there.

'We've got the Blazerpeople and TV was taking Blazerwoman to seventh heaven with his big wangly dangler! And she liked it, Bolt! That's life!'

Dr. Bolt quickly assessed what Freeda had blasted out, although he was concerned that he wouldn't have the judgment of a Dr. Lock in this tense standoff situation.

'It looks bad, Nurse Garotte! We all know what his seventh heaven means! He needs his new syrups! They both do! See if you can get to the boot, Nurse, to get my special syrup case out. Those new tutti-frutti ones! That I saved for later on!'

Lavender felt she needed to do it, for Julietta, so she inched towards the Mercedes' back boot. But that sex doll with the erect enormous penis. That was the problem with this TV. Yes, Lavender had a lot to get off her mind!

'The pervert put a sex doll in the garden and it looks just like him. God only knows where he got it from, Dr. Bolt. The sex maniac! That's what he is, Dr. Bolt! A sex maniac and we should have cut it off years ago and never mind that changing into a woman business. Murderer! Bastard! Murderer!'

With the second response team having arrived, the house was again fully covered with marksmen, but it was hoped there would be no more firing. This sort of thing never happened in relatively quiet Tennin and the police were still assessing what was an ongoing and fast-moving situation.

TV and Freeda put the doggy masks back on the Blazerpeople and once that mask was on Chaz, Freeda naturally thought it didn't look right, as he didn't have that hooter! It seemed that aesthetically speaking, the Blazerman needed that black cock on his nose.

'I fink he looks better with that big cock on his nose. I know what, TV! We can superglue it back on. Superglue always works, TV!'

Within a few moments they were hunting down the superglue which Chaz said was out the back in the drawer. TV covered the end of the black cock with glue and slapped it on the mask and held it for ten seconds. Chaz had his cock hooter again.

'I reckon it will be all right, Freeda!'

'Well, Dicky always had that funny nose, TV!'

TV unfastened Chaz's hands and then fastened them around his back as Freeda held the knife up to him. The fastenings on Chaz's legs were then released and Chaz stood up. TV had Chaz's keys and he had to take that money, all in the shopping bag with that kilo of coke. He laid a line out on the table and had a snort with a rolled-up note to fortify himself.

"Here, Freeda, have a line before we go out and down Fishgate! It'll make ya feel better, Freeda!' TV laid it out and Freeda, copying TV, snorted, at least they were strengthened for what was coming next. 'Now ya sure you know what to do, Freeda?'

Freeda knew, but she was fearing the worst now. She could see some of the implications of what was about to occur. Impending danger was concentrating her mind.

'Yeah, I got it, TV. But I'm scared, TV. I don't want to see you hurt.'

They would always be together, no matter what TV said. They were married now. He took her hand and touched her fingers softly on top of the wedding ring and sweetly kissed her, but it was all too overwhelming for Freeda and she broke down again, sobbing on his shoulder. But after a few moments of comforting, it was time to play the end games, TV and Freeda's end. TV turned to Chaz and gave his orders.

'We're going outside, Blazerman! We're gonna get in ya car and you're gonna drive us to Fishgate promenade, right! And any fucking funny business, you're fucking dead, right!'

Chaz nodded his head and Freeda was enthused now by TV's words and the euphoria of the coke. She still believed that TV would get them out of this fix. TV could do things, anything. He had come to that window and sawn it out in the middle of the night and nobody stopped him. He scared them all away.

'I knew we'd go to the seaside, TV! I knew we would be together at Fishgate!'

'We'll go to that place in your picture, Freeda, and have a soft Mr. Whippy cornet with loads of strawberry syrup, Freed!'

That made Freeda smile and feel happy again. To be there, holding TV's hand, a hand of somebody she loved and who really loved her. That would be better than anything, and it would be as husband and wife. They had to get to Fishgate! They had to!

TV and Freeda had Chaz and Linda up, and by the front door. Both had the bizarre doggy masks on and Chaz was in his pants, the bandage on his thigh soaked bloody red by now, and desperately in need of a change. He sported that hoodie with the carefully executed caricature of TV and Freeda on the back, a bizarre irony. TV held the knife at his throat and he put the plastic bag full of drugs and money over his wrist. He had the sawn-off shotgun in the left hand. Freeda had the big knife and TV was doing his best. He wanted the right effect because he thought it might just be possible to somehow get down there. It was a long shot but you never know. But it would be so fitting if they could get there and sit on the beach together, before it all came to its inevitable end. But he didn't want to see Linda hurt, nor Chaz.

'Remember, Freeda, only pretend. Linda is nice, Freeda. Don't hurt her. Do that for TV, Freed.'

'All right, TV,' she replied, and Linda prayed that she would stand by TV's word. The letterbox opened and the snake knocker seemed to spit out more of its endless furies.

'We're coming out! And we're gonna make our way to Blazerman's Jag! We've got knives at their throats and armed to the teeth! If you try anything, they're both dead, right!'

The officer in charge of the armed teams had everybody in position. This was it, the final moment! The Titanic was up vertical out of the water, hovering before that inevitable end.

'They're coming out! Get ready!' the officer said. The door gingerly opened and Chaz came out first, a bizarre sight with that penis mask, underpants and TV hoody, and that bloody bandage. The marksmen were on the order to shoot to kill, but at all costs attempt to ensure that the Barbers were safe. It was all a fine line.

The police officers looked in disbelief. Dr. Bolt behind the horse chestnut kept on that megaphone, making it up as he went along, watching them as they came out. He tried valiantly to calm the situation, manage it as best he could. The place was like a front-line war zone as it was.

'Now don't do anything silly, TV! Just put the weapons down, all of them, and let the Barbers go! And there'll be cigarettes and a great party!'

TV led Chaz a little way forward and then Freeda came forth too, with Linda in the trouser suit and doggy mask. It was twilight now with darkness very soon to descend.

Dan was only a couple of hundred yards away up the lane from the house. He heard that megaphone, and he knew it was Dr. Bolt. It was all about entering the lion's den now. He had held back because of the police cordon at the bottom of the lane, so he climbed the little railing fence awkwardly and with difficulty, and was walking on the edge of the rapeseed that would take him right down there. He was determined to make it down to that house, whatever he might come up against.

By the time TV had come out, the body of Dr. Lock had been recovered from the route that Nurse Garotte had taken, and was coming back through the woods, via a couple of paramedics. TV edged up the path slowly, looking around anxiously, wishing he still had that automatic shotgun loaded. Dr. Bolt was still exhorting them to put their weapons down.

'Fuck off, Bolt! We tricked you for fucking once, didn't we!' TV shouted.

'Yeah, we fucking tricked ya! So, fuck off, nuts and Bolt!' Freeda shouted, backing him up all the way. They edged out further and it gave time for a marksman to level up a sight on TV's forehead. There was another levelling up on Freeda and they were to be taken out if need be. TV spotted Bolt behind the horse chestnut and then there was an odd couple of seconds, where time itself seemed to stand still. A complete uncanny silence that gave a space, before a single rifle shot. A fraction of a second before it rang out, Freeda caught her Jesus's sandal on a burr in the pathway, which knocked her into Linda's back, and one of the marksmen refrained from pulling the trigger. However, the other one did and the shot hit TV bang in the center of his forehead, at the same time TV was firing the sawn-off shot gun at the tree, with Dr. Bolt taking some of the shot in his shoulder. For Freeda, the next few moments were like a slow-motion descent into her worst hell imaginable. Chaz instinctively fell down for cover and once he saw TV tottering and stumbling forward towards the fence, all he had in his mind was getting the bag! TV went down in the spring flowers, the white blazer covered with his blood. Freeda dropped her knife and ran to him screaming, the scream uncannily echoing that scream that Linda heard in the orchard. It reverberated through Linda eerily as TV writhed in his final death throes. Freeda was with him. She had her arms around him, trying to nigh will him back to life.

'TV! Freeda wants to be with you, TV! Freeda wants to be with, TV!' TV responded with his last words.

'Always, Freeda, always!'

'Don't die, TV! You can't die! Freeda wants to be with you, TV!'

TV hovered close to death and Dr. Bolt, whose jacket was stained with his blood, and nurse Garotte, with the help of a police officer or two, were trying to pull Freeda away. TV was dead now and Freeda began to struggle with them, but at least she had dropped that knife, when she had run over. Linda was with the paramedic team but Chaz just had to get that bag. As soon as his arms were unfastened, he sped across the garden and grabbed it, still with the doggy mask on, and muffled out his reasoning to a police officer, who saw him with it.

'Three grand he's got of mine in that bag! Nicked it out of a drawer!' Chaz took it around the back as more sirens were going off, and he sighed a deep sigh of relief. He had saved his bacon regarding the drugs thing. He got inside and reasoned it would be a search warrant out on the premises come six am. His mobile had been left on the coffee table and he gave Natasha a quick call. He started the call with the doggy mask on. Natasha was on a high-class liaison, a night with a late middle-aged, sixtyish, and wealthy couple in London. She was nigh naked and was just having her knickers pulled down when her father phoned.

'What's up with the line, Dad, I can't hear you properly. Your voice is muffled.'

Chaz realized he had the darn mask on, promptly pulled it off and told her the gist of what had gone on and said that he would be at the general as Linda had nigh passed out, under the strain of everything.

'Look, Nat, I'll lock the place up, leave the key under the mat but fuck get down here and hoover the place up, the creep dropped coke fucking everywhere! The pig will have a search warrant to get in here, before ya know it! So fucking get down here quick!'

Chaz kept repeating that they were all right. He had to go and he prayed for the best, and before leaving, he put the bag at the back of the fridge.

'The dough and coke are in the fridge, Nat.'

The police thought the disappearance of Chaz a bit odd, but they picked up the sawn-off shotgun and obviously, investigations would take place. While this was occurring, the hospital teams continued their struggle with Freeda.

'I wanna be free with TV! Freeda wants to be with TV!' Freeda exclaimed, while Nurse Lavender was giving Freeda her warm assurances.

'It's all going to be all right now, Freeda, once Dr. Bolt gives you your nice medicines and syrups.'

Dr. Bolt was feeling the strain with his wounding, but the call of duty pushed him onwards. He just had to sedate the mad witch. He looked positively manic and sighed a huge sense of relief from the great strains, when he inserted that needle and pushed in its pink contents.

'And I think we'll need a second nurse!' he suggested, knowing full well that the second would bring a horse down. But this was the psychotic

Freeda Huskit. She needed a whopping great dose and he couldn't wait to get that second in. Yet more relief from the strains was beckoning, and then he could feed her with some light boosters in the ambulance, on the way back, while she was zombie chilled. He would have to take her well out there, beyond 'zombie chill' into 'poleaxed', to prevent any more intransigence. Nurse Lavender couldn't restrain herself. TV had murdered Julietta, the bastard. She felt impelled to get a few knives in as revenge.

'Two at least, the little bitch! And your murderer lover boy is dead! Dead!'

Dr. Bolt looked even more overjoyed when he got Freeda with the second, as a paramedic begged him to allow the team to attend to his wounds. But in it went, a double dose of the pink, so it was all over now. Yet Freeda still wouldn't let TV go, even though he had passed away. She could never let him go. He was everything to her and without him, all there would be was the prison unit. She could see that clearly enough.

Before leaving the house, Chaz snorted a line, he just had to have something to calm him, and get him floating into the vibe he knew and loved. He had a pair of trousers on now and a bomber jacket, he couldn't have faced putting on a blazer, and he came from the house. He would phone Natasha again if he needed anything. But Chaz had underestimated the sheer stress of the ordeal and when he returned to the front of the house to board the ambulance, he came over all dizzy and everything was akin to being in a vague fog and he collapsed. Linda was now on a stretcher herself and she too was being sedated as the struggle in the garden paradise continued.

'Now you've got to let go of the corpse, Freeda. Let go! It's just a corpse, Freeda!' Nurse Lavender shouted angrily, but this Huskit was willful and the more she heard that big fat nurse, the more she held onto TV. She was never going to do what that big fat nurse told her to. She hated her!

After the second injection had been successfully administered, Nurse Lavender motioned for Dr. Bolt to get the straitjacket out of the medical bag. Now the Trust, had generally, declared the end of the use of straitjackets, due largely to the roaring success of Dr. Bolt's forced injection regime. Why struggle getting something on a client when a needle and syringe could be doubly effective? But Nurse Lavender Garotte felt vindictive. The bottom line was the syrups would take five to kick in, and by golly Lavender felt revengeful, nastily so, having lost her significant other and partner to these bastards. Freeda spat right in Lavender's face and in her anger Nurse Garotte punched Freeda right in the mouth. She hit her again as she was trying to get Freeda to release her grip from TV's body. Freeda just heard TV in her mind.

'We'll be in heaven together! They can never tear us apart, Freeda! Never!'

Freeda's mind cleared and there was only one thing that she was going to do, and nobody was going to stop her, nobody. She wanted to be with TV, not with that big fat nurse in the prison unit. She let go of TV, and with psychotic power pulled herself free from Nurse Lavender's hold as if it was a child's. She rushed across the garden, giving herself enough time to grab the pills that TV had given to her, which she had put down her cleavage in the polythene bag. Providence was with her as she managed to open the small bag and pour most of them down her throat. She was trying to get the last of them in too, and was desperately trying to swallow them as Nurse Garotte rushed across to stop her. It was obvious where this was going after those injections. Incredibly Freeda, who was hopeless at swallowing pills, nigh gulped the lot.

'No, you don't, young lady!'

Nurse Lavender made a determined and forceful lunge and managed to knock the last pills from Freeda's hand and managed to wrestle Freeda to the ground. She quickly trapped one of Freeda's arms and held her in a neck crank. Lavender had her now as this was one of her most powerful wrestling moves. She knew she had the upper hand; she had done a relentless Tennin Power Gym training schedule the last three months, and had been taking steroids in that period, under the close supervision of Dr. Lock. Chaz himself had used the gym a bit back in the day, buying steroids from the same dealer. He was recalling seeing a younger Nurse Lavender down there, as he came over dizzy and was put on a stretcher.

'Get away, oink, oink! I'm going to heaven with TV! Nasty fat nurse!' Then Freeda took a nasty, chomp into Lavender's strengthened arm, and she bite down so hard that Lavender had to let go.

'How dare you! You vixen!' Nurse Lavender screamed. She responded by whacking Freeda in the face a couple of times and Freeda struck her back in the face even harder. By now two police officers were trying to restrain Freeda as well, as she bawled for TV. Nurse Garotte was aware that she rather overstepped the mark and she tried to give a rationale for her actions.

'I know it doesn't look very pretty, Officer, but it's the only way to deal with this little heathen monster! The witch!'

Meanwhile, a paramedic had covered TV's body and while he was doing so, Dr. Bolt had returned to that medical bag inspired. He just had to get one more shot into Freeda. A nice tutti-frutti syrup would do it. He thought she needed it, just to end this continued recalcitrance, to give her that settled and peaceful 'poleaxed' vibe. By the time he came across the garden to get the next one in, Freeda's rage had finally relented, and she was left sobbing into Nurse Lavender's arms. The fight had ended and

Nurse Lavender smiled to Dr. Bolt, as if to say at last it was all over, with regard Freeda's kicking and raging end. She would soon be safely tucked up in the lock up unit.

But by now, Dan had appeared on the scene and he saw a route to get to that fence, as with all the commotion the police hadn't spotted him hiding behind one of the silver birches, that lined the road directly opposite. He had heard the shots and Freeda's scream and had been crying behind the tree trunk. But he felt compelled to get across to the bushes somehow, as he had seen the top half of Freeda in her wedding dress. He saw an opening and he took it. Freeda spotted him approaching and she burst away from Nurse Lavender with psychotic force. She rushed towards the fence to greet him. Her heart sang when she saw Dan, despite all the terrible things that were happening. Dan immediately realized that TV was dead. He prayed he was merely wounded but the paramedics were carrying TV on a stretcher to an ambulance, his green hair poking out from a cover. But Freeda was ecstatic.

'Dan! We did it, Dan! We got married and Freeda is in her wedding dress! And we're married forever! Freeda and TV are married forever, Dan!'

Dan reached the opening by a bush and they hugged each other.

'You look beautiful, Freeda! Beautiful! You're beautiful, Freeda!'

Dan burst into further tears as Freeda was pulled away. 'You were always beautiful, Freeda! You're a goddess, Freeda! You're beautiful!'

Freeda was gone now, so Dan turned and began walking away back up Holly Beach Lane, sobbing for Freeda and TV. He noticed the confetti on his clothes, and he looked at it on his hand, and sobbed the more. He was heartbroken. Dr. Bolt took his chance to get one more booster tutti fruity syrup in for keep's sake. Freeda didn't even register the needle, she was sobbing so much and the drugs had numbed her. There were four or five ambulances stacked up outside 'Chaz's Pad' now and Chaz and Linda were in one, both covered with blankets. They had both witnessed Dan coming to the fence but then Linda lost consciousness due to the extreme stress and sedation. There was a doggy hood on the seat.

Freeda was shepherded away from the garden towards the ambulances too and the last she saw of TV, was the stretcher going into another with Jesus's sandals poking from the blankets that covered his body. Freeda was breathing heavily and becoming increasingly unsteady as she was rapidly moving towards unconsciousness. She sensed where she was going, and she wanted to embrace it, as a release from all this pain and agony. Those sandals of TV's being the prompt.

'Collect us, Jesus, cos we had ya sandals and badges, collect me and TV,' she whispered, before she collapsed, as the doors closed on TV's stretcher. He had gone and Freeda was going too.

'Get her into the ambulance, quickly!' Dr. Bolt shouted, realizing that he might have been a bit over-zealous on the medication. He could have brought down an elephant let alone a horse.

Dan looked back as he could hear all the continued shouting and could see that Freeda was about to go into an ambulance on a stretcher. He was inconsolable as he continued walking back up the lane. He had always feared that something bad would come out of it all, and all his fears had been proven right. It was a tragedy.

Once inside the ambulance, Freeda was wired up to the monitors and she was still mumbling for TV, but was slipping in and out of consciousness. Back in the lounge the CD player was playing on, with all the hits of the old days. 'Moon River' was playing and there were the two remaining carp, looking out into the empty, but LED lit room. The two nigh finished bowls of strawberries and cream were upon the big coffee table and the bunting bearing their names, 'Freeda and TV' was caught in the soft light, and the small plastic angels with their pipes, seemed to be opening to the heavens. Freeda's *Sesame Street* record case, stood by the CD player, estranged from its loving owner. Her purse could be seen poking from Linda's handbag that was lain on the furry chair and there were three fags resting on the edge of the ashtray on the mashed-up arm. It was all over.

Freeda was soon in intensive care and she felt as if she was floating on the waters. There were still bits of confetti in her hair and all she could see were colors and angels and TV waiting for her on the beach by that café at Fishgate in his special white blazer, like when they got married. She was aware that nurses were around her and she could see her wedding dress, her beautiful blood-stained wedding dress, hung up in an opened cupboard. Then she heard something odd that became louder and clearer, and she could hear the sea in the background, and Freeda uttered the final words of her life to the two nurses with her.

'Donkeys! The donkeys have come for us!'

When she passed away her face seemed to settle in a smile. Her spirit was finally released from the torment of her tragic life and let us all pray that the Freedas of this world are finally embraced by some great, sublime, all-encompassing love.

CHAPTER TWENTY-FOUR

THE ORB, THE SNAKE AND THE FLYING SAUCER LAMPPOST

Natasha got the second distress S.O.S and as luck would have it, her evening's work had just come to an end. She had been the plaything of this couple with the bi-curious wife seven times now, and they had been working through the couple's bucket list of sexual fantasies. Nat gave them the porn star treatment and they couldn't get enough; they loved her high fashion, girl about London town look, and shameless and un-shockable attitude. Natasha had given them a free reign to express and discover their deepest desires, and she was getting a nice wad of cash for the trouble. But the couple sensed that something serious was up, by the urgency of Nat's responses as Chaz was filling her in with the details. He was in the toilets of the hospital and groggy and he told Nat that the crazies had got hold of all the guns and shot the fuck out of the police, and now Linda was fast asleep in her hospital bed on a drip, suffering from shock.

'Oh, you're fucking joking! Oh, fuck me, Dad. A fucking doctor dead in the front garden! Oh, fuck me and they shot him! No! What? Raped Mum! Oh, fucking hell!'

Natasha said she would be coming down to clean that house up immediately, even though it was half eleven. It would take her a good hour, with forty-five minutes of that on the motorway.

'I said it was divvy to keep those stupid fucking guns, Dad! You should have got rid of them after that fucking shoot out! But yes, of course I'll be down. I'll fucking hoover up every grain.'

Chaz was in the toilets standing by the basins, ready to cut the call short if anybody came in. The cubicles were all vacant.

'Look, Nat, I'm already in the shit over the guns, but there's another automatic shotgun in the cabinet. I want ya to get it out and I want ya to take the fucking thing, and ya know that chalk pit lake ya go past on the train to Foxdale?'

Natasha knew where he meant as you passed part of the lake on the train journey, although where Chaz wanted Nat to throw the gun was out of eyesight. He told her about the gaps in the fence where she could park up nearby and get to the steep chalk faces of Olwyn's lake. Nat could understand what he meant.

'Right, cover the fucker up with a blanket or something when you take it in there, and fuck don't go down there in ya stilettoes, wear something fucking practical, Nat. There shouldn't be anybody about. But keep an eye out and just throw it as far as you can out from high up there. Ten yards out and it's ninety foot! But make sure you don't get fucking seen doing it for fuck's sake. If there's people around, don't bung it in. And oh yeah, the Glock is in there too under the folders and for fuck's sake get all the ammo out!'

'All right, Dad, I'll do it all no problem, and I'll stick some boots on and wear a donkey jacket!'

Chaz laughed but there was more.

'Now listen. As I said the gear is in the fridge in a plastic bag with the dough, now I've phoned Gray, so go to Gray's, just go down there and give him the bag, he'll be up. I'll text ya his number. There's about a kilo or so, and we'll see you up here in the morning. I know I can trust ya Nat, because they'll have a warrant to search in the morning! We've gotta get that shit out, Nat! We gotta!'

Natasha popped back to her penthouse flat in her Porsche 911 convertible, that sported her personalized number plates 'Nat Fab1'. She filled up a hold all of clothes, as she was anticipating a couple of nights stay, so was hoping to catch up with her friend Zoe, with a Saturday night visit to 'Club Hollywood', in Tennin, although she had to get back for Tuesday's Uni exams. She fortified herself with a line of coke, before hitting the motorway to the strains of Oakenfield's Energy 52. As soon as she was on the motorway, she was on to Zoe, who was in a local bar with some friends. Zoe was a clubbing diehard and loved a party, and she was excited to hear that Nat would be about tomorrow night.

'Can't wait to see you, Nat. We'll have to have a party! How are ya fixed with gear?'

Zoe asked.

'My father's a drug dealer, Zoe!'

Zoe smiled and liked the idea of having copious amounts of free powder. 'We'll have to see if we can pull!'

'Fuck! I'm not going with the usual suspects. But I've got to fucking fly. We're expecting a search warrant on my old man at six in the morning. I'll keep in touch, Zoe!'

Zoe wondered what the heck was going on? She turned to her friend and said it looked like Nat's old man had been busted, or at least the police were on him.

With the line she had before she set off, and the high adrenaline, and the music blaring out the speakers, Nat didn't realize how fast she was going. In the next breath, she heard a Police siren and could see a car trying to keep up with her, flagging her down.

'Fuck!'

Nat slowed and pulled over onto the hard shoulder. She wound the window down and the Police wanted to know why she was moving at over a hundred and twenty miles an hour? Natasha was always non fazed in these situations. She was used to the hairy, and she was sharp and expressive as if she'd been to RADA.

'Now, I know you wouldn't believe it, Officer, but I am rushing to my parents' in Tennin Hospital, they were held hostage by a couple of fucking loonies and my mother's been repeatedly raped. I'm sorry, I know it sounds fucking mad but I just want to get up there quick. You can check it all out with Tennin Police, major incident in Holly Beach Lane.'

The two officers had been hearing about the incident all night long and they stopped an intended search of the car, and after seeing some ID they let Natasha go.

'But please, Ms. Barber, can you drive back there within the speed limit please?'

In a display of typical Barber defiance, Natasha quickly laid a line out on a Uni reader as the police car waited behind for her to pull away. She snorted with a rolled-up note and glanced behind before reentering the traffic stream.

'Fuck em!'

Now Gray lived in a semi-detached in Tennin and naturally he wanted to help out his drugs buddy in need. But a kilo, and a load of dough? Probably a hundred grand or something ridiculous he thought. If he got caught with that, it would be a big custodial. Gray fancied a cup of coffee but he was out of milk. He was single now after the divorce and his girlfriend wasn't around this evening, so he decided to take a quick one to the parade of shops on the estate, that was no more than four hundred yards away. He left the house, dressed in his normal combat fatigues and noticed those two guys again, parked up in a Ford Focus. He had seen them on three occasions now and he was sure they were the Tennin Police.

'Here he comes!' one of them said to the other in the car.

The two guys were exactly that, plain clothes police, and were part of a newly formed Tennin Drug detection unit. Their aim was to get to the heart of the Tennin drugs trade. They were after the bigger dealers and were sure that Gray was involved, after a group of youngsters, who were arrested on possession charges, squealed on him, apparently Chopper talked a bit too much. The unit had been following and watching Gray and were hoping to see him connect with somebody of importance along the hierarchy, and hopefully catch a big monster fish, red handed with a batch of cocaine. Gray came out of the convenience store with the four-pint carton and they were still there, parked on that down slope leading to the close where Gray lived. Gray sighed, as it was so obvious. He stopped by the car and tapped on the window. As Chaz had always said, the Tennin Police weren't the cleverest.

'Hullo, officers, trouble in the vicinity?'

When Gray got inside, he phoned Chaz, but Chaz had fallen asleep and his mobile was on answer. Gray gave him a message to contact him as quickly as possible.

'It's fucking urgent, mate!'

Gray came off the mobile and swore. It was Natasha. It wouldn't look too swell if she parked up in that fucking Porsche and came up to the door with a bag. He racked his brain thinking how he might get Nat's number, something that Chaz had forgotten to give him.

It was still pandemonium at 'Chaz's Pad'. The acting officer was hoping to get a quick search warrant but it would have to wait till morning. A window for opportune skullduggery presented itself to the Barber's. Nat arrived and harassed the police officers to move their car so that she could park up alongside her parents shredded Jeep. The Jag had its windscreen smashed out and had taken plenty of shots through its body too.

'Could you move, please! I'm Mr. and Mrs. Barber's daughter and I've been told the house is wrecked, so could you move, please.'

It was a complicated one, but the police didn't have that search warrant to enter the house as yet, so Nat strode up the path with her hold all. She was shocked to see the sex doll in the garden.

'What the fuck is that!'

She would get on the mobile to Chaz as soon as she was inside the house. She did so, when she got through the front door, but Chaz was fast asleep, after being heavily sedated himself. She would have to make it all up as she went along. She decided to bite the bullet and ask the police exactly what had occurred.

'The two clients of the asylum obtained what we think were illegal weapons from your father's house and subsequently shot dead a doctor and injured three police officers, and this is a site of a major crime. As soon as we obtain a warrant, we shall be searching your parents' house. One of our officers has been seriously wounded, Ms. Barber.'

'I don't know nothing about it, my dad's at the hospital and he wants some stuff up there to wear and that, but you ain't coming on our premises without a search warrant, mate.'

Natasha had a quick brain and had a criminal's courage. She would get those guns out via her bag, under the cover, of taking those provisions up the hospital. She got inside and made a beeline for the fridge and got the drugs and money. She got an incoming call and it was Gray. He had acquired her number from June.

'I can't have it down here, Nat. I've got a plain clothes team watching me fucking house. Can't you get it to somebody else?'

Natasha thought for a moment and knew immediately what she would do.

'Look it's no problem, Gray. I'll sort something else out. It's all right. But I gotta fly!'

She would take them down the traveler's camp at Fenton Hill, where Scamp presided; the police didn't like going in there. She got on well with Scamp, it was a case of 'friends with benefits', that relational New Age idea, that had become so popular. She was a chip off the old block, even sharper than Chaz. She gave him a ring; he was in a local pub. Scamp immediately hoped it was the benefits. Natasha sounded urgent.

'Me dad's in the shit; he's in hospital at the moment. I know it sounds fucking crazy Steve but he was taken hostage by two fucking loons from that fucking mental hospital and they had a shootout with the police with his fucking guns and he's likely to be searched in the morning. You couldn't keep some gear and that, until the thing blows over a bit could ya, Steve? But fucking keep it quiet!'

He knew that Chaz had illegal weapons but he couldn't very well say no; he had to help his drug supplier out, and he was more than sweet on Natasha. Natasha finally clinched it when she said she could stay for an hour or so. She would go to the hospital afterwards.

With that one sorted Natasha took the gun that had been discarded in the front room and she collected the other automatic shotgun and the stash of cash from the cabinet. But that Glock had slipped her mind. She packed the holdall full with the coke, money and two guns with some clothes on top and thought the situation through as she was playing high stakes. She could either go straight out the front. She reckoned she could deal with them, or alternatively, she could take the holdall out the back, over the wall, and hide it near the road. But then she would have to park up opposite as there were no slip roads and she might be seen hoping over the fence or something. She went with the first. She knew her rights. But fuck, the bag was heavy.

The police were parked up on the road and they spotted Natasha as she opened the gate. She had made sure she had backed in when parking and she had the boot open as the police confronted her. They hoped she was naïve.

'We are going to have to search that bag, Ms. Barber, as a precaution.'

'Fuck off! Do you think I'm some fucking greenhorn? You haven't got a search warrant and you need my consent. And I'm recording this conversation on my phone.'

They backed off and Natasha shut the boot. She was so relieved driving down Holly Beach Lane. She had avoided going down for God knows how long. But by the time she got down the Fenton site, another session of sex and with all the sorting of the guns and drugs, she was exhausted, and she decided she would just go back to Holly Beach Lane. She wanted to do a bit more hoovering too. She tried belling Chaz to tell him she had pursued a different ploy, but he was still spark out. While Nat was driving back to the house, there was a returning visitor to 'Chaz's Pad'. It was the black panther. It slipped across the back wall and positioned itself, up on his haunches in the old fruit garden, looking towards the house, with its piercing emerald eyes.

When Nat finally arrived back, the police vehicle was still there. She parked up her Porsche, the police could see who it was, and Nat entered the garden, but when she was nearly up the path, the dreaded fox scream, that one that sounded like a woman, rang out again. Nat was shocked, terrified, and she went back outside to speak to the Police, as she hadn't heard the story of that one from her parents. But the officer on duty had, it was Gabi.

'Can you check that woman screaming out the back please!'

'Your mother and father reported the scream recently, we investigated and there was nothing untoward out there. It was foxes,' Gabi said. Natasha persisted.

'Well it certainly sounds like a woman! I want it checked please!'

Gabi and the male officer relented and reluctantly went out the back with torches and Gabi shone her torch on that eerie, crazy sex doll. They were astounded and couldn't grasp what had gone on and then they made a brief and cursory search further into the orchard.

Nat went back inside and with that search warrant impending, she was focusing on looking for any signs of coke she had missed when she had whipped the hoover round earlier. She looked up on the wall, the Freeda loves TV bunting, and she had that down. She thought there might be some coke in the St. George trinket box. She would flush it down the toilet or snort it herself. But it was empty. She began hoovering around the chair again and focused on that coffee table as there was loads over it underneath that edition of *Big Jugs*. She could see that there were two carp missing, which she thought strange, and she wondered what the smell was, she noticed it earlier, as if something had been burning. She found out when she put some of the left-over food off the coffee table in the bin. Her mind registered that idea, the loonies had those carp out and cooked them! She worked for half an hour and then sat back in the Waldorf for a fag with its ripped-up arm, wondering what the fuck had gone on. She would be up that hospital first thing.

While she was sitting there thinking hard about the issues, that same terrifying fox scream went up again. Now Nat was of the same character as Chaz. There were guns in the house, and Nat knew plenty about them, through having a father obsessed with them. She was also a better clay pigeon and pistol shot than he ever was, even competing for the county, and she still shot regularly at the University. She realized she had forgotten to take out that pistol earlier so she grabbed the Glock, that had been hidden underneath some folders in the cabinet and loaded it with a magazine. Nat just had to take a look out in the Orchard and confirm in her mind there was nothing there. The police were of little help. Gabi had disturbing dreams after the last time she visited the house. They knocked at the front and said there was nothing out there and off they went to the car. But Natasha had to put her mind at rest. As soon as Nat opened that porch door the scream went up again. It had the same effect on Nat as Linda. She was sure it was a woman and it sounded like it came from just over that back wall. When Chaz brought her over to look at the house, when the papers were going through, she had walked out towards the wall talking with her father, then all of a sudden, she had become nauseous and violently sick. She thought she had picked up the norovirus and now out there in the dark with the mist swirling she was thinking about that moment. She shone the torch, a high powered one with a beam out there as she held the pistol readied in her other hand, she glanced behind her just in case the Police appeared suddenly from nowhere. Then there was a rustling, and Nat saw something moving out there, swiftly towards the back-boundary wall. It was something big and she managed to get the beam on it and saw a glimpse of the big cat slipping over the wall. She went further out into the garden with the torch as she felt impelled to investigate. It sounded as if Jack the Ripper was out there, the scream was that bloodcurdling. Bloody police are useless, she thought. What the fuck was it though? If he was out there, she would put half a dozen rounds in him.

The owls were hooting and it was quiet in the depths of that old orchard and there was atmosphere with that wispy mist swirling around. What Nat did notice were some small stones that Chaz hadn't noticed out there due to the long grass. She investigated and could see that they transcribed a small circle. It all seemed mysterious to her. Then something uncanny happened. Nat felt nauseous all of a sudden and was violently sick again. She heaved and expelled a couple of times and fuck this house, she thought, and turned back. She got inside and couldn't face the prospect of sleeping in the house all alone. The place was putting the fear of Christ up her. She gave Scamp another call.

'Steve! Can ya come over?'

'What's the problem?'

'It's just this fucking house. It's putting the willies up me.'

'Sure, babes.' Steve got up immediately and began to dress. He liked Natasha asking him like this. He was deeply in love with her, and had already asked her to marry him two years ago before she went to Uni. She declined and he took that really bad, but he could never let go of her. His mum bolstered him, by saying that it might be a case of her coming back to him in the end, and Nat phoning like this, seemed to suggest it might lead to that one day. Scamp as he was known by most, obviously knew that Chaz had moved in up Holly Beach Lane in that Ashcroft's old house. It was all before Steve's time but his mother had told him about the murder over the back, and the claims that Ashcroft had conducted all kinds of devil worshipping ceremonies in the house, and out there in the back orchard, so Steve could understand.

Within a matter of ten minutes he was pulling up Holly Beach Lane. He just managed to squeeze his car into the space left available, next to Nat's Cabriolet. Natasha rushed out to explain to Gabi and the other officer that it was her boyfriend. The streetlamp's light was sufficient for Scamp to notice the destruction of Chaz's Jag, with its windows largely shot out and its body riddled with blast damage. What the fuck had gone on, he thought?

'Oh, I'm so fucking glad you've come Steve, the place gives me the creeps!'

Nat used the opportunity to give him the Glock.

'Stick it in your car,' Nat whispered, knowing that Steve could leave early before there was any search warrant out on his vehicle.

Steve knew what it was and quickly put it under the front seat before locking up.

They opened the gate and came up the path and Steve spotted that doll in the back garden, standing up in the flowers. He was looking non-plussed but Scamp loved the fact that the situation allowed him to say something, that events had given him the context to say it.

'If you ask me for something, I'll always have time for ya, Nat. But what the fuck is that in the garden there, in that flowerbed?'

Nat brought it into the back porch with its green wig and white blazer. The Dragon Star cap had come off and was on the lawn.

'I don't know what went on, Steve, but the crazies probably took it from the room that Dad uses for sex films. And you know what, I saw a puma or something out the back there.'

There were no more screams overnight, and while they were lying in Chaz and Linda's double, early in the morning, Steve told Natasha what he knew about the house. The murder and those satanic activities. Nat didn't like what she was hearing. Steve had kept this quiet. He hadn't told Nat when she saw him a few months back. Steve got up with the worms and left early before that warrant came in.

Chaz and Linda were awaiting discharge from the general hospital. It had been a tough thirty-six hours up there. Linda was in a state of shock when they arrived and was maximum sedated. But now she had come around and they were seated in a quiet corner with Nat, who was now her usual catwalk looking, meets a porn star self, sporting a red newsboy hat, expensive patchwork jeans, red see-through top and micro bra and a bling studded belt. The look today, was finished off with her crystal and suede Christian Louboutin courts. She was a fan of the designer and swore by his shoes like Chaz swore by alligator. She certainly needed money to keep up with her clothing and lifestyle choices, tons of it, like her father, and by coincidence, she too was sporting a pair of cat-eye sun glasses, but these cost her well over the grand. Nat loved expensive fashion gimmicks, but today wasn't a day of gimmicks. Chaz was still clad in that uncustomary black bomber jacket as the white blazer was now somewhat tarnished. He was in subdued mood; everything was up in the air. He had more complications to deal with too, as Natasha had taken the automatic shotgun that TV had used to Scamps, as well as that other rifle and the handgun. Chaz was a bit concerned regarding Scamp but Nat assured him that he would do anything for her.

'He won't fuck up for his Natasha, Dad,' she said, and Chaz prayed that she was right with her faith.

Natasha was fuming that all this business had taken place. It was outrageous! How could they have been allowed to escape from a lock up unit! She was incensed. It helped ease the qualms about all the other issues.

'I just can't believe it! You've got to sue them, Dad! You'd have a cast iron case. They were negligent! And look at what those fucking nutters put you through!'

Chaz tried to put the glass up to half full, but it was difficult. The shooting and illegal guns had depressed him. One doctor dead, one policewoman in intensive care and a couple with life-changing injuries. Chaz knew it was a case of 'aggravated manslaughter' with those illegal guns and the best projection in his mind, was a Libran scale, rather optimistically balanced, weighted with money gained from suing the Trust, the other with a heap of litigation papers coming at him and a custodial. But he was Chaz Barber. He still felt obliged to sound confident. Chaz Barber always came up roses. Four years ago, when Chaz had his one and only big 'turf war' with the Albanians, he had the luck to get through it. Chaz threatened them with the full weight of his connections and the dispute ended up in a shootout at an address down by Fishgate, he was with Gray, he was more involved back then, and a couple of Alfredo heavies using powerful shotguns on the house. The sophisticated gang realized that the area was best left alone, and they moved back to London, but not before having two hitmen on motorbikes lying in wait for Chaz at Snakestone Corner with powerful handguns. A seventeen-year-old Nat was in the car that day too. It all happened quick that one, Chaz spotted them a moment before the shots rang out, and he swerved the Merc, he had back then, and the shots went through his screen, with Chaz ploughing into some bushes. It was a hairy period and Chaz took to carrying that loaded

Glock around with him, as he half expected something might occur. Chaz opened the door and fired shots back at them and the hitmen pissed off. They had missed their opportunity, and afterwards, Chaz quickly got onto a small remote lane, and parked up in some woods. Nobody had witnessed what had gone on as it all happened so quick. But Chaz had shot through the tanks of one of the motorbikes and that was left on the road, so eventually police checked it out, discovered it had been stolen and they didn't have any leads, apart from a farmer who had heard Chaz's shots. Back then Chaz naturally turned to Scamp. He was going out with Natasha and he came over to the woods with his pickup truck with a tarpaulin wrap. He took it away and they burnt the car out, with its bullet holes on the bonnet and wing, down by the estuary wall that night and incredibly the whole incident just blew over. The Merc went by way of a traveler friend scrapping the next day and the police never got a trail on the incident. Linda considered leaving him back then, but she didn't, as nothing else occurred. But she would have done if she knew what had really occurred with her daughter in the passenger seat being shot at. The Albanian gang was the reason why Chaz had the automatic guns, but there had been no more big turf wars in Chaz's little patch.

'We're take them to the cleaners! Make a right packet out of it!' Chaz exclaimed, although he didn't sound overly convincing. Linda felt she had been fed through a mangle thirty times and she couldn't get her head around anything. Her thoughts and feelings were all at sea, going up and down with the waves. It was a seasick Linda.

'Oh, do you have to speak like that Chaz after what we've been through! I'm just too traumatized!' The sheer tension and stress were beginning to bite. The dream house had ended up like a war zone and Linda didn't know how she would feel about anything anymore. But Chaz was certainly sure as to who came out worst.

'Well what do you think it's like for me then, for fuck's sake! I had to put with that bloody knife at me throat with her talking about chopping me fucking head off! Tuh!'

Wherever all this was going to lead, Natasha just couldn't put up with her parents rowing over the ordeal. She had to come in between them calling for calm.

'Fucking hell! You're doing me fucking brain in! It wasn't your fault! The hospital was negligent! Those two fucking loonies shouldn't have been roaming about.'

Before they were discharged, Chaz and Linda were to see a male psychologist and a female Dr. Patel. The Trust were trying to go out of their way, hoping that a litigation wouldn't be brought against them. The psychologist, a man in his early forties, was exceedingly professional in outlook and manner, and seemed to have a sensible, rational perspective, on how Chaz and Linda might proceed.

'What you should recognize Mr. and Mrs. Barber, is that it is perfectly normal in these abnormal circumstances that you will both feel incapacitated at times, when you return to your home, the site of your ordeal. Yet you are obviously going to have to face the house and we recommend that you do so immediately, so that you make that attempt to put this behind you very quickly.'

Dr. Patel added to the advice.

'Yes, we would strongly advise you to get back to your normal routines as much as possible. Although be sure not to overwork.'

Chaz listened appreciatively and fully recognized the difficulties that he and Linda were now facing, but in view of the conversation with Natasha earlier, he had to say his piece.

'I'm a builder, Doctor, working for a very sympathetic employer and a few weeks out won't do me any harm. And we can face our own house. It's a beautiful house. That's why we purchased the place.'

There was then a noticeable hunch and a lift of Chaz's shoulders as he intended to assert himself. By merely doing so, he felt better, it was the fact that he had lost control to those two nutters, strapped up in that darn bloody bondage chair, with that silly fucking mask on. It had deeply undermined his sense of self. He had to regain it, and quick.

'And I'll say, I'm bloody taking this case up with my solicitor! I've heard about all the agency workers and security procedures being flouted.'

Tennin General was under the same Trust and clearly, they had a massive case to answer for. But it was nothing to do with Dr. Patel.

'Well that's something that you will have to take up legally, Mr. Barber. I cannot comment further upon that issue.' The case was closed for a while until the next time. It wouldn't be very long.

On the way back home, there was a lot on the Barbers' minds. Chaz was trying to think around Nat, taking both the illegal shotguns to Scamps.

'What ya gonna do, Dad?' Nat asked.

'Well I can't really deny one wasn't in the house, can I? It'll have to re-appear in the back garden, that's credible.'

Chaz was thinking smartly but he was worried to heck. The police would be challenging him as soon as he arrived back.

'Are you sure ya hoovered all that coke up?'

Natasha tried to reassure him.

'We done everything, Dad, and as I keep saying when they searched it, it was only the guns.'

She parked up outside the gate and to keep matters away from the ordeal, Chaz began talking enthusiastically about what he was going to do to the house as soon as they had settled back into normality. Both cars had been towed away, the Jeep and the Jag, and there was a sparkling new Jeep out there. Nat had purchased that from the money that was in the plastic bag, or at least she set up a 0% finance deal and the agreement was, that she would pay the bill off so she had a nice wad of cash. She'd go furniture and clothes shopping on the weekend. There might be insurance complications due to the bizarre nature of the incident, but that hadn't prevented Chaz from having a money transfer from his Swiss accounts for a quick purchase. It would be the AD 2003 white Jag now. Nat had picked up that new Jeep, and the Jag would be ready in a couple of days when the money went through.

But Chaz was talking enthusiastically about future plans. He spoke about how he wanted to put a concrete drive from the road down the back, and build a big double garage to dispense with the front as a personal parking area. He was determined now that he would live in the darn house and the debacle wouldn't affect his life. To hell with the past but Nat could see how tense her mother looked about going on the premises. Chaz stopped for a few moments, and surveyed that shredded trunk of the horse chestnut. It didn't help matters, and there were capping stones dislodged from the pockmarked brick wall, hit with the shotgun blasts. He said he would go for an immediate full repair of the wall through Alan. It would give him a pretext to finally get those eagles. That made Chaz hunch up his shoulders with a shot of testosterone. It was like an act of defiance. He had always wanted eagles and now they would land when the chips were down. But the bravado couldn't hide the fact, that everywhere, there was evidence of what had taken place. Natasha done her best to reassure her mother.

'Don't worry, Mum! Me and Steve cleaned up everything. You won't know they were ever here, Mum. Promise!'

The three went through the gate and the Barbers were home, at the site of that terrible ordeal, but home nevertheless. Nat was still comforting her mother, knowing that she was taking it all so badly. Linda cast her eyes to the now bare patch, where TV had fallen, and she flashed back in her mind to a couple of days ago, TV lying there, blood-covered, dead in her front garden. Then she looked towards that horse chestnut with its shredded upper trunk. It was hard to imagine that it had all occurred in this now peaceful and idyllic setting. But it was all too much for Linda, and she broke down into tears and was comforted by Chaz and Natasha.

'Don't worry, babes. We'll put this all behind us in no time. We'll be like rocks in a storm! Rocks in a storm, girl!'

Things in the front lounge were looking nearly the same as prior to the arrival of TV and Freeda. Nat had replaced the big screen TV with the same model, and it was on the wall identically positioned. She had also, as requested by Chaz, purchased two new mirror carp to get the tanks back to their head of four. She had also purchased a brand-new Waldorf, from the High Grange shopping center and had it delivered within two hours. It had been a busy clean-up day. But the velvet chair was still there but now had freshly purple material patches on both arms. Natasha looked incongruously, or was it harmoniously placed, sitting underneath the naked painting. Chaz was looking at the new carp in his chair as Linda could be heard climbing the stairs and heading for the bathroom.

'I bought them where you said, Dad.'

'They're great, Nat, same kind of size. Luv um! Had to have the four again, had to. Help us get back to normal. Couldn't have forgotten the bastards if there were just two and an empty tank.' Natasha had a stressful couple of days to say the least, so she had the coke out, laying a line on the coffee table.

'Do you want one, Dad? Fuck it, I've just gotta have one!' Chaz was up for it. It would be the first for a couple of days. Why not? Natasha snorted the line and laid out another and looked at the chair. 'Made a fucking mess of that chair, didn't they? New one should be here tomorrow, Dad,' she said. Chaz smiled as he was thinking it was nice that Natasha had been so supportive like this. She was a great daughter.

'Oh, that's no fucking problem, Nat. Their ghosts are not going to fucking haunt us! I can tell ya!'

A small truck arrived outside and filled up the rest of the parking area. Chaz turned his head and could see it was Scamp with that military shotgun. The gun was in the bag on arrival and Scamp had only taken a brief glance of the weapon. Natasha went outside and before she took the weapon, she closely checked the road, the police were expected today. Chaz was grateful that Nat had been so sharp. She had made a point of picking the gun up with a tea towel wrapped around it so it was going to be TV's finger prints all over it. She thanked Steve who gave her back the money too. He hadn't touched it and none of the other travelers got wind of it all. He kept his counsel and would keep the kilo and Glock until things were calmer up Holly Beach Lane. He came inside the house as Chaz had something to say to him, regarding the other gun. Chaz thought the best place to dump it was that lake of Olwyn's that he had instructed Nat to do. Get it down about ninety foot deep. Chaz had the website of the place up on a laptop. Steve had been briefed by Nat but Chaz was obsessing.

'Yeah, I know the lake, Chaz. I've already spoken to Nat about it.'

'Well, park up, take a nosey and slip in that end, the fence is poor up there and fucking sling it out as far as you fucking can! And you can have five hundred for your troubles and another five for getting me out the shit.'

Scamp left soon after, and Nat and Chaz went out the back with the automatic shotgun. Nat was in the zone and on point as Chaz would have put it in the orchard.

'Would he have had enough time to have gone up there, Dad? It wants to look as if he maybe came out the back for a split second, saw there were so many of them, and just cast it away, landed somewhere awkward, and the police missed it when they had a look round.'

There was a water butt down by the compost heap with mildew on the surface of the water, Linda hadn't used it, she had used a hose, and they put the gun in there. They cleared out the mildew so that the gun was just about visible. Chaz would pre-empt the police and say they had found the weapon, and he would admit to having the two illegal weapons on site. It was all a case of damage limitation. They were sitting back in the lounge when the 'She's Not There' ringtone fired off on Chaz's mobile.

'Hullo, is that Mr. Barber, Charles Barber? I'm a sub editor of the *Daily Orb* and we would like to run a front page and exclusive on your ordeal!'

Chaz said '*The Orb*' with animation, and Natasha smiled, as she had put the wheels into motion for this. Natasha Barber was like a chip off the old block when it came to seeing financial opportunities. She wasn't doing too bad either, just turned twenty-two and a top end Porsche out the front there, bought with half her own money. Then she had plans to take up a mortgage on a penthouse flat as soon as she left Uni. Her dad was going to give her the deposit and once she had finished her degree, she would start up her very own hi-end escort agency. Nat had already discussed it with her father, and after having a year or so 'in the field', she knew what the rich clients wanted. You could say she thought like her father, with a rather more expanded mind and she had the sex on legs to sell as well. She had vowed to herself that she wouldn't go down his route with the drug dealing. But sometimes vows are hard to keep. Yet she was up for her dad's ideas about the porn channel though. It would suit her down to the ground, she reckoned.

'If we can get an exclusive in-depth, there will be a substantial payment, as we think it has the potential to be a big news and features item across a number of our publications.'

Chaz loved all this. After the long dark night, this was the light beginning to shine through again, oh ye of little faith!

'Er, I'd be delighted to help you. We think the case highlights some of the problems with the NHS at the present time, and being so bizarre, we think it would be an ideal scoop for *The Orb*!'

Suddenly Chaz's glass was more than half full again, and he was perking up, beginning to feel himself. This was his castle. It had been overrun by the barbarians for a spell, but Chaz was philosophical. How long did the Roman Empire last? All these things are sent to try us and now he was back at the helm, back in the driving seat, king of the citadel. There wouldn't be a TV Mk II, he was sure of that, and Chaz certainly wasn't going to be driven out of his Rome by a couple of nut crazies! The citadel he had created was full of money, and Chaz loved money and the more the merrier. What else is there to get out of bed for? Possibly an afternoon visit or three, to that young escort girl, Brooke, he had at the boxing show!

With this big money opportunity coming his way, Chaz realized, despite everything, he would be on his feet in no time. A few Erectafen, a few more lines of coke, a few more gold ingots for the Swiss accounts and some long weekends carping. As they say, you can't keep a good man down. He looked at Natasha and she could see that he was smoking hot for it.

'They reckon it's got the potential to go front page national and Sunday exclusive. Big bucks! It's a coming up those money spiders all over again. All over the Chazzy boy!'

Chaz felt transported. In these moments he saw everything one-sided, money-sided. With a lump sum of money, he and Miko could go ahead with that carp shop. They could even move, live close to the shop, in somewhere like Fishgate. There wasn't a big carp supermarket down there but there was a goodly number of carp lakes in the vicinity. Chaz lifted his shoulders, feeling new waves of energy pulsing through his veins. Natasha was pleased to see her dad looking happier with it all. For a moment or two he would just forget the implications of that vicious army shotgun. And could anyone plan for people like those two devils?

'I knew that e mail would work, Dad! Go for it! You might as well make something out of it all!' Chaz agreed with that sort of attitude.

'Fucking right, me little peach!'

Chaz rubbed his hands together. Things would be coming up the roses now for the Barbers!

A little while later, he was feeding the carp with the 'egg shells in' blues and reds, and beginning to get back in the groove, enthusing about his bright future. Linda had changed by now and was sitting on the new Waldorf, looking a little less stressed after the shower. Chaz dropped some more reds, observing how the new carp were reacting. It was a 'here come the new carp just like the old', as both newcomers were bang on Chaz's boilies. Chaz was sure his world would fall back together again, or at least until he had to phone 'pig' about that automatic gun out there in the water butt.

'Get on um, my sons! We'll make a killing out of this, Linda, a fucking killing!'

Linda wasn't ready for this kind of talk and especially the reference to killing with three dead and one still in intensive care after the fiasco. Everything was all too raw.

'Oh, Chaz! Do you have to talk like that?'

Chaz raised the testosterone levels a few more nanograms. It was his right to make as much money as he possibly could from all this.

'Come on, Linda! For fuck's sake! If that TV fucker had said a casual "yes" on a whim, my head would have been up on the fucking pole! Fucking charming, eh! Having to put up with that, when ya come home from work.'

Chaz's anger boiled over and he thumped the arm of the chair, three times, thwack, thwack, thwack, stoking up more adrenaline for the ensuing battles.

'I'll sue the fuckers to fuck! Sue um to fuck!'

But Linda dampened his ardor. He was going down and Chaz obviously knew it.

'You're not going to come up all roses, Chaz! Not this time!' she protested, but Natasha just couldn't put up with it, their continual arguing. She could see that there was a mighty lot of tension in the relationship now.

'For God's sake! You're doing my fucking brain in again!'

Chaz made that dreaded phone call to the police regarding the found automatic shotgun and they said they would be up to the house to collect the weapon, and a statement from Chaz, immediately. On the announcement of that, Chaz had another hoover around the front room, while Linda, quiet and morose, took to the bedroom to read a blockbuster.

This time it wasn't Gabi and Chris, it was PC Amelia Wainhurst and Chris. She tried to put up an excuse to a superior, about how it might disturb her going to the house, but it was flatly rejected. She was a policewoman, that was her job. She wasn't picking and choosing sweets, down at the supermarket. She knew that it was going to be uncomfortable, but she would just have to face it. Chaz saw the car arrive and looked out of the window and to his amusement and delight, it was that PC Angelica. It brought some much-needed humor to the grim proceedings.

'Well I never! We got PC legs-over-her-head, Nat, coming up the garden path! Get ya hairy fanny out!'

Chaz thought back to the little vow he made to himself, and he felt in need of a bit of comic relief. He went straight underneath the carp tanks and got the magazine, laying it out on the coffee table, arranging the newspaper to kind of slightly obscure it.

'Ya Dad might be on the rack, me little Peach, but why not have a bit of fun while they're flagellating him? Fuck um!'

Chris opened the gate and was still talking about the other week when he and Gabi investigated that terrible scream. Amelia was taking it all in, just eager to get it all over with, and get out of there. Chaz opened the door and said that the discarded gun was in the water butt in the garden.

'We didn't want to disturb it, Officer. We thought we might tamper with the mechanisms of the law, sir.'

They accompanied Chaz around the path to the back and Nat was by the water butt looking at the gun. Chris took the gun out and Natasha, to Chaz's amusement, played about with Amelia's uncomfortable situation.

'Oh, hullo! How's your glamour modelling and stuff going these days?'

PC Wainhurst recognized her immediately, she'd even spoke with Nat when she was on set. Natasha was doing a rather more hardcore film on the premises that day and 'Voluptuous Angelica' had gone on to greater, bigger and rather more explicit things than Natasha. After Chris had put the gun in a thick polythene bag, to avoid any more disquiet, PC Wainhurst asked Chris if she could speak to him for a moment out the front. Chaz smiled as he knew she was struggling to escape the embarrassment. Amelia came up with the excuse that she had a terrible migraine. She sat in the car and just had her head in her hands. It was a case of the fallout of that secret life meeting the upright police expectation. She couldn't verily say that those were the old days. She had worked on a film the other weekend, *Voluptuous Angelica, The Gang Bang Fiend*. She regretted getting deeper and deeper into it. But it was too late, she had.

Chris was led into the lounge for the statement and it became the most uncomfortable moment in his police life. Chaz was enjoying himself.

'Feel free to sit in the velvet chair, Officer, and then we'll deal with the statement from the settee.'

Chris brought the statement paper to the table, sat down, placed it on the coffee table and before him was that legs over the head photo of PC Amelia Wainhurst, with the newspaper only slightly obscuring. He could see who it was and he was shocked, not in terms of how terrible soft porn was, but it was just so unexpected. He tried to keep hold of the situation appropriately.

'Could you kindly remove the magazine while we're working on the statement, Mr. Barber.'

'Oh, sorry, Officer, but it's a New Age these days, isn't it? I'm always looking at them and my daughter here, Natasha, is always appearing in them.' Nat was sitting on the Waldorf, smiling, not giving a shit. Chaz took hold of the magazine and turned over a page and showed him a glance of Nat. Nat was sitting directly underneath the oil painting smirking. Chaz then quickly put the magazine underneath the carp tanks.

When Chris left the house with the statement, Chaz and Natasha had a good laugh. It helped to break that tense and morose atmosphere enveloping 'Chaz's Pad'.

They decided to get an Indian delivered so that they didn't have to cook, and Linda came down but remained sullen and didn't say much. She smiled at the animated telling of the PC Wainhurst tale, with Natasha saying, that Angelica, her sex industry moniker, was big on gang bang parties at sex clubs, as well as being with an escort agency that Nat had left way behind, now that she'd gone on to bigger and better things.

'You wouldn't believe what she gets up to.'

Chaz inevitably snorted a few more with Natasha, and Linda eventually relented and snorted one too, to try and get her head away from it all. Linda had read a piece on Iraq war veterans in the nineties around post-traumatic stress disorder, and she recognized all the symptoms in herself, so it was like a self-medication. Chaz loved to see Linda on the coke again. It reassured him. Gave him the impression that things would gradually come back into their natural shape.

'That's it, have a line of Charly Farley. He'll make ya feel better, Linda,' was Chaz's all-round prescription for her blues. It didn't really work, but she flew high for a few fleeting moments.

Later in the evening it was time for Natasha to go. She had to earn money, and there were University second year exams the following week, which she was ill prepared for. Before leaving they put one over to Steve, just to make sure, and the majority of the conversation was to be undertaken by Natasha.

'He won't fuck up on you, Nat, he's still besotted with ya.'

Nat asked him about the gun. Scamp said he was going to take it to the lake under cover of darkness. He had already told her, a couple of hours ago, although he still enjoyed speaking to her.

'Look, Steve, I need ya really badly to do this for me and do it right. No fuck ups. It's for me, do it for me! I won't forgot ya, Steve, if you do it for me, never.'

Chaz was smiling, listening to her, putting on the drama.

While she was asking him, she was holding her mobile and had a finger poking out the side, and was pretend winding something round it, from her right thumb and forefinger. Luckily, Steve had kept his counsel at the park and Nat reckoned her emotional hold over Steve would clinch it. Towards the end of the call, Chaz got on the blower and told him that he would give him some generous deals going forward as long as that kilo came back intact.

'Well do the business for us, Steve! Natasha is relying on ya here, mate.'

Natasha planned a return in a couple of weeks after her exams to help steady the ship. She was more than a little concerned about her mum though. She was looking and acting vacant and as Nat left, Linda was in the front lounge, staring into the deep abyss, somewhere in those carp tanks. There was something comforting about watching the subtle gill and tail movements of the carp, and Linda was smoking a joint now, to further augment the sense of escape she wanted to feel. Anything for a zombie chill.

It was another balmy warm evening, the high summer like weather, showing no signs of relenting just yet. Nat was in the driver's seat, the door open, with Chaz alongside, affording some father and daughter intimacy underneath the horse chestnut.

'Thanks for everything, Nat, you've been fucking blinding!' Chaz said. She had been a great daughter and had helped them no end over the past couple of days.

'It took some fucking bottle getting that coke and gun out of here, Nat.'

Nat hadn't given that a second thought. It was all part and parcel of being a Barber. 'I wished I could hang around, Dad, but you know how it is.'

Chaz certainly did, those exams had to be passed. She was a talented girl was his Natasha. He had high hopes for her.

'Look, don't worry yourself, Nat. You've got your own fucking life to lead now, babes, and we'll get over this. It's not likely to happen every fucking fortnight is it? And I'll squeeze that Trust's fucking lemon. I'll fucking crush the fucker!'

Natasha nodded her head in support but she could see the other side of the issue. Her mum on her own while he was in nick and visiting Chaz in prison for God knows how many years.

'I'm still worried about Mum though.'

'She'll be all right. I'll fuss around her. Chocolates, nice days out, plenty of presents, bit of charley. We could even have a week chilling. She'll be all right, Nat. Don't worry.'

'Well make sure you don't leave her stewing it all over while you fuck off for a weekend fishing, Dad.'

It was the time of the year for that, as Nat knew full well. Chaz promised that he would give it a while. He then raised himself, hung over the door and they kissed goodbye, rather a touch uncomfortably intimate for father and daughter, some might think. Natasha pulled away with a hoot, deeply worried. She hadn't said too much about it all, but it looked bad for her father. She had already spoken on the blower to an escort client of hers, a criminal lawyer, and he confirmed what she knew, there being a five-year minimum sentence for the possession of illegal firearms. Allied to that was a doctor dead, a police officer in intensive care and other injuries and all from the use of Chaz's illegal weapons. He suggested a definite ten-year sentence with Chaz serving at least five, and in his own calculation, Chaz thought he would serve five. Anything better would be a big result.

Natasha stopped the car about a mile from the village and parked up for five, as with all the stress of the past few days, she just had to have another one. She laid it out on a Uni reader, essays on feminist perspectives on the media industry, and snorted. But she wanted to get herself in the groove. She had an overnight appointment to prepare for. A couple of grand one from a rich Arab who she had been servicing every few weeks. He was a good little earner and one of her favorite, personal clients, and it suited the clients and Nat, that nothing went through the books. It was money she could stash away in her Swiss account as she saved up for furnishings for the new penthouse flat that was in the pipeline. She thought about her dad and shook her head, he was going down for some time, and a little thought crept into her mind. The business. She could drop that daft DVD thing he still kept up with, and just go internet with Miko and Viv and possibly take over and go with Alfredo, Steve could help her. He could be her right-hand man and that Jay seemed to be reliable and sensible for a young dealer. She thought a few more thoughts. She could supply the Uni as well as Tennin and this new Candy Foxes thing was promising. She even fancied the idea of opening a club herself. She had drifted into 'Club Hollywood' with Zoe and there was a desultory turnout down there. Maybe she could seek a meeting with the manager and owners. They also had another club down at Fishgate that was on the ropes. Chaz would be right up for it as an investment and they already had one over that Tennin Council leader, Sally Brockett. She was a big recreational user. Steve could organize the security down there. Strictly no drugs unless they're the firm's. She could keep her fingers in plenty of other pies too. She was like a chip off the old block like that. It had to be varied income streams in the New Age.

Chaz was rolling one joint up after another with a line of Charley in between. He just had to get out of it, and the drugs were convincing him that everything would eventually come up the roses. He looked in the tanks and watched the carp, and that simple pleasure and passion of sitting by a carp lake, seemed a long way off now. He would have to go in hard on the drug dealing for the next six months before the court case, and make sure it all went into his Swiss account. At least he would have something to fall back on down the line. He began thinking of Natasha. Maybe it was time to get that porn channel idea up and running, put a lump of money into it, Natasha could take up the Barber helm with Miko and Viv. But every toke of the joint seemed to have Chaz fluctuating between despair and hope. While he was deep in thought, Linda still looked sullen, and was monosyllabic, toking and staring into the abyss. She was away with the fairy's, with the cocaine supplementing an already drug and pain killing addled nervous system.

'You know, Chaz, I think all this was meant to be. It's as if there's a light coursing through my body and mind, and I'm like dissolving into the divine.'

'Hold on up, Linda! Hold on up! You're talking as if you need a fucking holiday! You need to get away from this place for a few weeks. Fucking dissolving into the fucking divine!'

Then the business of *The Orb* exclusive reared its confrontational head again. A quick financial kill and two or three weeks away, it was all there waiting for them.

'You'll be glad I got all this up and running, Linda, when we're on that Greek island sunning ourselves with a bottle of wine! Poker's white hot, so we've got to hit it big time! Fuck it! We've suffered enough.'

Linda was still morose and spaced out as she took another lug and kept quiet but felt an outburst was inevitably welling.

'Just keep a backseat, Linda. Chazzy boy will handle all this!'

Linda just had to protest. She didn't want any of *The Orb's* money. This was all too personal, and it would feel like dirty money to Linda. Fuck the holiday, she thought. She wanted peace of mind; a *new* peace of mind and she found a clarity when speaking about it.

'Oh, Chaz! I just don't like the idea of it being national news! They'll want all the lurid details! It's such an invasion of privacy.'

Chaz was determined to talk her round using all his powers of persuasion, so he thought he would toss the idea around a bit and come at it from another direction. A train of thought fell into place.

'Look! It's all up in the air at the moment, Linda! Jonathan will go all out for an "out of court", I know he will. There'll be good money in it for him. And he can use the threat of a full disclosure in *The Orb* as encouragement. That fucking Trust won't like that, will they?' Chaz was making it up as he went along with a joint on the go, but he liked the idea. It was intelligent. It would get that big, big payout from the Trust. Yes, Chaz liked this train of thought, he found it reassuring. He knew he had to be positive in these more than trying circumstances. Linda just looked at the Titanic ornament in the far carp tank.

'The Trust will pay us out a life-changing sum, Linda, to keep it all quiet. I'll have enough to go legit with the carp shop. And if its thirty odd miles away, well we can move, can't we? It would be a new start. You were only talking about that the other day! After the long dark night, the sun comes up! It always does, Linda. Always does! Believe me!' Linda knew about the illegal firearm custodial too. She knew it was a foregone conclusion.

'What about the guns! You'll get five years or even ten! And you can bet somebody is going to sue you, Chaz. It's a certainty, like that Titanic going down.'

Chaz toked on his joint, inhaled and then defended his more positive outlook again. For Chaz we've always got to accentuate the positive, always. That glass has always got to be half full. He knew he was going down, but get it half full and go down well.

'Look if it goes like that, I'll be out in two and a half. Half the sentence every time, I'll be out in the blink of an eye. And there's no better deal making solicitor than Jonathan. He'll get a million out of that Trust. And I promise I won't sign anything with *The Orb*, before I've had a meeting with him. He'll keep us quids in, Linda, quids in.'

Linda didn't like any of it. She was fully expecting him to do that time, and to face many a law suit. But Chaz's attention being a touch meditative due to the joints, was fixating now on the new carp and Chaz had been living in his own bubble for a long time now.

'I'm glad Nat bought us the carp. It wouldn't have looked right if there were just two. Yes, everything's getting back to normal, Linda. I can feel it. I can feel it, Linda!'

Linda was intending to go out in the four-wheel drive the following day, ostensibly for a trip to the big out of town shopping center. Chaz thought it would do her good to get her mind off things, while he visited Jonathan to talk through the issues. Nothing would be off the table. Chaz would say that he expected a sentence, and if the worse came to the worse, the pay out from the Trust could pay the law suits off. There'd still might be some cash left over from the newspaper scoops. It was all about getting that worst-case scenario in your mind, then it wouldn't be too hard to deal with. He was alive and strutting around like a cock again, so how bad is that and he had a new Jag, an AD 2003 model to pick up. You have to be philosophical about these things Chaz thought, and the Jag would keep him in the cocoon. He would feel like Chaz Barber in that new white chariot, firing again.

A taxi arrived to get Chaz to the garage, as Linda was taking a shower, and as soon as Chaz had gone, she quickly began to get ready. She wasn't intending to go to that shopping center though. She was going to Foxdale, to get those wedding photos of TV and Freeda developed. She had surreptitiously swapped over new films and placed them into the camera and made a show to Chaz, that she was binning the film. But in fact, she had hidden the roll and was off to the Foxdale Boots where they offered a one-hour service. She would hang around for a couple of coffees in the town, while they were being done, and she wouldn't be bumping into Chaz, who was in Tennin. Linda's handbag, that Freeda had wed to her shoulder before she got into her wedding dress, had been picked up by

Natasha during the clear up and was put in her mother's bedroom. Natasha took the contents for granted and hadn't looked inside and Linda hadn't bothered about it while in hospital and she went to collect it from her bedroom. She brought it downstairs and opened it and came across Freeda's novelty spotted purse, with its friendly cat face outlined on it in black. It was a both sides now moment, looking into that purse. There were those two pairs of novelty sunglasses that Freeda liked to pose with. Linda recalled her sitting on the furry chair trying on her different sun glasses, cat eyed and love hearts and putting on her lip glosses using that small make-up mirror. Linda had seen how much those things meant to her. The cheap lip glosses were there, and a cheap pound shop perfume that Freeda had worn before she had used Linda's. There were also her 'special' skin creams. All cheap, but all so cherished. There was also that money that Freeda had referred to a number of times which was some coppers and some small change silver. Linda was looking into the context and content of her life. There was another little compartment in the purse and Linda pushed it apart and there was a couple of old photos. She looked at the first one and it was of Freeda and TV, lain on a settee smiling, with TV's arm around her, and Freeda's head resting on TV's shoulder. Linda assumed that it was taken in that locked unit where they had first met. It looked like one of those photos from an instant camera and, had in fact, been taken by a Nigerian, who they used to call 'Tiny', who had long been transferred. There was also a crumpled postcard. Linda remembered Freeda referring to the picture in her purse before they took Chaz and Linda out to the car. It was a view of Fishgate beach and pier. Deep feelings welled up and she choked with tears in her eyes, as Linda realized this place was like a dream paradise in Freeda's eyes. The emotional significance was so great to Freeda that TV had tried in vain to get them down there, before they were apprehended. But then came the final revelation and she saw it all. There was a small color photo, creased and well-worn around the edges and some twenty-five years old, that had been taken on Fishgate beach by that cafeteria. A six-year-old or so Freeda was smiling, holding her mother's hand while licking her ice cream. Freeda's mother was looking particularly happy. Linda's heart was in her mouth, as she realized that her stepfather was probably abusing her at the time the photo was taken. Linda looked and thought again about the contents of the purse. Tears streamed from her eyes as she held the love heart sunglasses. It all gave testimony that Freeda's yearnings for love in her life were no different than any others. Linda took hold of the undeveloped film in her hand, and she reflected on the wedding, and it all took on greater emotional significance.

Linda sat in a quiet corner away from others in the coffee shop. It wasn't busy, and she just sat there, staring into her coffee, mulling over the events in her mind. She became emotional for a few moments with tears in her eyes. She looked down, so that nobody could see that she was crying, and she found it hard to regain composure, as the events were all so raw and deeply poignant and she was far from coming up out the other side.

She collected the photos. She had two lots developed as she had something in mind. She got back into the Jeep and took a look. There was something about them that Linda warmed to. The sheer joy of Freeda radiated from them and she was particularly taken by one of the pair together by the gate. Linda was smiling as she spoke on her mobile.

'Clarke is his surname, Linda,' June said. Linda hadn't said exactly why she was wanting to contact him, and she didn't disclose the issue any further. She just said that she wanted to talk to him to clear something up. June asked her to look after herself.

'Thanks, Ju, see you later.'

Linda smiled again at the photos, and she decided to head straight to the asylum. She felt she had to see Dan. Linda had been deeply moved by the way that Dan had greeted Freeda by the fence. She couldn't forget it. She felt obliged to give him the photos as a memento, and she soon found herself at the reception desk in the asylum.

'Hi, I've come to visit Dan Clarke. I'm a friend of the family's.'

It was enough to get the ward number and off Linda went. She approached a nurse as she gained entry to the ward.

'Dan? He's in the television room watching old movies. He's always doing that,' the nurse said. Linda felt awkward, but she was sure that he would warm to the photos. She knocked the door and then opened, and Dan was seated on the shabby looking settee watching an old film from the nineteen sixties, but staring into space really.

'Dan?' Linda tentatively asked.

'Who are you?' he replied. He had been depressed and withdrawn since the deaths of TV and Freeda. All he had engaged with was bigger and bigger doses of tranquilizer, and he would sit sullen and morose all day long. Zombie chilled was where he wanted to be right now.

'I've got some photos for you of TV and Freeda's marriage. I was the photographer they told you about. They're beautiful and they're yours, Dan.'

Linda passed him the photos and within a few moments any resistance Dan had to this stranger broke down. He was overwhelmed, as they looked so perfect together with the flowers around them.

'Their marriage was special, Dan. And I saw you outside the house when you came to Freeda.' Linda took his hand tenderly with tears coming down her cheeks as Dan sobbed, heartbroken.

The Trust weren't prepared to pay the type of settlement that Jonathan was after so Chaz dealt with *The Orb* and gave an account that didn't disclose everything, as Linda wouldn't speak about the events. Chaz just said that she had been tied up and repeatedly raped. *The Orb* wanted to speak to Linda but Chaz said that she was too deeply traumatized. But he gave them all the graphic details in terms of his experience. Jonathan believed that there would be a big settlement no matter what, and Chaz just couldn't resist the lure of a quick lump sum. So, in early June AD 2003 the events at Holly Beach Lane would be known all over the country, and Chaz said to Linda that he couldn't give a shit if the village knew all about their S&M leanings. They were the type of people who are outraged in public, then they wank in private, wishing they were doing it. Get over it! It's a new Age! But of course, it was the very talk of the village and convenience store, once those papers arrived, and the ordeal was splashed across the front. Tennin was on the map again. It had a habit of getting there with the unsavory or bizarre side of the human condition.

'You know, that bloke with the white blazer who drives the white Jag' was what they were all saying, and everybody had seen him and registered him. It was the talk of Tennin.

After another week or so Chaz was itching to get moving. There was a heap of cash in the bank but he wanted to re-establish himself. Become Chaz Barber again and get out on the rounds in that new AD 2003 Jag. It was sitting out there waiting for the king in the white blazer. He had ordered five new ones as a statement of intent and was gearing up for that full return to the fray. Linda suggested to take the old blazers to the charity shop but Chaz couldn't have the young Herbert's wearing his white blazers. Chaz was the man, the main man. He would trash them at the council dump. And better, sooner than later, was Chaz's approach to the matter. Get the memory and trace of that TV wanker out of his life for good and move on.

Chaz took the bull by the horns and got Scamp to bring up the kilo of coke and Glock. The vibe had cooled. Chaz gave him a freebie from it, and thanked him for getting him out of the shit. That shotgun was down at the bottom of that deep old blue lake of Olwyn's and nobody had seen Scamp dispose of it. Once Steve had left, Chaz had to get going. He had a full itinerary. He had to get to the solicitors first, regarding ongoing developments, and then there was the obligatory run to the carp shop. Chaz was in the process of planning a trip. This time a full weekend session at Joey Olwyn's lake. Linda would settle down again now the coke was back on the table. He had thought about the possibility of scoring another blank full of eels but it didn't bother him now. It would just be nice to sit by the lake, feel at one with the natural world and smoke a bit of weed. Have the craic with Miko. If a big carp came along so be it, and he could take his chance. Chaz felt more philosophical about life now and what was important for Chaz was getting back in character, back into the true self, back in control. Then there'd be a quick healing process.

It wouldn't have taken place if Dan hadn't garnered support from the other patients and Lorenzo, Cheryl, Drill-head and a few others accompanied Dan in a visit to the managing director. They said that Dan had the money in a special bank account, given to him by an aunt, and he wanted to spend it on a dual cremation. With the strength of feeling about, and a means of reducing the expenditure, the Trust authorities allowed it to pass, as long as there was no publicity, and it went off quietly. There were sensitivities around due to the loss of Dr. Lock. Linda met the Trust director under something of a disguise, Mrs. Davis, she introduced herself as, and it was left to Linda, to arrange the funeral at a local crematorium. Linda paid for everything with a few extras added, taking the money from the safe upstairs and Linda had plans.

It was decided they would use the marriage photo on the service sheet and the two songs to be played at the funeral were 'Come to my Window', it seemed appropriate, and 'At Last', Freeda's special song that they swayed and danced together to. A dozen photos had also been chosen and put on a loop projected on a screen, with the old snap of Freeda and TV in the lock up too. Linda had also seen the priest who would speak at the funeral. She told him of the circumstances of what she knew about their lives and emphasized how the symbolic marriage meant so much to them. She showed the priest the purse and spoke about its poignant contents and Linda tried to express her thoughts on the ambivalent meaning of their lives. After the meeting Linda went to the funeral directors and gave them the purse, and the Sesame Street record case that she had recovered from the bin outside, so that Freeda could be reunited with her prize possessions. She also took them a clean white blazer, trousers and shirt for TV, and a new wedding dress for Freeda, so they could be cremated together as newlyweds. She wanted to bypass too much interaction with the Trust over such issues. Everything was like an emotional catharsis for Linda to what were life-changing events. But she kept it all secret from Chaz, who was content that Linda was gradually getting back to some kind of routine and helping him recover his Chazzy Barber true self.

On the day of the cremation, Linda was lucky as Chaz wanted to make a quick one to the carp shop and as soon as Chaz was gone, Linda dressed quickly and came forth from the house, clad in black for the funeral. She was intending to get dressed in Tennin's shopping center precinct toilets, if Chaz didn't go out in the morning. But Chaz left with a full itinerary, carp shop and visit to the solicitors, so she had her chance. She took a quick change of clothes with her but it would be an odd day and she had told Chaz she was intending to go shopping at the High Grange center, as she would do, after the service.

There were a few nurses at the crematorium but no Dr. Bolt or Nurse Lavender, who was on compassionate sick leave. All the friends of Freeda and TV went in a couple of minibuses that Dan had paid for through Linda. A wake wasn't feasible but at least they were given an appropriate send off. Dan stood with the mysterious woman in black who wasn't recognized by anybody, and was just introduced as his Aunt Lydia. The priest found the ceremony more challenging than most with the double coffin behind him, with a wreath of red roses upon it.

'Freeda had a tragic life as many will know but she found a hope in Samuel, of whom we can see by the photos here, she loved so dearly. And let us not think of anything bad today. Let us think of the healing power of god's love and pray that TV, as he was known, and Freeda are together at last in that love. We commend the bodies and spirits of Freeda and Samuel to God.'

The coffin slipped away behind the curtain to the sound of Freeda's song and they were all tearful and they all voiced their goodbyes.

'Goodbye, Freeda, goodbye, TV.'

Linda and Cheryl were comforting a particularly distressed Dan, who tried to hold his tears back but inevitably broke down sobbing. It was the loss of such a great friend and the thought of that moment he had hugged Freeda, but he was so grateful that Linda made it happen.

'It's fitting for them,' Drill-head observed, and everybody agreed and all shed tears.

The double coffin was just so apt and there was a beautiful floral tribute to the couple in their allotted space stating, 'Freeda and TV' and they all gathered around reflecting in deep sorrow.

Meanwhile, Chaz pulled the new Jag up outside the carp supermarket. It had gone well with Jonathan who was really on the case, chasing the money. Chaz had also spoken to him about handling a future criminal proceedings defense. Jonathan was fully prepared to take it up and thought he could keep the sentence down to six or seven years, so Chaz was thinking three and a half and out. He was going to take up a clever defense in terms of emphasizing a macho gun culture that his client, regrettably, had been intoxicated by.

'We'll endeavor to take the heat off you by a third, Charles, and blame that bit on society's ills.'

It seemed rationale to Chaz, and Jonathan gave Chaz a feeling of hope. He was determined to be contrite and deeply apologetic in court, breaking down in tears would be effective he thought. He would even say that he deserved to be punished as he had done wrong. The tactics would procure leniency.

In terms of that negotiation with the Trust, Jonathan put in a suitable out of court settlement claim, otherwise he threatened a fuller disclosure.

They had rejected him flatly and now they had to accept the fall out and it was a big mistake. The chief executive was forced to resign and it seemed likely they would have to accept the original out of court settlement sum anyway. There were some very angry people at the Trust, who believed that error was being compounded by more. But for Chaz that life-changing sum of money would be coming his way for a spell before big sums went out the other way, via claims against him. But Chaz was still hoping that more would come in on the one hand than go out in the other. That was Chaz's natural way of thinking. The glass half full and eventually overflowing. Chaz had made a stack of cash through the bank holiday weekend, despite the debacle; stacks, and you don't do that if you live and breathe negative energy.

Linda was still standing around the remembrance flowers, thinking about many things when Chaz marched towards the entrance of the carp superstore, with more than a bit of the old panache back. He had the Nero's on, his expensive jeans with a pink carp T-shirt. He was the dog's bullocks again. Chaz was back with a wad of the *Orb's* money in his back pocket, and seemingly with the mojo. Kevin was on the tills, and had in fact been speaking about Chaz only a short while earlier with the manager, wondering, when or whether, Chaz Barber would show his face and grace them with his presence.

'Speak of the devil, he's bloody here! I wonder how he's feeling, Graham?' Kevin asked. However he felt, he would have plenty of dough, was Graham's reply. Almost everyone had seen and read the papers and people wanted more of the story.

'He'll spend some, before he goes down,' Kevin replied, in an empty shop.

It was common knowledge about the shoot-out with the guns and it seemed to Kevin that these two asylum patients were moving towards cult celebrity, as it was all the rage on the emerging blogging sites. Of course, none of that was going unnoticed by Chaz, when he held all the exclusive rights as it were. Chaz entered with his normal breezy demeanor, as if nothing at all had happened since he was last in the shop. Not a thing!

'Hullo, Mr. Barber! And how are you after all the kafuffle?' Kevin was trying to say the right thing. Chaz lifted his shoulders a few times, as the carp king persona was kicking in again. It was good to be back, thought Chaz.

'No problems now, the mad fuckers are dead and buried, Kevvy me boy!'

Nothing could keep Chazzy Barber down. He wasn't going to be haunted by them. Kevin smiled, but he didn't want to get involved anymore, regarding such a touchy subject. But after the morning's meeting with Jonathan, Chaz wanted to open up and boast a little.

'And between you and me and the deep blue lakes in these parts, they're coming up plenty of Adam and Eve juice, Kevvy me boy! We've made over a hundred grand on it already. And with my genius of a clever solicitor on the job, it looks like a very, very substantial damages payout from the Trust. The snakes have done their biting shall we say Kevvy, big nasty conger fuckers, not the bootlace fucking eels!'

Chaz was on a high this morning, the lawsuits hadn't come his way yet, and he had a couple of lines earlier too.

'The man with the golden fishing hook!' Kevin quipped.

'And I'll be getting the trademark blazer back on any day now, Kevvy!'

Chaz was firing on all cylinders, feeling his normal sense of self again. It was a wonderful feeling after the last few weeks trials and tribulations.

'Got a new batch on the way this week! It's twelve grand of blazer's day Wednesday. That mad fucker soiled the others we might say, mate.'

Kevin was treading as softly as he could here, so he thought he would bring the conversation back onto solid carping ground.

'June's a nice time to get back carping, Chazzy!'

Chaz raised his shoulders again and took a sly glance over to the photo board, and that pride of place, but very old photo of himself with the big 'Ressie' record carp. But it was a full-on bravado day today.

'Shot down in May but he'll be back on top in June, me boy! And I think I might try these Osaki efforts. Looking at a big weekend chilling down at Olwyn's lake after that fucking virgin. See if me and Miko can make a right old whore out of her, Kevvy boy! Ha, ha, ha!'

Chaz bellowed with laughter, but was also thinking that he just had to catch a decent carp, so that he had a fresh snap up on that wall. It was essential. Those divine blues and passion reds had to start working for him. But whether they did or they didn't, Chaz felt himself coming back to Chazzy Barber's rightful place and space in this here world. Kevin had been down to the lake the previous week checking out the water himself.

'We had a nosey down there last week. Come away with four punnets of jellied eels, Chaz. Joey said he's got traps all over the fucking lake. Bringing them out by the crate full. I shan't be joining quite yet!' By now the problem with eels was apparently getting around the local scene.

'Wriggling fucking bastards!' Chaz exclaimed, praying that he wouldn't have an entire weekend like that last trip to the water. 'If they get at me again, I'll snort a fucking horse bag up me hooter!' It appeared that Chaz was regaining that renowned wit and tendency to holler at his own jokes. But that was Chazzy Barber, fully back in character.

Chaz got his sacred blazers, and on the Friday, it was time to get back out there, knock it out and be the 'real' Chaz Barber again. And it was as if nothing had ever happened. The crows were kraaing out the back, the pile-drivers were pounding and even the big bluebottles were buzzing around the new shed. Linda was about to return to boilie making and she was back to feeding the four-great carp and ticking in the research data book. The old world had reasserted itself like the Old Roman Empire had done after the first rush of the barbarians. This wasn't the Visigoths. The white blazer, a brand new one, costing the usual two and a half, was on a hanger over the top of the door, immaculate and perfect. It was a momentous day and it was cloudless, yet another twenty-eight degrees on the mercury, and Chaz felt great! His injuries – that abdomen and the battered head – had healed, and he felt like a new man now. He had even brought a new twill shirt and tie and yet another pair of Blue Nero crocodile shoes. Chaz had regained that nigh blue blood perfection, that domain that he, and only he, had staked out in Tennin. He had even been doing early morning bicep workouts, before his first joint.

'A change is as good as a rest they say, Linda! See ya later, sweet alligator! Chaz is a crazy crocodile daddy these days, me Herberts!'

It was all in honor of the new Blue Nero's. He thought he would treat himself to a pair and by now that new velvet chair had replaced the patched up one, and all going through on the hospital insurance. But things had indeed come full circle and on the coffee table, there were a number of bags of coke, all weighed out and readied for the drop. Linda was relaxing as best she could on the new Waldorf, but she didn't have any inclination to go around the circle, to return to where she'd set off from.

'Do you have to, Chaz?' she asked.

'Look! It's only half a dozen big drops and I've made over five grand and I've got half a dozen porn drops to keep me eye in for the food bill. Have a couple of lines of Mr. Farley and chill out for the devil's sake. There's plenty of hoot in his trinket box. Get back on it! Bang on it, Linda!'

It was Chaz's philosophy that once you get into your 'true self' and the groove of that life mode, circumstance can only knock you down for a short while, before you simply have to get up, brush yourself off and carry on. As far as Chaz was concerned it was no different than somebody like Phelps, having to get back up and get on with it after being humiliated by that Cannibal. You've got to rise above failure and the negative and move on. Live life anew was Chaz's motto, and he chortled to himself as he began to stalk down that new pristine white blazer. This was the real deal moment. He was the man again! The main man, and there was only one white blazer king! He took it from its hanger, handling it with due reverence, before slipping it on. He shuffled about, admiring himself in the oval mirror, all as per normal. It was a big moment, that admiring himself in the oval mirror, as per normal. Chaz's world had come back to its right shape again. That thing with TV in the blazers merely showed how cool Chazzy Barber was, as others aspired to wear those blazers, just like him. Chaz was back in! And it was also all systems go for moving all assets into hidden Swiss places.

'It shall be big on ingots away, safe for a rainy day, just in case all assets are taken away! Ha, ha,' Chaz reflected a little jokingly.

It was the same old routine. He sprayed with the sweet breath spray, opening his mouth and flashing his whitened teeth, with the shiny gold cap. Yes, everything was coming up gold and Chaz thought he would buy at least three ingots worth with all that money they had up in the safe. 'Class!'

He stood back a touch and looked at himself in the mirror. It was new everything, even new Harrods socks and pants. What a lucky Brooke, he thought, because he would find time today. It was a matter of re-assertion. He also intended to really get back in and vowed to flirt with that Jessica on the phone about the forthcoming porn shoot proposed for the end of the week. Chaz had missed the casting due to unforeseen circumstances, but he sure wasn't going to miss the follow up shoot. 'Class!' he would also get down to the Waterside penthouse of that Angusia and deliver eight, and who knows what it might lead to, Chaz thought. He masturbated in the bath thinking about those tits of hers the previous night, so the hot libido was still intact.

Chaz sauntered up the path with a briefcase full of DVDs with the coke stash in one of its sleeves. Linda saw him off from the front door; no more depression anymore. Chaz had moved on. He was back in the vast continent that Chaz built.

'See if you can knock out twenty-five, Linda. There's plenty of fresh eggs! And there's ten kilos of orders to sort!'

Linda nodded dutifully, but she didn't intend to do any of it today. Not a thing. Linda's world hadn't gone full circle. It had spiraled off someplace other.

Chaz opened the door of the new Jag and he smiled as it was all behind him. That fucking 'nutty farmer' fiasco was all in the past. Today was the day of the return of the main man, the 'get high' boss of Tennin. He adjusted the rear mirror and lifted up his shoulders. He was reborn and the adrenaline was kicking in big. He hadn't really checked the porn site subscriptions for a week or so since the commotion, and he thought he would have a closer look now he felt his mind was clearer. The laptop was down a sleeve of the briefcase. He quickly logged on and went to the site and was astonished. Would you believe it! That Mrs. Greene-Burrows of Holly Beach Lane had paid a sub! 'Whoop-hay!'

Chaz always thought she was up for it, and she paid it up, despite the fiasco! Chaz knew things. People are never what they seem and he thought about all the times she had sent the 'come on' signals out. He opened the dashboard and took out a small bag of coke, a little 'Percy', that he had popped in there, when he picked the new Jag up. He had to have a line to celebrate. The sun was high up in the sky again, what a start to summer they were having, and it just had to be 'California Dreaming'. He sped down Holly Beach Lane, hollered as he passed Catherine Greene-Burrows' house and although he didn't see her, he dreamed of getting her in the Dark Room, any night soon! He wondered what kinky stuff she was into and he could now put in a cheeky innuendo or three across to her, playing around with them, as he pleased. It would be daily early morning walks to the paper shop to get *The Orb*! 'Sorted!' It would widen things out, liberate things a little, cos ya gotta let it all hang out in the New Age! That's what it's all about. Everybody's at it behind dark closed doors. Get on with it! And Linda would get into it all, eventually. It's 'California baby!' in crappy old Tennin. The porn, the drugs, the sun and the solar beds and hip dressing and big expensive sports cars. 'Get on it!' There was also the temperature rising matter of escorts, who would accommodate your every whim and kink. How about that eh? Exaltation across the nation! Paradise on earth! Adam and Eve juice in the garden and women get paid well for putting it about, don't they? And there are tons up for it in the New Age celebrations.

After the dreaming, he changed CD and had that track of the moment, 'Make Luv' on, a track that was rapidly becoming the new soundtrack to his cruising. It was a particularly pertinent one as the Saturday night thing from Oliver Cheatham had been 'the' track of Chaz's and Linda's early marriage days. He remembered it aligning with Nat's Christening all those years ago. It was the birth of hope and Chaz felt reborn! It was the new world! Pay them well and tease that whore out of them! It's the New Age!

The first drop on the agenda was Jay and Dai, up on the Temple Hive estate. Chaz had umpteen phone calls from them over the past couple of weeks. When ya gonna start dealing again, Chaz? All they could get hold of was the bashed-up crap. Dust that had hardly a trace. Jay and Dai liked to offer all different levels to their punters, with different prices and you couldn't do that with the bashed-up shite. Their business relied on Chaz's gear, big time, as did many others in the region. Thus, Jay and Dai were waiting eagerly, ever so eagerly and impatiently for the Second Coming, and it was a coming to them in a brand-new white Jag, the AD 2003 model. In fact, they were lucky that Chaz had that kilo held back at Scamps as Alfredo was still on holiday in Europe and not due back until the following week. He was staying in his second home, doing his yoga and sipping cocktails with his girlfriend, oblivious to what had occurred to Chaz.

Dai was at the window, looking out, waiting for that white Jag to arrive. With the cessation in dealing they were going in big with a triple order. The pair of them were also gagging for a line of Chaz's 'superior' themselves, after having crap for a few weeks and smoking themselves dopey with skunk. The Jag didn't disappoint. It finally arrived, sparkling in the early afternoon high sun, with the roof down as per usual. The Herbert's had suffered, but you never appreciate what you've got, until it's taken away.

'Here she comes! The White Blazerman is back in town, Jay!'

Anyone would think the Titanic had resurfaced as the pair hollered and hooted. Jay was smoking a joint at the table with a wad of notes in front of him. It was to be an all action weekend with another big dance event to cover down near Fishgate, as well as all the normal punters gagging for it. At least they could exploit their chance now, and it was Dai who had to catch up on his council tax this time. No problem now though.

'Thank fuck for that!' replied Jay with great relief.

'Yes! The bad motherfucker is back!' Dai joked.

Chaz loved it when they opened the door to him. The sheer joy on the Herbert's faces. He loved the idea that *he* was the man. The bringer of glad tidings. The 'special' one who brought the high as a fucking kite, and this week's money.

'The superior pop star dust man is back on the scene again, me Herberts!'

Dai looked him up and down.

'And new shoes!' Dai noticed them, and he added that it was fucking great to see him again as the inferior was rank bad.

'Crocodile, Bengali!' Chaz remarked. 'I like to bung a few quid to the undeveloped world, Dai. Do me bit! Local farmers in Tennin don't keep um as yet!' Chaz joked.

Everything was back as it should be, and Chaz strutted through the lounge full of it, as in that moment the glass was brimming, rather than half full.

'Well as you may have gathered, me and the Mrs. have been on a fucking roller coaster. And it's gonna be big. Looks like a big one, on the "out of court".' Chaz lifted a finger up triumphantly. 'That fucking solicitor of mine is a fucking genius! Should be through the books of the firm by the end of the summer! Fucking sorted or what! And don't worry if Chazzy boy disappears at Her Majesty's pleasure for a few as a little birdie has been singing in me ear, that Natasha might become head of the firm while I'm away! I tried to keep her out of it, Jay! I tried to keep her away from it!'

'Likes the filthy fucking lucre too much, Chaz!' Jay joked as he smiled knowing that the drug supply wouldn't abruptly come to a halt.

'Like us all, Jay! Like us all!'

That raised their eyebrows though. The thought of Natasha pulling up in that Porsche. Dai dreamed. Chaz then hunched his shoulders and delivered the goody bag on the table. The man was well and truly back in!

After the drop at Temple Hive, Chaz went down to the Waterside by the Creek and those new penthouse flats. There was no Angusia though. She phoned when he came out of Jay's and she said that a new guy would be at the flat to sort the cash out for the deal. Fair enough, Chaz thought, and that was another eight ounces knocked out. Then he had numerous smaller drops of two ounces and a number of ones. It was a busy day and with the heavy traffic around due to a road closure, Chaz wouldn't have any time for escort dalliances. He wanted that kilo out by tea time but he wouldn't be going near Gray's anymore. He would sort something different out for delivery there. Then he would concentrate on some bread and butter porn. He even joked to himself about catching up on 'Henry the cuckoo clock!' He just had to get that kinky German over to him. He promised it on a gentleman's handshake! Henry and his fucking Exocet missiles! Chaz chortled through his day, and how he liked being the real Chaz Barber. It was to be a five G day and everything was back in play, and possibly even the ducks would be flying.

But nothing was in place for Linda. By the time Chaz was running around dropping off films, Linda had readied herself to leave. She placed a letter underneath the trinket box on the coffee table, that pointed out a few things and concluded she had decided to live alone. Chaz would be devastated. She had taken thirty grand from upstairs and stated that on the letter, and hoped they could part amicably and settle their finances in the same way.

Something unusual occurred while she was up there poking around the lock up safe. There were many folders in there, and she out of interest, wondered what he had kept over the years. She opened one and it was a folder of Swiss banking information. She opened another, and there was nothing but Chaz with carp. Why on earth did he lock those up, she asked herself? But at the back, there was another, a thick one, that was a touch macabre. Chaz had oddly kept newspaper cuttings of that horrific unsolved murder. Why on earth had he done that? There weren't just clippings from the period, going back twenty-eight years, but others at a later date, about the fact that the murder had never been solved. It seemed that Chaz had some unfathomable secret obsession with the case. But it was one that he had never talked about to Linda. She walked up the pathway with a suitcase puzzled. Chaz said he would be out till gone ten, so she had plenty of time, even though it was twilight. It was like saying goodbye to a certain poisoned chalice and dream of a life. Maybe all our dreams are utopian, she thought. But how she would miss that garden. Despite everything, it was still beautiful. If Chaz did appear early, she would say that she was going over to Debs, because she so desperately, wanted to speak. That would really annoy him, but he wouldn't go with Linda, as he detested her. Linda had gathered up the strength of character to leave, but she hadn't the strength of character to actually confront Chaz and talk out her issues. He controlled her too much. She feared that she would be talked around and fall back down that snake pit. The letter done the talking and was a useful means to move the relationship to another place. It was all over for Linda though and the final decision was made when she had a realization, that she would never get out of that snake pit while she lived with Chaz, in this house. She just knew that, from something deep within her, that was saying leave. Those darn eagles he had just had stuck up on the piers, all said to Linda that it was Chaz's house, and Chaz's only, and that was that. But he could keep it and his solicitor would have to engage with her lawyer. And the gun business was nothing to do with her. She didn't even know he had illegal firearms, although she had seen those automatics.

As she was about to open the door of the new Jeep, she glanced across the road towards the lamplight. She looked at it for a few moments, and yes it did have an unusual aura quality about it. She was drawn across the road and peered up at the light, seemingly transfixed. It was a still night again and a fox screamed from deep down in the orchard at the back of the house. It sounded like a fox, but resonated with those screams that had brought the police up Holly Beach Lane, and it made her recall that horrific scream of Freeda's, when she realized TV was dead. Something stirred across the road by the Jeep and she turned her head and in clear sight was a snake, and this one was mysterious. It wasn't a native snake; it was an exotic one, whose colors and patterning were caught in the lamplight. Linda immediately thought about that Bryan Jonsen, and all the myths about his exotic animals escaping. But she wasn't afraid. She thought it quite beautiful and she slowly stepped forward to catch a closer look and then she had an epiphany. That snake seemed to be TV's snake and it made her think of that erotic high she had felt in the Dark Room. It was an uncanny moment, sublime and unfathomable. But the snake had some kind of odd correspondence within her, and she experienced it as a momentary split-second return to that orgasmic ecstasy, as if a snake driven by sex, had shot through her body into her deepest mind, setting it ablaze. The snake then slithered and spiraled its way into the bushes.

Chaz was at a set of traffic lights stuck for a few moments. It had been a blinding day. Every ounce had been dropped and all the money was either in the dash or in his pocket. He had taken a text from Alfredo that said he was back in the country and the sweet shop was open. With the orders he had already prepared for the morrow, Chaz would have another two kilos as he had to get that one to Candy Foxes. He was back big time!

He'd got his eye back in with the porn drops and had enjoyed some saucy text banter with Jessica too, and why not drop a blue one, yes get back on the Erectafen, and phone Linda to get ready for a session? The traffic lights turned green and he sped off, and was talking to Linda on the mobile while driving. Linda was still looking up at the lamp when she took the call, spaced out, seemingly intoxicated, in whatever it was that TV was seeing in it. She was talking to Chaz from a great distance and divide. Something had indeed moved in her mind, spiraling her elsewhere.

'Feeling my old self again, Linda. I've finished all the drops and I've taken a blue un so how about getting into the gear, and we get back in the Dark Room tonight, eh? We got to get back in there sometime, girl.'

Linda was still spaced out in the lamplight, intoxicated again, thinking about that snake and feeling those correspondences of orgasmic ecstasy.

'Yeah, as you say, Chaz.'

This was just what Chaz wanted to hear. What a day! Everything was resurfacing again. Everything was coming back neatly to where it should be. 'Sorted!'

'That's my Linda! Have a big little one or two! Free yourself up a bit, girl! It's a New Age! And we don't wanna miss out, Linda! Do we? See ya soon!'

Chaz's last drop had been near to the entry into the Triune Way so he thought he would whizz along it, and slide around that roundabout. He was in the new Jag, so why not, eh? He felt as if he was floating on air. There wasn't much on the road, so he could open the throttle up and give the new Jag a blowout. All new cars need one. He was buzzing, firing. He must have had five lines during the course of the day and he was out of his nut, eyes like flying black saucers with a star glinting in the middle. He had the Bowie Greatest Hits back on the CD and low and behold, he entered 'The Triune' with 'Starman' playing again. Chaz smiled to himself as whatever the déjà-vu might bring, it wouldn't bring that 'nutty farmer', back at the lamppost on the final roundabout. Chaz put the speed on and slid around the first and repeated the dose on the second, and for luck he thought he would increase speed into the third and slide it around as if he was on the racetrack, waiving a final goodbye to that fucking lamppost where it had all started. Why not, there was little on the road and my God, he was cooking! He felt he could do anything again! Back in or what! On the weekend he was bound to catch that pregnant virgin fucker. Make a whore out of her! New photos up on the wall! Ya gotta have it! And he would make a visit to that Brooke, for an aggressive kinky one, tomorrow afternoon! What a life! It's AD 2003 and it's a New Age, and Chaz Barber is 'the' Zeitgeist!

But when Chaz approached the roundabout that he met TV at, a big black cat ran across him, and this time he could see it was a big black cat, as its emerald eyes seemed to stare him down. Chaz automatically swerved, lost the back wheel and went careering, spinning at high speed, wallop, into that very lamppost that TV had met him at. The panther scampered off into the trees as if slipping back into a dark unconscious. There one moment and gone the next. Smoke billowed out of the crashed Jag. Back at Holly Beach Lane, the four-wheel drive had long since gone and there was that fox screeching again down in the old orchard, but this time it did sound like a woman. That darn fox needed shooting and that exotic snake slithered and spiraled its way back across the road, making its way to the Dragon Star's lamplight, looking like the true sign of the times.

Lightning Source UK Ltd.
Milton Keynes UK
UKHW011955090720
366299UK00008B/211